MW01641664

LENA KAIN

Lena Kain

Second Edition

Printed in the United States of America by Bang Printing
Edited by Eric Grekowicz
Cover and character illustrations by Stephanie Lesniak

Bang Printing
3323 Oak Street
P.O. Box 587
Brainerd, MN 56401

ISBN 978-0-9848735-0-0

Table of Contents

Bred HyCouncil Public Library
San Diego County Division

Original Transcript: 1550 B.C.E. King Lycaon
Translation by Damarchus Proudfoot 1880

The Gift of Change

On a land of one mass, an earth of one whole, life existed. No mountain nor river dared to separate the creatures that had since time everknown lived in harmony.

All in one, the world lived as desert, forest, and plain on a single continent. To be in a constant state of change, as it can no longer sustain, its mountains rose and flattened, while its rivers slithered in new directions like the very creatures of the land. Weather too brought the comings and goings of the seasons.

Shifting occurred among the animals as well and they had little to complain about. There were as many sunny days as there were rainy. Big or small; furred, feathered, or scaled; animals had a shared skin. When they wore this coat of flesh, they called themselves "the Commons," and it was used between kinds to settle conflicts that arose amongst differing groups.

Then a time for stability came. The earth was unfinished and sought completion. No more could the seasons come and go as quickly. A mountain altogether could be a tiresome thing to move, but if there was to be any rest for the earth, then it would have to make the land shape more permanent. But if there could only be one shape, then the earth had a difficult choice to make.

It did not wish to give up the deserts, forests, or grassy plains, but it could not keep them on one body. Unwilling to make a sacrifice among the lands, it used some of its rivers to break itself into regions which would then drift apart.

The animals did not know about this decision and were therefore separated not by kind but by perchance. Some of them did well in their regions or learned to live in a way that the land allowed them to. Others did not find adaptation so easily and put on their Common skins to enable their survival. Not all creatures found the form a preferable way to survive and went about in their flesh of fur, feathers, or scales. Then in choosing a way by which to live, the Commons and the animals forgot each other.

Some could not remember how to become Common, while others forgot how to become animal. Still, others saw the advantages in remembering both forms and continued to live in a manner that would require both a common and animal skin.

For those who did not, the gift of change was soon forgotten, never to be relearned.

This history of Hybrids has been taken from the San Diego County Division of the Bred HyCouncil Public Library databases and should not be distributed or re-printed without permission from the state council department.

1
A Spirit Changed

The weather had been beautiful all day for this time of year. Winter in San Diego, a city on the southern coastline of California, usually never yielded any sunlight. The day was drizzly, which is to say that the people carried around their umbrellas but did not open them. Not entirely overcast with a gray haze, the sky opened up in areas called "Heaven's light." The name had its inspiration from the manner in which the sun burst through the clouds in a smudge of golden rays.

In older times, people believed that angels gathered around these openings to smile upon the earth and a section of heaven truly did give itself to the planet. It was more of a Christian idea for anyone who believed. Achak, however, did not.

To be more accurate, Achak did not know what to believe in or if he believed in anything at all. By modern ideals, his religion was not recognized, though mainly because it did not have a name.

Fundamental to all religions, this one had a Story of Creation, an explanation of how the earth came about and was conceived. But unlike an organized religion, there were no gatherings and no churches. In his culture, the beliefs were passed from generation to generation and shared by the wisest and oldest of the tribe members, which in this era meant the senior family member. In Achak's tribe (household), the beliefs were passed down by Grandpa: Guyupi Twinfang, from his father's side.

Rituals were still held in the midst of the backyard with a bonfire. Grandpa gathered around the flames and threw into them a powder that would make them splash with sparks or rise in suspense. It had all been a very exciting event when Achak was a child. Grandpa's chanting voice, the dancing flames, the puppeteer shadows, and the stories, now, at the age of seventeen, had diminished to some effect.

Like any young spirit his age, Achak did not have time to think upon the Story of Creation which had occurred so many millennia ago while his own life—his own creation, youth, and growth—was happening here and now.

Quite happening, Achak thought bitterly and made a couple of swipes at the corner of his lip to check that there was no more blood dripping from his mouth. The spot where his thumb touched was dry, but he could feel the swelling skin that had closed the wound. It was a wonder none of his teeth had been knocked out when Donovan Parsons had landed the perfect punch.

Not alone in his misgivings, Sirena too had in some way incurred a fresh scratch down the side of her face. But unlike Achak, who had no intention of returning to the San Diego High campus at the end of the lunch break, Sirena kept up a cheerfulness that was not to be spoiled by her new blemish. Laughing and smiling, she tagged along with him down the streets of local neighborhoods and did not ask uncomfortable questions about why he was ditching the after-lunch class periods.

She was an odd girl, Achak could say in the least of Sirena's appearances. She always seemed to come out of nowhere, like she had just dropped from the sky. And indeed, their first meeting had been just as random a visit.

"Twinfang? I like it. The name's so expressive," Sirena had commented on Achak's surname after school on one miserable rainy Friday the previous month.

Not only had he been taken by surprise to hear it, but the idea that anyone—a girl—was standing right behind him while he was opening his school locker was something of a shocker as well.

His fingers slid off the binding of a book that he would be taking home for the weekend. He did not know what to expect when he turned around, but whatever he had imagined—in those brief moments it took his neck and body to react—Sirena did not meet those expectations.

Girl or not, the fact remained that her gender had not been the remotest of startling features for Achak to discover about Sirena. Yet, she must have had a bigger voice than body to have addressed him in such an outspoken manner. Still, the loudest of her features was not her voice, but her looks.

Achak's eyes leapt straight from Sirena's bright crimson hair, then on to the thick black layer of mascara around her eyes, to a silver chain of winged skulls, and so forth down her long black drapery of gothic material until they reached the tips of her black buckle boots.

"Why?" Achak had asked himself aloud, then quickly reformed the question in his head. "Why—if her hair was so vibrant with color—did she not incorporate those colors into her clothes?" But he had found his answer when he took a second look at her and caught sight of the dark layer of hair underlying the red.

She was not the type he would normally have talked with, but that did not keep him from feeling both the awkwardness and embarrassment of his silent response. As of yet, he had spoken no words to the girl who had addressed him even though she had clearly given him a compliment, as there could be no confusing his last name with those of his classmates surrounding him.

"Sirena." She stuck out her hand and introduced herself.

Achak shook it and introduced himself by his first name, which he hoped would stop her from addressing him as "Twinfang." He was not in the least bit taken in by her charm, but as she kept pursuing him with more interest than anyone else had ever shown him, he decided not to blow her off. This, of course, was Achak's biggest mistake—which he regretted later.

"What year are you?" he asked curiously of her. "I've never seen you in any of my classes."

"No? Well that's because I don't go here." Then before Achak could raise an eyebrow to wonder what a teenager was doing in the hall of a school she did not attend, Sirena hurriedly added, "I was meeting a friend."

Just who that friend was—as she did not speak the name—Achak never found out.

"Twinfang, have you ever considered what kind of an animal your name could be associated with?"

Achak continued to listen to Sirena while they walked down the hall together, despite his earlier hopes that she would stop calling him by his last name.

"Shouldn't we be looking out for your friend?" He had tried in vain to change the subject, but she either did not hear or ignored him in order to carry on the fascinating discussion of animal surnames.

"But then you get into expression like 'lion heart' and I just don't see the resemblance," Sirena argued on this Friday and continued making circles around Achak in the same manner she had on their first meeting. He had grown used to her doing this by now and did not dizzy himself in trying to keep his eyes upon her. Around and around she went, both on her feet and in her ramblings of bestial associations.

"I mean, I know lions are fierce and everything," she said, avoiding a woman with her poodle as she circled around to Achak's left.

They were walking alongside a green patch of grass that began a community park whose playground was desecrated with splinters.

"But they can also be brutish, can't they?" Sirena continued her rant of lions. "And wouldn't it make more sense for nobility to want to refer to themselves as being both strong and tame. I'd rather think that the eagle was a better choice, but something like a wolf has a better pack life than a lion's pride."

"Yes, but aren't wolves generally seen with a negative connotation to them?" Achak added to the discussion. "Little Red Ridinghood, the Three Little Pigs."

Sirena flapped her vibrant red hair from side to side impatiently and pulled Achak onto the grass towards the playground. "Not in your culture, though, are they?"

Achak hated when she referred to his bloodline so directly and did not answer. It was a difference in his roots that he himself did not give any special attention to and expected the same from other people. But Sirena always had a way of slipping in a comment or two about his roots that not only made him feel different, but that he should be locked up in a lab somewhere for study.

He knew better than to voice such feelings aloud as Sirena would only laugh at him—laugh in such a high pitched shrill as Achak wished she would cease from doing now.

They had both pulled off under the shade of a tree, where Sirena released the hand she had been holding and left Achak to watch her display.

Hearing her voice rise and crack, Achak had begun to wonder whether it hurt her stomach to shriek so hard. He could not explain the change that occurred in her. One minute she was bowing over—bawling in private amusement. Her mirth carried an icy blast over Achak's spine, then the next minute Achak was gaping upon the black feathers that sprouted from Sirena's pale neck and staring nearsighted at the red-headed vulture that drifted down in her place.

An impossible flicker of the skull neck charm flashed off of the vulture's chest, then Achak's vision went as black as the feathers he had just been staring at. And her laughter, a shriek from the buzzard's wide-open beak, died away with the sight of it.

One Week Previous

2
In the Beginning, there was Manu...

Sirena had hair of a vibrant red that clashed considerably with her long black drapery of clothing. Loose long sleeves hung from her wrists while chains jingled from each of her many pant pockets. Slowly, she pushed open a white door and stepped into a room of immense grandeur. In her arms purred a black cat that she hushed with a brief stroke. Someone was standing at the other end of the room and showed no signs of wanting to be interrupted. Sirena listened, but made no attempt to approach.

" 'Should the human race think itself so superior to bees, ants, and elephants as to be put in this unique relation to its maker?'" said the man, Manu Firdaus, while making an attempt to wipe away his own fingerprints from the silver tray in his hands.

Slowly, he rotated the tray with the cloth between his fingers and gazed down at his own reflection. Sirena went unnoticed as Manu continued his proclamations, unaware that there was anyone else around to hear him. A turban, the color of sandstone, crowned his head. His face was of smooth copper, but the decades had seeped through the corners of his eyes and mouth where they showed the creases of his mortality. However, age had not depreciated the appearance by which gold shined from the inner lining of his suit and flashed with excitement in the beads of his dark eyes as he spoke. It was with this sparkle anew that he had whispered the words with too much fervor to keep them to himself.

"Am I my brother's keeper?"

"I was under the impression that most people believed it was God or some other divinity to control the shape of this world."

Manu's turbaned head came up to meet the face that watched him.

Sirena smiled while Manu was made to stare at her first through the mirror, then to turn around to glimpse her in her entirety. She set the black cat on the floor, which scampered under one of the chairs, and strode forward. Her dark sleeves flapped eerily at her sides as she moved towards the center rug. From her red hair, black feathers were released and drifted in a spiral trail behind her. "I'm so glad that we can agree on who has the real power, but I might argue about this being wholly man's dominion."

"Always with the jokes," Manu hastened to disengage. He lowered the tray in his hands and began to move toward a dresser against the wall. "Where are the manners and modesties in a lady so young? Not so much as a knock and an 'excuse me' to announce your arrival."

Manu set the silver tray next to a vase. Disturbing the napery, he made to straighten the wrinkled fabric that lay beneath. When he turned around, Sirena grabbed the loose fabric of her pant legs and curtsied in the least of lady-like exaggerations that could be performed in her gothic attire.

"Charmed," Manu sneered. "Really, Sirena. I think you should make the change permanent if you're not going to make the slightest attempt to be human."

Sirena had to restrain herself from scoffing at the remark, not because she took any offense to it personally, but what did the Man before her really understand about being human while surrounded by all this luxury. She looked around at the grandness of the room where furnishings stood in their unused state. Even antiques of carved wood were polished and shined to a perfect finish.

"Sir-ree-na. Sirena," Manu cajoled to her with unnecessary repetition. "Look at you. Not so much as a breath of life within. I'd almost think you were suffocating."

Letting her voice be carried over the walls, Sirena shrieked a forceful laugh and stopped almost as abruptly as she had started. The room was left in a sudden ring that quickly dissolved.

Looking offended by her outburst, Manu at once readjusted himself to meet her again with a posture more befitting of one so nobly suited.

"Quiet already?" he smiled, having fully regained himself. "I see that you are not at all at your usual level of energy."

He turned back to the silver platter and began straightening out the cloth again, but there was a mirror set above the dresser by which he could continue to watch Sirena. She had not moved from the place she had taken in the center of the rug.

"Perhaps life does come in shorter breaths what with all the work you have taken. Or maybe you are deprived of sleep. The rings around your eyes get darker every time I see you."

Sirena tried to smile but she could not stop her lips from giving a slight quiver as they curved up her cheek. "It's mascara," she explained and Manu nodded.

"Granted," he replied. "I am relieved to hear that." Manu stayed near enough to his props to let the silence fill the distance and make the room appear even more immaculate.

Shifting herself, Sirena felt uncomfortably out of place. Draped in black, she stood as a caped phantom would in a masquerade ball. And it was true that there was something masquerade-ish about the room, which was not without a theme.

Upon the many foundations of wood, the fragile shapes of glass, mirror, and ivory, there were animal likenesses, either of the being itself or its coated patterns. Not just leopard and zebra, but there stood gigantic forms of elephant and rhino. Nor was the doorway near Manu of a usual shape. Its archway frames were actually supported by two oak giraffes whose necks intertwined at the top. Bear Claws balanced the wooden legs of chairs and desks, while the simpler plate-holders could have the support of hooves or horseshoes.

Sirena thought she had caught a glimpse of a unicorn in the dome mural above her, but did not make a second inspection after greeting Manu and gave up the idea to a hopeless romantic's portrayal of the Garden of Eden.

A very unpleasant and disquieting thought occurred to Sirena as she caught sight of the Ganesha statue, a four-armed god with an elephant head, propped in front of a gold-rimmed mirror hanging between two windows. She had just been trying to guess which of these most exotic creatures Manu might have kinship with when the vastness of her surroundings took effect and nearly drowned her. She suppressed a shiver before Manu could steal a glance back in the mirror.

So here she was: a scavenger of no particular talent in the trade, yet Sirena was standing in the presence of what was probably the wealthiest patron her sort could be affiliated with and she would be expected to act "the part." She had character, that much she was certain about herself. Her gothic attire and boisterous personality had in all likeliness earned her the place where she now stood and her first interview with Manu, but she would have to keep up appearances in order to receive the full payoff.

Sirena had thus far taken up a tone of indifference with Manu in all of her assignments, despite the unbelievable amount of money that lay in the balance. Having requested several progress reports with her, Manu had never shown her an inkling of disappointment.

Now was different. The room was different and Manu was quiet. But to find a more solid source for her discomfort, Sirena blamed the creeping goose-bumps more reasonably on the constant stares of animals glaring at her from their stationary posts.

It felt horribly like paranoia to have so many lifeless eyes upon her as if the decorations were comprised of mounted heads rather than art sculptures. The mirrors did not help to shorten the depth of the room or reduce the number of faces in it, which made Sirena grateful for when Manu finally moved away from one.

With a single tilt of his body, Manu had the whole of the room under his command, but he merely walked back towards his desk, still across the way from Sirena.

"Wine?" His hand gestured toward a bottle and two flipped glasses that sat on another silver platter on his desk.

Released from her spellbind, Sirena took a deep breath and let her heart rate slow. "No thanks. I'm underage."

"Exactly why I would not have expected you to refuse," Manu chortled. He poured a glass for himself and remained standing by his desk, then took a sip and said, "Oh well. Let's hear it then. How goes the relationship?"

Sirena made a few braver steps towards the desk and found a comfortable stance with her arms folded across her waist. Not wanting to look entirely on the defensive, she quickly stretched out her arm and picked up a geode paperweight only to switch it continuously between hands.

"I can get *him* to talk, but I don't think he's interested in a girl like me." She spoke of love and losses with no real emotion behind her voice, but simply impassivity.

"Maybe you could make more of an effort to see him as your type," Manu suggested with the slightest hint of conviction.

"As if!" Sirena reviled. "I've tried to kiss him. How much more compatible can I be?" She reached into the pockets of her loose dark pants and pulled out a brochure, which resulted in more droppings of feathers on the rich magenta carpet.

"I see you've found a location by which to proceed?" Manu looked upon the brochure in Sirena's hand eagerly.

"I thought you might like to have a look at it." Sirena dared to move into Manu's space. Placing the brochure in his hand, she closed his fist around it as though presenting a keepsake that would serve as a memento. "It might interest you," she said encouragingly.

Manu unfolded its pages to the feature centerfold. Text running up, down, and across, Manu even scanned over the map key looking for Sirena's promise of intrigue. Then in a harsh tone, he said:

"Sirena, I am already disappointed that I am reading through a brochure. Such marketables hint upon a tourist attraction and such places are not suitable for the more discretionary parts of business. I see, too, that this place is located right next to the 'World Famous' San Diego Zoo. Consider not including audiences, the next time you scour for locations."

Sirena's head shook from side to side, dropping feathers as she whipped her hair around.

"You're missing the beauty of it," she argued flatly.

"Beauty does not come in arrest warrants, which is exactly what will come out of—"

"Museums?" she twisted. "Or how about Museums of Man?"

Her words quieted Manu who took up the brochure again and re-examined the list of attractions. Sure enough, he found a Museum of Man under its headlines.

"Alright," he said. "If you think you can isolate him under that symbol, then I will not be of hindrance. Just don't make it public."

Sirena's face lit up. "Then it's settled?"

"It is decided," Manu corrected with a tone that suggested the agreement was to be described in different terms: his terms. But he looked at Sirena with a somewhat softer expression. "You are in rare form today to have put so much thought into this."

She turned her head away from Manu to make her lips unreadable behind a drape of crimson before smiling to herself.

"Now that's just rude!" Manu exhorted, his bemused face contorting into rage.

Sirena looked shocked then spun around on her heels. Fixed upon the door from which she had entered, she death-locked the intruder with a mad glint in her charcoal eyes.

Caped in a white labcoat, the bespectacled man approached. With his hair greased back, his forehead looked enormous under the widow's peak of receding gray strands.

"Sss-sorry," he hastened to say. His hands waved out apologetically.

"You have a way of slithering about here," Manu eyed him coldly. "Please excuse us, Sirena. I believe Dr. Coral has something important to say."

Both Sirena's and Manu's eyes were fixed on the doctor, hers gloweringly and his expectant.

"No-no," Dr. Coral said, unfastening a few buttons on his coat to let more of his day clothes show. They were not nearly as impressive as Manu's but were comprised of a simple red collar shirt and a black tie. He acted as though he had just come off the job somewhere and looked ready to loosen his collar, but refrained from doing so in front of Manu.

"Reeeally," Dr. Coral assured as he walked past the desk. "I have no intention of ssstaying. I just sssaw a few new facsses down the hall and thought I would meet more when I heard voicsses..."

Sirena looked to Manu sharply, her hair ablaze, but Manu waved his hand in dispassion, his eyes fixed on Coral.

"Now really, Ladon! You make my interviewees sound secretive, but I am none too interested in what you think about them. Listen in, if you would like, but first Sirena has some things to report."

There was a soft mew and Sirena found the unlucky cat twisting around her legs and affectionately rubbing. She bent over and scooped it up into her arms, stroked its shiny coat a few times, then ignored it.

"So is the myth true?" She stared into Manu's face with all seriousness in her narrowed black eyes. "An animal will always be able to recognize its own kind?"

The cat in her arms made a whine for attention and she pulled it away from herself staring at it mutinously, but did nothing more than examine it. "What if you're wrong? If he's not as ancient as you say, do we send him back?"

With her last words, Sirena released the cat from her hands and let it fall to the ground, only to land on all fours. It scrambled off and Sirena did not care to wonder which piece of furniture it would hide itself under this time.

"Careful!" Manu warned and out of nowhere a fluff of gray fur ran across the magenta carpet in pursuit of the cat. Try as it might, the pup could not dig its paws far enough under the armchair.

"What's that one for?!" Sirena shrieked and hurried over the armchair to reclaim her pet.

"That," Manu answered, while Sirena pulled the pup by the tail and reached out for the cat cowering under the recliner, "is for a retriever."

"Retriever?" Sirena exasperated as though she had been offended. "Am I not to be alone on this?"

Manu met the dark shadows of her eyes and answered in a single word: "No."

"Who—" She began but Manu held up his hand for her to stop speaking.

"You'll be introduced, but first I need to know what you've learned."

Uncertainty filled her mind as she wished to continue arguing, but looked instead to Dr. Coral out of discontent. Her worst fears were confirmed when she caught the good doctor's smile as he slinked towards the giraffe archway in his unnoticed exit.

Sirena scowled, but the hardness in her face vanished as she heard her name called again by Manu. She took a seat in the armchair from which the cat had sheltered and kept the feline purring under her arms.

"I've learned," she said in a tone that was unable to hide her scandalized feelings, "that he's not too fond of cats, even if they are of him. Or maybe he just doesn't like animals in general."

"I see," Manu commented patiently. "So the boy has about as much interest in preserving the wildlife on this planet as you do. You have something in common. This is good."

"I thought you wanted to know what I've learned about him," Sirena said behind gritted teeth.

"I do, but I am not so much interested in what he thinks about animals as I am in what animals think of him. Remember, he belongs to a species that has been absent from nature for some time, so his human interests are not as important to me. Tell me what an animal's instincts have told you about him."

Sirena looked down again at the cat in her arms. "*She* sort of hinted that he was a compatible sort. Rubbed around his legs and that sort of thing." Then Sirena's tone hardened as she said, "But I don't think it matters since this cat gets along with me as well."

"Not true." Manu grabbed the back of an armchair across from Sirena. "The feline only gets along with you because I made you spend some time with her. First impressions are different. She likes to be around her own kind."

"That still doesn't mean he's... you know." Unable to find the right words, Sirena muttered, "He could be anything cat-related."

"Yes," Manu acknowledged. "Bobcat, mountain lion—he could be any one of a number of species." Manu smiled over Sirena's frustration.

Her bottom lip was tucked away as she bit down on it.

"That is where you come in."

The direct mention aroused something inside of Sirena that made her sit up straight. Trying not to show herself as being too eager, she massaged the cat before staring up again at Manu.

"Surely, you can sense the domination of a species for yourself?" Manu excited hungrily. "His height, his weight, his build. It all generally gives you an inclination of his species. What of his appetite?"

"Big," Sirena answered. "Carnivorous."

"Yes," Manu encouraged. "You have gotten close to him, have you not? As well as a few other things I could mention, such as going on dates and holding hands.... He has trusted you."

"Yes," Sirena replied with bitter sarcasm in her air. "He's trusted me. But that is about all—And don't think I haven't tried. I put my arms around him and he pushes me away."

"Come now!" Manu bellowed. "Are you so timid of a mere lad?"

Manu moved out from behind his chair and came over to Sirena's. She froze up as quickly as though a cobra had made to strike at her.

"Sirena, please tell me that you do more than just make circles around your prey," he whispered harshly above her head.

At once, she winced but did not turn around in her chair to face Manu.

"I don't know what you expect me to tell you." Sirena did her best to stabilize her voice. "I've done what I can. You can't expect me to know what a potentially Jurassic being's tastes would be in."

Manu chuckled and pushed off the chair. Sirena was relieved to see him moving back towards his desk.

"Of course I would not expect you to know Jurassic tastes. Now, go wait in the other room for a moment. I am afraid that I have already left my other guest waiting for much too long—quite rude of me."

Manu pulled open a drawer in his desk, placed his wine glass inside, then pulled out a fresh one, which he tipped to make appear as unused on the platter as the one that Sirena had refused.

"Never mind Dr. Coral," he said in finality to Sirena's retreating back. "And do make yourself comfortable. I will call for you shortly."

No sooner had Sirena walked out than Dr. Coral walked back in, wanting to have a word with Manu. But as he stepped through the giraffe archway, so too did the new arrival come through the doors across and mirror the doctor's entrance. Both men paused to stare at each other, but Manu came between their gaze.

"I apologize for keeping you waiting, Mr. Gray, but this will only take a brief moment." Manu gestured for the arrival to take up an armchair, then turned his back to meet Dr. Coral.

"Lapidar would be fine," the guest called out to Manu's backside.

The new arrival was not particularly fond at being addressed by his surname, but he accepted Manu's token nonetheless. And anyway, he thought he would need some time to adjust to the room that he had entered. His first inclination while walking inside was the same as Sirena's had been:

He stared up at the ceiling and took in all the animals on the painted mural. Surrounded by just as many dimensionless eyes, he found his place on the rug as spellbinding as though he had just stepped onto the arena of an amphitheater. With his sideburns and lengthy browncoat, Lapidar knew he was out of place. He had the rugged looks of a Westerner, like someone who was perhaps still living in the golden era of mines and railroads. The room had even made him self-conscious about his own assortment of gray hair that had grown amidst the brown at the youthful age of twenty-nine.

Then Lapidar heard the whimpering by his feet and looked down to see the pup that had formerly pursued Sirena's cat. Knowing neither of Sirena or the cat, Lapidar bent down and petted the small creature over the head and it began to wag its tail. He glanced at Manu, who still had his back turned and looked nowhere near finishing his talk with the doctor. Lapidar lowered himself into a seated position on the rug. Crossing his legs, he took the pup into his lap and allowed it to playfully gnaw at his fingers.

The same assortment of brown and gray yielded itself around the pup's fur just as it did over Lapidar's thickly layered scalp.

“It was generousss of them to contribute a bit of the country'sss budget, wouldn't you sssay,” the man with a labcoat spoke.

“I did not need the government's funding,” came a voice of power. Manu stood opposite the doctor, his turban and black suit empowering when compared to the white labcoat. “But,” Manu continued, “I could not refuse the reputation that the government's funding gave me. After all, how efficient could Domestica really be with animal rights activists picketing in front of its yard?” A thoughtful smile crept over Manu's face.

“Shall we get on with businessss then?” the doctor proceeded with caution. He might have spat in his procession of hisses.

“Of course, doctor. Why else would I 'ave summoned my anthropologist?”

“What exactly is it that you need from my area of expertissse?”

“What percentage of accuracy can you guarantee me that *he* is the one?”

“I can almossst guarantee that—”

“I need a percentage!”

“Z-zero, sssir,” the doctor hesitated to answer. “It will always be zero when I am forcssed to work with un-dateable findingsss.” He leaned toward an apologetic tone, but his voice still came out firm and assertive, perhaps even daring to show some annoyance in the questioning of his research. "The bessst I can do is go by tribal locations and movementsss, but admittedly thisss name does show potential."

Manu held his hand up before the doctor could continue. "That is all." He turned his attention to the other individual in the room, and the doctor followed his eyes with as much interest all the way to the place where Lapidar had taken a seat on the carpet.

Lapidar's eyes were directed upon the pup as he pretended not to have overheard Manu's conversation, while in fact he had.

Setting the pup on the floor, Lapidar stood up to meet the approaching men. Manu reached him first and directed his attention to the doctor who shook Lapidar's hand.

"Mr. Gray, I would like you to meet Dr. Coral, a friend and my finest researcher here on Domestica Animal Sanctuary."

"*Ssso thisss* is our little bounty hunter," Dr. Coral spoke with some amusement that Lapidar found offensive. The doctor looked from Manu's nodding head back to Lapidar.

Noticing the colors Coral exhibited between the flaps of his labcoat, Lapidar began a rhyme that went with the doctor's striped tie.

"*If red touches yellow, it can kill a fellow...*" Lapidar muttered the riddle as far as he could remember, but when he stopped reciting, he knew he had the doctor's full attention.

Giving Lapidar a thorough look-over, Dr. Coral diagnosed his findings: "The mutt ssseems capable, ssso long as he can keep his tail from curling between his legs. Let'sss just hope the *missus* approves."

Lapidar had to restrain himself from lunging out at the doctor. Coral made a nodded bow and exited through the giraffe archway, while Lapidar puffed out his chest at once so as to relieve himself of the doctor's bitter presence. Left alone with Manu in the grand perimeters of the room, Lapidar shifted his weight to one side, loosening his stance in readiness for business talk.

Manu did not need to make nearly as much effort to assert his authoritative charm when a slight change of expression could silence a room full of board members. So his illustrious power again put a halt to Lapidar's re-positioning. A mere smile and a flicker of the eyes seemed to bring the vast domain of the room into a ringing silence.

Lapidar stared straight back into Manu's twinkling eyes, not daring to blink or focus elsewhere. At this moment, Lapidar knew that he would not be the one to break the silence, not when Manu could pace by him, breaking the gaze, only to meet it again at a further distance.

"You've heard of this place, correct?" Manu continued to eye Lapidar with interest.

"In brief," Lapidar admitted, scanning his environment as though he only just arrived. "I believe our earlier discussion enlightened me to the services I can provide for Domestica. I wasn't aware there was going to be a pop quiz."

"No, no. You misunderstood," Manu said in an unperturbed voice. His thick accent made it especially difficult to recognize a change in tone. "I only want to ensure that you know the standards of your mission."

"Even I have standards."

Manu ignored him. "The specimen is no good to me dead," he began.

"Then we're in agreement. I wouldn't kill a boy and I wouldn't capture one for someone else to either."

"I want him alive!" Manu interrupted the insolence. "Now, I knew what areas you specialized in before I made my offer. But as far as tracking people down, you were still 'World Famous.'"

"That's funny," Lapidar rebuffed. "I was only aware of being 'The best in the West.'"

"Word travels fast." Manu turned to his desk and removed a bottle of wine from the silver platter. Flipping over a couple of crystal goblets, he began pouring the wine into two glasses. He passed one over to Lapidar. After taking a sip out of his own, Manu continued to speak. "Just bring the boy here and I'll figure out the rest."

Lapidar nodded. "Then do I get a name?"

"Twinfang," Manu responded almost incomprehensibly.

Lapidar spat some wine back into his glass. "I thought you said he was human," his words rushed out with concern.

"Native American," Manu spoke sternly as though he too understood the important complications if his mission involved anything but a human. "Believe me, I am well aware of the risks if he were a Hybrid."

Lapidar left the rest of his concerns unspoken. He could not expect the man he dealt business with to have taken all matters into consideration. Manu was the sort of thick wallet figurehead that paid to have others think for him. And

Lapidar would be well paid—so much so that he did not mind working out the finer details himself—for such a simple task. The abduction of a mere human boy seemed so basic that Lapidar's only issues arose from his confidence—perhaps his overconfidence in having overlooked a problem that he might encounter. Stay in human form and hold the kid at gunpoint like a normal criminal and everything should run smoothly, he assured himself.

Yet summoning a renowned and costly bounty hunter of Lapidar's caliber exceeded the norm. The extent of measures that Manu took to keep this abduction between a select few could only mean that the assignment involved high risks. Perhaps Manu could be viewed as another over-cautious political figure that wasted no expense to protect his interests and reputation. After all, should the Bred HyCouncil or the Coexistence Coalition learn of Manu's involvement with the abduction of a human boy, the consequences would be severe and Manu's entire life's work, Domestica, would fall to ruins. Could this be Manu's reasoning for taking such overprotective measures in hiring Lapidar for the assignment or could Lapidar have been hired for other reasons?

Regardless of his suspicions, Lapidar shook on the closing deal: $2 million in exchange for one boy. Lapidar could count his blessings for a financially secure future. He made no effort to hide his pleasure from Manu once the first half of his non-negotiable rewards, stacked in hundred dollar bills, was passed over in a snakeskin briefcase.

Can't be real, Lapidar rubbed the sides of the briefcase affectionately. His smirk dwindled after counting and securing the funds. He returned to his professional composure to address Manu once more on a serious note.

"Shall I bring the boy here?" he asked, looking critically over the furnishings of the room which, in all its luxury, looked like an inappropriate location to conduct the messier parts of business. "You're not so fond of prisons or interrogation rooms are you?" Lapidar mocked the for-decoration-only appearance of the antique and fashionably outdated chairs that were pulled up to a short glass-top table.

Manu took brief amusement in his words before answering the question. "Yes, I'll await you here, but not in this room." Manu returned another smile. "There are one hundred and twenty rooms in this structure, Mr. Gray. What makes you think they all look identical to this one?"

"Then I only have one final question for you. Whom shall I meet at the door?"

"I've already arranged for someone," Manu quickly cut in. "Sirena!" he called out to the giraffe archway.

Lapidar expected to see a secretary, but his face was wiped clean of a smile when he saw that the woman who entered was no woman at all, but a young girl. The child who walked into the room did not carry herself like a secretary, which could only mean one other unthinkable arrangement.

With a sneer on his face, Lapidar met the new arrival and her swiftness on the job in the lowest of regards. He did not so much as utter a greeting or shake her hand when she reached Manu's side.

Her face held an expression that looked just as disgusted as Lapidar's. However, her nose un-scrunched and figure re-straightened itself before Manu could notice. From what Lapidar could tell, Manu had only seen a look of indifference steadied on the young girl's face.

"Mr. Gray, this is Sirena. She'll be accompanying you on this assignment."

In contrast to Lapidar's stout figure, Sirena was a short sixteen-year-old red-head with both the pale skin color and scrawny physique that said this girl had never worked out in the sun before. However, her dark layers beneath crimson hair and the gothic apparel, from skull-chain necklace to high-heeled combat boots, told Lapidar that this was no granddaughter of Manu's.

"Surely, you must be joking." Lapidar took one last look at the girl's rebellious appearance before meeting Manu's face. "Tell her to wait here until I return," he said irritably.

"You WILL take her along with you," Manu said sternly, leering in amusement at the command of his own voice.

"I will not baby-sit—"

"NO! But you will sit, heel, and heed my orders," Manu barked back. "This operation will run my way or not at all."

With Manu's cold eyes upon him, withdrew Lapidar like the unmistakable lapdog that he was.

"Are we clear on this issue?"

"Yes," Lapidar answered, his voice tart with annoyance.

"Good. Now get out of my sight."

Lapidar marched straight out with his briefcase, but Sirena hesitated to follow suit.

"THE BOTH OF YOU!"

In the hallway, Lapidar watched Sirena storm out of the room and slam the door with a momentary glower at the knob before turning away. As though she sensed his entertainment over her juvenile outburst, Sirena looked in Lapidar's direction with a piercing glare.

"What?!" she demanded, then rolled her eyes and shoved past. Lapidar followed her lead, but had barely moved six steps when he decided to walk at a slower pace.

"Youngins," Lapidar muttered while Sirena strolled away. He had had just about enough of keeping his remarks to himself or perhaps he just hoped that Sirena would overhear him. But she didn't. He looked at her backside some ways down the hall and frowned. Instead of keeping pace with her, he elected to pause rather than follow in her footsteps. Examining the corridor some more so that it would not be so obvious he wished to put some distance between himself and his partner, Lapidar caught sight of other figures waiting nearby.

Two boys of Sirena's age stood at attention against the wall. In their dark hair and copper-toned skin, they very nearly resembled the pottery plants that also lined the hallway. In over-hearing Lapidar's comment, they turned their keen eyes to him and flashed him a glowing set of yellow stares.

Something Lapidar had heard on the streets came back to him and he began reciting it aloud:

"If red touches yellow, it can kill a fellow. If red touches black, it's a friend of Jack."

The boys broke their postures and looked at each other with their grins, cackling all the while.

Lapidar spoke again, "Jack and Jill, went up the hill..."

Again the two boys went hysteric and began to converse with each other. Their language was not English, but they seemed to understand enough to have become excited with what Lapidar was saying.

"Know them?" Sirena asked. She had stopped some distance down the hallway and turned around to see what was keeping her "partner."

Lapidar did not expect her to be so informed, let alone formal, but Sirena went ahead and introduced him to the two boys.

"They're 'The Jacks.' The taller one is Ék (ache) Jack, or Jack Ék, I forget which. And the shorter one is Dô Jack."

Sirena turned on her heel and proceeded to the elevator. The red doors chimed and she entered. Lapidar, however, held behind for a brief few moments. He felt certain that the next time he would come across The Jacks, it would be on less friendly terms.

3
Tradition

Through the sliding glass door, Achak watched his mother sitting on a wooden chair on the back porch. He had excused himself from participating with Grandpa in the fire dance in order to get himself something to drink. Delaying his return time to its maximum potential, Achak sipped from his glass of soda at a modest pace. He was in no hurry to join what remained of his immediate family in the backyard. His little sister Tehya was wearing a paper bag over her head like a mask and twirling like an uncoordinated ballerina around the open flames. Grandpa, of course, stood on one side of the fire, raising his arms up and down, twisting his wrists so that his palms alternately faced toward then against the flames. Every now and then the old man would dig into a pouch strapped to his belt and pick out a fist-full of dirt, tossing it into the flames. His words were incomprehensible incantations of "Hey ya-e ye-ah yah yah," that he half sung for all the neighbors to hear and close their windows.

Achak felt embarrassed just watching his grandpa and sister dance and sing around a backyard bonfire, making him all the more grateful for the glass door that stood between him and the spectacle. Raising the soda to his lips as he watched, Achak noted how remarkable it was that no one ever complained about the noise or the fire. Achak couldn't be the only one to argue with his mother about the absurdity of lighting a fire in the backyard and dancing around it with feathers and face paint while other families were having barbeques. From this outlook, Achak frowned at his own reflection which stood out of the darkened glass door.

Gratefully, he did not have to stare back at a painted face, but there was still the matter of the silver chain around his neck. Grandpa had given him an arrowhead pendant upon arrival, which Achak felt obligated to wear to avoid offending him. The only other boy who wore jewelry that Achak could think of was a classmate named Donovan, whom Achak refused to impersonate. Donovan had his one pierced ear like a pirate and a tiger's-eye nugget fashioned on a class ring that bore the San Diego High crest engraved upon its gold band. Not that Achak was opposed to men wearing necklaces, earrings, or rings in general, but the arrowhead pendant was something of a cultural novelty that had lost its fashion since the coming of tennis shoes and digital watches into the modern world.

The arrowhead had been nicely adapted into the sense of modernity with carved obsidian and a silver casting that held the stone in place, but that was exactly what made it the kind of jewel that Achak would not want to be caught wearing. It called attention to itself and he would not fancy being called a preppy in front of his friend Anthony, or worse, in front of Kitti. So he glowered at his own reflection and beyond it at the bright yellow flames, the silhouette of his grandfather's figure, and the Little Flower dancing around it with her paper bag mask.

A Rain Dance seemed like a pointless ritual in San Diego where the sky was overcast 350 days out of the year. If it rained within the next three days, which it had a high probability of doing around this time of year, Tehya would write it in the books as another one of Grandpa's miracles. She had a knack for keeping record of the dates that the ancient magic had worked and then reciting them for Achak whenever he spoke ill of Grandpa's practices. This was not helped at all by their mother who invited Grandpa over quite as often as Tehya asked for, thereby encouraging the chanting and beliefs that had so often forced Achak to make up his own stories that he would be spending the night at Anthony's.

Still gazing out the sliding door, he was well beyond his own reflection in thought.

"Achak?"

He started at hearing his name. Ms. Twinfang was standing at his side looking at him, her head tilted curiously, and she was smiling at him.

"You've been here for a while. Don't you want to come back out for the end of the ritual?" Her words were only half spoken in innocence. She knew how Achak really felt about her father-in-law's rituals. She was also used to this routine of having to plead with her son to participate. So Achak knew that her kind tone was another attempt to get him to come back outside. For this, Achak felt bad, knowing that he caused his mom a lot of headache when she was just trying to keep the peace in the family.

Mother and son sighed in unison. Achak smiled with some amusement at having noticed the shared frustration. His mom was too engulfed with staring beyond the glass door to notice that Achak had made a brief connection with her.

The quiet understanding lingered as Achak tried to see the ritual from her perspective. He didn't think she actually believed in its powers as weather worker or healer, but he began to appreciate the small joy it brought her to watch her little girl dancing and laughing around the bonfire. Between all the fighting he did with Tehya, he forgot how much of a princess she could be or how he used to hold her as a baby and dance with her as a toddler.

If only he had not spoiled the moment for his mother so often in the past, every time he threw a tantrum about his grandfather's silly, make-believe rituals. It had not been fair to her, Achak decided, and nor did he think it fair to Tehya for him to complain when he had once found the evenings of Grandpa's visits as much fun as she now considered them. In seeing his past mistakes, Achak realized that it was time to "straighten-up" and act more tolerable towards these things now that he was almost eighteen. Besides, Grandpa would only stay over for another hour or two anyway.

Achak stepped through the frame of the sliding glass door. "Alright," he sighed, looking back at his mother. "May as well." He took satisfaction in her bewildered expression and walked out, sensing her grateful smile on the back of his head.

"Achak! Achak! Look! Grandpa gave me a stone to hold during the ritual!" Tehya came running up to him as he placed the glass of soda on a small table next to the wooden chair his mother had deserted. He was relieved to see that Tehya no longer wore the paper bag over her head as she approached. She opened her hand to reveal a green polished stone.

"That's a pretty rock." Achak took to sweet talk. Really, Achak just thought it looked like a fragment of his arrowhead.

"Not a rock!" Tehya grimaced. "A stone!" She turned her head away from Achak sharply, dropping her stone-gripping fist back to her side. "Grandpa! Achak thought it was a rock! What did you call the stone again?"

Whether the old man had heard the question or not, he didn't call the name back to her. Achak doubted whether Grandpa could shout out loud enough for Tehya to hear him regardless of whether or not he heard her. Tehya gave Achak one last reproachful look then ran off to ask Grandpa the question from a closer distance.

Achak let out another breath before shrugging off his sister's insult and followed her steps toward the old man, but not nearly at her eager pace.

Still standing by the fire with his mysterious hand gestures, Grandpa left off his chanting as Tehya came running towards him. He backed away from the fire and took to the log that had been set out as a bench. As the old man steadied himself on the log, Teyha opened her fist to him as though Grandpa would need to reexamine the rock to determine its name, while having forgot within the hour what he gave to his only granddaughter. Nevertheless, he looked carefully at the rock in her hand as Achak arrived at her side, then looked up at her face and said it was a "malachite."

Tehya held it between her thumb and forefinger, inspecting the rock for herself before turning to Achak. "See, Achak. It's a mal-a-kite."

He nodded. "I see that. But what does it do?" He tried to make his interest sincere.

Achak didn't think his kind attempts were going as well as he had planned. Tehya scowled at him and clicked her tongue.

"It has spiritual properties, of course," she answered in annoyance. "It brings good fortune and protects its holder—I think from most anything, but Grandpa might have mentioned something about evil spirits."

Achak had to hold his breath to keep from making a smart-aleck response. "So where are you going to keep it?"

"In my pocket. At least until Grandpa puts it onto a chain like yours."

Achak felt the heat come to his face. He didn't know why it had not occurred to him sooner that Grandpa had given him a pendant with particular magical properties—gifts that were probably intended to enhance Achak's skills, wisdom, strength, courage, or whatever else Grandpa felt Achak lacked.

It had never been Grandpa to tell him to tuck in his shirt or go back in the bathroom for a closer shave, but it had been Grandpa whose hand Achak's had bumped whenever Mom asked for help carrying in the groceries. And it had been Grandpa to help them settle into this house when they first moved to San Diego from northern Washington almost five years ago. The old man had spent countless nights staying over and had tucked Tehya into bed. Had Grandpa not still been around, it would have been up to Achak to take up the role as man of the house. Instead, Mom had never sought her son's ears as a source of counsel but always turned to Grandpa Guyapi for that comfort.

Achak had been thirteen at the time: a child, as he was still considered to be. Grandpa had taken to coming around more often than usual lately. Though Mom had said it was by Tehya's requests and good behavior that she was allowed to stay up so late for the bonfires, Achak had dropped down in the kitchen one night where his mother and grandpa were talking in low voices and distinctly overheard Guyapi say that his mother needed more hands around the house to help out. Just that day, they had called a plumber to repair the toilet, which had stopped flushing and it was with some validation that Achak believed Grandpa expected him to be the handyman and fix everything that went wrong around their new home.

The stone was not a token of affection in Achak's opinion, it was an amulet. Grandpa thought that Achak needed the luck or assistance of a stone to help improve some aspect of his life. But just what was that aspect that Grandpa found Achak's skills to be deficient in? It was clear that Grandpa did not consider him a man or an equal, but if there was one virtue connected to this stone that Grandpa felt was essential to his manhood, then Achak had to find out what it was. Pushing his resentfulness aside, Achak spoke again to his sister.

"And what properties does my rock—I mean—stone have?" He asked Tehya in as nonchalant a tone as he could. His voice, hopefully, sounded neither interested nor interrogative.

"Oh, I don't know. I didn't ask." Tehya replied as off-hand as Achak had attempted to sound. Where her attention had previously been focused on the fire, she now kept a peculiar watch on Achak. "Since when have stones interested you anyway?"

"Huh? They don't." Achak cocked his head to the side. If he couldn't get the answer he desired, he wasn't going to waste anymore time pretending to be interested in his sister's stone either. "I was simply inquiring," he said shortly.

"Well stop!" Tehya's voice had become as irksome as Achak's. "Stop acting interested and go play with your model cars or something." With that, she ran to the porch to grab at her mother and left Achak to ponder her outburst.

Now he had done it: he had upset her. "Hey! I was just—drr!" He was sure that she was going to tell Mom what a jerk he's being or something to that effect. Watching her, he waited to hear his mother call out his name, but Tehya appeared only to be showing off her rock. Well, that was a relief.

"Achak," he heard his name called out by a raspy and more elderly voice.

Catching his breath, Achak stood shocked by the voice. Had he been overheard? He forgot that Grandpa was close enough to have listened in on a better part of the argument. Sure he thought that the magical stones and mythology was rubbish, but he didn't really want Grandpa to hear him say it. Achak simply turned to the old man and let the guilt slip down his throat until it churned in his gut.

"Help an old man put out a fire, will you." Grandpa was bending over a bucket of water that had been set beside the log. Achak had the grudging feeling that Grandpa wasn't going to say anything about his remarks, but was going to let self-inflicted guilt eat "the boy" from the inside out. Achak would be left to wallow in regret, not knowing what Grandpa thought about his grandson's defiant words.

Making no apologetic attempt, Achak picked up the bucket without speaking and splashed the water over the fire, extinguishing the flame and it was done.

"Why does Tehya have to be that way?" Achak found himself pacing the living room from wall to wall while his mother sat quietly on the sofa watching the 10 o'clock news. "I mean, what did I say to make her go off on me like that?"

Achak threw out the question more to vent some frustration than to expect an actual answer. Nevertheless, he still expected his mother to come back with some kind of reaction, but the television answered him instead.

"It was more of a celebration today as animal rights activists gathered in front of Manu Firdaus's estates to congratulate him on the recent national approval of Domestica Animal Sanctuary's activities." For a news anchor, Brett Pryson's voice was as oily as his blonde hair. "As you know, Firdaus is the owner of Domestica which holds more than 1200 acres of land and more than 40 imported and endangered species."

"Mom, I'm serious," Achak asserted to the potentially breaking news issue. "Tehya is—"

"Your sister," Ms. Twinfang said in finality. This confirmed Achak's speculation that his mother knew something about the argument from Tehya's mouth and had already taken sides. If she was mad, then she had a funny way of showing it. Her eyes never left the television set.

Achak looked at the man on the screen who seemed to think everything was worth smiling about. "We'll be back with more news after a word from our sponsors."

A golden apple fell from a tree and into a body of water that rippled into the word "HydroMax." Achak saw the clear liquid fill a bottle of water with the golden apple still showing on the label and could not stop the words from spilling out of his mouth.

"I didn't say ANYTHING when she—"

"You didn't have to say anything!" At last, Ms. Twinfang was staring fixedly at her son. "And I'm not mad at you, but you have to understand that Tehya wasn't speaking out of the present moment. You've teased her for a long time about Grandpa's rituals." Achak opened his mouth to argue this, but his mother held up her hand. "And I know you didn't start anything, but that's what she's used to.

People in general aren't quick to forget the mean or hurtful things that others have done to them. It's not in their nature to forgive and forget so easily." His mother allowed a moment's pause. "You'll just have to choose your words a bit more carefully next time."

Despite his mother's considerate tone, Achak returned to his room with a heavy discomfort in his chest. He hadn't told his mother that Grandpa had overheard him deny his interest in magical stone properties. Well, it wasn't so much that Achak didn't take an interest in Grandpa's gift. On the contrary, he had shown the utmost surprise when Grandpa Guyapi had dangled the necklace in front of his face with an arrowhead hanging off its pendulum.

The necklace was the first affectionate deed in which Grandpa had made an offering to Achak, aside from the gifts he gave his grandchildren during birthdays. But outside of that occasion, Grandpa never gave cause to spoil his grandchildren, nor did he ever hug and embrace them. As Achak became older, he began to develop some discomfort with his grandpa's lack of bodily expression. The man was a rock, and poor Tehya, at the age of eight, had to learn the hard way when mother barked at her for trying to sit on Grandpa's lap. Mom passed off the reason for such a cry as: "Grandpa is too old and you're too heavy," but Achak always felt that there was a different understanding behind her words. And now that Achak's bitterness had found a voice, he was certain that the old man's behavior would be more estranged towards Achak than it had been before.

In high regret and future worry, Achak continued getting ready for bed in the usual manner. He was grateful not to have come across Tehya while entering and leaving the bathroom. Achak figured that Tehya must already be sound asleep in her room, or pretending to be. Meanwhile, his bedroom door remained peacefully open when he returned since no recent quarrels gave him reason to leave it otherwise. He flipped off the light switch as he entered the room and blindly found his way to his bed. Because he had never looked up from his pillow to keep watch on the hour, he did not know to what hour in the morning he had spent regretting the words he had spoken in front of Grandpa.

A small light sent elongated shadows over the walls of a dark corridor. Two figures followed the weakening glow of a flashlight. Lapidar shined the light on the walls which showed not only doorways but lockers stacked three rows high. His movements were brisk, but quieter than those of his female companion's. A loud click and snap of heels on a linoleum floor followed the silhouette of Sirena down the hallway. Her steps were shorter, but produced more of an echo under the weight of thick platform boots. Together, the pair made no attempt to be discrete while walking down the deserted hallway, as though neither reserved the fear of being discovered.

Sirena fell behind Lapidar in an uneager pace. "Is this necessary?" She stopped in annoyance. Her voice continued to carry down the hall with a repeating echo.

"I need his scent." Lapidar held up his stride to wait for the other. He shined the light on her where she stood with her arms crossed in a pout.

Sirena turned her face away from the light that threatened her eyes. "And how do you plan to get it?" she snapped with more disregard to any precautionary measures they might have taken to avoid discovery.

Lapidar lowered the light away from her, directing it along the walls in search for her answer. Aluminum lockers lined the wall-space between doors, giving him the answer he desired.

He moved closer to touch the cold metal of one of the lockers on the highest row. First he felt along the top of the locker in search of some clue as to whom the locker might belong. Then his hand came upon the combination lock that dangled from its handle. He flipped the rounded lock up, showing its backside, and found what he was looking for. Upside-down, the name "M. Blackbird" had been loosely engraved into the metal, likely by some school official. Moving over to the next locker, he flipped its lock over to find another name: A. Santiago.

Waiting for confirmation, Sirena continued to watch him proceed down a row of lockers with her eyes narrowly fixed. The time he spent examining each locker shortened.

"They're names," he declared. "Find him! Find him!"

4
Tardy and Feathered

Achak saw two shadows walking down a dark, but familiar hallway. The main building of his high school had three rows of lockers, the likes of which matched the ones surrounding him. Having no desire to dial into one of the lockers, Achak kept watch on the approaching figures. Their steps echoed along the walls, assuring Achak that they were not phantoms while also alerting him to the fact that he was not alone.

He could not tell whether they were coming toward him or moving away as the distance between never seemed to greaten or shorten. But their steps soon became louder over the linoleum, closing in around him. Achak pressed himself against the wall, but something dug into his back and the aluminum rang out behind him like a clash of cymbals. Knowing his position was up, Achak slid across the cold surface of metal lockers to recede deeper and deeper into the shadows.

The footsteps became louder and more hastened as if taken at a run. He pushed himself harder against the wall, rattling every set of combination locks that he brushed against. His arm hit particularly hard against a single metal dial which he reached up for and began to turn: first clockwise, then two times counter clockwise then once more over clockwise. He pulled down, but the lock would not budge. The metal loop clung stubbornly through the handle. As Achak frantically tugged, he knew the shadows would catch up to him before he could open the locker.

Soon his banging matched those of the footsteps. His heart lurched and he struck out at the locker with his fist, regretting the move the instant the cold metal stung against his knuckles.

Achak gasped as he shot awake in his room. The cool morning air penetrated his flesh as the comforters were tossed from his body. One clatter of silverware from down the hall sent Achak springing from his bed and clinging to the bulbs of his bedpost for quick support.

In the drama of last night, Achak had failed to set his alarm clock. Worse than Achak having only enough time to ready himself, he was pushing for minutes before the tardy bell. His mother had to scream for him from the kitchen before it occurred to Achak to question the sunbeams radiating through his curtains and interpret the glowing red numbers from the digital alarm clock set beside his bed at 7:28AM. It would take him 15 minutes to get to the campus, with or without a ride due to Monday morning traffic, and the tardy bell would ring at eight.

A glance past the mirror on his way out of the bathroom told him that it was going to be a bad day as he had no time to do anything more to his ruffled hair than wet it down, but that only made it flat and disorderly. The strands of black hair still seemed to dictate their own direction. Longer ones chose to tweak out at the ends, but Achak didn't have the time to argue with himself about whether his hair was decent enough. Besides, he thought he knew someone at school who could carry that argument for him.

Regrets from the night before only occurred to Achak as he was reaching for his set of house keys on top of the clothes drawer where the silver chain and arrowhead pendant stood outside of the norm. He couldn't be sure what made him grab the necklace but he stuffed it in his jean pocket along with his set of house keys and decided that he would put the necklace on later.

For one moment he seemed to amuse himself in the thought that Grandpa's necklace might change the course of events that Achak forecasted for the day. Perhaps he'd even get away with not completing his English paper.

Achak left the room with his schoolbag over his shoulder. He followed the hallway at a stride into the family living room, nearly flipping up the centerpiece rug as he made his way to the front door.

"Achak, you're running late!" He heard his mother cry out from the kitchen.

He was fighting to flatten the rug with his feet and trying to hold onto his backpack while under the tangle of his gray sweatshirt. Ms. Twinfang continued badgering him about breakfast and lunch money until he closed the door behind.

Stepping onto the front yard walkway, he met the cool San Diego breeze with little hope of prosperity to his day. Unlike the coastline, from this industrialized side of town, the salt air of the ocean could not be smelt. If freedom blew, it breezed by on the moist draft and slight drizzle of gray skies.

Despite the chill, Achak did not draw up the hood of his sweatshirt. Soon enough, he would be breaking a sweat beneath the cotton layers in a race against the tardy bell. He wondered how late he would be walking into class and hoped that he would have the company of other tardy peers if he stepped inside only a couple of minutes after the bell rang.

Achak felt a bit foolish as he picked up stride wondering if it would even make a difference. He determined that it would not when he reached the first stop-light and an old lady with her Scottish terrier whom he had passed along the way caught up to him before the pedestrian crosswalk blinked on.

He stepped off the sidewalk at a regular pace, but his heart did an unexpected summersault. When he reached the other sidewalk, he pulled his backpack in front of him and rummaged blindly for his planner. His friend Anthony would be expecting him by his locker if this was the morning they had agreed to meet for a drama rehearsal. If Achak had only one class with Anthony, he was glad it was Mrs. Hyde's Introduction to Stage Drama because Achak had at least one person that would not be so embarrassed by his performance to never speak to him again.

When Achak finally pulled out his planner and located the calendar for the month of May, to Achak's dismay, he found Anthony's name scrawled next to the date and felt the angry surge of guilt for having stood up his best friend.

"He's late!" Sirena sat on her perch atop a tree, despite the swings and jungle gyms from which she could have propped herself upon. "The first bell has already rung."

Big surprise, Lapidar did not even bother to look up at her from his seated position at the base of the tree trunk. He shrugged his shoulders, not caring whether Sirena had watched for his response. As if he would go out of his way to answer her question, but he knew he had a job to do.

"Are you sure he comes from this direction?" he asked accusingly.

"No-o-o." Sirena sarcastically elongated her response.

"Well, then why didn't you ever follow him home? It would have been easier to grab him from there."

Lapidar heard the swift rustle of Sirena's dark garments and knew that he had ruffled some feathers.

"Look, I'm not here to make your job easier."

"Oh, I know that," he barked amusedly. "So far, you've done anything but make my job easier. But since we are getting paid to get the same job done, you might want to put a little more effort towards completing that task."

"And how would you know what I'm getting paid to do?"

Lapidar looked up to see how credible he should consider Sirena's words. In seeing him react, Sirena broke into a fit of very loud and forced laughter. *All talk,* Lapidar criticized and leaned back against the tree. Lapidar might not have spoken to Sirena throughout the entire mission, but his curiosity had gotten the better of him.

"Any ideas how Manu's going to find out what the boy's species is?" he asked the pair of feet dangling over his head.

"No," Sirena answered. "But if I were you, I wouldn't go and try making it my business. Manu has enough power behind his sanctuary to afford some secrets."

"Oh?" Lapidar looked up again to see the pair of dangling legs. "And it hasn't interested you in the least?" He heard the branch above him creak, then a tangle of black descended upon him.

Sirena pulled her flapping red hair out of her face and gave it a little toss to blow behind her. She opened her mouth wide and Lapidar braced himself for the shriek but, instead, out came a yawn.

"Well, not that I haven't enjoyed our time together, but I'm bored," she chirped and, without another explanation, turned on the soles of her platform boots and began to walk away.

"Sirena!" Lapidar stared menacingly at her back and stood up by his tree. "We have a job to do, remember?"

Her hand went into the air and flicked him a little "so long" with the wrist. In a trail of feathers, Sirena was making her way across the field of grass.

Lapidar turned his head off to the side and spat. He allowed the distance to grow between him and his partner before shouting, "Sirena!" And he chased after her.

Sirena turned the corner by the houses, but by the time Lapidar reached the first of privately owned property, Sirena was nowhere in sight.

From his throat, Lapidar's vocals were torn into a beastly growl and he retired back to the tree to await Sirena's return. Twenty minutes passed before Lapidar was finally able to jump up from the root of the tree and lash at her.

"Well?" he growled.

"Well, what?" Sirena snapped. "No, I didn't see him. I guess we'll just have to wait for school to get out."

Lapidar snorted with more impatience. The idea of having to wait six hours to fulfill a mission was not the sort organization he was used to when he set out to complete a task.

"This is all your fault, you know," his gruff voice extended the accusation and Lapidar straightened up by his tree.

"My fault?" Sirena said shrilly and came to stand directly in front of Lapidar. "Weren't *you* supposed to be keeping an eye out for him?"

She cocked her head upward and, before Lapidar could make a come-back, she was back on her perch above him.

"Give it a rest, wolfy," she called down. "It's not like we don't know where he is."

Achak ran the back of his palm across his forehead where the longer strands of hair stuck to his sweaty skin. Crossing another busy intersection, the residential housing was replaced by a chainlink fence. Cars pulled in front of him to enter the parking lots. The high school would have been settled by this hour for the most part as there were not that many latecomers, but the first parking lot had around-the-clock activity since it belonged to the junior college campus that neighbored the high school.

This college campus was also the reason why Achak did not share the same graduation excitement as every other high school senior. How excited could a person be in knowing that he was only moving next door? Sure the campus was nicer and offered more courses, but as far as Achak could discern, he would not be making that big transition from high school to college that everyone spoke about.

He regretted having snuck off the high school campus many times before with Anthony to pretend to be one of the college students and to check out their facilities. The premature tour of the campus had spoiled much of the excitement that would normally have accompanied the great "college experience." Much of his familiarity with the campus was met with disappointment even though he knew that the college's facilities stood ten times better in comparison to those at San Diego High.

He wondered if Anthony was still sneaking into the college weight room, but then he wondered how his friend might have managed it with the student ID requirements that were recently installed. Campus Security must be working double-time at the college to prevent a number of high school students from loitering.

"The College Experience" was a chainlink fence away. Maybe the grass was greener on the other side, but what difference did that make to Achak if he still had to commute from the same home and walk the same streets? He did not even need to pack his bags or cross an extra block to get to where he was going after high school. In fact, the campus would be closer to home if he attended the college. What new challenges could possibly await him next door that he had not already encountered?

Leaving the college behind him, Achak cut through the high school parking lot, zigzagging between cars to get to a building behind the front offices. He approached the side door of the two-story building at base level. The handle he pulled down on was flecked with yellow paint that bubbled in some places. His classroom was the first door on the right, room 12B, though he knew that if he wanted to enter the classroom as discretely as possible, he would use the second door, opposite the side the teacher lectured from.

The second door was wide open letting Mrs. Hwang's English lecture on composition enter into the hallway for Achak to hear. He vaguely heard her mention something about the organization of their last essays, which—judging by her tone—did not sound like a compliment, before feet echoed in the hallway in front of him.

"Achak?" He heard the familiar accent of his friend Anthony's voice, which always made his name sound Spanish, and saw a figure running towards him. Anthony stopped short of exposing himself through the open doorway. His own sweatshirt hung off one of his shoulders, while beads of sweat ran down from his temples. He had a buzz-cut, making it seem like there was less hair on his head than on his face where he grew what he could of a mustache.

"Your locker" was all he managed to say.

"What?" Achak said automatically.

"Oh man, someone's broke into your locker." Anthony's voice shook in urgency.

Somehow the words did not quite register with Achak.

"What—how?" he posed stupidly.

"I don't know, dog, but you'd better get your stuff out before—" His eyes looked beyond Achak and he let the words hang there in mid-sentence.

"I was wondering who was making all the noise." Mrs. Hwang's figure was framed in the doorway. "Care to step inside, Mr. Twinfang?" However, her words seemed to have the opposite effect on Achak, locking him in place. Mrs. Hwang may have had a soft voice and a small profile, but she required little assistance when it came to putting force behind her words. She knew more about the potentials of the language than a grammatical understanding.

Mrs. Hwang's head tilted to the side, no longer staring upon Achak's paralyzed body. "Mr. Santiago, I think it's about time for you to be heading to class now too."

"Yes, Mrs. Hwang, but—"

"Mr. Santiago!"

"Achak's-locker's-been-broken-into." The words rushed out of Anthony's mouth so fast that Achak wondered if Mrs. Hwang had caught the meaning behind all of them, but then she was an English teacher.

In hearing the statement for a second time, Achak thought he could feel the reality take on a more solid form inside his gut. He felt sicker each time he met Mrs. Hwang's face. The whites of her eyes became a smaller sliver as she looked from Anthony to Achak in disbelief.

"We need to get his stuff out," Anthony burst into explanation, cutting off the circulation of oxygen into Achak's lungs.

Surprisingly, Mrs. Hwang's features loosened. She gave what might have been a slight nod. "Go then and report to the main office." Then she locked her eyes on Achak. "Afterwards, come straight back here." Looking past Achak, she added, "or to class."

"Yes, ma'am," Anthony answered.

She gave Achak one last glance that seemed to break him from the paralysis before walking back into the classroom.

Was that pity? Achak found himself thinking upon the last look Mrs. Hwang had given him. Speeding down the hallway ahead of Anthony, Achak could not put enough distance between himself and the open doorway of room 12B. The class must have overheard the entire conversation. Before the day was out, everyone who was anyone would know that Achak Twinfang's locker had been broken into.

"Sorry." Anthony seemed to have read his mind.

"Why, did you break into it?" Achak slowed down before some other teacher peeked his or her head into the hallway because of his noisy strides. He felt dazed and dreamy walking down the hallway at an unaccustomed hour. His head throbbed with multiple recounts of possessions kept in his locker. What would turn up missing?

The textbooks would be the priciest to replace, what with Pre-Calc and Biology still in his schedule. And then there was U.S. Government—that was a thick book too and likely expensive to replace.

"What did they take?"

"I don't know," Anthony answered mechanically. "I didn't want to draw too much attention to it. We were supposed to meet in front of there, remember?

So I was—"

"Yeah, I remember—thanks." Achak let the hollow silence fall between them again. He felt some hope in the thought of Anthony having arrived on the scene so early. Though, for someone to have gone through so much trouble to break into his locker, they knew what they were after and had probably already taken it.

Drawing himself into the mystery, Achak wondered if anyone saw the culprit, someone he would know by name. Maybe the motive was not an object, but an act. Revenge, perhaps?

"You know who it might have been?" Anthony blurted out suddenly, apparently still on Achak's thought pattern.

"Donovan?" Achak suggested without the same level of excitement.

Anthony looked crestfallen. "Well, I thought it was a good guess."

"It was." Though, it was a suspect that Achak did not try to encourage with his tone. The thought of Donovan Parsons having gotten the better of him was not something Achak was willing to easily accept.

However, when Achak saw the condition of his locker, he quickly swept away any grudges and suspicions he had reserved about Donovan.

The aluminum door had been kicked or pounded inward. Its metal was warped and the combination lock had been completely removed. Achak lifted up on the naked handle and pulled to no avail. Wiping his palms on his jeans, he pulled again, this time with his left hand pushing off his neighbor's locker for leverage. The metal separated and Achak stared at the destructive remnants of a mini-hurricane.

Anthony swore under his breath as shreds of paper fell to the floor like confetti. Traces of pre-calculus and blue-lined notebook paper reflected off the lighting.

Achak's black binder looked as plain as ever with all of its contents torn loose from the rings. He stuffed all of the spared paper into his folder. The torn hole-punches made it impossible for Achak attempt to reorganize the scattered assignments. He even found some textbook pages mixed in the debris, which he hoped could be taped back into their places. Seeing as how the books were borrowed from the school to begin with, he would still have to replace them, but that could wait until the end of the semester. For now, Achak just needed the books to be functional for studying purposes.

For the most part, they seemed pretty intact. He could find book covers in the stores to conceal the slash marks that now decorated the covers.

Anthony rubbed his fingers over the grooves curiously. Achak on the other hand was neither impressed nor interested with the knife work.

"Come on!" he urged impatiently, tucking all his books under one arm. The binder—being in the best condition—was kept on the outside.

"Shouldn't there have been a note or something?" Anthony folded his arms. "Maybe a signature." Apparently, he did not think that tearing pages and bending the locker door was enough damage.

Achak forced a laugh. "Yeah, maybe we can get the police over here to brush for fingerprints."

Anthony glowered. "No, dog, but I mean the person would have wanted to say something to you, right? I mean, what was the point?"

While there might have been some merit to Anthony's observations, Achak could think of one explanation that settled any unnatural circumstances.

"Maybe he didn't have time... or they."

Just as suddenly, Anthony bent over to pick up a piece of paper that had fallen from the locker. Two things were uncovered as he did this: the first being that the paper he held was actually a flyer promoting the next school play, "Romeo and Juliet" starring Donovan Parsons. The second discovery was that there was a long black feather lying underneath the flyer.

"What do you suppose..." But Achak only tore the flyer away from Anthony's hand and began to walk fiercely away with all of his books and papers tucked under his chin.

He was unwilling to accept any evidence that pointed to Donovan Parsons as the vandal. Achak departed with Anthony at the entrance to the front office. However, the principal, Miss Joyce Kimberly, looked at the evidence with more of Anthony's level of interest and speculation. She was a stern woman and, although in her late forties, Miss Kimberly held the coloring in her hair, vibrantly and artificially reddened to the roots, and suppressed her aging wrinkles to the far corners of her eyes and lips.

"Who do you know in this play, that would... well frankly, that would want to play with your mind?"

Achak wanted to deliver a quick answer but hesitated to do so as it would also involve the mention of the star actor, the one whose face most vividly appeared on the flyer. When he at last spoke up, Miss Kimberly's reaction was to be expected.

"Uh-huh?" she begged for more of an explanation. "And did you audition for this play?" she asked as though determined to find some source of jealousy that would stand to reason why Achak would dare to accuse the school's Romeo.

"By requirement for Mrs. Hyde's class," Achak's answer was "yes."

"And which part did you audition for?" Miss Kimberly looked sternly at him.

"Mercutio," Achak muttered.

Miss Kimberly's face relaxed and, to Achak's relief, she actually smiled.

"Well, rules out that one, doesn't it?" she said in a friendlier tone. "And here I thought I'd have a problem with two Romeo's competing for one Juliet. But now that we can scratch that one off the list of possibilities we're back to ground zero with finding out who the real perpetrator is."

Even when she paced her office, her red hair hung stiffly behind her shoulders. But Achak was most relieved to see her out from behind her desk which meant that he was not in any trouble.

"Now this flyer." She held it up and Achak tensed in his seat again. "It doesn't necessarily mean that Donovan is the one responsible. There could be others, especially with the number of students on the cast list, but his name has not been completely cleared, agreed?"

Achak merely stared at her. He was dumbfounded. Seeing as how he never wanted to accuse Donovan in the first place, Achak still could not bring himself to raise a voice against Miss Kimberly, even if she was—as he supposed—suggesting that he would make some rash decisions against Donovan before all the evidence was weighed in.

"Let's have a look at some of the other things they left behind," Miss Kimberly said and gestured to a clear space on her desk for Achak to set his binder and books upon. She picked up the first text, a slashed edition of Pre-Calculus and examined the cover closely.

While also biting her lip, Miss Kimberly shared in Anthony's reaction of wanting to trace the grooves with her fingertips. Achak could see the concern building in her creasing forehead. Not that he could blame her for overreacting while the evidence suggested that there were students bringing knives into the school, but Achak had sat at her desk long enough. He waited for her to say something, but when she did not, he decided to press for some resolution.

"Ah, Miss Kimberly? Could I—Do you think I could get another locker? Mine's been kinda pounded in."

The moment he began to speak, the principal looked up in surprise as though she had forgotten that anyone else was sitting in her office. She seemed to be looking at Achak from a new angle because her eyes would not settle over his features, but kept searching his face for a trace of something unfamiliar. It was then that she finally spoke up and asked, "Are you sure you're not of another kind?"

"Another kind of what?" Achak puzzled.

Miss Kimberly sighed. "Well, I suppose if you were, it would be on your school record. Alright," she said standing up. "Let's get you a new locker."

Achak could still hear excerpts from the principal's speech as he walked the deserted pathways of the Science and Social Studies building, the only other one apart from the English building that contained two stories, where Achak had his new locker.

The interior of the sciences building was fairly identical to the English building except that it had fewer doors and more student lockers lined against the walls. Anthony had his locker in this building as well, which would make it easier for him and Achak to meet in the mornings. Achak had learned long ago why so many students shared lockers in this building. Its abundance in wall space had to do with the fact that science labs required larger classroom space since the storage and equipment had to meet state health and safety regulations, so doorways were fewer in number and further apart.

Now that he had his books stored, Achak had only to go upstairs from his locker to attend his third period class with Mr. Benson, the U.S. Government teacher.

With all of the excitement of the early morning, Achak doubted he heard anything Mr. Benson had to say about the Supreme Court and its former Chief Justices.

For the past two hours, maybe longer, Lapidar did not have a watch on the time to know for sure, Sirena had taken to her perch on the tree and sat there wordlessly. Lapidar doubted it was patience that kept her so silent. Maybe it was fear, but he shook that idea instantly from his head. This fiery-eyed teenager could not be self-entertained after hours of eventless waiting, while Lapidar found his 29-year-old self restlessly pacing around the tree. What kept her so calm or pre-occupied?

She had been staring at a single sheet of paper since she had returned. Lapidar thought she had just picked a flyer off the ground from around the college campus or else peeled it off the wall, but his simple explanations began to deteriorate the longer Sirena held the sheet in front of her. A single-sided print could not be of that much interest to the average teenager, but she appeared to be setting a new record. Her eyes no longer scrolled across the page from left to right but stayed focused at its center—probably because she had memorized everything that had been typed across the page.

Lapidar made an aggressive clear at his throat. As if snapping out of a day-dream, Sirena looked sharply down upon the interruption. Lapidar smirked triumphantly, half expecting Sirena to crumple the paper into a wad and throw it at him.

She gave a frown, at best, and quietly looked down upon him.

"What is that thing, anyway?" Lapidar asked silkily, not at all impressed at the way Sirena had contained her temper.

"I got it from his locker." She held the paper out to her side, as if she meant for him to try to jump for it. Then, releasing the sheet, she let it flutter to the ground. Lapidar caught it in the air with a crumple. Smoothing it out, he read down the margins, letting the admiration creep up his face. Aloud, he read:

"Achak Twinfang—First Period—English 4B—Second Period—Pre-Calculus—Third Period—American Government."

Lapidar slowed his speech as he read further down the list. "Fourth Period—Intro to Stage Drama—Instructor—Mrs. Hyde—11:30 to 12:40 pm." He stopped and looked up at his not-so-useless partner.

For the first time, the vindictive pleasure behind her smile could be read with a clear purpose in mind. Sirena's head tilted, spilling the bright red strands of hair over her face and into the sunlight.

"What time is it now?"

Sirena giggled, tossing her head back. By this Lapidar knew that the hour to act upon must be drawing near.

Mrs. Hyde greeted her fourth period students with her voice majestically drawn to project across the vastness of both stage and audience.

"Mor-r-r-rning Cla-a-a-a-ass." Students entering from the back of the theatre could hear the echo of her greeting. Among them, Achak walked shoulder-to-shoulder with his friend Anthony. They could see Mrs. Hyde's blouse glittering with shiny little dots that caught the stage light.

Anthony raised his eyebrows to Achak, who could not offer him a better explanation for such adornments or glamour. He shrugged just as a few snickers erupted behind him then turned around to see a glint of gold dangling from one of the boy's earlobes. This particular rebel, and his pony-tailed friend, Achak knew by more than just a name. Identical to the face on the flyer, Donovan Parsons "as Romeo" stood height to height with the canary strands of Harvey.

It was not like Donovan to laugh at Mrs. Hyde, the teacher of his favorite subject. And as these matters are prone to work in reverse order as well, Donovan was Mrs. Hyde's favorite student—her best actor—or so it was written all over the beaming expression she wore for him as they all walked toward the stage. Donovan was wearing an unusual compilation of brown trousers with—if Achak was not mistaken—a pair of clip-on suspenders over his plaid shirt.

Down the slope of gray carpet, the class approached Mrs. Hyde on stage and began filing themselves into the first three rows of theatre seating. Achak followed Anthony into the second row. They had never sat in the first one, which was unofficially reserved for real lovers of the stage, those with the pipedream that they would someday be performing on Broadway or in Hollywood.

"Maybe on the streets," Anthony would say.

"Why do all the acting levels have to be mixed into one drama class?" Achak suddenly burst out while Mrs. Hyde continued to take role.

A hard kick came under his chair and Achak turned around in his seat to face up to the delinquent. Mrs. Hyde had them all sitting in the auditorium with red-cushioned theatre chairs instead of the normal blues and plastics found in classrooms. Donovan Parsons had the seat behind Achak and, behind Anthony, was Don's friend, Harvey. They were both leaning back in their cushioned seats and looking proud of themselves for being able to listen in on Achak and Anthony's conversations.

"Hey, what's Donovan wearing?" Achak turned to Anthony and asked with exaggerated curiosity.

Anthony got the hint and replied very loudly, "I don't know. Let's make a bet out of it and see whoever guesses closest."

Two of the boys in front of them began snorting in their hands, but a couple of the girls shot them nasty looks. Achak continued anyway.

"I dunno, but I'm gonna say he's Tom Sawyer."

Another hard kick was thrust under Achak's chair, but he felt satisfied.

"Okay then," Anthony replied. "I'm gonna say, he's Johnny Appleseed."

Achak doubled over with the other boys in laughter and even Anthony could not resist taking amusement at his own joke.

There were simmering murmurs and returning silence as Mrs. Hyde began to introduce the day's lesson.

"I have a very important announcement to make." Mrs. Hyde's already enormous blue eyes widened excitedly at her own voice.

Achak wondered if it was really necessary for stage performers to give such exaggerated expressions in order for people in the back rows to understand them or if it was just a habit of Mrs. Hyde's to always go to extremes.

"Well, it's more of an opportunity than an announcement, especially for all those who take their acting seriously and want to brush up their college applications with some real-life experience in the field."

"Who's she kidding," Anthony hissed. "Application dates are well overdue. Everyone's waiting for acceptance letters."

"Everyone but me!" Achak snapped. He did not need to be accepted to attend a junior college; he just needed to enroll in the required classes before they were all filled. Although certain that he would not be the only SDH senior to attend San Diego City College next year, he was determined to be the most bitter.

Anthony punched him on the shoulder. He usually did this when Achak sounded depressed and it almost always made him crack a smile. This time Anthony added more punch to Achak's dilemma by mimicking Mrs. Hyde's expression of: "Not so melo-o-odramatic, dear."

However, Mrs. Hyde's announcement cut over Anthony's impersonation as she had been holding out for the suspense. "This evening, as I'm sure you all remember, will be auditions for a TV commercial. The product line is very popular, not just here in the States, but it is gaining in international markets as well."

Achak let his eyes slip to the stage lights by Mrs. Hyde's feet so that when he looked up at her again, she was surrounded by balls of green and pink flashing in front of his dilated pupils. Anthony had probably done the same thing because Achak could see him rubbing his eyes from the side.

"HydroMax producers will be here auditioning teenagers for their next promotion and have—or so I am told by certain sources..." and Mrs. Hyde winked her eye to show that she had some inside connections. "I am told that they would prefer a candidate from our school to star in the lead role, seeing as how they will be doing the filming on our campus. So can I have a show of hands of who I can expect to see there?"

Nobody raised their hand, but those in the front row did turn in their seats to watch Donovan raise his.

Achak continued to stare forward and ignore the person that everyone's eyes met. To his disgust, he saw Mrs. Hyde's bulbous blue eyes swell with tears of delight and admiration. She flipped the attendance sheet over on her clipboard and scrawled on a separate underlying sheet of paper the names of those who would audition. A couple in the front row had lifted timid and half-raised hands after Donovan's. Neither Achak nor Anthony had any considerations to be among them, even if it did mean extra credit for the course.

"I'd rather drop down on one knee in front of Mariam during a pep rally," Anthony whispered, but Achak knew this to be more false than if he had said that he would rather "drop dead." Mariam Blackbird was a Junior classman whom Anthony had taken to liking since he had found her locker next to his two years ago.

She had long hair curling around her face and had a fetish for the color violet, which in complement to her hair, sometimes appeared to shimmer off her black strands when light was reflected. But she had always had a boyfriend and could be found with him, hand in hand, whenever walking down the halls. Her boyfriend was named Marcus and he played soccer at the varsity level. All this insight, Achak had heard from Anthony over the years while Mariam continued to walk around these chilly winter days with Marcus's purple letterman's jacket.

"Maybe she only keeps him around because she likes the color of the letterman's jacket," Achak had told Anthony in hopes of bringing up his spirits. He thought it might have been partially true too since Mariam often wore earrings or other gold apparels along with black trousers to match the other colors on the letterman's jacket. Gold and purple crowned the Wildcat that was San Diego High's mascot. An image of the school's feline could be seen above the alma mater where the wall took over stage right.

Anthony had not liked what Achak had to say about Mariam's infatuation with purple and the letterman's jacket, so there had been a serious challenge for Achak to restrain himself when Anthony told him last Winter that he had tried out for the soccer team. Achak knew it had all been for the letterman's jacket and for Mariam, but said nothing of it when Anthony mentioned the part about making junior varsity and his resignation from the team. After all, it was Anthony who had come to Achak's aid on this morning and alerted him to the broken locker.

Not that Achak's belongings frequently came under attack or got stolen, but it was on days like this that Anthony's friendship truly came through for him. Drama class too would have been a place of much drama this year—drama that did not concern the stage as much as it did Donovan Parsons—were it not for Anthony's company. Here again, Achak would have had to endure a whole 70 minutes with his chair being kicked from behind, but Anthony's companionship kept him under control.

"Won't she just call him up already?" Achak hissed as a particularly hard kick under his chair made him squint.

"Saves the best for last," Donovan cracked in Achak's ear.

Then Achak and Anthony both jumped out of their seats as Donovan let out a yell of fright.

Achak almost regretted his jumpiness as he thought the whole thing to be a hoax, but Donovan was really screaming. Some of the front row began to laugh but it quickly died away.

There was a head redder than the stage curtains, or Donovan's new blush, above the actor's chair. It had taken to the top of Donovan's seat like a perch.

Though it was not uncommon to see pigeons inside the auditorium every once in a while and sometimes startle to a flap of wings in the backstage areas, Achak could not think of one region where it was common to find a vulture on a person's backrest.

It was an ugly thing to be seen up close: the head wrinkled like a prune, the fuzzy ring around its neck, and the feathers a dull black that would not reflect any lighting, even though they were under the powerful watts of a theatre spotlight.

Achak did not like standing near to the buzzard any more than Donovan appeared to, but he could not help sharing a smirk with Anthony while the vulture took to death-gazing their most disliked classmate. He heard Mrs. Hyde scrambling off the stage and nudged Anthony to begin edging his way out of the second row.

"Cut! Cut!" Mrs. Hyde began shouting. It was her way of saying "hold it" or "settle down." She had not used the stairs to make her way down the stage right aisle but jumped from the ledge.

Anthony was moving away toward stage left and Achak followed him, though never fully taking his eyes off the vulture.

Its eyes were completely filled with a mercury black, but Achak could sense that its focus was caught on him.

"What is it? What is it?" Mrs. Hyde was shouting her way forward as though the whole ordeal was a silly matter involving a schoolgirl and an iddy-biddy spider. Those were other frequent visitors in an old auditorium. But spiders, like the rest of the invading critters, rats and bats, were prone to hiding in the backstage areas and not the audience seating.

Mrs. Hyde stopped herself short from coming into Donovan's row. This time Achak thought for sure her baby blues would pop right out of their sockets.

Donovan was on the aisle floor, clearly hoping that the bird would fly away on its own so that he would not have to crawl his way under the seating to reach the gray carpet. Harvey had somehow managed his way to the end of the row and now stood behind Mrs. Hyde.

The sight of Donovan on the floor, his hands on the sticky residue of candy, spit, and gum that students had left was definitely a moment Achak wished to hold as a freeze-frame in memory.

"Donovan!" Mrs. Hyde hissed, but no louder than a whisper. "Get out from under there! Over here, now!"

However, Donovan did not budge, the vulture on the other hand, did.

Donovan gasped and threw his hands over his head as the vulture launched itself from his seat, spreading two massive wings that took up the length of almost three chairs each. Everyone ducked, but the vulture soared high above them.

It looked like it was about to fly over Achak and Anthony, but then it made a great arch towards the stage, circling their heads. Gaining height, it flapped above the stage and disappeared into the rafters and beams of the stage lighting.

"Oh, for heaven's sake!" Mrs. Hyde breathed. "Is it still here?" She marched toward the stage, no longer looking as nervous with the gigantic bird out of sight. Bravely, she climbed onto the stage down-center and several students followed her. They all began pointing and whispering excitedly up at the lights.

Achak and Anthony were two of the last people to join Mrs. Hyde on stage, but they still felt proud enough to grin mockingly at the last person to reach Mrs. Hyde: Donovan Parsons, who was not looking so cool anymore with his sleek brown hair displaced.

"You know, I think it might be a California Condor," Mrs. Hyde began saying to her students. "Maybe it's loose from one of the animal parks."

"Maybe it's time to dismiss class," Anthony whispered to Achak. "I'm not about to perform under that thing."

Achak had nodded his head in agreement even before the "thing" began screeching.

It was a shrill sort of cluck that sounded from the throat. Achak did not know whether it was just painful to listen to or if the creature really was being strangled or choking.

"Alright!" Mrs. Hyde hid a better part of her frustration and sounded half amused. "Would anyone like to go fetch the principal and let her know what's going on?"

Achak, who had already seen the principal once today, did not volunteer.

"Yes, Jian? Good." Mrs. Hyde exclaimed.

A short girl with long black hair and wearing a pink sweater that matched her plaid skirt ran past Achak and down the stairs of the stage.

"Well, sit tight, everyone," Mrs. Hyde sighed.

Achak would rather they be dismissed, but when she did not excuse them, he took a seat with Anthony at the edge of the stage.

"Bet we could just walk out of here and she'd never notice," Anthony grumbled.

Achak looked back at where Mrs. Hyde was standing down-stage, her neck craned to see around the rafters.

"Donovan and Harvey have already bailed." Achak looked around again to confirm his friend's words. They were once more proven to be true. Achak didn't know how he had missed Donovan's exit, the Romeo was not exactly easy to ignore in those clip-on suspenders.

"I suppose we could," Achak agreed at last, but before they were given the chance to jump off the stage, a loud crack erupted in the theatre.

Anthony hastily nudged Achak's arm to indicate the side door for their ditch. Achak nodded so that they both pushed themselves off the stage, but just when their feet hit carpet, a second crack was issued and the doors at the height of the theatre-seating burst open. Two figures began to walk down the aisle.

"Great!" Anthony wailed and fell back to leaning against the stage. Achak stood motionless while the principal, Miss Kimberly, and the shorter Jian came strolling down. Anthony elbowed Achak again, but he didn't need to receive such a call to attention. His eyes had already located one head out of the more than twenty students that had come in behind another teacher.

"It's Ms. Oswell from Biology," Anthony exclaimed, but Achak wasn't looking at the dumpy and freckled woman who always reminded him of some sort of cranberry muffin. His attention was caught on the girl that Jian had fallen behind to walk with. She too had long black hair, but her strands shortened near the face where they circled around her narrower cheeks. Achak always liked the way she had a matching shade of eye shadow for every color of blouse she wore. Today, above the thinner eyes, it was a sky blue that made her light powdery cheeks look as soft as clouds.

"It's Kitti," Achak nudged Anthony back for the first time. In a lack of concern for his friend, he had missed Anthony's arm and lodged his elbow hard into Anthony's ribs.

Coughing and laughing, Anthony gave a "meow" tease and purred in Achak's ear. His stomach gave a sudden lurch as he heard the voices more clearly from among the approaching parties.

"They feed on carrion," Ms. Oswell was saying. "Now does anyone know what that means? Yes, that's right, it means dead animals." Ms. Oswell and her jittery tagalong of students were making such a ruckus over all the excitement that Achak could not believe it had taken Miss Kimberly so long to turn on them.

The principal only looked at Achak and Anthony as she passed. Then her hawk eyes drifted over the stage. In swift strides, she strode up the stairs on stage right. A few strands tweaked in separate ways from the rest of her red hair and Achak had never seen her looking so ruffled.

"Now everyone take careful observation of its features." The bird was not even in sight yet, but Ms. Oswell already had a homework assignment that involved drawing a picture of the said bird looming above stage. She was talking so fast to her students that it was a wonder she didn't get tongue-tied. "I'm sure you'll be able to identify it just by the shape of its beak. And it may even be one of our own California Condors. They're endangered, as you're all very aware."

With his arms folded around his waist, Achak was watching the passing feet and thinking of a million other places he would rather be than listening to Ms. Oswell lecture on birds. His stomach was at a continuous growl in the absence of food.

Glancing behind, he watched glittering Mrs. Hyde come forward to meet the principal, referring to her as "Joyce," and directing her to the vulture. She pointed to the third row seating and gobbled away over the details.

Ms. Oswell's voice boomed excitedly over Mrs. Hyde's dramatic one as she announced to her class the location of the buzzard on the rafters. All heads looked up.

"See how the curve of its beak is?" Ms. Oswell was saying to her students when the principal interrupted her to make an announcement.

"Animal Control has been called and should arrive shortly," Miss Kimberly put an end to the lectures, but added to the excitement.

Ms. Oswell began tapping on students' shoulders to tell them to get out a pen quickly and start jotting notes.

"Now you see the wing span," she continued. "There's white on the inside feathers, which may indicate a condor."

"It's a vulture!" Principal Kimberly snapped. "A Lappet-Faced one to be exact. Definitely not native to any part of this region or state, for that matter."

Achak stared at the principal, who had not taken her eyes off the vulture with the stage lights glinting in her eyes. Achak began to feel sorry for her after the long morning she had endured helping him sort out his locker situation and now having to contend with escaped birds. She would soon have Animal Control officers to speak with and reporters for the local papers. After all the trouble the vulture would cause, Achak could not blame Miss Kimberly for wanting to glower at the buzzard that would probably result in her having to fill out more paperwork.

"Who was the student that the vulture landed on his chair?" the principal asked suddenly.

"Oh, it was Donovan Parsons," Mrs. Hyde answered in surprise. "He's..." she broke off, unable to find Donovan's head among her students.

"Never mind," Principal Kimberly snapped. "Who else was sitting in the third row?"

"Well, that would be Harvey." Mrs. Hyde began searching heads again but turned up no results.

"Come on," Anthony hissed. "Let's go before she starts asking for people from the second row."

Achak nodded and followed him to the door on stage left. Two girls had descended the stairs and had their heads bent close so as not to be overheard. One threw her long hair back and her head fell forward again in a fit of giggles. By the shorter strands that curtained her face, Achak saw that it was Kitti.

His heart skipped a pulse, then as though Kitti could hear the drumbeats from within his chest, she turned her head and landed her eyes on Achak. When he froze, Anthony held up with him.

Kitti gave him a polite smile, then went back talking to Jian. "So you think I should say 'yes?'"

Achak thought he might never move again, but then Anthony grabbed his elbow and pulled him along. He walked alongside Kitti, but his neck could not turn to continue watching her as he departed. Instead, it was Kitti that stepped back into his line of sight.

"Ooh, wait," she chimed. Her face was lit with delight, but her friend Jian wore a tempered expression that asked the same question Kitti voiced:

"Is that new?"

"What?" Achak could not grasp Kitti's field of vision fast enough to know what she was talking about.

Then Kitti's finger pressed up against his chest and he remembered the obsidian pendant hanging from its chain. "Pretty," she sighed and looked up into Achak's face.

He supposed that the fact that a girl found interest in his jewelry should have been considered an insult, but the compliment had come from Kitti Kitono, who to him was the most beautiful girl to walk around the campus.

"Thanks—um..." Achak stiffened. What else should he tell her, maybe who gave it to him? Or should he just return a compliment? Instead, he aimed for more neutral ground. "It's something of a good luck charm."

"Oh?" Her eyes brightened with intrigue. "Does it work?"

"Not really," he laughed truthfully, his nerves relaxing somewhat.

But the moment was too good to last as Jian tugged at Kitti's sleeve. Kitti looked at her friend sharply.

"Well, I have to get back to class," she excused herself with the softest of tones, presenting Achak with two things he could be grateful for: her departing smile and a hint of reluctance to her departure.

As an afterthought, Achak felt that maybe Grandpa's good luck charm did have something to offer him, at least if it could arrange more encounters like that with Kitti Kitono.

"Nice," Anthony commended, taking hold of Achak's arm again.

However, the side-door opened before they could reach it and two blue-suited men came in with their rods and hook-ended poles. Kitti and Jian leapt out of their way as they marched up the stairs that led to the stage.

From the ends of their poles, they began to pull out extensions that made the poles reach as high as the rafters. The vulture gave an angry flutter every time the hooks moved too close. It lifted one of its legs as a pole came edging near. Animal Control officers very nearly hooked it around the one claw, but the buzzard skipped happily away on one leg and hopped further along the rafter, where the pole could not reach without demanding some movement from the little man below.

Achak watched as the two hooks were made to miss time and again, at one point clipping onto each other during one of the vulture's narrower dodges. The vulture appeared rather clever and intentional with its dancing feet. But that was about the most entertainment Achak could hope to gain by watching a vulture and a pair of Animal Control officers. He left the auditorium shortly after.

Without a chance he would be caught in his ditch attempt, Achak held the door open for a gray man that was trying to make his way inside the auditorium through the side door. In a fierce tug, the man took the door handle out of Achak's hand and continued to hold the door open without so much as a thank you to Achak for admitting him inside.

If this man was a school official, Achak's ditch attempt would have landed him in detention, but whoever entered the auditorium Achak could not even be certain knew his way around. As the man stood in the doorway, hesitating his entrance, Achak caught a glimpse of his sideburns, then noticed with a longer hold up, the length of the man's browncoat, which trailed as low as his ankles. Achak's scope-out did not go unnoticed as the man returned the examination by glancing down Achak's profile in return. This held up Achak just long enough for Anthony to begin shouting at him to hurry along.

"Hey, Achak!" he called again from the walkways.

Lapidar looked to the first of boy's shouting, then narrowed his eyes on the one standing in his entrance way, but the next minute, he brushed aside "Achak" Twinfang with a glance and redirected himself towards the stage where vulture, classes, and Animal Control officers were still assembled.

From one detached building, Anthony went straight for the next and led the way to the neighboring gymnasium. Without asking Achak, he made a detour stop inside where "soda" machines became the only new installations added to the sports center. Really, they were just drink dispensers with splashy slogans written across them to promote non- carbonated beverages. Anthony bought a bottle of HydroMax Citrus mineral water and complained that "they" were all out of the cider flavor. It was common knowledge that apple was the best, but Achak shrugged off the complaint.

He had just let his eyes wonder around the campus when he looked back at the auditorium and saw the long-coated man reemerge from the side door. Leaning on the frame, the man was prepared to hold the door open for someone. But it was not student, nor teacher, principal, or Animal Control officer that stepped out. Rather, like the unexpected manner in which a paper wad strikes the head of a student, the enormous black vulture flew out.

It flew high and Achak saw two more black streaks tear loose after it across the sky. There were angry kaws and the vulture made a wild dive with the two other blackbirds streaking after it. They descended behind the science building, while the man with a long brown coat followed on foot in the direction the birds had spiraled.

Lapidar came around the corner of the two-story building, but did not come to Sirena's aid. Instead, he moved slowly along the stucco and found a square gap he could hide himself between windows. The voices came in clearly from around the wall as both had risen to the level of shouting.

"Don't you dare threaten me, small feather!" Sirena stood a head taller than the other girl, whose hair was naturally dark and raven-like.

Lapidar peered around the edge and saw that the other girl was wearing a velvet blouse that shimmered the color of plums in the sun. She had next to her a young man who had equally dark skin, but was standing quietly to the side of the girls' argument.

"I want you away from here," Sirena's competition had lowered her voice to a dangerous temperament.

Lapidar heard Sirena's shrill laughter and knew that she was about to take flight. There was a loud kaw and a burst of black feathers into the sun. He waited for the small feather to pass with her boyfriend before stepping out of his hiding place and crossing the street. Ahead of him, Achak and Anthony made their way past the Wildcat Café.

It did not even occur to Achak to ask Anthony about their destination now that they were officially playing hookie.

Anthony had already crossed over into a shopping center parking lot before opening with the question: "Pac-man?"

Achak did not give it any thought and simply nodded. The Pac-man Arcade stood four blocks from the campus and was probably the only place that any unlicensed student could find amusement without a car.

The arcade was a large yellow slab connected to the strip outlet stores. Its walls were singularly painted to be as loud spoken as a taxi cab. A few tinted window panes protruded from the left side of the door, but only from the inside could Achak see that sitting behind the glass were diners. Achak walked straight up to the food court, a motion that was also favored by Anthony. A large soda, two hotdogs, and a side of nachos later, Achak found his appetite satisfied and his jean pockets weighed down with quarters.

He waited while Anthony scraped out his coins from the change machine, giving it one last rub down to ensure he had not missed a single quarter, then put the fist-full into his pocket.

They took their time walking around the arcade, keeping an eye open for any new arcade games, then settled in front of a machine titled "No Remorse" and duked out their frustrations between their favorite fighters.

Achak watched his character, a masked samurai, sway in place for the last time waiting for Anthony's Viking she-warrior to bring on the finishing move. He watched on helplessly and then the screen went black.

"Hey, what gives?" Anthony slammed his fist over the second player controllers.

"Whoa. Careful there, Mr. Santiago," came a would-be casual voice. Immediately Achak knew the source of the problem to be anything but electrical. "You wouldn't want to get caught vandalizing, would you?"

"Speak for yourself, Don." Achak stepped back from the machine and turned around to see the boy with a gold loop earring and suspenders standing. The power cable was dangling from one hand. Donovan Parsons was the sort of thespian that had attempted to revive every archaic and prehistoric fashion trend since the invention of cotton. Though, because of his popularity, nobody else seemed to mind that his clothes were fashionably outdated. One day it might be a red cowboy handkerchief around the neck, today it was a pair of clip-on overalls strapped above brown plaid. In Achak's opinion, a thistle of wheat from Donovan's mouth would have completed the costume.

"Where's the straw hat?" Achak heard Anthony speak under his breath. He laughed aloud.

"Don, why don't you refund our quarters and go back to 'em rehearsals," Anthony mocked. "I bleeve Oz is missing its scarecrow."

Too late to react, Dovovan's fist cracked into Anthony's face. Achak grabbed around Donovan's arm to prevent him from coming down on Anthony's fallen body. Then Achak's own arm was pulled back. He felt his skull being bashed open as a hammer came over the top of his head. Harvey had stepped in to form the two-on-two. Eyes tearing over, Achak could barely make out the face of his assailant and he was too slow to raise a hand against the oncoming fist that struck unhindered with the side of his jaw. Releasing a cry as his back fell onto the game stick, Achak caught a glimpse of the shadow that stepped out from behind Harvey.

The next minute he felt a tight grip come over his shoulder and swung out blindly at it.

"Relax!" He heard the unfamiliar tone of a man's voice speak. "They're gone."

Achak pushed off with his elbows where his fall had been broken by the arcade game and not on the floor on which he had seen Anthony land upon.

"Anthony?" he began, but left off any questions as he met only one eye glaring back at him from the opposite arcade. The other eye was hidden behind a lump of swelling and purple flesh.

"Here." The man passed Achak a white handkerchief and indicated to his lip.

Dabbing the cloth at the corner of his mouth, Achak took a good look at the man that had intervened with the fight. It was the same westerner as before, the one who had had stepped inside the auditorium with his long coat.

Giving his sideburns and browncoat another look-over, Achak came to the same conclusion: that this fellow looked like he was from the old country.

"I'm going to get your friend some ice," the westerner stated as he departed, making one sharp turn of the heel. And Achak had the faintest impression that the man was as rough around the edges as the stubble on his mug.

"Ah—thanks," Achak called out to the retreating backside. He looked back at Anthony guiltily. "You alright, man?"

"Yeah, just don't look at me like that."

Achak could not blame Anthony for sounding so angry. Not only did he give consideration for the pain that must be pulsating from the bulbous eye, but he also had to admit that between the two, Anthony bore the more serious marks of a scuffle. While both a black eye and cut lip would be obvious signs of losing a fight and embarrassing enough to have to show in front of peers, having to hide behind a pair of dark sunglasses seemed like the raw end of the deal.

The westerner came back with the ice pack before Achak and Anthony could carry out any more of a conversation. Achak doubled over Anthony's gratitude, thanking the man for all his help, but noticed that the man did not look very appreciated. He failed to return so much as a "your welcome" to indicate that he had heard their thanks where even a nod or smile would have sufficed. When the westerner spoke to them again, it was to tell them to get on home.

Leaving the arcade in worse spirits and with so many curious eyes at their backs, Achak and Anthony walked toward the school. They would have to split up once they reached the corner of Park Boulevard, where Anthony would be carrying on east and Achak would travel west alongside the campuses. It would not be long before the remaining periods released students by the dismissal bell, but hopefully Achak would have put enough distance between himself and the high school before the majority of students began spilling onto the walkways.

When they reached the street corner, Anthony flung Achak back a quick wave and hurried to cross over to the other sidewalk. Sharing his side of the street, the outdoor tables of a small cafe sat their capacity-worth of students.

Achak had no intention of dropping in on any of the tables to find out if there was anyone around he knew, but he would still have to stop by the corner in order to reach the campus side of the boulevard. Instead of watching the faces conversing over the tabletops, Achak kept his eyes on his destination across the way, watching the front steps of the main building for students.

Classes were still in session so the walkways and lawns remained relatively clear. A couple of ravens hopped and skipped over the grass, and Achak wondered which of these had chased the vulture and whether that vulture really deserved the gang up or if ravens were no better than a flock of Donovans.

Waiting for the crosswalk to come on, he listened for any gossip from the cafe, though nothing caught his interest. Another student was waiting on the other side of the crosswalk and it occurred to Achak that he was familiar with the girl. She had Spanish hair and skin tone, hazel eyes, and the darkest clothes Achak had ever known a girl to wear with the exception of one other he could think of. As dark as she could dress without going totally black, the girl named Mariam wore violent shades of purple and fluorite, as well as having a bit of a design fetish with roses. Her velvet blouse was covered with them, though only visibly so with the reflection of light.

"That's right, girl!" Running across the street, Mariam exploded from Achak's side before he could even step off the curb. "You'd better leave. Back to your territory!" He turned around to see who she was yelling at and saw the Goth girl to whom he had referred to as the most darkly dressed. He had not known that Sirena had been sitting at one of the tables, nor if he had would he have joined her.

Black hair, black tank top, black pants, and combat boots contrasted with the palest face Achak had ever had the displeasure of meeting. The Goth girl had, on several occasions, taken to walking alongside Achak and asking him to accompany her to places. But she was much too concerned with Mariam now to pay Achak any heed.

Her chair had fallen behind her in what must have been an aggressive push off from her seat. Eyes ablaze, she glared across the table at the approaching Mariam. Everyone seated around the patio had pressed their heads closer together to both watch and commentate.

"Fly home, buzzard!" Mariam marched forward, looking ready to engage with the gothic rival. Sirena laughed as she stepped out from behind her table to meet Mariam in the walkway. Hands on her hips, she stood at equal terms with Mariam. Both were in each other's path.

"Well?" Mariam scowled. "What are you waiting for? I said, 'Fly home.'" Mariam may not have understood why Sirena was not obeying, but Achak could see clearly how Sirena was enjoying the show. She was at least a head taller than Mariam.

None to Achak's surprise, Sirena did what anyone with the advantage would have done. She walked straight up to Mariam, whose eyes measured only to the height of Sirena's skull choker.

"Move it, small feather!" Sirena demanded. She did not wait to repeat herself, and instead shoved pass Mariam, who stumbled back against the short wall. Leaving the cafe, Sirena then grabbed Achak by the arm and pulled him across the street with her.

"Come on, Achak," she delegated, looking over her shoulder to watch Mariam.

His face burned as he wondered what rumors were spreading behind him. He wrenched his arm from hers. "What was that about?"

As angry and humiliated as he was, he did not think he would release the pressure just by meeting Sirena's face. But as soon as she looked upon him and he saw the fresh gash on her cheek, he could not help sympathizing with what had just occurred. Could he really be so hypocritical when he knew that neither one of them had done anything within the moment to deserve a beating or threatening? He looked upon her cheek and related that Sirena must have endured as much as he had this day.

Achak felt kind of bad that he had not noticed her injury sooner.

Some day this was turning out to be, Achak thought bitterly and made a couple of swipes at the corner of his lip to check that there was no more blood dripping from his mouth.

The spot where his thumb touched was dry, but he could feel the swelling skin that had closed over the wound. It was a wonder none of his teeth had been knocked out when Harvey had landed the perfect punch.

Sirena reached her hand out and gently touched the corner of his lip, slightly smiling in the process. "I've been thinking about you, Achak."

Thinking it rude to say, "I haven't" in response, Achak searched for nicer way around the topic. "You okay?" he asked with at least some sincere concern.

"Yes-yes." She waved her hand airily. He was pleased to see that she was still smiling, but did not want to mislead her into believing that he shared any intimate feelings for her. "Come with me this time," she beamed. "It'll be fun."

"I've ah—I've got homework."

"Yeah right," she laughed. "You never even attended classes to know what your homework is. I saw you leave the grounds."

To this, he was stumped. "Shouldn't we get cleaned up and—"

"And it's Sirena so don't let me ever find out again that you've forgotten my name." Her voice was still a tease.

Achak did not argue with her accusation, even though his failure to mention her name had more to do with the fact that he did not want to let on that he had overheard her being called "buzzard," than it had with a failure in his memory.

"Right, well, Sirena," he put emphasis on her name. "Then I guess there's only one thing to decide upon."

"Forget it. I've already decided for us." She reached for his hand again and walked him away.

Achak stuck with her, if only because his reluctance was weakening because of his curiosity. Though, now it could be determined that Achak was not alone in his misgivings, as Sirena too had in some way, possibly through Mariam, incurred a fresh scratch down the side of her face. But unlike Achak, who had no intention of returning to the San Diego High campus at the end of the lunch break, Sirena kept up a cheerfulness that was not to be spoiled by her new blemish. Laughing and smiling, she tagged along with Achak down the streets of local neighborhoods and did not ask him uncomfortable questions about why he was ditching the after-lunch class periods.

All the while, Sirena seemed to be carrying on a one-sided conversation, talking on random issues, usually on what she picked up from her surroundings. Spotting a thin-ankled woman with her poodle trotting ahead by leash, Sirena found another source of inspiration.

"I think it's hilarious when people look like their pets," she began. "It's also funny to think of people as being related to certain animals and then when you get to know them better, it turns out that their personality is also representative of that animal. It's like that pair over there." And she pointed to the woman and her poodle as if it had not occurred to Achak where she might have come up with such a bizarre topic. "Did you ever watch those dog shows on TV and notice the uncanny resemblance between mutt and master?"

Achak thought this over for a minute, trying to relate the subject matter to someone he knew personally, but he could only think of Kitti's name and perhaps the slant in her eyes as being something feline. The ridiculous idea was swiped from his head when he realized that not all Asians are cat-lovers and so began to wonder whether Kitti owned any cats, or if she even liked them. He had never spoken to her about pets, which gave him the idea that he could work that topic into the conversation when next they met. Yet the more he thought about it, the more pathetic the conversation sounded as he rehearsed it in his head. "Do you have any pets?" he could ask. "I don't own any pets myself, but if I did..."-urg! Whoever said talking with girls comes natural never experienced it for himself, Achak thought, giving up on the preparation of conversation topics. With cats fresh on his mind, Achak was back at square one of the discussion, hardly aware that Sirena was deeper into thought than Achak had stayed along to follow.

"...But then you get into expressions like 'lion heart'." Sirena's speech began to slow down. She steered Achak aside, pushing him onto the fields of grass that began a small community park, which showed little up-keep on the swing set or monkey bars.

"...And I just don't see the resemblance." With her closing thoughts, she released Achak's hand. He dwelled for a moment in the shade, but Sirena kept her feet and mouth moving by circling him.

"I mean, I know lions are fierce and everything. But they can also be brutish, can't they?" Sirena continued her rant of lions. Around and around she went, both in conversation and on her feet. It was the creaking of the nearby swings hanging off their rusted chains that brought Achak out of the circle. He wanted to take a seat somewhere and Sirena seemed to move right along with him as he drifted further across the empty playground. However, every available bench he spotted was desecrated with splinters. Then Sirena had the idea of moving back toward the trees, probably the only healthy wood in the park.

"And lions live in prides. I know it's just a name, but for royalty to prefer to associate themselves with prides rather than a colony, clowder, rookery, or tribe. I'd rather think that the eagle was a better choice, but wolves can be loyal predators too."

"Yes, but aren't wolves generally seen with a negative connotation to them?" Achak challenged, having interested himself enough in the conversation to comment. "I'm not so sure kings and such want to be remembered as the boy who cried wolf."

"Negative stereotypes!" Sirena said hotly and flapped her vibrant red hair around. "Wolves are misunderstood, don't you think so?"

Achak shrugged. He had a reluctant idea in mind about where this conversation was going. And he wondered what, if anything, did wolves have to do with Native Americans, but the answer was out before he could distract her.

"Wolves were friends to the people of your tribe, weren't they?" Sirena imparted.

Achak remained silent while Sirena broke into a fit of laughter as she sometimes did when things became too quiet between them. She had spotted a fine shade tree of high branches and pulled Achak under.

Drifting closer to the tree, she backed into the shadows in her state of giggles. Her throat chimed melodiously as if she only just realized the absurdity of everything she had been talking about. She let her fingers slip from Achak's hand, fingers that he never realized he had still been holding onto. Taking a couple of paces back with her eyes intently on Achak, Sirena began to transform.

Achak watched from a foot away the stages of evolution occur like a video about the seasons being thrust into fast-forward. A smooth complexion turned bald, red, and wrinkled, while the black material of her outfit frilled out into feathers. A thin layer of fog began to overtake Achak's vision. The feathery creature became framed in white, almost like a wide-screen movie caption, blurred, and then Achak lost reception.

"Where've you been all this time?" Sirena looked from Achak's unconscious body to the man approaching.

"Around," Lapidar replied. "I don't mingle." He looked down at Achak. "You really shouldn't have done that. I don't suppose you plan to carry him back to Domestica?"

"No," she sighed in conclusion.

"...Manu's a nut."

"Yes. But a very rich one."

-●○●○●-

5
Master and Mutt

Weak and nauseous, Achak thought he saw a hazy walkway of stairs leading up to a structure of immense height for only a two story building. Round cement columns stood near the entrance. A smear of vertical lettering came down from the portico as it was engraved in one of the cemented pillars, and spelled out perhaps not an English word:

D-O-M-E-S-T-I-C-A

"It could've been you."

"No—I'm not extinct," Sirena's high-pitched vocals answered to a man's voice.

Then a new voice of heavy accent began to speak with some fatherly concern. "What did you give him?"

"A sneak peek into this year's coming attractions," answered Sirena with her usual charming level of energy.

"Then he's not ready?"

"How's that?"

The clicking of heals on a hard surface floor, maybe tiles, told Achak that the man was walking. He could hear someone's heavy breathing and worried that it might be his own until it became a self-discouraging whisper of "no, no, no, no."

"It'll be too much of a shock. Take him back."

"After—"

"You'll be paid. But I'm expanding the contract."

"To?"

"You and Lapidar—"

"I haven't agreed to the terms of this revised contract YET," barked in retaliation a fierce voice that Achak thought was likely to belong to the said "Lapidar."

"Easy, boy. It'll be worth your interest. Adaptation can be taught; it just takes consistent reiteration. Bring him back when he is able to stay awake. And make sure nothing happens to him in the mean time. And use caution."

"What does he add to your collection?" Lapidar growled, unsatisfied.

"The last prehistoric mammal."

"They're extinct."

"No, no, my boy—just forgotten."

Sirena looked from the doorway then back to Lapidar in an anxious desire to leave. The room of immense scale, even if its décor included the exhibition of art, which it did, would surpass the human capacity of most exhibit galleries in the world. Like any place of business, it lacked the comforts of informality with its custom-made furniture, so perfectly angled with the art pieces that they became a part of the display, not to be touched. She looked over to Lapidar who continued his talk with Manu, apparently unaware of her efforts to get his attention.

"I'll get the boy for you, but will that be enough?" Lapidar took a defensive stance, removing some of the weight from his front and putting it onto his hind leg, which would allow him to sustain balance when put against any frontal attacks.

Manu laughed. "And why should that matter concern you?"

"Because I want to know the probability of me being placed into one of your collections. I want to ensure that after my job's done, you won't go stray on your bargain and put me into your little petting zoo."

This time Manu restrained his amusement to a contorted smile. "*Do* stop calling my sanctuary a petting zoo. I'm not in it for the money, but I would like some appreciation for my efforts. There is no public admittance into my facility for such a materialized purpose to befall the creatures I'm protecting."

Sirena glanced up at the chandelier above her as one of the tiny lights flickered in a crystal bulb, and rolled her eyes away, again glimpsing the doorway before returning her gaze to Lapidar.

"I am trying to prevent endangered species from extinction and you are accusing me of running a circus act!"

This is likely to turn into a circus if someone doesn't give, Sirena thought. She'd get a headache if they didn't stop arguing soon. "Lapidar," she interjected, and at last he saw the sternness in her face.

"Just one more thing," Lapidar spoke more to Manu than to Sirena. "You told us to use caution around the boy. What exactly can we expect from his transmogrification. We're not talking about dinosaurs here, are we?"

"No, they are indeed extinct. We are speaking of mammals, my boy—one of the oldest no longer known to man." Manu thought a moment. "His premature transmogrification could turn up very bad results indeed. Should this happen, he will have the potential to shatter skulls in a single bite. You will be looking face to face with a creature possessing more than your share of strength or speed, as nothing in this remaining animal kingdom could dare match: a smilodon with 11,000 years of unpredictable evolutionary changes."

Lapidar came out of the meeting looking very harassed. He had had about enough of riddles and secrecy.

Shooting only a glance at Sirena, he muttered, "Smilodon, sure. I'll have to look that one up."

"Hey! Hey! Lapidar!" Sirena called after him. When she reached him, she dug her claws into his arm and jerked him back. "Just what do you think you're doing?" The shrieking began again. "Bad mouthing Domestica in Manu's face! Are you crazy?!"

"And what about you?" Lapidar yanked his arm free from her grip.

"Wha—"

"I saw you! I saw you and that Twinfang boy!" The blood was rushing to Lapidar's brain. "You knew him," he barked accusingly. "You knew him before I pointed him out. You've made contact with him before!" Lapidar paced back and forth in the hallway, indecisive about whether he should tear Sirena apart. "Is this a game?!" Lapidar barked for all his flying spit was worth. When next he stopped in his tracks, his face ignited with rage. "Just what did Manu want me as a huntsman for if he already knew where the boy was located?"

"Well," Sirena pretended to ponder over. "He didn't need you to track down what Dr. Coral already found." From under her dangling strands of red hair, she gleamed at Lapidar with a superior smile. His temper no doubt amused her. She simply shrugged her shoulders in response to Lapidar's question. "I suppose Manu feared that the boy might run."

"Were there others?" Lapidar maintained a degree of distrust. Sirena's brief responses still carried with them a tone of secrecy that Lapidar could not allow to slip by unchecked.

"Others? Before you? Why yes." Sirena spoke in a tone of indifference.

"And?"

"And nothing," she said sternly.

"They're dead?!"

Sirena broke into a fit of hysterical and mirthful laughter, an eerie combination of amusement and ill wishes.

"Oh my! Is the big bad wolf scared?" She couldn't go on to say more for lack of breath. Every time she opened her mouth, another fit of laughter broke out. She grabbed around her waist, clutching her mid-section as though a kidney might burst.

"You're asking for it, Little Red," Lapidar snarled.

She ran the tips of her fingers through crimson hair and grasped the Red Riding-Hood connection. Then Sirena clutched her hair into pigtails and laughed harder. Swishing the two ends around like a jump rope, she began hopping in place and making a horrible shrill. When the jumping ceased, she twirled several times in place before stopping with a famished look and panting. Lapidar could not put words to what he had just witnessed.

"Oh, don't look at me that way," Sirena breathed. "And you can stop... worrying about Manu." Though spoken with amusement, her words sounded sincere. "He's not going to kill you," she panted a slight laugh. Her breaths shortened.

Bowed over her knees, she appeared to be struggling with her self-containment. It was hard to believe that she was talking about serious issues in such a hyperactive manner. The amount of pleasure she took in discussing matters of life and death was quite disturbing in Lapidar's opinion. Yet this reaction, he knew, was all in the nature of a scavenger—one who waits around for the death of her prey, following her victims to the end.

"I—I think he likes you," she mocked.

"I'm not so sure I want to be liked by him," Lapidar grumbled, moving away to disassociate himself from Sirena.

"Ya-ya." She rolled her eyes and followed him. "You're not the first. Just don't let *Him* hear you say that."

6
Survival of the Fittest

A mist overhung the lampposts in an early morning haze. Adding to that visible murk of air was Sirena's steaming coffee drink.

Her eyes unfocused, Sirena watched the vapors whirl from the Styro-foam. Darker rings shadowed her eyes even though the mascara was limited to only the skin beneath her lashes. She slouched back in the armless steel chair at a table in front of the Wildcat Café. Her head kept sagging as she tried to keep taking sips from her coffee drink to keep herself awake.

"What are you doing here!"

Sirena looked up from her drink to see the small feather and her taller handsomer boyfriend Marcus. The noise was too appallingly loud to be tolerated at this early hour. Then there was also the pride of her kind that Sirena had to standup for and defend, but she stayed put.

"Excuse me." Mariam came bustling over to Sirena's table until she stood right up against the metal. "I asked you what you are doing here after I specifically told you to stay clear, buzzard."

Sirena shrugged and took another sip of her mocha. There was still some whipped cream on the top that she decided to lick off.

"Look at me when I'm talking to you!" Mariam screeched. The table shook under her slamming hands. "You don't belong here and you know it."

"Quiet down, small feather," Sirena said, licking the cream off her lips.

Marcus put his arm on Mariam's shoulder to stop her from leaping over the table and began pleading with her in a low voice.

"Come on, Mariam. This isn't worth it. Just leave the buzzard alone." He grabbed both of the small feather's shoulders and turned her around towards him. "She's just out to find trouble. Don't get involved."

"You should listen to him, small feather," Sirena blurted. "He's a smart boy."

"Let go, Marcus!" Mariam pulled her arms free and Marcus withdrew. "Who are you waiting for, buzzard?" She turned her attention back to Sirena.

Sirena shrugged again and responded with, "Can't a girl sit?"

"As if that was all you're doing, but I know you're waiting for someone!" Mariam turned swiftly to her tugging boyfriend. "Alright!" she exclaimed, then shot Sirena a final look. "Don't get too comfortable in that chair. You haven't built your nest in this neighborhood."

Achak felt someone pull on his arm, attempting to lift him from a cold surface. His body gave a jolt in retaliation, then the sense of struggle occurred to him and he bolted upright, eyes wide. He expected to meet face to face with the one responsible for his startling arrival into consciousness. Instead, his eyes met only darkness, so impenetrable that he had only his mind through which to navigate.

Then his eyes adjusted, the black wall eroded and shapes began to emerge. The rounded bulbs of his bedposts came into view, and beyond them, stood his dresser and open closet, with collar-less shirts dangling from their hangers.

The coldness—it became clear to him—had come from the sweat soaking up his clothes while his uncovered body lay exposed to the draft coming through his open window. His bed sheets and blankets, now visible in the moonlit room, rested at the foot of his bed in a bundled heap.

How had he come to this? Try as he might to remember, Achak still ended his recount of events at the Wildcat Cafe. Whenever he tried to recall anything beyond that, his mind ventured into the fantastical visions of black feathers sprouting from the palest of human flesh. This, of course, was unreasonable: milk-white skin being feathered with the color of night like some horrible omen of death.

His afternoon must have fallen to forgettable trivialities, but Achak could not be satisfied with the idea that his most recent and wakening moments had vanished from memory, however insignificant they might be. He knew his short-term memory had its flaws, but even flaws had limits, which could not explain the suddenness of his memory failure.

Conceivably, Achak could forget how he had spent his evening from three days passed—maybe even two—but his last evening, only a few hours gone—according to the digital alarm clock's 4AM display—should still appear in his mind with traces of details that could speak some truth to its occurrences. Yet, Achak could not create at least one familiar scenario that would have landed him fully clothed in daytime wear on his bed. His shoes were still on and he could not remember ever having opened the window.

He would have to consult "someone" about his arrival home, his first choice being his mother. Although he did not want to come off to her sounding like a child asking about a scary dream, Achak did want some reassurance that he had not gone barking mad. These days, not even Tehya woke up Mom in the middle of the night. Frozen in his doorway, Achak had to convince himself that it was not the dream that scared him, but the missing time.

After resting his head against the woodwork, Achak left the doorframe and entered into the hallway. His chest tightened with guilt, though he was not yet sure what he should be regretting. Facing the hall's end, Tehya's room stood to the left and Mom's room to the right. Achak's arm entered the room first, flicking over the light-switch to reveal a made-up bed and a tidy room. Achak's heart raced, not out of concern for the absence of his mother, who must have been assigned the late shift at the Peshewa Casino, but at the lost prospect of being able to find closure to his concerns. Without thinking, he ran into Tehya's room and straight up to her empty bed, patting down its sheets as though his eyes were playing tricks on him.

In panic, he had turned on every light in the house before settling in the kitchen, staring at a flat sheet of paper resting by the toaster and coffee maker. The letter read:

Achak,
Sorry I missed you. Wish you had called, I was starting to worry though I know you're a big boy now. I have to work late tonight. Grandpa came to pick up Tehya at five. I hope you can manage on your own this one night, though I suppose you already ate out with your friends.

Take care,
XXXOOO' Mom
619...

The numbers to his mom's work phone never finished translating before Achak's mind dropped off. No one knew where he had been, or the approximate time of his return.

He put his head on the counter top, pushing the letter away and trying to strain his mind for the answers. Worse than finding no answers, Achak felt his recollection slipping further and further into fantasy. This time, he not only saw feathers but also felt the prickle of grass that he could have only known if his face had been laying upon the ground. He recalled voices, muffled and now untranslatable. Achak could not have realized that the harder he tried to concentrate, the harder the memory worked against him. He needed to relax in order to let his mind chase after the images that flooded his memory but instead he was like a scientist struggling to interpret a painting by focusing too hard on what he saw and not what he felt.

Silent, Achak stood in the dim light of the kitchen. Slivers of light crept through the window blinds above the sink and cast bar-like shadows over the counter top. Achak stared long enough to watch the bars shift, until it occurred to him that he had been measuring time. He looked at the numbers on the microwave clock, which said 7:15 in their green digits. The hour finally registered, pulling Achak back into the present. Dazed and slow in his movements, he rubbed his hands over his face, allowing his feet to blindly walk him down the hallway toward the bathroom.

With his head bent over the faucet, Achak splashed water on his face and scrubbed, unable to cleanse himself of feathers entirely. Then at last, the straggling images were rubbed from his eyelids. When he finished washing up, only his reflection looked back at him from the mirror—just the familiar contours of his face and two dark eyes and his partial upper body, hidden under yesterday's clothes. Achak wet his hair down with a promise to his reflection that he could present a better version of himself than on the previous day.

The time he spent combing his hair down became the first step toward a new day. He left the house with the determination to attend all of his classes. Remembering how Donovan Parsons had fought with him, Achak would also have to get through this day without conflict. But mainly, he would pay careful attention to each detail, knowing how he had spent each hour. He would even talk to his mom about his day when he returned home, just to prove to himself that he was not amnesiac.

As a change of routine, and because there appeared to be nothing readily edible around the kitchen, Achak planned to stop at the Wildcat Cafe near the school for breakfast before heading to his first period class.

-●-○-●-○-●-

At the low wall of the cafe's courtyard stood a man in his late twenties with ruffled hair and two fashionably outdated sideburns running down his face. Achak recognized the browncoat and ruggedness of the man who had rescued both him and Anthony from a serious beating in the arcade. Though Achak felt he had not given the man a satisfactory thanks in his own conscience, he did not think, after recalling the way in which the man had curtly brushed him aside last time, that a second attempt would give better results. So he was relieved to see that he would not have to walk in front of the man to enter the cafe.

Achak moved through the break in the waist-high wall with the continuous pavement leading him to the entrance of the cafe. He had not realized how long his hunger had been lingering until his stomach gave a painful jolt as the scent of sugar melted warm in pastries and coffee beans under the brew taunted his empty intestines.

Leaving the cafe, Achak had already crammed one of two glazed donuts into his mouth before leaving the doorway. He took a little more time with the second as he walked to the end of the patio, ready to make his way across the street and to the campus. It had not taken him nearly as much time as he had given himself, so he would not have to go to Mrs. Hwang's class immediately. Perhaps, he could check in on Anthony and his black eye before retiring to his desk in 12B, then he might be able to sort out a few things.

But before he could do that, he distinctly heard two voices call out his name in unison. First, Achak came face to face with Sirena who, having walked off one side of the curb, would meet him at some point over the crosswalk. Without so much as a "hello" to Sirena, Achak sought out the second voice and shot a look back in the direction of the man leaning against the cafe wall, but his place had been deserted, except for a stray dog that was sniffing along the wall and putting its nose into empty wrappers. Achak turned his whole body around, but could see no sign of the browncoat.

"Are you okay?" He felt a gentle hand come over his shoulder.

Achak turned to meet Sirena and expected to find her with a worried expression like some girls will at the merest startle in an individual. But then, as he found, Sirena was not the type to overreact. Kitti might have shown more concern, but Sirena smiled either with narrowing eyes or more mascara set above them than Achak was used to seeing at this close range, for when she beamed at him, she also glowered. He was about to return the formal greetings when he realized that a single red strand he thought had settled on her cheek was really a scratch mark. His mind raced... because the slash on Sirena's cheek was so familiar, she had been with him the day before... during the time period he could not quite remember. Yet, he did not want to sound too cheerful about finding Sirena in such a state, which would have been similar to her pointing at the swollen corner of his lip and shouting: "You still got it! You still got it!"

"Urm, I'm good. And... what about you?" He took as much time saying these words as his concerns would allow. Achak had some uncertainties about whether or not he should be glad to see Sirena. There was an eerie darkness about her that not even the skull around her neck could explain.

However, if anyone was to be his source of information, it would have to be Sirena, who he last remembered spending his time with.

"You look seriously strung over," Sirena laughed.

"Oh, um—couldn't sleep," Achak lied.

"I see. Well, we did have a long night, but wasn't it fun?" Sirena grabbed Achak's arm and dragged him along with her.

"What?" Achak could not believe what he was hearing. The image of Sirena and him locked together, arm-in-arm, and staring into each other's eyes haunted his mind so vividly that he pulled away as soon as Sirena had wrapped her hands around him. But the reality of the situation took hold of him as he began to slowly accept the possibility that he may have spent a better part of the night in the company of the darkness, the stars, the moon, and Sirena. "You and I hung out? Where—What did we do—"

Two separate laughs broke out: one, the high-pitched cawing of Sirena, but the other, a much deeper bark from behind. Achak whirled around to see the man with the browncoat standing in the same spot against the patio wall. The stray dog had disappeared. Achak gaped at the mangy appearance of the man who took on more mutt-like characteristics than the dog had while sniffing into empty food wrappers. It must have been the sideburns and stubble that made him more squalid than any stray Achak had seen wandering along the gutters.

If this was an opportune moment for Achak to offer the man his gratitude for the previous day's rescue, then why did he feel a cold block of ice roll over in his stomach? He backed up into Sirena and, by doing so, saw the movement within the browncoat as the man pulled out his hand. It was not empty.

From behind the sleeve of his other hand, he tried to conceal a gun. Its black metal gleamed with the rim of the muzzle now pointing directly at Achak. To his and Sirena's eyes alone, Achak knew that nobody else around could see the threat as the revolver did not leave the shadow of the draping fabric.

"Go!" Achak hissed to Sirena, but he sensed only a slight shift in body movement from his side. "Sir— " he meant to say her name, but his voice cracked and faltered. Then an arm came around his and jerked him from his frozen place.

Together, he and Sirena took to the street that ran alongside the school, passing the fencing around the track and field. Achak listened for any sounds of bullets that would crack the air, but nothing beyond the hammering of his chest and feet reached his ears.

Sirena was largely responsible for the escape. Setting the pace and leading Achak at the turns, she brought both of them back on the main street without hearing any gunfire. Achak did not know why they headed away from the school instead of seeking protection in it. Though, at this point, he did not care to put his trust into logic or reason, not when deliberating might mean the difference between life and death. It was easier to leave his fate in Sirena's hands than to wonder what might become of them if he were to take it upon himself to decide on the course of action. Then it occurred to him that Sirena might not know where she was going but could be running them ragged out of pure shock. Both the stitch at his side and his estimation of the lapsing time put the fear back into his chest, now heaving for oxygen.

Looking around himself, Achak saw no familiar residences, but had crossed a freeway on the overpass where their surroundings changed completely on the other side. The street curved into open landscape where a community park spread wide and far. To Achak's alarm, they would not have any cover for what appeared to be another half mile. Any experienced gunman would have welcomed a chance like this to shoot while there was an opening, but Sirena appeared to have no intention of altering her direction or taking cover.

"Sirena!" Achak pleaded.

She shook her head and Achak knew that she would not respond.

"Where are we going?"

Still Sirena ran onward without speaking, yet had the sense to raise her right arm and point to their destination ahead. Achak watched for the rising palm trees and white tower before protesting. He knew that just beyond the clock tower was the San Diego Zoo, and before it, with free admission, was Balboa Park—both attractions being concealed with the heavy greenery of the most tropic and exotic of plant life.

Achak could think of a dozen other public areas where he and Sirena could have stopped at along the way and used as a hideout without having to come this far, but none would have been nearly as populated or renowned. Already, Achak could see a couple of yellow school buses poking their rears at the back end of the parking lot. The idea half upset and half elated him. For one thing he could be confident of their hiding spot. For another, it would be a long journey home without a taxi.

Across the grass, short black rails began to prevent them from taking any shortcuts and took them instead around the walkway.

"We're going to Balboa Park," Sirena stated at long last, slowing down as she came up to the parking lot.

The news did not surprise Achak, who had already crossed off the zoo as an option because of its admission fees. For instances such as now, he regretted not having bought an Annual Student Pass or taking advantage of the local discounts, but then again, Balboa Park would provide them with more than enough cover to serve as an ideal hideout.

Weaving in and out between cars, Achak followed Sirena to a break in the greenery where a stone walkway opened up. The path was tiled by square-cut rocks and painted in the reds, turquoises, and yellows of a Spanish Village. He came upon tapestries and beads hanging from the windows of small adobe huts. The atmosphere of people flocking from one station to another and circling the courtyard put Achak's nerves at ease. He made one last look down the pathway behind them, assuring himself that it was vacant of any browncoats.

"So where to now?" he burst out with the promise of life. He knew the desire to kiss the ground had to be restrained. But he had to admit that it was exhilarating to be alive after being so close to death.

"Oh, you'll see," Sirena came back with the tease of a temptress. She too sounded only too grateful to have escaped a horrible fate at the hands of a gunman.

"Alright, I'll play along, but can I ask you something about yesterday?"

"Ah-ah-ah." She stopped him from pressing forward, teetering her finger in front of his face.

"Well then, what do you want to talk about?" Achak was still panting. He almost wished he hadn't asked the question because, in truth, he was in no state of mind to want to talk.

"What would you say about going to the Museum of Man?" Sirena voiced in a kind and hopeful manner.

"Yeah, okay." Achak didn't think it made much of a difference which museum within the park they visited.

"Isn't it ironic that the zoo is next to the Museum of Man?" She became excited with this bit of factual coincidence. "I mean, one place teaches you about animals, but then you have to enter a separate park to learn about man!"

"Yeah, uh—so?" Achak wasn't sure he really wanted to hear about it. His mind was busy reeling over images of the encounter with the gunman, while Sirena found it interesting to plunge into a discussion about the location of museums.

"So basically we're manifesting a hierarchy in which man must remain separate from the animal kingdom, no matter how much we resemble other mammals anatomically."

"And?"

Sirena became determinedly set on drawing an opinion out of Achak, no matter how argumentatively she had to treat the subject. "Oh, come on! You can't be that arrogant. I mean, to keep facts about man and animals in a separate park is like denying your ancestry and lineage."

Achak shrugged good-naturedly. "Well, we were kicked out of Eden. Maybe that's the difference between the zoo and this place."

Monuments overtook every courtyard and garden. Faces carved over the entrances overshadowed everything that might have been considered natural, where no overgrowth could intrude upon the inventions of man. With the exception of the botanical garden, which still bore signs of man's influence, the museums gave tribute to him and his inventions, where stone and statue prevailed. Trains and steam engines were commemorated through one door, while modern photography could be glimpsed and snapshot through the next.

Achak walked with Sirena down the outer corridors of the yellow stone buildings and looked out the archways that he never seemed capable of memorizing. The bell tower that marked the Museum of Man was a haunting protrusion of needle on top of dome—bone white upon the horizon. Neoclassical and cathedral-like, the Museum of Man was encased in a square courtyard, which had to be entered by walking under one of two superior archways. Carved overhead, a draped woman gracefully tipped her vase, spilling water down the sides of the archway.

Achak was prepared to walk up the stone steps and pay the admission fee, but Sirena pulled back on his arm. She had her attention elsewhere and, as Achak looked around, he realized that they had the whole courtyard to themselves. It was open-hours and the square was almost never deserted. Normally couples would wait around the fountain and watch the blue sky settle over the white tower, but maybe they preferred to watch from the bridge that crossed into the Gaslamp District.

Walking more towards the center of the square, Achak peered through the archway that led out onto the bridge where he saw one darkened silhouette coming forth. Already it was too late to move unnoticed. The man with the gun raised his hand and took aim.

"Did you have a nice time?" He wasted no time putting himself within speaking range.

"What do you want?" Achak found the courage to say.

"Shut up. I wasn't talking to you," the man spat, upon which Sirena came forward. "Well, Sirena?"

"Lovely," she chimed.

Achak could not believe what he was hearing. Did Sirena really mean to be so cool in front of the gunman, or was it simply an attempt at bravery?

"You're late," she remarked.

"Yeah, well, I'm sorry to keep you waiting." The gunman added an unnatural kindness to his voice.

"Me waiting?" Sirena puffed up. "What about *him?*" And she directed her hand back at Achak. "Or there's Manu to consider as well. I doubt he'll approve. You should be so lucky, Lapidar. Let me handle this and I'll spare you cleanup."

The chills reverberated from Achak's spine. While listening to the informalities, a lump caught in Achak's throat, making it hard for him to swallow the possibility that Sirena and the gunman were in together.

"My, aren't you feeling generous today." The gunman held the mockery in his tone. "But don't forget who the real gentleman is here. Ladies first." He gestured for Sirena to join him at his side. And she did.

With her back to Achak, Sirena walked forward and did not meet Achak's face again until she was positioned by the gunman's right hand. It looked a lot like picking teams and clearly Achak was the odd man out. Sirena gave him a little wave from the other side, which, in Achak's mind, did more damage than any wisecrack remark from the gunman. At last, he seemed to comprehend and yield to the direness of the situation.

"Now what?" He found the only two words that would make him sound like neither a hero nor a coward.

"I thought you wanted me tell you about yesterday?"

But behind Sirena's taunting play, Achak could detect a hint of impatience. In some way, he knew that she was not enjoying this as much as she let on.

"So tell."

Again his response had pushed her into uneasiness. Tugging at the loose black material at her sides, Sirena hesitated—her shifty movement displaying the anxiety.

However unsteady her body language was, she retained control over her vocals. "What's there to tell?" Her own words brought back the vibrancy of her persona. When her eyes flickered, they dropped into a darker shadow. The red dyes of her hair ignited in the blue sky. "I'm more of a visual person anyway. Let me show you."

Then Achak witnessed evolution, these being the last of human words spoken before she transformed.

He watched the pigments of her hair bleed into her face, which, shortly afterward, shriveled, thinning and stretching the neck. She went bald, then the black fabrics tore apart as strips frilled into feathers.

•○•○•

7
The Hot and Cold-Blooded

Achak could not keep his eyes from darting between Lapidar's browncoat, visible to him only from the furthest corner of his eye, and what glimpses he could catch of Sirena's face. Whereas his first instincts were to try to catch Sirena's attention, expecting her to give him some sign of recognition, ultimately, he would have settled for any small level of eye contact. In repay for all of his attempts to force their eyes to meet, Sirena would not give him so much as a glance in return.

Sirena kept her back to him, which was mostly because Achak was kept restrained by the gunman with his hands handcuffed to his back and the revolver sticking into his side. Achak moved at a slow pace, which every once in a while would be hastened by the gunman's harsh prod into his ribs. This way, he had no chance to move alongside Sirena and refamiliarize himself with her.

But the real reason Achak moved so dispiritedly behind her was when he had made an attempt to open his mouth and call for Sirena, but closed it again after it occurred to him that "Sirena" might not be her name after all. She had probably never shown Achak her true self and would have to start out by shaking hands if they talked. And so after making his many vain attempts to seek comfort in her company, Achak turned his head away from her as well.

He faced no walls or enclosures yet, just the earth and the sky. Mostly though, he faced the sky.

San Diego was the least of flat counties in Southern California, which became more visible to Achak while traipsing over the slope of one hillside and looking out upon the slopes of the many others. Hilltops rolled away his view of what might have been Downtown San Diego, or the ocean.

He had no clear sense of direction from this altitude, only that up was forward and down was behind; and green was at his feet and blue was at his head. Whatever else remained hidden to him visibly, Achak pondered over when was the last time he had seen it and if he would ever be able to see it again.

This was true of a lot of things, Achak surmised: Tehya, his mom, his grandpa, Anthony. Would he see them again?

He had been collected by a vulture and a gunman, two distinct representations of death, but neither of them had attempted to carry out his murder, or, at least, not in any way Achak could imagine it. There were no bullets fired and no obvious circling over his scalp, which meant that he must be of some use to them alive.

Achak's pace began to lag while he shook his head in denial. It was so easy for him to convince himself that no one wanted him dead if he too wanted the same outcome. Lapidar nudged the revolver into Achak to keep him moving.

What became of hope and sky bowed itself in an instant. As though the heavens really could diminish and black steel bars could separate the clouds, Achak was led onto Death's private property.

Before him, rose the great broad wall and pillars of a mansion, white—and yet, grayer to him all the same.

There was no more incline to the path he walked, but rather, he began to know the smooth and even surface of a plateau. His feet learned of cement and not of the asphalt of roadway, which spiraled around the hillside, while his eyes too had to meet the vertical surface of stone—so refined in texture that it defied nature's beauty. And what of the grass around him? Normal for these hilltops, and yet they yielded no signs of nature's influence as every blade was trimmed to equal height and perfection.

Sculptures stood their guard along the walkway and prevented guests from setting foot on the grass. Even Sirena held a tight course over the pathway's center, the furthest she could come from either side of grass fields, and from the eyes of Aphrodite, Zeus, Shiva, reincarnation, and Karma.

Achak was not sure what shadow movement or change of pace made him believe that Sirena was trembling in front of him. Maybe it was his own set of fears that he wished to have shared by another, but whatever the cause, he called to her like an intuitive fool.

"You don't have to!" Achak broke the silence between them. He had surprised his own body with the tearing of vocals. "You can turn back."

Landing a hand on Achak's shoulder, the gunman jerked him back into a standstill. Sirena stopped walking ahead as well and turned around.

Unlike what Achak had expected, her cheeks were not tearstained, nor her lips unreadable. Her dark pupils met him for the first time since she had changed back from being a vulture. Then her red eyebrows came down over them and moved closer together.

"What are you talking about?" she screeched.

Achak stared down her long dark veil of gothic drapery and thought of what consequences he would face if he had interpreted Sirena's movements incorrectly.

"Sirena?" a deeper voice erupted behind Achak's head and unnerved him.

"And what do you want, Lapidar?"

"For you to keep moving. I'd like to get this job over with." The moodier voice behind Achak was almost a growl. Achak had the image of a beast before he came to realize that it was only his gunman speaking.

"It'll be over with soon enough," Sirena said smartly. "I want to know what he meant, right here and right now. Well?!" She focused in on Achak.

"The boy's talking nonsense. Just ignore him."

Sirena shook her head and gazed once more from the gunman, Lapidar, to Achak. Her eyes went seemingly darker as the black rings of mascara closed in around them.

"You'd rather not do it." Then knowing that he would not be shot, Achak struggled with the cuffs and grip that Lapidar had fastened around his wrists. And just as Achak had anticipated, his struggle had caught both his captors off guard, which gave them each a new reaction.

Lapidar became more violent as he wrestled for a grip around Achak. His arms wrapped around Achak's neck in a chokehold. The gun fell to the ground without going off and Lapidar began shouting at Sirena to pick it up. She was panting in her small movements toward them, then stopped and did not proceed in her approach.

Achak used the delay to locate the revolver with his feet and, when he heard the metal scrape against the concrete, he kicked it across the grass. Lapidar squeezed tighter with his arms and Achak gasped for breath.

"Great!" Lapidar cried angrily, but Sirena had too much of her misty eyes fixed upon Achak to notice Lapidar's frustrations. "Well? Fetch it, would you? Come on! I'm not bringing him in like this!"

Sirena ignored him and began again her slow approach. Achak's struggling had ceased since he had been taken into the chokehold, but somehow Sirena's attention had riveted in him a new desire to fight for his survival.

His elbow went into Lapidar's ribs, but in return came a fist into Achak's side. He was no longer in a complete chokehold, but no longer could he keep up the struggle while he was withering in pain.

"Don't," Sirena shouted.

"I've got to!"

"No, we've got to bring him in conscious, remember! Not like last time."

Achak landed on his knees and, there, he looked up and saw the familiar angle of a great cement-caste building. Like out of a dream, it came back to him: the solid white textiles and pillars. It stood at twice the height of any ordinary two-story building, but there were just two windows lined vertically along the walls and Achak doubted that there was a third windowless floor squeezed between them.

The nearest of pillars came around the walkway, before the stairs that led to the entrance. Their rounded fronts were engraved with descending Roman lettering, also familiar to Achak from a not too distant dream.

"D-O-M-E-S-T-I-C-A"

"Get up! Get up!" Lapidar was yanking Achak by the collar to obey. "Sirena? What's wrong with you? Stop staring at him and get my gun!"

"No. He's different."

Because Sirena's word made as little sense to Achak as the inscriptions on the pillars, he was able to turn his mind and eyes towards them.

"I'm diff-rent?" Achak stared up and saw Sirena tilting her head and trying to make sense of him.

"Why should it matter?" Lapidar growled to her. "Who cares, as long as we bring him alive and conscious to Manu?"

"He's fighting. Don't you see? It's not like him."

"Forget it," Lapidar yelled. "The fact that you're 'questioning' isn't like you either."

Sirena scoffed. "This is different!"

There was a growl and Achak was knocked sideways onto the cement. His face hit stone and he watched, from the ground, Lapidar swish his browncoat and storm off over the grass to retrieve his gun.

Achak did not make an attempt to bring himself up further than on his knees. Meanwhile, Lapidar already had his weapon in his hand and was aiming it once more at Achak before his feet returned to the sidewalk.

"You want to play, little boy?" The mad glint shined once more in the gunman's eyes. "Sirena, get moving! You can assess his behavior later all to your liking, but not on my watch."

She glared at him. "Don't you get it? Your rage—his rage. It's as if he could already be..."

"Be what?!"

"Smilodon."

A rattle like none Lapidar had issued before came from his throat. "Enough with the riddles. 'Smilodian—smilopé.' Just what you're all talking about, I don't care. But if you're suggesting he transmogrify himself, right here right now, then you're a very long way from understanding the human species.

"He's an arrogant little boy. That's all. He's just messing with your head."

Lapidar's words may have shaken the vulture, but Sirena stood her ground.

"You didn't see his eyes just a moment ago."

"What about them?"

"They changed. They were brown and then they were flashing green. But maybe if you weren't too busy wrestling with him, you'd have noticed."

"Hey, little missy, you'd better watch what you're accusing me of." The growl returned to Lapidar's voice. "So the boy's got a little fire. So what?"

A strange snicker and rattle came into Lapidar's throat. "I bet if you were to hang out with the opposite sex more often, you wouldn't find it so surprising."

Achak could see by the tightening of Sirena's shoulders that she was not enjoying being made a fool out of.

"He had eyes like yours, you fleabag!"

In Lapidar's halting laughter, Achak was taken up with a painful tug into Lapidar's clawing grip. When Achak was once more standing, Lapidar released his arm and took hold of his throat.

Achak thought his lungs would be punctured. Sirena shrieked.

"You're pitiful, small feather, even for a Hybrid. Yes, it can happen. The hungry glow in a set of young eyes. Don't you know anything about our becoming?

But he's generations with the forgotten and no more nearer to summoning his own cross-being than he is to becoming an Olympic athlete. Get it?"

"No," Sirena said heatedly. "You sound like you know a lot about this human transmogrification business. So are you telling me that humans can meronize themselves by accident?"

"Well, I wouldn't call it 'meronizing' just because his eyes glowed. Now, had he summoned a pair of fangs, I might reconsider the term, but he's not about to make the full or even a percentage of transmogrification."

Lapidar held up his hand to gesture to the mansion and Achak was surprised to see him smiling, but he could see the mockery in pointing it out for Sirena.

She frowned and gazed upward. The building was waiting and Achak knew that from somewhere within waited the person who commanded his abductors.

Like eyes, two grand windows stared down at them from above the portico. The monster awaited. Its mouth shaped the entrance: its teeth made the pillars, it tongue made the stairs; and Achak felt the nudge of the revolver in his back that would lead him on to be swallowed by Moby Dick.

Up the stairs, Achak resolved to silence, He could have appealed to Sirena for more of a conversation, but the fact remained that she seemed to have more to discuss with Lapidar than with Achak. But that did not stop his eyes from straying feet ahead to where Sirena walked erect and in human form, her hair flapping behind her like a scarlet banner. She came up to the center of the wide oak doors and tested their handles.

"Locked," she said and turned around to inquire to Lapidar.

He tugged Achak along with him towards the portal. "Knock," he suggested, then without waiting threw up one of his fists against the wooden panel.

Turned around, Achak had the reflection of stone statues to stare upon. The visions of sculptors stood mounted in their cement castings. Across the lawns, their figures eloquently conveyed a myth over the fields of grass. The beauty of Creation came forth from their intricate poses, displaying moments of birth or rebirth as could only be told by the goddess Venus, a pearl in the oyster's shell, the doe's first teardrops, or by a feathered scuffle between the brolga and the emu egg.

All the figures reminded Achak of his English class and how Donovan Parson's would soon be dressed in the role of Shakespeare's Romeo, but he was no Romeo outside of costume or the classroom. Why drama and literature seemed to come together, Achak pondered as two subjects of distinction that paired together in obscure partnership: like the rough layers of Lapidar versus those of feather and grace belonging to Sirena. Should pouring over books in English and masquerading on stage in Introduction to Drama always go together?

"Can a vulture and a human be friends?" Achak verbalized. When turned around by Lapidar, he tried to meet Sirena's eyes, but she looked away. Instead, he caught the gunman's unflinching features.

"Lionhearted, aren't we?" Lapidar mused.

Sirena gasped and turned to him while having realized, along with Achak, that their conversation at school had not had as much privacy as she assumed.

"You filthy, eavesdropping—"

"Silence!" Lapidar barked. "I'm starting to like the boy. If only for his tongue. But I'm starting to hate these riddles. Really, kid, don't ask such stupid questions or you'll come across as a poet. However, if you really want an answer, the correct multi-choice would be: *it depends*—on the person, yes, but on the species, even more. There's no such thing as humans for one thing. We all belong to another kind. But to answer your question, cats can get along with birds, but in your case, a captive can't get along with his captors. How's that for explanations?"

Then without waiting for a response, Lapidar presented Achak to the large oak doors. Achak half wondered if he should feel elated to be standing there, where he thought it was possible to march in two elephants side by side. Though, unceremoniously, Lapidar stepped out from behind Achak and knocked again, or did what Achak might otherwise have described as laying two hard punches against the woodwork.

Sirena revived her first show of pleasure by laughing, something that she had not done since her transformation into a vulturous creature.

"You don't expect him to hear us, do you?" She flipped her index finger skyward. "Who knows what room—"

She broke off as a loud moan signaled the opening of the doors. Achak did not need to be prodded with the revolver to know he needed to stand back. Lapidar grabbed his wrist to make sure he would not make a run for it. The thought had not occurred to Achak since the distant front gates had closed behind them. Achak recalled the chime of steel bars, and the imprisoning effect of the front gates coming together.

As the doors before him parted, light was cast over Achak and washed upon the shaded portico. His eyes adjusted and he saw, standing against the doorframe, two black bearded men with ornate robes. Each wore a sash, while their dark hair was hidden under gold headdresses wrapped around their scalps like a towel. Neither spoke nor breathed too heavily, though Achak could see the beads of sweat that glittered from under their turbans from the effort it must have taken for each man to have opened his own door.

Each man had the same copper skin and dark eyes. For a uniform, they had gold sashes tied around their waists and paisley designs woven into their vests.

Without speaking, the doormen walked Achak and his two kidnappers across the carpet and to an elevator, giving Achak the impression that he was in a hotel lobby as opposed to a crime base. But if one pair of turbans impressed Achak, it was nothing compared to the one worn on the head of the man who greeted them once the elevator doors opened on the second landing. The cloth was as unadorned as the others, but wrapped around in such a way that each fold was well-balanced to noble perfectionism. The man was dark skinned, bannered, but tux-suited. As smooth as cream, the ivory of his head wrap matched the inner lining of his coat. The sweetened perfumes of the room only worked further to soften his appearance. This old, yet well-preserved man, looked as fragile as the antiques displayed around his quarters, from the most delicate of hand-painted vases to the miniature details of the smallest figurine. Each item was themed appropriately as a tribute to animals. To this, Achak hoped that the man's nature was as foam soft as the creamy colors he preferred.

"How creative, Mr. Gray. I asked you to bring the young man here conscious and you bring him at gunpoint. Not only that, but you parade into my mansion through the front door."

"Yeah, well, as rich as you are, you could have laid out the red carpet."

"Your humor can be tiresome."

"As can your lectures on endangered species. Now do you want the boy or not? Because if you find my methods tactless, I could always throw the boy back into the sea and have you fish him out by some other means."

Lapidar pulled irritably at Achak's collar, forcing him to the ground and causing the elder to cry out in a shift of power. Achak felt that if the gunman moved again, it would be to put a bullet into his head.

"He's here. He maintains consciousness, just like you asked. And look—" Lapidar pulled down on Achak's hair to exhibit more authority, "he's even unharmed."

"What about his lip?"

Lapidar laughed. "Yes, well, high school can be a rough experience."

"Do not bother me with trivialities. It is not this young man that is really bothering you, is it?"

"And what's that supposed to mean?"

Manu looked triumphant, pulling on his words like he would a choke collar. "Well, you are quite the family man, are you not? But do not let these matters concern you. There are more important obligations in your life, which is why you accepted my offer in the first place. Now leave Mr. Twinfang with me."

"Yeah, I'm sure he'll make a nice pet." And Achak distinctly heard an inhuman growl issue from the gunman's throat. Lapidar released Achak's hair and stepped aside.

Achak's unease grew as both men fell into a quiet surveillance of the room. The gunman refused to look at the turbaned elder at all, while the elder merely glanced over from time to time, occasionally letting his eyes rest on Achak. More to the captive's discomfort, Achak found that the extended break in conversation tended to cause both men's eyes to wander over to where he kneeled.

Between his two male abductors, Achak preferred the man with the gun for reasons that he knew to be irrational. But he could not argue with the foreboding that followed each contact he made with the elder. From beneath the turban, a set of eyes squinted with signs of pleasure. Though warmly placed, the elder's smile did not welcome. He appeared more self-satisfied, whereas his gunman was bitter and aggressive and, in Achak's opinion, preferably predictable.

"You disapprove of my plans for this facility?" The turbaned elder had not changed tones, but Achak had caught the flash in his eyes that showed the elder was angry.

Lapidar must have sensed it too because he backed down, but it could not have been in a worse position that he placed himself. As his arms crossed, he cocked his head in an aloof manner to show that he had not been completely put out by the question and so he answered it.

"Don't act so offended," sneered Lapidar. "I'm not even sure what your intentions are with this place."

"No?" Manu spoke quietly. "I think you do."

The gunman stared, but Achak saw a flicker of surprise and shared the anxieties.

Were it not for the shadow that came between them, Lapidar may have pulled the gun on Manu. However, Sirena had come between them, not taking sight of either man as she held out her arms in a halting gesture and stared across at Achak. She was smiling at him in a way that told him that he ought to be more concerned with his own wellbeing.

When both men cooperated, Sirena straightened her posture and re-fixed her preying eyes on Achak. Manu and Lapidar's attention followed hers and there drew an awkward moment when it seemed that no amount of background noise, not even the ring of the elevator doors opening or the alleluia of a grandfather clock, could delay Achak's fate much longer.

Then someone's clearing of the throat broke the silence—someone, who up until this moment, had not been in the room, yet now stood illuminated beside a tiffany lamp with his arms folded over impatiently as though he had been kept waiting all this time.

Sirena shrieked—as Achak tended to describe her startles or outbursts of glee as something that resembled more of what one tended expect to hear from the mouth of a carcass-devouring bird, or a banshee at best.

Nobody else said anything in the ear-ringing moment but they seemed no less surprised to see the new arrival than what Sirena had expressed in non-verbal hysterics. Yet, Sirena's scream did not go entirely unchallenged as it appeared on the looks of the men's faces alone that a startle or horror could be spotted in the whites of their eyes or between their tightened lips.

Close at hand was the impatient man that had snuck in on them: a gangly figure with a narrow face and sharp features. Perhaps once handsome in his youth, he had the receding gray by which his eyeglasses could only divide as a forehead as equally large and bald as the mug below it. In fact, the only hair that attempted to stay in shape was his widow's peak, which still fell back a ways and looked like a balanced point that needed to be glued into place to hold up the rest of his crowned hair.

Then there was his face, composed of pointed edges that were as sharp as the diamonds in his eyes, which when staring longer into, Achak realized were really in the shape of diamonds. But Achak sensed the same slits form in every man and vulture's eye against this stranger in their company. Yes, Achak looked to see the fierce stare of Lapidar. The wolf was practically growling in place. But of all the people Achak expected to see blatant with their temper, he did not expect to see

Manu compose himself as the least of happy persons to see this slender intruder take shape by the lamp.

"Ladon!" he exclaimed in haughty voice. "How nice of you to slither in, doctor."

Achak did not wait for Manu to give mention to a title before certifying the intruder with a profession. The man was not modest about his work while adorned in his white labcoat and with thin-lenses to his spectacles. His gray hair only reaffirmed what Achak had already thought to expect from a man who had taken no less than eight years of college to earn his certification as a practitioner.

Just what kind of doctor this man was or what medicines he specialized in, Achak could only guess. It was his measuring stare that led Achak to believe that this doctor had anything to do with medicine and chemicals at all.

"Forgive my protrusion," the doctor hissed and Achak was not sure what the man meant by his words since the correct word would have been "intrusion."

"Yes, you have quite the neck for that," Manu remarked and Achak felt even more out of the loop in his understanding of the discussion. "But I suppose, I can give you a moment."

When Manu turned around, his eyes fell immediately upon Achak. "The young man isn't going anywhere." Then he nodded to Sirena and held out his hand for the doctor to proceed out the door to which he indicated. "Excuse me for the moment," came his last words to those that remained.

Without Manu to watch out for, Achak cast his eyes on Lapidar. He caught the change in the gunman's face, who kept his eyes on the elders' backs as they left the room through the giraffe archway. The doctor was striding proudly alongside Manu and for the first time Achak noticed that the doctor stood taller by comparison, even without the crown of a turban.

An undeniable grumble issued from Lapidar's throat, then two wooden doors closed between the archway.

Achak tried to hide his gaze before the gunman could turn back around, but their eyes met before he could bring them to the floor. Yet, the matter that most concerned Achak, and now his abductors, neared its deciding hour, and that was to learn why he had been brought to this mansion. Perhaps even the lapdog gunman did not know the answer to this question. The longer Lapidar stood motionless, staring at Achak, the more reasons Achak found to believe that his abductor knew nothing of what would become of things.

Perhaps the turbaned elder was wrong in his suspicions and his gunman really did know very little of his mission or of the roof over his head. What had they called this place, Achak struggled to recall. *Domestica?*

"My, aren't you quiet." Sirena gleefully took charge. "Now, where do I begin? I hate introductions." But once her feet began to move, it was hard to separate her words from the course she had taken in circling around Achak. "...You already know me for who and what I am."

Achak turned his head away and chose a random item from the décor to focus on, settling on a victorian armchair, instead of Sirena's endless rambling. He found it difficult to ignore her words, realizing that at some point he would be expected to answer back. And what would he say then?

"Hey, don't look away. I thought we were friends."

Achak could hear the false anguish in Sirena's voice and wondered how he had ever been convinced by it before. She was a good actress, he thought bitterly, better at her improv than any performance Donovan Parsons could deliver, even after rehearsal.

"Come on. Don't you want to hear what I have to say?"

He felt ready to tell her "not really" after falling victim to so many of her lies, but lie or no lie, he wanted an explanation, no matter how far from the truth it might be. It took some hesitation, but eventually Achak was able to direct his eyes back on Sirena.

Her expression was livid—amused, but dangerously ill-formed, like the eternal grin of a skull. How she had ever put on the charm of a humming bird while wearing the feathers of a vulture, Achak could only wonder loathingly.

He felt the color drain from his flesh as he met not the face of a young woman, but of a scavenger. Sirena's body may have been concealed in human flesh, but behind her black and hating eyes Achak saw the cold, blank stare of a creature that does not hunt for the meat it devours. It waits and follows death like a moth attracted to light.

"What do you think we'll do to you?" Sirena put on a lofty air. She was just about bouncing on her heels before Achak could answer her.

"I don't know." He concealed his fear as best he could, forcing both voice and body to stay firm.

Sirena's penetrating gaze in all likeliness saw through the attempted bravery.

"Lionhearted, are we? Don't act so tough. You've got the wrong species."

"And what species would that be?" Lapidar interjected.

"You'll know soon enough." Sirena beamed at Lapidar. "But first, I want to know what he thinks before it all takes place. Now come on Achak, think we'll kill you?"

"Not you personally," Achak retorted and was relieved to hear the coolness in his tone, which he believed he owed to Lapidar—to Lapidar and his insane level of boldness in speaking out against his employer.

"And why not me?"

"You'll be flying in circles by the time I die."

Lapidar barked in laughter. "Useless banter," he critiqued, then his sharp ears turned toward the archway.

The turbaned elder and his lab-coated doctor began to re-emerge into the room. Then Lapidar interrupted the exchange of smiles. "Now, how do you expect to contain him in one form without his morphing into the other?"

His words, as far as Achak could discern, had been intended for the turbaned elder. Achak had been using ignorance to his advantage, pushing for time by keeping up the conversation, but Lapidar's question demanded a direct answer. No more circling for time by appealing to Sirena's jest, Achak would be forced to hear his fate. Already, he could hear the meaning of "containment" echoing a million possibilities of imprisonment.

"Don't you think that once he has one transmogrification figured out, he'd be able to work out the other for himself?"

"I think it's time we brought forward Dr. Coral."

The turban man's answer was not to the gunman's liking, who through quick questions had probably hoped for an easy to understand answer. Lapidar growled at the invitation. Already, Achak knew that the doctor was not someone he wanted to meet.

Dr. Coral was a slouch-shouldered man with a sense for his laboratory written all over his long white coat. He had a widow's peak of slick gray hair and spectacles that cropped his eyes just as his head was cropped by the receding hairline. Dr. Coral was less like an equal and more like a subordinate, no matter how respectfully Manu spoke to him or offered to bring out servants to his aid.

"No, no," the doctor refused each time. "There will be no need."

Manu was sashed with a royal purple, while the doctor had no more elegance than an un-torn pair of slacks.

"I am most eager to begin this, Manu." Curt and hard-spoken, the doctor went straight to business, expressing yet another sign of their hollow partnership.

Manu nodded graciously and turned to his mercenaries. "If you will excuse us," he spoke more directly to Lapidar than Sirena. "This will only take a few minutes."

"What? We don't get to see him change?" Lapidar was looking outraged as if he had just been thoroughly mal-critiqued on the job.

"I'm very sorry, Mr. Gray." Manu smirked in as un-sorrowful a manner as he could provide. "But my procedures are a crucial asset to Domestica. They are as classified and protected as any trade secret."

Lapidar shot a side-glance at Sirena, grunted, and trailed away.

"Are you ready to evolve?" Manu eyed Achak possessively.

"What am I?"

"Extinct... forgotten."

In the two words, Achak was given all he wanted to know of his being. Lapidar was right to be disgusted: this man was a collector.

Achak had the sudden urge to be ferocious. He wanted to pass himself off as the most dangerous and untamable of species. Anything with teeth and claws would do.

"Are you sure you want to change me like this? Unchained?" Achak thought along the lines of werewolves, ready for the moment when he might no longer stand on two feet.

"I can't promise you that I won't bite," he threatened, wondering if he could be both tall and venomous.

Dr. Coral laughed—his chuckle was as intellectually short and malicious as it was inappropriate.

Even Manu gave a soft cackle. "Young man, I am that by which you pale in comparison to. I am descendent of the very first..."

"The first what?!" Achak pulled the fire from his chest. He wanted to infuriate this self-proclaimed Deity, just as Lapidar had done, and hopefully see the towel dishevel and fall from his head. And what better way to offend him than by attacking the pride and soul of his species, or at least by putting a hammer to Domestica.

"The first?" Achak mocked. "So would that make you a unicorn or dragon?"

Manu wrenched a smile. "Yes. I think it is about time we got on with it." He straightened his suit and sash while speaking to Coral. "Doctor, if you would?"

"Certainly."

"Don't say I didn't warn you," Achak stammered as the doctor moved toward him.

A syringe was gleaming from the doctor's outstretched hand. Achak sought to move, but couldn't. He had no choice but to let the doctor come behind him while the gunman stood just outside the door. Meanwhile, he had his hands still handcuffed to his back.

"I know it looks murky," the doctor soothed falsely. "But it'll only be a little hyssop and nepeta."

Might it hurt? Achak wondered as he felt two fingers come up his neck, counting the distance from his collar. Then he felt a horrible twinge as a needle was sent into his spine. A shock went from the top of his brain and dispersed itself into every nerve that ran down the length of his body.

His knees buckled and crashed instantly, and he could do nothing to catch himself as he fell down face forward.

"Uncuff him!" Manu bellowed, but Achak never felt the touch that released his arms.

Warm tingles that felt like an army of ants crawled over his skin, yet he could see nothing through the lids of his eyes to know what spasms or thrashing his limbs had undergone. He would have screamed, but the muscles of his jaws did not respond. The ringing in his ears put him far out of contact with the rest of his body and for a split instant, he concluded that he had been decapitated. Then just when he thought that he would be swallowed whole, the darkness released him.

Feeling like his body had been un-numbed, Achak willed his mind to call out to his furthest joints. Fingers and toes, he felt them become animate. Then he turned his focus to the larger regions of his body. Naturally, his head came up first, his neck wholly intact.

His last thoughts returned to him as he recalled the grin on Manu's face and the sensations of Coral's fingers over his neck. "I'm going to bite your head off," he dazedly remembered vowing to himself. But between his body's perspiration and trembling, the idea did not seem so appealing to him now.

Sickly, he hesitated to take his eyes off the carpet, knowing that he possessed neither the strength of mind nor body to face Manu. He could wait until they dragged him from the floor, but before then he thought he should at least confirm that all of his body parts were functioning before they carried him away.

His arms held beneath him, though they seemed somehow shorter than he knew them to be, and his body hung low to the ground. Perhaps he had only lifted from the elbows, but, no, the hairs of carpet could still be felt beneath his palms.

"He's kinda small for a saber cat, ain't he?"

Lapidar's voice came as a shock to Achak, who had no recollection of him or Sirena reentering the room.

"He is young," Manu suggested.

Achak looked from one curious face to the next. There were no signs of concern as they watched him on the floor.

"That or he's not pure bred." Lapidar shrugged. "But maybe you could do an x-ray just to find out how he compares to what remains of prehistoric fossils."

"Believe me, I intend to."

For the first time, Lapidar looked at the elder incredulously, his suggestion perhaps having only been intended as a joke. He gaped at the elder, unblinking in his silent shift of thoughts.

Achak did not understand a word spoken between the men, but it all sounded like madness in Achak's opinion. He had shaken himself loose of the fear that had originally paralyzed him. With more certainty, he thought willfully that despite his rapid heart rate, his nerves had stabilized enough to be able to stand up and speak.

However, Achak found that as he tried to lift off the ground with his hands, his forearms were already stretched to their limit despite the fact that he remained close to the carpet. Feeling panicky, he thought he might have lost the muscle control to bend and straighten his joints. He could only feel the balls of his fingertips. When Achak looked down, he saw no limbs that he could recognize. Instead of hands, he saw two hairy yellow paws, matted and scruffy strands growing downward over his elbows which were now pointing in the wrong direction. The angle of his arms looked awkward and he came to the rash conclusion that they were broken. Then Achak made an attempt to rediscover the use of his right arm and found that the paw lifted with it.

"This can't be real," he tried to say, but his throat produced a groan that was followed by a longer whimper he hoped no one heard, but he knew it was already too late. Three sets of eyes were upon him.

"What did he say?" Sirena beamed at Lapidar.

"Who knows." Lapidar smiled back and stared down at Achak, who looked undecidedly from one face to the other.

Their gaze brought Achak lower to the ground as he fought to maintain the support of his legs. What could he do now that he had lost human speech? This could be a trick, he speculated, hoping more than fearing the possibility. They might have drugged him with a type of hallucinogen, he entertained the idea further, relieved by the prospect that the effects of a drug might soon wear off.

He had no such luck because he was led in dogcatcher-style as both Lapidar and Dr. Coral had him by the catch-pole. With the wiry ends noosed around his neck, Achak was brought dragging and growling to the outside of the mansion, where lay not the fabulous gardens he had seen out front but a furious tangle of jungle.

Life sprang from life. Moss and vines clung to branches, mushrooms sprouted from roots, and shortly therein, a fortress of stone emerged. It had the large dirt stones of the Amazon, but Achak could tell it was a fake. No temple of the gods had ever been created to look so flat and square, while a timeline of carvings united cultures across the outside of its clay surface, by which circular calendars accompanied Egyptian hieroglyphics. There was a totem perched at its front and across the entrance way from that, an apple tree. A short memorial went under the tree, but Achak had no chance to read the subject as he was forcibly pushed by.

Entering the temple, Achak gaped as if it had all been an illusion and what lay within was nothing more than a kennel of animals—two to every cell. He now saw the bar windows high above the walls for ventilation and to the very end of corridor an office stood with its far window open as not many glass windows came to be during this time of year. Achak breathed in an unclean odor, a mixture of wet fur and newly marked territory. Then the sounds issued from rows of bars down the corridor, though unless a bark or meow could be heard, Achak had no clue as to what species inhabited any one cell without first peering into them.

Taking the opportunity to familiarize himself with his new roommates, Achak accounted for every species and their number in each of the occupied cells. He found the first few empty, but knew that beyond the trees and overgrowth he had passed by, there must be dozens, if not hundreds, of animal holdings, each with an outdoor replica of the animal's native habitat and ecology. This meant little in making Achak feel right at home since any wilderness would take about as much getting used to as his newly acquired mammalian body.

He felt every bit abused and "animal" knowing as he did that he would soon be penned up like every other four-legged creature in the vicinity. Achak felt responsible for his capture: he had not fought or struggled, or at least not to any extent that his grandpa or family could be proud of. What would he say to them should he ever manage his way out of the facility?

Steel bars were locked into place as Achak found himself between brick and the brink of freedom. He let his eyes drift from Lapidar and the brown-coat, plunging down, down, down, until the last thing he heard was, "Keep your tail un-tucked from between your legs, kid."

Day 4, Thursday

8 Wolf Pact
Part I

"Look at the gray fur that overlays the gold. Such camouflage! I imagine that the region he dwelled in consisted of both desert and forest—not like it is today."

Achak's chin rested hard on a rough surface, a floor seeded with dirt and other debris. As he lifted his head, it felt as though pebbles had imbedded themselves into his skin. In that instant of raising a hand to brush off the irritation, Achak knew the nightmare to be real. The closest he could come to carrying out the sweeping gesture was to meet his chin halfway with the back of a forepaw.

All the remaining parts of his body ached with the discomfort of having slept in the worst possible position. His arms and legs, having rested under him, were tingling off the troublesome weight of his body.

Realization came again to Achak in the nightmarish form of finding himself in a hairy body. But it was a mild shock Achak experienced in learning about the two fangs that extended well beyond the hairs of his chin. Then again, after overcoming the first shock of finding himself clothed in fur with one-inch nails coming out of his toes, he supposed it just didn't get much worse than that to cope with the changes. His adjustments could also be explained by the fact that he had not spent nearly as much time unconscious as everyone believed him to have spent. He had, after all, only feinted sleep in the beginning to persuade Manu and all the rest to leave, or to overhear the things that Manu normally would not have allowed to be discussed if he knew Achak to be awake and listening. But at some point, he had drifted off into sleep and not caught the reasons for which he had been captured and brought to this facility.

At least now, alone in the dim early hours of day break, Achak had all the time he needed to familiarize himself with himself—with his new body, that is, as well as with his surroundings. He noticed that the cell across from his was now empty where previously a large red elk had been caged.

The beast's fur had been dark around the hooves and its antlers had bore fingers-worth of sharp extensions. Its dominant features had indicated to Achak that the specimen had been male. The smaller points of the partner's antlers suggested that it was female. Yet, Achak had also learned from their behavior that they had never before been human. The male's eyes spread wide with alarm at the sight of Achak, whose fangs were at least as long as one of its antler extensions. When it began to snort and to clatter its hooves over the concrete, Achak knew that he was dealing with just an elk—primitive and instinctive—and not a former human being.

Sure, it would be natural for anyone or thing to be alarmed by Achak now that he weighed about two tons combined with the artillery of claws and fangs, but it also would have been within human capacity not be as alarmed by something that was separated by two sets of steel bars.

So far, Achak had found the bars to be the most useful, yet trapping, of company he had within the kennels. Not only did the bars protect him from the antlers of hot-headed elk that jumped instinctively into defense mode, but Achak had also found it useful to stare into the bars' shiny surface and examine his reflection.

He had two all-mighty fangs that would put Dracula to shame, but these he had already discovered. Then he learned to like his claws even less when he not so wisely put them up to the brick wall and found that they made a sound like nails on a chalkboard when met with a hard surface. The blame he also put on the sensitivity that his eardrums now appropriated.

While he had a new amount of control over the movement and perkiness of his ears, Achak found the feline joints to be inferiorly limited to a dog's. For one thing, he could not bring his ears all the way down to block out any annoying sounds, such as those incessantly echoing down the corridor from other animal cells. Achak could appreciate a taxidermist as he would have loved to stuff some of the beasts that seemed to find all hours of the day and night the most arousing hours to kick their dish trays repeatedly into the bars.

The other problem with his ears was that not only did they alert him to the approximate direction of the sound, which in an echoing corridor meant that he could pinpoint almost the exact brick the sound waves were to rebound off of, but his ears also told him the exact distance of the noise maker. But this knowledge of sound and distance was what Achak thought to be too much information as he found himself mentally trying to refuse the processing of such data.

It was very distracting to have to think about how far away a machizma was when it skidded its foot on a section of loose gravel inside the kennel. The only extra sense he had to be grateful for was his keen sense of smell which, apart from being in a contained facility among other unwashed animals and their excrements, turned out to be his most useful foresight into the emotional state of other beings.

He could smell the sweat running down Dr. Coral's temple. This at least would warn him about those who intended to do him harm versus those who feared harm being done onto them—a devise he hoped would be useful in catching Manu or Dr. Coral at their weakest state of mind. If he could detect fear or influence such paralyzing emotions at just the right time, he may actually stand a chance of escaping.

Achak doubted he had many more hours to become familiar with himself. He took one last look at the protruding region of his mouth, visible to him even without the reflective bars, and noted the length of his whiskers—that was, to think of them as more facial hair than he could grow in human form.

Expecting Dr. Coral to pay him a visit, Achak decided to do for himself what was probably most expected of him and attempt to transform back into his original state of being. He had to admit that, in having no idea of the methods to go about transforming, his attempts were about as productive as trying to fly. The changes that he tried to call to his body parts and sensations he tried to replicate often translated to a stretch of the leg here or tensing of the muscle there, but seldom anything that produced results.

He spread his paws only to learn that they each came up one toe short of the norm. The idea baffled him. How was he supposed to extract a fifth finger out of thin air? This he pondered until he looked between his legs and found a tail that could not be pulled back in.

"Well, aren't you the lively one," Dr. Coral lisped with his overzealous tongue. His throat was hissing with the extra saliva. "As a tip off: no amount of anatomical underssstanding will tell you what you need to know. And I don't care if you know the placessment of every bone, mussscle, and tendon. It's not for mortalsss to underssstand the basisss of living matter. To expect to behave within the Lawsss of Matter or equal exchange is to deny the fact that a hundred and thirty poundsss of human matter has just been changed into two tons of prehissstoric carnage.

"It'sss not what you are by physicsss, boy; it'sss what you are by nature. And at thisss point, there isn't enough humanity left within that petulant mind of yours to ever return to itsss form."

Achak snarled through the bars. He went so far as to snap at the doctor that dare attack his humanity when what acts could be less human than those committed by Coral and Manu's imprisoning of Achak without just cause?

"And I ressst my case ssss." Dr. Coral busied himself with some medical instruments: dabbing at various vials, all of which were filled with a thick red liquid Achak knew to be blood. The doctor then took out a black pen and began to put marks on a few unlabeled samples. Sparing a glance away from his work, he looked to Achak's cell where he would meet the only set of curious and mindful eyes there was along the aisle of specimens.

"Be grateful for what you are, boy. Were you ssstill human, you'd have your life to worry about and not your appearanssce. I will be only too glad when the time comesss to abandon thisss ssskin forever. It will be like shedding my sssnakessskin, though humanssskin, I should sssay."

Achak stared dryly through the bars at the man speaking. He had no human say over which direction this conversation went and was therefore reduced to listening only. Had his ears been a bit more flexible, he might have been inclined to turn them away completely.

"Humansss disssgussst me. They ssspend, consssume sssome more, then litter. Exssspand, develop, breed, and overpopulate. But do you know what I find to be the mossst pathetic of their ssspecies? Their attemptsss to clean up after themssselves. Biodegradable is rubbish. Do you think what they use to break down a sssubssstance would be sssafe for thisss planet? It takesss one toxin to dessstroy another. It'sss like building on the sssame ssstain. But I sssay the desssspoiled layer has to be ssscratched off the sssurface."

In truth, Achak was only mildly interested in what the doctor was saying. Thus, he kept twitching his ear towards the other end of the kennel, wanting to listen at the door for any approaching footsteps. His tail flicked if he felt even the slightest excitement over a new sound. Most of the time though, he was startled by the chattering of the meercats and kit foxes, among the other smaller and quieter animals, but every once in a while, Achak could catch the distant cry of something much larger—something not encaged in this kennel.

"I developed a product, you know. To ssscratch the humansss off thisss sssurface. You may have heard of it. I held auditions at your ssschool for TV commercials."

Coral turned away from his blood-filled vials to reach into a crate tucked under the counter and removed a water bottle. Then carrying the bottle out to Achak, he turned out the label for Achak to read off the brand name: HydroMax. And he had finally caught Achak's interest, which although Achak didn't drink the brand personally, he knew plenty of people from school that did - not limited to his friend Anthony.

"You're probably wondering why I'm telling you all thisss, but I don't sssuppose it matters what I tell you sssince even if you do ever walk again as a human, what are the odds that another human would believe anything you'd have to tell them about your disssappearance?"

Coral laughed to himself. "By the way, we won't be needing a blood sssample from you, in case you were wondering, but Manu has asssked that I remove a sssample of bone marrow for the fossil comparissson. You know, just to sssee if you're the sure thing. As if your fangs don't already prove—"

Through Dr. Coral's interrupted speech, Achak heard it too—a distinctive howl, as only a wolf might perform for the moon, had aroused the animals both inside and out of the kennels. Perhaps the most profound of cries came from an aviary where the squawks and shrieks of birds competed from one breed to the next.

"Wolf tramp!" Dr. Coral cursed. He threw down the clipboard he had been reading from and launched himself past Achak's cell only to freeze up as the door opened before he could reach it.

Turbaned and suited, Manu beamed inside with a smile like no other. "The Jacks are on it," he informed, his face of ravished amusement as though he had not had a day like this in a long while.

"And I suppose it doesn't concern you that he's gotten in this far?" Dr. Coral inquired crossly.

"Yes—yes," Manu brushed off. "So you were right about him."

"As always, I am! I told you he was a werewolf."

Almost choked up with laughter, Manu consented, "Well, that may very well be. But you know how fascinating their like are and how many generations they go back. He may very well be—"

"Your downfall!" Dr. Coral finished. "If ever he went to the Bred HyCouncil with this info..."

Manu laughed harder at these cautions. "Except that he's in no position to make himself known to them either."

Dr. Coral pulled himself up for a vicious strike. "I still feel we should have—"

"It will be done soon enough, Sirena will be delighted to know," Manu assured.

"Yes, another mention of one of your more excellent ssselectionsss."

"Are you insulting my hires!"

Achak was amazed at how quickly Manu altered his lungs from laughter to vindiction.

"I have fair cause to debunk your desscisions," Dr. Coral replied. "Yesss, Sirena. Quite the character. Another unusually rare form. No doubt a coming member of your collection."

"I have no interest in her specifically," Manu snapped, "just in her lure."

"Then you'd just better hope you don't become too attached to these hands or they'll be ssso much the worssse under my charge. And the sssame goes for The Jacksss, as well."

"Ladon, you have such a cold-blooded nature," Manu decried, returning some cheer into his voice. "But trust me on this matter, Lapidar is no threat to our goal. Nor, will you see, is the Bred HyCouncil."

"A most reassuring ssspeech," Dr. Coral scoffed in his persistent de-fiance. "At leassst you've managed to preserve the interessst—and with sssome angst to ssspare. I'd rather thought you'd have lossst your passion by now and become bored with the plan."

Manu took the compliment well and failed to restrain a smile. "Ah! And I see you were showing off your latest invention to the young man," Manu remarked of the bottle in Coral's hand.

The sudden change in Manu's tone troubled Achak, who understood the bottle of HydroMax to be poison, a substance of no delight. As if Coral too had suddenly gone soft, Achak watched the doctor hold out the plastic bottle in his hand in gracious presentation.

Achak would have liked to puncture the bottle with one of his fangs and drain HydroMax of all its contents, but Manu showed no concern over the liquid in the bottle, which only moments before was presented to Achak as a toxin.

More because of the way in which Manu resigned himself to invitations did Achak believe that he was seeing two people for the first time in a clear hierarchy of man and servant. Unable to distinguish the pair between leader and follower, Achak resolved—to no comfort—that he was indeed losing his human instincts. If he was to ever decide the motive of these two men, he must first decide which of them is giving orders and which of them is taking them.

Achak arched his head closer to the bars to watch more carefully in hopes of seeing what could not be heard.

Stepping aside, Dr. Coral gestured for Manu to come through the kennels. "Shall we have a look?" he said, offering Manu passage.

Manu delicately shook his head. "No, I think not now. I have other matters to see through, but I trust you to manage things at this end."

With a departing look into Achak's cell, Manu turned heel and let himself out with the weight of steel naturally bringing the door to a close behind him.

"And ssso walksss the firssst and the lassst of Man-eew."

From watching the door, Achak snapped his head towards the doctor.

Coral eyed him back complacently. "Oh what do I care? You'll never ssspeak again."

His gleam triumphant, he stepped in front of the bars grabbing hold with his left hand for support as he kneeled down. His right hand went straight through the bars as he reached out for a collar-like trinket that had been dangling from Achak's fur.

"Let'sss remove thisss then, shall we?" His fingers touched the arrowhead pendant and Achak bounded back. At second reflex, but already too late in his response time, Achak snapped at the arm that had safely receded behind the bars.

"Very nice sss," Dr. Coral appraised, watching Achak's two most succulent fangs. "Though you would do well to take it under clear advisement that your pride wavers on the extensions of cartilage, which is to sssay that biting into bone will have itsss detrimental effectsss on your fangs."

Achak wondered if he had any reason to doubt the truth behind Dr. Coral's words. While knowing that the acceptance of such information would put Achak at a disadvantage, he did not think that rebuking them was worth busting his teeth over. The limited use of his fangs did not leave him completely defenseless while he still had his claws.

With a broader smile than before, Dr. Coral drew up his hand to the space between his eyes and pushed back on his glasses to straighten them.

"You know, when I transmogrify, there is one thing I always leave behind as well." He tapped the lens frame. "Even after ssso many years of being pressscribed them, I can't get used to this accessory of metal and glassss. The weight of it, the pressure—it jussst never wantsss to come along."

His lips twitched, incapable of holding either smile or frown. But Dr. Coral was resolute on twisting over a grimace, something that in its forced compromise looked deranged.

"Well, in your case sss, I sssuppose we can let the little accessory ssslide." He rubbed at the hand that Achak had set out to amputate. "It ssserves as sssuch an appropriate dog tag, don't you think? Ssso Neanderthal to have an arrowhead around the neck of a sssabertooth tiger..."

Dr. Coral's voice trailed off, and while he let his thoughts hang, another man elsewhere and true to his form was holding his position behind the leaves of a cedar tree.

Lapidar had his chest against the tree branch where he could peer over the edge to observe the predators hot on his scent. His position was well-suited for a swift take-off in the event that his location should be discovered.

He knew that the jackals below were still sniffing out a wolf's scent which had lost its potency the moment Lapidar had returned to human form. Watching The Jacks bound into the bushes and squander off in separate directions assured Lapidar that he had the ground covered. His unease then was stimulated not by The Jacks but by the cautious glances he shot above. All he needed was a vulture like Sirena to fly overhead and spot him, and his position would be up.

No one but Sirena would have expected him to climb to this height. While Lapidar would have liked to believe that Sirena went home upon receiving her pay, he was more inclined to believe that Manu had kept someone of Sirena's class around with an extended contract. While she had shown little in the way of manners or maturity, her wits and wings were two features that even Manu could recognize as assets.

...how do you know what I'm being paid to do?

Lapidar clung to Sirena's former words as proof of her employment. Contrary to having few reasons to believe her words then, Lapidar gave them every cautionary bit of merit now that he was playing against her. He would not allow himself to be caught by underestimating those he would be opposing.

Then there was the issue that if all were loyal to Manu, Lapidar was outnumbered at least five to one. He had no way of accounting for those that might be under Manu's employ whom he had not met inside Domestica.

Gradually, Lapidar leaned his body over the branch while trying not to scrape off the bark beneath him. Then letting gravity take hold, he released his grip and tumbled in the air, landing at the bottom of the tree trunk. He resumed his hairiness on all-fours.

His nose came up, sniffed, then with a growl, Lapidar made a mad dash through the shrubbery.

A stone building appeared in front of him and Lapidar's concealment was lost in the clearing of an apple orchard. Hoping not to be seen, he ran faster towards the stone building. Lapidar could not hope to find camouflage because of all his white fur. If The Jacks were looking anywhere around the building, he would surely be seen unless he could reach some of the alpine bushes that dispersed themselves around the wall.

Dr. Coral had stopped his hearty banter. He now looked particularly disgruntled while leaning out of a small water-stained windowsill in his office. His unease was revealed through the twitching nerve above his brow and the tightening between his lips.

From Achak's angle, all he could see of the outdoors was a few orchards divided between a pathway that was eventually swallowed by forest.

He watched the door where everything remained quiet beyond the dulcet chirping of birds. Outside, he saw the forest beyond the window, the picturesque scene of trees and a soft breeze to rattle the leaves from their branches. He tried to imagine Manu's men among them, a band of turbaned scouts placing each foot carefully in front of the other while moving along the forest. Then Achak wondered about the one Manu had called a "wolf" and what that was intended to mean about who they were pursuing.

There was a rap at the door which put an end to Achak's waiting. He moved along the bars for a closer look. This could be a status report, Achak thought as he watched with eagerness the sight of Dr. Coral and his labcoat swishing passed his bars to answer the incessant knocking.

Achak did not understand why the person did not just admit himself as Manu had done, but Achak looked to servitude as the most likely explanation. He thought otherwise once the door was opened. There stood not two turbaned henchmen but two teenage boys, no older than Achak, and both with equally black hair worn to their shoulders.

The lankier of the two already had his head inside with his right hand acting as a doorstop in case Dr. Coral were to have any ideas about slamming the door in his face. He looked past the white-haired doctor, glancing between cells, and to the far end office space, the window, and finally returned his gaze to Dr. Coral.

"Jack," the doctor reproofed, looking from one to the other. "Leave now. You have no businessss here—and, I take it, no sucsscessss in finding the wolf." He slapped his hand across the doorframe, putting his arm in front of the shorter boy who looked ready to enter.

The boy ducked under it and prattled from behind the doctor as though laughing. He walked with a hunch, ready to approach on all fours and, in this partially human posture, met Achak at the bars, bringing his face level with the sabertooth tiger. Achak jumped back. Another cackle, this one softer than the former, issued from the boy.

"Dô! Get back here. Jack Dô!"

It was the smaller boy Coral was referring to, but Achak looked to the larger boy at the doorway and saw him grinning. Beyond Achak's bars, a stranger grin was forming on Dô's face. Salivating all the while, Dô's mouth hung open, his lips stretched across, and his cheeks looked as though the skin was tearing apart. Then came the fur and whiskers, and Achak didn't care how many times he saw it, he could not get used to the sight of human-to-animal change.

Nothing could reduce the shock and slight disgust he experienced while watching so animated a transformation take place in front of him. As though his eyes were blinking quickly, the sight of Dô's body seemed to come and go in brief flashes: extensions here, bending there, growing, shrinking, until it found the happy medium. Dô became a jackal.

Achak felt dazed by the close up, and maybe motion-sick as well. As though the world might just blink out at any moment, he steadied his eyes on the new form that stood before him.

Tramped with a brown mangle of fur, the boy had a starved look. The boy-turned-dog was not the least bit ashamed of his ragged appearance, though it may be that he was not even aware of the condition of his animal form. His coat was much thinner than Achak's with hair that, while shorter, could not be tamed. Achak wondered if such gangly fur amounted to skin irritations, but then he remembered that such animals played host to fleas and Achak shuddered at the thought that this jackal could pass some along to him.

Dô was not at all quiet about his mischief, which from the very deep of his throat could be heard gurgling a soft cackle. His brother Jack made a similar noise from the door. Changing as the younger had done, Jack Ék came down on his forepaws and Coral went hysterical.

He grabbed a dog pole from its wall hook and swung it.

Claws scraping over cement could be heard as Jack Ék scrambled from the doorway and off into the forestry. The decision being too abrupt for Dô to follow, the smaller brother lingered in front of Achak's cell, tail wagging and tongue hanging. When he looked at Achak, his dog panting ceased as he brought his tongue back in, forcing a single fang to stay behind. With a deliberate gesture, he shook his body from nose to tail, loosening fur and flinging dirt, among other small particles that Achak did not want to know about. Fleas and ticks, like lice, were the last of mammalian worries Achak wanted to experience.

Dr. Coral kicked at Dô's rear as it too followed the brother's mad dash out of the kennel and into the trees. Although The Jacks left, having never spoken a word by human standards, in Achak's opinion they had said more about Domestica than either Manu or Dr. Coral had conveyed through their elaborate speeches.

Their behavior alone had shown Achak that the typical shapeshifter is proudest and most comfortable while in its animal form. Where The Jacks were speechless as two obedient school boys, their true personalities were unleashed upon transmogrification. Their departure only served to further unnerve Achak as he came to understand more vividly what it meant to be both man and beast, and wondered how much more of his own humanity would be foregone the longer he stayed in this wild form. Surely, he could not hope to maintain a sense of human behavior and mannerisms if he was expected to remain on all-fours where he must drink from water dishes with his tongue and sleep on the floor near his own filth, and bath by his own saliva, and toss in the night to the biting of his own fleas.

Once more, Achak found himself pleading against all doubt that this was just a cruel hoax, a nightmare that he would soon part with upon awakening. But no higher state of consciousness ever came and Achak had to accept that this was the best reality he could hope to reach.

Fangs, tail, fur, and fleas summed up all he knew and all that there was to be learned of life as a smilodon. And from what Achak had seen of The Jacks, he did not find it of particular interest to meet the expectations that the barbaric and untamed wild had in store for him. Could he once have imagined himself as the free spirit that his years as a teenage boy had taught him to seek while succumbing to his longing for independence? Yes, but in his longing to be wild and free and sprout wings, he had not wished to do so literally, much less to sprout fur and fangs among the other parts that were never essential to human existence.

If Achak thought he had endured harassment by The Jacks, it was nothing compared to how Dr. Coral must have felt fuming loud enough to hear his breaths.

"Mangy... Warm-blooded nefarious... mammals... and Manu. They were much better off as mere dogs!"

Achak moved a forepaw to bring himself closer to the bars and filling the gap that had been forged when Dô had advanced on him. His untucked claws moved against the pavement, issuing a scratching noise that he knew would draw Dr. Coral's attention. He had only to hope that Dr. Coral would think nothing of it but, as always, he was wrong to assume that any part of him could go unnoticed.

"Ssso you want to listen in, do you, boy?" Dr. Coral smiled with his convictions. "You're not in want of food, are you, then? Hungry for knowledge, inssstead?" His face became sour with his tone. "As amiable as that is, I have no ressspect for sssuch chivalries. Play the detective, if you must. It will pay out little in the end."

Coral came to stand in front of Achak and hissed in soft inhales of victory. "As I've already sssaid, there will be a time for all to give up their human ssskins if they wish to sssurvive. And I myssself will be only too happy to return to what is natural and sssinlessss."

He had what looked like a can of soup in his hand, which he then threw at Achak's bars. It bounced off with a loud thud and rolled away—cells away from his.

Achak had bounded back before the projectile could threaten his nose, but in doing so he watched hungrily as the instant-ready dish was taken out of his reach.

Dr. Coral was on his way to the door when Achak made a spontaneous lash at the doctor's legs with one of his claws. The doctor reacted with enough time to avoid having his legs torn to shreds. He stumbled safely to the other side of Achak's bars and looked fiercely back.

"Too bad." He tried to sound clever but Achak could tell that he was furious. "You're not a fighter, but I'll commend you for ssspirit. You're not as pathetic as you look."

Achak chuffled and spat, baring more than just a single pair of fangs.

"Do not get crossss with me, boy!" Dr. Coral was well beyond the level of self-containment. "I gave you what you asssked for. Fed you loads of info, enough to choke you with the entrails. Anyone could have had more than his fill of information. But I sssupose that'sss the primitive mind-frame of your ssspecies that is working now. I doubt that if you had any sssense about you at all, you would have become extinct."

Coral's antagonism was quickly becoming his confidence and strength. Inhaling a few deep breaths brought him back into a controlled tone.

"But I'll share with you one lassst bit of information for what good it will do your puny mind. As I've already explained how you came to be, I'll tell you a little sssomething about The Jacksss. I gather you've already noticed how little they ssspeak and how much they prefer their mutt ssskins? No? Oh well, I'll tell you anyway.

"The Jacksss are the opposssite of what you are. Imagine persssuading two wild dogs to turn human. Well, they were only pupsss at the time, really. Orphaned... you can't exactly blame them for wanting to exissst in likenessss to the only being to fossster them. But they were already the equivalent of ssseven human years at the time they took form—a little late to understand a human life, and let'sss face it, they'll never be able to live out as many years as the average perssson, having only the lifesssspan of a dog. But that'sss evolution for you. They're born, bred and will die jackalsss."

All through his speech, Dr. Coral had been backing his way towards the door. One simple turn of the heel when he was finished speaking and he was gone. Loneliness filled the corridor in his absence. Achak paced his cell. He had no way of keeping himself still while his brain was racked with information.

The last news concerning The Jacks left his mind staggering under its weighty meaning. Over and over again, Achak found himself speculating that, if The Jacks were just the opposite of him, then Manu must have planned for the two species to meet halfway. Was it his intention then to make humans into animals and animals into humans?

In whichever way Achak looked at it, he could not get both sides of his brain to agree on why Manu would want to arrange for the species to trade places. He could be planning his own enlightenment by trying to get one species to understand the other, but again Manu's methods of going about this demonstrated little in the way of world peace.

Determinately, Achak was ready to accept that Manu was a collector, a man too rich and too bored to know what to do with his substantial wealth. It must be a challenge to collect from the living, but then Manu had pursued Achak as a researcher might dig up fossils. Yet, maybe to Manu, the process of finding rare creatures in humans was much more a sport than research, like hunting. To Achak, it was more like buying a box of cereal just to try to draw out a particular toy. Manu was shaking the contents out of humans just to find something rare, something collectable. He must truly have nothing better to do with his money, Achak decided. What else would lead a man to track down a being that has been extinct for 8,000 years? Achak felt like a Cracker Jack prize.

Then he had to consider the fact that to find a treasure meant that the person would either share their findings or brag about them. In Manu's case, he not only had something to brag about, but something that he could use to intimidate. It would frighten people out of their skins to know that Manu had the power to change them into a creature that they knew nothing about.

Achak's head throbbed with his theories over the matters. He still had not come to grips with how he had been transmogrified. Between his struggles to comprehend a species of two forms and the purpose of Domestica, Achak laid his overloaded mind to rest. He was no more certain of Manu's plans than he was of his own feline existence.

It was a while before Achak could comprehend what he had seen moving by the window. A dog had popped its head in, taken a sniff, and then ducked back out. Achak might have passed it off as an illusion in his exhausted state of mind, but then the same creature put its head in again. Only this time, its paws were hanging over the windowsill and Achak had a better look at its head. It appeared not to be an ordinary run-of-the-mill dog, but another wild breed, possibly a foreign to North America.

Achak might have gone on the defensive, but this mutt was not a Jack. It was a lighter, gray and white canine. The hair around its face was so long that Achak could have mistaken it for a lion's mane, except that the snout was definitely of a doggish length. From a second impression, the mutt's behavior was too happy-go-lucky for Achak to feel threatened by it.

The wolf pulled itself all the way through the open window. Tail wagging, it began its exploration by sniffing around the office, momentarily disappearing around the corner, then coming back into view at the doorway.

Sure the wolf had its freedom now, but Achak was just counting the minutes until Dr. Coral returned, at which time, Achak would not want to trade places with it. If he could communicate with it, he would tell the wolf to go straight back out the way it came. However, the dumb dog seemed completely unaware of even the slightest peril that awaited it were it to get caught running loose on the Domestica premises. The wolf seemed interested in the other animals, well enough, having walked up to the bars of two snoozing lama and stuck its nose in, but it remained clueless to the understanding of prisons and captives. Instead of leaving, the wolf excited over each new inmate and kept its tail wagging. It was a hopelessly incompetent animal, Achak thought miserably as he watched and waited for the worst to happen.

The wolf found Achak's dinner, a curious, shiny tin can and practically barked in playfulness as the can rolled away from his paw. Yes, it was a male, Achak determined, though he could not explain how exactly he had come across this information. Then the observation struck him that this mutt was much too old to want play like a pup, and as he thought this over, he saw the wolf pick up the can between its teeth. Carrying the can in his mouth, the wolf brought it over to Achak, passing it between the bars.

How had it known? Achak's eyes widened to the wolf. He looked from the can now rolling by his paws, then up at the wolf who had sat himself in front of Achak's bars. No longer grinning and drooling, the wolf held a mild expression with its fangs hidden inside its closed trap. He was looking back at Achak and meeting his intense stare with one of equal focus. This was deliberate, and Achak thought that the wolf really did want him to have the food. However, the first thing in Achak's mind was not to take up the can and eat, but to wonder whether this mutt would be there to help him in other ways.

Impatiently, the wolf growled and Achak set to work at opening the can between his teeth. First, Achak tried to puncture the can with a single fang but that only resulted in a toothache. Then he took the can between both his fangs and made a similar attempt to pierce through the tin with a shorter set of molars. With better results, he chewed his way into the lid successfully.

All the while, the wolf was watching him patiently. Achak tried not to notice the wolf too much as it made him nervous to have a pair of fiery yellow eyes and black rings staring into him.

Taking the mulled can into his mouth, Achak tipped it over, spilling all of the contents onto the concrete. He wasn't going to be picky about eating off the floor when he was hungry enough to eat the contents raw. Although consumed by his appetite, Achak could not ignore his new wolf companion, which he could not be entirely certain was to be trusted.

As much as the companionship elated him to know that there was someone on his side, the jaded green glow that reflected in the wolf's eyes unnerved him.

He had finished scarfing down the pile of cold diced meat, in a matter of seconds and was back to studying the wolf with mixed feelings of appreciation and distrust. The wolf hung out its tongue in friendliness.

Jumping to his paws, the wolf made a dash back into the office space. The excitement alarmed Achak, who almost thought bitterly that the wolf would bail on him until he heard the squeaking of chairs being moved and drawers opening.

Achak had his nose peeking further between the bars than ever. His vision could not have felt more limited than it did while watching the wolf shuffle between corners. His neck was aching for a better view inside the office.

In a matter of minutes, Achak heard the jingle of keys and saw the wolf padding his way back toward the bars with a shiny ring clamped between his teeth. Three silver pendants dangled from the ring, their heads flat and rectangular. Achak had the foolish idea that the wolf was going to hold the keys one by one between his teeth and attempt to unlock the door while balancing on his hind legs. But that was not how it would be done.

When the wolf raised his forepaws, like one might beg, it was not to reach the keyhole, but to become a man.

Lapidar, newly clothed in a dark navy collared shirt under his browncoat but still with his khakis, stood in front of Achak's bars.

-●○●○●-

8
Wolf Pact
Part II

Spitting the ring of keys into his left hand, Lapidar drew himself closer to the cell and locked his hands around separate bars in front of Achak. He leaned in to study the sabertooth tiger carefully then pulled himself straight.

"Listen up," Lapidar spoke in a hushed tone and dangled the keys in front of Achak as though he wished to bargain with them. "When I let you out, you follow me through the window and keep up. Once we're off the property, don't even think about going your separate way. I can't tell you how many hounds Manu has after us, so to go stray is risking your own hide. Agreed?"

Achak nodded and Lapidar pushed one of the keys through the lock. It was a lucky guess too, as he turned the pivot over once only to hear it click on the first try and the door was free to slide open.

In what looked like a collapse, Lapidar fell to the floor on his hands and knees, but Achak noticed a blink later that his arms had been layered with fur and his hands were really paws. Achak had no more than the instant to think on this as Lapidar bounded toward the office. He peaked once out the window before leaping through and Achak followed.

Already Achak was falling behind in the short period of playing "Follow the Leader." Lapidar was quicker on his feet than Achak could possibly have imagined. However equipped with the perfect body as Achak thought himself to be, he had taken few opportunities as a human to become much of an athlete. His lack of endurance was beginning to show as he began to struggle with his breathing. Although he made it his best effort to keep Lapidar in sight, he had the obstacles of the Domestica jungle to contend with. Soon, all Achak could make out of Lapidar was the wolf's tail dancing between the trees. Though he quickly lost out on the visual, Achak had his keen ears to keep a sense of Lapidar's direction.

It amazed Achak how quickly he was adapting to his new senses. He seemed to have a better control over his nose and ears than over any other bodily function. His fore legs, especially, felt beyond his control, having never before used his arms for such a purpose, except on the few occasions he had given Tehya piggy back rides when she was younger. This was different and Achak's arms ached under the strain. The only thing keeping him from giving into the pull on his muscles was the amount of attention he had to divide between what he smelled and what he heard.

There was ruffling in leaves of trees and bushes all around him, the constant crackling of brush snapping beneath his feet, and always a new scent, be it a friendly pollen or a stench of something caged and unclean, reaching Achak's nostrils. Only with careful deliberation could Achak avoid the distraction of one of these aromas and keep on Lapidar's trail. It became more apparent and crucial to Achak that he not allow his senses to wander unless he could be certain that a blind race forward would lead him safely out of Domestica. But Achak did not have confidence in his direction, which was proven to be less dependable as Achak stayed longer with the chase and he had to weave at odd angles to follow Lapidar's breaking branches. He received his largest surprise when he almost ran head long into the railings of what must have been a larger animal confine.

While avoiding the tangles was one thing, Achak's body and physical shape was working against him on other levels. He supposed that being cramped in a kennel for so many hours had taken its toll as he had been given no opportunity before hand to stretch out his legs. But Achak did what he could under the circumstances and, when there was not so much as a fleeting glimpse of Lapidar, Achak tweaked his ears ahead for any sounds of panting or the thumps of paws.

He had tried to resort to his sense of smell, but he was too overwhelmed with keeping the oxygen in his lungs so that he could not spare a sniff for Lapidar. When he caught a sudden whiff of dank leather and thought he had Lapidar by the tail, by no will of his own, he was sent rolling through the tuft of the nearest hedgerows.

Achak hit the steel rails that were hidden behind the branches and heard a squeal issue from the other side. Whatever it was he had startled, he doubted it would give him trouble now that he could hear it running to the other end of the enclosure.

Left, right, scanning the trees around him, Achak caught sight of a bushy tail flicking from view before realizing that his own tail was being gnawed by a set of pointed fangs.

By reflex alone, he kicked the muzzle of his assailant and yelped as a fresh grip took hold around the back of his neck. Both Jacks were upon him. The one on his back especially had a tight hold on his flesh. Forcing Achak down with its body weight, neither fangs nor claws went unused.

Achak had no choice but to roll with the weight and hope that one of The Jacks would release his grip. There was no whine as his body crushed over the Jack, but there was no getting up either. Jack Dô had used the moment to wrap around Achak with a bear-hug which could not be so easily squirmed out of. Worse, by rolling as he did, Achak had allowed his vulnerable chest and stomach areas to remain in the open.

With Dô holding him down, the other was slinking around to Achak's exposed side. Heaving in noisy intakes of breath, Jack Ék moved into sight. His pause was brief before he began lunging toward Achak.

Spit flying—Achak was surprised to see that the fangs never reached him as a gray streak caught Ék in midair and both blurred figures were sent scrambling in opposite directions. Before Achak could wonder where they had gone, they were back in view and tearing at each other's flesh.

Lapidar, being of a larger size and build, appeared to hold the advantage. His slashes had much more noticeable effects over Ék, who, when struck, would have his head tossed to the side where his fangs were no longer of any threat. What impressed Achak the most was the sort of grip that Lapidar could manage by locking his jaws around any part of the jackal's body and then dragging it around like it was nothing more than a rag doll. With one such attack, Lapidar had whirled Ék so wildly around with his teeth that releasing his grip had forced the mutt sidelong against the trunk of a tree.

Buying himself a few moments for Jack Ék to recover, Lapidar took on Dô who had snagged Achak with the bear-hug. As soon as Dô saw the wolf leap, his grip loosened around Achak, who tried tugging away before Lapidar could land on top of the both of them.

Three figures tumbling over one another, Achak broke free, though not without some painful consequences clawing into his sides. The sting was crippling but not to the extent of what Ék must have endured as he limped away from the tree. Of a merciful mind, Achak did not pursue the injured Jack, but continued to watch the foam and gnaws of Lapidar's fight.

Achak wanted to help but saw no opportunity to step in with Lapidar always on the attack. He would have let slide the idea of doubling up with the wolf, but an unanswerable thought came to mind: where had the other Jack gone?

Two things were certain: the roots of the tree where Ék had landed were abandoned and the jackal was no longer in sight.

Following the hedgerows that led him closer to Lapidar's scuffle, Achak saw a distinctive tail among them and guessed where Ék must have gotten off to. He moved in and found that shadowed amongst the leaves, the jackal had arched its back in a sure attempt to pounce. Before Ék could launch in Lapidar's direction, Achak leapt forward and put himself between the ambush. However, size alone could not secure a victory for Achak.

Ék went through with the pounce in spite of Achak having done the same thing, which resulted in neither figure knowing how to avoid the other. Achak tried to put as much force into his leap as Ék, but he lost as much balance in the impact as he had intended for the Jack to lose. It was only through luck that Achak did not experience a concussion upon landing. He got up and made many furious swipes at Ék with his claws, but he did not dare snap out with his fangs. The thought of taking the Jack's fur and skin into his mouth on top of Dr. Coral's earlier caution about his two most powerful teeth being fragile did not encourage Achak to put them to use immediately—or at all, if he could avoid it.

Of course, he did not want Ék to know that he had no intention of using his fangs. Snapping at air, Achak could not bear the thought of holding himself back, even if his misses were not completely intentional. Still, he felt shame in his reluctance to bite down on his opponent. But the fact remained that even while in the heat of battle, Achak did not like the idea of having to sink his teeth into the flesh of another living being.

All Achak could see as he snapped blindly around himself was a smear of mangled fur. He felt dizzy and foolish and always at the receiving end of a blow. He was *losing,* the word aroused his mind with a thrashing of its own. Just then, he received the mother of all pangs to swipe across his face. He was disoriented by the strike and probably would have been taken down had it not been for Lapidar's intervention.

Ék was knocked aside as Lapidar stood over Achak with a vicious glint in his eyes. He growled severely for Achak to follow and ran into the thicket.

Achak had an easier time keeping up with Lapidar, though this was more likely due to an intentional flagging in Lapidar's pace than an improvement in Achak's.

All criticism aside, Achak was pleased to see that at the end of the jungle, there was only a fence of taller steel rails that stood in their way and Lapidar had already dug a means of going under.

Because Lapidar was no ordinary sized wolf, Achak had no problem slipping through the hole Lapidar had dug for both of them. The problem lie ahead in finding a safe haven when they reached the other side. They were shooting straight down the slope of one of San Diego's many rolling hills and, as far as Achak could tell, the greenery offered little in the way of cover or camouflage. Anyone looking down could have spotted their location.

If Lapidar had worked out an escape route, he chose not to share that information with Achak. However, as Achak kept speed with Lapdiar, his confidence in the wolf grew.

This was it, Achak thought as he looked ahead at the final threshold. A train was making its way straight into the tunnel of a hillside. Squeals and whistles issued from its engine. There were tunnels beneath the train tracks where water run-off could pass through and, further along, short bridges held the track level. The words "Santa Fe" could be read from many of the freight carts. Slowly, the train appeared to be moving along the green hillocks from a distance.

Achak did not mind the screeches and hollers of its passing as it resounded the cries of freedom hammering in his chest. The throbs were both painful and welcomed. His head might explode with the blaring noise, but his heart would burst out of joy.

The sight of the train brought with it numerous possibilities for escape of which Lapidar had to choose from. Achak wondered which of the bridges and tunnels he would choose. Only later could he come back to admit that the choice made was the last one that he could have come to expect. It just went to show how little Achak knew about mercenaries. Or maybe it was just the way of the Hybrid to always choose the most lethal route.

As they approached closer to the train tracks and the oncoming engine, Achak's relief was quickly becoming a sense of foreboding.

Louder and louder, the engine roared, filling Achak's ears with sharp pulses. The screeching metal beneath the wheels was magnified by Achak's keen, yet sensitive eardrums. His physical discomforts were then elevated by Lapidar's behavior in producing the mental tension of chasing down a train.

In wolf's form, Lapidar was not running across the train tracks or under, or in the direction of the tunnel, or any other sensible escape route. Contrary to reason, he was running alongside the train and looking up at the many passing cars, most of which held storage units. Achak knew what was on his mind, but that did not make him feel any less anxious about what they were about to do.

If Lapidar had planned this stow-away all along, the timing had been very poorly managed as the train was quickly building up speed. With each passing car, Achak was certain that they would not be able to hop aboard before they saw the caboose. Achak might even welcome that outcome, if only to be spared the leap of faith into the freight car.

Lapidar made his assent up the slope of the tracks and, before Achak caught on to the initiative, the wolf had disappeared inside the sliding door of an open unit. He had made the process look too simple, which proved to be otherwise when attempted by Achak. As he ran up the slope, Achak lost valuable timing and the unit he was aiming for moved ahead of him. He descended the slope to regain his distance with the car that Lapidar had boarded.

Giving himself some leeway, Achak held off his ascent until he had spaced himself in front of the sliding door and then charged the incline with all his might. When he reached the top, he was again in line with the door and had only to jump in. However, even the last hurtle had its particulars as Achak came to realize the excruciating role that gravity had to play when he launched himself from the ground.

Once in the air, he had no control over the speed at which he came towards the door. Moving at a slower speed than the actual train, Achak went halfway in and was hit sidelong by the door, which gratefully knocked him inside the unit instead of tumbling him down the slope.

Immediately, he heard Lapidar bark out in laughter and raised his bruised body to see the wolf sitting against a crate as a man and watching him. Achak's narrowed eyes met Lapidar's.

Contrary to Achak's darkened gaze, Lapidar did not share the same distain. "Don't be too angered, kid," he said. "I'm actually impressed you were able to board at all." To this, he added sincerely, "It's not in every agile being to attempt a jump like that onto a moving train."

Those were all the thoughts he shared before closing his eyes and taking in deep breaths. Achak too was heavily exhausted as he found a place near the other end of the car to sit. His legs were ready to give-way beneath him, but he did not let them come down so easily when he knew they would cramp upon lying if he did not loosen them with some stretches first. He envied Lapidar's sitting position, which Achak could not arrive at when he sat down in the typical feline manner.

His knees always up and to the side, Achak tried to ignore the cramps that were building around his joints and instead quieted his mind by listening to the steady rumbling of the train beneath his paws. The vibrations were subtle enough not to bang him around, yet strong enough to busy his mind on the various rattles around the unit. At least the sounds and odors that surrounded the train could not be compared to those of Domestica, and the animal kennels that included neither baths nor sanitation.

Achak closed his eyes and allowed himself to be gently rocked with the rhythm of the train. It had been the longest of days for him, and trying not to think on it too much, he could scarcely believe that only 36 hours had passed since he had worn human flesh.

Giving his ears a twitch, Achak opened his eyes, his arrival into the present was instigated by Lapidar's voice.

"I suppose you want an explanation? Seems only natural," Lapidar shrugged.

Achak kept an eye on him but did not give him any affirmations that he had guessed right.

"I probably won't be able to answer everything that's on your mind seeing as how you can't even speak what questions you may have, but there'll be more time to talk once we set you right."

Achak wagged his tail to the promise. He could not have imagined a more welcomed response than that which assured him that he would soon be returned to a normal life.

Lapidar kept silent for a while, keeping one arm wrapped rather tensely around a knee. He looked very much the part of an assassin in his corner. Not at all the tail-wagging mutt Achak had seen in the kennel, but as a man of business, Lapidar kept his distance.

"You'll have your human body back, yes," he confirmed on a serious note. "But not your life."

He scanned around the car for a point of reference or perhaps just for an excuse not to meet Achak's face.

"You're a Hybrid now and, well... I guess—I can't explain the difference, but to exist as two forms instead of one requires some changes in lifestyle, and not just physical. That's just the surface level of what it means to be Hybrid. And while it may not be a requirement to utilize both forms, which is why most humans and animals remain separate species today, in your case, your transmogrifications will be vital if you want to keep clear of menageries like Manu's. You won't be able to keep your species a secret, and once word gets out, you'll be popular among the Hybrid kind. And I guarantee that your popularity will be more attributed to animal collectors, than the regulars."

He stared down Achak.

"You understand what I'm telling you about your kind? You can't hope that people will just forget about you and let you alone.

"Not even the best of us," he said in an afterthought. "I'd even bet the bounty on my head that the breeds coming after you will be constantly on your tail with negotiations and bargains, none of which they'll hold up to. Oh yes, they will resort to some desperate measures to hold you by the collar." And there was amusement in his words as he spoke them.

Achak didn't need a voice to ask for an explanation, Lapidar was enjoying the subject much more than him.

"I shouldn't have to explain to you that your kind is supposed to be extinct and that exclusiveness is going to be what lures people's interest. You're going to attract a lot of attention, most of which will be of the unwanted kind."

For a lone wolf, Lapidar was quickly becoming a fast talker. It surprised Achak to hear him ramble on a topic for so long.

"But..." he sounded ready to end the discussion. "I don't want to get too much into this. There are a lot of unknowns and I can't say exactly what's going to happen when word gets around. There are a lot of other things to consider—other involved parties—the Bred HyCouncil for one." He stopped after mention of such an organization and fixed upon Achak's clueless expression.

Sighing, he talked himself down. "I forgot how much there was to explain."

However, if he was as bothered by the explanations as he claimed to be, he did not allow his frustrations to reach his tone. He was still attempting to be as soft-spoken and light-hearted as he could with the subject.

"My wife could probably offer a better introduction, having been through this once herself.

"Alright," he began again. "The Bred HyCouncil is something like a government body that the Hybrids cooperate with—or at least most of them do. Any Hybrid that wants to become a citizen of the United States had better register with the Bred HyCouncil as well as obtaining his green card. Makes sense, right? We have to answer to two governments. Do you know how many illegals would be crossing our boarders if the Bred HyCouncil did not keep tabs on the Hybrid populace?

"Well, you can get a sense of where I'm going and how things get complicated. Not only do members of the Bred HyCouncil have to forge laws that will keep Hybrids from exposing themselves to or endangering or threatening the human public, but they also have the responsibility to see that those laws are enforced. This means the council members are comprised of police, detectives, criminologists, as well as the politicians and what not. The department titles... I can get into that later."

Lapidar made a shift that looked like he was about ready to stand up, but decided against it.

"This train makes a stop at L.A. Union Station. It's a rough neighborhood but the risk is probably worth the time for recovery," he said and Achak thought he heard him mutter something about werewolves. "Besides, I'd rather not make it back on the first train. If Manu is keeping an eye on us, he'll have trouble following our route if we keep switching trains."

Achak had so far avoided thinking about their destination. It being Los Angeles, he did know the city too well, but he was familiar with its reputation of high rises and crowded streets. The city worried him. He could not expect to move along unnoticed in his current state. Achak doubted the city dwellers were accustomed to seeing big cats walk around the streets.

Lapidar sensed Achak's doubt. "Don't look so worried. It'll be dark by the time we get there."

The car became quiet as Lapidar had talked about all he could of Hybrid existence for one day. This suited Achak fine as he thought he had heard about all he could absorb of this new world. His eyes sagged and he found it harder to stay watching the landscapes.

As the train rumbled on, Achak lay down on his side, the one opposite of that which he had most recently bruised against the door.

No measurable length of time had passed before he was blinking blearily around the empty car in an answer to Lapidar's prods and whispers.

Lapidar was directing him to the doorway which now looked like a dark curtain with little hole punctures that emitted light. Achak realized that they were stars. He was even more surprised to learn that only about half of the dots belonged to the sky and that those bundled near the bottom were city lights.

The stars overhead began to disappear as the earthbound and artificial lighting dominated the sky. Lapidar moved in front of the twilight in human form. Tightening his grip on the doorframe, he stuck his head out, allowing the draft to untidy his hair, and then pulled himself back in.

"We're coming up to the station, but prepare yourself in case we need to make a jump."

Achak nodded to show that he understood. Then raising his body, he began to yawn and stretch as he had known cats to do, lowering his front and cranking up his rear end. He paced around the car until he heard the brakes squeal and felt the train skidding on its tracks. Looking to Lapidar, he found the man still standing by the door and periodically glancing ahead of the train.

"It looks fairly quiet," he said and Achak moved closer to the opening. "Must be a slow night."

The train was gradually losing speed as Achak saw the first of the buildings come past.

"Don't stand in the doorway," Lapidar cautioned. "You'll be seen."

Light was reflecting inside the car as they passed lampposts and squat buildings. With a long screech on its tracks, the train made a complete stop.

Lapidar popped his head out, then transmogrified. Muzzle first, then tail, he leapt off and vanished into the shadows. Achak thought he should look around too before going blindly into the darkness. He heard small voices a ways ahead, near the engine, and scampered out as Lapidar had done.

Achak stumbled upon the wolf at a chainlink fence. Lapidar was already fast at work digging a hole to pass under. Achak joined him and stuck his larger paws into the ditch.

The wolf growled when there was a large enough gap to move under and went through first.

Stiff in the legs, Achak worried that he might move too slowly, but Lapidar had reduced the pace, making an effort to be cautious.

Dogs barked at them as they passed through run-down communities, but no lights came on from the houses. The inhabitants were either asleep or they did not often respond to their watchdog alerts. A surprising amount of stragglers were silhouetted near the houses, forcing Lapidar to cut around streets and dip into lawns to make frequent detours.

When the blocks turned more commercial, Achak thought for sure they were moments away from discovery. The streetlamps chased away any shadows and cars were frequently pulling in and out of gas stations. While crossing the roads may not have proven difficult since there was no traffic at this hour, the problem always remained at the other end of the block where many of the bars and small markets still appeared to be operating within their business hours. The night must still be young, Achak concluded as he scrambled past the glass windows and doors where he could look upon clerks and customers.

His only perchance was that the people inside had their attention elsewhere as he passed. Lapidar, on the other hand, did not appear conscious of this concern as he kept running along the sidewalk without a thought spared for the people indoors. He pulled into an alley just as a young and flirtatious couple was coming up the street toward them. The pair were too engrossed in each other to notice the creatures that had slipped into the shadows in front of them.

The alley they had slipped into was the quietest area Achak had been since leaving home two days before. As much as he longed for peace after having spent his last hours in a bumpy freight car and an even longer period among the unhappy animals kenneled in Domestica, Achak felt that the alley exceeded his ideal location of undisturbed silence. The piles of trash bags especially gave Achak the sense that in its shapeless form, there could be someone lurking under its heap.

Instead of being able to leave the area right away, Lapidar took his time sniffing along the bricks and dumpsters. Before Achak could wonder what he was on about, Lapidar lifted one of his legs and Achak turned around.

"Hey," he heard Lapidar call him in human form. "No—no, this isn't camp out, but I'm warning you beforehand that we'll shortly be entering Hybrid territory. I'll be able to get us a motel there, but there are certain customs or honorable behaviors that Hybrids live by. Not that I want you seen," he hastened to say, "but in the event—"

Lapidar's voice was cut out by his transmogrification. His chin fell forward and out came the snout and snarl of a wolf. When his glowing green eyes peered upward, Achak moved aside to avoid them, but then he realized that it was not him that Lapidar was glaring at.

The wolf ran past Achak and took a seperate tug of fur and flesh into his mouth.

Achak was frozen in step at the sight of the two blurred figures in the heat of battle—a much more terrifying display than it had been back in Domestica. Maybe it was the fatigue that made Achak more jumpy at this hour or maybe The Jacks had been forced to hold back and restrain themselves from doing him too much injury.

From what Achak could tell, Lapidar had engaged with a wolf much like himself, only shorter, though not necessarily younger. The beast was foaming at the mouth and making noisy wrasps when it was on the attack. Lapidar too was behaving more rabid with a mad glint to his yellow eyes and a fang-exposing snarl that had Achak frozen in place.

His feet unlodged only when a brisk cackle of laughter sounded from somewhere overhead. Achak found himself retreating from the dumpster, where above, standing on the lid, was a man of his midyears. The crack of his striking voice came from behind a gruff red beard. He had a lumberjack face that definitely looked mishandled in the forest, with a scar that traveled from one earlobe to the innermost corner of his eye.

Even less flattering to his features was the way he puckered his lips, raised his head, and gave a howl at the moon. Achak could smell the liquor and cigarette from the wolfman's clothes. The stench almost made Achak forget about the fear. This man stood pedestalled above Achak, looking down with the least of friendly expressions—looking hungry.

Achak heard the clatter of an aluminum can separate from any of the sparring noises in Lapidar's direction and turned around to see three more wolves standing by the entrance to the alley. Had the howl called them here?

They were watching Lapidar. Moving in, they began circling the fight. Achak could not stand aside and wait as no fewer than four wolves moved around Lapidar. He turned away from the dumpster, but the wolfman made a clearing of the throat that kept Achak in his place. Rendered helpless, Achak began pacing the dumpster. He watched the circle of wolves enclose the arena by which Lapidar and his opponent would fight.

As the brawl carried on and the wolves pacing around moved in closer, Achak saw Lapidar get shoved into one of the barriers, which bit back and used its claws to force Lapidar toward the center of the ring and into his opponent's ready-jaws.

Braised by the back attack, Lapidar immediately crumbled to the fresh assault of his opponent. The wolf came on top of him, pinning him to the ground and relentlessly scratching at his face.

Achak could no longer stand by and watch. He made a leap toward the center of the ring and was dragged out by the next available barrier. It might have been the same wolf that had disoriented Lapidar, but Achak could not be certain as his head was banged against the pavement. He returned to his feet quickly, then down jumped the wolfman from the dumpster, directly in front of him.

"You know the rules, kid," he mused. "Where's your honor?"

Achak would have tossed aside the man's words and gone through with the rescue attempt anyway, but in hearing them, they had echoed what Achak had remembered Lapidar briefly mentioning about certain acceptable behaviors that Hybrids lived by. He knew he would come to hate these rules, like he hated the hypocrisy of the wolfman's gang up. Of course it wasn't fair, Achak growled to himself, they had bullied Lapidar with a back-attack and that would not be the last of honor codes they would breech. Yet, Achak knew he should not attack the wolfman, at least not while he was a man. He would have to put off a fight with the ringleader until both fighters wore their animal skins.

"Do you want to save your friend?" the wolfman taunted. Achak looked up into his bearded face to see the sharp teeth and sallow eyes that made this man more wolf than human. The small pupils of his eyes were fixing themselves around Achak's own face. Their interest, from what Achak could tell, was on his fangs.

If he had figured out Achak's species, he showed no surprise over the discovery. This concerned Achak. One thing he had hoped he could count on was that anyone with the mishap to come across him would turn-tail and run as soon as glimpsing his fangs. When this did not happen, Achak had to wonder what kind of beasts would stick around to challenge a sabertooth tiger. Did they really mean to fight him? Achak could only think that this pack of wolves was looking for a challenge, and were hoping to have found that match in Achak. But if they only knew how he had come to be, they would not feel so threatened by him. They might even take pity on him. But instead, Achak was asked to do the impossible.

"Come on, kid. Stand up. Let's talk." The pack leader was gesturing for Achak to meet him face-to-face and bipedal.

Achak didn't know what to do. The man would surely find it offensive if Achak did not do as he was told. Cooperation seemed like the only way of getting back to Lapidars side, but transmogrification was out of Achak's abilities. Would he have to play tough guy despite it all? He could think of no other alternatives to avoiding the issue of transmogrification. To act defiant would at least be a brave way of going about the encounter, though it was not really a matter of foolish heroics for Achak, it seemed like the only way for him to go.

"Well? Get up!" Robbed of his smile, the pack leader was vividly losing his patience. All his circling minions had stopped in their tracks to watch. They moved in closer and Achak became very uneasy, but he could give no other response than his defiance. He looked from the three wolves approaching, then up at the pack leader and met all of their faces. Then the most absurd idea crossed into his head.

Given only the use of animal tongue and body language, Achak had the option either to growl, whimper, or wag his tail.

Raising his head to the pack leader, he hung out his tongue and wagged his tail doggy style. The grin, he found to be the hardest to control, seeing as how he was neither dog nor sincerely happy with the situation. His nerves were more inclined to tremble his body like a cornered rabbit.

"What's this?" the wolfman growled, though Achak could see that he was trying hard to hide his amusement. "What's the meaning of this, boy?! Do you—dare you mock me?"

He might have continued the outrage, but another louder crash in the alley turned everyone's attention away. With a following of bangs and several clatters, a wolf was thrown into the trash heap. Cardboard boxes exploded of their contents and trash bags tumbled from their pyramid.

Before anyone could stop him, Lapidar had forced his way through the pack and was standing between Achak and the wolfman.

Growling and threatening, Lapidar was spared from the pack by the hand and will of their leader. The wolf from the trash heap had slumped from its pile and staggered forward only to be halted by its master as well.

"This is interesting," the pack leader commented.

The companionship of wolf and sabertooth tiger was becoming more and more awkward in Achak's mind as well.

"But come now! He's no pup. What right have you to defend him?"

Lapidar did not yield, which seemed to mystify more than upset the pack leader.

"I can keep them off so long as you humor me. But don't try my patience. If you have something to say, then bring those human lips of yours up here and say it."

The growling ceased. Lapidar's fur retracted and he slowly brought himself up from his hands and knees. This was unlike him, but Achak could see that he was panting as he wavered for a moment in his standing. Achak could not tell whether he was severely hurt or just swaying under the fatigue.

"No," Lapidar breathed. "The boy is no pup. But he's no Hybrid either."

"I said, 'Don't try me!'" he snapped. "I know a Hybrid when I see one. I can sense a human mind behind any layer of fur or scale or feather. And this one is no exception!" He pointed at Achak as he said this.

"Yes," Lapidar admitted. "He's human, and I was about to tell you as much too. I never said that he was sabertooth, you were the one who jumped to that conclusion."

Achak did not think it was wise to point out any of the pack leader's assumptions, but then this was Lapidar—the man who would protest a change of contract with Manu and then break the contract.

The pack leader was not taking Lapidar's impudence any better than Manu would have.

"You're not making a lot of sense here." He attempted to control his tone, but the muscles in his face were tightening around his brows. "If he's not sabertooth and he's not in human form, then what does that make him?"

"Human," Lapidar said again as if that settled the matter and Achak could hear in his voice that he was taking some amusement over the conversation. "Or at least he would be, if he could change himself back."

The pack leader looked ready to tear at Lapidar but remained silent and human waiting for the rest of the explanation.

"It was an accident," Lapidar lied. "And now the boy can't change back into his original self. You've seen it for yourself, right? You asked him to change? I assure you that he would have obeyed if he could. In fact," Lapidar emphasized, "you would have never found him in this form if he could manage any other."

Turning his head from his minions to Lapidar with a most uncertain expression, the pack leader looked torn between shock and amusement. In the end, he filled the alley with a most obscene crack of mirth, barking himself hoarse. His minions were looking undecidedly from one to the next, and shifted around in their wolf skins wondering whether they should still have them on.

When the laughter died down, the pack leader spoke to Achak. "Is this true, boy? Are you stuck?"

Achak felt the heat come to his face, but nodded obligingly with Lapidar's story.

The pack leader burst out again with his crackling fit. He became up-roarious, trying to produce more noise and hollering greater than before.

Apart from feeling the embarrassment, Achak did not think the wolfman would buy into the story so easily. But after asking Achak whether he could transmogrify a few more times, the pack leader gave up on the questions.

"Take a stand, boys," he commanded and four other men stood in the wolves' places. Three of equal height and age, and one, shorter than the rest, emerged from the place of Lapidar's opponent. They had no color to their outfits, but wore a common dress of gray shirt topped with a black jean jacket, and as Achak thought about this, it made sense that they would clothe themselves in black and white shades since as wolves, they could see no other hues.

After greeting his wolfmen, the pack leader turned around to meet Lapidar again. "And might we meet again, lone wolf?"

Lapidar shrugged, giving out his usual lack of social exchange, except that he offered his name. Then looking down at Achak, introduced him as well. The feelings of danger dissipated with the introductions.

"And which werewolf bunch would you be?" Lapidar asked.

"Lunar," the pack leader replied.

"Eclipse?" Lapidar counter-balanced and there was surprise in his voice.

The pack leader smiled and nodded. Achak did not understand the exchange that had been made, but made a mental note to ask about it later.

Lapidar inclined his head to the pack leader and patted his thighs for Achak to follow. When they reached the end of the alley, he held Achak off as he peered around the corner, his old precautions returning.

"Oi!" The pack leader halted their departure. "You knew Vargulf?"

Lapidar turned his head back to meet the werewolf once more. "No, who's that?" he asked, but Achak was not entirely convinced of his uncertainty and by the looks of it, neither was the pack leader.

The question hung in the air until Lapidar gave the man a final look and walked out of the alley with Achak at his heels.

"It's Clayborn now!" The pack leader's voice followed them out of the alley.

The streets had become deserted since their werewolf encounter and Achak could not help but suspect that it had something to do with the Lunar pack. Stranger still was the fact that Lapidar continued walking while in human form and had not returned to his wolf skin. Maybe he really was badly injured, Achak began to worry before remembering what Lapidar had told him about crossing over into Hybrid territory. It seemed like an hour had gone by before he finally spoke up.

"Listen, Achak."

Hearing his name as opposed to "boy" surprised him, so he did what he was asked.

"If you meet anymore wolves," Lapidar warned, "wait for one of the Lunar pack before you do anything stupid. There's at least one following behind us and I doubt he means to attack."

Achak wheeled around, piercing the darkness and every street corner with his eyes.

"I'm not finished," Lapidar snapped and Achak brought back his full attention. "Wait here!" Lapidar indicated the nearest doorway to a closed bank, then pointed across the way to a plain looking motel. He explained, "When I give the signal come and meet me across the street."

Achak nodded and backed his way into the shadows of the doorway, never taking his eyes off Lapidar's back. He felt nervous as he found himself making frequent glances in the direction they had come from to see about the stalking werewolf, but always he stared down an empty walkway.

"Psst, kid!"

He nearly tore out of his skin before turning around. There, standing before him was one of the men Achak had seen emerge from the pack. He had a long drawn face, bonier still under his shag and the least of facial hair, though he was not without his sideburns, which Achak was beginning to think of as a common fashion trend among wolves.

"Here," he said and held in his hand an offering of fair size. The bulk was wrapped in a brown cloth. "For your friend." The werewolf gave him a last piece of instruction.

Achak nodded and took the gift in his mouth, careful not to rest it against his two larger fangs.

The werewolf walked again in his own direction and disappeared around the street corner. It was only a few minutes longer before Achak, while watching the other side of the street, saw Lapidar summoning him to come over.

After looking both ways, he padded across, following Lapidar who had already turned his back and was leading the way to their motel room. He climbed the steps to the second landing and ushered Achak around the L-shaped corner, pausing at the second room. Holding the door open, he made Achak enter first.

Bolting the door tight, Lapidar used every lock and chain available to seal the door. When he turned around to claim a seat on the nearest bed, Achak brought the package over.

"Oh great!" he snarled. "Gifts. I should have warned you not to accept any. Though, I guess you didn't have much of a choice."

Unwrapping the cloth, he continued his banter. "Couldn't they wait a day or two before making an offering? Oh how nice, a first aid kit." And he held it up for Achak to see. "And this is why I hate the city. Everyone's always in a rush. A rush to go places. A rush to get married. A rush to send invitations."

Lapidar removed his coat and Achak saw the scratches and stains that were making him angry. Wherever there were torn shreds of material across his shirt, dark stains appeared around the wound. It made Achak feel guilty not to have a share of injuries and, because he could think of nothing else to make himself useful, he went into the bathroom and brought out some complimentary towels.

"Thanks," Lapidar muttered and, seeing Achak's welcoming swish of the tail, decided to continue speaking in a softer tone. He pulled out an envelope from the first aid kit and began reading its contents aloud:

"*In the day there is a man. In the night there is a wolf. Where a full moon is halfway, an eclipse overpowers. Like minutes in the hour, Earth's shadow will devour and those whose howl remains will surely own the night.*"

Lapidar stopped reading and chuckled to himself. "My aren't they swell poets!" He looked across at Achak, who had his head tilted to one side.

"This is an invitation to join the pack," Lapidar offered the simple explanation, then finished reading the card silently. "Basically what this card says is 'Join us or die.' But no worries. It's not the first one I've rejected nor death threat I've received."

He stuffed the card back in its envelope and began tearing it into shreds. As Achak watched Lapidar, he could not bring himself to take the threats so lightly, even if Lapidar's gestures were genuine. For one thing, he had the bandaged arms to consider. Whether or not the gashes were serious, Achak looked at Lapidar's bare arms with all his concerns. He wanted to say how sorry he was, at least in the case of not being much help during either scuffle with The Jacks and Lunar Pack.

"I think I would have preferred it if they had sent me a beer," Lapidar said, not taking his eye off his bandages as he tightened them. He spoke as if no change in mood had come between him and Achak. "Some food wouldn't have been so bad either, huh?"

When he looked at Achak and found him sitting in the same spot on the carpet, he frowned. "And will you stop looking at me like that! *I'm fine.*"

Achak stayed watching just long enough to see Lapidar roll his eyes, then hopped on the second bed—a more painful process than he could have imagined. He curled himself on the bed cat-like. Each shift brought out a new ache around his body. Sharp pangs ran through every tendon in his arms and legs. He would have rested his chin on the bedspread if his fangs did not get in the way.

Instead, he turned his head around the room for something to watch other than Lapidar. Without the television on, he had only a bland table with two wooden chairs near the bathroom and framed copies of paintings by unknown artists. He was staring into one of the framed canvases, whose garden had an archway of cement and vines, behind which there were maze pathways of rose bushes receding endlessly into the background. A chuckle made by Lapidar pulled Achak out of his stupor.

"You know, I never would have believed you'd of had it in you to wag your tail in the face of the pack leader OF A WEREWOLF CLAN."

Achak remained still and Lapidar did not give up on him.

"But seriously, we can start transmogrification lessons tomorrow. And if you speak like you do rebel, I can't wait to hear the first words out of your mouth."

9
Transmogrification
Part I

Manu had asked Sirena to make frequent checks around the San Diego High campus and Lund Street to see if Achak had returned. She now waited on the stem of an overhanging power-line and loomed over the Twinfang house. A police patrol car was parked in front and two uniformed men with their black suits and gold badges were walking up to the doorstep. She waited for the front door to open and took flight. Achak was being missed at the Twinfang residency where a missing persons report would soon be filed for his sake.

Her wings were tired. Sirena had spent most of the day circling over the San Diego High campus and, with nothing more than a sea breeze, she had not been able to keep soaring on the winds, but flapped with her massive wings. Hours had passed since she last perched.

Unseen in the dark sky, Sirena made one last loop around the campus and saw a figure walking across the grounds. It was well after the school hours for even sports teams to be out practicing, which eliminated those possibilities. It was for this sort of lone trespasser that Manu had sent her and for whom she had been watching.

She could not quite make out his features from her current elevation and so began to soar lower. He looked just like Lapidar, a long coat trailing from his backside.

The lone figure had been making circles on a lighted patch of gravel near the locker rooms in much the same manner that Sirena had been circling the school thirty feet above. This was not normal behavior for someone of mere human characteristics so when Sirena made her descent it was to land in the same patch of light that the nighttime stroller had deserted.

Her claws touched the cool earth and became instantly warmed by a pair of black platform boots that sprouted over them. The vulture's hair once again rested on her shoulders.

Now that she was behind him, she recognized the male student by the back of his head. She had once found a perch on his chair in the auditorium. It would be fun to see the startled look on his face again should she spring on him a second time.

Sirena crept forward in the darkness, making her feet as quiet and light as... the feathers on her back. She was drifting toward the student like some horrible creature of the night whose black cape or cloak was renowned for billowing behind its prey.

"I've been waiting for you!" the darkness called out to her.

Sirena stopped and squinted her eyes angrily into the shadows to see a familiar silhouette.

"What do you want, small feather?" Sirena scowled: her sneak-up plan ruined. The boy was already staring at the pair of them with his wide gray eyes. He backed away and ran into a doorway not far along that was propped open with yellow light streaming out.

"I want to know what you're still doing around here after I told you to leave." Mariam held her place with her body of a shorter frame than even that of Sirena.

Drawing herself to her full height, plus platform stilts, Sirena opened her mouth in a toothy grin that she knew Mariam would be able to see.

"Not so brave without your boyfriend, are you, small feather?"

Mariam huffed. "Marcus doesn't think you concern us, but I think otherwise. Trying to take another boy, are you?"

"Take?" Sirena inquired and kept her smile broad. She had not expected any such suspicions to reach her, but Mariam seemed a tad more clued in than the other vertebrate.

"Where's Achak?" Mariam burst. "What have you done with him? He's missing!"

"Achak-who?" Sirena mused.

"Don't Achak-who me!" Mariam bellowed. "I've seen you with him! You were the last person with him before he disappeared."

Sirena shrugged and watched a few feathers drop from Mariam's hair.

"What do you want with Donovan, buzzard?" Mariam closed a fist demandingly in front of her.

"Dono-what?" Sirena tilted her head, then looked from the light-streaming doorway and back to Mariam. Connecting the boy with the name, she broke out into shrill laughter.

"Oh, you small feather!" Sirena wailed. "You have no idea what you're getting into. Keep your feathers clean and go home."

Mariam stayed put and Sirena approached the small feather to test how well her courage held. It molted almost instantly with Mariam giving a startled jump back from the larger scavenger. Sirena let out another howl of delight and turned away.

"Bravery dwindles without numbers," she hollered back over her shoulder. Her figure was taken into the light of the doorway. When she took one last glance behind, the small feather had left.

The entrance hall was a ridiculously narrow room with an even punier space against the wall serving as a ticket booth. The box was empty and dark, but there were flyers taped everywhere around its glass window that listed the next sporting events. There was an ad for volleyball games, but next to that, an out-of-place flyer announced that tickets to *Romeo and Juliet* starring Donovan Parsons could be purchased at the Front Office or through Mrs. Hyde.

Sirena smirked and turned around, but something not so pleasantly discovered was waiting for her against the opposite wall. They looked like nothing more than a pair of vending machines that dispensed energy drinks and water bottles, but Sirena knew otherwise.

She took a step nearer to the machine with the golden apple gleaming from its front and the fruit rising from a sea of deep blue.

"But that's Coral's product," she muttered to herself, but there were voices overpowering hers. She looked back to the doorway right of the ticket booth.

"Check the camera," a man's voice shouted.

"Come on! Let's get the lighting set up."

Sirena edged nearer to the door and peered inside. Her eyes narrowed on one individual that was strolling around the basketball courts from crew member to crew member. It was none other than Dr. Coral, looking more out of place in the gymnasium than he had in any room inside the Domestica mansion.

"Donovan!" Coral called and the boy Sirena had been stalking in the darkness walked over to the only person wearing a white labcoat and holding a clipboard.

Sirena kept half her body behind the door. She wished that she had not tired her wings out when now more than ever she needed to fly in for a closer watch. It was only with some fortune that their voices echoed across the hollow gym.

Coral's voice went unnaturally gentle and Sirena's eyes filled themselves with black ink as she tried to focus in on him whom Manu trusted.

"What'sss with the tired look today?" Coral briefed a glance over his clipboard. No one else seemed to pay Coral and the boy any heed as they were all too busy adjusting the more unusual aspects of camera and lighting equipment. The basketball court had all the scuffmarks and worn polish of a typical high school gym, but the walls at least were free from chipping or peeling.

Above the bench seating, a mural depicted the school mascot of a "wildcat" in a fierce roar over what normally would have been the screaming heads of spectators. Tonight those stands were empty for the exclusiveness of this film shoot.

Donovan stood by the doctor and Sirena could see him trembling with nerves. His eyes avoided the camera crew and equipment. It was a very familiar setting for him to be in, this being his high school and all, but somehow the presence of only a few nameless faces, seven or so light stands with their long necks, and one black camera mounted on what looked like a motorized trolley cart, had transmogrified the atmosphere.

"I—I'm just a little nervous," Donovan said and that was an understatement, Sirena thought as she watched him rub his left arm as though chilled by something.

Dr. Coral looked up from his clipboard again, this time staring up long enough to take in the boy's appearance.

Sirena smiled maliciously.

Donovan had come dressed in a long browncoat that brought out the golden streaks of his hair. With a darker collared shirt underneath and a handkerchief peeking out of one of his jean pockets, the attire had a western feel to it. Dr. Coral's lip curled as he shot a glance back in the direction of the school mural. Sirena too looked back at the mascot.

"What are you wearing?" he said with a startling coarseness.

Donovan straightened up, but did not look offended. He had given a nervous laugh before answering. "Ah-oh, just a—just a new fashion I thought I'd try." His voice rose and fell unsteadily. "I like to try to impersonate people I see—MEET, I mean. Maybe I'll try wearing a labcoat some time." He laughed again.

Sirena stifled her cackle. She had not expected Coral to take so much personal offense to the Lapidar resemblance.

Coral's eyes narrowed. His voice cut across Donovan's banter. "Well never mind, we've got to get you in cossstume. Over there," he snapped.

Following where Dr. Coral had pointed, Donovan walked toward where a woman in business jacket and skirt was laying out a basketball jersey and shorts over the lower benches.

"Propsss, please." Sirena heard Dr. Coral shout out with his back to her. Moving her full body through the doorway, Sirena dared to enter the gymnasium. There was squealing as a cart of basketballs was wheeled onto the courts.

"Now," Dr. Coral muttered and began picking up balls to examine them one by one. He dribbled a few to test their inflation. After bouncing away a series of rejects, he held out a single basketball and announced his selection: "Thisss one."

Sputtering and whines forced all heads around, first, to see what Coral had done to the basketball, then further toward the entryway of gym where a short dark figure stood with something orange and no longer round compressed between her two hands. Her fingernails had clawed their way through the deflated basketball.

A high pitch and piercing laugh burst from Sirena's mouth before she could string two words together. Donovan especially had a startled expression on his face that made Sirena feel even more mysterious around all the unfamiliar faces.

"Ssirena!" Coral exclaimed in a not so welcoming voice. "How nicsse of you to drop in."

"Been here all this time," she said in reply, not laughing but smiling. "Boring, really."

"Yesss, well this isn't exactly your area of expertissse now is it?" Dr. Coral reflected curtly and there was a definite hint in wanting Sirena to leave. She did not, but was only further convinced by his tone that there was something worth staying around to watch.

"I like your coat," she shouted across Coral to the young actor that was now getting into his sports wear. With that comment, Dr. Coral shot a disgusted look back at Donovan, who went scarlet, then turned again to Sirena.

"I'd really rather you not ssstay and watch thisss," Coral spoke again and he struggled to keep the rattle from appearing between his words. "We've got a lot of trial runs to do before we shoot and I'd rather not have you ssswooping around and damaging more propsss."

He stared down at the deflated basketball that she still carried around. Most of the film crew had returned to their task of adjusting the lights and camera equipment, but Dr. Coral had no time to issue them any more instructions before Sirena spoke again.

"I know what you're up to," she whispered. Her eyes narrowed, but Coral glittered back his own pair of gleaming diamonds.

"I don't know what you're raving about," Dr. Coral hissed under a quieter breath.

"You!" Sirena accused in triumph. "That drink," she accused again. "Water and all the minerals a body needs. What's the catch? How does it work?"

As she pursued, Dr. Coral let the features in his face become more relaxed, but she had caught the first flicker in his expression and went on.

"How does it kill?"

Dr. Coral's features went rigid and he rung his arm out so fast toward Sirena's neck that she did not have time to avoid his hand completely.

Grabbing onto her shoulder, he buried his fingers into her bare skin.

"Sssilence," he spat. His nails pinched her deeper into her collarbone to prevent her from freeing herself. "I don't know how a little girl like you found out but the sssecret dies here."

Fortunately as he pulled her closer, she pulled away and Dr. Coral was left with nothing but a bundle of black feathers bunched between his clenching fist.

"Don't," she said darkly. "I dare say you won't."

"Ssscavenger!" Coral came forth, but Sirena held up her hand to stop Coral from lunging at her.

"Silly serpent. I'm not about to tell."

Unblinking and staring, Coral had paused in his assault. Some of the rage in his expression had actually dissolved into curiosity.

"I just want to know how it works."

Dr. Coral forced the shapes of his eyes back into diamonds. "And why should I tell you?" he struck out with venom.

"An easier thing to do than murder," Sirena answered. "But I shouldn't have to remind you. You know what I am and what I must eat to survive."

Foreseeing his reaction, Sirena watched as Dr. Coral glanced behind himself—at his camera crew—searching for any alternatives, then resigned.

"Find out for yourssself!" he hissed decidedly. "You'll need proof to convincsse Manu and I'm not about to jussst hand it over and give you sssome leverage over me. Blackmail won't work on sssuch complicated groundsss."

"Fine," Sirena shrugged, glided on her heels, and began to walk towards the door.

So clearly the purple showed in Dr. Coral's pale cheeks that it came as no surprise to any of his crew members that he tore loose one of the six water bottles from a ringlet pack and threw it at Sirena's retreating backside.

With haunting grace, she spun around, her black drapes all aflutter, and caught the bottle in midair. Arms out and bowing so that the billows of garments looked even more wing-like, Sirena grinned. She rotated the bottle in her hand, recognized the golden apple on the label, and brisked away, never to catch the distortion in Coral's face as she departed in her satisfied swoop out the door.

Day 5, Friday

"One other thing I forgot to mention the other night, kid, transmogrification is easiest when you think about what keeps you human."

In the motel room, Lapidar had the curtains drawn with only natural light radiating through the window. The beds were left unmade and he had taken a moment to flop the "Do Not Disturb" sign over the door handle for any housekeeping to see and bypass.

"It's all about finding out why you need to transmogrify into a particular form, and I can't put enough stress on the 'NEED' aspect of becoming human—the answer isn't: because you were born that way. There are a lot of folks out there that would do better to stay as beasts than humans but they're able to utilize both forms."

Taking a seat on the bed while in deep thought, Lapidar already looked worn by the day's lesson. Though his eyes still glittered with life and his voice held strong, Lapidar's appearance was in less remarkable condition. Apart from the bandages, his ruffled and gray saturated hair had the matted look of something horribly dyed.

"Okay, now what you'll see and what you'll feel when you transmogrify are two distinctly different things. What you'll see—and I know you've already experienced it once when you were forced into a Sabertooth's skin—is some parts being torn away from your body while other parts seem to be taking on more weight. It probably looked something like extendable fur coming out of your skin. And when you transmogrify into a human, it will look like your fur is retracting under the many layers of skin and who knows where, but that's not what it feels like.

"Seriously, do you think you could hide that much hair under a thin layer of flesh? No, that's not possible. Science and the Laws of Matter make it impossible. You're not tucking this part of yourself away or flipping your skin inside out. In actuality, it is the motion of change that is occurring: the moving out of one skin and into another. But don't think of it like evolution, or it'll take you years to master it.

"You're not aging. There is more than one clock in our bodies: there's the one that tells us how old we are, and there's another that knows of neither past nor future, young nor old, and runs neither forward nor backward, up nor down, north nor south, but moves left and right, east and west. It's hard to think of it as a clock when you look at it that way."

Achak didn't think he understood, especially after six hours of virtually no progress. He wore as thick of a fur coat as ever over his skin. The sun was setting by the time Achak's spirits began to lag, not so much from exertion as from sheer frustration.

If he had managed anything within the past hours, it was putting his legs to sleep. All he could think about was standing on two hind legs again. Lapidar perceived as much about Achak's shallow focus, telling him that it would do him no good to only think about the physical elements of his transmogrification

"Do you want a human body back or do you want your humanity?" Lapidar finally had the nerve to ask.

This only made matters worse for Achak, who, in his short life span as a Sabertooth Tiger, had adopted some of its more aggressive habits. When it became apparent that Lapidar really wanted Achak to consider his answer to the question, Achak snarled in wild indignation. As if Achak would want anything less than complete humanity.

Every time Achak let the growl slip through his throat and vibrate in his chest, he had the feeling that he was moving one step away from becoming human. And all the while he had Dr. Coral's haunting words to go by:

There isn't enough humanity left within that petulant mind of yours to return to its form.

Could the amount of time he spent as a Sabertooth really be affecting his ability to think humanly? If so, then every moment Achak spent inhabiting a prehistoric body took him further and further away from his goal, and maybe there was a time limit to how long he could remain in his sabertooth form before it became permanent.

"Hey, come on!" Lapidar shouted a stir into Achak's motionless body. "I want to see some effort!"

Achak shot him a glower before cocking his head low, again with every thought fixed on becoming human. He had stopped watching his limbs and forepaws when he realized that the lookout for hairless changes was making it impossible for him to concentrate or even fathom the human transmogrification. Every furry feature and irregular joint on his body put his mind on the loops of *why* and *how.*

He closed his eyes, pretending not to see or accept the shapes of his body. If he could imagine it the way it ought to be and move his limbs the way they should then maybe when he opened his eyes, he would find them just as he had remembered them.

"Humanity isn't about the way you look, it's about how you think. So think already!"

Achak didn't *think* all of Lapidar's disruptive comments were helping.

"Watch the paw!" Lapidar growled, forcing Achak to jump as though it might be stepped on. "No, I mean it. Keep you eyes on your paw."

Achak did what he was told despite wanting to account for the order as another useless instruction. He looked down at his paw, saw the brown fur and tucked away his nails, preparing himself to be disappointed.

"Now try to spread your fingers," Lapidar further instructed. "Spread them like only a human can do... and maybe a few gifted apes."

Achak could not do more than point out his claws. The skin and lack of flexibility between his toes prevented him from doing much more. Not to mention, it hurt. He thought it must have been a lot like separating webbed toes as he felt like there was skin to be pulled apart. Then he realized that he had been visualizing the separation of toes and began to imagine how it would look with human fingers. But the result was the same no matter how he envisioned it.

For an instant, and a momentary relief from the pressure, his mind left the focus of his paw and transmogrification. He remembered giving Tehya piggy-back rides and thought how much more she would enjoy it if she could have a go on him now. Riding on the back of a Sabertooth Tiger, he could hear Tehya's squeamish glee, even if she was almost eleven.

The feeling was distinct, like removing a tightened layer of fabric away from the skin, or pulling off spandex sleeves. It did not hurt, but felt refreshing as his skin was being allowed to breathe again, except that it was only occurring to him in his hand.

His eyes were still open but as he had been so immersed in his thoughts, he did not comprehend the visual until it was already over. He could only take notice of the sensation, but it had startled him so much to feel the tingling that he let the fur pull back over his skin just to end it.

Achak had lost the sensation, but not without first elating to his small victory. Lapidar howled with equal excitement. Achak had seen it too and there could be no denying what he had done with his right paw. He had seen five short toes elongate themselves and claws recede into fingernails above the skin. There was a thumb, but more importantly, there was hope, Achak told himself.

Hours later, that hope began to diminish and Lapidar asked Achak to start from the beginning. As the day shortened, so did Lapidar's temper. The only thing growing between the two Hybrids was the tension.

"Okay," the wolf sighed grievously. "From the top. The first thing to know about transmogrification is that it does not depend on equal body mass to make the change. And, the change it involves is more of a mental shift than a physical one."

Achak stared again at his paw, but the best he could do to change it back into a hand was to squint his tiger eyes until they blurred the shape of his paw. However, each time he stared clearly upon his feet, they still had the hairy and round appearance of a sabertooth cat's.

"Would you stop closing your eyes, kid, and watch for the changes?! Wishing inside your head isn't going to make it happen."

But Achak seemed to have developed a block for everything that Lapidar was saying, or maybe it was just the wolf's temper that made him less keen to listen and follow Lapidar's advice.

"Spread you fingers! Spread 'em!" he barked.

Achak would much rather have summoned fingers from his fur just to ball them into a fist and send them straight into the side of Lapidar's face.

"It's not about being human, kid. If that was the case then all you would have to do is attempt to stand on you hind legs. A begging dog could do that!" Then he began shouting, "Don't think: 'bipedal.' Think: 'humanity!' I've said this before. It's not about being human; it's about your humanity. What thought makes you human?!"

Lapidar's words were booming in Achak's sensitive feline ears, causing him more pain than his already aching body could endure. He roared at Lapidar for silence.

The wolf gave him a terrorized look, then resorted back to his shouting.

"Don't roar at me! DON'T YOU DARE—" The wolf spat, and he really did transmogrify himself into that form of his nature. Coated in gray fur, his dark strands streamed from his backside until they merged into the white of his belly. Lapidar faced Achak with his fangs bared. His mouth foamed and growled as he approached.

He snapped, and Achak had to back away to keep his nose from being gnawed off. Lapidar bounded forward as Achak tried to avoid him again, but the wolf had sunk his teeth into the back of Achak's neck and, with the fold of skin between his teeth, flung Achak sideways onto the carpet.

Achak was growling too now, but before he had had the chance to lift himself up, Lapidar leapt on him, pinning Achak to the floor with his claws. His nails sank deeper and Achak chuffled loudly in a cry of pain.

Lapidar snarled in his face sending spit around Achak's eyes.

As the pinned sabertooth, Achak became scared while the wolf moved one of its pressing paws closer to his neck, but then a human hand wrapped around Achak's throat and Lapidar was sitting on top of him, wearing his browncoat once more.

"I'm trying to help you!" he growled, and Achak noticed that his voice still had not been restored to the one of a completely human Lapidar. "And I'm telling you that it's your attitude that keeps you this way! Anger makes you stupid, do you understand me? It makes you reckless and it's the most primitive state of mind you can ask for if you want to stay animal. But if nothing else I've said goes through your head or makes any sense to you, then let it be this: I'm the only friend you've got in this part of the neighborhood."

His hand released the pressure from Achak's throat and he stood up. Lapidar began to straighten his browncoat, then walked towards the door. Before his departure, he announced in one last croak that he would be at a bar down the street if Achak needed him.

"Don't come in anything but a human's skin!" He told Achak and snapped the door behind him.

Manu walked into a room with ample recliners to sit upon. Their cushions lavished ornate designs of magenta and gold, but even at the outlandish level of comfort it yielded, the room was still a recognizable feature of Domestica as giraffes framed one of the archways.

In fact, the moment Manu had opened the door, The Jacks had run in on his heels and leapt into two identical armchairs to curl up. Manu made a faint attempt to smile at the wagging tails of his loyal hounds, but managed only a grimace.

At the room's center was a large column where built-in shelves and cabinets came around its cylindrical base. As though this was the highlight of the room, a crescent of recliners came around its other side. Though not seen from Manu's angle, a flat screen TV waited on the other side with its screen painted black until the master would face it. The Jacks had no sense of how to turn it on, even though they had seen their master do it many times in the past.

Their master was never as quick to enter a room as they were, and The Jacks could not help but notice the shorter steps he made towards them.

Ék Jack held his tongue in and stared. The strangest thought had occurred to him in seeing his master hunch on a limp leg, but surely he had only imagined it. He knew his master to be a straight walker who always stood up tall on his hind legs.

The Jack also knew that light would not come into the black box until master stood in front of it. He also new that there was a long gray bone that master liked to pick up and take with him to the sofa.

Master had a way of taming the room and knew exactly when to touch the spot on the wall the exact moment the room became brighter. And at this moment, master picked up a new stick from a canister that stood next to the central column. It was a long stick—a fine stick—for master to keep the lower end of it touching the ground with every step so as to tame the carpet.

"You don't look so well," Sirena said from her perch on the open window. Both legs were hanging from the sill and into Manu's guestroom. The Jacks growled as she brought both feet onto the gold carpet. Sirena eyed the cane between Manu's legs as he sat himself down on the sofa between The Jacks.

"Don't you have a nutritionist to keep your muscles strong?"

"I have," Manu inhaled, "Dr. Coral."

Sirena's eyes darkened but she made no comment on the matter.

"He's nowhere in San Diego from what I can tell," Sirena reported instead.

Manu took another deep breath. "These dealings make an old man feel much-much older," he sighed and placed two fingers between his eyes as he rested his head over the cane.

"Judging by the train they took, I'd say they headed into L.A.—"

"Sirena, could you get me some water?"

She turned around to see where Manu was waving his hand and saw a short refrigerator under a narrow table. It had made the wooden table look like a cabinet because its outside was designed with the same bamboo appearance.

When she opened the door, she called out the names of flavors to Manu. "Cider, Citrus, Tropic Berry, Coconut..." Sirena looked around with a smile to see which additive would be Manu's favorite.

He scarcely heard her as he waved his hand away for Sirena to decide for him. She frowned and grabbed the first bottle of cider she could wrap her fingers around.

Before handing it over, her thumb stroked across the label, past the apple, and glided to the finishing touches of the letters: "H-y-d-r-o-M-a-x."

"Coral's quite successful with this product, isn't he?" Sirena said, handing Manu the water and falling back into one of the armchairs where she could continue to face him.

Manu didn't answer her, but drank deeply from the bottle until he was nearly finished.

How he might choke! if she were to say anything obscene to him at the moment. Sirena reserved the temptation.

"Flavored mineral water," she mused. "He's not the first to invent it, but he certainly has done a great job marketing it... adding flavors without diminishing the nutritional value."

Manu studied Sirena. "He has ingeniously discovered how to extract the vitamins from their natural source." Manu placed the bottle down on the coffee table between them, where beneath its smooth glass surface showed the on-going stack of bamboo rods.

Ignoring etitiquete, Sirena retrieved the bottle into her own hands.

" 'Course he has," Sirena said. "It's on the label." And she pointed to the "100% all natural" stamp that appeared on the cover.

"Then what are you on about?" Manu demanded, his temper and energy restored to full power.

Sirena merely shrugged and took the empty bottle into her hand where she slowly revolved it between her palms.

Manu began to chuckle and Sirena looked up. "Oh, I understand completely," he exclaimed and held the amusement on his tongue where it annoyed Sirena the most. "You think Ladon has somehow poisoned the supply of water and means to do away with me. Is that not it? Well, I hate to disappoint you, missy, but what Dr. Coral has done to this water is nothing more than to enable our existence. What with our lakes and rivers polluted, acid rain, and depleted ground sources, we can hope for no clearer liquid than that which has been taken into the refineries, properly cleaned, and then packaged for us to be able to take back to our homes."

There was a knock on the door panel and Sirena steered wildly around in her chair to see Dr. Coral standing there in his white labcoat.

"Excuse me," he hissed in a low voice. He was looking directly at Manu. "I will be in my lab for a few hoursss."

Manu flushed at being caught in a complete spew about Ladon's research in front of the very man himself.

"Yes," Manu said with a humble nod. "Do take some time to carry on with your own work."

"Thank you," Coral bowed and left the doorway.

Sirena chased after him. Doors on both sides of her lined the hallway she ran down.

"Where is this lab?" she asked brightly and Coral cast himself around wearing a hardened expression. His eyes narrowed into slits, then he released her from his gaze and smiled.

"Yesss, you can come and sssee it," Coral hissed delicately and Sirena drew back as though he meant to strike at her. "Did you think I would sssay 'no,' little birdie?

Come if you like. There'sss nothing you will dissscover in my lab if you do not know what you are looking for."

He cackled and led the way down the hall, stopping in front of two flat and shapeless doors.

"What's this?" Sirena asked.

"An elevator," Coral explained. His hand reached into his labcoat pocket and drew out a chain of keys, one of which fit into the keyhole beside the doors. Then the floor beneath their feet began to rumble.

"But there was an elevator back there," Sirena exclaimed and pointed back to the other end of the hallway.

"Yesss," Coral confirmed. "But that one does not go all the way down. My lab is in a basement of sssortsss." He looked at Sirena for some kind of response, then added, "Are you sure you ssstill want to come along?"

Sirena nodded her head firmly and gave Coral the nastiest pair of eyes she could fix him with.

The doors opened for a second time some feet below the earth's crust and Domestica. Sirena followed Coral out of the elevator and into a single room that was filled with lab equipment of every size and shape, most of which was made of glass. She was particularly lured to the flasks that were suspended with tubes coming out of their ends and colored liquids that filled vials. In the corners were stacks and stacks of crates that certainly were filled to the brims with assorted fruits. That ruled out the theory that HydroMax may not have been produced with natural materials, but Sirena still began to question the nutrients.

She went over to where Coral had begun picking up and tapping the contents of a beaker. His eyes narrowed through the spectacles in careful observation. He shuffled around through a few clipboards and when he had found the right one, he began making check marks and jotting down notes that only he could understand.

"pH 4, DCIP, Blue - inefficient vitamin C," Sirena read loudly over his shoulder. "A bad apple, eh?"

He turned around to look at her, but his face was not filled with contempt.

"Please do not contaminate my sssamplesss with your ssspit," he said with a broad grin.

"Heh!" Sirena sneered and flipped her hair back, releasing a few feathers from the black underlying strands.

"Or with your feathersss," Coral hissed and turned his back on her.

Sirena stuck her tongue out and did not follow as Coral moved away. She backed into a cleared counter space and took a seat on its black marble surface. Her hand touched the clipboards that rested beside her and she began flipping through the doctor's notes.

"What's Hyssop?" she cried out.

"That'sss an almost seizure-inducssing herb to clear the mind," Coral answered her from behind one of the sinks. "It does not belong with HydroMax. But if you were to read the top, you'd have already known that. Hyssssop is what I used to transmogrify Achak."

When he looked up it was with a livid expression of disgust, which Sirena understood as the memory of the boy's escape.

"As a chemical, it goes ssstraight to the brain and nerves, you sssee." Coral went back to his cleaning. "I alssso used Nepeta in that sssolution, that'sss a non-toxic herb that can only become hallucinogenic in large quantitiesss."

Sirena put the one clipboard down only to pick up another and begin flipping through its pages. She glanced up at Coral's back to see him shaking his head.

"What was the first flavor you came out with?"

Coral turned away from the sink and this time Sirena was certain it was not entirely because his work was done, despite the fact that he moved away with a clean flask in his hand. He had not grabbed a paper towel or drying cloth.

"Cssider," he said indifferently.

"Cider, as in apple?" Sirena asked and allowed a smirk to creep up one side of her face.

"Would there be another kind?" Coral hissed.

"Grape," Sirena said and shrugged as though Coral's first choice did not matter to her.

"I like what you've done with this place," she remarked. "It's soooo..."

"Plain?" Coral finished. "Yesss, I know itsss not of homely decors, but were you the interior decorator, there would be no lightsss for me to sssee what resultsss my work produssced. I sssee the way you dressss yourssself for a funeral."

Sirena smiled placidly, then jumped off the counter. "Alright," she announced. "I'll be going now. Thanks for showing me around."

"Leaving ssso sssoon?" Coral gave her a cold quizzical look.

She nodded and walked back towards the elevator. There was no key required for admittance on this end. The doors opened when she pushed the button and she stepped inside them. Facing the lab with a last examination, she held off on pushing the 2nd floor button.

"Hey, Coral!" she called out. "Are you as good at extracting poisons as you are at injecting them?"

Coral just stared up at her from his clipboard, then the doors closed and Sirena was satisfactorily heading back to the earth's surface.

-●○●○●-

9
Transmogrification
Part II

More than once, Achak poked his head between the drapes to wonder both if he would see Lapidar coming up the street or if he might chance going out himself when the coast was clear. He did not like the idea of walking out alone in a Saber-tooth Tiger's skin and in a Hybrid neighborhood. The safer option would be to wait for Lapidar. Achak's build up of worry settled most uncomfortably in his stomach, where soft rumbles told him it was nearing suppertime.

Out of loneliness through the hours, Achak had actually begun to develop some concern for Lapidar. The hour was such that no bar would still be open, but there was the possibility that Lapidar had moved on to a club to do some more drinking.

He could have brooded over the matter throughout Lapidar's entire absence, but then he may never see his human self again. Though his odds for success in becoming a self-trained Hybrid were few, Achak practiced his transmogrification. He had nothing to gain and everything to lose if he failed. At least he could always blame it on Lapidar should he fail and lack a good teacher.

Left to his own judgments, Achak positioned himself on the carpet where he had left off. He stared at his paw and imaged the change that was to occur in its appearance. But he could feel nothing as he tried to reconstruct the sensations with his mind. As he caught on to a tingling in his ankle, he was disappointed to learn that it was only his foot falling asleep.

When all seemed futile, he started from the beginning, attempting to do nothing more than spread his toes. He thought about them as fingers, but they hurt as inflexible members of the feline body.

He was still pulling apart his toes when he began thinking about how much he longed for home and school. For three days, he had been missing, though possibly four days for all his family knew of his disappearance since neither Mom nor Tehya had been home since he arrived late on Tuesday night. He wondered what his family might be speculating about his absence. Did they think him dead? Murdered? Kidnapped?

The last of these was partially true, or at least he had been kidnapped, even if he was not being held against his will now. He would like to believe that he could go home and return to life as it was before Manu, but even from here, he could see that there would be a lot to answer for once he made it back. And what would he tell them? He doubted Mom and Tehya would believe the part about the Goth girl-turned-vulture, or especially the part about him being turned into a Sabertooth. They would have to see it for themselves... but would he really want to show them? After everything he had seen of Hybrids, and the dangers they encountered with werewolves and supposedly vampires as well, Achak could not convince himself to introduce his family into such a world.

His ears tweaked as he heard the television come on in the room next door. The noise called him back to the present where Achak found that he had managed nothing more in the last hour than to engrave his paw imprint in the carpet. His legs were cramping beneath him, to add more to the rumbling discomfort in his stomach.

Boredom and fatigue set over him. Achak moved himself on top of the bed, lying with his legs off to the side where they could not be squashed or put to sleep and gazed lazily at his paw. It was all he could do to keep his eyes open, but through it, he was seeing his sister Tehya alone in front of the backyard bonfire and holding her paperbag mask up to the licking flames, preparing to throw it in. The bag caught fire and Achak snapped awake.

He rolled over on his stomach. There was still no Lapidar, but Achak swallowed back any worries about the wolf's wellbeing and concentrated on his own. He thought he may have even liked the idea that Lapidar had over-drunk himself and gotten lost. Achak's only sympathies were to himself and the fact that without hands, he could not turn on any lights in the room. He was certain that this would not be the last time he wished ill upon Lapidar for abandoning him.

Achak could see in the dark well enough without the need for lights, but the quiet of the night would surely drive him mad if he did not create some sense of having company in the room with him. The loneliness subsided as he pressed his nose to the TV power button to turn it on.

Shadows given off by the TV were dancing around Achak's legs, which ultimately frustrated him by the distortion of their shapes. He wished the changes were real and not just a play off the light over his fur. Struggling with his concentration, he tried to keep his eyes steady and focused but kept following the movement of shadow off to the side.

The illumination of the television set kept projecting dark and shifting stretches across the walls and beneath him. It reminded him of the light that flashed upon Grandpa and Tehya when they moved around the fire. He could almost hear the crackling as he imagined himself stepping into Tehya's shadow to go see the rock in her hand. If he could do it all over again, he would have been interested. In his mind, he was burning to hear what the stone was used for, but not to disregard it or mock it as he had done. He wanted to know how it would protect her when he told her...

...He would sit by her bedside as he had done many times before when they were both younger and he had wanted to play the big brother role of reading to her at bedtime. There were times when she had asked him to make up a story, complaining that Mom had read to her all the children's books on the shelf. Achak had never refused her request, but sometimes he left the room a little heavy hearted when he had disappointed her and she had told him that his story wasn't as good as Grandpa's. Achak could never come up with the endings, many times adding the "happily ever after" just to please Tehya because Mom would have a fit if he told her anything that gave her nightmares.

Is this how he would tell her? One night when she was all tucked into bed and probably too sleepy to understand, he would make the whole confession about his disappearance and hope that she believed it to be a fascinating piece of fiction.

It was laughable to think about. He had almost forgotten how much of a busy-body she could be when it came to rambling over creatures of folklore and to think that Achak could even explain the mystery of werewolves.

His fingers tingled but he held onto his thoughts about Tehya. He saw the fur on his arm receding, yet he was still trying to decide what about Hybrids would impress Tehya the most. Thinking not just of vultures, but how any bird could grant a human with the ability of flight....

Then he caught onto the tingling and realized what was taking place. But the moment he became excited over the change, it stopped. He stared where the transmogrification had reached his elbow and watched as the fur slid back down his arm as though he was only rolling down a long sleeve.

The door clicked and opened. Just as Achak had restored the last of his fur into place and seen his fingers ball into a paw, he looked up to see Lapidar walk in. Nothing about the wolf's ragged appearance looked any worse than it had before with the exception of the bandages that were brown stained with liquor. A strong whiff of alcohol and cigarettes came into the room with him, but he was accompanied by a tasty smell of something warm and seasoned. He moved without trouble near the bed, Achak observed all he could find of sobriety.

Lapidar took one look at Achak as he tipped a couple of bags onto the bed and sniffed his disapproval, cocking his head away from a despicable sight of an untrained Hybrid. He busied himself with untying the handles of the plastic bags and cast Achak with the aroma of peppery spices and jalapeños.

"I won't apologize, but if you want any of this, you'll swear not to tell my wife about me losing my patience with you. Deal?"

Achak was taken aback as he gave Lapidar an eager nod. He could not have been more pleased to receive both human company and food as he approached the wolf's side. Flicking his tail over a few times, he had both the accomplished feelings of transmogrification to be grateful for and the initial signs of partnership. He thought of even performing for Lapidar, who was busy opening containers and spilling food onto a plate. By the time he noticed Achak's head resting under his arm, Lapidar let out a yelp and shouted.

"Wo!" Lapidar nearly lost the fork in his hand. Then he smashed his palm into Achak's nose and pushed the sabertooth away, saying, "Get off me, you meathead."

Achak did what any toddler would do when he wanted something that he couldn't ask for and pulled on Lapidar's shirt. With the fabric between his teeth, Achak was careful not to tear the threads as he gave a brief tug. He kept at it until he was certain Lapidar would not be distracted by the food that was no longer within arm's reach.

Achak wandered a couple more feet away, putting himself closer to the bathroom than his own bed. He stomped his forepaw twice so that Lapidar would know where to focus, then with every bit of confidence began his partial transmogrification. Adjusted to and expectant of the tingling, he endured the sensations without anymore of his fearful discomforts. When he thought of it like rolling up his sleeves, the change happened like before: his fingers stretched and his fur retreated up his arm, frilling just beyond the elbow then settled back down his forearm and wrist.

Shaking his head rather amusedly, Lapidar gave a slight, yet approving smile. He seemed to be trying to prevent Achak from feeling too accomplished as he turned his attention back toward the food.

Even without the congratulations, Achak could sense that Lapidar was proud of him. Before, it had appeared that Lapidar was slapping food onto his tray like a dog dish, but now as Achak sniffed at the tray in front of him, the assortments of rice, beans, tortilla chips, and enchilada were kept to their separate sides and not being served to him as a big pile of mush. He ate each portion happily, and did not realize until he was finished that Lapidar had taken to his wolf's form to eat without hands or utensils as well.

"You've made decent progress," Lapidar began telling Achak after dinner, "but there's still a great deal you need to know about... well, about Hybrids in general and the life as one. It's not enough that you simply learn to become human, otherwise Manu can just use his devices again to force you back."

Achak watched Lapidar closely. So far everything that Lapidar mentioned was something that Achak had already given considerable thought to. Now he only had to wait for him to speak beyond those concerns. He waited.

"Well, the good news is that it won't be long now before you're able to stand erect. Once we've gotten you past the shoulders, there's just the neck and the head, or as is normally the case, the point of no return. Transmogrification is quicker from this end. Sort of like jumping into a pool: you jump in feet first and sometimes you don't go all the way under, which is why there are centaurs, berserkers, and other men (horses and goats) who stop their changes midway at the torso. To move around as such—half and half, I mean—is to be a 'merow.' But if you dive in head first, then everything just follows in right after, and you won't meronize your body."

Achak kept his head nodding and waited for Lapidar to continue.

"With transmogrification out of the way, I needn't remind you that there is currently a bounty on our heads and that it would be best for us to move on as soon as possible. So once you're human, we make for the hills and it'll be back to Union Station where hopefully Manu has yet to station a postman.

"You'll be more vulnerable in human form, but at least you won't stand out so much. We've been lucky so far. Everyone that's seen you in a Sabertooth's skin poses too high of a risk against themselves to be able to report you. Manu can't go around with search flyers for an escaped, dangerous, and would-be extinct specimen and anyone from the Lunars wouldn't dare show their face to the Authorities."

Catching his breath, Lapidar paused. "I think I've already run through our biggest threats. Just concentrate on changing back into human and forget about the other stuff."

Day 6, Saturday

In flicking over the light switches, Lapidar turned himself off to any more explanations. But the next morning was to be a disappointment as Achak appeared to have reached his limit on transmogrification, having barely made much progress by nightfall. Lapidar had said that he expected Achak to be licking from his fingers by suppertime.

Worse still, the TV had been on all day and Achak had tried very hard to draw Lapidar's attention to the HydroMax commercials every time they came on, but Lapidar had never understood him. Achak had also received a nasty shock on the nose by putting it to the static screen.

It wasn't fair, he shivered as the last of the tingles trickled down his neck. He had taken his transmogrifications up his spine before he had to release it under the overwhelming chills that followed his neck. Were Hybrids not ticklish?

Lapidar was none too supportive through the process either, each time asking if Achak wanted his coat to keep warm. Achak would have liked to comeback to him with something about having enough of a fur coat, but could not manage it without his human speech. By the time it was clear to Lapidar that Achak was not going to make any more progress that night, the liquor bars had opened for Lapidar to be able to cool his temper with another "cold one."

When Lapidar returned, he collapsed immediately on his own bed without saying a word to Achak.

As the sound of heavy snores grew from Lapidar's side of the room, Achak decided to continue practicing his transmogrification somewhere that would not disturb Lapidar. The bathroom seemed like the only non-disruptive place where he could change quietly.

He had remembered comforting himself by the tub only one other time before this: when he had first checked into the room with Lapidar. Now he faced the same white polished surface. Both times in the bathroom, he had been avoiding Lapidar, only this time it was not with bitterness that he had left the wolf to snooze in a quiet room. But there was a personal gain to be had as well as Achak recognized the moment as a perfect opportunity to take a bath.

In the midst of all the excitement and endless worry, he had forgotten about all the other concerns of ordinary human existence. He thought of the easiest way to go about washing himself and determined that he could spill a bottle of shampoo into the tub and fill the bath with the soapy water. It seemed easy enough in his head. He didn't exactly have to turn the cap off to open the tiny complements of the motel shampoo bottle when biting off the top would work just as well. He spilt the shampoo over the base of the tub, away from the drain, which he plugged easily with one of those drain clogs that looked like a cork on a chain.

For the last step, Achak had only to turn over the tap a few times. He managed with not too much difficulty to put his jaw around the dial and turn it over without hitting his fangs against anything. However, the water was steaming in the tub and he only had one tap to work with. He could deal with a cold bath, but a hot one would boil him alive. To adjust the temperature, he needed to move the tiny lever under the dial more over to the right, but the faucet got in his way and he could not fit his muzzle close enough to shift it with his nose. He tried using his paw, but to keep balance involved placing one foot in the steaming water below. His shampoo was giving off a perfume as it evaporated from liquid to gas.

He thought of waiting for the tub to fill and then letting it cool off before he hopped in. Achak knew he had the time for it, but he could not let the job sit when he still had one more crazy idea to try out. As in any case when long sleeves tended to get in a person's way, Achak thought of rolling them up.

At least with human hands at his disposal, Achak could keep his balance over the tub and use his fingers to move the lever over. He had yet to try flexing his limbs during his partial transmogrifications, having done nothing more with them than verify that they were in fact attached to him by mere twitch and twiddle trials. The idea he had now astounded him as much as horrified him. He had to try it—though, away from the hot water, first.

Pulling away from the steaming tub, he stood nearer to the sink and began rolling up his smilodon sleeves to his elbows. He twiddled and curled his fingers to test their flexibility and control. After his hands obeyed his wishes, he returned them to paws. He did not want to flex more than he absolutely needed, in case the change in bone and nerve shape between species caused something to break. Knowing exactly how he would go about the transmogrification, he put both forepaws on the side of the tub and rolled up his sleeves to his shoulders. One hand gripped the edge and the other reached out slowly toward the tap, which was not far enough to require all of his arm length so he had to bend his elbow. His fingers touched the cold metal dial, then lowered to where he was able to bring the lever toward him and cool off the water.

The plan went unhitched and when the water was high enough, he shut off the tap with his hand thinking how normal it felt to see only human limbs performing the bodily functions he wanted. A *chill* crept over him from the steam as he readied himself to get into the tub.

Pushing himself away from the bath and using the toilet seat for balance, he raised himself from a crouched position. His hind leg hit the water first and he wobbled in place.

A terrible sensation came over his body causing him to tremble in place. He was chilled despite being under a sweat while in the steam-filled bathroom. Then Achak had the slush of water around his one ankle that had been immersed in the tub. When he looked down, he gasped and with a loud splash knocked himself sideways into the tub. His jeans and shirt became soaked, but he did not care as he went right along laughing. His right leg still hung over the side of the tub.

He splashed some more with his arms and could not stop. "Human again." The sound of his own voice shocked him.

Lifting up his soaked body, he leapt out and reached for the door handle stopping himself just short of opening it. Lapidar was still asleep, he recalled. Achak's clothes were dripping everywhere reminding him of what he had come into the bathroom to do in the first place. He carried on with his bath and hung his jeans and shirt on the towel rack to dry as he showered.

Although he tried to take as much time as possible, he doubtfully managed to slow himself longer than ten minutes more than what his normal timing would be on a school morning. Even after it came to drying himself, Achak had nothing else to put on but a pair of sopping wet jeans. It was useless to argue with himself when he knew that he would not be willing to walk out with only a towel draped around him. Taking up his jeans and putting them on, he left the shirt to drip-dry on the towel rack.

Achak ran over to Lapidar's bedside and began shaking him awake. The wolf was still groaning like he was caught in the haunts of one nasty nightmare so Achak did not feel too guilty about pulling him from his fitful sleep. When the shaking alone did not work, he began hissing in the wolf's ear for some response.

Lapidar gave a pained moan, blinked his eyes a few times in the darkness, and let out a yell as he threw Achak back to the other bed with one shove.

It hurt but Achak's mood was not spoiled by the sudden outlash as he tried to calm Lapidar.

His words repeated with cycles of: "It's me, Lapidar. It's okay." He could not help but add, "My what big teeth you have."

Even with the joke, it took Lapidar a few minutes to settle down as he had scrambled to the end of the bed, moving as close to the door as possible. There were a few moments of silence as he studied Achak.

He untangled the blankets from his body and threw them on the bed in a heap. "Very funny, kid," he growled, standing beside the clump of blankets that was once his bed. His throat continued to rumble long after he was finished speaking. "I'll congratulate you for giving me a fright but my wife was able to transmogrify in half the time you took."

"Not that I'm very offended, but was your wife forced to deal with you skirting off lessons to go to a bar?"

"Peh!" Lapidar walked off toward the bathroom.

Achak was just about to slump over on the bed appreciating the full use of his body again when Lapidar came rushing out of the bathroom. He paused just short of Achak's bed, stared and cackled in mirth. Before Achak could wonder what had amused him so, Lapidar was pointing at his bare chest, only just realizing why a T-shirt was dripping wet in the bathroom. Achak did not mind being laughed at, even though he knew Lapidar meant to mock him by it as he carried the joke with him all the way back into the bathroom.

"So this 'need' thing," Achak spoke to Lapidar through the bathroom door. "Does it only imply a physical desire to accomplish something?"

"You mean like taking a bath?" Lapidar barked in laughter. "No."

When he emerged again, his smile had faded, replaced by his usual somber reserve. "Now get your shirt and let's go," the wolf instructed, speaking once more of serious matters.

"What? Leave?" Achak protested as he was being pulled towards the door still shirtless. His entire being caved in on itself. It was as though he was caught in the process of transmogrifying without knowing what changes his body wanted to make. Would he remain boy or become tiger?

"We can't go now." Achak declared hoarsely.

"And why not?" Lapidar challenged.

"Because I've only just changed back. I'm not ready. I haven't—"

Lapidar rolled his eyes and pushed the door open with his foot, dragging and tugging Achak along all the while.

"No!" Achak cried angrily and forced his arm away from Lapidar. He stared into the wolf's cold eyes and appealed to any human compassion that lay within. "We're not finished here yet."

"We are if I say we are," the wolf growled.

"No!" Achak cried fiercely again. "You can't send me home yet. There are still some things to clean up."

But even as Achak made the declaration, he was not entirely certain why either Manu's animal collections or Coral's plan for human mass murders should become a concern for Lapidar, who was now glaring at him.

"Don't preach to me, kid! I did my part. Freed you, didn't I? I even got you back into your human form. My conscience is clear. Now, I don't care what problems await you at home, but it's not my problem to solve them. Understand?"

"Get your hair out of a tangled wad!" Achak yelled back. "I'm not talking about my home. I'm talking about that mad scientist freak called Coral."

Achak could not believe he was raising his voice to a gunman, but it was like being pushed down a hill and he knew he would just keep tumbling until he hit the bottom.

"And!" Achak stormed. "You're not through with me if Manu can just pick another bounty hunter and come after me."

"If it hadn't been me coming after you in the first place," Lapidar wailed, "then it'd just have been someone else. Not my problem." His voice lowered. "And as to Coral, he's just some quack working under Manu and is no more a threat than a single thorn on a rose bush. He's talk, kid."

"He owns HydroMax!" Achak bellowed.

Lapidar stared at him, then chuckled. "So he makes a few buck off people who are too paranoid to drink from the tap or who are obsessed with watching their cholesterol. Big deal."

"Yes, it is," Achak surged, "...when you consider the global distribution and popularity of his product."

"Boy, what has Dr. Coral been telling you that has you so riled up?" Lapidar cackled some more, but Achak wouldn't stand for it.

His voice boomed. "He's told me of the numbers he's reached through his distribution—of the poisons humans have put into the planet and of the new chemicals we use to try to clean up old wastes but we wind up adding to them—"

"So he's an environmentalist nutter."

"—OF the way the world would be better off without humans. And of the human's dependency on a drink like HydroMax and their inability to live without."

Lapidar had gone rigid with Achak's words and was certain to be shouting his "not my problem" argument back, but he stayed quiet.

"What else did he say?" Lapidar said slowly and Achak was taken aback by his sedate tone.

"He—he said that Hybrids and humans were never able to co-exist. He made a comment behind Manu's back—something about being 'the first and the last.' He also said that human antibodies—those things that fight off germs—had become weaker over the centuries as—as we've tried to make things easier for ourselves. And that's when he started rambling on about the purpose of HydroMax. 'Said I was lucky to no longer be human. I think he means to eradicate..."

Achak stopped himself abruptly. He did not want to make any grand theories for Lapidar to be skeptical of and laugh at; he wanted to be taken seriously.

Lapidar kept to his study of Achak and his face bore a look of scrutiny that was certain to result in a sarcastic remark. Then he said, "Alright," and turned outside the door again.

The word formed soundlessly again between Achak's lips and his eyes fell. He had known that the wolf would not take him seriously, but to cut him off completely inflicted a deeper wound than if Lapidar had just broken out into laughter. Achak sought out his shirt from the bathroom and dragged his feet behind Lapidar's. He did not want to go home, but maybe when the wolf took him back to San Diego, he would find a cheap place to stay in a hotel, instead of returning immediately to his family.

Sliding his fingers over the stair rails, Achak let them chime over each bar that aligned with the descending step until Lapidar shushed him. His feet and hands went quiet while Lapidar walked over to drop the motel key in the "Quick-Return" box by the check-out office. Then the two went walking down dark and deserted neighborhoods again.

Achak shivered in his damp clothes, but he did not speak up to complain. They were headed for the train station again.

Lapidar stopped at the first red light they had come to on the market street and, though there were no cars, waited for the pedestrian cross-signal to come on.

"It'll be another four hours by train to my place," Lapidar said suddenly. His voice was low, as though to give some courtesy to the night. "No one I ever did business for will know where that is."

The shock Achak felt in that moment was nothing compared to what he would receive afterward.

"I have a wife and two kids," Lapidar continued to describe his home. "Son's eight. Daughter's six. Their names are Tyler and Lacie, by the way. The wife's Vivian. And I think that's about it. Neighborhood's clean. Wife cooks. And I can't think of anything else you need to know to be accommodated."

Lapidar looked at Achak and frowned. "What's the matter?"

Achak had distanced himself in thought and did not even have enough sense to thank Lapidar for his gesture.

"Wha—? Sorry—I mean, thank you."

Lapidar paused and Achak was forced to stop too.

"You'll need a place, won't you?" the wolf exclaimed.

"Y-yes," Achak stammered. The question posed had him searching for his wallet and when he could not find it, he gave Lapidar a quick and meaningful "thank you."

Lapidar shook his head. "I knew I couldn't just send you back to your family. You were right. Manu would have sent someone else to come after you and I never should have brought you to him in the first place. I have my limits, you know. 'Turned down jobs that didn't fit well with my ethics, and I had the instinct to decline this one, but it would have been my last had I only sucked up the guilt and followed through with it, then gone on with my life."

Achak looked at the wolf with a deeper sense and empathy for his disposition.

"Moral obligations," Lapidar snorted. "My dad used to say they're things that will kill you in this line of work. But he didn't last so long even without owing up to them."

Intermission

The silhouette of a bird was encased in the moon. Its black wings and feathers were spread in a steady glide on the chill night's current.

Gradually and in circles, it began to descend upon the buildings. Its raven talons stretched for the branch of a tree near one of the rounded roof-tops.

The preference was understandable. There was hardly an inch of grass for the raven to make its landing softly on the earth. So by the perch of a tree it balanced and watched.

Reflected in its beady black eyes was a lit doorway. Just feet outside that and under a lamppost, two students sat at a wooden table—their hands busy with the collecting and distributing of money and tickets. In other instances, they consulted a clipboard onto which a checkmark would be placed next to the student's name before he or she entered the auditorium.

A crowd was forming around the table as audience members—mostly fellow students—hastened to get away from the cold and darkness and to be able to take their seats inside the heated theatre.

Mariam waited.

It would be no good to her to leave her branch now and stand in line with the rest of the crowd. To do so meant that she would have to become human and her feathers provided much more protection against the bitter cold than her blouse or string-tied sweater. She was also able to find better cover while under the thick of leaves and branches than if she was down in the open.

There were no corners to hide around by the booth, just the warmth of student bodies cluttered and teenage adrenaline. As the last of the buildings before the outdoor basketball courts and athletics fields, the theatre had but one twin neighbor—the gymnasium: another rounded rooftop that could have made the building look like a barn if painted red.

Of a more interesting view to Mariam was: the walkway that led to the parking lots. Because of the theatre's isolation, Mariam found it easy to observe the approximate number of ticket holders coming up the path. The faces much too distant and shadowed for Mariam to identify, she eyed the bodies with a reluctance of hope.

Would Marcus come? Would Marcus come?!

Mariam's feathery head tucked closer to her body. Maybe she had been stupid to wait for him. What with their argument the night before, she had a number of reasons to question their togetherness.

He had not only discovered Mariam's interrogation of Sirena, Marcus had witnessed it as well. Not so much concerned about a vulture's well-being, Marcus as it turned out was more upset about the fact that Mariam had approached Sirena alone and at all.

If 'alone' is how you want to do things then you can continue to do things without me! Those had been Marcus's words that had left Mariam without a date to tonight's drama production: "Romeo and Juliet."

And what if Marcus didn't show up tonight? Would this lead to their official breakup?

Loosening her claws' grip on the branch, Mariam fell back, first as a spiraling distortion of feathers, then with a soft-footed landing on her hands and feet.

Rising, she felt erect with the tree. Her first hunch was to light up her digital watch and see how close she was coming to show-time.

"Five-til."

That was no comfort to her as she wanted to give Marcus a little more time to make amends.

Even so, she knew that she would be giving Marcus more than just a "little" time, but that she would boggle her mind for days or weeks—however long it took him to speak with her again. Whether at fault or not for their most recent squabble, she—Mariam—would take the fall-out... like she always did.

It could also be that Marcus had every intention of coming to the performance, but "no" intention of sitting next to her.

Mariam brushed up: physically with her hands straightening out her blouse, and mentally. Her arms, not wings, once again did a little flap at her sides as she strode towards the ticket booth.

The crowds were clearing as it neared show-time. Just a handful of students stood between her and admittance.

She reached into her sweater pocket and pulled out two bookmark-size printouts of colored paper.

The ticket stubs had a nice calligraphy and title-wrap around the words: "Romeo and Juliet."

To Mariam, it was like staring at the tragedy of her and Marcus's relationship. How ironic it would be to end it on a night like this, a certainly diary-worthy occasion for love-drama.

In a surge of anger, Mariam nearly tore the second ticket in half. She thought better of waiting outside all night for Marcus, but then she did not want to let the second ticket go to waste. If a familiar face turned up, she could always offer a free show in exchange for some human company.

Mariam looked around, only to notice that every student already held a ticket in his or her hand. The queue moved steadily towards the doors with Mariam closing off the rear.

As every delay was welcomed, Mariam had to wonder whether she had turned out for the sole purpose of seeing a school performance or if it was for the off-chance of seeing Marcus that beckoned her to the campus grounds.

When Mariam could no longer depend on the number of ticket holders to slow down the line, she began to hope that, somewhere in front of her, there was a student without a ticket.

It was wishful thinking until just such a student did come to the front of the queue. And the student's sassy voice carried over to the back of the line, where Mariam stood waiting.

"I forgot it."

"I'm sorry, ma'am. But I need to see your I.D."

Mariam's ears natural tuned into the convenient delay. The lady at the front of the line was squawking her sob story for all ticket holders and collectors to hear.

"My boyfriend has our tickets, but we got in a fight!"

How like her own story, Mariam related as she listened, except that she held the tickets instead of Marcus. Mariam straightened out the guilty smile that had curled over her face when she imagined Marcus coming to the booth with what she hoped would be an equally wailing tone. Yet, there was a definite high-pitched scratch to this young lady's weeping that made Mariam more irritated than empathetic to her cries—a seemingly natural and instinctive spitefulness towards a common-feathered enemy.

"I doubt he'll use them so couldn't you let me in without them?" the damsel cawed. "This play is really important to me and I need to write a paper on it for extra credit in a class."

Mariam saw the red hair swish before rolling her eyes away.

The ticket boy was being more than generous and courteous to the young lady, who seemed incapable of standing still or listening. Her voice became so fretful that the boy had to repeatedly refer to her as "Ma'am" before offering another solution.

"Okay, ma'am. What's your boyfriend's name? I may have already seen him come through. And are you sure the tickets were for tonight?"

"Yes!" she squealed. "And his name's Achak Twinfang."

Mariam's eyes darted forward with merciless hostility. The red hair and scandalous cries amounted to the one feather that Mariam least expected to run into.

Pushing her way towards the booth, she nudged the shoulders of each ticket holder to clear her path to Sirena. Mariam's eyes penetratedthe crowds with the force of daggers and talons. But if Mariam was prepared to make a scene, she could not hope to have the element of surprise as Sirena was staring straight back at her.

It occurred to Mariam that the encounter might not have been a coincidence at all but that somehow the vulture had made it her mission to know who was standing in line behind her and how to call her attention forward.

Her plan a' soar, Sirena's expression grew ever more gleeful as she approached Mariam. The tips of her very red lips beckoned for more blood.

Of all Sirena's outfits, Mariam had never seen one that looked more like a witch-robe of curses than tonight's, which jingled many chains from choke-collar to bust. There were black crisscrossing laces over the bodice, and sleeves whose silk connected only at the armpit, hanging from Sirena's bare shoulders like torn rags. Her pant-legs remained inseparable from each baggy side.

"How nice!" Sirena exclaimed, her arms held out wide as if to embrace Mariam. "My savior!"

"Yeah right, buzzard," Mariam shushed. "If you think I'm giving you my extra ticket—"

"You have an extra ticket?!" Sirena excited. "And here I was just going to ask to borrow a couple of bucks."

"As if! ...I'd loan, let alone give you anything."

"Well, if you don't let me in, I can't tell you where to find Achak," Sirena said and held up a gleaming sealed test tube.

Mariam put a hand safely against the tickets in her sweater pocket before speculating: "And why should I trust anything you have to say. For all I know, that bottle could be filled with apple juice."

"Funny you should mention that," Sirena replied. "But how about I tell you what it does first and then drink it to show you? ...After the show, of course."

"You'll need a ticket or student I.D.," Mariam recited like a true ticket collector.

"Clever," Sirena remarked. "But just hand the spare ticket over. Is it really worth jeopardizing Achak's life over?"

Mariam frowned. A wiser self told her not to buy into Sirena's guilt-play, but a nobler self told her to fork it over for the life and well-being of another.

She gave in to the self-sacrificing gesture and removed the extra ticket from her pocket to hand over to Sirena, even before the vulture could say: "You want Hybrid company now, don't you?"

Worse than having to give away Marcus's ticket was the awareness that Sirena's last comment rang true to her. Mariam did want Hybrid company, though now was the first time that she realized that she had no other Hybrid friends outside of Marcus and her flock. It wasn't customary for ravens to fly about making friends with every species there was Hybrid. In fact, Mariam didn't even think it was allowed because their nest was never greeted by any family less related than the crow. Furthermore, it was just that sort of illicit socializing (with Sirena) that made Marcus fight with Mariam in the first place.

So why do it again? There was a chance that Marcus might still show up—late in the first act perhaps, yet punctual enough to see Mariam and Sirena sitting together.

Mariam had to admit to herself that she had more questions than she had answers for her own behaviors. But if the choice came between saving Achak or making amends with Marcus, then Mariam knew which would be the nobler choice. Mariam's only concern was that she didn't know what sitting next to Sirena meant. It could just mean: giving a vulture a free night's-worth of entertainment.

"Okay," Mariam resigned. "Where do you want to sit?" She reduced herself into complete submission and followed Sirena into the auditorium.

"You're not like the others," Sirena remarked. Her sleeves were catching air as she swooped down the center aisle.

Mariam stayed quiet and hoped that Sirena would not lead her all the way down to the front row. Coming to a few vacant seats, Sirena seated herself at their center, distancing herself equally from humans and aisle-way. The preference was shared as Mariam took the seat next to her, but as she did so she thought repulsively of her own behavior. Why else would a bird build its nest on a tree, except to be left alone?

Two seats away from humans in any direction, Mariam searched the aisles for the familiar silhouette of Marcus but found no one of his profile amidst the occupied rows. A lot of parents had turned out to see their sons' and daughters' opening night performance.

"What did you mean by me not being like the others?" Mariam began her interrogation of Sirena casually. She turned to watch the side of Sirena's face.

"I meant that you're open and willing to interact, nothing more." Sirena hung her thoughts as equally casual and joined in the chorus of audience members that let out a "shush" to indicate the beginning of the show.

Then the theatre darkened, the stage lights lit up, and collective silence followed the opening lines.

The dividing act finished with a balcony-climb performed by the most Romeo-like Donovan. Upon which, for the sake of love, Romeo had denied his name before the curtains could fall.

Mrs. Hyde took the podium to announce the intermission. Neither Mariam or Sirena stood up to re-freshen themselves, but guarded their seats as though their were eggs in the nest. Mariam had the slight intuition that if one of them were to stand, the other would naturally follow in order to keep an eye on.

"Now for the real show," Sirena nudged Mariam and stood up. The liquid-filled test tube was visible beneath her silk sleeves.

"Where are we going?" Mariam hissed, her voice heightened with alarm.

"To catch a breath of fresh a—" Sirena's voice caught in her throat as she made an abrupt stop on the aisle stairway.

Her eyes lingered on the uncommon sight of ushers making their way between seats. Boxes were stacked alongside the door, where trays of water bottles were being loaded for the ushers to carry against their stomachs and pass around the theatre.

"Are they giving samples?"

Mariam had no time to react to the first question before Sirena surprised her with another.

"And is this normal?"

True Mariam had never seen student ushers passing out bottles before during a performance, but she did not feel that the event warranted so much excitement over. Indeed, they were just water bottles. She laughed off the tension.

"It's not a big deal. It's a promotion."

"It's HydroMax!" Sirena specified with a high note of insinuation.

Mariam only rolled her eyes. Sirena was clearly trying to play up something insignificant in order to distract her from asking questions about Achak.

"Look, buzzard! Either you speak to me about Achak or we take this outside!" Mariam said in vehement breaths. "You owe me a favor and I'm calling it in!"

"Shut up! Or the only favor you'll be calling in is for me to spare your life!" As she spoke the dark contrast between Sirena's eyes became deadly serious. Then as one of the ushers approached, Sirena's fiery hair ignited with feathers. She took one of the bottles into her hands and with a worshiping voice said, "I expected something like this!"

"You expected free samples of water?" Mariam derided.

Ignoring her, Sirena marched her way up the stairs and out of the auditorium.

Once outside, Mariam immediately began her interrogation.

"Where is Achak?!" she shouted and Sirena hastily pulled her further away from the door without concern for which way she twisted Mariam's wrist.

"The twin-fanged boy has changed." Sirena again jingled the test tube that was supposed to explain more than what words could.

"Changed into what?"

" 'More than prince of cats, I can tell you...' " Sirena laughed.

The answer did not perturb Mariam who was already preparing to submerge herself completely in truth... no matter how far it took her away from her flock.

Mariam straightened her posture and spoke. "Then can you tell me where you took him and where he is now without quoting Shakespeare?"

"I can." Sirena smiled. "...but he's no longer there."

"So where do I begin?" Mariam finally understood that Sirena did not know the current location of Achak and that he had somehow escaped or gotten away from her and whoever else was involved.

"A missing person's report went out on him," Sirena stated. "So, like a human, you can begin with the police, or like a Hybrid, you can begin with the Museum of Man... eww."

In a flash of reflected light, Sirena raised the test tube. Mariam opened her mouth to protest, but the contents left the vial and entered Sirena's mouth. Sirena drank and then she gagged before covering her mouth. Paler than ever, her face illuminated in the moonlight and glistened with sweat.

"Sirena?" Mariam breathed the name as she reached out to her rival who collapsed face forward into the dirt.

"Sirena!" she cried again. Mariam trembled as she watched in horror the body contort into fits and seizure-like spasms. But before she could scream, the body began to whither and to molt with black feathers that overtook every inch of flesh.

Once whole, the vulture hobbled itself upright, fluttered its feathers, and, in one push-off, lifted herself into the air with just a few massive strokes of her wings. Before long, Sirena was nothing more than a faint speck against an equally black sky.

Day 7, Sunday

10
Blood Ties
Family

A flapping billow of black cloth trailed from Sirena's back as she ran down one of the familiar corridors of Domestica. Infinitely, she seemed to be running through landscapes as the walls beside her changed. Their portraits and pottery plants took her from coniferous forest to beach to desert, but her eyes were cast on the white cloak trailing ahead of her that soon vanished through a doorway.

Two flat doors were sliding together when Sirena put her hands between them to stop the silver-haired man from disappearing, and the doors slid open again.

Sirena struck her arms across the doorway to prevent it from trying to close in upon her. Dr. Coral smiled at her from inside the elevator.

"Sssirena!" he exclaimed in false delight. "How's the invessstigation going?"

Sirena held up the promo-bottle in her hand. A golden apple and the word: "HydroMax," gleamed from the label.

"Well, at least I know where you were last night," Coral conceded. "Did you enjoy the play?"

"I've come to two conclusions," Sirena insinuated.

Coral frowned, but his expression became less upset as he said, "Jussst two?"

Sirena jerked her head impatiently and a few black feathers fell out from under her vibrant red strands. Her cold, dead eyes strayed into the shadows of Coral's blue ones.

"You're either going to overload the human body with minerals and poison them with metals such as iron. Or you have no intention of supplying them forever with the body's necessary essentials and, once grown dependent on the freeload, you intend to withhold the nutrients, leaving the bodies without fuel."

Coral reached out a finger and stroked the silver skull that rested over Sirena's chest. Hands pushing off the doorframe, Sirena propelled herself back outside the elevator and looked scathingly upon Coral.

Instead of allowing the doors to close on her, Coral stepped between them. Then the finger that had touched Sirena's skull necklace now rubbed with the grease of his thumb. He looked up from his hand and smiled gloriously at Sirena.

"And which do you believe it is?" he asked, and his wondering eyes forced Sirena to throw an arm in front of herself defensively.

"Personally," she said in a low voice. "I'm inclined to believe the latter. It's less detectable."

The steadiness behind Sirena's words brought her at ease, and she tossed her hair back so that it swung around her face. Then she put her hands on her hips.

"We're a lot like cars, eh?" She returned the grin that Coral had provided her. "Dependent on..."

"Our fossssil fuels" Coral finished for her. "And always out to find that miracle pill that will give usss a daily dose of everything we might need," Coral extended. "Yet, we alssso contradict our own desires and want to go on dietsss ssso that we are dependent on lessss. Well, I've anssswered that problem haven't, I? Not that I could deliver all of the fat the body needsss ssso people ssstill have to eat, but all the vitamins are in thisss one drink."

Sirena traced her own finger around her necklace: the skull and its wings. "Then," she clarified, "the body forgets how to collect these nutrients on its own and you cut off the supply?"

"We like short cutsss. Our bodies are like our minds, they are controlled by our minds—the same minds that tell usss where to ssset the TV remote ssso that the next time we walk into the room, it will be easier to reach. Humans are lazy and ssso are their bodies. Why balancsse your meals when you can take a pill or drink a bottle of mineral water. The body thinksss the sssame way too: why break apart foods and gather nutrientsss when one can jussst wait for the pill or liquid that'll do it for him."

"Is this a Hybrid neighborhood?" Achak asked when he first saw the row of identical houses. It looked to be a planned effort by all members of the community to keep the rooftops red and the walls sandstone. Each estate had two-stories;

one garage; a green lawn; and a white mailbox, paired with its neighbor's.

"No," Lapidar answered before he raised his knuckle to the front door. "And I hope no other Hybrid finds his way here."

Achak nodded with comprehension.

The woman who opened the door let out a shriek of surprise. She threw her arms around Lapidar then quickly retreated when she saw Achak.

She was tall and magnificent. Dark hair that was beaded and braided crowned her head and highlights shimmered around her coppertoned face. While her loose v-top was none too flattering, Achak could still detect a thinner figure that the orange fabric did not conform to.

There was a moment when Achak thought he saw a flicker of fear in her eyes, but that was all lost when she projected her voice into the house.

"Kids! Your father's home!"

Achak heard the laughter from upstairs, then any number of feet padded upon the ceiling above and down the steps behind Lapidar's wife. The first eight pairs of feet belonged to two family dogs—pups, really—that scampered down the stairs, the smallest trailing and stumbling on the bottom step. As Lapidar rushed past his wife and into the living room, he threw himself to his knees. Achak received the shock of his life upon seeing the three figures that collided with each other and Lapidar being tackled to the ground. From there, the resemblance became apparent between wolf and cubs. All gray fur meshed and Achak knew that he was looking at Lapidar's children.

Mother wolf had forgotten all about Achak as she too watched her husband and children at play on the carpet. Her enjoyment came to a bitter and unfortunate end when she distinguished the long white cloth that one of her children had snagged from Lapidar's arm.

"Alright, that's enough! Get off your father. There'll be no more rough-housing."

She made a threatening step toward the scuffle when she remembered why she was still holding the door open.

"Oh my! Hi, I'm sorry. I'm Vivian, but please just call me Viv." She turned a swift eye on Lapidar. "Darling, don't you think you'd be more polite to introduce your friend before playing?"

When she turned back around, she wore a generous smile. Achak did not know what else to do with himself except offer her his name. He had yet to be invited inside; the delay seemed to be pending on Lapidar.

"Achak Twinfang." With what he could control of his jaw muscles and his throat still dry from the journey, he managed to return a halfway formal introduction. "Nice to meet you ma'am—Viv."

He might have stood in that position forever were it not for Lapidar's second transmogrification that occurred beyond Viv's shoulder. Lapidar reappeared as the bandaged man while his children took to their human forms at his sides.

To Lapidar's right, a boy appeared, looking more like his mother with skin as dark as his hair. The little girl on the other hand had a fairer tone and hair that naturally held gold streaks under the light.

This time, it was Achak who forgot his place as he shamelessly watched the figures that stood in the living room.

"You can come in if you like." Viv hurried Achak over the threshold so that she could finally close the door. "Come. Sit."

She did not release Achak's arm until he was standing in front of one of the sofas and could take his own seat.

"Kiddies, let go of your father. He and I need to go in the next room and have a talk about some things."

Lapidar gave a fleeting look around, which Achak pretended not to be aware of as the wolf followed his wife around the stairs. Achak felt that now was a good time to go deaf and blind, while Lapidar's children flopped themselves on the carpet and began waiting.

"You're one for surprises," Viv began the argument before they were out of earshot. "Then this is *the boy,* I take it?"

"Yes," Lapidar answered her.

Achak was relieved to hear a door snap shut from underneath the stairs which made their voices dissipate.

In the time Lapidar spent in the garage with his wife, Achak familiarized himself with the living room. Aware that two sets of eyes were upon him, he remained seated quietly on the couch and avoided the children's faces.

Everything in the room had the familiar touch of home, which meant that nothing—not even the shade of wood from coffee table to cabinet—matched. It was a nice living room, one not themed to look like someplace you weren't supposed to sit in for long periods of time. The recliners included two couches, the only pair of anything in the room, and were fully comforted with pillows, some of which had floral patterns while others were simply a solid shade of lavender.

Achak liked the fact that the entertainment center did not fit well with the shelf that held movies despite the fact that they were both assembled out of wood.

Photographs on the fireplace mantel and above the television set had their personalized frames that were representative of the member they held. The boy must have played soccer as he had plastic balls engraved with polygons glued to everything from his picture frames to the small trophies that sat in the glass case of the entertainment center. Achak could not tell what the girl was interested in, but in one photograph, contrary to the flower dresses she wore in many of the others, the daughter had a wooden toy gun and a sheriff's star badge.

Straight away, he determined that the mother was a teacher—elementary, by the looks of it. There were knick-knacks of #1 Teacher and a little glass apple next to a teddy bear. In Achak's opinion, each oddity had "Teacher's Pet" written all over it.

He would have liked to analyze the room further, but at that moment Lapidar's son chose to step between Achak and his view of the movie shelf. *Just like his father,* Achak thought.

"Who are you?" the boy probed, careful not to sound too coarse in his inquiry.

"A friend." Achak delayed having to give out any details that might lead to any questions about his species. Wondering how long he would have to play the entertainer, he looked around the stairs, but could not see hope in Lapidar emerging from there soon.

"I've never seen you here before."

"I'm new," Achak humored. "Actually, I'm more of a student than a friend."

This sparked the little girl's interest who bobbed her head at once to stare down Achak.

"Daddy's not a teacher. Mommy is, though. You don't seem like one of her students."

"Yeah, because they're all your age, Lacie," the boy chided to his sister. She stuck her tongue out at him so that he smiled and looked back at Achak.

"Hey, mister? I'm Tyler. Who are you?"

"Achak Twinfang."

Both children looked taken aback.

"Ajack?" the littlest came out with quickly.

"Lacie!" he brother shushed. "Okay, mister, but—um what are you?"

Achak thought that this must be the equivalent of what species are you, but he was not sure if he should give an exact answer. After all, he supposed his nature was already causing problems in the next room over with Lapidar.

Not wanting to cause more family conflict, Achak responded with a generic answer. "I'm a cat," he understated, and this seemed to create enough excitement among the young ones.

"Really?" Lacie squealed. "Dad's never brought one of them around."

"What kind of cat?" Tyler demanded.

"Not a common one." Achak was spared the un-pleasantries of the children's pouts as Viv's voice came through the walls.

"THIS IS WHY I tell you to look into these things. You never think ahead."

"There's nothing to think about," Lapidar barked back. "It was 'yes' or 'no.'"

"How about a background check."

"Viv—hon, these men don't have backgrounds."

"Can't you at least ask about the job before taking it?" Viv sounded almost hysterical.

"For the hundredth time—no! There's nothing good about what these men want. If you refused the work, they'd have to pay you to keep your mouth shut—or kill you."

"Lapidar please! Don't try to blindside me with your protectiveness. This isn't about the boy, is it? This is about your father. But this isn't the same! This isn't about some boy forced to follow in his father's footsteps."

"No, it was the boy forced into a lifestyle he couldn't get out of!"

"Darnit, Lapidar! You're still venting it! Things are different now. You're different. You have a family."

"Viv, stop! This isn't worth it. The mistake is done. I made a bad decision that I'm trying to fix. Please, just..." His voice faded back behind the walls.

Achak felt the misery of the guilty intruder. At least none of the children minded him anymore. They both had their heads sagging over their knees with Lacie appearing to be on the verge of tears.

"Hey—hey. What's all this?" Lapidar exclaimed and came over to his youngest, taking her up in his arms. "Tyler, you know better than to let your sister listen in. You should have taken her upstairs."

Tyler shrugged, while Achak swallowed the guilt in feeling equally responsible for the children.

"Don't you kids have some Saturday Morning Cartoons or something to watch?"

Tyler shook his head. "Dad, it's Sunday."

Lapidar turned to Achak with Lacie still around his neck. "Come on. I'll take you *all* upstairs. Achak, you're going to be in Tyler's room. Tyler, you're going to share with Lacie for the next few days."

Achak stood up just as Lapidar turned again to his son.

"You mean he's staying over THAT long?" Tyler rushed over to his father's side. "But we still don't even know what he is."

Lapidar barked out a laugh. "Oh? Isn't it obvious? He's a Sabertooth Tiger."

"What? Nu-ah!" Both kids blurted in unison. Lacie was looking straight over Lapidar's shoulder at Achak and staring as though she doubted her father's words.

Not sure whether to be angry or indifferent, Achak froze at the announcement of his species. He felt slightly betrayed.

"Prove it," Tyler shouted at Achak.

"Hey, not now," Lapidar scolded. "It's rude."

"You're bluffing."

"Am not." Lapidar looked at his son sternly. This ended the argument for the remainder of the morning.

At the top of the stairs, Lapidar sent Achak with some fresh blankets into the first room to the left and shut the door behind him telling him to get some rest until he was called down for brunch. Tyler meanwhile had gathered a bundle of toys and games under his arms that he thought he might like to play with for the day and brought them into Lacie's room.

It was Lapidar's request that the children not come around bothering Achak. He did his best to keep them separated and forced the children to have their brunch first so that they would leave the table before he called Achak down.

Apart from keeping the children away, every other one of Lapidar's behaviors suggested that Achak was a welcomed guest. There could be no more arguments overheard between him and Viv, and the wife herself seemed keen on making Achak's stay in her home the best it could possibly be.

"Just let me know if there's anything I can do for you," Viv had made a point of saying as much on more than one account.

When she wasn't asking Achak if he wanted something, she was making light talk of the things he did in San Diego, after having learned that that was where he was from. It always put Achak in an awkward position to talk of home or school where he was being missed. Plus the formality of the topic made him feel more like he was talking to Lapidar's mother than wife.

He went upstairs for a two-hour nap after brunch, then came back downstairs to find the house bustling with activity. Achak had long since lost track of the days, but with the kids still at home and running about the house and Viv chasing them down at one point to ask if they needed anything for school, it felt like a Sunday afternoon.

"Pencils, Lacie? Paper, Tyler?"

"No, Mom," they chorused.

Lapidar was not showing his face around the house much, though every now and then he would pop his head in from the garage or backyard, kiss his wife, and grab something to drink from the kitchen before going back out. Achak had absolutely no chance to grab him and pull him aside between chores. Instead, he gave up on the wolf for the moment in hopes of being able to chat over dinner.

Between the two parents, Achak felt useless and sometimes got in the way when Viv was preparing to vacuum in a certain area. When he thought he should make it a point of staying upstairs as a shut-in and pretending to nap, there was Viv's voice again telling everyone to "vamoose" into the living room until she had finished vacuuming the bedrooms.

Achak thought that he should just sit down and watch TV like any other good over-the-night houseguest. This might have given him a chance to relax a little. It sure seemed easier than trying to offer a hand that was refused for every chore. However, when he reached the room and turned back around to face the inner wall and the television, it was already on with two bobbing heads in front of it.

Undecidedly, Tyler flipped through the channels with the television remote. Lacie was telling him to slow down so that she could see what was on. Tyler went to the extreme of making her sit through entire commercial breaks and she complained each time that he changed the channel.

"Tyler, turn it back—No, stop, that's too far! Mom!" Lacie screamed. "Tyler's not changing the channels properly."

However, Viv still had the vacuum on upstairs and could not hear the screams of her daughter. But when they saw Achak walk in, both children fell to heavy whispers and there was no getting Lacie to understand that her words could be overheard.

"Tyler! The man's in here! What do you s'ppose he is?"

Achak took a seat on the couch and stared at the flashing images on the TV. It really didn't matter to him what was being shown on the screen, his eyes were too captivated in the images that ran through the most recent parts of his memory. He seemed to be stuck with reliving the encounter with Dr. Coral as he was meant to overhear secrets through the bars and then told that he would never be able to speak them as a human. If Achak had not shared these with Lapidar, would he have been sent home and allowed to return to life as usual?

Of course not, Achak answered his own question. He remembered how it had felt to walk on fours and how it had felt different to think and move on a sabertooth's level. The beast was a part of his entire being now, whether in human skin or tiger's. Somehow it was there now, telling him that he wanted to scratch the itch on his back with a hind leg or that he would really like to sharpen his nails on a fine piece of recliner. Absent mindedly, his fingers had been digging into the couch and he had had to ease them.

Sirena walked up to Achak in a room lavished with animal collectibles and asked him if he thought he would die. Achak nearly said yes.

The memories going through his mind had become so vivid that he thought himself on another mad flashback when he heard "HydroMax" spoken aloud.

The living room came back into focus and a commercial was showing Achak his high school gym and a sports jock was drinking from the clear bottle. His eyes fell upon the gold apple on the mineral water label and Donovan Parsons putting his lips to the toxin. The commercial ended and Achak stared once more at the heads of Lapidar's children. They were staring right back at him as though they thought he was ill and maybe he looked it too.

"Hey, mister?" Lacie spoke up with a tongue that kept moisturizing her lips. "Mister—" she paused in her forgetfulness. Tyler whispered in her ear. "Mr.

Twinfang, we were wondering if you could tell us what you really are?"

Achak stared at her blankly and looked at Tyler who was nodding his head un-helpfully as a backup to Lacie's question.

"What I am?" Achak asked puzzled.

"You know. What's in your blood?"

"He knows that, Lacie!" Tyler hissed at his sister. "He's just playing with you."

"What's in my blood? Well, I'm Native American." Achak put his fingers on the chain around his neck and held up the pendant as though that proved his ancestry.

Lacie was drawn into it as Achak expected most girls would be because of its shiny stone and silver grips, but Tyler scowled and pushed his sister down. She began yelling but Tyler's words were still heard over the name-calls and wails.

"Not that! Your other kind!"

At last, Achak understood. He had not given Hybrid mannerisms much thought, but perhaps he had been rude before in not showing himself to the family in animal form. Is this why Vivian was arguing with Lapidar earlier? Had his introduction offended her and should he have made his first appearance on all-fours?

"I mean, you're not really extinct are you?" Tyler said. "The Bred HyCouncil would know. Would they really keep it hush-hush?"

"I have no idea," Achak said aghast, feeling his head spin. "What's the Bred HyCouncil?"

It was the children's turn to exasperate. "You mean you don't know?!"

Achak would have given anything to be able to take back the last question. He wished he had taken more time to extract information from Lapidar.

"You're not really a cat, are you?"

"Is that a problem?" In Achak's eagerness to learn some of the social norms of Hybrids, he forgot that he was being questioned by an eight-year-old child.

"No," Lacie answered hurriedly, sounding very apologetic for her brother's indiscretion.

"Yes," Tyler contradicted her. "Well, it is!" he reaffirmed. "Dad never mingles."

"How would you know?" Lacie argued. "Dad doesn't bring all of his friends home."

"I heard him and Mom say so before brunch."

"You were upstairs!"

"Yeah, but then I went to get a drink, remember? And I heard them in the kitchen before I walked in."

Lacie jumped up and stood over him. "You were spying!"

"Not spying—listening," Tyler corrected.

"I'm telling Mom." She threw down the TV remote that she had claimed while Tyler wasn't looking. Pausing by the stairs, she looked back, not yet sure about leaving until she could be certain Tyler believed that she would tattle.

Achak did not like where this argument was going. He looked from one sibling to the other wondering how best to end the fight. His only certainty over the matter was that if he let Lacie go to her parents, he would again be the subject of a heated discussion, something that he had had enough of for one day.

"Alright. Hey, cut it out, both of you," he said weakly and tried to think of a resolve. "Let's just go back to watching TV." He picked up the remote from the carpet to hand to Lacie. "And Tyler, don't repeat things your father says without knowing where they come from."

He could not be sure if the last bit was a good moral or not to pass along to Lapidar's kids, but at least it pleased Lacie to hear Tyler thoroughly rebuked. She sat down by Achak on the couch and began flipping through channels again.

Achak could tell that Tyler was not about to hang around after being told off. He got to his feet and pulled on his un-tucked shirt. "Fine," he said, implying that things were just the opposite. "I've had enough."

Kicking at the carpet along the way, he stormed toward the stairs and stomped all the way to the top. Viv must have finished vacuuming because Achak could no longer hear the whine of the motor. When a door slammed closed, he had to guess it belonged to Tyler's bedroom, which he supposed had been reclaimed by its owner.

"Ignore him," Lacie advised, but Achak had to admit that the conversations had worn out for him as well.

"I'll be back," Achak excused himself to go find Lapidar, but left Lacie as casually as if he was just going to find the restroom. Straightening up, he began his search towards the sliding-glass door that led to the backyard.

"Garage." He heard Lacie's voice direct him and turned back to round the corner for the stairs and meet the door beneath them.

The garage was open with the family car pulled out and jacked. Lapidar's lower half could be seen with his legs sticking out from under the driver's side of the vehicle. Judging by the empty filter nearby and a few rags lying around with black stains, Lapidar was changing the oil.

Achak walked into the fresh air and stood at the edge of the garage. Lapidar had already noticed his presence before Achak could speak up and call him from under the car.

"So why don't you take the car to work?" Achak had tried to imagine Lapidar pulling off more abductions in a narrow Accord. "It's a hybrid, right?"

Lapidar laughed and began wiping his hands with one of the rags. "Yeah, I suppose Hybrids behind the wheels of hybrids is a trend. But I couldn't risk letting Manu or the others having my license plate number, now could I?"

"So you don't drive at all?" Achak did not know how quite to approach Lapidar with questions about the sacrifices he would make to protect his family. "Do all Hybrid—"

"No—and I only try not to drive around. But I can't argue with the wife when there are errands to be run, stores to shop, and kids to take to soccer practice."

Achak waved all that aside. "It's not exactly your model. I'd of thought you'd be driving something bigger," he stated.

"It's a car," Lapidar replied. "And it's small enough for the wife, big enough for the kids—and stop harassing me if you're bored and go find something else to do." He reached back under the car and pulled out a blue bucket filled with oil.

Achak did not budge. "You know, I think your son really wants to see a Sabertooth."

Lapidar returned the grin. "Yes, I get the picture. You want to know when we'll train. Well, it'll have to wait," he said looking at the sun barely visible over the Tehachapi foothills.

"After dinner then?" Achak asked.

His face with a look of sincere distress, Lapidar sighed. "It's family night." Making a clear at his throat, he pleaded, "The kids will be expecting some games."

Thinking back to how he had upset Tyler, Achak sighed at the prospect of what another family gathering would bring. He walked the length of the driveway and stood at the mailbox corner to look down the neighborhood. At least the children could leave their tricycles in the yard without being ticketed, Achak commented on every perfectly green lawn. He was beginning to hate the order and structure that accompanied such a peaceful neighborhood. Why couldn't Lapidar's life be as rebellious as he dressed?

Achak watched as a bald and suited man waddled by with the Sunday paper tucked under one arm and a brass-handled cane under the other. The man took one look at Achak and seemed to think better of ever looking back.

"Evening," Achak greeted, but received no response.

Lapidar barked out with a laugh and came over to stand beside Achak with a grin. "I'd run too if I didn't know you. Have you seen yourself in the mirror recently?"

Achak shook his head and looked down almost dreading what he'd see. His shirt was stained beyond the grease worn by Lapidar. Visible scrapes could be seen on his arms, though the bruises were of a lesser degree. From there, he gained an idea of what the disaster of his face and hair must look like. His jeans looked to be about the only things to survive the trip.

Scratches he had not treated after cleaning had become inflated with dry blood.

"Got a towel?" he said.

Lapidar shook his head and threw him a rag. "Ever hear of a shower?"

"No, but how about lending me a change of clothes, grease monkey."

Lapidar shrugged. "I thought my son would have offered you something by now."

"Tyler did, but I prefer cowboy boots to baseball caps."

A half hour later, Lapidar had fitted Achak with a white polo shirt, striped with gray and black across the chest. His jeans were slightly large, but tastefully baggy, even if they had to be held up with a belt.

"Aren't you gonna tuck in your shirt?" Lapidar sniffed before admitting Achak into the kitchen where the rest of the family had gathered for dinner.

The family looked in much better shape with everyone sitting at the table at the same time. Viv had put out all the food in large dishes for everyone to scoop onto their own plates in the portions they wanted.

If it was uncomfortable for Achak to be among so large and complete a family setting, he quickly lost himself to the table talk. Even Viv did little formalizing and only stood up from the table once to pile her children's plates with a first serving. She offered to do the same for Achak, but he declined and added a compliment of her cooking.

Maybe it was Lapidar who finally convinced Viv to sit down and began the banqueting by opening up to Achak with his questions about why that Donovan classmate wore overalls at the arcade.

Achak laughed and explained to him how Donovan was a drama-freak and loved to create his own fashion trends. He ended by telling Lapidar what a fashion inspiration he must have been and that he expected a few more browncoats to be spotted around the campus when he returned.

Though nobody else at the table seemed to be able to keep up with their conversation, Lapidar was himself a good audience. He wanted to know what Achak's first impressions were of the kidnapping from the time Sirena first transmogrified for him on Tuesday to finding himself in his own bed and then undergoing the very same abduction the next day. Achak doubted that Lapidar had ever had the opportunity before to interview his victims as he was particularly amused when Achak admitted that he had been convinced that the first abduction was only a dream.

The response embarrassed Achak a little, but he went on to talk more comfortably about Sirena's performance as a vulture in the auditorium. About how Lapidar looked to him for the first time, Achak lied and said that he wasn't sure if the gun was real or if it was part of the costume.

"You said that Sirena had been around before?" Lapidar changed his tone to one of more concern.

Achak nodded. "Weeks before," he informed. And Lapidar breathed in heavily his consideration over the news, but did not share his thoughts.

Letting the issue slide, he included the rest of the family in their conversation over dessert, chocolate brownies, when he started posing questions to everyone at the table about what kind of game they would like to play. Achak waved his hands away from giving out any suggestions and said that he would rather let the kids decide. They of course wanted any game that would force Achak to transmogrify, including freeze-tag and hide-n-seek. Lapidar caught on to their ploy and suggested an indoor game that would require less running around because he was tired and had had a long trip. Achak did not doubt the truth behind either excuse.

Day 8, Monday

10
Blood Ties
Class

The next day, Lapidar began coaching Achak through his transmogrification and excersized a little more patience than he had before. The difference it made showed visibly in Achak's quick progression of the reverse transmogrification. He found it easier to think in the mind frame of a Sabertooth Tiger when he was not protecting his human dignity from an onslaught of insults. By lunch, he managed to meronize his body with a set of forepaws, but that was only the beginning of his training.

"Maybe we should start on all fours before continuing," Lapidar suggested after watching Achak summon the fur only up to his elbows in the last two hours. "I think the heights are distracting you."

"Heights?" Achak looked to the outdoor freezer that Lapidar was sitting on in the garage. There were no vehicles parked inside as Lapidar had arranged space for them by pulling the car out onto the driveway and shutting them both in for some privacy.

"Yes, heights," Lapidar repeated. "You're standing upright, which won't be a very stable position once you do transmogrify."

"Yeah, but won't I just fall forward? You do." Achak was not really seeking an argument out of the instruction, but he had been taking orders without questioning them long enough. After all, he never had the opportunity to do so when he was obeying as a Sabertooth Tiger, whereas now he could question how things worked. "Come on," he encouraged Lapidar. "Why wouldn't I just land forward when I changed?"

"And so you would." Lapidar slid off the freezer and into a more comfortable position leaning against it. "But that isn't the issue. I'm not teaching you how to land on all-fours. I'm teaching you how to transmogrify and I don't need you distracted by a bunch of other factors that we can worry about later."

"How is it 'worrying' if you said I would naturally fall forward?" Achak argued.

"Because you're thinking about it," Lapidar snapped. "If you try to envision the change, it'll scare you too much from doing it. Now get down on your hands and stop thinking about what happens when your feet become paws and you lose your balance."

"Alright, I got it." Achak waved for Lapidar to sit back down. "If I'm already on the ground, then I can't worry about falling forward." He brought his hands and knees to the concrete and added, "I just hope you know how ridiculous I feel being down here."

This seemed to be all Lapidar could tolerate of Achak's backtalk. His throat cracked with a snarl. "Then your attitude is the first thing that needs to change before your body can! The least you could do is have some pride for your species."

"I have pride," Achak replied, uncertain about what set Lapidar's temper off. All he received was a snort in return. "I just think it's embarrassing for a human to be on the ground like this."

"A brotherhood of mammals takes on the same stance without complaint. And you're not trying to be human, if I needn't remind you."

"No, you needn't," Achak scoffed. "But I wouldn't be Hybrid if I wasn't going to account for my human emotions as well."

Surging forward, Lapidar grabbed Achak by the shirt collar and pulled him up. "Listen up, human. Being Hybrid isn't just about your petty insecurities. It's about having enough dignity to preserve both species and not forsaking one form because you don't like your nose so close to the ground! Maybe if your confidence wasn't already run through the mud then you wouldn't mind bringing the rest of your body so close to it."

"If you're saying I'm ashamed!" Achak moved on the defensive.

"I'm saying that you take your kind for granted. You're a Sabertooth Tiger. What more could you want out of your kind?"

"I didn't want any of it! And it wasn't until you showed up—I was fine with myself as a boy—as a man," Achak corrected his final declaration.

"Well, I hope you're listening, *boy*," Lapidar mocked.

"It's MAN!" Achak puffed out his chest.

"It isn't *man* until you can stand short of one and still feel like his equal. And that goes for standing on all-fours as well."

Lapidar raised his hand and Achak flinched as though he was about to be smacked. To shield himself against the attack, he brought up one of his arms which Lapidar grabbed hold of. With Achak's wrist, Lapidar pulled him toward the kitchen door and slapped the remote next to it that would open the garage. Achak had to duck to avoid hitting his head on the rising metal surface. Lapidar shoved him toward the passenger side of the little gray Accord.

"Get in," he commanded.

Lapidar rejoined Achak in the driver's seat, started the ignition, and began pulling out.

"Where are we going?" Achak snapped in his seatbelt. He was not the only one who demanded to know as Viv came running out the front door and across the lawn flailing her arms at the vehicle.

"Lapidar! Stop!" She reached the passenger side first then marched her way around the front of the car looking very stricken. "Where?!" she demanded to know. "I have to pick up the kids after school. You know, that place you never attended?"

Her glare was equal to Lapidar's which still presented itself from his argument with Achak.

"I have to take *this* kid to some places!" He briefed Achak with a corner glance.

Viv folded her arms and waited, at which time Lapidar repented slightly by speaking in a softer tone to his wife.

"The city," he explained and Achak direly hoped that he was not referring to the same city that entailed werewolves and Hybrid motels. "I'll be back by dinner time."

She looked across at Achak whose frown must have appeared no better than her own and softened her expression. Biting her lip, she nodded back at Lapidar. "None of that tough guy attitude, I'd better not hear of. It always gets you into trouble."

When she next made eye contact with Achak it was as if to say that she expected a full report on Lapidar's behavior when they returned.

Achak waved goodbye as the Gray's residence was taken from his view by the car in motion. He watched the other houses of the neighborhood go by. Before long, he had nothing more to occupy himself with than the tumbleweed of desert and green road signs.

All he knew of Lapidar's hometown as they distanced themselves from it was that there were an awful lot of planned communities with identical adobe rooftops made of red shingles. He finally had a name for the place when Lapidar passed a billboard to a fast-food hamburger and felt intrigued.

"Tehachapi?" he inquired.

Lapidar turned his head to Achak incredulously. "You mean all this weekend you never knew where you were?"

Achak shook his head and laughed even though Lapidar's surprise was one of less amusement.

"Angeles Forest Highway?" Grabbing the door handle, Achak caught only a glimpse of the Exit sign as Lapidar veered the car with a hard right to the nearest off-ramp. "That wouldn't be the same 'Angeles" as in 'Los Angeles,' would it?"

"Could be," Lapidar shrugged.

It was a curt answer that could have drawn into a very long trip, but the atmosphere was soon dictated by the sights and smells of the Angeles Forest. Achak could taste the sweet nectars of the forest as he rolled down his window.

With his heart hammering inside his chest, he stuck his head out against the breeze and longed for nothing more than to run amongst the trees and park himself under the fruits and shade of the most enticing. If there was ever a point that he had wanted to become animal, now was that moment when his instinct told him to follow. Most of what nature had to offer was being whipped away by the car's momentum and Achak had no opportunity to appreciate the divine scents and noises of a land so un-tampered with by man.

He felt restless with his bottom cramping in the car seat. Zooming by him were the short steel rails that protected drivers from steering their cars over the cliff side. Every time a passing zone came up and the lanes widened, Achak had the urge to jump out of the vehicle. But the roads were windy with every bend looking like another close call to going over the edge. Achak did not dare make his jump while he could not see what was around the next corner. He was again trying to plan just the right timing for a safe landing, like he had with the freight train.

Looking over the gorge, Achak stared down at a creek flowing through the mountain pass. He frightened himself with ideas about losing his patience enough to want to jump out, which if taken at the present moment would mean free-falling to hundreds of feet below. Unable to trust his instincts, Achak forced his eyes back on the road. Closing his eyes, he wished for the forest passage to end.

By the time his stomach began to churn and complain of the zigzagging turns, he opened his eyes only to learn that the cliffs had moved over to Lapidar's side. This put Achak level with the hillside and greenery. Although placed with less peril on his side, Achak continued to feel his heart beating rapidly over the landscape. Instead of heights to fear, he had temptation. He saw shade tree after shade tree whiz by; bark of which nails could be sharpened and trimmed; branches low enough to climb and perch; and high, thickened tree tops, the likes of which he could observe the comings and goings of others.

"STOP!" he cried. The ideas were like a buzzing in his ear that he hoped to put out with the sound of his voice.

Lapidar looked at him, then his rearview mirror, and began pulling the car to the side.

"Why? Are you sick?" he mused. Lapidar had placed more attention on turning the wheel and applying the brakes than what he could notice of Achak's desperate leap out of the vehicle. "Hey! Where're you going?" he called after Achak's fleeting backside.

Achak was already forcing his way uphill and around trees by the time Lapidar had put the car into park and began to chase after him. He reached a plateau and grabbed onto the nearest tree, decided he didn't like it, and pushed himself over to the next one. This Douglas-fir was more to his liking with low branches that were sturdy enough to support him and even higher branches to climb, although it did present some pine needles to prickle him along the way.

He dug his fingers into it and could not decide what had brought him to such measures until it was already too late. Falling to the ground, caught in the mix of twigs and leaves, Achak trembled at the thought of what he had tried to become. He could not shake free of his desires so that the tingles of his transmogrification overpowered the trembles. Fur crawled up his arms and body until there could be no more bare skin.

At first, he seemed to think the change to be okay and went back to his tree. When he put his paws against the bark and began to claw through, he thought better of what he had done. He would have to change back, but his ears were twitching as never before to the small noises from around the trees. It excited him to hear so many bustling activities at once. Birds in the trees and rodents scurrying, the life of the forest turned Achak in circles.

Crunching the brush directly behind him, Lapidar took no precautions in approaching Achak, the Sabertooth. Each pant between his breaths carried a soft chuckle. His presence stirred more of Achak's human instincts as he was beginning to think that Lapidar had intended for this to happen.

"Why are you giving me that look?" Lapidar crouched over to Achak's level. He glanced up at the tree that Achak had chosen and sat down in the brush under its shade. Comfortable with his position, having an arm wrapped around one knee and his other leg tucked under, he continued to survey Achak in silence.

Achak chose instead to worry about the fluttering in his chest. His heart refused to yield as it hammered through the smallest hums of a beetle's wings to the cooing of a local mother's nest.

"Is this what you wanted?" Lapidar broke the silence. Achak turned his head, but saw that the lone wolf was merely taking in his surroundings. "I used to take the kids up here all the time. Well, not here exactly. There are more secluded areas around the park." He met Achak head-on. "If you're done here, we should really go."

Achak looked down at his paws knowing that what Lapidar asked for was easier said than done. He flipped through his memories, trying to pick out the most human among them. First he tried thinking about school, but for one reason or another, each classroom setting was interrupted by the thought that he might act upon an instinct or whim that would have the other students talking. He might perk his ears more towards the gossip around the class instead of the teacher's lecture or be lured by the green lawn outside the window.

"Most Hybrids get along with their fighting spirits, but I'll leave it to you to want more of what nature intended out of play." Lapidar studied his nails as if he wished to turn them into claws. "I guess jumping aboard trains wasn't enough excitement for you?" he leered.

This Achak knew to be untrue of himself. He was not some action-seeking stuntman who thrived on these life-and-death adrenaline rushes. Infuriated with Lapidar, he turned his ears away from the accusing words. He knew of only one person who could pull him out of the slums, and she was closer to his mind because Lacie had reminded him so much of her.

If Tehya was here to laugh at him, he might not feel so offended by the wolf. She, he thought, could serve as his human purpose, but he needed one more piece of leverage, like when he was trying to fill up the bathtub at the motel, except he didn't think that there were any faucets around in the forest. He wondered what petty task he could roll up his sleeves for and set his hands to work on when he spotted the pendulum swaying from his neck. Shimmering off its silver chain, the arrowhead had again not been carried over.

He remembered the night it had been given to him and the way it sat in the palm of his hand, or the reflection of it he had despised in the sliding glass door. Before he could hear Dr. Coral repeat his commentary about the stone being appropriately Neanderthal, Achak reached toward his collar to close his hands around the arrowhead.

The small fragment of obsidian was cold; it's texture smooth and eternally chilled like the weather that must have compounded the minerals to hold its shape. Maybe Achak needed to think more upon the stone whenever he wanted his human form. He found that sometimes it was necessary to take a step back before proceeding forward.

Lapidar pulled Achak to his feet and gave him a slap on the shoulder. Achak's knees buckled but he did not bother to brush Lapidar away as he stared at the pendant in his palm. Its presence and guide was bothering him more than ever.

"Why doesn't this come with me when I transmogrify?"

Lapidar winced as though someone had just screamed in his ear. Taking his hand off Achak's shoulder, he stepped back with a measure of uncertainty.

"What?" Achak questioned the look. "What's wrong with my necklace?" He tried to sound serious, but the notion of superstition was a bit too farfetched to hide any amusement. Besides, jewelry was always a funny topic when it came from a guy's mouth. Even those who were big on jewelry did not go around complimenting each other's earring studs.

Trying to keep an eye on the car downhill, Lapidar pretended not to hear Achak. He only acknowledged him when he meant to give out a warning.

"I think we should move out before we meet any vampires."

"Vampires?" Achak exclaimed. The subject was far more interesting than his necklace. "You mean like werewolves, there are vampires as well? Clans of bats and rats that go around drinking people's blood?"

Still walking, Lapidar did his best to restrain his interest with a shrug. "They enjoy the fiction behind their species, or at least, they enjoy inspiring the fiction."

He looked at Achak's hunger and decided that he would explain more on the walk downhill.

"Werewolves are no exception to that mythical pride. They're deluded into believing that myths make them powerful. The whole lot of them are troublesome beings that want to instill fear by the masses, reminding those of how long they've existed as a culture—if one can call upon their behavior as a so-called 'tradition.'"

Lapidar humored the subject further by adding, "I have no idea where all the silver bullet and garlic stuff came from though. Maybe we'll come across them again and you could ask." His face paled. "It's nothing to be proud of. They strive to be monsters."

In Achak's opinion, Lapidar wasn't giving out any new information about the two legendary horrors, but his rising tone was at least making the topic an interesting one to pursue.

"They're a threat to the Coexistence Coalition with a large quantity of their dealings having to be cleaned up and covered by members of the Bred HyCouncil."

"Were you ever one?" Achak boldly tried to unravel the personal details behind Lapidar's opinions.

"One what?" Lapidar growled. "HyCouncil member?"

"No." Achak honestly did not think that Lapidar could have anything to do with law enforcement. "A werewolf?" he clarified and watched as Lapidar's chest swelled.

"I would never!" Spit tangled in Lapidar's words. His eyes widened with rage and teeth began to show more and more like fangs.

"Okay, alright. Down boy." Achak hurried to open the passenger side door but it was locked. The windows too had all been rolled up since Achak had bailed out of the vehicle. "Okay so you were never a werewolf," he said as Lapidar approached with the keys. "Then what exactly were you?"

"A lone," Lapidar snapped, forcing the door open for Achak to get inside.

"Alone?" Achak pondered to himself since Lapidar had already closed the door in his face.

For twenty more miles of forest, Lapidar drove in silence and Achak watched the city unfold from the clouds and hover in a thin layer of mist. It would be a dreary overcast day in the city. High rises that would normally have glistened off the sun were as dull and gray as the fog from which they sprouted.

Picking up speed on the downhill, they were descending upon the city faster than Achak had hoped for. He would much rather have stayed in the national forest admiring the industries and architecture from afar.

"You don't like cats, do you?" Achak's words were swallowed by the whipping breeze passing through his window.

"What?" Lapidar bellowed back.

"I said, 'What city is that? L.A.?'"

"Maybe L.A. County," Lapidar replied, not taking his eyes off the road. "But thee L.A.? Well, I'm sure it's around there somewhere."

"So then which city do we make port at?"

Lapidar took a few minutes to think it over. In the meantime, he rolled up the windows and turned on the AC as they no longer had the refreshing breeze of the mountains. At last, he decided on: "San Marino. I'd hate to take you someplace rough from the get-go. It's a nice area to start in—upper scale, but at least the only thing you have to be careful of are the peahens. There's sort of a city ordinance that protects them."

"Are they Hybrids?" Achak asked glumly. His first impression of cross-natured beings had left him somewhat scarred, though not to the same visible extent as the claw marks seen on Lapidar's arms.

"Hybrids? Yeah, some of them will be, but you won't be able to tell which are and which aren't. They've had a lot of practice at blending themselves with the others."

"How do you people sleep at night!" Achak dropped his forehead against the window.

At a change of heart, Lapidar pulled his hand away from the radio having not yet turned it on.

"It's not as dangerous as it seems. Hybrids don't exactly break in people's houses and start pecking their eyes out while they sleep or gouge out intestines."

Achak looked at him revoltingly for the unpleasant visual.

"Most Hybrids have a greater respect and appreciation for life." Lapidar opened and closed his fist as if to emphasize the change that occurred during transmogrification.

"Greater than whose?" Achak asked, although he already knew what the answer would be.

"Greater than human beings," Lapidar said and Achak hated the glorification in his voice. "It's why we've been able to live so long."

"Typical," Achak critiqued.

"What is?"

"Your belief system," he finalized and decided not to elaborate on the subject anymore. Only in his mind did he further evaluate the paradox. Comparing the two races, he saw humans and Hybrids under the same lens. There were humans who esteemed themselves to be greater than animals, while Hybrids esteemed themselves to be greater than humans.

He wondered if it was within a Hybrid's right to value himself greater since it was a fact that within a Hybrid's body there were preserved two organisms of human and animal. From an ecological standpoint, the Hybrid might have a higher purpose in balancing out nature and preserving it. But Achak came from a human bias and no matter how much he tried to see humans and animals on an equal scale, even Hybrids he judged to be primarily of a human mind. Because of their lack of technology, animals always wound up on the lower end of the hierarchy. While in Achak's mind, human and Hybrid were equal, but he didn't dare tell Lapidar he thought as much.

Keeping his mouth shut, he watched the freeways, then paid careful attention to the neighborhoods. His eyes scouted around houses in search of any peahens. Twice he had to glance at a short brick wall before realizing the thing perched on top of it was not a statue.

"There's one!" he cried out for Lapidar to see.

"No need to sound so alarmed. I told you they're not all Hybrid. And even the ones that are can be reasonable. They just want to keep their neighborhood safe from any Hybrid that would threaten their territory."

Achak relaxed a little now that he knew the local Hybrid were not out to collect on their scalps. As he further studied the neighborhood, he realized that Lapidar had made a point in calling the city "upper class." The houses certainly met the criteria as each was entitled to its own garden, French windows, and ivory carved doors.

No one was allowed to park on the side streets as Lapidar was intending to do. He pulled over in front of a house and instructed Achak to roll down his window. Achak did, while Lapidar immediately began speaking to—as far as Achak could see—no one.

"Where can I park my car?"

Achak didn't expect anyone to answer until he noticed that there was a peahen, a bird whose brown feathers and size resembled those of a turkey, nesting in the lawn. It raised itself up then altered its feathers so that it was no longer a peahen but a beautiful woman standing in the peahen's place, in all shades of brown. She had a flattering tiara not of jewels, but beaded tips bobbing over her head. Curly locks of hair framed her face and, while they did not particularly go well with the colors on her suit, she still looked exquisite.

"I can take it," she said taking out a small notepad and pen. Only then did Achak notice the nameplate on her breast. "Your name please?"

"Gray," Lapidar called out as he put the car into park and turned off the ignition.

Stepping out of the car, Achak waited by the lady wondering where to go and what to do. Lapidar came around from the driver's side and handed her the keys.

"Have a pleasant afternoon at The Changeling," she replied and let the two be on their way.

Lapidar led off up the driveway, then took the path to the front door and rang the doorbell. "The Changeling" did not sound like somebody's house, but the exterior was deceiving like that.

When the door was answered, both the man that was behind it and the room took Achak by surprise. There was no guestroom and where there should have been a second floor or at least a ceiling, there was a large red curtain drawn from wall to wall. The doorman blazed in a shirt of orange and yellow. He nodded for them to proceed on through as he shined radiantly in front of the backdrop of a red curtain. Another man standing directly in front of the curtain stepped forward and was about to speak to Achak when he changed course to talk to Lapidar instead.

"Any reservation, sir?"

"No."

"Then carry on through," he said and gestured his hand toward the curtains.

Achak pulled an opening in the red cloth and stepped through. For one breathless moment, he thought he had been transported. The polished wood under his feet made him feel like he had been pushed onto stage, while a performer danced in front of him.

Not facing him, but with his back turned away, the shirtless man made some elaborate gestures with his hands for the diners at the nearest table. He did not look at all naked with the amount of body paint that had been applied to his arms and torso. The two gentlemen sitting there gazed at the dancer mildly impressed and continued their conversation over dinner. Taking no offense, the dancer continued moving on to other tables.

Achak stared both intrigued and embarrassed by the dancer. Crossing Achak to reach the tables at his other side, the performer spun around and Achak saw the full extent of the costuming, which was not limited to synthetic fur and thin fabric dyed to the pattern of a white snow leopard. Achak knew he had gaped too long when he caught the dancer's eye in the passing.

The performer's face flickered into cat shape, but Achak blinked and the face appeared human again. Lost for words, Achak had no intention of pondering over the transfiguration.

"Why are you just standing here," Lapidar growled and pulled at Achak's arm to have him follow.

It relieved Achak to see that Lapidar had chosen a table in the middle section as the aisle seats seemed to receive more of the dancers' attention since they were easier to get to. Achak had more time to observe his surroundings once he took a seat.

Toward the back end of the room, Achak noticed that there really was a stage, which eased him to know that he had not been standing on it. Although, he now understood why passing through the curtains had made him feel as if he were standing in front of an audience. Nearly everything, including the tables, was draped in red cloth. At the foot of the stage, two more dancers, looking as shirtless as the first, moved in step with each other. Achak could not discern their species from a distance, or determine the patterns on their animal skins, but something about their movements made him think of two predators devouring a carcass as opposed to coordinated dancers.

Far from exotic, Achak found the range of native instruments and dance to be an unusual combination of both the modern drumbeat and the archaic flute. They may very well have taken some routines from Hawaiian fire-dancers. Of course, through their costumes, they gave homage to predatory land mammals, but if they represented a more exclusive group than what Achak had observed, he was not one to ask what the animals might be limited to. He was just relieved to see that cats and dogs could dine and dance together, or by his interpretation, that he and Lapidar were not doomed to become enemies by nature.

"We can't help showing off our colors," Lapidar whispered across the table to Achak. Smiling, he seemed happy about Achak's reaction to the place.

"You don't see many feathers here do you?" Lapidar pointed out with a know-it-all grin.

Achak had not really given it much thought, but he glanced around and said, "No."

"That's because we're only in league with flightless birds," Lapidar explained. "Most avian beings are too proud to want to mingle with grounded mammals. But I guess we can be the same way with our fur coats." He looked to the dancers near the stage as he went on speaking. "You see all sorts around here. Not just those with patterns—though I will admit that they are the proudest of their coats—but even other breeds have fur of different lengths to which they'll flaunt."

Achak looked to the dancers to see if he could watch them with the same admiration that Lapidar spoke of. He supposed their costumes deserved the recognition for sheer craftsmanship. They were better than Tehya's paper bag masks at any rate.

Reaching for the glass of water that had been placed in front of him, Achak stopped short of it and rested his hand on the table. His fingers reflected off the glass, which in their squat distortion looked like the stubby joints of his paws. The illusion was so captivating that he imagined them becoming so, and they did to his astonishment. He was just beginning to feel the warmth spread up his arm when pain was hammered onto his hand.

Lapidar's fist had come over his hand in a single strike. "Not here!" He looked furious, his face scarlet.

Achak glanced around to see if anyone else might have noticed a change in him. From the nearest table to his left, a lone man, copper toned and silver bearded, watched him with mild interest. But Achak could see that the man had been reading a newspaper which had held his interest prior to any distractions. He returned to his reading once Achak caught his eye.

No one else seemed the least bit attentive to what Achak had almost done. This made him angry with Lapidar for resorting to such unnecessary reprimand. He rubbed his sore fingers and stared back at the wolf.

"What was all that for?" he demanded.

"You were about to transmogrify!" Lapidar hissed.

"Still..." Achak continued to rub the back of his hand. He did not feel as careless about the situation as Lapidar's tone suggested and reasoned that he was at least partially in control of his changes, even if not entirely. "A simple 'hey' or 'cut it out' would have grabbed my attention."

Lapidar growled in discontent and Achak could tell that the argument was going nowhere. Wanting to break the moody atmosphere, he stood up from the table and excused himself.

"I'm going to the restroom," he said and walked toward stage-right. Behind the curtain were a payphone and the bathrooms for women and men. He might have proceeded into the men's, but he did not expect to be confronted with the temptation to call home. He stared longingly at the payphone, then reached into his pockets and found a few quarters left over from the arcade. Dropping them into the machine, his heart leapt as the phone began to ring on the other side of the line. He had no idea what he was going to tell any of them if they picked up. Maybe the answering machine would pick up and he could just tell them that he was okay.

Achak felt the red curtain behind him move, but did not give any consideration to who might have been passing through when a hand came down on the receiver. The dial tone filled Achak's ears and produced a buzzing that manifested his anger.

"Now what?" He slammed the phone into the receiver and turned on Lapidar. "What am I? A prison—"

Lapidar caught him up by the collar. The wolf's eyes flashed yellow. "Do you insist on being so naive! What if Manu had picked up? Or one of The Jacks? What would you have done then? You'd have worried yourself right into a trap!"

He let go of Achak and let him think upon the words. They worried him more than anything he had stopped to think over.

"What would he do to my family?" Achak asked in urgency.

"Whatever it'd take to get to you, I'd imagine," Lapidar delivered the words without emotion—their meaning as clear as ever, regardless.

"Then why shouldn't I call them to see that they're okay?"

"Because there's nothing you can do about it, if they're not." Lapidar spoke the one truth that Achak did not want to hear.

He was helpless and he couldn't accept it. "Of course, you could care less either way," he accused Lapidar.

"I wouldn't be here if I didn't care!" Lapidar took the offense personally. "I'd have left you to Manu or the werewolves," he added tartly.

The bathroom door opened to the men's and Lapidar quieted down as the fellow walked out and back through the curtain.

His voice became more controlled. "I'm trying to help you, but you need more time. You don't even know how to transmogrify."

Achak closed his eyes, tightening them until he could see spots. "Alright," he said, looking at Lapidar with a clearer vision of the way things would work.

Lapidar led him back to the table where the centerpiece candelabrum had been replaced by a rotisserie...

"Duck?" Achak questioned the obvious as the carcass on the table still had all of its distinctive characters, including the beak. The creature looked as though it had been cooked alive.

"Dig in." Lapidar laughed while taking a seat.

"This is one of those animal instinct things, right?" Achak moved around the table to his own chair and waited for Lapidar to surrender the serving knife. It surprised Achak to see the wolf using silverware, but he looked down at his own plate and the silverware that lined it. Noticing the sides of tabooli and rice on his dish, he decided to take his chances with the main course.

10
Blood Ties
Order

Splintering picket fences and degrading lawns, Achak thought this new neighborhood looked as run down as the one in which he had encountered around the train station of werewolf-central. Only this time they had left the skyscrapers behind, though not far behind as they could still be seen above the houses. Achak stood on another doorstep with Lapidar and remained less impressed with the upkeep than he had been with The Changeling.

"What's this one called?" Achak asked before the door could be answered.

"The Basement. It's a bar, and obviously a bit underground, if you know what I mean."

Achak nodded as Lapidar opened the door, which turned out not to be locked. The living room vaguely resembled a typical living room with its recliners and a big screen TV, but Achak could tell by the squatters that it served as something more like a lounge. Down the hall, there were more rooms, which also tended to function better as lounges than as living quarters. Between doors there were candy and keno machines, which Achak noticed all happened to be out of order.

At its end, the last door was not a room but a descent of stairs leading into the cellar. Wooden steps creaked under Achak and Lapidar's feet until they reached the dusty and clouded depths of an otherwise normal bar. It was a larger space than any Achak had ever seen utilized for such a business. Much better maintained than its exterior, the place had booths, tables, and a center bar of polished wood. The seats were cushioned and matching, as red as any cheap wine or ale.

However the next thing Achak was to notice was less appealing or comforting to him.

"Everybody's looking," he hissed to Lapidar at his side.

"That's because you're under age. They'll ignore you in a minute," Lapidar assured, but Achak was not so sure.

He was looking around anxiously at all the eyes that were upon him and the people who had stopped sipping from their drinks to stare.

"Does it always have to be a bar?" Achak remarked at the remembrance of all the times Lapidar had ditched him at the motel.

"Hey, it's the best place for information," Lapidar defended. "Try to go somewhere nice and the informants will start taking down your profile. Here, lots of people come and go with information and nobody raises an eyebrow."

"So we're going to interview?" Achak asked while looking around and wondering who they would even begin to approach with a question.

"No," Lapidar said fiercely. "Let everyone in on your business and you may as well send Manu an invite to meet you here. Word travels fast among Hybrid. Question the wrong person and you can expect to see Manu's hounds here in as little as a day."

"Then where do you suppose we start?" Achak wanted his answer quick and direct.

"With the auctioneer." Lapidar nodded to the central bar, where a tender and several cocktail waitresses were serving drinks from within the oval counter.

Achak's cheeks turned to ice at the thought of conversing with the bartenders. He hoped that Lapidar would make his pleas as quick as possible. Between the tall, lanky and crudely shaven man and the long-haired waitresses, who almost pushed themselves as far over the countertop as the drinks they served, Achak did not like to think of either caterer as being a reliable source for information.

Before they could reach the bar, a tailcoat walked across. To Achak, he was nothing more than a man with a drink and a classy business jacket walking over to one of the booths, but to Lapidar he was much more threatening. The wolf half-froze as the tailcoat passed by as though his path had just been crossed over by a black cat.

Lapidar's eyes followed the navy tailcoat all the way to the entrance where he took a seat at the booth closest to the stairs.

"Do you know him?" Achak breathed as he fed off the tension building in Lapidar's face.

Snapping out of his trance, Lapidar let the sight of the tailcoat fall from his gaze as he met back with Achak. "I hope not," was all he replied.

He continued back toward the bar and Achak followed, though dragging a couple of paces behind to avoid speaking with the bartender.

"Have a seat," Lapidar growled when they reached the bar so that Achak would take up the stool next to him.

The bartender came immediately over to take their orders and Achak did not like the way the man gave him a double glance-over. Suspicion put Achak in a tense sitting position, but he had Lapidar next to him to bring the room's atmosphere down to one of moderate trust. Having a mercenary at his side, Achak could be expected to feel as secure as anyone who traveled with a personal bodyguard.

Relaxing a little, he took his time taking in his surroundings and Achak found that the people around him were of the most interest. He had still yet to learn how to distinguish the features of a regular human versus a Hybrid.

Upon closer inspection, the bartender had little hair by which to hide his age. He appeared to be of his mid-forties with patches of hair missing from his brown shag. Achak could tell by the creases and bags around the man's eyes that the alcohol addiction had done little to preserve his youth.

"One Old Fashioned and make it a bottle of the commonest for the little one, Giles," Lapidar said to the bartender and Achak couldn't tell if he was ordering or interviewing. Whatever he had said, the bartender had walked away and made no objections to Achak being underage.

"Sorry." Lapidar turned to Achak while Giles busied himself further along the counter mixing drinks. "You can order what you want next round. It's best not to start out with complicated orders. Plus we don't want to be loaded with a strong substance since information can be just as easily taken as it is given."

"Right," Achak confirmed, though not sure if he had followed Lapidar completely. Before he could clarify, Giles returned with one ice-glass for Lapidar and a brown bottle.

The tender gripped the counter firmly and stared over from one to the other, then settled with speaking directly to Lapidar.

"So can I persuade you to take a match today? You always bring me a good sum."

Lapidar smirked and took a glance over Achak's shoulder who turned around to see what they were both referring to.

Beyond the booths, there remained what would have been an open floor space, something that Achak would have expected to be utilized as a dance floor, but the people standing around it were not moving their feet. Nor was a game of spin the bottle about to take place at the center of their ring.

Achak swallowed hard and did not think he could hold down the drink he had just taken. A large enclosure of Hybrids formed the arena. The difference between this instance and a similar one involving werewolves was one of human behavior. These spectators watched and placed bets instead of circling the fighters like a pack of wolves.

Caught off-guard, Achak was made to choke as Lapidar elbowed him in the arm.

"Stare at it too long and you may find yourself a participant," Lapidar taunted. Giles laughed.

"Ha, right." Achak was nowhere near laughing at the idea. He had had enough experience with jackals and werewolves than to think of Hybrid sparring as just any laughing matter.

"Domestica?" Giles exclaimed in a loud whisper.

While Achak's attention had been focused on the arena, he had not realized there was already an exchange occurring between Lapidar and the bartender.

"I have not heard a thing of any direct affiliation to the place," Giles said in a lowered voice. Seeing Lapidar's disappointment he hastened to add, "But I have reason to suspect some of the rumors here have been of some connection. The mere mention of the place gives me the creeps, so I would remember any mention of it. No other Hybrid would dare house a pet, let alone a zoo of them."

"Why not?" Achak asked and both men looked at him as though he had just said something derogatory.

Giles glanced at Lapidar, then returned to Achak. "Because we are animals and to keep them, even as pets, would be to imprison your own kind or kin species." His eyes remained keen and focused. "How is it that you don't know?"

Lapidar was about to intrude with a bluff, but Achak thought he could come up with a better one.

"I grew up on a reservation," Achak lied. "I suppose our customs are somewhat different in that we believe animals are our brothers and are therefore free to find a home with us should they choose. But I think I understand the situation you speak of, in which animals are not kept of their own freewill."

"Fascinating," Giles remarked.

Achak took a swig of his bottle to let Lapidar know that he was through talking and would think better before opening his mouth again.

"Oh, but I have heard an interesting rumor about a certain free-agent."

"Hmm. And what's that," Lapidar encouraged Giles to continue.

"There are few cults and I will tune into their affairs, but something as big as the Lunars is bound to catch my ears."

"Oh, that." Lapidar sank into his pint glumly.

"But it gets even better," Giles said brightly. "The Solars are in direct competition with new recruits and will compete for any potential. They're the ones who have your name. I would not speak, but there are others here who would."

"Perfect," Lapidar remarked. "But I don't really have time to be concerned with them now. I really need Manu."

Giles winced. "You're desperate tonight. I could tell you of another who let the name slip—but wait just a moment."

A waitress grabbed his sleeve and he walked off to go cater to others. Achak had barely taken two sips from his drink, but Lapidar's glass was down to its last quarter.

He looked at Achak's bottle and his comment was to be expected.

"What's wrong with you?"

Achak shrugged.

"It's just beer. Nuth'n to it, eh? Just being one with the men." Lapidar chuckled as he held up his glass. "A toast, eh!"

"To what?" Achak laughed.

"To animal pride and freedom—we drink." Lapidar chugged, while Achak merely sipped at the bitter contents that touched his lips from the bottle's throat.

"TRY IT—" Lapidar bounded off his chair toward Achak, but he made contact with another man's left arm. "—and I'll rip you to pieces." He tightened his grip around the man's wrist suspended in front of Achak's face. Achak noticed the arm was unusually hairy. The man was still in human form, but his features held such a beastly nature to them that Achak felt certain that the man had not transmogrified correctly into human or had been caught in the process of changing. The wrist belonged to man whose face was hidden behind a rag of matted hair.

"Eeey only wanted to get the bartender's attention," the man as good as squealed. He rubbed at his noise with the back of his other hand, and snorted as he scrunched the nostrils in a sniffle.

"Then I suggest you go around us and not in between. But allow me," Lapidar said tersely and called to Giles. "We have a customer over here."

Achak was brushed against as the swine moved behind him and away from Lapidar. He hated knowing that the beast was at his back and wished that Giles would hurry over. When Giles did come, all the swine requested was a cold draft, which even by the annoyed expression on the tender's face sounded like a drink that was not to be bothered with. Giles seemed eager to get the man to leave and gave him a bottle straight away.

When it was all done with, Achak sighed over his drink, then cried out as a force struck the small of his back. His chest hit the bar counter, then the stool was kicked out from under him and he fell back. The pain from his spine sent a charge up and into skull, which triggered the transmogrification.

Trying to sit up like a human, the nerve forced Achak to arch his head back. With his eyes on the ceiling, he felt the change come over him like an electric shock. His mouth stretched across his cheeks with the numbing sensation of having one's skin torn apart. Two of his eyeteeth grew over his bottom lips and proceeded past his chin. His hind legs could no longer support his arch up which put his back to the floor.

Before Achak could roll over, a boar, reeking of alcohol came over him. Lapidar in wolf's form pulled him off, but the boar had managed to lodge one of his tusks into Lapidar's throat. Lapidar could no more breathe than attempt to lock his jaws over the boar. Bounding, Achak pulled the two apart and immediately put space between himself and the boar. He thought that if he kept some distance away from the tusks that would be his best defense, but the boar was a charger. Bowing his head, the boar was redirecting his tusks to hook Achak from under. Achak dodged but his paws did not have a firm enough grip on the tiles to turn the attack around. His adversary was quicker on hooves.

The entire bar broke into a concert of screams and shouts. They were moving toward the arena and everyone gathered around to watch.

Through all the movement, Achak lost sight of the boar. He made a wild circle looking for the swine that had forced him into this form. But instead of sighting the creature, Achak's muzzle hit against the snout of his opponent. Two tusks pointed in the opposite direction of Achak's fangs: up.

The boar scratched his front hoof at the wooden floor, and thrust his tusk under Achak's muzzle. Its point of impact hurt worse than any strangle, like having something very long and sharp lodged in his throat. Achak could not breathe right away, but still managed to hold his own from a further distance.

Lowering his head so as not to present the enemy with the same target, Achak hissed at the boar as more shrieks and shouts followed. Some men began to shout their wagers. They were all rooting for him, but Achak did not know how to fight, especially not with the use of fangs. He readied himself to make an attack anyway, trying to recall the stance he had seen cat-like animals take on any number of nature television shows. There must be an appropriate launching position that he could use to pounce on the boar while avoiding any contact with the tusks.

"If a lion can do it, a sabertooth should have no problem," he heard one of the men say while placing a wager. But Achak did not think himself capable of killing a boar with a spear, let alone with a pair of fangs attached to his jawbone.

Every thought about sinking his teeth into another man's skin unnerved Achak. All that childhood talk about hygiene and barbaric behavior now competed with his instincts. He might taste sweat, salt, or blood, but there were no alternatives to what he had to do. His claws would be of some use, but he still had the tusks to worry about. To really stand a fighting chance, he would have to bring the fight to an end in as short a time possible. The fact remained that despite his obvious physical advantages, he was reluctant to use them. What good is a sword to a warrior if he's too afraid to swing it?

Achak kept his front body low and at the ready, confident that the closer he kept his chin to the ground the less chance the boar had of jabbing one tusk or the other under his throat. He needed to keep his fangs up and pointed to attack, but Achak kept finding himself preparing for the defensive.

"Rip him! Tear him!" Achak heard from the nearby voices. The boar swung his tusks in the air with a jerk of the head as if gesturing what he would do once the tusks had been hooked or lodged into Achak's flesh.

"Rip him! Tear him!" The words came with a breeze into Achak's right ear—a whisper from a seashell. Off to the side, he saw the overlaying gray fur and yellow eyes of a wolf.

Had Lapidar managed human speech in his wolf's form or had it only been his imagination, or maybe an echo off the crowd?

The moment the boar began the charge, Achak leapt and saw the tusks go under his feet. Without a neck to crane, the boar had no means of reaching Achak in mid-air. There was just a propelled sabertooth and the presented rear of the boar's backside. Together, they tumbled and rolled. Risen and twisted, the boar presented its neck and Achak took the opportunity into his mouth.

He gagged as the warm blood slid down his throat. Achak could not avoid the taste of it coming through his fangs. It stuck to his tongue and gums. Hacking and sputtering like a cat, he released his grip on the hog.

The boar did not make another attack against him, nor had Achak expected it to. Rather, the beast stood paralyzed with the blood dripping from its neck and onto the tiled floor. Achak had not driven his fangs far into the boar's flesh, or to any fatal depths, but he imagined that the shock of being bitten had done more than enough for the boar. He doubted the beast had ever met another creature with fangs bigger than his tusks.

Taking steps away from the boar, Achak growled his way outside of the peopled ring. At the same time, saliva dripped from his mouth as he tried to part himself with the blood he had swallowed. Red was oozing down his fur, but he did not care what the crowd thought of him as its spectators backed away. The boar may have been scared, but Achak had a worse feeling of terror from the experience at the taste of carnage and blood. The ability to take life rested at the peak of a single pointed fang, and with Death so close to Achak's lips, he could taste the murderous intent from within.

What if he had—could he have? He did not know the answer. Many times before he had been told by his grandfather's stories of heroes and convinced by his mother that killing could be justified under the right circumstances—and in instances of self-defense. Now, he wondered if he could ever count on such reasoning to clear his conscience. Were he to have killed the Hybrid would he have come to accept it as a just and fair defense?

He moved toward the bar, away from any occupied stools, and waited for Lapidar to join him. The wolf came to his side with a jingle of silver hanging from his mouth. Achak saw the arrowhead pendant and remembered the young man it had belonged to. Who was he now? He could not see the meaning behind old habits, like the way he would always tuck the jewel under his sweatshirt. If he could go back to being oblivious to the rest of the animal kingdom, then he could have his old life once more, but that was not likely to happen.

Lapidar became man and dropped the necklace in his own hand for Achak to take. However, Achak doubted his instincts would permit him to meet Lapidar on the same level. He still felt the rapid heart rate and answered to the pulse of a hunter.

Catching on to Achak's unwillingness to transmogrify, Lapidar stuffed the necklace into one of his coat pockets for safekeeping. He began speaking over the counter to Giles the bartender. Whatever he asked first, Giles shook his head "no" to. Then Achak distinctly heard Lapidar say something about "tailcoat" and saw Giles look over Lapidar's shoulder to the mentioned corner. Giles shook his head again. His lips moved, but it was in brief and Achak could not hear what was said.

Lapidar nodded and seemed to be content enough with the information to thank Giles.

He moved from between the barstools and led the way to the stairs. Achak looked back to see his stool lying on the floor with the broken glass. Puddles of alcohol were surrounded by yellow signs asking for people to watch their step, which made the remnants of their bar fight look as insignificant as a janitor's regular cleanup.

The back end of Achak's fur was damp from the spills. Slight stings occurred around the wet spots where Achak assumed his skin had been scraped by the glass shards. His back paws followed gingerly behind his front as he was careful not to stretch the broken skin too much in his movements. However, his efforts were lost when he reached the stairs.

Lapidar climbed ahead of him, but kept shooting nervous glances back as though he expected Achak to suddenly tumble down the stairs from behind.

When they reached the top, people who were cluttered on the sofas and around the big screen TV all looked at Achak as he walked past them. Some of them looked ready to stand up and engage, but the most one jerseyed young man did was to move behind them and make his way to the basement. Achak suspected that he was going downstairs to ask about him and would find the mess around the bar and the bidders of sufficient resource.

As they stepped outside, Achak began to worry himself more practically about what Lapidar would say to him. He was sure there would be reprimand for revealing his extinct form to the public, and he would continue to do so if he did not transmogrify soon. Once they reached the boulevard, they were bound to meet some more people, not all of them Hybrid.

Achak had little to worry about in the current run-down neighborhood they traveled through. It was dark and no one but the smokers outside The Basement were around to see them walk away. Occasionally, he checked his back to see that no one was following but, in finding no one there, he knew that Lapidar too had his senses keened in to detect any stalkers.

There were no detours as Lapidar kept to the most direct streets that would lead them back to the main boulevard. This would become problematic when they reached the downtown district with Achak on his paws in front of the non-Hybrid public. As it was, they were already approaching the first of businesses, most of which had closed signs over their windows.

Achak saw a homeless man sitting on the curb ahead. The sidewalk was glowing brighter now that the streetlamps were guiding pedestrians. He knew he would be seen if he continued on the same path, but Lapidar did not alter their course. Placing himself on the outside, Lapidar walked between Achak and the homeless. He said nothing to the bum who likewise did nothing in return but stare.

Next on their encounter, three fellows from the local bar walked toward them.

"Move in front," Lapidar whispered and Achak did as instructed, making room for the men to walk right by.

Those passing were loud and coarse to other couples around the area. They laughed and belched and even hollered to a woman across the street who was with her boyfriend or lover, but when they neared Achak they quieted down. First whispering, then stopping entirely, they gawked at the pair.

"Is that?" they asked each other.

"Barnum and Bailey?"

"No, it's the Ringling Brothers!"

"You mean Sigfried and Roy."

One fellow was too busy clearing at his eyes and wiping away with his hands to say anything. Achak supposed that this must have been the most sober of the three to have noticed his abnormal extension of fangs.

To Achak's relief, no one did anything more than admire him. Although the men were rude and drunk, Achak appreciated the fact that he did not have to resort to any defensive measures to avoid them.

From out of a coffee shop stepped a corporate employee whose eyes were misted over with fog building up on the lenses of his glasses. He looked desperate for the caffeine that was simmering out of his foam cup. It must have been a late night at the office turned later by the sight of the gigantic feline that he had almost hit with the coffee shop door.

Achak may have growled, but he distinctly thought he heard Lapidar say, "What's your problem?" after making the customer spill his coffee.

Light flashed and Achak turned around. He saw the businessman dialing on his cell phone. However, Lapidar pushed with his knees to guide Achak into a walkway between buildings before either could hear any of the phone conversation that was to occur.

The passage they arrived in was not like any dumpster lot Achak had seen. Rather, there were a few more businesses operating to the sides of the two buildings, except that they had been closed for the night. Achak could see clear down the path and into something like a courtyard, but it appeared vacant from his end.

"Come here for a moment," Lapidar called to Achak before letting him slip away. He bent over and drew Achak's necklace out of his pocket. "There!" he exclaimed, clipping the arrowhead around his neck. "That should help you change, eh?"

Achak's eyes fell over the pendant, but then he slinked to a corner away from Lapidar. Looking back, he saw the wolf lean against the wall and fold his arms over each other.

Lapidar cocked his head back and said with a gentle air, "Whenever your ready. Just don't try to rush it."

Taking a seat near one of the pottery plants that framed a doorway, Achak stared at Lapidar wondering how to take his words. He certainly seemed patient, but in the past, it had never lasted long. If Achak approached Lapidar again without having transmogrified, would he still be as lenient with the sabertooth's presence as he had in allowing that factor to go amiss thus far? He was sure he would have his answer soon as he would likely fail to manage another transmogrification in the same day.

Already so many changes had occurred since his practice session that morning. It almost felt too tiring to manage another change. If it was not physical exhaustion, then it was a mental one that discouraged him from making the attempt.

He hated the rapid transition into alternating species. To him, change was meant to be gradual, something he could break into steps or phases, but for a Hybrid, there was only one step, one phase, one act.

Unable to change his options, he looked down at the necklace that had restored him safely to his human form earlier that day and wondered if he could work its magic yet again. He was not confident in its power as he remained seated for the attempt.

Rolling up his sleeve, he reached up for the amulet, or in this case, the arrowhead. It felt uncomfortable to change, more so than even his first attempt at it. Not so much the tingle, but a chill, from the inside not the out, was rooted and transgressed through the very depth of his bone. He thought his arm would shatter before he reached the pendant, but after the slow and agonizing start, the speed of change kicked in and like a wave of panic, rippled through his every nerve.

Finding himself both crouched and human, he straightened out his legs and raised his body. His head felt light and his legs wobbly, but, one foot after another, he stepped toward Lapidar.

"Is there anyone?" His voice came out distant, but tickled his throat like a purr. He coughed.

"No," Lapidar responded. "Just people." He looked over Achak carefully. "Are you alright."

"No," Achak answered honestly. Then finding only a bit of his more cheerful self to cling to added, "Viv will torture us for missing dinner, won't she?"

"Yeah, but that's what the beer at The Basement was for."

Achak frowned.

"Do we just walk? I don't remember where we parked." Achak was eager to have them leave off the topic and move on.

"A couple blocks more... I think." Lapidar rubbed his forehead and began leading out.

They continued walking in the same direction as before where the tall corporate buildings and apartment complexes towered above the smaller businesses. Achak distinguished the two building types by their windows, in which the corporate ones had tinted and dark panes while the apartments' were exposed with lights and thin curtains.

Achak kept rubbing his shoulder where his fall from the stool had been broken. His ribs underneath ached, but he could not avoid rotating his body out of caution. His worst fears realized, a voice called out to them from the shadows.

"Excuse me, boys!"

Achak leapt in a secondary beat while Lapidar snarled.

Darkened from the inside, the spokesman stood in the open doorway of a bar. It seemed a regular place for humans. The sound of pool tables cracking and televised sports commentary could be heard from behind the silhouette. He stepped out further and allowed more light to come across his features.

"You two fellas look like you've had a rough night. Why don't I buy you two a drink?" The fuzzy brows of the spokesman twitched. Partially under shadow, they looked as dark as the hair atop his head. His whiskers on the other hand, gray and white, were the only thing to add variety to his otherwise monotonous face.

"Sorry, not interested," Lapidar said forcefully from Achak's side.

He nudged Achak's arm, but neither took the initiative to move from the spot before the spokesman could continue his offer.

"*Wait a second,*" his voice almost whined. "You haven't even heard my bargain."

"No deal," Lapidar snapped. As though this was all he was waiting for the spokesman to say, he took a step back.

"Now hold on. Doesn't the boy get a say in this? It's a school night. Shouldn't he be in school?"

Achak was attracted to the movement of the spokesman's hands where he was turning over every jewel-encrusted ring on his finger.

"You must be very stupid to approach us like this after you saw what happened back there." Lapidar's lowered tone was more dangerous than the spokesman's rising one.

"Stupid, eh? I wouldn't be the one who brought such a species into a duelist's bar."

"That's right," Lapidar further provoked. "Not without a contract at hand."

The spokesman removed two rings from his right hand and began to toss them up with his left, playing them like dice. Achak could tell that he was trying to distract Lapidar.

"You're all the same," the wolf growled and made no effort to pull away. "You don't care how young you contract them." And Achak thought this was a personal remark considering Lapidar's young age and dangerous career path.

"As young as they come, right? Forget about their future. There's profit to be had!"

"No one around The Basement has a future, or did you forget your place, wolfy? Anyone with a future would not have come to this area. They'd know better."

"You should know that The Basement isn't just popular for its cheap drinks and games." Lapidar's voice had slightly cooled since he had released the bulk of his pressure.

"I know." The spokesman smiled wryly. "It's good for its business ventures too. Or don't you think I know how you've been traded along?" He was gleaming in a dangerously superior manner.

"You and Morgan used to have quite the show around here."

"Don't you mention that name again!"

Lapidar pulled Achak back, doing the opposite of what it looked like he had wanted to do with his closed fists. His force caused Achak to lose his balance and stumble back, which was probably the one factor that ultimately protected him.

"We'll be leaving."

"Of Course!"

A fork edged claw extended from the spokesman's right hand as he lunged forward, not at Lapidar, but at Achak.

Piercing, warmth, then agony reached into Achak's shoulder collar. The warmth was oozing down his front, then chilling against his clothes, but the real injury only occurred to him when he felt the cotton material stick uncomfortably against his skin and burn.

"Run! Now!" He heard Lapidar shout. Wondering why his legs were so bent, he hadn't realized that he was on the ground until he tried to move them. He turned over onto his hands and attempted to push off like a sprinter. After only a couple of steps, his hands met the cement again. He thought it was the pain that had brought him to the ground, but instead saw that his arms had been covered in fur.

It seemed out of reason that his instincts would have brought him to his saber-tooth form. Or at least they were not very good instincts to suggest Achak run with one bad leg instead of two good ones.

However, the three-legged handicap was not to be so crippling as the saber-tooth's legs turned out to be better than two human ones. Lapidar raced in front of him and darted into a parking structure.

Tucking his claw back under his sleeve, the spokesman picked himself back up from where Lapidar had mauled him. He was just wiping the blood from his scalp when a shrill laughter shattered the darkness.

Whom he spoke to, he did not know, but the girl had a young voice and very short figure.

the same share doing a regular man's work."

Next to Lapidar, Achak thought he had it easy, even on matters concerning Manu. When compared to having a lifetime of threats, Achak felt guilty for the amount of fear and cowardice he built up over having only one.

"Don't look too sad," Lapidar said. "Not all the work has been bad. Giles was always good to me."

Day 9, Tuesday

11
The Hunt is On

Off the air, Manu was not so friendly to reporters as he made his way outside the studio. Around every corner of the studio halls, an eager journalist was waiting to ambush him with a few questions. His suit had acquired many creases in the avoidance, but under his eyes were a greater number of folds.

Among the questions reporters asked was whether they could get an exclusive to talk with Manu, one-on-one, about his research that lead to the discovery of a sabertooth tiger. Many, including a young man that carried only a portable voice recorder and a clipboard as an intern, heckled Manu with more direct questions, such as: "are you concerned about the accusations that will arise from conspiracy theorists" and "how long do you suppose it will take you to find the creature again?"

"No comment!" Manu knocked the recorder out of the intern's hand.

Grumblings followed his back as more studio employees peered outside their office doors and cubicles.

At the tenth floor, Manu boarded the elevator that would take him down to the first parking level.

"Mr. Firdaus!"

He was greeted by an excited and timely talk-show host as the elevator doors opened again only one floor in the descent.

"We should have a chat sometime. By the way, I was told by some of the studio executives that they'd like to bring you back to do a report on the Atlas Channel for their 'Primeval' special."

Manu kept his side to the host, fortunately never turning his head back to see the talk show celebrity as he left the elevator and spared himself the sight of any hand-gestured obscenities.

As black gowned as ever, Sirena came out from between a pair of parked cars in the underground structure to meet Manu.

"I am surprised by your patience," Manu said silkily.

"You needn't be," Sirena lofted. "I'm quite capable of entertaining myself."

"Indeed."

Manu carried on down the rows of parked cars without taking further notice of Sirena. She, on the other hand, skipped along beside him, fighting back the urge to smile.

"Where did you park?"

"Not here," Manu said shortly.

"Where's Ladon?" Sirena tried again to engage.

"With the car."

At the corner, near the stairs of a fire escape, Manu and Sirena walked through the exit and stepped onto the sidewalks of a downtown neighborhood.

"So he was spotted right in front of the studio?" Sirena looked down both directions of the boulevard where shops lined the district.

"Yes, by a man with a camera in his cell phone," Manu finally answered directly. "Not only that, but surveliance cameras were rolling as well in front of the businesses."

Manu's face filled with disgust at the mere sight and sheer number of shoppers that populated the sidewalks. When he spoke up again, he over exaggerated the competing noise of traffic by yelling back his answer to Sirena. "I would not have bothered with the interview were it not of such convenience and resource!"

"I see."

But just when Sirena thought she had seen and heard all there was to Manu's mentality, she began spotting peculiar gray-suited individuals among the crowds and the occasional black van parked at every street corner.

"WHO ARE THEY?" she demanded at once.

"Just some actors." Manu marveled at the nearest pair of agent-looking figures. "The Bred HyCouncil felt that I should take some 'human' methods to show my recovery efforts. They suggested that I hire a real batch of non-Hybrid search parties to demonstrate to members of the community that I have confidence in the human race's technological innovations. But, I'd rather keep this project exclusive."

"Thanks for the membership," Sirena attached with an air of sarcasm.

"So what do you think? How could a Sabertooth Tiger appear and disappear without anyone knowing where he came from or went?"

"Transmogrified," Sirena answered briskly. "He's a lost cause now. So do the Bred HyCouncil speculate as much?"

"They'll be here in a short while to ask questions. I want you gone before then."

Manu stopped again to look around at the neighboring businesses, but Sirena kept walking down the lane without a glance back.

Only minutes after Sirena's disappearance, Manu was approached by another man, slender and refined in appearance. His black hair was of a glossy shine and matched the inner trimmings of his tailcoat.

Achak was glad to be sitting back on the couch of the Grays' living room. He had slept all through the previous evening, when they had first arrived, and into the morning. Although always meeting him with piteous stares, Viv was slightly less awkward to be around now that she had dropped the formal talk and only spoke to him on matters that involved the activities of the household. While he enjoyed hearing about the kids; Tyler's ability to roller blade with two sets of skates over his paws and Lacie's knack for tracking down certain house pests with her nose before they have a chance to invade any storage cupboards, Achak wanted to see more of Lapidar. Unfortunately, the wolf still appeared to be playing the guilt trip as he avoided the living room and most places where Achak would lounge at, even the children's rooms when it came down to it.

When he could finally stand no more of Lapidar's avoidance game, Achak took the first opportunity he had to call the wolf over. He waited at the kitchen counter and when Lapidar came in from the garage for a drink, he called out for his attention.

"Lapidar?"

He hardly meant to sound rude or make the wolf choke over his drink, but his patience was running low.

"You can't keep avoiding me. We need to talk."

Patting down the counter top with a paper towel where he had spilt some of his drink, Lapidar remained silent and did not attempt to deny the accusation.

"It's been almost a week away from home... away from Domestica. I need to visit home."

Nodding, Lapidar looked up from his cup. "I wondered when you might ask. How does tomorrow work for you?"

Achak flushed. He had not expected Lapidar to agree, let alone suggest the following day for a visit. Tomorrow sounded almost too good to be true.

Day 10, Wednesday

Lapidar saw Achak to the Amtrak station early the next morning. It would be almost midday before the train arrived at the downtown station in San Diego.

"Sorry, I can't come with you," Lapidar said the moment Achak's train began to board passengers.

"There's no need. This is something I have to do. Call me if anything comes up." Achak handed him a folded sheet of paper with his phone number written down on it and shook his hand goodbye.

Achak gazed nervously out the window as his train rolled away, removing Lapidar from his sight.

There were pay phones in the rear of each passenger car and, without having a real plan about what he would say, he began dialing home to let his family know he would be arriving shortly.

"Hello?" Achak barely recognized the voice that came over the receiver. But it was his mother's, however grim and low it had spoken.

"Mom?" He cried back, too happy to worry about what she might think of his absence.

"Achak!" Her voice was a wail and it was joined by at least two other outcries in the background.

So they were all there: Mom, Tehya, and Grandpa. They must have been sitting at the table having breakfast, Achak tried to interpret by the amount of chattering. He had the visual of every detail in the house running through his mind.

"Dear, where are you? Where've you—What's all that noise in the background."

"The train." Achak tensed as the first of questions was asked.

"The train?! Where are you going?"

"Home," he replied and he liked hearing the effects of that single word upon all of his family.

"When will you arrive?" his mother squealed.

"At about eleven. The downtown station."

"We'll be there!" Every word he said he could hear being repeated to Tehya and Grandpa.

A brief silence fell between them.

"You can't talk long now, can you?"

"Well, I could, but it would be kind of expensive."

"Right," Mom said. " Then I guess I'll see you at the station. Bye, dearest. I—"

"Mom?"

"Yes?"

"I missed you." Achak put the phone back into its holster feeling a little lonelier than he had before making the call. Even with his final words, there was still a lot he had reluctantly left unsaid.

Achak had expected Mom, Grandpa, and Tehya to be there when he arrived, but not a couple of patrol cars pulled up at the front of his house. There was an officer in black and another wearing day clothes.

"This is your son, ma'am?" The uniformed officer asked of Ms. Twinfang.

"Yes. He's here safely now. I appreciate all you've done to help."

"I'm afraid that's not all, ma'am. You filed a police report for this missing person case and it's our job to follow up on all the details of his disappearance."

Without responding, Ms. Twinfang put her hands to Achak's shoulders as if to steer him away. Then she asked, "What is Achak going to expect as punishment? We're not talking of prison time, are we?"

"Is he over eighteen, ma'am?"

"No, not until June ninth."

"Yakima," Tehya hissed in an undertone and Ms. Twinfang scowled at her.

"What was that?"

"Oh, nothing," Ms. Twinfang answered. "It'll be graduation too, you know, on that day for Achak."

"Very well. And congratulations, son. There will be no civil offense made against his case, ma'am. But we'll still need his statement for our files."

Achak would have been more comfortable giving it to them with his family not around, but as the two officers met with Achak around the kitchen table, everyone stood by the counters listening. He didn't want to tell a delinquent's run-away story in front of his mother, who already appeared to have lost some weight in the short time he had been away. He couldn't tell the truth, but even limiting his story to kidnapping would produce some very awkward questions that he could not answer. Who would be his abductor? Lapidar was innocent, Sirena and the Jacks too young, and Manu too wealthy.

No, there appeared no way around the lie. He had to tell the authorities something that did not involve Hybrids. Neither of the officers looked anything more than human to have believed his story anyway.

Futher questioning continued as the uniformed officer took a seat in front of Achak.

"I'm Sergeant McCormack and this is Detective Hunter," the former introduced. "Hunter's name is a derivative of his work," McCormack chuckled.

"Hello, " Achak did not warm up to their icebreaker. He could already see that convincing a man of McCormack's years and experience would be difficult without having to resort to some extreme measures of fabrication.

"So I understand you've spent some time away from home for awhile, yes?" McCormack was careful not to suggest anything in his tone, but Achak could hear the calculations of a mind at work even without the feverish scratching of a pen by Detective Hunter.

"Yes," Achak replied. He gave a nervous glance at his mother who was unconsciously making a lot of noise with her fingernails under the counter top.

Tensing not only to the answers he gave McCormack, Achak began to feel a certain amount of pressure radiating from the direction of the younger detective.

Detective Hunter had handsome features and looked to be about the same age as Achak. However, beneath a harmless layer of brown curls and blue eyes, the kid was a prodigy of good looks and a successful career path. He was the talk and boast of a household. While only a case reporter, this young man held a place beside his superiors that Achak could never hope to acquire in the short amount of time there was between their ages.

"You're aware that a missing person's report has been filed on you?" McCormack continued.

"I am now, thanks."

"Now? Did you expect anything less from your family?"

"No, but it wasn't my intent to make them worry." Achak lost his patience and rambled on for too long.

"Ah! And so here we are then. And just what was your intent? No phone calls. No note. How is it you let your departure slip for so long without telling anyone?"

Achak distinctly remembered his phone call from The Changeling two days ago, but decided not to mention that.

"My intent? I just wanted to do some traveling, I haven't seen much outside of San Diego." Achak tried to run with the story of a restless teenager, but couldn't be too sure how to pull it off. Not that he hadn't been restless before he left, but trying to imagine himself taking his distress to the extreme of a runaway was not something he thought himself capable of.

"I suppose it was just sort of spur of the moment, so I really couldn't tell anyone beforehand."

"Why not after? Why not after you left or when you first reached your destination?"

"I just didn't want anyone to know where I was going or where I was. They might try to come for me." Achak's excuse was falling apart faster than his mother, whom he could hear stifle a sob every now and then.

"And just where did you go?"

"The only direction a person can go when they live on the south coast. I went North: L.A., San Francisco, Sacramento. " He listed the biggest city names he could think of and refused to include Tehachapi among his mentions.

"Well, let's see now," McCormack was careful to put each and every one of the names and places under scrutiny. " L.A., yes, that's typical of tourists, though I wonder why not Hollywood while you are at it?" San Francisco, yes. And then Sacramento, our state's capital. But I imagine you were a little disappointed with that one. There isn't much more than a government building."

Achak shrugged.

"Alright, so let me see if I can add this up," McCormack explained. "You clearly took a rail that would take you along the coast, but you didn't stop to go to Anaheim. See Disneyland or another theme park. You went straight to L.A. to do a little shopping, maybe? Where are your bags? Then up to San Francisco, perhaps to do a little more shopping and see the Golden Gate Bridge. And then finally to Sacramento to see—well, to see..."

"To see how close I could get to the remnants of my tribe in Washington," Achak answered before any more of his destinations could be scrutinized.

"Okay!" Mrs. Twinfang broke in. "I think that's enough. Gentlemen, if you please." She waved her hand toward the walkway that led out of the kitchen. "My son needs some rest. He's had a long trip. We can do this another time."

And by "another time" Achak knew that she meant after she's had a good long talk with him. Her voice was crisp and decisive, no longer filled with the tearful breakups of a mother gladdened by her son's safe return.

The kitchen went quiet as Ms. Twinfang followed the officers out and showed them to the door. They walked through the living room and left Achak in the quiet presence of Tehya and Grandpa.

With one elbow on the table, Achak balanced his head against his hand and massaged his forehead.

He knew he had come off as a liar to both the officers and his family, and he was guilty of it too. Even though he didn't consider himself a "bad" liar, one who was intentionally out to hurt people with his lies, he knew that he had still done a number on his family, which explained why Tehya was leaning against the fridge, occasionally moving the magnets with her finger and not rushing over with a hug.

After all the time he had spent thinking about his return home, the prolonged silence was not what he had imagined. Yet there was Grandpa pouring himself a cup of coffee from the carafe. Achak began to feel as uncomfortable around the normal activity as he did around the abnormal.

Tehya was dressed for school, a different sight from the last image he had of her in a flowery dress outfitted for picture day. Achak stared at the "Lucky Cat" depiction at the center of her shirt.

Bored with her magnets, Tehya appeared to be waiting, and now was as good a time as any to speak to her.

Achak gulped. "You're not going to school today?"

"I don't want to," she huffed and Achak's heart leapt.

He could read past her pouty lips and see that what she really meant to say was that she didn't want to leave if Achak wasn't going to.

"Did your pictures come in?" he started out slow. She looked shocked by his outspokenness but nodded.

"They're wretched. I hated that dress and some of the ribbons came untied on the basketball courts and looked shriveled on the photo."

She went suddenly silent. One of the magnets she had been flipping over fell to the floor.

As Ms. Twinfang walked back into the kitchen, Achak thought he saw his mother glimpse him before she set to work in front of the dish rack drying plates with a towel, a different approach from letting them drip-dry. Beginning to stack the plates in their appropriate cupboards, she breezed by Tehya and her feet kicked the magnet across the linoleum.

"Your bag was brought back," she said without turning around. "One of your classmates named Sirena brought it over—interesting girl."

That was an understatement, Achak analyzed his mother's words. What with Sirena's red hair and black wardrobe, she was bound to earn any mother's disapproval. But another thought had crept into Achak's mind, a more frightening one. So Lapidar was right to believe that Manu would be sending people over to check on Achak's family. Sirena had come by with the excuse of returning Achak's backpack, but it could have been worse, as Achak could only imagine the million and one possibilities Manu could have used to get Achak's family involved.

"Are you ready to tell me what you've really been up to?"

Achak looked up from his hands on the table and stared upon his mother's back. He thought of all people, his mother was sure to believe his story, but perhaps that would have been an insult to her wisdom. Knowing that he couldn't cover one lie with another, and that an attempt at it would only hurt his mother more, Achak gave into the only truth he could afford to speak.

"No," he answered her.

"Then go. Just go."

Achak did as told, stood up from the table and left. Back in his bedroom, he groaned. He could almost bang his head against the dresser for not planning ahead of time. And while Achak might have developed the perfect lie, he had never given the matter any thought.

Pacing his room, Achak took notice of his bland furniture and empty wall space and began to wonder what he had done with himself for all these years. Looking at the standard T-shirts in his closet, he knew there would have to be a change in his wardrobe now that he had borrowed a second polo shirt from Lapidar.

His room had been tidied up since he had left. Comic books were stacked neatly beside his bed dresser. Shoeboxes filled with cards and action figures, while another which held his markers, rulers, and stencils were tucked under his bed.

Achak loosened the bed sheets and pulled the covers over himself as he lay down. He had barely closed his eyes when he heard the door to his bedroom creak open. Expecting to see his mother Achak's body arched up, but it was Tehya he found standing in the open doorway and waiting to be invited in.

"Kind of early for sleep, isn't it?" she commented on observing Achak all wrapped under his bed sheets.

"I guess," he replied. "But I've had a long trip."

"Oh—yeah," Tehya struggled with her words "then I shouldn't bother you."

"Wait—yeah! You can stay if you want. Stay—please," he offered then begged.

"Really?" Tehya remained by the door. Her eyes were bright with surprise, but her smile: modest and suppressed.

"Yeah," Achak again felt the ripple in his throat like a pur.

Tehya ran over and sat beside him on the bed.

"That Sirena girl really creeped me out," she said in a whispered but urgent tone.

"She scares me too." Achak looked at his sister and saw the perfect opportunity to put his arm around her in comfort.

"She's not your type," Tehya said and put her head against Achak's shoulder.

Ms. Twinfang's face came down heavy in her hands.

"Kachina, you're in circles." Grandpa had come over to her right and took up a seat. He tried again to bring her hands away from her face and hold them on the table but they were locked with her elbows. "Already you have told as much of your mind."

"I know, Guyupi." She looked up to meet her father-in-law. "I just keep thinking about what could I have done—did I miss the signs to be able to prevent something like this from ever happening?"

"Something like what?" Guyapi pleaded for reason. "Nothing has happened. Achak is home safely."

"Achak is not home!" Her voice cracked under the implications. "I don't know where he is."

"Home and home the way you want him to be are not same thing." Guyapi kept his eyes staring into hers. "No mother has ever asked for more than her child's safe return and good health, but what more would you ask of him? If you are waiting for things to return to the way they were—"

"But that's just it!" Kachina wailed. "They can't. And I'm stuck with the way they are now. And I..."

"Kachina, you don't even know what you are crying about!"

This time Ms. Twinfang's hands did come down into Grandpa's.

"You don't know what changes have come about, but you cry over the worst of them."

"Guyupi, weren't you listening?" Kachina's voice came out frantic. "The way he spoke to the police? His lies? He couldn't even give a straight answer."

"So he still has some room to grow," Guyupi softened. "But I think I saw a few more inches." As he glanced around the room, his lips came up to form a subtle smile. "I can't remember the last time I saw him with collars on his shirt."

Tehya was busy showing off a friendship bracelet she had made with one of her classmates. Held in place with braids and little knots, there was a colored pattern of beads, except for one seashell that sat alone at its center.

"You didn't buy that did you?" Achak asked, thinking how silly it would be to purchase a bag of shells from a store when the beach was practically next-door.

"No, Mory and I found these. They already had the holes for us to run our strings through."

Achak studied the pattern before the subject of jewelry inspired a thought.

"Hey, wasn't Grandpa gonna—"

Tehya had already guessed what he was going to ask before he finished the question and pulled out a thin silver chain from under her shirt collar.

"Why is it under there?" he asked, but wished he hadn't.

"Because I thought it might upset Mom to see it." She went suddenly quiet. Tehya had so far avoided asking Achak any awkward questions, but now the subject was in the air again. She stopped looking at Achak and stared down at the necklace, then decided to remove it altogether.

Sliding her hands beneath her hair, she unclipped the chain and held it up for

Achak to examine. He took the pendant in his hand, immediately noticing that it was not in the shape of an arrowhead, but a yin and yang of the sun and the crescent moon. The silver backing only showed on the sun's half where part of it extended into rays.

"Can I see yours?" she asked, and reached out toward his collar.

"Sure." Achak moved to give back her necklace, which caused Tehya to bump his shoulder with her outstretched hand. He groaned and Tehya jumped back.

"What's the matter?"

But it was too late for Achak to cover up as his right hand immediately went toward his shoulder to soothe.

"I sort of..." He paused to think of an excuse but his mind drew a blank.

"You're hurt?" Tehya hissed in a whisper. "Let me see!"

"Oh, all right," Achak gave up on the lies, but was determined not to let his sister see underneath the bandages.

He took his left arm out of his sleeve and lifted up one side of his shirt for her to look at the bandages that ran around his chest and crossed over his shoulder.

"No, it's not serious. It's just stitches," he said in response to the concerned narrow of Tehya's eyes.

"How?"

"Three pointed claws." That was the most Achak was willing to elaborate on his wound, and Tehya seemed to except it without further question. "Just please don't tell Mom."

She nodded and Achak knew he could trust her, but before they could exchange another share of topics, Ms. Twinfang walked past the door and looked in. Her eyes were puffy underneath, and the tips of her frowning lips were pointing down at both Achak and Tehya on the carpet. They sat waiting for the drumbeat, but it never came. Ms. Twinfang proceeded past and into her own room. Eyes still fixed on the doorway, Achak and Tehya glanced each other knowingly. Without a word, Tehya collected up her necklace and bracelet and left the room.

Alone on his bed again, Achak waited for maybe a half hour before determining that Ms. Twinfang was not going to come in. He searched the room for any areas to clean up, but everything had already been straightened out. Even the floor was spotless of debris. Since he could not make anything tidier than it already was, he opened two of his drawers from the bedside dresser and decided he would switch some of their contents around, putting his pencil box, calculator, and trading cards in one drawer, while mixing headphones, charger cables, and sunglasses in the other.

The process should not have taken more than fifteen minutes, but he stretched it through the hour by shifting items around to see what would look best when the drawer first opened.

When he heard a soft tap, he turned around to see Grandpa standing in the doorway.

From his knees, Achak stooped and then stood. "Grandpa?"

Instead of a verbal explanation, the old man walked straight up to Achak and pulled aside his shirt collar.

"Hey, what?" Achak wrestled with him, but he knew what Grandpa was looking for. "Where's Mom," he asked at once before he would even agree to pulling up his shirt.

"She has gone out for some groceries." Grandpa drew back his hands and Achak lifted up his shirt.

"Look, I know what you're going to say." Achak hated the silent build up that his Grandpa always used to emphasize a point. "I know it looks bad, but I've already been in the hospital and treated for it, see." Achak reached into his left front pocket and pulled out a bottle of some antibiotics.

Grandpa hardly pretended to look at the bottle while his attention was on Achak's shoulder.

"Isn't a scratch to worry over."

His words, which were of no comfort to Achak, implied that he was not the one they were meant for. Achak suspected that Tehya stood within earshot just outside the room.

"Come into the kitchen," Grandpa said in the same dry tone. "The light in here is poor." He put the sterile pad back over the wound with minimal wrapping to hold it in place and allowed Achak's shirt to fall over it.

Achak let out a tiresome groan. He knew Grandpa had not heard anything he had said, but he would not let Grandpa go without hearing his frustration.

He watched as Grandpa left the room, grateful that there was a wall between him and the kitchen, as he swore loudly under his breath. A brush by the door side, and Achak shot a glance back into the hallway just in time to see a swish of long black hair flee in the other direction. But Achak did not have enough sympathy for Tehya to call her back.

Taking one last look at the prescription in his hand, Achak tucked the bottle away and walked out toward the kitchen.

Grandpa had not only seated himself at the square table but had a strange display of oddities laid out in front of him, including jars of herbs and a stone mortar that was not without its pestle. He had a journal open and was reading off the ingredients list, adding a leaf or a flour or yellowish sand that looked like pollen.

Achak came over to his side and sat down. He watched as the mortar was filled to the brim with different herbs and spices and had a few stems and long grass hairs sticking over the top. Grandpa then picked up the pestle, a long smooth rock with a rounded bulbous bottom, and began grinding the different plants inside the mortar. He mashed them down until there was nothing but a quarter of the mortar filled with an algae green paste. Achak could smell the incense of the flowers and tart dry grains and hoped that he would not have to eat it.

"Your shirt," Grandpa indicated for Achak to take it off.

"You don't know how it'll mix with the stuff they've already provided me," Achak offered his last bit of caution before cooperating.

Grandpa's deafness could not have been more obvious behind the low humming tune he worked by.

Achak gave up on him and unraveled the loose bandages before removing the sterile pad. He heard one of the stools creak behind the counter and guessed that Tehya had ducked herself out of sight again.

"Ollie ollie oxen free free free," Achak called in as little enthusiasm as possible and Tehya's head came up from behind the counter. "Want to watch?"

She nodded and walked around to sit on the other side of Achak. Reaching for different jars around the table, she turned their hand written labels toward her.

"Smell this one." Achak grabbed one of the pre-grinded powders and pushed it toward Tehya before Grandpa could complain about his movement.

Achak could smell the contents from his distance, but laughed as Tehya still brought the jar close to her nose for a stronger whiff.

"I can taste it," she coughed morosely.

"Whelp, now we're even."

Grandpa lifted a brush from the utensils and took up some of the balm into its bristles then painted it over Achak's stitches.

Achak was surprised for it not to have burned him, but it felt cool and refreshing over his skin.

"What's it like?" Tehya asked.

"Salty," Achak said frankly sticking his tongue out and trying to scrape off the taste with his teeth. He wiped at his mouth with the back of his hand and turned to Grandpa. Achak considered pleading with Grandpa not to tell Mom about his injury, but decided against it and instead asked, "Where did you write down the stories?" Achak hoped that the answer was as simple as flipping over to the next page in the journal.

"I did not write these. They were passed down by my grandfather."

Achak stared at his grandpa and tried to imagine the number of "great's" he would have to say in front of such a title.

"So were the stories ever written?"

"Some yes, but never the same way they were told from the beginning." His words rang a kind of pleasant memory and he smiled. "Ah—yes, the beginning. I doubt you remember how fond you were of that story."

Achak remained speechless. Of course it would be rude to say that he had forgotten each and every one of Grandpa's stories.

"You liked Grandpa's stories?" Tehya exclaimed in such an awe-struck manner that even Grandpa had to laugh.

"Liked them? He wouldn't go to bed without them."

At least one story, Grandpa, at least one.

"The Beginning?" Achak thought aloud. "That wasn't really its title, was it?"

"No, you're right, Achak. The story was given a name, just like all the creatures in it. Its name was something like *Animal People.*"

"Are those two words supposed to be together or apart," Tehya asked for she too had no recollection of the story ever having been told to her.

"That is one of the great mysteries of the story. You see, the story begins with the people and animals being together, but it ends with them apart and divided under different natures."

"So humans came from animals?" Tehya asked.

"No, I think he means: humans were considered to be animals. Or at least in how we lived barbarically among them."

Grandpa listened and only smiled at their theories. Achak saw Grandpa's eyes close and knew that he was listening for other inviting sounds.

"She gave them all a common skin to wear," Grandpa said suddenly.

Achak and Tehya both wheeled in their chairs to look for the "*she*" they expected to see standing with a bag of groceries, but there was no one there for Grandpa to have alluded to.

"She was created by Old One." His voice resounded from behind.

"Jeez, Grandpa, I thought you were talking about Mom," Achak straightened himself in his chair.

Grandpa hummed a few notes into his words.

"I am talking about Mom."

"Yes, but not *our* Mom," Achak clarified. "Mother Earth, right?"

"She is," Grandpa emphasized, "mother of all life."

> "...*A mother* whose oceans and seas came to touch at a single mass of land. One continent to support all life that was to dwell on dry shores and let thrive the life that was to flourish beneath the waves. Mother loved all her creatures and their nature—be it fur, or fin, or scale, or feather. But there rose the competition for her nurture.
>
> Of those with flippers or fins, the sea dwellers began to talk amongst themselves, saying such things as 'Home beneath the waves is biggest. Mother must love us more.'
>
> Then their words floated to the surface in bubbles and were heard by the seafaring birds that fished beyond the shores.
>
> 'Do you hear them talk?' The feathered flocks met in a council.
>
> 'They think Mother would favor them, but do we not fly over their heads? We soar above their seas and the soils of the land dwellers. You see, it is us who Mother would favor with our wings. And so colorful are our feathers!'
>
> The birds deemed themselves to be the favorite of beings. They might have kept their proud secrets since the winds always blew in their favor and would not let fall their words to the land beasts, but those of feathers were not the only to glide on the winds.

Bats did not have feathers, and nor should they want them, but they did not like to think of themselves less beautiful for it. They took the words down to their fellow furry and featherless friends. When the land dwellers received this message, they became angry. They had allowed the birds to nest and feed on their lands but here was proof of the feathers' betrayal. In their own council, they agreed to tear out any nests from their trees and pluck the feathers from wings until the birds were too afraid to touch ground. Then the land dwellers would show the proud feathers what fruitful gifts Mother had bestowed upon them.

However, before the lands could be covered in feathers, another whisper reached the ears of the land dwellers. Alligators, frogs, and snakes came up to the strongest of furry creatures and told all they had heard rising from the bubbles. These messengers had to hold their breath under water and could not swim out as far as those of fin or feather.

'They dared us to swim out to them and jeered us when some drowned before turning back to shore.'

All the scales on the snakes frilled up as they told the lions and wolves in a hiss, 'We were mocked above all for not having feet or fins.'

Just when the fur was beginning to stand on end for all land dwellers, the peas and turkeys came with more talk from the feathers.

'They scoff at our wings because no amount of flapping will lift us into the air.'

The land dwellers formed a mixed group of flightless feathers and furless, even slimy and scaly, skin types when they confronted Mother.

'Give the furless separate waters to swim in and let the birds nest elsewhere or we shall all go to war,' the wolf spoke to Mother for the sake of all land crawlers, and those that hopped or slithered.

However, Mother did not understand the conflict and refused the demand. She also thought the wolf to be cunning in his approach and wondered what she should do about it. For now, she left the wolf alone and let his warning slide by her.

The lands did not continue for even a day of peace before there came a disturbance. Trees were being shaken from their roots, while nests lost their eggs. The waters too suffered as dirt and feathers fell to their surface and put their inhabitants amidst a blind cloud of brown murk.

Mother cried when she saw the bald patches on the backs of the land dwellers and the missing feathers lying askew over the shores. All fighting ceased as Mother listened to their stories. She still did not wish to divide the lands and sea and so decided on an alternative. If all the fighting had begun from differences of skin, she would have to unite them all under one. More agreeable to the animals was the fact that they would not have to forego their feathers, or scales, or fins, or fur, but that they could share in their alternative form that she called 'people.'

When all the animals stood upright for the first time wearing the skin of people, they celebrated. With the common tongue and hands of people they could come together as no other form had ever allowed them. They shared a language, and learned to love most what they had never been able to do, and danced. But the dancing did not last, since to be of people was only one of two forms, and they were still just as much animal as they were people. Old differences arose and new battles were fought over them.

The wolf came to mother again and repeated his plea:

'Divide the waters and the lands so that there can be no more arguing over who has the most.'

Mother frowned at the wolf and said, 'You who has come to speak out for all, will be the most distrusted of all.' Yet she considered wolf's words and broke apart the lands, which in turn, divided the seas.

One result she had not considered was the weather and how the shape of the land would affect the lives of the dwellers. Some braved cold weather; others desert and mountains, while others still almost drowned in the heavy rains. She thought each land piece could hold the same number and type of animal, but she had miscalculated, and some died when they could not withstand the changes.

Mother wept as more became sick, or hungered, or over-exhausted in harsh lands. She thought many more animals would be lost as the land fought for stability. Then those animals that appeared to be struggling the most with their survival became people and were able to cope with the changes much more easily. Mother was happy to be able to look upon the survivors.

As a consequence, the animals and people who could sustain their form went on doing so and forgot that they had each possessed a second skin. Between the coming people and animals, their relationship still lacked peace. Their ways of life grew more and more distant until the bond they had shared as the animal people was lost. Although fights continued to arise because of their differences, people and animals no longer strove for complete division among their kinds and settled for coexistence."

Lying on his back, Achak stared at the ceiling from his pillow. He moved one hand out from under his head to raise up the pendant that had remained against his chest. His eyes traced around the silver edges of the arrowhead while his mind tossed over the similarities between the animal people and Hybrids. What if not all "animals" had been forced to give up their human forms and likewise "the people" of some lands were able to keep their alternative forms? He knew the answer was a Hybrid, what remained of the animal people. That was what he believed in. It was his only explanation for what he was now.

But even with a cultural understanding, he didn't know what to do about this nature. He had the Coming People for his family and could not decide how, if at all, he would begin to tell them about Hybrids.

Day 11, Thursday

Nudged and shook, Achak opened his eyes never realizing they had closed for the night.

"Achak?" He heard Tehya's voice and blinked a few times to bring her into focus. "Someone's here to see you."

He looked at his alarm clock and saw that it was already nine in the morning. He would normally have already been awoken for school, but he supposed Grandpa had made up some excuse as to why Achak needed to stay home and recover.

"Mother earth to Achak, you have a visitor," Tehya said again impatiently.

"What? Who?"

"I don't know, but he won't leave. I already tried slamming the door on him."

Achak shuttered at the thought of a guest being so un-welcomed. Would Manu or Coral have come? He ran out to see.

Still wearing his previous day's clothes, he headed straight to the front door and swung it open.

"Lapidar?"

"Can I come in?" the wolf asked gruffly. "You have quite the suspicious household. Have you told them?"

"No."

The answer Lapidar would have preferred was indicated by his frown.

"I didn't expect to see you again so soon."

"Nor I you, but we have new things to consider."

Achak opened the door wide enough for Lapidar to enter and gestured for him to have a seat on the couch. "Is everything okay?" seemed like the considerate thing to ask.

"Turn on your TV and find out." Lapidar swept into the living room with a fierce breeze trailing off his browncoat.

Tehya moved away from the coffee table set by the couch and took the armchair across the room.

"Why aren't you in school?" Lapidar growled at her.

She narrowed her eyes at him.

"What about the news?" Achak pushed on for more details.

"You were seen!"

Achak quickly grabbed for the TV remote on the coffee table and searched for any news station. SoCal News, or SCN, had an aerial view of Domestica from on their news copters and were talking about Manu's facility and a speech he had given earlier that morning. Then he distinctly heard the headlines "Sabertooth Tiger sighting in Los Angeles."

"There still have been no further sightings of the primeval feline in these parts of the city," a live reporter said from her field location on the downtown streets of Los Angeles.

The cameraman filmed sidewalks of casual shoppers and busy intersections.

"What we do know," the reporter continued without her face in the spotlight, "is that Manu Firdaus, founder and president of Domestica, an animal sanctuary for endangered species, is taking full responsibility for the creature at large. He is looking for anyone with any information and cautioning locals against approaching the beast, which is an obvious threat to anyone who draws too near. But the real question on everyone's mind out here is how on earth did a Sabertooth Tiger come into the city, or into this century for that matter? For an answer to this question, I turn things back to you, Brett, in the studio."

"And we're back in the studio with exclusive coverage of Mr. Firdaus's explanation for these strange reports." Brett Pryson's jaunty voice took over. "Sabertooth Tiger at large! Scientists are baffled by the reports coming in and eye witness accounts of one of history's—prehistory's—most fascinating creatures to walk the earth since the dinosaurs. But one man has the explanation for the colossal feline. The man behind the behemoth's re-entrance into the world: Manu Firdaus of the world-renowned animal sanctuary, Domestica. We turn now to our video coverage of that report."

Achak stared in horror at the television as Manu's face filled the screen. He hardly saw the leaps in footage between Manu and the photographic stills of himself in Sabertooth Tiger skin, but the words would replay in his ears for hours after the film bite had ended:

"When I started Domestica, I set out with one goal in mind, to restore the numbers of any species that dwindled close to extinction. But in that purpose, I found a curiosity to perhaps rediscover in nature what I thought had been lost to the world—to the eyes of man—forever.

"Everyday, we are making discoveries of new species: some in the deepest parts of the oceans; others, in the densest tangles of the jungle. In my quest to put an end to extinction, I also sought a means of reversing the bind it had taken on many a prosperous species. I sought to track down the beings that had all but fallen from the ends of the earth."

"Yeah, that's one way of looking at the west coast," Achak remarked in the middle of the speech, unable to contain his rage.

Manu's voice continued regardless of Achak's off the air rants. His tone was rapidly becoming more illustrious as he spoke.

"And so, I am not ashamed of the comments that have been made about my facility, but rather, I am pleased by the shock that has gripped the nation... and soon the world. For when I set out to rediscover a banished life form, I tracked down every rumor and every myth and every urban legend right down to the tales of the Loch Ness, and I stand here today to tell you that I found what I went in search of. And the first of all extinct beings to reenter our world is a Sabertooth Tiger, a being that has been missing from our bestiaries for more than 11,000 years."

Brett Pryson's face came back on the television and Achak shut it off, then immediately shot his concerns toward Lapidar.

"You think he'll look for me here?" Achak fought not to move his eyes so hurriedly over to Tehya.

"It's a possibility," Lapidar answered gravely. "But it's probably best that he doesn't find you here."

"You found me."

"Yes, but I mean Manu won't want to get anyone else involved if he can avoid it. He's already facing inquiries by the Bred HyCouncil for Domestica operations. The newscasters aren't going to be the only one's asking him how a Sabertooth Tiger appears and then disappears."

"So where do we go now?" Achak took a deep breath of the problems that lay ahead.

"You're not leaving again, are you?"

Achak was cut short of his answer by Tehya standing at the kitchen corner and looking in on the living room. Her eyes were relentlessly pressed into Achak's.

As if only realizing there was someone else in the room, her next gaze she fixed on Lapidar.

"Who're you? And what's with the clothes? Are you Achak's spirit guide?"

"No, he is not my *spirit guide,*" Achak cracked with sarcasm. "He's a friend."

"Spirit guide?" Lapidar cut in.

Achak ignored him. "I won't be gone long." But even Achak did not believe his promise. Forced into Tehya's narrowed eyes, Achak's emotions swelled inside of him as well. "What do you want? Would you rather me lie?"

"I wanted my brother, but I guess he's not here." Tehya reignited the fire between them.

"No, or at least not for long."

"So you are leaving again!" she cried. "Why? What's so important that you can't include your family? You're going off to do something bad, aren't you?"

"Woah," Lapidar intercepted. "You seem like a bright girl. You should know your brother better than that—than to think the worst of him."

Tehya looked off to the side, then back.

Lapidar redirected the conversation. "And what's all this stuff about spirit guides?"

"Grandpa's stories." Achak brushed the question aside.

"They're not just stories!" Tehya yelled. "Their legends. And they were once the beliefs of a proud race."

Achak didn't have the nerve to argue with Tehya after hearing Grandpa retell his version of Creation. The story was all too similar to the Hybrid's existence.

Next, Tehya turned to Lapidar, ready to yell at him too. "A spirit guide is a person or animal that leads his charge through a journey of enlightenment and helps him seek knowledge and wisdom, but none of which has happened in Achak's case."

"Oh," Lapidar said, making Achak want to crack out in laughter. "Well, if that's all it is, then, yes, I'm him, or it. I hope that I haven't disappointed you, little lady. Am I what you would expect?"

"You're not animal," she said straight off. "And you're not very smooth talking."

"Yes, well wolves generally tend not to be."

"Wolves?" Tehya raised an eyebrow and looked to Achak, who was too busy gaping at Lapidar to give her any regard. "You're the most hairless wolf I've ever seen." She pursued Lapidar for more information.

"You've seen wolves?" Lapidar returned cleverly.

"Yes, well, you know what I mean."

"Alright. But I can't very well follow my—um, charge if I walk around like that, so I have to borrow the skin of my brother... kin."

"So you're telling me that you can take on a wolf's form?" Tehya made sure that she had understood Lapidar correctly.

"I most certainly can," Lapidar said with a broad grin.

"Prove it." Tehya smiled back.

Both challengers thought they had the better of each other, but only Achak seemed to know who was really on top.

"NO!!!" he screamed and ran over to grab Lapidar's arm. "Don't show her!"

"Why not?" He pulled out of Achak's grip.

"Because it could get her involved." Achak still spoke with the strangle of his heartbeat caught in his throat. "Please. Let's just go."

Lapidar looked at him sadly, scaling every contour, then he turned to Tehya with the same sorry expression.

Her eyes wide, she was looking terrorized from one to the other, not sure whether she had understood them at all.

"Please excuse us, little lady," Lapidar said to her. "I do hope I have the chance to meet with you again soon."

He went first to the door and held it open for Achak.

Standing on the front step, Achak grabbed the knob to close the door behind him. He gave one last look at Tehya who remained standing in the same place and said, "Goodbye, little flower." Hating himself for leaving her so paralyzed, he marched across the lawn without following the paved path to the driveway. At the corner, he met up with Lapidar and followed him down the street.

"Did you bring the car?"

"Yes, but hush," Lapidar whispered. "Let's just go."

Ignoring the order, Achak whispered back. "Where? To your place."

"No, we face Manu in his own backyard. That's why I don't want you staying here."

-●○●○●-

12
Scavenging Resources

Domestica was perched on one of the many "emerald" hills that rippled through the San Diego county. The kennels being the only landmark visible to her from above the sanctuary, Sirena landed near the stone walls. It was one jungle clearing that she could easily glide her wings through without clipping them on a branch or becoming entangled in the vines. Some orchards were nearby and Sirena walked up to the first apple tree and picked out a fruit. She did not think Manu would appreciate her taking without permission, but she savored that first bite even more knowing that Manu would not approve.

"Shame I didn't poison those!" A voice hissed from behind.

Sirena turned around and saw Dr. Coral stepping out of the trees. She took another bite of the apple and crunched it loudly for him to see the red particles on her tongue.

"Is it meaningful that a serpent should appear before me under an apple tree?" Sirena chimed. "It's why you hate him, isn't it?"

"Who?"

"Man-ew."

"No," Coral answered, but Sirena saw the balls of his pupils shrink. Then his hand withdrew from his coat pocket and he pointed a tranquilizer at her. "But don't ever let me find you around my film shootsss or factories or ssso help me, you'll wind up in my lab as a tessst sssubject worssse than Manu, underssstand?"

The trigger finger tightened closer to his hand. "You want evidenssce to present to Manu, then you may jussst have to demonssstrate the effectsss of HydroMaxss to him insssteead."

Coral's spectacles were ready to slide off his nose as he gazed at Sirena with two diamond pupils. Sirena threw the apple and knocked the tranquilizer out of his hand. Her talons closed around both collars of his labcoat and she was upon him.

"Fool!" she shrieked in his face. "What do I care?"

Coral was caught and not listening. "Why don't you tell Manu?" he spat. "I'm sure he'd love to hear about it. He's out to sssave endangered ssspecies and I'm trying to make the human racsse into one."

Allowing the fibers of his shirt to tear, Coral tried to bend over for his tranquilizer, but Sirena held and shook him. Two fangs extended from Coral's mouth and Sirena pushed him away, releasing his labcoat before he could spit any venom on her. He lost his balance and fell into the thicket.

Sirena stood and laughed over him. "Oh, I'm not entirely in doubt to your scheme. I look forward to munching on the number of human carcasses it will leave for me. For me and my kind, I mean. Scavengers, you know."

Coral stared at her silently in his fallen position. His pupils danced in and out of focus. Sirena stayed silent for the moment, but Coral said nothing as he stood up and began to wipe his lenses clean with the sleeves of his coat. In a nonchalant way, he appeared to be ignoring Sirena. Any moment, he would turn his back and walk towards the kennels.

"I have a plan to retrieve the smilodon," Sirena blurted before her meeting lost all purpose.

Coral's eyes flickered but then a shadow came over them that dulled his interest.

"Why not use the Jacks?" he remarked as though responding to an invitation.

"They're not allowed outside. And besides, I can't carry two jackals with my set of wings?"

"Carry?" Coral mused with intrigue.

"Flying is essential. I need to keep my eyes on the duel master," Sirena explained vaguely.

"Duel masssster?" Coral inquired further and Sirena could not help but broaden her grin as she lullied over the details, which Coral had all but demanded.

"I get tired of these extended life expectancies. Humans get older and older, not dying as often as they should and what's a vulture to eat? They age, they overpopulate, and I can't even bank on the possibility that they'll all grow intolerable of their bustling streets and compact parking spaces to just go mad and start killing each other. Not even with nuclear warfare can I hope to be left an uncontaminated corpse to feed upon.

"We scavengers get a raw deal—literally. So you see, I'm in favor of shortening their numbers. And I know that in the mass quantaties that they'll drop because of HydroMax, there won't be enough gravediggers to keep up with the incoming bodies. I imagine that the pits will look something like those of the Black Plague or of the Nazi concentration camps."

Only minutes away from home and into the downtown sector of San Diego, Achak squeezed his sweaty palms around his jeans. Sitting, tense in the passenger seat, he had remained silent through the entire drive. They would be pursuing Manu, but Achak could only imagine what a face-to-face encounter would result in. With only himself and Lapidar, they were weak on numbers. Achak wondered about the sort of fighting that would be involved with the encounter and he saw a Hybrid's method of sparring—of bared fangs and the thunderous slashing of claws. His ears filled with the sounds of growls and snarls echoing to him across time. And he could not stop the shaking in his legs no matter how tightly he clutched the material around them.

"Where are we going?" he asked again, although it could not have been clearer to him that Lapidar meant to take some immediate counteraction against Manu.

"We're going to speak with some of the Bred HyCouncil." Lapidar spoke in absolutes. "I think it's about time they knew about you and started to consider how they will treat your case. It will take some of the pressure off you when it comes to adjusting to life... as a Hybrid." His words were assuring, but his jaw muscles did not relax as he moved them.

Speaking up again, Lapidar added, "I don't know what help they'll be against Manu. They, the Bred HyCouncil, I mean." Lapidar hesitated. "I've never been able to turn to them myself and I don't know how they respond to prominence, but I don't suppose they'll arrest you for making a report, or at least, not after everything else you'll tell them."

Achak looked nervously over to Lapidar's side, afraid of what he would be expected to do.

"And you'll have to go into their station alone. I'm afraid I can't come in with you, if you can understand that."

Achak nodded, but his better instincts would have told him to run while he had the chance.

"This is it." Lapidar parked his little silver Accord in front of a stately building. It looked just like a city council center with stone carvings along the walkway. Achak glanced across a grassy lawn and caught sight of the separate building attachments with pillars between the arched walkways. An American flag was mounted on a pole mid-field. There appeared to be memorials engraved on the walls and sidewalks with the exception that there was no sign posted to tell anyone what business they had circled upon.

Achak walked up the main steps beneath a low portico to the door, which he hesitated to open in thinking that he might need to wait for the doormen. Lapidar had not given him any special instruction so he tested the handle to see if it was locked and proceeded to walk in. Nobody stopped him. Achak thought he had stepped into a private bank. There were phone dispatch personnel waiting for calls at their desks. Their office remained separated from Achak by glass windows. The furthest end of the room was lined with a counter where several clerks waited at their stations in a narrow area set between the wall. Achak went up to one of these individuals and began speaking.

"Excuse me."

"How can I help you, sir?" The clerk looked dimly upon Achak as though nothing he heard could come as a surprise to him.

Maybe his story would, Achak thought nervously, but then he recognized the clerk's features, the young curly haired detective that had interrogated Achak inside his own home. There was mutual recognition as the clerk's lips folded when he regarded Achak thoroughly over the counter. He looked ready to speak to Achak more tryingly when he was cut off by the sound of gunfire.

The door banged open across the hall. Most everyone turned around for no more than a glance, but Achak stared horror-stricken as two officers came in like dog catchers with a mongrel noosed at the end of their two sticks. The fox, orange and white-bellied, was putting up a good fight and trying to get the officers to bang rods. They had to stop in the center to try to regain control over the animal.

"Brady, you've deceived children for the last time with your follow-the-leader gimmick," the officer on the left began speaking while he wrestled with the pole. "Stop luring them away from campsites and getting them lost. I don't know what you intended to do in San Diego, but that last child in Yosemite died."

In a blink of an eye, the offices no longer battled with a fox but a full-grown man. Their poles went up as the man with vibrant orange hair stooped upright.

He was young and short, younger than Achak, and his face was only slightly freckled around the nose. There was nothing disturbing at all about his pale features except the proud grin he wore for the officers.

"Aw, Roy," Brady's slender voice spoke up to the left officer. "It warn't but in my nature."

"Then let me introduce you to my new partner, the hound. Silent and certainly square-jawed, the other office stood. "I'm sure you'll remember how the story goes," Roy continued.

"That ain't right," Brady pouted and began pulling the nooses over his head.

Roy, followed by the hound shortly after, pulled out his revolver and aimed it at the quite foxy Brady, who raised his hands into the air.

Before Achak could hear the remainder of the arrest, the clerk cried out a very angry, "Sir?"

Jilted back into focus, Achak did not even wait to apologize to the detective behind the counter before racing into his story.

"Yes, look, I haven't been a Hybrid for very long. Just over a week. But this man, well I don't know what species he is—Manu Firdaus, I mean, forced me into animal form, but that's not the issue anymore since I know how to change back and forth between species. But two problems: Manu is still after me and I don't know what his plans are, but secondly, I'm supposed to be extinct."

"Morning, Hunter," the one outspoken officer, Roy, greeted Achak's clerk as he passed by. He let the fox, Brady, continue onward through another door led by the hound. "How's the early shift," he asked formally but after looking over Achak asked more directly: "Who's this?"

Hunter opened and closed his mouth taken aback by the question. "Achak Twinfang," he answered at last and raised an eyebrow. "Says he has a complaint to make against Manu Firdaus." Hunter glanced at Achak before continuing. "Says Manu changed him into something, bu—"

"I'll see him," Roy said decidedly.

Achak looked at the peek-lined black hair of the officer and his sharp pointed noise and wondered whether he should feel entirely better off with this one-on-one invitation.

Lost for words, the clerk stuttered, then announced more clearly: "Surely you have other claims to handle? The boy has only just walked in."

"Yes," Roy expressed himself with more finality, "but I would like to speak with the boy. Surely you know about all of the inquiries on Manu's discrepancies."

Hunter nodded and said, "Take him." His hand indicated that Achak should follow the officer into the back room.

Achak stepped into a hall where a lane of private offices were set like picture frames in a walkway surrounded by glass windows. He saw no more of the hound and the fox, but in walking around one of the corners, could not see through the dark tinted glass of some frames.

Roy led him feet from a blacked out window and stopped in front of another private office. The window upon the door was transparent enough to see the stacks of papers and files upon a desk and bookshelves in the office.

"Come in." Roy opened the door and directed Achak before he could read the nameplate. Luckily there was another one propped on the desk and Achak read the title: Detective R. Hutchinson. "Sit down," Roy continued his curt tone of instruction.

Achak took the nearest seat in front of the desk, while Roy walked behind him to open a window before taking the business seat.

"Manu has discrepancies?" Achak asked while remembering what Lapidar had said earlier about the Bred HyCouncil and with Manu facing something of an inquiry.

"Our investigations are not open to public hearing." Roy sat down and cleared away a few papers that were laid out in front of him until he had nothing but clear desk space.

"But if my information is somehow related," Achak began to argue.

"That remains to be determined." Roy leaned back in his chair and kept Achak in focus. "Let's begin from the beginning. Who are you?"

"My name is Achak Twinfang and I was once, as of last Tuesday, only human." Achak stated, putting what he deemed to be his two most important characteristics out first. "I am a local of San Diego and come from a long line of Native American decent that migrated from the North. I suppose, the most relevant thing I can say about my lineage is that I am Sabertooth Tiger."

"Pedigree," Roy said blandly.

"What?"

"The appropriate term for your animal ancestry is not 'lineage' it is 'pedigree.'"

"Whatever." Achak could not believe how lightly the detective was treating the matter. He could care less what the appropriate terminology was for talking about his ancestors if his present situation was going to be ignored.

"Ajack."

"Achak"

"Let me make one thing clear. If you're going to walk into my office exclaiming 'whatever' to everything we discuss, then maybe you should come back when you're ready to consider things more seriously."

"I'm sorry, sir."

"That's better."

Achak turned his head away before the detective could notice his scowl. He stared out a window beside Roy's desk where bushes lined the lower half while further out a courtyard of pathways led to separate archways. Meanwhile, Achak was considering the open window behind him and whether it would prove necessary to have to use it.

"Do you have a friend outside?" Roy guessed correctly, his tone polite and inquiring.

"No. I just can't be sure I have a friend inside either."

"Hmm, well, I guess I'll have to work on that." He put on a mild apology. "Now what were you saying earlier about Manu having changed you into something?" Even in the detective's deep voice, the words sounded stupid.

"Look." Achak shook away his frustration. "All this talk you've been hearing about a sabertooth tiger running loose in L.A., it's all true."

"We have yet to locate the beast."

"It's me."

Roy folded his arms, bending his chair back further.

"You realized there are penalties for causing a public disturbance."

"I didn't do it on purpose!" Achak's voice rose more out of fear than anger as he tried to defend himself. He had the alarming vision of being arrested on the spot and placed inside a prison for Lapidar to bail him out.

"Why are you confessing this?" Roy stared at his desk phone as it began to ring with a single red light blinking on one of the extensions.

"I haven't confessed my guilt to anything yet," Achak said in a low and steady voice. "I can hardly be held responsible for my transformations if I have no control over them."

"What do you mean?" Roy's chair came up a notch or two.

"I mean, I'm not supposed to be Hybrid. I was human until the day I met Manu and Domestica."

"How did that happen?"

This time Achak heard the amusement in the detective's tone and knew that his next answer would be treated as something more ludicrous.

"I was kidnapped."

The phone on Roy's desk rang for a second time, but again the officer let it continue unanswered.

"It's true." Achak wanted to get his point across before the phone could ring a third time. He knew that Lapidar had a better sense of how things were running on a time-basis and would try to reach him if things did not go as smoothly as they had planned. But before all of Achak's efforts could go to waste, he was determined to have someone hear out his story.

"You can check with the San Diego police department. I had a missing person's report go out on me."

"And what will that tell us?" Roy raised his eyebrows in surprise. "You told police that you were kidnapped by Manu Firdaus?"

"No, I told them I ran away for a week."

"A week? Did Manu hold you for so long? You were kidnapped and yet I thought I saw you hanging out in The Basement and drinking with friends three days ago."

Achak dropped back in his chair. The facts were proving too hard to swallow as he tried to connect all the pieces together. Then he noticed the coat rack on the wall and saw to his own disbelief the familiar navy tailcoat Lapidar had pointed out to him in the bar. The phone rang a third time and Roy hit the speaker button.

"If I transmogrified for you now to prove what I am," Achak argued.

"I would arrest you on the spot—hello, Hunter," Roy said over the loud speaker.

"You have a visitor," Hunter's voice returned. "Mr. Lapidar Gray." Achak shifted uneasily, but his movement had not diverted Roy's attention away from the phone.

"Who?"

"A Lapidar Gray," Hunter repeated no longer sounding so sure of himself.

"Alright, I'll be out to see in a minute." He stood up and began walking around the desk toward the door. Opening it, he paused before leaving. "Lapidar?" he repeated under his breath, then shot a back glance toward Achak who was edging his chair away from the desk. "Hold it!" His shout was set free in the hall. But too late, Achak sprouted fur over his skin and leapt out the open window. He heard more shouts follow his escape, but he had safely reached the Mansfield Arch, returned human, and walked with the pedestrians down a block. The Accord pulled over for him at the corner, and Lapidar drove them both out of the vicinity.

"Not so well, eh?" he said.

"No," Achak sulked.

"I was amazed you got to speak to a detective."

"It wasn't by my request," Achak explained with a sour disclaimer. "He invited me. It was Mr. Tailcoat from The Basement."

"You serious?" Lapidar smirked. "Maybe we're not so lost after all."

"How do you mean?" Achak pulled hard on the door handle to force it closed all the way. "He wanted to arrest me on the spot. Thinks I intentionally caused a public disturbance."

"Yes, but don't you see. Manu's already made a claim about you and even though L.A. was out of his jurisdiction, as a San Diego detective, the tailcoat was close to the scene the day it happened. He'll have his personal reasons for wanting to look into the matter further."

"Personal?" Achak put the question out doubtfully. "The only thing Detective Hutchinson seemed adamant about was arresting me."

"You transmogrified in front of him, didn't you?"

"I had the option not to?" Achak said wryly. "And besides, I'm not sure it's a good idea to have the Bred HyCouncil coming after us among all the other bounty men."

"First of all, they're not after us, they're after you," Lapidar corrected. "And secondly, there's nothing better than putting two sides at odds with each other." Lapidar gazed up at the higher levels of buildings while he drove. "With some luck, both sides will impede the other's plans."

Achak began to mellow with the drive. His eyes skimmed lazily around the familiar businesses of San Diego's Gaslamp District. All the downtown buildings were as gray as the overcast sky, but the displays of their windows were full of color. He spotted a couple of wig shops with their retro displays of hot pinks and purples around the empty mannequin faces. Then he saw the crimson length of Sirena's. It was a heart beat before he remembered that Sirena didn't wear a wig, but colored it for a natural look.

"Aren't there any bars around here?" Lapidar growled as he almost turned the wrong way down a one-way street.

"Lots of them," Achak shrugged.

"You know the kind I mean," Lapidar snapped. "Oh, forget it. I'll have to pull over to find one."

Achak came down the stairs of a parking structure and stepped onto the boulevard, looking from one end of the block to the other.

"How do you spot a Hybrid business?"

"Look for what you typically would not see around that type of business. And don't worry about the closed sign, they're most always open 24-hours."

"Alright, how about that place." Achak pointed to something called, "Down Under." Nothing around the letters or windows said what sort of business it was, but a small sign posted at the corner said, "Must have Mallard or Ugly Duckling membership."

"Good eye," Lapidar said. "I'm sure they won't be too happy about me going in, but I'll be back out with directions." He returned outside and pointed toward some construction zones. "Two blocks that way."

Under scaffolds of remodeling, the building they came to resembled a sloppily pieced together monument of popsicles sticks. Somewhere within the poster labeled walls that were collaged with advertisements, a single doorway led them into an active business. Of course, no one would have thought to walk in so trampled a place, whose architecture appeared less stable or operational than a woodpile.

Yet inside, Achak had stepped into a business with both the class of The Changeling and alcoholic provisions of The Basement.

Lapidar moved over to the left facing the bar, but Achak eyed longingly at the wooden panel to the right where a waitress was directing a customer to his seat at a restaurant section called *Reds and Greens.*

When he turned around to keep up with Lapidar, Achak ran shoulder long into a woman his age.

"Excuse me," he pardoned himself.

The girl, however, shrieked and for a moment, Achak thought he was being yelled at for bumping into her. Then he came to understand the commotion.

"Achak?"

He translated his name from her emotional outburst. Gaping at the woman his age, he recognized her by the violet designs of her blouse. Not only was she topped with roses, but Achak thought he could see the sparkling of body glitter below her neck and he knew that he had run face to face with Mariam.

Her name reached his lips with surprise and anguish. For the first time, he had found someone who was both his age and Hybrid.

As her eyes lit up to him, he thought the purple of her mascara had bled into her pupils. She was a stunning glitter of twilight with the incense of flowers.

"I didn't know you were a Hybrid!" The loneliness left Achak but then his own words backfired as he found Mariam staring back at him with a peculiar frown.

He had clearly given Mariam insight into his ignorance of Hybrids. Ignoring her boyfriend Marcus and his smirk, Achak proceeded directly into providing an explanation for his awkward comment.

"I guess, I don't come to these places often enough," he laughed. Then he looked at Marcus, who was not laughing, but standing with his arms folded and his head turned away. Mariam too had a look that was no where near smiling.

"I thought you were..." Mariam began, but she fell short of saying what was on her mind and Achak watched the changes in moods transition over her face. Startledness became concern—became relief—became joy.

"Have you been here all this time?" she hammered. "No one knew—I mean everyone was worried."

Marcus was the first to snort before Achak could begin to doubt Mariam's words. He knew that this "everyone" had to be an over-exaggeration.

"What do you mean by worried?" Achak aimed to carry on the conversation longer.

"I mean," she retraced her words, "That no one—not even the principal, Miss Kimberly, knows where you are. I had to give a witness statement telling her and police that I was the last person to see you on the café corner with that Sirena girl."

"You did what?" Both Achak and Marcus cried out. Then Marcus's eyes narrowed upon Achak and he jerked his head awkwardly away.

Mariam ignored both their responses.

"You've been gone for nearly two weeks. And there hasn't been so much as a feather seen of Sirena either."

This was probably true as far as Achak knew because, in fact, he knew nothing about the incident in which Mariam had vouched a ticket for Sirena to sit with her in a school production of *Romeo and Juliet.*

"I can't believe—You and her!" Mariam said with disgusted hypocrisy. "Whatever you see in a girl like that, I'm sure I don't want to know."

But Achak knew what kind of girl she was talking about—a vulture—and felt compelled to explain these accusations.

"Woah-ah!" Achak had to step back and take a glance at the bar to see how occupied Lapidar was being kept before he could justify his actions to Mariam. When he saw the back of the wolf sitting on a stool, he safely continued, "If you think Sirena and I..." Achak shuddered to finish. "I would never date—it was a mistake to even follow her. Had I not, I wouldn't be in the mess I'm in—"

Achak broke off, wondering how much he could or should tell Mariam about that day he had followed Sirena away from the WildCat Café. He found himself again watching Lapidar's backside at the bar and thought it best that he should tell Mariam as much as he dared while in, and not in absence of, the presence of an experienced mercenary.

Mariam was now gazing at him with as much suspicion furrowed over her brows as Achak wished he could redirect over to her boyfriend Marcus.

He regretfully sighed loud enough to be heard before becoming wary of how his careless words—sighs, groans, and all—could bring about more curiosity from the others. All the while, Achak was beginning to sense a mounting degree of distrust that had not been there when he had first bumped Mariam's shoulder. He was hesitant and Mariam and Marcus could sense that. Achak knew, as with all social situations, that the longer he tried to hide truth or deny it, the less patient the listeners would become and sooner or later they would make up an excuse of why they had to leave, and Achak didn't want his Hybrid classmates to leave.

He did not want to bore them with excuses and *changes of subject.* Not that it really mattered to him whether Marcus left—the guy was clearly a jerk—but Mariam, on the other hand, seemed nice and genuinely concerned about Achak's absence. However, there was Lapidar's feelings to consider as well, and Achak did not want the wolf upset with him for spilling the beans to some soft-spoken, cute-faced high school classmate—or however the wolf would choose to narrow-mindedly describe Mariam.

Speaking directly to her, Achak said very forth-coming and politely that: "I'd like to tell you, but maybe we should sit down." Achak avoided adding "together" to his invitation in Marcus's earshot. "Long story," he finished in a rush of breath.

Mariam's lips parted, but it was Marcus who answered first... and not with spoken words either.

Achak was thrown back by the force that had smashed into his chest. When he threw his arms out to shield himself, Marcus's fist cracked against his wrist.

The face of the boy that could call Mariam *his* was red from forehead to chin.

"Marcus!" Mariam shouted. "He didn't mean it *like that*!"

But there was no taking back Achak's words or talking Marcus down with an explanation. Achak could see that the gel-spiked black hair of Mariam's boyfriend had frilled out into raven-black feathers.

"Whatever you are, you should know better than to cross breed!" Marcus bellowed from the other side of his fists.

Achak raised his hands to block and to remain on the defensive side of the argument.

"What are you talking about?"

Hidden behind his arms, Achak could no longer read off the face of his attacker to know what was on Marcus's mind.

"Get off him!" Mariam shrieked and Achak could finally bring down his defenses while Mariam held one of Marcus's wrists back.

However, already the brief scuffle had caused enough of a scene to bring some behind-the-counter employees out onto the floor. Without looking, Achak could hear the squeaks of bar stools as some observers made their way over, which—without a doubt—included Lapidar among them.

"Achak?" he heard the familiar gruff voice call his name.

There was no more need to keep his eyes on Marcus, who by now would have noticed the amount of attention his fury had brought the three of them.

"I—" Achak began to explain.

"Forget it," Lapidar said. "I'm just grateful you didn't transmogrify."

Achak could not resist the slight urge to smile in relief as he mentally agreed that transmogrification was the worst counter-action he could have taken against Marcus, especially while in public domain.

How wrong he and the wolf both were, while in fact the worst case scenario had just stepped through the door while they both had their backs turned to reface the bar.

Employees too were making their way back behind the counters, and likewise customers who had gotten up to assist in the break-up of a fight were returning to their seats.

All peace was restored until Mariam let out another shriek. Achak turned sharply around. Expecting to catch Marcus by the fist, Achak's hands dropped when he saw that no one was racing towards him.

Falling in front of Mariam and raining down like a splash of confetti, black feathers drifted to the ground. Behind a layer of their sparkling downpour stood Sirena in their midst.

Lapidar growled beside Achak, but it was all over before any more transmogrifications could take place.

"Give this to Achak, messenger girl." And Sirena tossed an envelope Frisbee-like into Mariam's unready hands.

It fell to the floor for Mariam to pickup at which time Sirena became a shadow in the doorframe, seeming to disappear in the washout of light before anyone could think to do anything about it. They were all staring at the envelope.

"If I were you, I'd tear that up," Marcus said while standing off to the side—a distance that Achak could not explain by any boyfriend account. There was a smile on his face and he seemed generally amused for a guy who had just seen someone treat his girlfriend like the lowdown feathery plague-carrier of a messenger pigeon. No gentleman in the world would have just stood back and watched while his girlfriend was made to bow-down and pickup something another person had thrown at her.

Some boyfriend he was, Achak thought before putting his criticisms aside to attend to the letter that Sirena had delivered.

The envelope that was supposed to reach Achak's hands remained in Mariam's.

Achak took a couple of brave steps toward her, but stopped as he remembered the assault he had suffered only minutes ago while trying to be polite to Mariam.

He worried also that Mariam might be considering Marcus's words to have the letter torn apart, but her fingertips never whitened in so threatening a manner.

In her gaze over the envelope, Achak saw again the concern that only a woman of true kindness and caring could express so openly. Overriding his eagerness to wonder what Sirena could possibly have to write to him about, Achak wanted to relieve the envelope from Mariam's hands solely to take the pressure off the kinder of Hybrid classmates.

He took another step forward then froze to another one of Mariam's changes in expression.

"Liar!" The tears swelled in her eyes. "I actually went on a limb for you! And here you were all along! Safe and sound—AND BAR HOPPING!" she shrieked and threw the envelope at Achak's feet. With feather's surrounding her own face, she flew out the door with Marcus trailing after her so that Achak did not dare pursue.

Apart from any boyfriend barriers, Achak had Lapidar to prevent him from leaving the building. The wolf had already placed a hand on Achak's shoulder to stop him from behaving as rash as Mariam had. This gesture, along with the envelope at his feet, had reminded Achak of what should have been most important to him just now, and Achak wondered whether there would ever be another time in his life when friends (and family) could be the one thing that mattered most.

Achak bent down to retrieve the envelope and his hands trembled as he slid his finger between the fold to open it.

—●○●○●—

13
Fight or Flight

Lapidar and Achak shared a table at a restaurant in San Marino—the most prosperous Hybrid restaurant in L.A. County to be exact—125 miles from Reds and Greens—a distance that would have been easier to manage with a set of wings. Reading Lapidar's expression behind the candelabra, Achak confirmed, "You're still angry with me aren't you?"

"I don't have any right to be," he said, but he barely looked over the paper he was reading, where his temperament remained hidden behind the newsprint.

Achak slammed a fist on his fork and knife. "I should have been able to catch her!" he flustered. "And why are we here again?"

He was looking around at the tall crimson drapes of The Changeling. This time he hardly found any interest in the dancers. Their constant movement around the room and jingling costumes were distracting to him and he was becoming annoyed with the way they would sporadically shift between faces, from human to animal, a change that would make Achak jump if performed too close.

"Just relax," Lapidar said, but he himself took a few glances around the restaurant. "We're here because this is where Sirena's invitation told us to meet."

"And you're okay with that?" Achak bellowed. He could not believe Lapidar would allow them both to be led around on a game of note passing. "Why answer this invitation and not the werewolves'?"

"Because with the werewolves, I knew what they wanted," Lapidar snapped. "With Sirena, I can only guess."

"She could still be with Manu." Achak bared his teeth back.

"Good. Maybe she could take us to him." Lapidar fell back in his chair with a mad grin and Achak could see that he was serious with his words.

"Or him to us!"

"Then why not have brought him to us back there? Why ask to meet us alone? Look at it this way, Achak. Sirena's a mercenary. She goes for the greatest dollar amount and if it's a deal she's after, we'll hear it out. Decline it, if it's no good."

Achak turned his head away. "She just likes playing games," he muttered. He had not really expected to find comfort in Lapidar's words, but he did not expect to be made to feel so foolish by their implication.

Keeping his eyes away from the wolf, Achak caught those of a female dancer and soon had to remind himself how to blink.

She wore all leopard-print and had hair that possessed the same matching shades of brown and gold twined together. Across her chest, a vest was interlaced with leather straps. From somewhere behind her legs, a tail flicked and she dropped a few feathers from her waist belt. Then her green eyes flashed and Achak found himself again sitting in a chair across from Lapidar.

He gave up on the dancer's enchantment and stared around at all the other tables. Their occupants were all business personnel suited for interviews and clients. It was no wonder Achak felt out of place without a tie. Had it not been for the invitation and reservation, they would not have been seated until after three o'clock as walk-ins. The guest list was full and still there was no sign of Sirena.

"This isn't really her kind of place." Achak looked impatiently over to the red curtain where all arriving guests could be expected to walk through, but no one except for the raccoon-faced maitre d' ever seemed to peek his head in. The only suspicions came from the waiter who, each time he came around, tended to walk less and less patiently away from their table after having caught sight of their unopened menus. Meanwhile, Achak met glimpse by glimpse the white rings around the maitre d's eyes peering between the curtains, only this time the raccoon seemed to be calling to one of the dancers.

The nearest one, the leopardess Achak had been watching earlier, came to the curtain and put her face right up to the raccoon's. There was a brief exchange between their moving lips, then the raccoon's white-gloved hand came through the curtain and passed something over to the dancer. She closed her hand around it, then went back to dancing.

Lapidar gave an obnoxiously wide yawn. "Well, if she's gonna keep us waiting, I say we order." He opened the menu in front of him and scanned over his options.

Achak hardly cared what his finger pointed to when he gave the waiter his order. He knew it was under the pasta section, but could not recognize or pronounce half the seasonings, except for the mushrooms and red peppers. Were his appetite more savage and his nerves less jittery, he might have complained when the dish brought out to him resembled the form of salad more than any type of pasta. However, the bland noodles worked well to settle the leapfrogs in his stomach and he was able to think better with some food inside him.

Achak did his best to ignore the repugnant glances Lapidar shot at his plate and instead went back to combing the other tables with his eyes. With each talking pair, Achak could not help but imagine the next table would hold that one isolated individual, who would have her glowing eyes fixed upon him. He knew the plates would be cleared away soon and then it would be time for Sirena to show herself.

A whistling made Achak turn back around where he found Lapidar wearing a broad grin and just staring at him.

"Excuse me?" a voice peeped and Achak stared dumbstruck into the leopardess's green eyes.

Her cinnamon locks were even more beautifully wrapped around her face up close. Achak thought he could smell the sugared perfume that held the curls.

She could not have been older than Achak, but as she passed him the note that was in her hand, her mouth moved inaudibly. Then she skirted away from him as though out of embarrassment.

Achak looked down at the folded paper she had handed him and began to open it. The edges were bent and there were creases where several of its folds had been undone. Achak's hands were shaking but that did not stop him from noticing that the paper had been formerly read and tampered with.

He scanned the lines quickly then lurched over the table. Barely able to hold himself with his one arm, he tried to lean his head against the rounded edge for support, while the tablecloth moved under his fingers. Wherever the note had gone, it was no longer in his sight, but from somewhere above Lapidar projected its message.

Dear primordial friend,
If you ever want to see your sister again, you will come to the Beasts of Burden by eight o'clock.

--The Graveler

"Sounds like our friend, the mole," Lapidar commented.

When Achak finally came up for air, he had no idea where he was to understand why the waiter was asking if he was through with his plate. His eyes strayed to the least of complex items in front of him, which for him came as the few silent and endless moments that he spent watching drop after drop slide down his cup. The damp surface around his glass became a darker red than the tablecloth. Once Achak understood that it was the water creating the illusion of a shadow, he spoke up.

"So where is this place?" His voice came out steadier than he felt.

"Let's find out," Lapidar said easily and turned around in his chair to find someone, "Hmm..." he mumbled in mild disappointment. "Your dancer seems to have gotten away from us. I'll just ask the waiter."

Feet below them, the café cart rumbled; but they were on the deck above it, sitting in the unreserved seating of the Amtrak. Occupying the window seat, Achak looked out and upon the Oceanside where waves crashed against the sandy beaches.

"I think the car will be okay at the station," Lapidar muttered to himself. He made frequent glances in Achak's direction, but Achak was in no mood for talking. If there was something to be discussed, it could wait until after Achak's little sister had been returned to him.

Disregarding Achak, Lapidar continued to carry his one-sided conversation.

"Ingenious plan." Lapidar remarked "I don't think I gave them enough credit for it. They sent us from San Diego to L.A. and back again. All the time, they knew where we'd be and controlled our arrival time by leading us out of the city. We have no time to plan because by the time we get back to San Diego, it'll almost be time for you to meet them."

Achak interrupted his banter with a fierce chuffle from his throat. "Maybe if we hadn't wasted an hour at the metro station!"

Lapidar cracked out with laughter. "Then we'd be spending an extra hour in traffic. No, this way is better. At least it gives us some time to relax and think."

"Think?" Achak growled. "I don't want to think! I want to rip that sh-shyster apart!" He came very close to swearing on the train, but stopped himself short in light of the other passengers, especially the children. Falling back into his seat, Achak stared out the window. While his insides were on fire, he knew he could not keep his eyes from flashing their green and black diamonds, which he had to keep hidden.

"Just don't go gett'n yourself motion sickness looking out that thing," Lapidar said gruffly and readjusted his own seat. "I like your sister so don't go letting her down." He bowed his head and pretended to fall asleep.

As they left the station from downtown San Diego and began walking Broadway Street, Achak simplified what he saw of the tower businesses into a manageable conversation.

"So worst comes to worst, you're there, right?" Achak's brief laughter shook. He did not know how else to act positive except to try to be funny.

Lapidar grimaced. "If the worst comes to you, then, no. But for your sister, I'll be there."

Achak waited on a street corner of San Diego's downtown metropolitan while Lapidar went on to check out a few places. Unless Achak knew how to recognize a Hybrid, there was no use in the two of them splitting up to double their search. He had the useless task of standing watch, but as a postman his mind was not kept busy enough to prevent him from making a nervous count of the passing minutes. Achak thought he should have arrived at the Beasts of Burden at least an hour beforehand, however, that hour was quickly coming upon him. It had to be at least after 6pm and they were still no closer to finding the place they were to meet at.

"I'm going to circle around these two blocks," Lapidar finished telling Achak when both sides of a one-way street called "Wyvern" turned up a series of closed bars, none of which could be the Beasts of Burden.

Left alone on the corner, Achak had no watch on the hour, but felt the value of each precious minute as he waited for Lapidar. He had the entire voice of nature telling him that he would not make it to the Beasts of Burden on time. From whatever side of him the jungle of towers let up, the wind blew upon him a cold draft to prick at his arms and cheeks. He felt like a flock of buzzards were tearing away at pieces of visible flesh and pecking apart his certainties.

Achak kept his eyes west where the sky was beginning to turn red. Its devil skin was high enough to be seen over the buildings and not just between or as a gory reflection in their windows. But the colors stopped short of Achak and met the gray flat clouds looming overhead. High above, the clouds scattered and drifted so that every now and then a darker shadow would float across Achak. There remained patches of sunlight, but his corner was the only one denied any illuminations of hope.

The people passing by were as invisible to him as he was to them. And despite the drifts and heavy shuffling of feet that came over the occasional crosswalk, Achak could not be touched by their presence.

He wanted to tilt his head back and look up at the sky, but was afraid of letting his eyes roll into his head where they might not return.

Through a torrent of rushing air, Achak's cheek was slashed. With a pang, the same shoulder dropped under a new load, which rolled down his back like a piece of metal cord.

People around him stopped moving and stared. Achak put his hand near the shoulder, where another weight had perched itself. His fingers tapped the spot where fire rose. There he felt the talons of a bird digging into his flesh. On his cheek, the heat of another's breath kept him from turning his head.

"Sirena," he whispered low enough so that no one around except for him and the vulture could hear.

Red and crinkled, Sirena coiled her long neck so that her head was aligned with Achak's eye. The blackness of her beak arched into a hook that threatened to rob Achak of daylight with a single jab into his socket.

Achak sensed a grim smile where the beak curved into the red creases of her face. Then where Sirena could not have launched herself, Achak's left calf singed as a needle struck into it. He cried out and lurched himself forward, but Sirena did not release her grip upon his rocking body. His left leg dragged, then he unmistakably saw, the black, red, and yellow stripes of a serpent roll away from his feet and slither into a sewer gutter.

Warmth crept up from its bite melting Achak's knee in place, but he could not fall while the vulture on his shoulder opened a wide span of wings. Sirena forced everyone around Achak to clear away and pulled him nearer to the building where he could not be seen by the crowd. There, Sirena released Achak's shoulder, now as excruciating as the pain crawling up his leg, and took her human form. She whisked herself immediately under Achak's left arm.

Acting like a crutch, Sirena dragged Achak along the sidewalk. She kept his weight on her. Helplessly, he left her arm around his waist as the rush of poison spilled into his midsection and, like the backwards drumming of a waterfall, reached into his heart. He thought he would lose consciousness but only went down in truth when his body was shoved into a doorway. Unable to catch himself, he fell right through the entrance where his collapse never broke until he hit the floor.

Feeling another set of talons grab onto his shoulder, Achak was dragged across the empty shop space.

The windows were boarded to keep people from breaking their glass panes while no security devices were in place, and the only misty light came from a gas lamp that had been propped upon a short ladder. Some refurbishment appeared to be under process with bits of sandpaper lying about and portions of the walls stripped of paint.

Unfortunately, Achak never quite got a grip on all of his surroundings. His eyes bleared the sight of his abductors as the poison finished running its course through his body. Seemingly dying, Achak found no other matter of more importance to focus on than his heavy strains of breath.

Sirena nudged him with her foot. "Don't worry. If you were dying, I'd still be circling you."

Finding it hard to move his lips in so much pain, Achak could not comment between her words. He looked at the outline of Dr. Coral who still had the draping of a labcoat by which he could be recognized no matter how dim the lighting. His glasses too gave off a hostile glint by the gaslamp and produced pointed shadows across his face.

Sirena laughed. "You were so easy to trap. The smallest threat to your family had you rushing back down here."

"Where's my sis'er?" Achak ground the words between his teeth.

"Still with the mole, I believe."

"At the Beasts of Burden," Achak's teeth clattered. "I have to go there. I have to—"

"And what do I care what happens to your sister?" Sirena's voice was surmounted with an anger and impatience that Achak had never heard before. "I set the whole thing up. I gave the duel master your address after his first encounter with you. He seemed so set on having you fight for him that I knew he would go to some extreme measures to get to you."

Her voice rose with pride, while the crimson lips broadened her face with shear delight.

"Not even Manu could have laid out so clever a plan. There wasn't even a need to get anyone's hands dirty since it could all be dealt with by the duel master."

"Have to get 'her!" Achak gasped. He tried to raise his body, but like a turtle, remained feebly on his backside.

"As if you could in the ssstate you're in now." Dr. Coral took amusement in his diagnosis.

Turning himself over, Achak tore the skin inside his throat with a pained gasp. His eyes were clamped as the water burned from their corners. He raised his knee and dragged himself a few paces-worth on one elbow.

"You realize there's only one of two ways we can shut you up?" Dr. Coral carried on. The clicking of his feet made slow progression towards Achak. "We could—"

"Kill you," Sirena finished. "Here and now," she added more hungrily, stepping on Achak's hand.

"But then Manu would be miserable without his pet sssabertooth." Dr. Coral took over again.

"And we wouldn't want to see the boss upset." Sirena continued the alternating lines. "On the other hand, it would put your kind where it belongs on the extinction list."

"But our other option would be to give you another dose of thisss." Dr. Coral held up a vial of murky brown liquid. "Then keep administering you regular amounts of the serum so that you never reemerge in human form again. Not that you'd want to anyway. You see, I have my own plans for the human race. So regardless of whether or not you save your sister today, the end to her and all other human existence is inevitably drawing near."

"Paleease." Sirena rolled her eyes and walked around to the door. "Just give him the stuff and let's go."

"And how would we drag a ton of sssabertooth with usss if we changed him now?" Dr. Coral snapped. "We have to wait for the effectsss of the venom to wear off a bit."

"And how do we control a ton of sabertooth once that happens?" Sirena shrieked back.

"We lead him to the Beastsss of Burden sssince he has no idea where it is."

"Are you crazy! He'll unleash himself on us there!"

"He'll have other priorities to contend with firssst." Dr. Coral gave a strong delineation. "When it'sss all settled, we'll leave the mole to The Jacksss."

"And what about Lapi-dog?"

"Give him reason to be more consscerned over the sssister if he doesssn't already have one." Dr. Coral hung his words to give them their true power before continuing. "Oh, and don't go back to worrying over a sssabertooth. My venom is mossst effective when used a sssecond time, but we will require The Jacksss help when it comes to heavy lifting."

"And you think we'll be able to just walk right out of there with all those Hybrids around?"

"It'sss a sssimple matter of hysssteria as you've already observed on the human ssstreetsss. Let the fearful ssscatter. They'll be no worssse than a bunch of chickensss running around with their headsss cut off."

The sweat ran down Achak's cheeks, but he lifted himself completely upright regardless. His arms shook violently under him, yet he was prepared to push off from the floor no matter their state or penalty to his own health. Crouching himself slowly upward, he looked into both preying sets of eyes that were upon him and said, "Take me."

Achak was lead down a couple of blocks and steered into a nude doorway. Between the wooden frames, he walked into an abyss of rallied chanting so that it almost seemed that the darkness itself was comprised of it. Anger and excitement, all the emotions of the crowds reached his ears at once, though he could not yet see by what numbers they came.

Dr. Coral's fingers pressed into Achak's arm and prodded him forward in a few sharp jabs. Achak could see the syringe shining from the doctor's other hand, ready to stick him with it when the moment was right.

Sirena caught Achak by the bandaged shoulder when he almost missed a step going down into the depths. He still had the effects of the venom weakening his coordination and somewhat obscuring his vision.

The yellow spotlights overhead came like streaks across the ceiling. Meanwhile, the crowds and shadows were standing over a great pit where rails prevented anyone from falling in.

None of the wide-mouthed faces had yet guessed it was Achak coming into the arena, at which point, he searched for his sister. He sorted through the heads for the one smaller outline of Tehya, but the bodies packed around seemed so much taller, especially once Achak was brought to the stairwell that would take him into the pit.

His hand touched another's on the rail as he prepared himself to make the descent. When he looked up into the person's face, his pardon was cut short in his throat as he gasped for Mariam. But the next moment she was swept into the tide of spectators, who realized that their sabertooth duelist had arrived.

Dr. Coral played the part of a good coach and walked behind Achak into the pit, his syringe kept out of the sight of any who would call the foul.

Glass shattered at Achak's feet against the cement steps and the crowd above him went wild.

"Watch your head," Dr. Coral said jovially.

Achak looked up to see if any more bottles would be raining down on him. The rails were being rattled and dust kicked up by the shuffling of feet. Harmful faces were worn by all those he could see calling for blood.

Then Achak saw the one soul who did not want him in the arena—saw and heard his own voice cry the name of an ally. Achak shouted out to Lapidar who was squeezing his way between spectators to get to the rails. Even with the wolf out of his hearing range, Achak knew that Lapidar had found out something about his sister. Pointing and hollering, Lapidar was trying to get Achak to look to the other side of the pit.

Focusing too high at first, his eyes landed on a stuffed ox head that was mounted above the arena on a wooden beam. Achak's eyes followed it to the crowds below where a glass case of animal skulls was propped. Their heads were positioned upright with a gold plaque set in front of their teeth like trophies.

Achak had only a brief moment to wonder if the skull of the loser would become the trophy of the winner when he saw Tehya standing by the display. Her cheeks looked moist with her hands cupped so tightly near together that they looked as white as the bones beneath the skin. Beside her was the mole Achak suspected was responsible for her abduction. Tehya had not yet seen her brother, but Achak could tell her eyes were traveling around and looking for the source of the new hysteria. He tried to call out to her, but knew without discouragement that his words had been drowned out by the chanting.

Tehya lowered her head down into the pit, a feature that was understandably building tension in her, resembling a deep empty swimming pool. She cast her eyes around the steep walls and saw Achak standing in front of the steps with Dr. Coral. Her cheeks were immediately splashed with tears as her lips cried out with a sure call of recognition.

Achak waved his hand and called back to her to show that he had seen her.

She ran up to the rails and the mole immediately lunged after her to stop her from going over. Achak's cheeks burned as he watched the mole wrestle with Tehya to try to force her away from the bars. She appeared to be screaming at the top of her lungs while her arms swat back and wrapped around the rails which she refused to let go of.

The image of her struggle burned into Achak's eyelids even after Dr. Coral nudged him forward and broke the sight of Tehya. Across the pit, Achak's opponent was coming around the corner of the second stairwell. The man had to duck under a beam to step onto the arena. His grizzly hair was wild and black. The fact that there was enough of it to cover his broad shoulders was no light matter. Achak could hardly make out more than glows of silver between the tangles that were the grizzly's eyes.

"Try not to let him break too many bones," Dr. Coral said from Achak's side. "I doubt Manu will pay a ssstrenuous amount to have them mended."

Achak shot the doctor with a flash of the eyes and was given a dose of venom back in the form of a syringe. His eyes held their gleam of yellow while the rest of his body conformed into sabertooth and he dropped to his paws.

Following Achak's example, his opponent put on his own layers of fur which appeared to just extend from his already worn strands of grizzly hair. The enormous bear made the first approach and Achak could sense Dr. Coral disappear from his side.

Achak's ears were popping at the sounds of spectators. It was as though he could hear nothing at all.

Believing he still had more space to prepare a counter defensive, Achak did not move immediately while the grizzly stood feet away and received a nasty shock when a claw came within a hairline of taking off his nose. Achak began by scampering to the other side of the arena and found that the grizzly could run almost as fast as he could. Leaping out of harm's way, he spent a better part of his concentration avoiding and ducking the lash-outs of his opponent. Unfortunately, in a small and plain arena, there were no obstacles by which his superior agility skills could come into play.

He knew that one good hit by the grizzly's mighty paws would knock him into a critical position for the deathblow. Achak's fangs didn't feel so long when thinking about all the tangles of hair he would have to pierce through just to get to the flesh. Getting on top of the bear might be his best chance, but it was a matter of being presented with the backside by which to leap on. Only then would he be able to drive his fangs into the vulnerable side of the neck.

Trying to get around the creature itself was enough of a challenge without opting for a particular target. The grizzly was not especially quick at turning, but Achak could not draw close enough for the delay to provide him with any opportunities to attack. At some point, their fur would have to touch, but while the grizzly still presented a mouth bigger than Achak's and two able forepaws, Achak was determined not to let that moment of engagement begin until he could secure some kind of opening.

He danced around the beast and tried not to let himself be chased too close to the walls where he might not be able to move around the flail of claws.

The audience was becoming particularly restless with the run around as Achak heard the booing and jeers rise from the uproar every time another strike was dodged. The fans wanted bloodshed, which came in its small doses when Achak stumbled over the grizzly's paw, having leapt too close and was clipped in the tail by one of its claws.

This change was a distraction to both duelists who stalled in their next move. When the blood registered with the grizzly, it fumbled in its next zealous swipe. Poorly aimed, the sway of fur was dodged with ease by Achak. With a running start, Achak launched himself on the beam that preceded the stairwell and, before the grizzly knew where he had gone to, landed on its back. Achak clawed away until neither fur nor flesh was left un-torn.

The grizzly wheeled around and Achak was halfway between being thrown and bailed off its back. He landed awkwardly from a rebound with the wall and thought how crippling it would be to have twisted or sprained an ankle.

Something certainly seemed to be jammed as he avoided the next onslaught and found that one of his hindlegs would not give him the effective push-off from the ground that he required. The result was one brutal swipe across the side that sent him back against the wall.

Lapidar edged his way between shoulders. He had gotten behind a girl with a feisty temper who was fighting her way between people for him. She seemed to be heading up to the rails from the grizzly's side of the arena, which conveniently enough for Lapidar was exactly where he needed to go to get to the Graveler and Tehya.

The decision was already made up for him. He would spare no mercy for the mole if met with resistance in the take-back of Achak's sister. If it were on the damnation of his own soul, Lapidar would not allow the cycle to repeat itself with the loss of another youth being forced into a hostile life.

Someone was on his tail, but Lapidar did not care for the repercussions of his actions when his goal was so near. He knew the tailcoat was following, but it was at a distance by which he could not be stopped.

"Lead me on, little feather," he whispered to the back of the young woman to whom had lead him thus far.

She reached the glass trophy case and worked her way around it, pausing only when she saw the younger and equally dark-haired girl that was Achak's sister. Eyeing the gap of rail that the Graveler was fighting to keep Tehya away from, she, Mariam, filled in the gap. But staring only momentarily down into the pit, Mariam turned around on the bars and continued to lean on them while watching not the fight, but a struggle.

Lapidar leapt on top of the display case and when he bounded off he was no longer a man, but a wolf arching for the Graveler.

Glass rained down on both the grizzly and Achak, who was being pinned under its massive paw. All Achak knew was that a fight was going on above him as well as in the arena where his own life was being pressed out of him by the crushing weight the grizzly was slowly applying to his chest.

He wondered if people were becoming outraged at having hung around to witness such a weak battle between a grizzly and a sabertooth tiger. He doubted any duelist before him had ever lost so easily.

"I'll take her," Mariam said and grabbed for Tehya's hand.

"What?" Lapidar growled. He moved in to tear the two apart when he realized that the small feather was no longer paying any attention to him.

Mariam leaned her head to look back over the rails. She came back up with an urgent look towards Lapidar.

"Go! He needs you!"

Lapidar did not need further explaining before he came back down on all fours and, in one bound, hurtled himself over the rails to save Achak.

He fell into the pit, not as one, but with three other figures chasing after him. All jumped over the rails and descended upon the arena in Lapidar's likeness.

The two that fell together were a welcome of familiar hounds to be hand-trained by Manu and sent to escort Dr. Coral. He recognized The Jacks on sight, but the third was a more domesticated breed with the glossy black coat of a Doberman Pinscher. But Lapidar could care less about the Bred HyCouncil's affairs when Achak was his first priority.

His first notion when he hit the basin was to get on top of the grizzly bear without forcing any more pressure on Achak. He managed only a moment's disturbance to the grizzly's ankle by which he could divert its attention before the jackals interfered.

They were hardly the ground wrestlers he had known them to be on Domestica terrain, but each sinking gesture of their fangs was intended to kill or cripple. Both hungry sets of eyes were on his throat. For Lapidar to have locked his teeth on one for too long a period would leave him open for an attack by the other. Then there was Achak, whom he knew remained held under the weight of the grizzly. The only person Lapidar left to mystery was the status of the Bred HyCouncil member whom he had lost track of in the arena.

But all that came to an end when Lapidar expected to lock jaws with one of The Jacks and instead came nose to cheek with the Doberman Pinscher. Growling, the large black canine forced him and The Jacks into temporary retreat. Lapidar saw from above the foaming jaws, the cackling smiles of The Jacks as they edged nearer to the stairwell, only to hold back until Lapidar made another attempt to reach Achak.

He shot a glance in Achak's unchanged position and growled at the Doberman as if he wished to explain the direness of the situation. The Doberman growled back, never giving a look in Achak's direction. By this, Lapidar knew he would have to fight through the HyCouncil member to get to the grizzly.

Craning, Lapidar lowered his head to cover the softer tissues of his neck and readied himself for the fangs of a Doberman, who, in a last hurl of spit and foam, lunged after him.

Lapidar kept his head low and his jaws lower so as to bring them together. It would mean grabbing less flesh, but the smaller pinch would draw blood much faster than if he were to try to put puncture marks over a larger hold of flesh. The wiser attack was based on the knowledge that the first few moves had to be quick and damaging.

His Doberman counterpart had the same ready stance. Only when he barked a few swears at spitting length did he show the full reach of his jaws, which surpassed Lapidar's. The Doberman left off his threatening booms and charged.

He ran straight for Lapidar, eyes wide, but in a last draw, changed his course toward the grizzly and leapt.

The great bear roared and stood on two to knock the creature off its back. But the Doberman had already managed a secure grip on the grizzly's flesh and forced all of its attention to the task of shaking him off.

In the moments the two began their waltz, Achak limped out from under the bear, certain that in the next instant he would be flattened under it again when it fell forward. But if he thought his part in the fighting had ended, he could not have been more wrong as The Jacks came upon both him and Lapidar. Not quite the manageable pair to wrestle with, Achak slashed blindly as he watched Lapidar's increasing peril when the grizzly flung the Doberman to the side and begun its rampage on the entire arena.

Achak pulled away from The Jacks in time to put himself between the grizzly's arm before the full force of its claw could swipe Lapidar. He took the hit and landed on his side, feet away, but knew the true disaster had been prevented. As Achak staggered upright again, the grizzly already had a killer's stance over him.

He opened his fangs, but knew that even his two most powerful weapons would bust when the full weight of the grizzly came down on him.

From his side, a black streak whizzed by and in a flash the Doberman was back and dangling like a fishhook under the grizzly's mouth.

Achak backed away and felt a slender creature rub up against his foot. A chill ran over his fur as the serpent slithered past his leg and toward the bear.

The Doberman was being shaken like a rag doll while the grizzly tried to free itself from its pincher. Achak watched the chaos reach its conclusion as the serpent slithered near the grizzly's leg. Dr. Coral settled the drama with one venom-filled bite and the grizzly staggered sideways, brushing against the wall, before making its final rest near the stairwell.

Staring at the mound of fur, Achak lost sight of Lapidar and The Jacks. A simple "kah-kah" brought him into wake. In the space around his head, a raven was flapping violently for his attention. He snapped at the halo and it took off toward the stairwell behind him urging him with its cries.

"Kah-Kaugh!" The raven loomed above the stairs, where with or without its advice, Achak knew that was where he needed to go. Then the aggressive barking turned him around to face the pit where Lapidar and the Doberman were still engaging The Jacks.

"Kah-Kaugh!" The crowing not only grew louder but was right up against Achak's ear where the raven nipped him.

He chuffled, but heard something less pleasant come his way—something like a soft hissing. Jumping over the first step, he heard the violent "kesha" of a snake striking air. Achak ran up the rest of the steps without looking back. Because of Dr. Coral's serum, he still had to wear his sabertooth's skin and take the stairs four at a time, but could not have been more grateful for its ability to tear through the crowds when he reached the top.

Following the set of black wings, Achak set his eyes on the exit. Light flooded the doorway from the street and Achak met the cool and refreshing breeze of the outdoors. He lingered near the entrance, ignoring the kaws of the raven. His mind could not be at ease while his friend remained somewhere back in the darkness and alone with The Jacks, a Doberman and a serpent. Achak wondered if he had not left too soon.

Lapidar, as it turned out, had fared better against The Jacks having not been reduced to fighting them alone. Holding one hairy leg between his teeth, Lapidar pulled the Jack away from the stairs. It had not even occurred to him that he had voluntarily took on the larger man-beast of the duo when the Doberman came up behind them. Even with a mouth full of fur, Lapidar still took the moment to watch the Doberman at his fight. Like before, the Doberman was a wildly aggressive and tight-skinned cerebus. He had the foam and mad glint of any beast set to guard the gates of the underworld.

His tears at the Jack were brutal as he would not hesitate to pull on the tail were it the only available target to him. He bit high, low, and mercilessly at the ears, removing from the Jack a part of the lobe. Any blood to smear across the Doberman's black coat would shine like the rest of his fur under direct light.

Pinning down his Jack with a paw against the cleft, Lapidar lowered his fangs toward the throat to end life the way he knew was quick and best. His nose brushed up against the fur, then he opened his jaws wide for the kill. Closing them was just a matter of lowering himself an inch or two, but a faint breathing came to his ears. Raising his head, Lapidar perked his ears and listened for it. The breathing came with a rattle, not like a fly or a bug would buzz its wings, but like the flapping of a snake's tongue. Caught by his senses, Lapidar raised his eyes across the floor and saw the weaving scales of danger slithering towards him.

Striped red, yellow, black—Lapidar jumped back from the Jack's un-punctured neck. His head hit against something in air making him see green spots and a shower of feathers. The creature shrieked its cry of pain but not without hooking its claws into Lapidar's collar of fur.

Dazed and unknowing, Lapidar shook himself of the pain and continued to back away from the Jack and the serpent. Only when he tried to move toward the stairs did he realize that a force was working against him. His paws slid back on the concrete, but he found that the pull was not from behind and attached to his tail, it was above and flapping away with its enormous wing span.

For someone so short as a human, Sirena was large and powerful as a vulture. Her great wings were enough to hold Lapidar from his escape.

He tried clawing his way forward but found no grip along the concrete. His paws moved toward the snake. He was taken back steps at a time and dragged in the last direction he wanted to go. Sirena knew what she was doing and it was just a matter of waiting for Dr. Coral to slither within striking distance before she released him.

Meanwhile, the Doberman was still fighting his own battle with no inclination of the peril that was coming their way. If he had, he would not be wasting any more time with the jackal while there was a venomous creature in the vicinity.

Lapidar alone heard the soft hissing approach. His hind legs were clawing away at the floor as he struggled to break free from Sirena's talons. His throat was at a continuous growl while he gave away all of his breath to his last attempts.

Clambering down the stairs in his haste, Achak made a final desperate leap off the steps and tore the wings above Lapidar's head. Achak had one of Sirena's wings clamped between his teeth when he landed.Jerking his head irritably, Achak tried to throw her off, but. had trouble releasing her. She flapped madly, an attempt that only drew Achak's fangs further into her flesh, where her wing stayed caught.

Achak wanted her off as much as she did. For him, the pain was only the unpleasantness of having both feather and blood come into his mouth. But he swallowed no guilt from it, until he had wrung her to the ground where her mortality showed in the face of a young girl bleeding and screaming on her back. Life was oozing from her left arm and turning even the blackest strands of her hair a deeper red. Dr. Coral was the one to shut her up when, instead of leaving her to wail in a pool of blood, put an end to her misery with one swipe at her neck.

Both bodies went as rigid as a stick—Dr. Coral's being of the more literal resemblance—then Sirena convulsed, then stopped and Achak knew she was dead.

Dr. Coral released her and his straightened body recoiled. His black void eyes were deep inside Achak's and his head was raised, bobbing in air over Sirena's body. From her neck, he began to slither over her, taking the shortest pathway over her body to get to Achak.

Paralyzed to the spot, Achak could not have known whether it was all over for him or not. His feet moved when he heard the wolf's howl and he jumped over Sirena's stilled legs to join Lapidar at the stairs.

Together they ascended and Achak could feel the hot breaths that chased them up the stairs. Achak's hind leg was pulled away from him and, when he turned on the catcher, he met not a Jack but the Doberman. He made as if to snap at it, but with its hold on his leg, the Doberman had meant for him to be dragged and propelled elsewhere.

Achak was not the target, but Lapidar was and took the challenge.

Ready to pounce on the Doberman, Achak was not about to let the two go at it, but before he could do anything to stop them, he heard his name called.

Mariam stood by the doorway waving her hand for him to come. He shook his sabertooth head, but kept his attention long enough to see her become more insistent with her gestures.

"Come on!" she shrilled.

Achak hesitated a few beats then ran up to Mariam. He did not expect to come near her as she was normally good at keeping the distance between them, but he came to her waist while her arm was caught up by another.

Marcus held up her wrist and would not release it. He looked from her to Achak. His face was covered with pure anger, the type that only a Hybrid could fabricate with their changing eyes. Feathers fell from his dark hair as Achak had known Hybrids to do when excited. In this instance, Achak thought for certain his feather's had been ruffled. Feathers stuck out in all directions even though his hair was greased back.

Mariam's mood changed full-circle and her eyes filled with water. To whatever difference it would make, she said, "Marcus, I'll only be a minute. It's nothing," she added more pleadingly.

Without possibly knowing what effect these words could have had on Marcus, she grabbed Achak behind the neck and ran with him up the stairs.

"Come on! Come on! Come on!" She was both urging and cursing him.

Achak did not have the faintest idea of what was going on. All he knew was that when he reached the streets and the night drew coldly upon him, he again had the urge to turn back around where something had gone amiss. More to his grievance, the last person he could help was the one to take up so much of what was on his mind: Sirena.

Did she really have to die? He could not be too sure he had wanted her dead, even if he did feel certain about wanting revenge. And he did have his vengeance—*like he wanted*—impaling her wing and bringing her to that helpless state on the floor. He had put her there, where she bled, Dr. Coral bit, and she died. It had been one thing to see her as a vulture, but entirely another to see her as a woman. Lapidar would not have seen the difference.

Mariam, the girl now running ahead of Achak, meant the same as Sirena to him: both girls comprised of dark layers and vivacious personalities. He could not have wanted her to come to so irreversible a fate.

Now leaving behind a trail of black feathers, Mariam slowed down and turned into the gated court of a closed restaurant. Achak entered between the dark rails while Mariam took flight.

All the tables and chairs had been stacked away and locked unless mounted into the cement. He saw in one corner near the display window a small figure huddled.

"Achak!"

14
Dog, Cat, and Bird

Teyha squealed a small burst of glee and Achak felt her arms wrap around his furry neck. He could smell everything he knew of her, including the whiff of floral-scented body spray, and let the moments pass in her arms.

She gasped in his fur and he turned around to see Lapidar standing alone by the rails. He had a worn expression but looked pleased with himself. Achak was glad to see him alright and for the most part held together with the exception that a few sections of his shirt were torn.

"How about if we get the two of you home?" Lapidar let his folded arms drop and motioned for them to follow.

Tehya took a step ahead to walk in front of Achak, but he brushed against her leg to stop her. She gave him an inquiring look by her side, but he could only bump her again to communicate what he wanted. Lapidar turned around to see what was the hold up and told Tehya to "Get on." Achak nodded fervently, grateful that Lapidar had understood and translated, then allowed Tehya to put one leg over him with much nervous hesitation.

"Won't I be too heavy?"

Achak and Lapidar both shook their heads with Lapidar adding, "We need to leave the area as quickly as possible."

"So you didn't intend to stay in San Diego?" Tehya combed the hair behind Achak's head and found the silver chain belonging to his pendant. But before her question could be answered, Lapidar transmogrified and no longer could his human voice be heard beneath his snout.

Achak felt Tehya bury her face into his fur as though the sight of Lapidar's change was too much for her to witness. Sympathizing with her shock, Achak began the journey home at a slow trot, then picked up pace when he thought she could hold on tighter.

They stood at the front door of 1842 Lund Street. Not man, girl, nor saber-tooth knew what to do next, then Lapidar rapped his fist on the door. Things remained quiet as each waited in their own uncertainty for the knock to be answered. The house stood in complete silence so that even the windows were devoid of light and life. Lapidar looked down at Achak with a thoughtful squint.

Then Tehya climbed off her brother's back and stared from one to the other. But Achak's only resolution to either's contemplation was to check the kitchen window. He brought his forepaws against the stucco and leaned in for a better look. However, the house remained dark and, even with his keen ears, Achak could not hear anyone stirring around the other rooms.

He lowered himself and shook his head for Lapidar to see what he had learned.

"It's okay you guys," Tehya spoke out with her first relaxed expression. "I have the keys."

No matter the steadiness in her voice when she held out the key from her pocket to unlock the door, her hand trembled.

She pushed the door open and began to walk in, but Achak forced his way in front of her and she cried out at being shoved into the doorframe. Achak gave no notice as he began compulsively poking his head around the room, under the pillows of every recliner, and down the hall.

"It's okay," Lapidar assured Tehya. "Let him be protective."

"Yeah, but..." Tehya rushed to cut in, then shook her head. She raced down the hall. "Achak, wait! Mom and Grandpa could be sleeping and you'll scare them in that skin!"

Lapidar sighed and turned around to secure the door. He walked around the room and flicked over a switch, as well as the knob under a lampshade to bring some light into the space. When he was through, he went into the kitchen and brought out an assortment of cups, including two water glasses and one tin bowl filled halfway. He sat on the smaller sofa and waited for the others to rejoin him, which they did in due time. Achak found the water dish waiting for him on the rug, while Tehya took sips from her glass and watched the sad sight of brother having to draw up water with his tongue.

She changed her face before Achak could look up from his bowl and wonder what she had been thinking. Lapidar saw it but said nothing and hoped that she would keep silent as well. He did not understand the shame and humility that went on in human minds when it came to walking on fours.

Achak, he was sure, no longer minded the sabertooth tiger's wear. He was as natural in his movements as though he had practiced them all his life. From lying near his water dish, Achak stood up, stretched, then found a comfortable place against sofa by his sister's feet.

Tehya leaned forward and looked down at him. Her head above his, Achak raised his eyes and flicked his tail, a behavior that without flaw, forced her to smile.

Just then, Lapidar began choking on his water and Achak jingled his pendant to look at him.

"S-sorry," the wolf-man coughed. "Maybe I'm better off drinking water without ice." He hit his fist a couple of times against his ribs then swallowed hard. Achak and Tehya both relaxed again.

"You want to know what I think?" Lapidar began again. "Dr. Coral's mad if he thinks he's going to kill a bunch of people by bottling this stuff."

Lapidar swished around what water was left in his glass, but Achak just shook his head less assuredly. Trying to follow their conversation, Tehya leaned over him with a puzzled look, but Achak stood up. He trotted to the corner and rounded into the kitchen. Opening the refrigerator with his teeth, he knocked off a few magnets and proceeded to rummage inside nose first.

He found what he was looking for and kept the neck between his teeth while he carried it back with him into the living room. Lapidar took the plastic from Achak's mouth and read the label. He turned the HydroMax bottle for Tehya to see and searched for clarification from Achak.

"This is the brand?" Lapidar studied the bottle more closely. "The stuff that kills humans," he stated nonplussed. As though in denial, he rotated the bottle a few times in his hand searching for a warning label. When he found none, he began to read the ingredients. Finding nothing, he dropped his hand over the arm of his sofa and let the bottle fall to the carpet.

Tehya stared at it with a slightly repulsed expression. "You said 'kills' people, right?"

"Apparently," Lapidar answered. "Enough people get taken into this nutritional hype and it won't matter whether they've all bought into it or not. It'll be global panic for all those who survive."

"How?"

"What I don't get is: why is Dr. Coral with Manu if he wants to genocide humans? Manu is trying to save species from becoming extinct, but Coral wants just the opposite."

Achak yawned and put his head back down by Tehya's feet and between his forepaws. Tehya had already stretched herself across the sofa and was lying down with one arm hanging over the ledge. Her fingers were stroking Achak's fur.

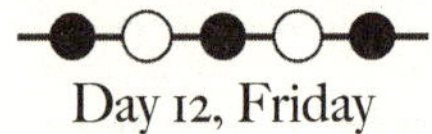

Day 12, Friday

Lapidar stared at the pale ceiling and into space before daylight and morning occurred to him. He sat up on the couch and focused on the digital timer on the VCR until its numbers too were understood. When he looked back at the other resting bodies he saw not a girl and a sabertooth, but Tehya laying sound asleep on the couch with Achak below her, as equally sound and human as she was.

Some aspect of Lapidar's stirring was heard by Achak, who began to struggle with the morning as Lapidar had done. He rolled over and rested on his elbows to check on both his sister and Lapidar. Then Achak sat up all the way and stayed leaning against the sofa. There was a bothered look in his face that told Lapidar he had not quite come to grips with the previous day's events.

"Sirena," Achak said before Lapidar could ask. He had detected the wolf's concern even without having turned to see it with his eyes. "Is..." he hesitated. "Is she really dead?"

"If not by poison, then having bled to death." Though spoken softly, Lapidar said these words with no true remorse but out of courtesy to Tehya, who was still breathing heavily in sleep.

Achak tried again for a more heart filled response. "Should I be—"

"No," Lapidar cut him short of the guilt. "You didn't kill her and what do you think she was trying to do to you by holding you back?"

Achak fell silent, though not out of the sleepiness he had succumbed to before.

"I'll say this much for her," Lapidar began his eulogy. "She was no amateur mercenary. Manu hit gold when he found her. I would have bought her out if I could have afforded to out-pay what Manu offered. Having an avian is advantage enough, but she had the feather type and personality to intimidate. She could play with your head, as well as make circles around it.

"But no, I can't say I'm going to miss her. No, we were better off without her."

Lapidar banged his fist on the arm of his chair and Tehya slept away.

"But we sure could use a pair of wings." The longer Lapidar was free to speak the more agitated he became. "I don't know any avians, other than the one now lying six feet under, do you? What am I talking about? Of course, you don't."

"No—no, I do!" Achak's head shot up from his hands and knees.

Lapidar looked at him skeptically.

"You met her."

"Who?"

"Mariam. Oh man, her and Sirena used to get into some rows—" Achak stopped himself as the mention of Sirena brought him a haunt of painful images. Lapidar waited for him to continue. "She goes to my school."

There was a rap at the front door and everyone fell silent. Achak knew his last bit about Mariam had been overheard by whoever was standing out there waiting for an answer.

"Tehya, no!" Achak moved to stop her from peering out the living room window, but she had already turned herself around on the sofa and parted the curtains.

"He's got dark hair and a blue tailcoat," she called from the other side of the curtain. Lapidar and Achak both looked at each other.

"Tehya, you're in no danger." Achak cleared his throat. "The guy is a member of the Bred HyCouncil and can't harm you. He's like the police. But Lapidar and I will be in trouble if we're found here."

Tehya rushed over and threw her arms around her brother.

On the San Diego High campus, Achak was far from forgotten as every one of his classmates seemed to have noticed his extended absence. Maybe some word of his Missing Person Report had reached their ears, and if that was the case, it was more than likely that they had later learned of the statement by which he said he had run away. He even saw Donovan Parsons dressed like someone who just came from a safari. His brown vest beheld more loops and pockets than a person could put to use and Achak knew then that he was no Hybrid. Anyone as in touch with the animal kingdom as a Hybrid would not have acknowledged that such an industry as zoos, wild animal parks, or safaris existed. They would have preferred to get in touch with fellow animal kin through another means.

The differences Achak picked up between humans and Hybrid helped him to walk away from the situation. But Donovan's laughter still carried down the hall as he called out to ask whether Achak had been punched too hard in the lip to graduate.

Achak ignored this and kept his eyes out for Mariam. He could not be sure whether she had even come back to school after the previous night but, if he still could not find her during the lunch break, he knew where her locker was to await her there. Achak knew of only one set of eyes who could spot Mariam's head in a crowd better than he could.

"Anthony!"

His friend froze with his back to Achak. Some people around the lockers stopped to watch but most were lower classmen who could not tell the difference between a reunion and an everyday callout. They kept to their business in the halls and did not even realize when the person Achak was trying to reach did the least of compassionate things. Anthony walked on as though he had not heard his name at all.

It was Achak who made the pause this time when his second call went unanswered. He began using both the first and last name to address his friend, which succeeded in catching both the attention of the upper and lower classmen so that everyone but Anthony was acknowledging Achak.

"Santiago!" Achak tried all combinations of both name and initial to get through to his friend. He could have caught up to him, he could have kept up the pursuit, he could have pulled in front of him or intentionally have caused a collision, he could have even grabbed at his friend's shoulders and forced eye contact with his sabertooth strength, but Achak did not think of mistreating his friend like that would help him to win their relationship back after weeks without speaking to him.

Instead, Achak took a different sidewalk from Anthony when he reached the end of the hall. He could take comfort in the fact that he had finally reached the quad where most of the students sat on the grass with their lunches. Mariam's flock was bound to have found a nice shade tree to nestle under or so Achak hoped when he began checking out the groups that had gathered.

His eyes searched for the metallic purple that reflected off her black wings, but he could see no one with the oily colors. One opportunity remained open to Achak as he identified the cluster of young men that were walking toward him. Marcus, whose shirt also reflected intricate designs of purple, was among the group. There could be no denying that he had seen Achak in return as his voice began to rise with the gossip.

"Yeah!" Marcus pretended to agree with one of his friends. "I don't know why anyone would want to run away." He passed by Achak with an all-knowing glance. "I guess even 18-year-olds can behave like children."

"Talking about yourself again, Marcus?" Achak hissed in the passing so that only the group could overhear him. He heard the scuffle take place behind him as Marcus was held back by his friends. But Achak could care less how he offended Marcus if Mariam was not around.

Unfortunately, with Marcus's departure, Achak also had seen leave the last of people who could help him find Mariam.

Achak paused near a wooden bench to observe for a while. He had come to the crossroads and chose a path that would lead him to the football field. Many students found it the ideal hangout spot to meet either on top of or under the bleachers. Campus security was always monitoring the area and telling students to get off the bleachers when they began climbing them from the support beams underneath.

For this reason, Achak was not sure he wanted to go in that direction and decided to stay above the bleachers. Any disturbance would lead to some type of suspension, as was called for in the "No Tolerance" Policy, and would bring Principal Joyce Kimberly down to the field to suspend the individual. With the principal on site, Achak would be recognized and duly penalized for his misconduct. At the very least he would have to answer for two weeks-worth of unexcused absences.

He continued slowly on the same path so that if he heard a commotion, he might at least stand a chance at turning back around and going unnoticed.

His passage did not go without its false alarms and disappointments. The first of startling cries woke up another string of possibilities to Mariam's whereabouts as a blackbird went streaking across the sky. Shrieks and kaws followed its dives. Achak looked up at the noisy buzzard and realized that it could be Mariam mocking him. He knew her to be a raven but without his tiger's nose, he could not hope to identify her in that form.

Neither could Achak depend on the finer senses of his hearing when it came to detecting those nearest to him. The form of Lapidar took him by surprise when he suddenly found the wolf's loyal companionship by his leg.

"Do you think she could be hiding out as a raven?" Achak asked when he saw that Lapidar was not about to leave his side any time soon.

The wolf shook like it was wringing out its fur and Achak took that to be a general show of doubt.

"I don't know if this should concern us or not, but she's almost always with Marcus and some of the other guys. But I saw them back there."

Lapidar looked up with his trap closed, which was the opposite of what he would have done as a man. Because of his changes in expression, Achak could always determine when the two had made a connection or shared a thought. Lapidar went back to sniffing and wagging like an ordinary stray. Achak could tell when Lapidar had picked up an unusual scent which Achak hoped each time belonged to Mariam.

But Achak heard the most trail-cutting alarms when they reached the bleachers. The warning bell rang out from the building behind them and students would now only have five minutes to get to their next class.

He could not explain his angst in wanting to find Mariam sooner rather than later, but he was not ready to turn back even while all the other students from the bleachers were making their way toward the buildings. He scanned heads, but there were hardly any girls to look over since most were boys who had been using the support beams beneath the bleachers as a jungle gym.

The bleachers had already been empty except for the few climbing down their steps. Achak did the opposite of any students and walked up the clinking and rickety seats. Without protest, Lapidar followed him. At this animal, the students stared, but they took no extraordinary fascination with the creature, which to them was just a dog. Or at least, no one ran off shouting, "Wolf!"

Achak reached the top and stared back down where the last of the students were clearing off the field.

"I should be waiting by her locker," he voiced to Lapidar.

The wolf took a seat beside him but, in his current state, could not offer Achak any advice.

Sighing, Achak gazed across the way where another set of bleachers walled in the track and field from the city street. Some trees planted along the walkway also formed the barrier that prevented students from climbing over the chain-link fence and off the campus. These narrow pines Achak tended to watch closer than any other as they were the source of frequent chirping and some blackbirds even dived to and from their branches.

It was there in his half stupor that Achak saw the greatest of all divers swoop in and out of the pine needles. Following its take off was an assembly of at least a dozen others. With much kawing they would jumble like a dust devil in the air and engulf the first of divers in a sea of black feathers, then release it where it would fall a few feet in the air before all would move in for another assault on one of their own kind.

Achak was already running down the bleachers and yelling for them to stop. Lapidar faced the harder challenge of bounding from one bench to the next on four legs, but he had an easier time hurtling himself over the rails that prevented spectators from walking onto the track.

The whirlwind of ravens was no longer looming over the school property but made their way over the residential neighborhood behind the campus. Then Achak saw the entire flock go down in one swoop at the lone black speck falling from the sky. A block away, maybe two, he could still hear the shrieking kaws of a ravaging and flung himself over the chain-link fence before Lapidar had the chance to transmogrify and keep up.

He did not need to search the front yards or gardens of houses while the screeching commenced unmistakably ahead of him. The ravens had all converged into an alleyway between houses and, unlike werewolves, were willing to carry a fight even if the odds were unfairly set at a dozen to one. Their prey cried loudest of all while the others dived, pecked, and tore its feathers. Achak could hardly make out what they were attacking since the cloud of wings made it impossible to see past their numbers. They chased it up against the wooden fence of someone's backyard where it could not have become anymore cornered and the indecipherable kawing became vivid cries of "Stop it!" and "Go away!" from amidst the onslaught.

Achak ran forward and swung out his arms to prevent whoever was in that circle from being torn apart by the buzzards.

"Mariam?" He found her balled behind her arms and legs. Her cheeks were flushed and a thin slit under her eye was bleeding. She stared silently for a moment at Achak as if struggling to place him.

When he had pulled Mariam to her feet, she was not at all ready to meet Achak with gratitude or relief, but with fury.

"Let go!" she wailed and stumbled back ways into the fence.

"Mariam, are you—"

"Go away. Can't you see you've done enough?"

Achak took a couple of steps back to bring more distance between them, but this proved unwise as a few ravens resumed taking dives at her. Screaming, she threw her arms over her face again and Achak ran up to fight them off. He grabbed her shoulders and pulled her away from the fence, but she fought with him more than the ravens.

"No," she cried. "I won't mingle. I won't do it. Not for you, a stupid cat—I'm not with you!"

The ravens swooped in near both their heads and Mariam gave in to Achak's draw in. At first he fought them with hands alone and tried to swat them away while he walked Mariam outside of the alley, then Lapidar came. As wolf, he began snapping at their wings until they all scattered in their flight and slowly dispersed.

Mariam appeared to be drifting with shock written all over her vacant expression while she stayed beside Achak and Lapidar back towards the campus. Achak too was at a loss for words. Wondering what could have led Mariam's own kind to turn against her like that, Achak walked her back on the school grounds and into the first building where she and Anthony had neighboring lockers. Indoors, she made her way quietly to her locker but shot anxious looks at Achak and the wolf.

Achak waited for her to stop before he began speaking. The proposal was awkward, but he came forward with it anyway.

"Mariam, I came to talk to you, I—" He looked down at Lapidar. "Well, we need your help."

She stopped turning the dial to her combination.

"I told you, I don't mingle." Although her face was hidden behind her long strands of black hair, Achak could see the tenseness building around her figure. "You earthbound sorts can find the answers to your own problems."

Lapidar ripped out with a growl but Achak moved in front of him. "What was so different about yesterday then?"

"I wasn't helping *you*," she turned around and declared. But when she looked at Achak the swelling in her eyes told him that she had meant to help him.

"Thank you," he said and Mariam looked taken aback by his sudden change in approach. He reached out for Mariam's hand and she flung herself against the lockers.

Achak saw the wince of pain and terror in her face, but did no more than raise her hand to his lips and kiss it. "Thank you. For whatever trouble it's caused, you saved my sister."

He released her and began to walk down the long hall of classrooms and lockers. Lapidar followed him with much growling and protest, even going so far as to tug Achak by the shirt.

Behind, Achak could hear the sniffling that made him feel worse for walking away. There was a thud and Achak looked back to see Mariam on the floor, hands and knees to the cold surface, and crying. Lapidar made the first run toward her, but Achak was not far behind.

She took one look at those coming at her and stood up. Making a dash at the door, she released feathers from her hair and in the next minute was all bird caught in a windy updraft.

Staring skywards, Achak watched as Mariam made a long arch in the direction of the downtown district and confirmed with Lapidar that they should follow her.

Lapidar stood up as a man to give instruction. "Stay human, and I'll follow her scent." He transmogrified again and chased after the small black dot that was now vanishing over the building tops.

Wondering whether he could keep up, Achak ran after Lapidar and felt the harder strain on his longer legs.

There would be no scent of Mariam while she was in the air and Achak knew that until she landed he would have a better chance at following her with his human eyes than Lapidar could crane his wolfish neck to see.

Mariam did not soar far and maybe it was a bad thing for Achak to be grateful for, but he was relieved to see her come down and into the crowds.

Lapidar moved ahead of him and Achak noticed with some amusement the black feather he was holding in his mouth.

"I've been exiled! What do you think!" Mariam sobbed in her hands again.

Lapidar put a soft foot forward. "He doesn't think, Mariam. Achak's not accustomed to Hybrids."

Then Lapidar tried to keep his voice low as he explained things to Achak.

"The avians have customs that keep them loyal to their flock. It's something like being asked to be a werewolf only you're born into these principles. If you're caught associating yourself too closely with other species, especially those of the opposite, then you're banished from your tribe. Just like I've chosen the life of a lone wolf, by straying away from weres, Mariam will never again be admitted into another flock of her own kind."

"AND IT'S ALL YOUR FAULT!" She ran up to Achak and began beating his chest while also sobbing into it.

"Don't take it personal!" Lapidar called over her wails.

Achak took the abuse in good stride and after some hard blows, including one that she had landed on his stitched shoulder, Mariam discontinued.

"Can we take you someplace safe? Do you need anything?" Achak began offering her before she could become angry with him again.

Mariam stared at him, first with a suspicious gaze, then with a softening in her features. "I—" she hesitated. "I am hungry." The words were out before she could stop herself and she covered her face with her hands in shame.

"Alright," Achak said cheerfully. "Where to?"

Lowering her hands from her eyes, she said, "There is a place," then stopped to hiccup. "Not here, but 'round the beaches."

"Let's go then," Lapidar resigned. "What's it called?"

Coastliner Diner

Achak read the immense wooden sign that had been carved below the torso of a mermaid that would normally have come off the bow of a ship. The front of the restaurant looked very bow-like despite the fact that it was perched at the end of a very wide pier that went some 1600 feet into the ocean. It had been a very long and troublesome trip to have to switch several buses to get there, but it was probably an easier journey for someone like Mariam to make owing to her set of wings.

However, Achak still wondered why she would want to come all this way to get a bite to eat when there were plenty of seafood restaurants around the downtown sector, but then he noticed the less obvious attraction of the coastline: the absence of ravens. Birds here consisted primarily of pigeons and seagulls, the usual beggars of picnicking families. It now made sense to Achak for Mariam to want to go someplace where she was least likely to come across someone she knew or even a member of her own kind.

They stood in front of a panel decorated with seashells and waited to be seated.

After a few minutes, a man with silver hair tied back in a ponytail and wearing a vest that folded like two black flippers over his white belly came with menus in his arms.

"How many?" he chorused and there was a definite deep throatiness to his voice that could have belonged to an opera singer.

"Three," Lapidar said, but Mariam reached her hand between him and Achak and grabbed the waiter by the shoulder.

"Pelican seating," she hissed to the man and Achak thought it was a rather rude thing to say to a waiter in demanding seats to a particular table or section.

The man merely glanced back with a sigh. "Should've guessed," he said in an undertone. "Can't tell with the way young folk dress these days."

Achak kept his eyes moving around the booths and tables to wonder what he would find special about the pelican seating. When they turned around a corner, Achak saw a flight of stairs that they then began to ascend. From the outside look of the place, he hadn't expected there to be a second floor, let alone a third.

As they walked past a door on the first landing, Achak peeked into a dining room with a number of Hybrid with either a wing or a flipper *meronized* from their arm and showing off fin and feather to their partners. They were all engaged in lively discussions—none of which could have been conducted on a private level as there was a sense of community in which Hybrid from one table would turn around in their chairs to talk with those at another.

Given that Achak's thoughts were deeply engrossed in matters concerning Manu and Coral, he thought he could have used that sort of positive and inclusive atmosphere, but up he was lead over the second flight of stairs. He reached the third floor and held in a gasp.

Glass windows all around the room like a lighthouse revealed the ocean with the exception of the angle in which they had just climbed, which had to be supported by a non-transparent wall. The painting on that wall would have suggested that they were in a fish aquarium, but the window view was like a pelican would see in its flight, gliding toward the endless sea.

Needing to say something about the world he had just walked into, Achak pulled up behind Lapidar and whispered, "Can we afford this?"

Before Lapidar could give him a response, the waiter was sitting them at a table around the center. Achak noticed that all the tables against the windows tended to be draped in white satin and had only two chairs. He was okay with having a seat not entirely next to the window since most were angled to provide spectacular views of the ocean anyway. He watched the small rolling and tumbling of the waves coming in, which were disturbed only by the passing jet skies and sailboats.

When seated, Mariam immediately got to ordering them appetizers: shrimp salads, but Achak's stomach was tied in so many knots that he took no more than a few bites. Mariam, whom Achak had guessed must have been struggling for days with little food, pulled Achak's salad plate in front of herself and began devouring.

He found it somewhat awkward to be sitting there between a man who had once held a gun to his back and a woman too busy gorging herself with food to notice that there were two other people sitting with her. Edgily, he sipped from his water glass, having ordered nothing else to drink. It was a lot like standing in front of a crowd of people and trying to find something to do with his hands.

Having eaten twice her normal share of salad and bread compliments, Mariam wiped her face with her napkin and exclaimed, "This place is great. They even bring the tab out in a message bottle."

Then the entrees came out and Achak let his dish sit without interest. Mariam had already finished three-forths of her catfish before Achak had stuck his fork into his halibut. He had ordered his fish broiled so as to be lighter in taste and easier on his stomach, but with each bite, he heard Dr. Coral hiss in his ear and wondered what the mad scientist was experimenting with now in his lab.

Achak thought that there might even be a snake lurking under his table, but as he looked by his ankles for the proof, he found that he was nothing short of paranoid.

What had happened to make him think that he was in constant danger of being under attack? Well, he could answer that question only too simply: after having had a serpent fall from the sky and land right on top of him, after having had a boar knock the stool right out from under him to start a bar fight, and after having a werewolf pack surround him in an alleyway with the pack leader demanding that he transmogrify.

And now he had the waiter, the silver-haired man who bustled over to the table with a glass bottle in his hand.

"Excuse me, sirs, ma'am. Would any of you happen to be Ajack Twin-fang?"

Six eyes landed upon Achak and before he could consider denying the claims, the bottle was placed at the center of the table in front of him with the waiter's announcement of what was: "A message, sir."

Achak took the bottle and uncorked it, already able to see the paper that was stuffed within its transparent hold. He turned the bottle upright over his lap knowing full well that there was no liquid inside. In removing its contents, he pulled out a scroll made out of fine white paper. He broke the wax seal, unraveled it, and read silently, each sentence awakening a little more of his horror.

To: The boy that evolved,

I see now that you have learned to transmogrify and congratulate you on your progress. My ears are also not deaf to the rumours that you have recently undergone some trouble with duel masters that have sought out your unique classification and agility for their sport. The changes that I have brought you are without question troublesome.

Undoubtedly, you are a good investment for these men who pursue you and for anyone who wishes to be held in the mass of public spotlight. I, however, do not wish for this media furor. The rumours that have reached my quarters have done more harm than good. Domestica, I fear, will no longer be able to fulfill its purpose while the public perceives the breakout of one of its inhabitants as a failure to keep rescued species under safe confines.

Furthermore, I no longer have interest in you as a relic of my animal sanctuary now that you can alter your form. In asking for you to visit, I am in no way asking you to surrender yourself, but to negotiate a truce by which we may both get on with our affairs.

The proposed resolution would require you to make a temporary change into sabertooth tiger skin and to be filmed inside one of my enclosed habitats. You are to appear as a rescued salvage in front of the human news media.

This of course would mean putting yourself in a locked compound for a series of what could be hours, but I have no intention of holding you beyond the contract. I simply ask that you work with me to clear up these discrepancies, after which you will be free to leave.

Your hate and anger towards me are understandable and justly felt, but do not underestimate what this bargain can do for you should you have the desire to decline it. Clearing up the situation will result in alleviated charges and fines that the Bred HyCouncilmen have placed upon you for the little public disturbance misunderstanding. I am giving you a chance to clear up your name against all legal inquiries, to stop those who would pursue you to their own ends, and to allow you to get on with your life.

And feel free to bring that stupid dog of yours along with you, should you feel the need to have protection.

Please send your response via the messenger.

In humble submission,

Manu Firdaus

In heavy thought, Achak fell back in his chair staring at Lapidar.

"Think it's a trap?" he asked the question upright, but in his mind he was already constructing a million ways in which Manu could lure and trap him on the Domestica premises. It wasn't a real question he had asked, but what Achak really wanted to know was how Manu and Coral were going to get him. Had they booby-trapped the entire facility or would they employ dozens of the most vicious animals known—and maybe some that weren't—to ambush him?

"I think it sounds fair." Lapidar stared down at the note after having already read it silently. He seemed to be examining it line-by-line to read between the words but, in Achak's opinion, his partner was applying a little too much concentration and Manu's traps were not about to be laid out through the loops or slants of his calligraphy.

"Yeah," Achak muttered. "Sounds too fair."

Lapidar shrugged. "He doesn't seem to be offering you anything for pain and suffering though."

"Because he knows he has me cornered," Achak snapped. "There's even a partial threat in there. 'Do not underestimate,'" Achak said in a would-be Manu accent.

He turned sharply away to force his attention out the window, though saw only his own reflection in the glass, and couldn't help but notice that Mariam was watching him now. She had stopped her savage gorging over her plate of catfish to listen in on their conversation. Her eyes were caught on the scroll. When nobody made any attempts to enlighten her, she grabbed the bottle that stood empty on the table and turned it over a few times to read the label.

Crystal clear as it was Achak had not bothered to examine the bottle at all, but if he had, he would have known exactly who the message had come from before he even uncorked it to retrieve the letter. So clear and obvious the label shone that Achak could not understand why it had not drawn more attention to itself, but there, printed in gold letters around the bottle, were the words: HydroMax Euphoria, an apparently more sophisticated spin on the original brand.

The bottle was of no more interest to Mariam as she was now gaping at the scroll that Lapidar had set on the table beside his own plate of fish.

"Is this the same guy who always appears on the news?" she asked, now staring at the wax seal with the red encasing of "M."

Achak and Lapidar both looked at her in surprise and did not stop her from conveying all she knew.

"Local guy—millionaire. Has an animal ranch or something built behind his mansion?" She kept her thumb moving over the bottle label as though impressed by its gold shine.

"How did you know that?" Achak exclaimed, aghast.

"I didn't know he was Hybrid." Her eyebrows raised in their usual show of surprise. "But how can anyone not know about him. He's all over the news." Mariam turned her attention to Lapidar. "Can I see that letter," she asked.

Lapidar handed the rolled up piece of paper to her with his eyes intensely upon her face.

Achak felt the heat rise in his own cheeks. He did not mind so much that Mariam would be reading the letter or that she would soon know of his dealings, but he did mind the manner in which Lapidar looked at her. Achak could already see the wolf calculating and, if Lapidar wanted Mariam's help, he had better ask for it like a gentleman. Remembering only too well how Sirena had been paid and used by Manu, then made to suffer a tragic fate, Achak did not want to see Mariam become the raven-equivalent of that sort of subordination.

When Mariam finished reading, her eyes came over the top of the paper and bored into Achak's. She was staring at him as though she had never seen him before and he was an alarming thing to look at.

"I hadn't realized," she gasped. "Of course! You: the rampaging sabertooth. And Manu—Manu wanted to collect you!"

She seemed to be aware that some dark amusement had escaped her tone as she began sipping her water in a manner not sufficient for satiating thirst.

"Who else is involved?"

Achak could still hear the excitement in her voice as she went on speaking.

"Not—oh dear—not the vulture?" Mariam's eyes widened. "She was working for *him*? And I interfered. I knew she was just scouring around to make trouble, but I never would have guessed she was in league with—and her so young."

"Young and ambitious," Lapidar said flatly and Mariam gazed at him. "I myself was finding work in as dangerous an employment as she was at that age. I doubt she was older than sixteen."

Achak's chest tightened and he stared down at his half-eaten plate. Even fish was looking too heavy a food for him to digest with the weak feeling inside himself. Sirena had been impaled by his fang and cast to the floor where the coral snake struck her with its own set of venomous fangs. For all it numbed him, he could not erase the image behind those two facts.

Lapidar was not the only one to read the guilt off Achak's face as Mariam said assuredly, "She was a bad egg."

"That's no reason—" Achak could not finish his statement and had to swallow the last of his words. He took a drink from his water glass as Mariam had done to feel it cool fluid wash back his emotion.

Mariam smiled pleasantly at Achak, which he found bizarre given that she never liked Sirena and could care even less for her demise.

"Of course I didn't mean that she deserved it," Mariam said soothingly. "I only wanted to say that it was not your fault and that—" She quickly turned back to Lapidar with another look of inquiry. "That other man—that snake—he was working for Manu as well, wasn't he?"

"I don't think it's that simple," Lapidar answered her and went on to explain the potential effects of HydroMax, using the bottle in demonstration, and how he suspected Coral is hiding his greatest weapon to eradicate humanity right under Manu's restoration devices.

Mariam's lips fell further and further apart as she listened to everything Lapidar had to tell her about the two masters' plans.

"Well that settles it," she said when Lapidar was through explaining. "I'm in."

"What?" Achak blurted, losing interest in the droplets that were sliding down his glass.

"I said, I'm coming with you. You could use a smaller set of eyes and a pair of wings."

"No," Achak said at once. His outburst shocked all, including himself since he had been the one who had proposed recruiting Mariam in the first place. Now he was regretting ever mentioning her to Lapidar, even if their timing of arrival had saved her from a ruthless flaying by her own kind.

"No?" Mariam puffed out and feathers flared from the loose strands of black hair around her face. "I believe it is my decision to make. As if! You could stop me from tagging along."

She looked as dangerous in her sternness as Achak had known his mother to come down on him.

"Look," he said, hitting on a note of practicality. "What's the point in getting you involved? You already have the worries of your own kind turned against you and we are dealing with a man that is both powerful and influential, and who probably has the authority within himself to turn the whole world against anyone who helps us."

"Are you through?" Mariam asked, her expression calm. "I'm glad you have some ideas about how Manu can turn his invitation against you so that way we don't walk into his place completely off our guard. But! when you're through worrying *for* me, you'll be able see what insight I can lend you, including: aerial view of Domestica and maybe some foresight into the traps he may have laid around the property. I'll be able to inspect this so-called 'enclosed habitat' before he puts you in there and ensure that there are no threats lying within."

Lapidar's lips curled higher with each considered measure Mariam gave under advisement.

"I can even locate the weakest points for us to escape should things go bad."

"Alright!" Achak stopped her before she gave Lapidar anymore ideas and volunteered for another life-risky procedure. He thought that maybe Mariam might be throwing herself in the face of danger to eagerly place herself among another group after losing connections with her flock or else adopting new worries simply to bury her own.

Mariam gave a satisfied smile at Achak's submission, but he was none-too assured by her show of enthusiasm.

Achak's hardening gaze upon her reached his tone. "You can scout the grounds, but the first thing you are to watch for are sharpshooters."

"Agreed," Lapidar said. "Snipers were something I had anticipated as well, but let's not forget the use of tranquilizers while we're on the topic of being shot at. Manu may not want all of us dead."

Lapidar stared profoundly at Achak and continued. "I've been thinking a lot about that serum you told me about: the one in which Dr. Coral used to make you transmogrify in the first place and the one he used on you to force you to face the grizzly. If he keeps that going in your bloodstream, you'll never be able to turn human and it could be that Manu may not have entirely lost interest in you as a 'salvage,' to put it in his terms."

Achak had not thought about Manu's interest in him as a collection since he had left the facility. And he definitely had not given any more thought to the serum. It was not in his mind-frame of theory to think that Manu could want anything other than to kill him to keep him from blabbing. The idea sent a fresh wave of chills up Achak's spine.

Mariam looked uncertainly from one to the other waiting for an explanation. Lapidar had not bothered to include the full details of how Manu and Coral had managed the task of securing Achak in his animal form.

"Did I hear you correctly?" Mariam implored. "Not able to change back into human?"

"Yes," Lapidar answered in a rising voice. "It's how Manu discovered Achak's nature. I imagine it has a 6-hour course of working its way through the body system, but in an everyday situation, its effects would be more permanent and that person wouldn't remember how to change back in the long-run."

"Why?" Mariam kept her head shaking in disbelief. Her eyes were out of focus as she repeated the question in lowering whispers.

Lapidar shrugged and tilted his head back over his chair to gaze up at the ceiling. To Achak, the explanation had added nothing new to his concerns as he had already guessed the worst of serum uses that Manu could apply to him. Somehow, it was less frightening to think that Manu might want him alive. This meant that Mariam might not be in as much danger as Achak originally foresaw.

After all, Manu would have to resort to traps that would have less detrimental effects on the animal that was ensnared.

Achak looked down at his plate and began cutting into portions of fish again with the side of his fork. Then, taking them into his mouth, he chewed with less difficulty. No longer as terrified of what lay ahead, he went on eating, aware of having both other sets of eyes upon him. When his fork went down a third time, another set of fork talons came crashing into his.

Mariam had stabbed her end into the portion that Achak had just cut for himself and taken the chunk of fish into her mouth.

"Thanks," she said while tearing the bits between her teeth for Achak to see.

Lapidar laughed and Achak was relieved to see them both in higher spirits. By the time they left the Coastliner Diner, none of their plates showed signs of a faltering appetite as they had all eaten, within reason, a good portion of their meals.

Achak passed the letter back to the messenger as they walked out with the word "agreed" scrawled at the bottom along with his signature. He had asked Lapidar to sign it as well so that it was clear to Manu that he would not be entirely trusted to keep his end of the deal. However, Mariam's name was kept off the letter in hopes that word would not reach Manu that she had joined up with their party.

After reading Achak's answer, the messenger passed Achak another scroll, which he tucked away in his pocket, having no desire to spoil the easy-going conversation that had started between the three.

The mood was shaken only temporarily when Mariam asked the question, "Where're you two staying tonight?" after they had traveled some blocks down the Gaslamp District, away from the bus stop. Achak and Lapidar were both walking habitually back in the direction of their hotel.

"We have a room checked out in a travel resort just down the way," Lapidar said. "I don't know if there are anymore vacancies, but there are two beds and I don't mind pulling together a couple of chairs for myself."

"Okay," Mariam said, she did not need to say that it was a good arrangement when the pleasantness of her voice was enough to express her thanks.

Achak was looking forward so much to them sharing a room together and ordering pizza that he did not want to open the second letter and would have let it wait for morning, but had he slept in, he might have missed the appointment that was scheduled for:

Noon, tomorrow.

Day 13, Saturday

15
The Man and the Serpent

"Wonder what's keeping Mariam," Lapidar said and Achak looked anxiously up at the sky to wonder if she would be flying back anytime soon.

The scouting was in progress and each passing minute that kept Mariam away filled Achak's mind with worry as he imagined spotting one of the Jacks with Mariam's wing clipped between its teeth.

They were nearly at the front gates and she still had not returned. The timing could speak for itself given that they had hailed a taxi that would take them up the wrong side of the hill forcing them to walk where the roundabout ended their roadway, some distance down the green slope—down a ways from Domestica.

Steep as it was, Lapidar had refused to allow Achak to transmogrify to make the climb easier. He speculated that the circumstances had been arranged that way and to watch out for further temptation Manu might have laid out in hopes of persuading Achak to change into sabertooth tiger well before the agreed upon time.

Following the long, tall, and dark front gates that graced their side-view of the Domestica terrace, Lapidar opened again with his suspicions.

"Where're the news vans?" he said, staring around the pavement that ran down the other side of the hill.

Achak was thoroughly out of breath and didn't think that he cared to make any observations unless it was one about Mariam, but then he found another.

"There's Roy." He jerked his head over his shoulder where a small dark figure could be seen emerging along the green pathway from the roundabout that they had just taken. "Yep, he's got an invitation too! Here to clean up the inquiry, I bet."

"Yeah, probably paid off," Lapidar snapped.

"He helped save our lives," Achak said in a reminder of the grizzly incident.

"Heh! You didn't brawl with him afterwards," Lapidar huffed while still catching his breath. "Wanted to rip my throat out. Violent breed—Doberman—and he's got a badge to hide his bloodlust. Makes him more dangerous, if you ask me."

Achak said nothing in response but inwardly hoped that the detective would again be on their side should things turn ugly and that Roy was not, as Lapidar had suggested, paid off.

"Ring it," Lapidar barked now that they were standing at the gateway to the mansion.

"What about Mariam?" Achak argued, but this only made Lapidar more agitated.

"There are security cameras everywhere! If you don't ring it, Manu's going to wonder why we're just standing here."

"We could pretend to be waiting up for Roy."

Lapidar's growl did nothing to steady Achak's hand as he pushed the intercom button on the side. It buzzed like a doorbell and they waited.

Dr. Coral's voice, receiving more friction than his rapid tongue could produce, answered with a hiss: "Enter."

There was another buzz and the front gates began to swing open electronically.

Lapidar hurried down the long pathway cut through the lawn and led on to the grand doors of Manu's palace and Domestica. He hardly spared a glance for the elegant statues of mythology that ornamented the grass fields or even the stone pillars that began their ascent up the front steps.

"Hey, slow down," Achak muttered. "I thought you wanted to be on the lookout for traps."

But he did not need to hear Lapidar's snort to tell that the wolf would much rather avoid the detective than anything Manu had to throw his way. Achak gave the skies one last look before entering. The door was left wide open to admit them and Achak was not surprised to see two doormen waiting on the other side of the entrance and standing as still as dolls with their turbans.

No one bothered pointing them in any one direction or leading them to the elevator as an escort, which Achak thought was most unhelpful to someone who would likely lose himself in search of a restroom in such a large estate.

"Why are they so quiet? The question was pouring out of Achak's mouth before he could give it any thought. He had spoken while the doormen were still in earshot.

One shot a glance and Achak saw with growing unease that the doorman flashed him a yellow eye from which came a diamond pupil. He was not comfortable with showing his back to the turbaned men after that.

The elevator doors closed and Achak had a final look at the two doormen resuming their posts at the entrance. They stood as still and narrow as the doorframe itself.

"Like charmed cobras," Lapidar muttered.

"What?" Achak doubted they had been watching the same thing. Contrary to Lapidar's remark, he did not think the doormen looked anything like cobras, but more like stone statues.

"Oh, come on!" Lapidar growled. "I told you to be on the alert."

Achak was staring as Lapidar moved his finger across the elevator wallpaper and clawed his name, followed by "was here."

"What was obvious?" Achak asked, as irritated with himself as he was at Lapidar's unwillingness to explain things better.

Bringing his voice lower to enacted the words, Lapidar said it was "*The hissing*!"

"You can hear it under their breath." His voice restored to the same wolfish growl. "Or at least you can if you're listening."

"Didn't think to," Achak said truthfully. "They were being too quiet."

"That's 'cause they were irritated with something. A snake goes quietest just before it strikes. Keep your eyes on the prowl."

Achak felt the slipperiness of his sweaty palms and rubbed them against his pant legs. Trying to air out the space between his fingers, he noticed that they were less willing to cooperate and move apart. *As long as they function better as paws,* Achak thought to himself.

Then the red doors broke apart with a decisiveness that Achak only wished he had. Lapidar too left the elevator with as much certainty and boldness in his step as the mechanical doors. Achak edged out behind and came to Lapidar's side.

Deserted though the hallway was, they both treated it like a booby-trapped temple. Both stood on and shared the first square and looked down their separate pathways, not daring to take another step unless they were sure of its safety.

Achak had never really looked at the hallway before. The first time through, he had been dragged down it and barely conscious of his surroundings, while the second time, he had been more enveloped in the presence of his abductors: Sirena and Lapidar, who had a gun, than to notice anything outside the dangers of his situation.

No postmen awaited them in this corridor. Its remoteness was only loosely inhabited by the small paintings along the walls and their accompanying pottery plants that resembled those framed in their likeness. The more astonishing aspect of these features was how the different plant life could be made to blend with those of other terrain so that a desert Joshua with its sharp bristles could neighbor a palm tree nearing the ocean.

Lapidar stared down Achak's pathway with a disappointed frown.

"Desert, Tundra, or Arctic?" he asked dryly.

Achak took a glance down Lapidar's lane while his own was being examined, but could not distinguish anything more attractive about Lapidar's direction from his own.

"Coniferous forest?" he suggested as lamely as Lapidar. The two shared a brief smirk then restored their serious expressions.

Remembering what Lapidar had said about keeping up his guard, especially when things got too quiet, Achak resorted to the use of his other senses.

He took a deep breath, not as a normal human would ventilate but one filling his nostrils with a taste—many of which he could identify. There was a perfume or incense which if he had to guess its name would have thought it an ambrosia of lily and rosemary. The scent was labeled thus before Achak could take another inhale, this time catching a mange of animal: dirty and potent, like the smell of leather when its wet, and definitely carnivorous with breath of recent devour. *The Jacks,* Achak concluded and labeled that smell too before reaching out with his senses again, this time catching one both toxic and crippling. He gagged and Lapidar stared at him. Achak tried to lower his level of breathing, but once the smell had penetrated his senses, he could not rid himself of it. There was no denying that something fowl had polluted the air.

Lapidar took two careful sniffs in the direction Achak had been staring down, but even the gradualness of his intakes could not spare him. Before Achak could warn Lapidar, the wolf was on his knees choking and gasping.

Achak bent over to check on him, only to prevent his own crumbling by holding in his breath. He touched Lapidar on the shoulder and felt the trembling muscle. Making up his mind to proceed alone, Achak crouched to Lapidar's front and mouthed him a "wait here" while pointing in the direction of the fumes.

Standing upright, he snorted another breath to reduce the smell, fumbled for a moment, and walked down the hall of tropical forest, certain that he would find whatever he was looking for at the heart of the rainforest.

The door came on his right, singular and wooden as any of the others. It had a lever handle of silver that he pushed down on to open, but there was a furious padding at his back. Achak released the handle, letting the door drift open on its hinges, and spun around, expecting to be toppled over by a rampaging predator. Instead, he saw Lapidar in human form and staggering to catch up.

"What did I tell you about using your senses!" he growled. In a sudden stop, he caught himself on the other doorframe.

"I was!" Achak bellowed. "Following my nose, but I'm not about to smell my way through that rot."

"There are other senses!" Lapidar said vehemently.

Achak turned his head back into the doorway to see what Lapidar had worried over and discovered that he had not been the only one to hear Lapidar's lecture about the proper use of animal senses. The Jacks were staring at them from odd cubbies. Ék Jack had come between one of the armchairs and the sofa, neither of which faced Achak, while Dô Jack could be seen off the other side of the sofa and tucked under a desk that leaned against the wall.

Neither looked pleased and both had their tails curled up between their legs. Continuous growls issued from their throats, but they made no further movements to approach than to leave their cubbies. They merely kept at a constant watch and flashed a blue glint from their eyes as Achak crossed the doorway. Lapidar joined him while holding one hand over his mouth. The Jacks reacted to any sudden movements, which kept them moving at a very slow pace across the room.

Slumping his shoulders, Ék Jack began to pace around the armchair, then distanced himself by going around the sofa and coffee table as well. All the while, he kept his flashing eyes on Achak. Dô Jack watched his brother, but shortly changed his growls to whimpers and did not join in the pacing.

Achak continued glancing over his shoulder to see that The Jacks were keeping their distance, but he was being drawn to the door that held its own off to the side where two wooden giraffes curled their necks to form an archway.

He had nearly reached their double doors when, at a last backward glance, he paused to study another figure he had overlooked.

Someone was slumped in the armchair Ék Jack had been circling and his arm hung limply over the side.

Edging toward the giraffe doors as Achak had done, Lapidar paused too and, in allowing his eyes to wander, struck upon the same curiosity. He took the first regretful steps toward the body.

Ék Jack spotted him and his growl rose with more conviction as he scrambled in front of the chair and bared his fangs.

Achak startled to how quickly foam begun to bubble around the Jack's mouth, which was then joined tooth and spit by his brother. Responding to this defense, Achak strode to Lapidar's side as well.

"I'll distract them," Lapidar instructed, but before Achak could contest, he was watching a wolf get chased down by two jackals.

Achak did not need to be told what he was expected to do in the meanwhile. He had already jumped to the conclusion that Lapidar was taking as much interest in the slouched figure as he found in its identity. However, he would rather be standing back a good ten feet with Lapidar and taking turns guessing than to be the one whose hands would unveil the tanned cloth that fell over the victim's face.

It would not have been much of a guessing game, Achak thought as he took a step forward with a hunch in his higher consciousness. The "MF" initials were gleaming off a ruby opal broach that was clipped to the veil. Achak's arm reached towards it and he tried not to think too much about how a turban could come to be so unraveled.

Too late, Achak drew back from the chair before Ék Jack could sink his teeth into a part of him. Falling to all-fours, Achak changed and ran, the warm breath nearly closing over his tail. There began the chase.

They were clumsier with their movements, but in that same regard, they were also more aggressive as they sprang from one end of the room to the next without concern for the objects that stood in their way.

Achak watched the way one of the pair rode up an antique shelf. In the passing, the Jack would drive a pair of claws into his back if Achak was not careful.

Lapidar, however, did not see the perch Ék Jack had taken and raced forward with as much speed as he could gain to make an impact with Dô Jack. The one above chose at that moment to descend on him and dived from the bookshelf while Achak made a lunge with the same intervention in mind.

The two met with a bone fracturing snap in midair and went crashing over the glass tabletop. Achak, who had been on top, endured the least of cuts as the glass shattered beneath them. He heard the Jack let out an ear-splitting yipe and Achak wished to make one as well—the glass shards cut into his fur from all sides.

Though he hardly knew the extent of his injuries then, he had been aware of enough glass flying past his face than to think that he had escaped with only minor cuts. The problem was that there was so much blood. He could not determine how much of it belonged to him or if it had mainly leaked from the body that was lying limp beneath him.

Two hands came around his waist and tried to help him up.

He was human again, but he had detached his cheek from a chest of wet and matted fur. Dampness that was neither his nor the sweat that dripped off him. The only pain he was aware of came around his front jaw where he felt an injury the size of a toothache bruise his upper lip. Then there was the coldness of moist droplets soaking into his collar.

Achak turned around to the nursing of his wounds by Mariam. Late in the action, Mariam's gestures begged forgiveness. In her face, Achak read the guilt by which Mariam must surely perceive the cause of his current bloody state to be the result of her own tardy arrival.

"There were no empty animal confines—no habitats labeled: 'smilodon' or 'sabertooth tiger.'" Mariam brought a towel to his face and dabbed at his cheeks. Her face could never go pale, but it looked a few shades lighter and her hands quivered slightly as she cleaned him.

"It's okay," he assured her, but his voice sounded distant and rather un-like his own. He hoped she heard his words as he took the towel from her.

Unfortunately, without the job of cleaning him, Mariam stood with an unfocused look in her eyes as she scaled the room for something else to busy herself with.

Achak heard glass shards cracking under pressure, but did not care to turn around to see what Lapidar was doing with the Jack's body. The scraping ceased and glass began to crunch back in the direction of Achak.

He pretended not to see Lapidar come around his front as he held the towel against his lip. Some other parts of his arms had begun to bleed freely as he finished wiping away the confusion of flowing streams.

Lapidar held out something red and white in one of his hands. Achak expected to be handed a handkerchief, just as Mariam had given him a towel, but the object was hard and wet. Clutching the offer, Achak stared down at something that was neither cloth nor sterile, but a piece of sharp, jaggedness and blood.

His heart hammered before he had even consciously recognized the portion of fang. He brought his finger up to his mouth and felt between the cut of his lip to find one tooth of broken edges.

"I'm sure it can be fixed," Lapidar said, though there could be little hope found in his voice.

Achak stared at it, not yet sure how he felt as he had never before appreciated being sabertooth or fanged.

"Um," Mariam began to peep, but before Achak could hear what she had to offer him in counsel, he stuffed the marrow chunk into his pocket and she went silent.

Because anything seemed like an easier thing to talk about than his fang, Achak walked between them and forced open a window. Then turning his back away from the fresh air, he moved toward the armchair without speaking a word to his two companions.

There's nothing to say, he insisted to himself while extending his right arm toward the slumped body. Pinching his fingers over the broach, he flung off the veil like he was performing some sort of magic trick.

Thinner and sorrier than Achak had known, it was Manu's face. His lips were as colorless as they were expressionless. He may have just drifted to sleep and let old age carry him away, but Achak thought he knew the likelier cause of death.

Mariam gasped and covered her mouth. This definitely had been the source of smell Achak was trying to locate.

"I guess we're done here," Achak said nonplussed.

"No, we're not," Lapidar breathed. "Decayed bodies don't send you letters in a bottle."

"Especially not in ones labeled: HydroMax," Achak said, astounded, picking up on Lapidar's implication. He was watching Mariam, who through nodding showed that she too understood the conflicting circumstances.

Achak's senses were quickly going back on the alert. But what he trusted most was his eyes as he sought out the faces of his companions. All heads accounted for except one. In his dental trauma, he had forgotten the reason for which he had fought and killed, but now he remembered and wondered what the wolf had done with Dô Jack. In haste, Achak began a search for the missing carcass.

The giraffe doors had been flung open and a trail of blood led to their entrance. As Achak came nearer to the slithers of blood, he was willing to bet with more certainty that the Jack was still alive. There was not a lot of what Manu would have called "life" spilled over the carpet and Achak did not think Dô to have as much will power as his brother after their master's death.

He came between giraffes and saw with some sympathetic relief that there the boy was: dark haired, human, and sniffling on the magenta carpet. The room was square and simple, but more welcoming in décor than Achak had known any of the others to be. Instead of isolated Victorian chairs, there were sofas on which a rump could find comfort. As magenta as the carpet, the cushions were laced with gold trimmings that matched the tassels hanging from the lampshades. Shelves were filled with books instead of antiques. And there were magazines resting on a coffee table. There were other doors as well, including one that stood slightly ajar through which Achak could see the carpet change design and become a reversed out gray from the magenta pattern.

From the center floor space, the boy's eyes widened upon seeing Achak, who crouched down to the Jack's level to show that he was friendly.

"Lay-done," Dô muttered to which Achak could not understand.

"Lay down?" Achak clarified.

"Lay-DONE," he repeated, this time nodding towards Achak.

Shrugging his shoulders, Achak shook his head without comprehension, but the Jack stared back at him with a meaningful bulge in his eyes and repeated the word. Then Achak heard Lapidar's voice break out from behind.

"I'd have thought there'd be bite marks," he commented. "Wonder what Coral meant by it."

"Where is Coral?" Achak took his eyes out of the waiting room and turned back to see Lapidar standing over Manu's body.

"Dunno," Lapidar shirked. Mariam stood next to him, which made Achak annoyed with the pair of them as neither had lost interest in the body. He was ready to speak to Jack again when he saw a third figure come down on all-fours like a shadow rotating across the doorway.

Roy's body collapsed into a canine.

Lapidar and Mariam stood guiltily in their blood stained clothes with two corpses visible. Though perhaps the scene was more clearly drawn from Achak's angle, he had the impression that the detective had enough incriminating evidence to act upon.

Given no opportunity to declare innocence, Achak let out a cry and transmogrified. He could feel the off-balance of his jaws with only one fang, but was charging toward the Doberman as though he had a complete pair. The detective made a clear avoidance of Achak.

Locked in the silver flash of two dark eyes, Achak could read into them and know that the detective was trying to get around him.

Mariam was shrieking behind them, but Achak had the impression that Lapidar was holding her back. Achak concentrated hard to block out Mariam's shrills and keep his attention on the detective.

It was in this intuitive listening that he heard something he had not intended to. He listened for breath and instead he heard a rattle, or rather a hiss.

Detective Hutchinson had his claws lashing out at Achak's face, but Achak leapt far enough back to spare a glance away from him. In a blur of hurried seeking, he saw the small squirm of reptile slithering toward Mariam's feet.

Unplanned and unpredictable, he made a move toward the Doberman's out-raised claw and swatted it away. The canine detective looked ready to accept any bite Achak had to deliver, but Achak turned his tail on the dog and lunged towards Mariam's feet.

She shrieked and jumped away, but Achak caught the neck of the serpent beneath his paw before it could extend to strike her ankle. Beautiful and deadly, its colors striped the scales in red, yellow, and black.

"Coral!" Lapidar bellowed and pulled Mariam away from the snake, Manu, and the armchair. "Roy, it's Coral! Dr. Coral."

Achak could not come to grips with what Lapidar was shouting about because he was too busy making sure that the serpent did not turn its fangs towards him next.

"Ajack, release him!"

It surprised Achak to hear that the detective had returned to human form and was issuing him orders.

Having not yet grasped the situation, Achak backed away all the same. He did not like leaving the snake, but instead of going back to its prowl, it common'ized itself into human flesh. Achak stood back on his hind paws and watched Dr. Coral's labcoat materialize out of the brilliant scheme of colors. He snarled as a sabertooth and returned to human form.

"You've been caught in violation of Cold-Blooded code 7:14 concerning neurotoxic snakes behavior code and have the right to remain silent," Roy recited. "Anything you say can and will..."

"Oh, shut up!" Coral spat, raised the small point of a gun from his coat pocket and pulled the silver trigger.

A miniature syringe stuck out of Roy's shoulder until his eyes widened. He fell backwards and landed in a fit of convulsions. With a clatter the syringe rolled away while Roy's breathing leveled out until he lay very still.

Dr. Coral threw the medical weapon over his shoulder and smiled, not his usual toothy grin, but one extended with the madness of two gleaming fangs.

"Mariam, see what you can do for the detective." Lapidar waved her off without looking.

She glanced back and forth between Achak and Lapidar without moving.

"Mariam, please!" Lapidar growled and she obeyed.

Coral meanwhile was staring across at Roy's limp body. Through diamond-pupils and thin squints, Coral's eyes still bore an unmistakable yearning for warm flesh. His poised fangs made him look all the more ready to strike.

"Too bad," his tongue slurred behind his fangs. "I was hoping to kill him, but I hadn't counted on there being four of you." He shined a cold gaze upon Mariam who was now on her knees and tending to Roy.

Achak could hear a "thi-thi-thi" crackling between the doctor's words and knew that humanity was rapidly leaving the serpent's thoughts. It was only a matter of time before the real tyrant showed its true colors under the shedding of skin.

"Too bad for you," Lapidar mocked. "We know about HydroMax and the human genocide."

"Courssse you do," Coral hissed and fixed his narrow eyes on Achak. "I told him and he was bound to have told you. Sssirena knew as well—figured out on her own, that one—but as you can sssee, she's no longer with usss."

"Is that why you killed her?!" Achak roared.

"Ssslow, aren't you?" Coral chuckled.

"He's not slow," Lapidar retaliated. "I don't know anyone who's transmogrified faster."

Achak flushed as the doctor guffawed.

"Taken a liking to him, have you? How touching." Coral said scathingly. "It'sss not normal to mingle with sssomeone ssso far from your breed. But every now and then I sssuppose oppositesss attract. Though Hybrid generally have a tendency to favor their own kind. It ssseems you've evolved, Lapdog."

"Heh! As if I'd fancy your approval," Lapidar spat on the carpet.

"But a little too warm-blooded, I sssee," Coral twisted. "Loyalty towards a Hybrid's own kind is his greatessst inssstinct, pride, biasss and ignorancsse, you know?"

"And what's that supposed to mean!" barked Lapidar.

"That humanity, the common ssskin, is ignorance. And not as Manu—man—has presssumed to be in likenessss of the creator, or the apple ssseed of wisdom."

"You know it'll never work, Coral!"

"And why not?"

Contrary to the doctor's crackling chortles, Lapidar's were crisp and booming. Achak looked at his tall companion and saw that he stood as confidently as he spoke. The grays of his hair were shining more in compliment with his brown strands, taking years off the stubble and grunge of his features. He resembled a college boy laughing in the face of an enemy.

"'Why not?'" he cried back. "Because we know. The Bred HyCouncil knows."

"*Do they*?" Dr. Coral spoke darkly. "I was under the impression that all who knew would be at my door by now." His eyes were drawing back on the unconscious detective. "Where is the back-up?" he sighed reprovingly. "Caught in traffic then?"

Returning a smile to Lapidar, Coral waited to watch the affects of his words over the wolf.

Lapidar's tone hardened as he replied, "Speaking of back-up, where's yours? Stupid enough to initiate the 'great' plan alone?"

"Alone?"

And this time Coral's face truly lit up with delight.

"Not at all. But I thought you'd have noticsssed the commonessss of our ssspecies by now."

"Our?" Lapidar questioned.

"*Our,*" Coral reemphasized and, although his gaze did not break from Lapidar's, he had implied a look-out-from-behind in his daring.

Lapidar did and the moment the wolf had his attention off of the doctor, there was an almighty "kasha!" then Achak found his palm pushing beneath the chin of a fanged man.

Neither had fallen to the floor, but Achak's right arm was bound to his side by Dr. Coral's body lock. Achak was cranking his own neck back from the pointed tips while trying to simultaneously force the doctor's neck away.

Their throats sputtered with the struggle. But it was Coral who had the fangs dripping with venom—toxic droplets that fell to the carpet between them. Achak had to move his fingers out of the way, lest death should be absorbed through the pores of his skin. Each dodge cost him as the fangs drew steadily nearer.

All the while, his knees were buckling and shaking until that point in which he could feel the hot breath blowing against his collar. Then an icy-burn splashed and dripped from his adam's apple and Achak panicked, letting a yelp unhinge his grip on the doctor's chin.

Falling back, he saw the gray streak come between his and Coral's collapse.

Two transmogrifications occurred simultaneously: the first being Dr. Coral's complete change as he dropped down in the form of a smaller and more slippery target. Then, having missed his man, Lapidar went tumbling and rolling away on the carpet as a wolf. Getting to his feet, Coral stood up again in human form—the labcoat hanging from his shoulders—Lapidar, however, did not.

"No!" was being shouted over and over again and all Achak could decipher from it was that Mariam was screaming.

"Thanks," Achak panted over his knees as he looked at the unstirring body of his partner. He didn't know why he was smiling, but the fact that he was still alive was something that was too good to take for granted.

He waited for his partner to come to his senses and when it did not happen—for he could still see Lapidar's chest rise and fall—he continued to watch and wait without concern.

Walking over, Achak called out. "Lapidar? Alright there?" He smiled between breaths.

Dr. Coral was doing something like wiping the corners of his mouth, but also rasping out of deep famish for Achak to spare more than a cautionary glance towards.

Still feeling of ease, Achak bent over his lying friend and saw the small speckles of red fur upon his leg. For the first time, Achak became aware of the way Mariam was wailing.

The sounds hurt more than his ears but felt like a seismic quaking that began in his chest. Every nerve seemed to startle to it and send electric shocks through his body.

He wanted to turn around and yell at Mariam to stop her piercing shrieks, but for all the ear-throbbing pain she caused, Achak knew that it was really the sight of Lapidar causing him the greater pangs.

Stiff and shaking in his joints, Achak had trouble lowering to his knees to bend over Lapidar. His fingers touched the long gray fur of his back and sent prickles through his hand and up his wrist. He then moved them across the shorter white hairs of his chest.

Lapidar's eyes were tightly closed and his breathing heavy. The pink tongue was lost somewhere in his open and almost quiet jaws. What life remained came in small twitches of his angled paws. He almost looked to be running, perhaps harmlessly chasing after rabbits in a dream he was having. But then his chest fell in succession with the shallowest and most final breath.

In that moment, Achak stopped breathing too. He kept trying to say something, but none of the right words came to his head and instead he was left with pointless utterings of "please" and "no."

The fur beneath Achak's fingers was fast becoming cold. Achak bent his head down until his forehead touched the silver strands atop the wolf's.

"Now, let'sss sssee. That'sss one down."

Achak eyes shot up from Lapidar as he turned to face Coral.

No longer wearing his spectacles, the glasses around doctor's eyes were black and pearly. His tongue came out to taste the air and Achak saw its two pointy tips instead of one rounded pink muscle. He looked disgustedly into the doctor's not so humane face and felt the shape change in his own eyes as he tried to match them unblinking against the serpent's.

"I sssuggest you leave here, boy. There's the flavor of fear in the air." His tongue flapped in front of his nose again. "And I can ssswallow feathers whole."

The diamond pupils rolled briefly over to Mariam before fixing themselves on Achak, who held fast. He found himself not petrified in the gaze of the serpent, but fire-blazed with life and raring for revenge.

When Coral's lips curled, the skin creased and split like rubber up the sides of his face, higher than a human could manage. His once bony cheeks became deformed with the mouth spanning from ear to ear, but no visible lips as though tucked away.

"Ssso angry, but it'sss not as though I did anyone a disssservicsse. The wolf murdered too, you know?"

"Not like you!" chuffled Achak.

"Do the sscircumssstances really matter?" Coral exclaimed, but the look on Achak's face must have told him that circumstances did matter because he carried on justifiably. "I'm trying to preserve a planet!"

"By killing off one of its creatures?" Achak declared in outrage.

"Man was never meant to dominate. Paradissse flourished without him and he dessstroyed it from the outssside, just as he does now, ssseparate from animals and nature. Sssuperior and oppresssively ranked above all life and matter. Expelled from paradissse for his hubrisss and sssoon the world."

Getting to his feet, Achak began to make changes in the way he presented himself to the doctor. He was determined not to show any surprise at anything the doctor might say or do. He had expected this, hadn't he? He just had not expected himself to be alone, but if he hoped for an ally, they were both lying on the floor.

Coral did not seem to mind that Achak was being quiet and continued to wait in his half-formed self. Then Achak noticed that the diamonds were gliding in the doctor's sockets back toward Mariam who was still kneeling on the floor next to Roy. She was oblivious to being watched while her eyes overflowed with tears and all that lay before her was a blurred heap.

Achak took a daring step toward the doctor which was tested by his reflexes when a wad of yellowish filling soared in his direction. Having steered himself out of harm's way, he felt the excitement double-up in his chest. His eyes flashed at the doctor.

"Come on, boy!" Coral bellowed. "Thisss is sssilly. You againssst me?" Bursting in high mirth, Coral shook his head. "I don't care what the wolf might have thought of you, you're ssstill nothing more than a ssscaredy cat. You've got a long way to go before you come to facsse me. Now go home." He made a particular show of his fangs.

"I have them too," Achak said at once.

"Have what?" Coral spat. His face rid of pleasure in a wide frown.

"Fangs." Achak stated. And there was a piercing echo as the doctor broke into glee.

Achak knew this was the time to summon his renowned weapon. Though Lapidar would not have approved of Achak's amateur meronization, he knew that it was the only sure way to fight. Not quite human, not completely animal, this was the middle livelihood by which all Hybrid accepted their two natures.

He had never imagined what meronizing might feel like, but he was not ready for the tightening pressure around his mouth and let out a yelp that was about as inhuman as the one elongated tooth that pointed beneath his chin.

The other fang stopped expanding about halfway and left off where a series of jagged edges lined the molar.

Coral went quiet and his eyes narrowed without blinking.

It did not matter that his one fang had snapped, Achak had threatened more in his change than Coral could with all his venom-filled speech.

"Ssso thisss is how it is?" Coral hissed while he began flexing the muscle of his jaws.

"Your doing," Achak slurred behind his fangs and looked down at Lapidar. "It'll be your undoing."

Dr. Coral put his tongue out. "I've ssstill got the extra hand on this, boy, and you've got to watch out for bone unless you don't mind losing the other fang."

"Do you think a lack of venom is going to matter once I've pinned you with this fang?" Achak asked rhetorically.

Dr. Coral hid his fangs behind his lips and watched Achak, the diamond outlining his profile and sizing him up.

Achak did not need to take any body measurements of the doctor. His eyes had mislead him once before, when he thought to estimate through size alone, but by species, a snake had a body comprised mainly of muscle. How else could Coral have restrained a teenager of almost twice his size? Though perhaps had Achak learned to meronize his sabertooth strength, he could have overpowered the doctor without Lapidar's sacrifice.

He knew the wolf would not approve of his merow tactics now, but his friend was no longer here to show him how to fight with honor and his murderer stood as the insidious challenger. *Run or be killed:* Lapidar would not have turned his back on such a threat.

There was Coral's unblinking diamonds, where Achak could see the blood circulating as cold as the man himself.

He charged at the eyes with the desire to puncture one blind and heard Coral shout something like "Neanderthal" before receiving one of the doctor's swinging arms in the pit of his stomach.

Both hissed and bared their fangs at a distance to show that neither had anticipated the other's move. Mariam was quiet again, but Achak could sense her dark beads following his back.

He felt more animal now than ever in full skin as he could not ignore the slinks he made with his legs that felt more like a prowl. The instinct even occurred to him to circle the serpent before attacking next. Coral remained in one spot with his heading bobbing in a ready strike.

A rush of wind grazed Achak's right cheek and he found Dr. Coral's face next to his.

"Careful, kitty," he hissed into Achak's ear and recoiled back to the center of the undefined circle.

Achak fumbled to grasp the speed at which Coral had struck. He circled him all the same. His eyes focused on the humanoid flesh of the serpent's neck where the veins bulged as the head rocked. He saw the throat roll as the doctor swallowed and leapt back to avoid what he thought would come to be another strike.

"Jumpy?" Coral laughed.

Enraged, Achak bounded forward then changed his mind and stopped himself before his rashness got the better of him. However, Dr. Coral responded in full extension of his body, lashing air. It must have been a second that the serpent's trap hung when Achak saw the limit of its reach and threw himself at the doctor's feet. He sunk his teeth and fang into the doctor's ankle.

The dive had not been well planned which was beginning to feel like fractures in his elbow, but the pangs only made Achak cling harder with his teeth.

His eyes were streaming as his teeth met bone. Coral let out a yell with a twist of his ankle inside Achak's mouth and managed to unwedge himself free. Achak backed away on all fours having come to full sabertooth sometime during his ankle-hold.

The doctor had moved away so quickly that Achak made a blind lunge to find his target. But his teeth closed around nothing and he came up empty clawed.

Beneath him lay the small coiled serpent. Its tongue was breezing under his neck, flapping and cackling. A hard stroke came across Achak's face in what he was sure had been a venomous strike and he toppled the opposite way.

Screeching heard now, Achak held his breath for the second coming. When it did not, he blinked and saw the black feathers falling, followed by the snap of a tail being whipped around in air.

Mariam had Coral clenched between her claws and looked to be struggling to keep him lifted by the neck. He was squirming and hissing so that Mariam had to concentrate both on flapping and avoiding the flailing tail.

Achak changed to his human hands and legs and stood up. He felt the side of his face and was ready to bet that it was Mariam who had grazed past him.

Before he could wonder what Mariam intended to do with the twisting bundle of serpent, she back-flapped nearer to one of the open windows. Then Achak watched her drop about a foot under her heavy and struggling load so that she was no longer aligned with the window but with the wall.

"No, no, no!" Achak shouted.

Mariam steadily regained her height, but the snake was becoming trickier to manage. Coral was now making snaps and lashes to clip Mariam's wings.

When Achak saw them crossing over the windowsill, he ran forward. Mariam made a heavy thrust with her wings before releasing the serpent and Coral made one more very powerful whip with his tail before dropping and snagged Mariam by the tail feathers. Both figures descended and Achak threw his whole upper body out the window. Arms outstretched, he caught Mariam before she could fall to the great distance at which Coral spiraled. His limbless body disappeared in a patch of shrubbery that grew along the Domestica walls.

Achak pulled himself and Mariam inside and set her down on the carpet. She rose with black feathers drifting from her velvet sleeves. Her lips looked colorless but she was beaming at Achak in a way that countered his unease. Without so much as a wail or shriek, she threw her arms around him. He shook under her as she clicked her heels with no consideration for the pressure and body weight she forced on Achak.

Despite the strain on his shoulders, his heart fluttered as he hugged back. He was sure nothing could change the way he felt but that was before his eyes fell again upon the broken glass.

Achak let his arms fall from Mariam as he followed the trail of shards to where Lapidar lay. Mariam pulled away, grabbed Achak's hand, and walked him over. He bent over and stared down at his departed friend. It was a moment that Achak held onto long enough to hear Roy moan his way back into consiousness. All feelings of victory and resolve had left him.

Meanwhile, two turbans lay empty-headed by the double doors some distance from the elevator. Beneath the back fence rails of the Domestica terrace, three serpents slithered under and out of the property. The one centered and leading had a striped backside of red, yellow, and black. Those of the less impressive scales with brown backsides disappeared in the greenery with the former.

Loyalty towards a Hybrid's own kind is his greatest instinct, pride, bias and ignorance, you know?

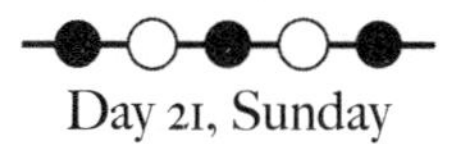

Day 21, Sunday

16
An Answer to the Wolf's Cry

Mariam was without her purple blouse. Somehow the sight of her in all black and without the proudest of raven colors shook Achak more than the sobs he could hear issuing from the kitchen as Viv tried to pull herself together before her children came down from the upstairs. Both Achak and Mariam had had to go shopping the previous evening for something suitable to wear and no matter how often Achak had reminded himself why he needed a black suit, Lapidar's death never seemed quite real.

Now that Achak wore the suit, his breath felt a little heavier however often he pulled at his collar and loosened the tie.

"Stop doing that," Mariam had said and walked over to readjust his suit each time.

Achak had liked it better when she was scolding him. The grief was building in her silence and Achak knew he would do something stupid if he could not find a better place for himself. From sitting at the base of the staircase, he had stood up several times to stroll around the Gray's living room and had never taken up a seat. Maybe he was just waiting for someone to tell him to sit down.

He stood up from the stairs again as he heard the small footsteps padding down in their dress shoes. Achak turned around to see Lapidar's children walking side by side with Lacie's hand in her big brother's. With them, came down Tehya.

Holding off his pacing in the living room, Achak continued to watch the children's descent. Even Mariam had ceased her sniffling to watch those more rightfully at a loss.

Tehya had stopped on the last step where she stared uncertainly at Achak. But having no clearer notion with what to do with himself, Achak had no directive with which to give her on appropriate conduct. Instead, he went on to notice how her long black hair, now shorter in the front, was looking more like Sirena's had, except that there was no red. She even had a very long black skirt that billowed behind her when she walked.

"Oh," Viv choked. "Don't you two look handsome." She rushed over to hug her children who were standing mournfully by the stairs and waiting for some instruction.

Achak saw the faintest glint of a tear run down Tyler's face and fought to hold in the burning from his own eyes when he felt a tug on his pant leg. Mariam was gesturing for him to sit down, her face ashen.

He sat down beside her as her tug had suggested and looked at the face between her hands expectantly. But there was disappointment in his waiting as Mariam spoke no more. Tehya rushed to sit quietly at his other side. When Achak glanced up again, it was to find all three Grays standing together in the living room walkway and in that motionless state that told Achak they were ready.

Achak stood up and reached his hand out for one of Mariam's to help her up. She walked forward and let go of him.

Arriving first at the front door, Mariam opened it and let everyone pass. Achak was the second to last and held the door open for Viv, but she would be the one with the keys to stay behind and lock the door.

Apart from being made useless, Achak felt down right comfortless in the back seat of the car with Lapidar's children. He knew the siblings would find surer consolation in each other than with Achak between them. Still, Achak felt a closer connection with the children, especially with Tyler, than he could express.

Tehya, meanwhile, was at the window seat with Lacie next to her and making small braids in the child's lighter hair. Every once in a while, she would glance up from her braiding hands to look at Achak, who seldom acknowledged the eye contact.

And before Achak had the time to understand the relationship he had with the Grays, Mariam's voice came from his side. "Achak," she whispered as though they were already in the procession chapel and indeed she was holding the passenger door open.

Achak got out of the car and looked at the short white walls and triangular rooftop and noticed how far it seemed from the curb. Or maybe it was just the scale that made all funeral chapels look a great deal further down a long pathway surrounded by grass than they actually were. But even the walk to the inside felt a timelier distance than one would normally have to travel to go from one end of the sidewalk to the other. Of course, with all things considered, Achak was not taking strides towards the open doors in his usual hurried pace or with the hustle of students trying to avoid the tardy bell.

Rather, he was keeping at a slow pace side by side with Mariam, behind the Grays and his sister. And no matter how resentful he was of Mariam's silence, he was at least grateful for her company. Without her, he would be forced to walk the distance to the chapel alone, as the sole witness to Lapidar's death, unless Detective Hutchinson did not object to accompanying him in the same way as Mariam. He had to remind himself that the whole procession would not have been possible without the help of the detective and that the man probably had more important jobs to take care of than being an escort for a 17-year-old boy.

Thankfully the detective had become involved as Achak did not know how to set up funeral arrangements for those Hybrid who had died in their animal skins. If it was not for Mr. Hutchinson, Lapidar probably would have wound up in some pet cemetery or else thrown in a ditch somewhere with the rest of the day's trash for all Achak knew of how to go about treating Hybrid bodies. Vivian had actually cried at the top of her lungs in wondering how she would get a priest to speak on behalf of a wolf, for she too had not learned all there was to living amongst Hybrid.

Then at the end of all that walking, there was nothing more splendid than a small plain room. Neither bright nor dim, the lighting cast a pastel of blue over the walls. It bounced off everything colorless except for the casket, which had to be kept closed under the circumstances. Purest in the room, it had only the black adornments of the attendees' clothing raging war against the blue lights. The windows were not stained glass, but the crisscross of their panes inevitably made them impossible to see out of and emitted only obscure amounts of light through their blurry transparencies.

Achak stopped to look at all those who had congregated in the pews. Left and center sat Giles from The Basement and an older woman with gray curls and pearls that must have been his wife. Two girls that looked like they could have been tenders at the bar sat with them, but they were so much identical in hair color and black skirts that Achak had to assume they were the daughters. To Achak's right and almost at a blind spot, he saw the man to whom he owed the most: Detective Hutchinson.

The Doberman did not look as slick or interrogative now that his tailcoat was replaced by a more modern black jacket, but the attire he had fitted was none-theless as glossy and authoritative as the primness of his straight-combed hair. Next to him was the most restless teenager Achak had ever set his eyes upon. The dark boy was more than fidgety in his suit, while his behavior bore more resemblance to a puppy that has known the attention of a dozen children's hands coming to pet him. He looked positively joyful to be in a funeral chapel.

"Dô?" Achak mouthed.

The detective tilted his head with a grim smile and Achak nodded back before speeding up to rejoin Mariam and taking a seat with the Grays in the front pews. Sitting at the end of the row, Achak suddenly became aware of how many and yet how few people there were in the chapel.

A slow and elderly man, who had only just made his arrival, began to walk forward down the aisle. He came to stand only a few strides in front of Achak and to the center of the upraised floor.

"Loyal husband and protective father," the minister began. "These are noble purposes in the Lord's eyes, but too often they are missed by one member of the family or another. The man who lies before you was not among these. He served his duty.

"Strangest of all in this instance, we shall find that he performed his duty not with a familiarity shown to him, but with his own sense of what husbandry and fatherhood should entail. He was not given the most nurturing or even sheltered of upbringings and so to have provided as much for his children was his own prevalence out of the darkness. And it just goes to show you how one man can make a difference.

"How one man striving to break away from a vicious cycle can change and shape a better path for his children and their children, and all generations to come thereafter."

Almost half an hour past and Achak could still feel the throbbing ache in his chest of the minister's continued speech.

"Lapidar Gray's death was not a tragedy of careless undertakings..."

No, it was a murder, Achak thought instinctively.

"It was a sacrifice. And to all those attending his farewell today, you do so as more than his family and friends, but as those who experienced his greatest impacts on life. You see, all of you have been changed—not so much by his death, as by his life.

"He has done more than leave behind a spirit by which we can remember him;

he has left behind traces of himself that each one of you sitting here today will carry out with you when you leave and take with you into the world. In the faces of his children alone, you can see the changes that his protection, his compassion, and of course the not so agreeable effects of his fleas and table manners have brought into each one of us."

Achak broke his eyes away from the white coffin for the first time to stifle a laugh and look at Mariam, who was struggling not to grin back.

"So when you leave here today, do not forget that although you are leaving with one less member of your life, you are taking with you every positive change that person has made to your life... and perhaps one more flea by which to remember him by."

The last of smiles were shared as the minister walked back down the short aisle of pews. Letting his cold sweaty hands slide off his lap, Achak stood up and watched the Grays grieve first over the casket. He had been dreading the moment when the minister would bring closure to his eulogy and ask that the others wait as immediate family pay their respects.

Achak stood back and, with some discomfort, Mariam stood slightly apart from even him.

As he was about to break the distance, a hand came upon his left shoulder.

"How did you like him?" Detective Hutchinson asked. His eyes were glinting at Achak, who straightened himself to thank the detective properly.

"Yes," Achak said. "He was just that sort of man that I think Lapidar would have hired himself."

The detective smiled. "I think it's a little too early for you to be telling jokes."

Achak attempted to laugh when his face went suddenly rigid. He had not intended to bring up the discussion, but he had been biting his tongue for a week, attending school like there had been no interruption in his lessons, and waiting for a phone call that never came from the Bred HyCouncil. The words were spilling from his mouth as though the matter concerned another face in the room.

"What's the news?" he whispered fiercely. "Manu? Domestica? CORAL?"

The last name came out from his mouth with such feisty demand that even the nearby Jack turned his ears toward the name and re-echoed it as, "Ladon."

Roy nodded to the Jack as though trying to quiet the boy down, but he made the same request less subtly to Achak. "Ladon Coral was indeed the inventor and owner of HydroMax industries. And no body, snake or otherwise, was ever recovered. But this is not the place to discuss these matters. We'll save our chat for a more appropriate time."

Achak turned around to see Mariam's lean figure standing near the casket. Tehya was wiping her eyes and muttering a little chant that she had asked Grandpa to teach her. When her voice cracked, there was an even more anguished sob to follow and she went dashing off away from Mariam. More than Achak's arm received a pang as Tehya ran past him, grazing him by the sleeve as she went. And he knew that he had done something wrong by not talking to her. Very likely, she was taking Lapidar's death more personally than Achak and he would have to convince her otherwise.

Roy must have had a sense for Achak's distress, for his next condolence was not spoken in words but in a gesture of clamping Achak on the shoulder. He turned and began to walk down the aisle.

"Don't let the fleas get you down."

Roy's callback was something of a wind-carried whisper. Achak could not be certain it was spoken. In the next minute, Roy had disappeared from the doorframe.

"Was that the detective who helped you?"

Achak was surprised to find anyone at his side, but Viv was not sounding as mournful now that she was looking away from the casket.

"I had hoped to thank him personally for... for everything."

"Um, I'm sure he'll be at the burial," he told her assuredly.

"Oh, right—well..." Viv's eyes filled with water, which put Achak in a tight spot to wonder how best to console her.

"Achak."

Relief came as he heard his name hissed and saw Mariam trying to get him to come over by the casket. It could not have been a better reason to give Viv her space. He stepped onto the elevated floor space and walked over beside Mariam.

Not sure what to do, think, or how close his relationship to Lapidar permitted him to stand near the casket, Achak kept about a foot of space between it.

"Oh, come off it," Mariam hissed furiously at his side and grabbed his arm to pull him closer. "He's not going to curse you."

"Alright," Achak said, but his immobile position, while inches from the casket, still did not satisfy Mariam.

She forced one of his hands to come on top of the casket and the surface came coldly to Achak's fingers.

"Well?" Mariam raised her eyebrows to him.

He would have preferred to shrug his shoulders than to tell her what was really going on inside his mind at the touch of his friend's casket with the lifeless body lying beneath the layers of paint, wood, and cushion. However, finding neither shrug nor corpse description a very sensitive response to her question, he said, "I think I can feel him kicking."

"Oh, you two! Honestly!" Mariam made a feeble attempt to glower at him while fighting off a smile then stormed off toward the back end of the chapel.

Achak beamed at her back, but when he returned his hand on top of the casket, his mind was filled with anything but jokes. In his head flashed all the visual re-creations of that day to make him want to wish that he was doing nothing more than recalling a bad dream. It all burned in the pupils of his eyes with the word: "unfair," cycling through each and every one of his relapses.

Wanting more than anything to tell Lapidar something of assurance as though he was doing nothing more than wishing his friend a good night's sleep, he spoke under his breath. "I'll find him." Then, moving his hand across the polished surface, he let it fall to his side.

In his mind, he was giving repeated thanks and commending Lapidar for both the friend and man—and unforgettably, the wolf—he had been. When he moved away, Giles and his wife stepped forward to visit the casket next.

Achak came up grimly beside Mariam at the back of the chapel. She gave him a braver smirk and teasingly poked him on the left shoulder, which in all likeliness, she did not know had the stitched punctures of a mole's claws.

"Hey," he said, rubbing over the bandages, but Mariam did not take that to mean "ouch."

She shrugged in explanation and Achak stayed beside her. He did not want to leave the chapel, which to him meant leaving Lapidar behind as well.

Yet, he found himself walking across the field of slender green grass and forced to stand above the ground where Lapidar would soon be laid to rest. This was not the field in front of the chapel, but another distant undisturbed land where no amount of traffic or street noise could come past the trees that formed a barrier around the park. Achak looked around at all the other tombstones and wondered how Lapidar's would look among these.

He felt a hand slide into his and squeezed Tehya's fingers tightly to show just how much he wanted her hand to stay there.

When he could no longer stand in his quiet thoughts, Achak again looked around at all those who had come to show their lowered heads. He might have returned his own head to face the earth, but the dog that sniffed around headstones was bringing him a sense of peace that he never thought he could know again. There were other things he needed to ask Roy about.

"So what are you going to do with him?" Achak drifted near that man and looked back at the jackal he had released like a pet dog. Dô was sniffing at the flowers near Lapidar's casket.

"Dunno," Roy answered. "To be honest, the kid's starting to grow on me." He smirked as he watched the Jack go from being a jackal to a 14-year-old boy and then back again.

Achak could hear Tehya giggle from some observed position nearer to the gathering.

"The HyCouncil would like me to put him back into the wild," Roy continued. "But I'm not too sure about that. He's been domesticated—wouldn't be able to survive on his own."

Roy looked at Achak with a saddening expression that Achak worried would result in a comment about Lapidar. It didn't.

"I've been reading through some of the documents that Manu and Coral left behind." Roy frowned some more. "It turns out that the lad won't be able to live out as many human years and he'll grow fast. I know he looks about your age, but he's really only two-years-old."

Achak inclined his head. He had already known about The Jacks' shortened life span from Coral, but he had spoken none of those details to Roy. The memories of Coral angered Achak, who had not wanted the serpent to survive, let alone to have escaped. Achak remembered only too well that day in which Coral had confessed most of his plans to Achak because he thought the "boy" would never speak again, only to have Lapidar free him moments later.

It was a painful memory to reflect upon, as any reminders of Lapidar tended to be. They always filled Achak's throat with fiery stings that he had to cool off by taking a drink of water. And any time he picked up that glass of clear liquid, no matter what faucet it came from, there was Hydro-Max swirling maliciously in the glass under his nose: telling him that his best friend had been murdered and the one responsible had escaped.

He had not yet asked the detective what had been done about HydroMax, but now, in Lapidar's non-living presence, it seemed like the appropriate time.

"I've asked the boy to come work with some of the HyCouncil as a search dog, you know, to keep him out of trouble." Roy chuckled. "He got excited when I explained the job to him, though I'm not entirely sure he understood me." Shaking his head, Roy concluded, "I think I'll just adopt him."

Achak was looking back in the direction of the Jack, who was staring at his new master with his tail wagging. The sight of the new pair made it difficult for Achak to bring up what he needed to ask, but he forced himself to mention it anyway.

"What's going to happen with HydroMax?" his eyes stayed on Roy even as he heard Tehya gasp, eavesdropping. Mariam too had choked over a sob while drifting nearer for Achak's company.

"To be honest," Roy sighed. "I just don't know. It's now in the government's hands to look into the matter, collect whatever scientific evidence they can find, and delegate how to remove the product from the market without killing people."

"I'm sure they'll find a way," Mariam said, wrapping her arm around Achak.

He remembered there was a time when that arm once wrapped around Marcus and how much Anthony had wanted to feel it around him. But Mariam had drawn herself nearer to Achak enough times in the past week not to alarm Achak by doing it now.

"Mariam's right," Roy seconded. "The treatment for those dependent on Hydro-Max may be as simple to cure as removing the product from their diet gradually so that the body relearns how to collect nutrients on its own."

"I suppose." Achak looked at Roy with a weary eye. "I just don't want—"

"To let *him* down." Mariam finished and she pulled Achak towards her. She took both his hands into hers and Achak had never stared into a pair of warmer eyes. "You won't."

"He'd have been proud to see all the things you did at Domestica... and that you've been checking in on his family," Roy added.

Achak smiled bleakly.

"Hey, come on!" Tehya said, pulling one of Achak's arms away from Mariam. "I have something to show you."

Achak stared at her blankly, but he was being forced to follow by the hand she tugged along.

"Where are we going?"

Tehya didn't answer and instead led Achak away from the field and took him nearer to the trees that lined the roadway. He knew of only one other person that would have pulled him aside and dragged him under a tree like this, and she—like Lapidar—was no longer with him. He could remember the first Hybrid to show him transmogrification, a girl with crimson hair and an even fierier blaze of spirit.

Under the shade of a cedar, Tehya released Achak's hand and let him wait for her as she went on giggling in private and excited humor.

"Okay, you ready?"

"I am," Achak answered her.

There was a moment when it looked like Tehya was holding her breath as though under water, then Achak watched her exhale and there was no recognizable form of Tehya left to stare at. But Achak knew it was her, even if her head now only came up past his knees.

GW01606066

BRITAIN'S FOREIGN POLICY *in* EGYPT AND SUDAN *1947–1956*

BRITAIN'S FOREIGN POLICY *in* EGYPT AND SUDAN 1947–1956

J. A. HAIL

BRITAIN'S FOREIGN POLICY IN EGYPT AND SUDAN
1947–1956

Ithaca Press is an imprint of Garnet Publishing Limited

Published by
Garnet Publishing Limited
8 Southern Court
South Street
Reading
Berkshire RG1 4QS
UK

First edition

ISBN 0 86372 206 7

British Library Cataloguing-in-Publication Data
A catalogue record for this book is available from the British Library

Jacket and book design by David Rose
Typeset by Samantha Abley

Printed in Lebanon

CONTENTS

Introduction

This study aims to provide for the general reader a chronological account of Anglo-Egyptian political relations from 1947 to 1956. I consider these years to be the most crucial period in the more than 70 years of the British involvement in Egypt for they marked a turning-point in the political relations between the two countries. The study begins with a description of the historical background in order to set the events in context and give some understanding of the complex issues at stake in Anglo-Egyptian relations during the period under consideration. The conclusion also describes briefly post-1954 events that illustrate the collapse of Anglo-Egyptian relations.

Egypt was of great importance to the British Empire for many years. This was due to its strategic geographical position at the crossroads between East and West. Egypt's significance to the British Empire was reinforced after the opening of the Suez Canal in 1869. The canal became vital to British commerce and mobility. Many British political figures publicly acknowledged that Britain had a strategic and commercial interest in Egypt. The opening of the canal made Egypt the gateway to British India and East Africa; the canal route was also the shortest route to the British colonies in Australia and New Zealand. In consequence, Britain became the largest user and greatest beneficiary of the canal. At any given time, more than 80 per cent of the canal traffic was British, and Britain became the largest shareholder in the Suez Canal Company.

The increased economic and strategic importance of the canal to Britain, together with the failure of the Egyptian government to meet its obligations and to pay its financial debt to Britain, eventually led to the occupation of Egypt by British armed forces. This was in 1882, when Britain established control of the canal. The legitimacy of the British action was questioned and the Egyptians objected to the occupation.

Egypt was still part of the Ottoman Empire and remained so until 1914 when Britain ended Ottoman sovereignty over Egypt and declared it a British protectorate. This marked Britain's first attempt to base its presence in Egypt on legal grounds. Nevertheless, the Egyptians continued to resist British occupation: soon after Britain signed the armistice in November 1918 serious disturbances took place in Egypt. The Egyptians had hoped that the end of the First World War would mark the end of British occupation. This did not happen, however, and in early 1919 Britain used its armed forces to crush the Egyptian nationalist revolt and set up the Milner Mission to investigate the problem. The Milner Mission concluded that Britain should commence negotiations with Egypt.

Subsequently, in February 1922, Britain unilaterally issued a declaration of Egyptian independence but reserved to itself certain rights related to: (1) the security of British communications; (2) the defence of Egypt against foreign aggression; (3) the protection of foreign interests and minorities in Egypt; and (4) the Sudan.

In the following fourteen years, political relations between Britain and Egypt left much to be desired. The two countries made eight unsuccessful attempts at negotiating a treaty in order to resolve their differences. Finally, on 26 August 1936, the Anglo-Egyptian Treaty of Friendship and Alliance was agreed, recognizing Egypt as a sovereign state but legalizing the presence of British troops in the Suez Canal Zone. Britain claimed to have given Egypt full independence, but the 1936 treaty "reserved" only the question of Sudan. All the other points were abandoned or, in the case of point one, confined to the Suez Canal. Egyptian nationalists considered that, by this, and by maintaining a large number of troops in Egypt, Britain had imposed severe restrictions upon Egypt's real independence.

A major issue in the Anglo-Egyptian dispute was the question of Sudan. The 1936 treaty implied joint administration of Sudan by Egypt and Britain. However, the British governor-general of the Sudan was recognized as having absolute and undisputed power. He was given full authority for all official and non-official appointments and promotions in the country. Despite Egyptian discontent and the disturbances, it can be said that the treaty worked well for Britain during the Second World War. Afterwards the Egyptians stepped up the pressure, demanding a revision of the 1936 treaty and hoping to redefine Anglo-Egyptian relations and to secure the unity of Egypt and Sudan. Again Britain refused to satisfy Egyptian demands. Britain was convinced that, despite the defeat of the Axis powers, the security threat had not entirely disappeared. This time it was the Soviet Union that emerged as a threat. The United States and the Soviet Union had become superpowers with global interests and were just beginning to compete in this critical area. While Britain still depended on Egypt because of the Suez route to India, both the United States and the Soviet Union wanted Britain to leave India and neither power was happy about the British presence in Egypt. Britain, though its empire was in decline, still had extensive commitments worldwide. Despite Britain's dwindling resources and its inability to meet its commitments fully, it still wanted to hold on to its interests in the region and protect them. Egypt, on the other hand, wanted nothing less than the attainment of full independence and unity with neighbouring Sudan. It therefore gave this goal its undivided attention.

With such divergent aims, and the imbalance in their priorities, the two parties entered again into protracted negotiations in 1946. A draft agreement, the Sidky–Bevin agreement, was produced in November 1946. The following year Sidky's successor, Nokrashy Pasha, abandoned the Sidky–Bevin agreement and referred the Anglo-Egyptian dispute to the United Nations. After the matter had been debated in the UN Security Council, bilateral negotiations resumed between Britain and Egypt but were interrupted once again by a new obstacle. Between 1946 and 1948 Britain was preoccupied with the Palestine question. As the mandatory power since 1920, it had tried to hold the balance between Arab and Jewish claims. After the Second World War, however, the Jews were determined to reclaim Palestine as their homeland. The Arab states, including Egypt, resisted this claim and the first Arab–Israeli war resulted.

This caused Egypt to confront Britain on new grounds and further complicated Anglo-Egyptian relations.

The years after 1947 show only that neither country was able to meet the other's expectations and demands. In 1950, the Egyptian Wafdist government, which had concluded the 1936 treaty, returned to power and resumed negotiations for the revision of that treaty. The negotiations again failed to progress, however. As a result, and under pressure from the Egyptian nationalists, the Muslim Brotherhood, and other anti-British demonstrators, the Wafdist government was compelled to unilaterally abrogate the 1936 Anglo-Egyptian Treaty of Friendship and Alliance. Britain challenged the legality of the Wafdist government's action and refused to withdraw its forces from Egypt. Hostilities among the various conflicting parties heightened and there was a blatant show of public discontent not only against Britain but also against the Egyptian Wafdist government. Thus 1951 marked not only the beginning of the decline of British supremacy in Egypt, but also the decline of the Egyptian monarchy and its traditional government. Ultimately, the Egyptian government failed to contain or divert the rising tide of discontent, which led to a military *coup d'état* on 23 July 1952.

The Free Officers' movement conducted its *coup* under the leadership of General Muhammad Naguib and succeeded in overthrowing the Egyptian monarchy. After a while, General Naguib was replaced by Colonel Gamal Abdel Nasser, an earlier leader of the Free Officers' movement. On assuming power, the new Egyptian regime expressed its willingness to solve the existing disagreements between Britain and Egypt. Britain welcomed the gesture and, accordingly, negotiations again took place in Cairo. As a result the new Egyptian regime signed an agreement with Britain in 1953 regarding the future of the Sudan which had been a major stumbling-block in previous negotiations. This agreement provided for Sudanese self-determination in a free atmosphere and led to Sudan's emergence as an independent state. In the following year, President Nasser of Egypt signed the historic treaty of 1954 concerning the evacuation of British troops from Egypt, so marking the end of British military occupation. Unfortunately, this agreement was relatively short-lived.

In 1956, new economic and political challenges caused confrontations between Britain and Egypt leading Britain to plan and conspire with France and Israel in the invasion of the Suez Canal Zone.

This brief introduction describes Anglo-Egyptian political relations in general terms, beginning with the British interest in, and then occupation of, Egypt, and ending with the British evacuation in 1954. This book focuses on the crucial period from 1946 to 1954 but it also includes a complete survey of the events which preceded, and those which immediately followed, the focal period as this was considered important to an understanding of the roots of the conflict and to further evaluation of its consequences.

In the remaining part of this introduction, I shall describe the purpose of the study, the organization of the research, and raise some research questions. Towards the end of this part I shall advance my argument and discuss my research method.

The general purpose of this work is to examine and explain the developments and processes involved in Anglo-Egyptian political relations during the period under study. Specifically, the investigation focuses on the factors that produced both threats and opportunities, resulting in strife at one time and harmony at another. More particularly, it focuses on those political attitudes, conflicts and pressures which determined certain political negotiating positions and strategies and produced particular results.

The book is divided into seven chapters, each of which examines a different aspect of Anglo-Egyptian relations. Chapter One provides the historical background and covers in detail events from 1882 to the end of 1946.

Although the main aim is to study specific political events in their specific political context, it also proved useful to consider their broader context as well. Thus, in Chapters Two and Three, I examine the effects of external factors on the issues under study. In Chapter Two, I look at the role played by the United Nations with respect to several issues which complicated the Anglo-Egyptian dispute. I examine the opinions of members of the UN Security Council and their recommendations with regard to solving Anglo-Egyptian disagreements. In Chapter Three, I briefly examine another factor from the external political environment which played a significant role in delaying the negotiation of a settlement between Britain and Egypt. This chapter addresses the Palestine War of 1948. Chapter Four moves into one of the most critical times in the history of Anglo-Egyptian relations: the last unsuccessful set of Anglo-Egyptian negotiations is discussed and I examine in detail the factors leading to the abrogation of the 1936 treaty of friendship and alliance. In Chapter Five, I examine the political events leading to the Egyptian military *coup d'état* of 1952. Chapter Six discusses the Anglo-Egyptian settlement of 1954 and the events leading to it. The final chapter takes us beyond the focal period under study and analyses the factors which contributed to the collapse of the 1954 agreement and the events which led to the Suez crisis of 1956.

An early review of the relevant literature generated two sets of research questions. The first set was broad and general in nature. It helped me to identify the issues and guided my selection and organization of sources. The second set of questions was more narrow and specific. It led to a searching exploration of the issues, and the answers to these specific questions laid the groundwork for my argument.

The two sets of research questions – general and specific – are described below. First, three general questions facilitated the selection and organization of sources at an early phase of the research:

1. Following examination of the development and processes involved in Anglo-Egyptian political relations during the last decade of British occupation in Egypt, how in general terms may the nature of these relations be characterized?
2. After evaluating the internal political situation in both countries, what internal political factors and/or forces have most affected the nature of Anglo-Egyptian political relations during the period under study?
3. After evaluation of the external political environment, what external factors are seen to have played a significant role in determining Anglo-Egyptian political relations during the period under study?

I also raised six specific questions. The answers to these, along with the answers obtained for the general questions, helped me greatly to draw conclusions and advance an argument. The questions were:

1. What specific issues, pressures, and attitudes affected the strategies and negotiating positions of the Anglo-Egyptian negotiators during the 1946, 1947, 1950 and 1953 negotiations?
2. Why at a specific time did the Egyptian government refer the dispute to the United Nations? What benefits, or lessons, if any, were gained from the Security Council decision?
3. Did Egypt's involvement in the Palestine War of 1948 help to delay the Anglo-Egyptian negotiations or was its involvement an effect of the delayed negotiations? What effects, if any, did the Palestine issue have on Anglo-Egyptian political relations?
4. What caused the Egyptian government to abrogate the only existing treaty, that of 1936, without having an alternative? What effects did this have on Anglo-Egyptian relations?
5. Why did the two monarchies – Britain and Egypt – fail to reach an agreement whereas Britain and the Egyptian revolutionary regime were able to reach an agreement without similar difficulties?
6. Did it make any difference to Anglo-Egyptian relations whether the Conservatives or the Labour Party were in power?

Of course, many other questions were raised during the course of the research. However, the questions listed here were of special value to the research. The facts that were revealed as a result of examining these questions provided enough information for some objective conclusions to be drawn. These conclusions are presented in the last section.

I argue several general points which are believed to have affected Anglo-Egyptian political relations throughout the decade preceding the final settlement. These general points and other specific points of argument are examined carefully in the text. The general points of argument are as follows:

Considering the general course of events in Anglo-Egyptian political relations, it is apparent that during the 1947–54 period the inconsistent and uncompromising attitudes which led to unilateral initiatives only created obstacles preventing a mutually satisfactory settlement between Britain and Egypt. I argue that the failure to conclude a settlement, the interruptions of negotiations, and the abrogation of an existing treaty, among other issues and reasons for dispute, cannot be attributed to one or other of the parties to the dispute. At the same time I argue that the Egyptian government failed to realize the need to separate the issue of Egypt's union with Sudan from the other issues concerning its own independence, especially with regard to the evacuation of British forces from Egypt. The failure to distinguish between the two sets of demands created a major barrier to a settlement.

Although this book deals broadly with the major historical events, I focus particularly on the reasons behind the breakdown of Anglo-Egyptian political relations.

1

Anglo-Egyptian Political Relations 1882–1946: Historical Background

Napoleon Bonaparte's expedition to Egypt in 1798 opened up the country for the first time to the possibility of European dominance. Britain, then a powerful country, was in an advantageous position to establish control over this strategic land. For the British Empire, Egypt would become a staging post for Britain's possessions in India and Australia. The opening of the Suez Canal in 1869 increased Britain's interest in Egypt for this vital waterway formed a link between Britain and its vast network of colonies covering the globe. The strategic importance of Egypt led Britain to give serious consideration to the problem of preventing other powers from dominating it. With this in mind, in 1878 Britain occupied Cyprus – the closest and most convenient point to the Suez Canal.[1]

The British government, under the Conservatives, became interested in bringing the canal under its own control but it wished to do this in a legal and regular manner. Its first move was to acquire an investment in the canal which it did by purchasing a majority share in the Suez Canal Company. At that time, Egypt was under the rule of Muhammad Ali's successors whose extravagant tastes left Egypt unable to meet its financial obligations towards its creditors resulting in the suspension of the repayment of its debts. Britain and France were the countries most affected by this and they therefore decided to introduce an Anglo-French commission in Egypt known as the "Dual Control". The role of this commission, whose members acted in the names of the British and French governments, was to supervise Egypt's economy and control its budget and expenditure as well as to protect European creditors.[2] The result of this dual control system was strong Anglo-French influence over Egypt and the destruction of Egypt's hopes of keeping European influence out of the country.[3] A few years later, in 1882, the minister of war Colonel Ahmad Orabi Pasha led an uprising in Egypt targeted against the foreign exploitation of the country by the dual control system and Khedive Tawfiq. During the revolt some Europeans were killed in Alexandria. In response to the riots in Alexandria and a perceived threat to the Suez Canal, Britain landed its troops on Egyptian soil. Despite crushing Orabi's revolt the British forces remained in Egypt. As a result, Egypt came under the direct political rule of Britain and Egyptian affairs and destiny were no longer in the hands of the Egyptians. Khedive Tawfiq who replaced his father, Ismail, in late 1879 due to European pressure on the Porte but possessed neither his father's qualities nor administrative abilities, seemed to be a more pliant instrument of Anglo-French policy in Egypt than his father had been. The British became the absolute and undisputed masters of Egypt and Britain began its 73-year occupation of Egypt.[4]

The British Liberal government under William Ewart Gladstone announced that its sole purpose was to restore the power of the Khedive and that Britain would withdraw its troops as soon as order and the maintenance of the Khedive's authority were restored in Egypt. It remained Gladstone's policy to withdraw British troops from Egypt as soon as the situation allowed, but when the Conservatives regained power in 1885 under the leadership of Lord Salisbury, Gladstone's policy of early withdrawal was replaced by a policy of delay. One of Salisbury's aims was to bring down the Sudanese Mahdist rebels and to bring the Sudan under the domination of the British Empire. Salisbury successfully accomplished this with General Sir Horatio Herbert Kitchener's 1898 campaign in the Sudan which crushed the Mahdist rebels.[5] Sudan was subsequently governed as an Anglo-Egyptian condominium which was provided for by the Anglo-Egyptian convention of 1899. The convention stated that, by right of conquest, Britain was entitled to share the administration of the Sudan with Egypt.[6] In fact, the Condominium Agreement was not put into effect. Nor did it guarantee Egypt a strong share in the administration of the Sudan.

The Sudan was also important to the British Empire because it was believed that control of the headwaters of the Nile (in Sudan) ensured control of Egypt. This was emphasized by Sir Patrick William Donner, a leading Conservative, who told the British House of Commons:

> Whoever holds the Upper Nile has Egypt in the hollow of his hand. When the British flag was hoisted in the Sudan we not only secured our positions in Egypt but we also undertook responsibility for the civilization and good government of those vast regions on which we cannot turn our back. While we hold the Sudan, and we must hold it, we cannot get out of Egypt even if Egypt ceased to be the stepping-stone to India.[7]

So the British military occupation of the Sudan assumed over the years the shape of a "veiled protectorate"[8] without legal international status since neither Turkey (nominally the sovereign power in Egypt) nor any other country recognized the British occupation of Egypt.

In 1904, Britain succeeded in evicting France from the Egyptian scene through the signing of the *Entente Cordiale* between the two countries on 8 April under which France gave Britain a free hand in Egypt, while Britain gave France the same in Morocco.[9] The British occupation continued unchanged and unchallenged until the outbreak of the First World War in July 1914 and Egypt's political status underwent a significant change. Britain's declaration of war against Germany on 4 August 1914 placed Egypt in an extremely awkward legal position. Egypt was still officially a part of the Ottoman Empire, which joined the war on Germany's side.[10] As a result, all the Ottoman sultan's subjects, including the Egyptians, were in theory at war with Britain. All the hostile acts of the Egyptians during the war were to find legal justification in this fact.

According to the British Cabinet, the situation in Egypt made it imperative to legitimize Britain's anomalous position in both Egypt and the Sudan. The British foreign secretary, Edward Grey, announced that the Cabinet was seriously considering the outright annexation of Egypt to the British Empire.[11] But Britain's acting consul-general in Egypt, Milne Cheetham, pressed the government to decide instead in favour of declaring Egypt a protectorate. He argued that such an approach would be the natural sequence, unassailable logically, of the policy of the Earl of Cromer (British agent and consul-general in Egypt until 1907).

Britain wished to avoid annexing territory while hostilities continued.[12] Thus, on 18 December 1914, the British government declared a protectorate over Egypt rather than annexation. The following day Khedive Abbas II, then in Constantinople, was deposed by the British government on the grounds that, since the outbreak of the war with Germany, His Highness had most evidently thrown in his lot with His Majesty's enemies. Prince Hussein Kamel Pasha, the eldest living prince of the family of Mohammed Ali Pasha, was appointed as his successor and given the title of sultan of Egypt.[13]

In a note to the sultan, the British Foreign Office enumerated the reasons for proclaiming a protectorate and declared that the British government would henceforth regard itself as a trustee for the Egyptian people. It promised to defend Egyptian territory against all aggression, wherever it came from, and to protect Egyptian subjects, wherever they might be. All relations between the Egyptian government and other countries were to be conducted through the British high commissioner in Cairo. The Capitulations[14] were condemned as being "no longer in harmony with the development of the country" but their modification was postponed until the end of the war.[15]

Thus, the veiled protectorate which Britain had in fact exercised for over 30 years became an open protectorate. Its questionable legal position in Egypt was unilaterally regularized.[16] Yet such action was questionable in international law, as it was accepted practice that protectorates must be based on joint agreement between the protector and protected. Egyptians had, however, little choice but to accept the fact and hope that it would turn out to be a temporary war measure on the part of the British government.[17]

Soon after the armistice was signed in November 1918 Egyptians began to demand an end to the protectorate and complete independence for Egypt. On 13 November 1918, Egyptian nationalists formed a delegation ("The Wafd")[18] under the leadership of Saad Zaghlul to demand independence through legal means and peaceful negotiations with the British government. At the same time, the Wafd Party[19] sought permission from Sir Reginald Wingate, the British high commissioner in Egypt, for its representatives to go to Paris and London to present the case for Egyptian independence. The Wafd's request was, however, refused resulting in violent demonstrations by the Wafdists against the British government which led to the resignation of the Egyptian prime minister, Rushdi Pasha.[20]

In early March 1919, the nationalist Wafd Party leader, Zaghlul Pasha, announced that he would go to Paris in person to lay Egyptian demands before the peace conference. But before he could leave, he and three of his colleagues were arrested by the British authorities in Egypt and deported to Malta. The deportation of the Wafdist leaders led to a serious outbreak of violence and strikes in Egypt, with frequent attacks on British soldiers, a development which seriously disturbed the British prime minister, Lloyd George, who was in Paris at that time. Without consulting his foreign secretary, Arthur James Balfour, he removed the serving British high commissioner from office. General E. Allenby who was appointed in his place was directed to exercise supreme military and civil authority and to take all measures necessary to maintain the British protectorate over Egypt on a secure and equitable basis.[21]

On 25 March 1919 General Allenby arrived in Cairo. Deciding to try to deal with the Egyptian problem by conciliation rather than by force, he released Zaghlul Pasha and his associates and allowed them to go to Paris to present their case before the peace conference. Zaghlul, however, was not well received there. Shortly after his arrival, the US president, Woodrow Wilson, recognized the British protectorate over Egypt.[22] However, Wilson's "Fourteen Points" were widely publicized in Egypt and elsewhere, because they emphasized the principle of the right of national self-determination. Egyptians amongst others interpreted these ideas as a further harbinger of hope in the achievement of their nationalist goal of reducing the dominance of foreign powers over them.

Despite the emergence of this new ray of hope, American recognition of the British protectorate in fact led to further disorders in Egypt and Allenby found himself forced to exercise his authority under the provisions of martial law which had existed in Egypt since 1914. Strict enforcement of martial law, however, failed to improve the situation in Egypt and disorders continued. Finally, in May 1919, the British government announced the appointment of a mission to Egypt headed by the British secretary of state for the colonies, Lord Milner. Milner, who had served in Egypt during the time of Lord Cromer, had always been sympathetic towards the Egyptians.[23] Before proceeding to Egypt Milner described the aims of his mission:

> To enquire into the causes of the late disorder in Egypt, and to report on the existing situation in the country and the form of constitution which, under the protectorate, will be best calculated to promote its peace and prosperity, the progressive development of self-governing institutions and the protection of foreign interests.[24]

In other words, the mission was to operate on the assumption that the protectorate was to continue and that Britain would not abandon its right to protect foreign interests in Egypt. This was reiterated by Balfour in the House of Commons on 12 November 1919:

> Let me, therefore, say that in our view, the question of Egypt, the question of the Sudan and the question of the Canal, form an organic and individual whole, and that neither in Egypt nor in the Sudan, nor in connection with Egypt, is England going to give up any of her responsibilities. British supremacy is going to be maintained and let nobody either in Egypt or out of Egypt make any mistake upon that cardinal principle of His Majesty's Government.[25]

Statements of this sort sent a clear signal to the Egyptians that the main intention of the British was to maintain Egypt and Sudan under British control. When the mission's terms of reference became known, Zaghlul Pasha, the leader of the Egyptian nationalists, ordered his countrymen to boycott the mission completely, so that when the mission arrived in Egypt on 7 December 1919, Egypt was in turmoil: strikes, demonstrations, telegrams of protest, bitter articles in the press followed one another in an unending stream of protest against the mission. Even the sultan and his more moderate ministers adopted an attitude of marked reservation and refused to express their opinions to the mission.[26] Agitation against the mission continued until March 1920; schools and colleges closed and there were threats of an impending railway strike as well as strikes by government officials. Large crowds appeared in the streets of Cairo and Alexandria, among whom were teachers and students of al-Azhar University. By the end of December 1919, the situation had taken a more serious turn: a mob attacked and set fire to a police station close to the government palace, and on 26 December 1919, two British soldiers were attacked in Cairo and severely wounded.[27] The Milner Mission came thus to the conclusion that a legal settlement between Britain and Egypt was essential for both countries. The settlement should not be dictated by the British to the Egyptians and the mission suggested a bilateral agreement between the two countries. It decided to invite Zaghlul Pasha, who was then in Paris, for an exchange of views. The mission's judicial adviser, Sir Cecil Hurst, was sent to Paris to invite Zaghlul Pasha to London.[28] Zaghlul accepted and arrived in London in June 1920, entering immediately into negotiation with Milner. Consequently, by the end of 1920, the British government indicated its willingness to abolish the protectorate over Egypt and Egypt was declared an independent country on 28 February 1922. Khedive Fuad became king of Egypt and a new constitution was immediately proclaimed which established a bicameral parliamentary system of government for the first time in Egypt's history. This system gave the king considerable powers but it also kept the new kingdom of Egypt under the influence of Britain. The British were still controlling Egypt's communications, the defence of Egypt and the Sudan, the protection of foreign interests and the minorities as well as Egyptian foreign affairs.[29]

On 19 November 1924, Sir Lee Stack, governor-general of the Sudan and sirdar (inspector general) of the Egyptian army, was assassinated in Cairo. Despite the fact that King Fuad and his prime minister, Zaghlul Pasha, expressed their deep regret for this heinous crime, the British high commissioner in Egypt presented an ultimatum demanding:

a. An ample apology.
b. The energetic prosecution and drastic punishment of the authors of the crime.
c. The prohibition of all popular demonstrations.
d. An indemnity of £500,000.
e. The withdrawal within 24 hours of the Egyptian army from Sudan.
f. The right to increase the irrigated area in the Gezira (Sudan) from 300,000 acres to an unlimited figure.
g. The withdrawal of all opposition to British government wishes to protect foreign interests in Egypt.

In his reply the prime minister accepted the extended apologies and indemnity of £500,000 but protested against the withdrawal of the Egyptian army from Sudan and the alteration of the agreement regarding the cultivated area in the Gezira. This response was considered a refusal to meet British demands and the British government sent orders to the acting governor of the Sudan to expel all Egyptian officers and Egyptian army units.[30] On 25 November the Egyptian government received a despatch from the officer in command of Egypt's troops in Khartoum stating that his forces had been surrounded and asking for instructions to avoid bloodshed. The troops were ordered to return to Egypt, so marking the end of Egyptian administration of Sudan's affairs, and resulting in the resignation of Zaghlul Pasha as prime minister.[31]

The years 1925–35 witnessed attempts by the Egyptian government to accelerate Anglo-Egyptian negotiations to enable it to achieve greater independence for Egypt. But domestic Egyptian politics during this period were characterized by the continuous struggle between Egyptian party leaders after the death of Saad Zaghlul Pasha in early 1927. This created a deadlock in the settlement between Britain and Egypt. However, when the British position in the Mediterranean came under threat, especially with Italy's invasion of Ethiopia in 1935 and the outbreak of the Spanish Civil War in 1936 added to the European crisis, the British government realized the importance of negotiating with the Egyptian government.[32]

It would be difficult to give an account of Anglo-Egyptian relations after 1935 without mentioning briefly the role played by the new young British foreign secretary, Sir Anthony Eden. Eden discussed the Anglo-Egyptian question with his colleagues in the Cabinet on 15 January 1936, expressing the opinion that because of the Italian threat to East Africa, the time was then opportune for a resumption of negotiations with the Egyptians in order to obtain a treaty consenting to the British presence in Egypt. Accordingly, on 10 February 1936 a pre-negotiation formula was finally agreed on by the British high commissioner in Egypt Sir Miles Lampson and Ali Maher Pasha, the Egyptian prime minister, which reflected Egyptian concern that if the ensuing negotiations failed to produce a result, it would be difficult to maintain the status quo in Anglo-Egyptian relations. In consequence, Egypt informed Britain that it was ready to begin treaty talks, and on 13 February 1936 an Egyptian Royal Decree was issued appointing the Egyptian delegation for the coming negotiations. It consisted of 13 members, including Mustafa Nahhas Pasha (who had succeeded Saad Zaghlul as leader of the Wafd Party in 1928) as chairman of the delegation. The Wafd was the best organized party at that time and the most popular political party in the country, with an extensive network in the towns and countryside. It had immense patronage power over the massive state bureaucracy and over local and provincial officials and village headmen.[33]

The British delegation was to be headed by Sir Miles Lampson, assisted by the local British military chief, Sir George Weir, the commanding officer of British troops in Egypt. The formal talks between the two official delegations opened on 2 March 1936 in Cairo and continued intermittently for a long time ending eventually in deadlock which led to the resignation of Ali Maher Pasha's government in May 1936. He was succeeded as prime minister by the new

Wafd leader, Nahhas Pasha, whose approach was quite different from that of Saad Zaghlul. He had softened his attitude towards Britain and became more friendly while in office than he had been in opposition. After taking office he agreed to a treaty with Britain, and so negotiations were immediately resumed and both parties were able to patch up their differences and sign the treaty on 28 August 1936. It should be noted that the 1936 treaty was concluded at a time when the security of Egypt was threatened by Mussolini's activities in Ethiopia. Known as a "Treaty of Friendship and Alliance between Britain and Egypt"[34] – similar to the Anglo-Iraqi treaty of 1930 – it legalized the hitherto undefined and anomalous position of Britain in Egypt, but it nevertheless left the Sudan question unsettled. In fact, more "Sudanization" was introduced in the administration of the country. This in turn led to the rise and evolution of local Sudanese nationalism especially in the years after the Second World War.

The treaty provided for mutual support in the event of war. Egyptian aid to Britain was to include the use of Egyptian ports, aerodromes and all other means of communication. In peacetime Britain would have the right to maintain 10,000 infantrymen and 400 airmen in the Suez Canal area for the defence of the canal. The treaty also defined the aim of the joint Anglo-Egyptian administration in the Sudan, which should provide for the welfare of the Sudanese.[35] It was further provided that in addition to the Sudanese troops, both British and Egyptian troops should be placed at the disposal of the British governor-general for the defence of Sudan. This treaty did not settle the question of Egypt's sovereignty over Sudan, but Egypt maintained that its sovereignty over Sudan was not divisible.

As regards the Capitulations, Britain agreed to help Egypt abolish them and promised to help Egypt join the League of Nations. The treaty was to remain in force for twenty years but could be revised after ten years by mutual consent.[36] Finally, the treaty formally recognized Egypt as a sovereign state and allowed Egyptian troops to return to the Sudan, from where they had been expelled in 1924. Egyptian foreign relations were to remain under the control and guidance of the British authorities in Cairo in consultation with the

Foreign Office in London and the British high commissioner in Egypt, Sir Miles Lampson, who was given the new status of ambassador.

An opportunity to test the terms of the treaty came when Britain declared war against Germany in 1939. The treaty's military clauses were immediately put into effect and, at Britain's request, Egypt was divided into four military districts; its ports, aerodromes, and communications were put at Britain's disposal and a state of siege was established. However, Egyptian cooperation under the second government of Ali Maher Pasha (1939–40) was minimal. Further, King Farouk showed sympathy for the Axis cause.

The king's pro-Axis leanings made it necessary for Sir Miles Lampson (later Lord Killearn, British ambassador in Egypt until 1946) to intervene frequently in the internal affairs of Egypt in the name of the treaty.[37] Lampson also installed Mustafa Nahhas Pasha, the chief Egyptian architect of the 1936 treaty, by forcing the king's hand on 4 February 1942, having surrounded his palace with British troops. Nahhas Pasha proved to be pro-British while in office. Following the installation of the Wafdist government[38] Britain received full access to military facilities in Egypt. Britain's action encouraged Nahhas's opponents to rally around King Farouk, so that as soon as the war in Africa ended in 1943 the political forces critical of Britain gathered momentum, and Nahhas's position became vulnerable.

By the end of 1944, when Killearn was out of Egypt, the king was able to replace Nahhas with Ahmad Maher Pasha – brother of Ali Maher. Thus Ahmad Maher as the Saadist leader formed a Saadist government. The Saadist Party had been founded by Ahmad Maher Pasha and Nokrashy Pasha in 1938 as a result of differences with Nahhas Pasha. The Saadists accused Nahhas Pasha of not upholding the true traditional policy of Saad Zaghlul Pasha. In order to strengthen his government's position Ahmad Maher Pasha asked for a general election which was held on 8 January 1945 and in which all the political parties except the Wafd – the biggest party in the country – took part. The Wafd refused to participate because it foresaw possible defeat at the polls as a result of Nahhas's pro-British stand during the February *coup* of 1942, against the king's wishes.

Consequently the Saadists won 125 seats against 74 for the liberals, 29 for the Kotla (the name means bloc and it was formed in 1943 by the Christian nationalist Makram Ebeid Pasha, minister of finance, as a result of a dispute with Nahhas Pasha), 7 for the Watanists (or nationalists) and 29 for independents. As the Saadists failed to win an outright majority, Ahmad Maher Pasha was forced to form a coalition Cabinet with the support of the liberals and the Kotla.[39]

Nevertheless, the new Saadist government soon began (on 18 January 1945) to demand the revision of the 1936 treaty, particularly when the king, in a speech from the throne, made reference to Egypt's interests in the Sudan as well as to the desire for complete independence after the war. Ahmad Maher Pasha endorsed the king's views in a speech to parliament, and stated that there was no justification for the treaty's restrictions since Egypt had fulfilled its obligations in the war.

Outside parliament, the Watanists took up the treaty issue seriously, and on 19 January submitted a note to the British embassy asking for the unification of the Sudan and Egypt, as well as the withdrawal of British troops from Egyptian territory. However, when it became clear that the Axis powers would be defeated, Ahmad Maher Pasha, at Britain's request, declared war against the Axis powers so that Egypt could become a founder member of the proposed United Nations and so establish its identity as an independent nation. But Ahmad Maher Pasha's decision cost him his life: he was shot dead by Mahmoud Issawi, a young member of the Misr al-Fatah Party (the "Young Egypt Society").[40] Following Ahmad Maher's death his chief deputy and the foreign minister in the Cabinet, Mahmoud Nokrashy Pasha, formed a government on 25 February 1945.[41]

The new prime minister, following the policy of his predecessor, declared a defensive war against Germany and Japan on 26 February and Nokrashy Pasha appointed Abdel-Hamid Badawi Pasha – a professional lawyer and a strong nationalist – as minister for foreign affairs, and also to lead the Egyptian delegation at the San Francisco Conference. In addition he appointed a consultative council to advise the government about the conference as well as about the forthcoming Anglo-Egyptian negotiations.[42]

Nokrashy's appointment of a consultative council alarmed Killearn who thought the Egyptians might submit a demand for the revision of the 1936 treaty to the British government before the San Francisco Conference. Britain argued that this conference had nothing to do with the revision of any treaty and that its main business was to work out a formula for international peace and security. Moreover, the question of treaty revision would also raise the issue of the security of the Suez Canal, which the British government did not want discussed. The Suez Canal area had become the largest British base in the region and was vital to the empire mostly because of the presence there of massive military depots. These contained base workshops, ammunition and medical supplies, petrol reserves and mobilization stores built up during the Second World War.[43]

On 17 March 1945 Killearn had spoken to Nokrashy Pasha regarding the possibility of treaty revision talks and the problem of Egypt's defence. The prime minister avoided replying to Killearn's query regarding the defence of Egypt, and on 30 March Nokrashy declared in the senate that his government's policy was to eliminate all treaty restrictions which might become a source of confrontation between Egypt and Britain.[44] On 28 April Abdel-Hamid Badawi Pasha, to the annoyance of the British government, raised the question of treaty revision at a preliminary session of the San Francisco Conference:

> We suggest it is a duty of the conference to prescribe principles for the revision of treaties which have became inconsistent with the new concept of world conditions and collective security and might therefore become irritants and possible sources of conflicts.[45]

The British Foreign Office now became more flexible on the issue of treaty revision, but Killearn, the chief architect of the 1936 treaty, did not believe that His Majesty's Government was ready to negotiate revisions as the military authorities in London were still undecided about their military requirements in Egypt.[46]

It was in fact Killearn himself who was trying to delay the negotiation of the revision of the 1936 treaty. Besides being ambassador in Cairo, Killearn was also the high commissioner in Egypt for the Sudan and had the British embassy maintain a large staff in Cairo to liaise with Sudan's affairs, maintained through the Sudan agent in Cairo, for the purposes of protecting the British Empire's strategic interests in the Sudan as well as guarding against the manœuvres of both King Farouk and the Sudanese political parties. It was the British ambassador who had the upper hand in dealing with Egyptian affairs. The relationship between Killearn and King Farouk was in fact less than cordial because of Killearn's support for Nahhas Pasha and because Killearn had forced the king himself to appoint Nahhas as Egyptian premier on 4 February 1942 against the king's wishes.[47]

Undoubtedly Killearn was also powerful enough to interfere in internal Egyptian affairs and to obstruct the king's function in Egypt itself. However, the king was believed at that time to command the affection and support of the majority of the people. He not only enjoyed the power to appoint the prime minister, but also had the right to dismiss the Cabinet and prorogue or adjourn the parliament which consisted of a senate and a chamber of deputies. The chamber was an elected body while the senate was composed of members, two-fifths of whom were nominated by the king, the rest being elected. Legislation could be initiated in either House, but it had to be confirmed by the king.[48]

The king's relations with Nahhas Pasha had always been unfriendly, due partly to Nahhas's dictatorial tendency and also to the fact that the Wafd Party, which regarded Nahhas as its leader, was the only one in Egypt that could form a government without palace backing. This was exactly what happened in the 1949 general election when the Wafd won and Nahhas Pasha became prime minister for the third time – his period of office extending until January 1952.

After the Second World War, Egyptian public opinion came increasingly to demand British evacuation from Egypt, as well as the unification of the Sudan and Egypt. These demands were particularly strident since Egypt had manifested its loyalty to Britain's cause and had been a main supply centre for food and manpower to the allied forces in North Africa and elsewhere.[49]

On 26 July 1945, the Labour Party formed a new government in Britain under the leadership of Clement Attlee. The Labour Party's declaration of policy in favour of a "better world of peace for all" and its promise to work out "the greatest common measure of agreement with other countries"[50] encouraged the Egyptian government to hope for the fulfilment of its national aspirations. On 1 August Nokrashy held a special Cabinet meeting to discuss Anglo-Egyptian relations, and the Cabinet considered the moment especially propitious for treaty revision. The treaty itself could be revised after ten years from the first signing and the moment seemed appropriate in view of the Labour victory in Britain.[51] The king, who disliked Nahhas for turning against him during the 1942 political crisis in Cairo, still wanted to avoid any steps which might lead to Nahhas's eventual return to power. He therefore advised Nokrashy Pasha to proceed slowly in putting forward Egyptian demands. Thus the prime minister delayed sending any formal note to Britain as he wanted to avoid any hasty revisions of the treaty on the one hand and the risk of the Wafd's return to power on the other. This coincided with the British Foreign Office's wish to delay the negotiations until the authorities in London had made up their minds regarding British military requirements in Egypt. At the same time, discontent with Nokrashy's reticence regarding the treaty negotiations had increased opposition against him from Egyptian parties. This resulted mainly from a speech by Ernest Bevin, the British foreign secretary, who told the British parliament on 23 October 1945 that no formal Egyptian representations had been received concerning treaty revision.[52] Bevin's declaration suggested that the Egyptian prime minister had done nothing to further new Anglo-Egyptian negotiations.

In early December 1945, Egypt sent a memorandum to Britain expressing its willingness to discuss revision of the 1936 treaty. Britain postponed action on Egypt's note on the pretext that it was busy with pending questions of international settlement resulting from the end of the war. Meanwhile, the press publicized Britain's unwillingness to negotiate the evacuation of the British base in Egypt.

This justified the claims of the Egyptian opposition that Nokrashy's government was ineffective in dealing with Britain and several protest strikes took place in Egypt.[53] One of these was held on 9 February 1946 when several thousand strikers, including Cairo University students and supporters of the Wafdists, marched from the university grounds in Giza to the Abdin Palace. They shouted slogans about British evacuation and the unity of the Nile Valley. When the demonstrators reached the Abbas Bridge on their way to the palace, their route was blocked by a strong police presence. In the resulting clash scores of people were injured. The demonstrations and strikes continued, compelling the Egyptian prime minister to resign on 15 February 1946.[54] Nokrashy Pasha was replaced by an old Egyptian politician, Ismail Sidky Pasha. The king's popularity in the country began to decline, however, as he was the only person left to blame for the delay in reaching an agreement with Britain.

The king immediately directed his new prime minister to declare Egyptian readiness to engage in Anglo-Egyptian talks.[55] On the king's orders an Egyptian delegation was formed under Sidky's direction, while the British delegation was placed under the leadership of Ernest Bevin. The latter was in fact sympathetic to Egyptian aspirations and wanted to achieve a peaceful settlement of Anglo-Egyptian differences through negotiation. Sidky Pasha lost no time in resuming talks with Britain, and after preliminary discussions in Cairo and London which lasted for almost nine months, the two parties reached a settlement of sorts through hard bargaining and extensive negotiation.

An agreement on the withdrawal of British forces was drawn up over a ten-day period during Sidky Pasha's mission to London in October 1946.[56] Unfortunately the agreement was never ratified: neither party was able to agree on a final solution to the Sudan issue or to compromise over the future independence of the Sudan. Egypt insisted that Egyptian sovereignty should continue over the Sudan and that the Sudan should unite with Egypt under the Egyptian crown. The British government maintained its declared policy of no change in the status of the Sudan. It also argued that the Sudanese had the right of self-determination leading to independence. So the

Sidky–Bevin draft agreement on troop withdrawal, which was initiated in London by the two men on 24 October 1946, did not survive Sidky Pasha's subsequent resignation.[57]

The protocol had brought the two countries near to agreement on Britain finally withdrawing its troops from Cairo, Alexandria and the Delta by the end of 1947 and from the remainder of Egyptian territory by the end of 1949.[58] The Sidky–Bevin draft agreement had also brought Britain and Egypt close to a mutual understanding and a state of goodwill. But it collapsed and was abandoned because Sidky Pasha was forced by King Farouk to tender his resignation in early December 1946 as the king believed that his prime minister had failed to win Egyptian sovereignty over the Sudan from the British government.[59] In fact it was the king who failed to grasp this golden opportunity to bring an end to Anglo-Egyptian disagreements through the Sidky–Bevin protocol. From the beginning of the talks in London, some members of the Sidky delegation who had been directly appointed by the king had been unhelpful in the negotiations. They were jealous of Sidky's successful handling of the negotiations and wished to deprive him of the honour of appearing as the chief architect of an Anglo-Egyptian settlement.[60] The dismissal of Sidky Pasha inevitably led to the breaking off of negotiations with Britain. The collapse of this agreement enabled Britain to maintain its forces in the Suez Canal Zone for a further ten years, which it justified by reference to the legal rights accorded to it by the terms of the 1936 treaty. It also enabled Britain to encourage the Sudanese to demand complete freedom from Egyptian interference and the right to self-determination.

Nokrashy Pasha replaced Sidky Pasha on 8 December 1946 and completely refused to compromise over the Sudan's future independence.[61] He was convinced that transferring the dispute to the United Nations would put extra pressure on Britain and enable Egypt to obtain a satisfactory solution. In this he was backed by King Farouk who believed that, by taking the dispute to the United Nations, he would be able to weaken Egyptian opposition and contain public opinion in the country and divert it to issues other than British evacuation and the Sudan question. Consequently, in January 1947 the Egyptian premier declared: "We have taken this course with full faith in the Charter of the United Nations; we are availing ourselves of a small nation's privilege to appeal to the Council against one of the greatest powers on a footing of perfect equality."[62] The Egyptian government viewed the United Nations as a great source of hope for the upholding of the freedom and dignity of all nations. The UN Charter, the Egyptians believed, might provide Egypt with a new framework for revising and recasting its relations with Britain on the basis of mutual respect and friendly cooperation.[63] The appearance of the Anglo-Egyptian case before the United Nations and the results obtained will be discussed in Chapter Two.

This historical overview has shown that in 1936 Britain and Egypt reached an historic agreement and signed a treaty of friendship and alliance. By signing this treaty Britain legalized its presence in Egypt. Egypt, on the other hand, won British recognition of its independence and a plan to gradually satisfy most of the Egyptian demands. In the ensuing years the terms of the 1936 treaty were subjected to a series of tests and Egypt's alliance with Britain was fulfilled. However, the dispute over Egypt's sovereignty over Sudan and the increased and impatient demand for the evacuation of British forces from Egypt weakened the 1936 agreement. The continuous demands for negotiations to revise the treaty were destined to fail until the treaty's ten-year provision allowed the revision to take place. In 1946 the Sidky–Bevin negotiations made it possible for Egypt to settle its dispute with Britain with respect to British evacuation from Egypt. However, the king's wish to bring Sudan under his rule and gain sovereignty over the Nile Valley was not accepted as a condition of the Sidky–Bevin agreement. By failing to fulfil the king's dream, Sidky was forced to resign and his negotiations with Bevin consequently collapsed.

During the decade after 1936, internal divisions developed within Egypt's most powerful party, the Wafd. Taking advantage of this split, Britain gained the sympathy of Nahhas, the Wafd leader, whereas his hard-line rival, Nokrashy confronted Britain at any opportunity. This was not overlooked by the king who, after Sidky's failure to fulfil his wishes, accepted Nokrashy as prime minister.

Nokrashy hoped to gain better results from negotiating the revision of the 1936 treaty which had been concluded by his rival, Nahhas. Accordingly, Nokrashy adopted an uncompromising attitude towards the Sudan issue and came to an agreement with the king that taking the issue to the United Nations would be advantageous to the king's wishes. Therefore, as the 1936 treaty concluded a decade of its life, Anglo-Egyptian relations entered a new era clouded with uncertainties dominated by the Egyptian demands for the evacuation of the British from Egypt and the unification of Egypt with the Sudan.

Notes

1. P. J. Vatikiotis, *A History of Egypt from Muhammad Ali to Sadat* (Baltimore, Johns Hopkins, 1980), pp. 127–8. See also J. Marlowe, *A History of Modern Egypt and Anglo-Egyptian Relations, 1800–1956,* 2nd edn (Hamden, Conn., Archon Books, 1965). Also W. R. Louis, *The British Empire in the Middle East 1945–1951* (Oxford, Clarendon Press, 1984).
2. John Marlowe, *Four Aspects of Egypt* (London, George Allen and Unwin, 1966), pp. 264–8.
3. *Ibid.*
4. The Earl of Cromer, *Modern Egypt*, vol. I (New York, Macmillan, 1909), pp. 165–73.
5. *Ibid.*, pp. 225–35.
6. Ronald Robinson and John Gallagher, *Africa and the Victorians* (London, Macmillan, 1981), pp. 110–22.
7. A. B. Theobald, *The Mahdiya* (London, Longmans, 1951), pp. 210–3.
8. *The Times*, 29 November 1914. See also J. Darwin, *Britain, Egypt and the Middle East: Imperial Policy in the Aftermath of War 1918–1922*, (London, Macmillan, 1981).
9. Brian Lapping, *End of Empire* (London, Paladin, 1985), p. 234.
10. *The Times*, 17 January 1915.
11. *Ibid.*
12. *Ibid.*
13. Muhammad Heikal, *Mudhakkirat fi'l-siyasah al-misriyya*, vol. I (Cairo, 1980), pp. 137–43.
14. The "Capitulations" was the name given by Europeans to concessions which the early sultans of Turkey granted to foreigners residing there. They were primarily intended to enable Christians to trade and reside in the territories of the Ottoman Empire. The "Capitulations" in Egypt included: immunity from personal taxation without the assent of their governments; inviolability of domicile; protection from arbitrary arrest; and exemption from the jurisdiction of the local courts. See Jasper Y. Brinton, *The Mixed Courts of Egypt* (New Haven, Yale University Press, 1930).

15. *al-Ahram* (Egyptian newspaper, Cairo), 15 December 1918.
16. *Ibid.*
17. Yahya Jalal, *al-Wafd al-Masri 1919–1952* (Cairo, 1981), pp. 137–43.
18. In English *Wafd* means "delegation". Saad Zaghul Pasha, an Egyptian lawyer and former minister of education, formed a political party know as the Wafd Party and became its first leader.
19. *Ibid.*
20. *Ibid.*
21. *al-Ahram*, 19 March 1919.
22. George A. Lloyd, *Egypt since Cromer*, vol. II (New York, H. Fertig, 1933), pp. 11–7.
23. *Ibid.*, pp. 19–23.
24. *Ibid.*, pp. 36–40.
25. Parliamentary Debates [Commons] 1919, 5th series, vol. 15, col. 1888–9.
26. *al-Ahram*, 17 December 1919.
27. *Ibid.*, 9 January 1920.
28. George A. Lloyd, *Egypt since Cromer*, pp. 19–22.
29. Foreign Office Research, January 1946, PRO/FO 371/62944.
30. *Ibid.*
31. *Ibid.*
32. P. J. Vatikiotis, *Conflict in the Middle East* (London, Allen and Unwin, 1971), pp. 47–8. See also Habibur Rahman, 'Aspects of Anglo-Egyptian Negotiations 1920–36' (MA Thesis, University of Ottawa, 1977), pp. 17–22.
33. *Ibid.*
34. *al-Ahram*, 22 September 1936. See also Hassan Yusuf, *Mudhakkirat al-qasr wa dauruhu fi al-siyasa al-misriyya*, 1922–1952 (Cairo, 1982), pp. 137–40.
35. Hassan Ahmad, *The 1936 Anglo-Egyptian Treaty* (Cairo), pp. 83–5.
36. *Ibid.*, pp. 90–1.
37. British Ambassador Minute in Cairo, 5 January 1946, PRO/FO 371/62937.
38. H. Rahman, 'Aspects of Anglo-Egyptian Negotiations', pp. 25–8.
39. *Ibid.* See also Anthony Nutting, *Nasser* (London, Constable, 1972), pp. 1–17.
40. The Misr al-Fatah Party was Egypt's earliest youth movement, but after the Second World War it became a socialist party, changing its name first (in 1940) to the National Islamic Party and then (in 1945) to the Socialist Party. See Chapter Five. For the assassination of Ahmad Maher Pasha, see the British Embassy Report to the Foreign Office, 7 February 1946, PRO/FO 371/62938. See also *al-Ahram*, 4 March 1945.
41. *Ibid.*
42. *Ibid.*
43. Cabinet Discussion, February 1946, PRO/FO 371/62952.
44. *al-Akhbar*, 3 April 1945.
45. Tariq al-Bishri, *Tarikh al-harakat al-siyasiyya fi Misr, 1945–1952* (Cairo, 1970), pp. 275–81.
46. *al-Ahram*, 3 May 1946.
47. Foreign Office Minutes, March 1947, PRO/FO 371/73574.
48. *Ibid.*
49. *al-Wafd al-Masri* (Egyptian newspaper, Cairo), 17 May 1947.
50. *Ibid.* See also *al-Ahram*, 23 June 1947.

51. British Embassy in Cairo Secret Report, September 1946, PRO/FO 371/62979.
52. Ernest Bevin Papers 1945–51: Egypt, PRO/FO/800-435-445.
53. Top Secret British Ambassador Report in Cairo, August 1947, PRO/FO 371/69192.
54. *al-Akhbar* (Egyptian newspaper, Cairo), 10 February 1946.
55. British Embassy Cairo, Tel. 513, 15 February 1946, PRO/FO 371/62957.
56. Ernest Bevin Papers, 1945–51: Egypt, PRO/FO/800-435-445.
57. Ismail Sidky Pasha, *Mudhakkirat* [Memoirs] (Cairo, 1950), pp. 31–9.
58. *Ibid.* See also PRO/FO 371/96845.
59. Sidky, *op. cit.*
60. *Ibid.*
61. *al-Akhbar*, 29–30 December 1946.
62. British Ambassador Minutes, Cairo, February 1947, PRO/FO 371/62977.
63. *al-Ahram*, 27 January 1947.

2

The Anglo-Egyptian Dispute and the United Nations

In July 1947, the Egyptian government referred its dispute with Britain to the UN Security Council. In this chapter I will attempt to explain why Egypt did this and to analyse the lessons that could have been learned from it by Egypt or Britain. By submitting its case to the United Nations, Egypt asked the Security Council to produce a resolution against Britain and to demand the total and immediate withdrawal of British forces from Egypt and Sudan. The Egyptian request also included the demand to terminate the British administrative regime in Sudan. Britain challenged the Egyptian demands and justified its presence in the Nile Valley on the basis of the Anglo-Egyptian legal agreement.

Although the Security Council could not agree on any resolution and decided to suspend its discussion of the Anglo-Egyptian dispute, the various presentations of the Security Council members are included here because their arguments, suggestions, and opinions have proved to be a valuable outcome of this study.

Chapter One showed that the Egyptians referred their case to the United Nations basically because the British, in the Sidky–Bevin negotiations, did not grant the king's wish to secure Egyptian sovereignty over Sudan. This Sudan controversy in Anglo-Egyptian relations has not been fully explained. In order to examine Anglo-Egyptian views on the Sudan fairly, it is necessary to consider the controversy in more detail. Therefore, before examining the proceedings of the United Nations, I shall start by locating the Sudan issue in its historical perspective.

The Sudan became part of Egypt during Muhammad Ali Pasha's rule (1805–49). Muhammad Ali is considered the founder of modern Egypt. He annexed Sudan to bring it under his authority in 1821 while his army was fighting campaigns in Arabia, Greece and Syria.[1] Muhammad Ali's ambition was to throw off the rule of the sultan of Turkey and to establish an independent empire in Egypt but the intervention of the European powers prevented him from accomplishing this. However, by the end of 1840 the whole Nile Valley was united under the Egyptian dynasty which was recognized by the Ottoman Empire and the European powers. According to the Convention of London in July 1840, and as confirmed by the Porte in June 1841, Muhammad Ali's family was given hereditary rights to rule Egypt to which Sudan had been annexed in 1821.

Muhammad Ali's interests in Sudan were both economic and political. He expected to find an abundance of gold – which was not found – to increase Egypt's economic power; he needed to increase his army's manpower with the slaves who then existed in the southern part of Sudan, and he wanted to build up his naval power from Sudan's rich supplies of timber.[2]

The authority of Muhammad Ali's dynasty in Sudan began to face problems in the early 1870s. The mismanagement of Sudan led to the growth of a Sudanese Islamic religious movement under the leadership of Muhammad Ali Mahdi. A decade later this religious movement influenced the collapse of the Egyptian authority in Sudan and began to threaten Upper Egypt as well. This coincided with the moment when Britain began its occupation of Egypt in 1882. Afterwards Egypt, with Britain's help, started the reconquest of Sudan. After a series of campaigns in Sudan, the Anglo-Egyptian forces decisively defeated the Mahdists at the battle of Omdurman and entered the Sudanese capital Khartoum in September 1898.

This joint Anglo-Egyptian military operation in Sudan was under the command of Sir Horatio Herbert Kitchener, who received the order from London to hoist the British flag beside the Egyptian flag in Sudan.[3] At that time, an agreement on the Sudan issue had already been prepared and was submitted and signed on 19 January 1899. The agreement delimited Sudan's frontiers and vested the civil and military powers in the Sudan in a British governor-general. This, however, had to be confirmed by an Egyptian Khedival decree on the recommendation of the British government.[4]

This agreement was known as the "Anglo-Egyptian Condominium Agreement", or the Butros–Cromer Agreement of 1899, which defined Sudan's status under joint British and Egyptian government. As noted in Chapter One, this resulted in the severance of Sudan from the central Egyptian government in Cairo and led gradually to the collapse of the Egyptian administration in Sudan. Nevertheless, Britain claimed that its presence in Sudan was only to support the Khedive's authority there,[5] as the British had similarly claimed in 1882 that their presence in Egypt was only to restore the Khedive's authority in the country. The Condominium Agreement of 1899 did not in fact make explicit mention of Egyptian sovereignty in Sudan, so leaving the issue open to various interpretations. On the one hand, the appointment of the governor of Sudan by Khedival decree could be interpreted as an acknowledgement of Egyptian sovereignty. On the other hand, the practice of having the appointment of the governor-general of Sudan always made by Britain and without consultation with the Egyptian government could be interpreted as an indication of the absence of Egypt's sovereignty over Sudan.

During the condominium Britain seized every opportunity to strengthen its direct hold on Sudan and, in the meantime, gradually removed Egyptian influence from the country.[6] Nevertheless, the continued Egyptian demand for sovereignty over Sudan caused the failure of eight attempts at Anglo-Egyptian negotiation. It was not until the 1936 Treaty of Friendship and Alliance, that Britain and Egypt established an understanding of their relationship.

In 1946, when the ten-year revision date of the 1936 treaty fell due, dispute over the Sudan issue continued. Negotiations again failed to secure Egyptian sovereignty over Sudan.[7] During the 1946 Sidky–Bevin negotiations the British objection on the Sudan issue was based on new arguments. Although the British negotiators recognized Egypt's right to assure an adequate supply of water from the Nile in Sudan, Britain denied Egypt's claim to sovereignty over Sudan on the grounds that the right to determine the future status of the country should be reserved to the Sudanese themselves who should decide whether they would prefer unity with Egypt or independence.[8]

In the meantime, in an attempt to justify its own presence in Sudan, Britain reiterated that its role there was as that of protector and to prepare Sudan for self-determination and eventually full independence. This definition of the British role in Sudan was accompanied by frequent public statements, in 1944–5, to the effect that the Sudanese were not yet ready either for self-determination or self-government. Britain contended that such a state would not be reached for another generation.[9] This made Egypt aware of the British intention of remaining in Sudan even after it left Egypt. This line of reasoning and these declarations made Egypt insist on its demand for unity with Sudan using the slogan that Sudan and Egypt were a single country and that the Nile was the "life of the nation" without which neither Egypt nor Sudan could survive.

Although Britain and Egypt seem to have shown favourable intentions towards Sudan, the evidence suggests that each had its own political aim there. Egypt's government and king wanted to expand their rule and dominance over Sudan and Britain wanted to strengthen its defence network and grip on the region so as to protect its interests in the Nile Valley.[10]

The Anglo-Egyptian conflict over the Sudan was reflected in the intense political developments which took place in Sudan between 1936 and 1946. In February 1938, the Sudanese Graduates Congress was formed. This congress of the Sudanese intellectual class gradually split into two factions during the allied victory in Africa in 1943–4 and led to the formation of two political parties.[11] One group came under the leadership of Ismail al-Azhari, and was called the Ashiqqa (Brothers) Party. This party allied itself with Egypt, favouring full autonomy for the Sudan under the Egyptian crown. The other group formed the Umma (or Nation) Party under the patronage of Abdel-Rahman al-Mahdi – the posthumous son of Muhammad al-Mahdi. The Umma Party advocated complete independence for Sudan with Britain's support. It wanted Sudan to be separated from Egypt and favoured the British administration because it considered that this would give them self-government through which Sudan could move to ultimate independence and possibly be able to seek membership of the British Commonwealth.[12]

This political difference among the Sudanese themselves encouraged Egypt and Britain as the condominium powers to interfere in Sudanese affairs and delayed the process of self-determination, with both Britain and Egypt seeking advantage over Sudan. The formation of the two major political parties in Sudan encouraged the establishment of several other political parties. Some of these were small, had little influence and lacked mass support (for example: the Khatmiyya, a Sudanese religious group; the Southern Democratic Party; and the Nile Party).[13] Others (such as the Muslim Sudanese Brothers Society and the Sudan Communist Party) were, however, more influential. The former became an active party as a result of the growing power of the Muslim Brothers Society in Egypt in 1939–49 of which it was an extension. Many Sudanese students at that time had studied in Egyptian educational institutions, particularly al-Azhar University in Cairo.[14] Some had joined the Egyptian Muslim organization and, on their return home, had begun to spread the principles and teaching of the Muslim Society in Sudan. Since Islamic principles make no separation between religion and politics, the Muslim Brothers advocated the revival of Muslim society and tried to establish an Islamic political party in each Muslim country to struggle against non-Muslim authority in their homelands.[15]

The Sudanese Communist Party was also an extension of a similar organization in Egypt known as the Egyptian Democratic Communist Party. The members of these Sudanese communists who were also students, had gone to Egypt for their higher education and on their return home began to pursue communist activities and demanded the right of self-determination for the Sudanese people. Meanwhile, the Egyptians were using the Sudanese communists with the other Sudanese parties to help Egypt's struggle against imperialism in the region.[16]

Although the two major Sudanese political parties and the other smaller ones remained divided, they temporarily resolved their differences by making a common alliance when the British foreign secretary, Ernest Bevin, stated in the House of Commons on 26 March 1946:

> His Majesty's Government look forward to the day when the Sudanese will be able finally to decide their political future for themselves and the welfare of the Sudanese cannot be secured unless a stable and disinterested administration is maintained in the Sudan . . . In the meantime, His Majesty's Government consider that no change should be made in the status of the Sudan until the Sudanese have been consulted through constitutional channels.[17]

This incident prompted the Sudanese political leader, Ismail al-Azhari, to send a note to both the British and Egyptian governments demanding the right of self-determination for Sudan.

The development of the Sudanese nationalist movement accelerated the formation of the Sudanese delegation to the United Nations. However, it went only as an observer not as an offical delegation, under the direction of Ismail al-Azhari.[18] This political experience and the publicity given to the Sudan question in the United Nations during the discussion of the Anglo-Egyptian dispute increased the power of the Sudanese political parties, particularly the Ashiqqa and the Umma, and increased their awareness of their importance to the future of their country. It also encouraged Sudanese public opinion to support the slogan: "Sudan for the Sudanese"; and they began to demand the right of self-determination. This resulted in the weakening of Egypt's propaganda in Sudan for the unification of the two countries.[19]

In the last few pages, I have reflected upon the Sudan question as it related to the Anglo-Egyptian dispute. Actually Nokrashy Pasha, the Egyptian premier, adopted an uncompromising attitude towards Britain with regard to the future of Anglo-Egyptian relations in general and the question of Sudan in particular. This was despite the British ambassador's efforts to break the deadlock in the negotiations. On 21 January 1947, Killearn asked Nokrashy to accept Britain's latest offer made by the Sidky–Bevin protocol. Killearn also advised Nokrashy that the United Nations had nothing to do with the Anglo-Egyptian disagreements and that Egypt might not gain a favourable settlement at the UN.[20]

The British ambassador was not successful in dissuading Nokrashy from his determination to appeal to world opinion. Nokrashy's stubbornness over Britain's latest proposal made the British ambassador realize that his efforts at negotiations with Egypt had been entirely fruitless, and he believed that with the support of King Farouk, Nokrashy would take the contest to the international arena.[21]

In the remainder of this chapter I shall examine the United Nation's treatment of the Sudan issue. First, I shall introduce the Egyptian argument presented to the United Nations. Second, I shall examine the British response to Egypt's claims, and finally I shall look at the reactions, opinions, suggestions and recommendations that the United Nations produced with respect to this case.

On 27 January 1947, Nokrashy Pasha announced to the Egyptian parliament that the negotiations with Britain had failed again and that Egypt intended to refer the issue to the United Nations. There was considerable delay in proceeding with Nokrashy's proposal as the Egyptian opposition, the Wafdists, objected to the official referral of the Anglo-Egyptian dispute to the United Nations.[22] It was six months before Egypt finally decided to send a letter to Trygve Lie, the Norwegian secretary-general of the United Nations. On 8 July, Nokrashy Pasha and his minister of foreign affairs, Abdel-Hamid Badawi Pasha, despatched a letter setting out the Egyptian claims and grievances against British forces in Egypt and Sudan.[23]

Egypt's decision to refer the matter to the United Nations was merely an attempt to divert Egyptian public attention from Egypt to an international arena despite the fact that Killearn had advised Nokrashy Pasha that the United Nations had nothing to do with the Anglo-Egyptian settlement.[24] It was, however, Nokrashy's firm belief that the British would not leave Egypt unless they were pressured by world opinion or a consensus of member states of the UN Security Council. Besides, this stand, he reckoned, would keep him in power longer.

On 5 August 1947, however, the Egyptian case against Britain appeared on the agenda of the UN Security Council. Egypt's letter to the UN secretary-general had stated that the British forces were maintained in Egyptian territories against the wishes of the Egyptian people. The presence of foreign troops within the territories of a member country of the United Nations in times of peace and without that country's free consent constituted an offence to its dignity and a hindrance to its normal development. This occupation was also an infringement of the fundamental principle of sovereign equality. It was therefore contrary to the spirit of the United Nations and the Charter, particularly to Articles 33 and 37. The British occupation of Egypt also contradicted the UN resolution, adopted unanimously by the General Assembly on 14 December 1946, which requested all member states to withdraw their armed forces stationed in the territory of any other member country of the United Nations. Meanwhile, Nokrashy Pasha cited a statement made by Bevin in the House of Commons on 16 May 1947 to show that Britain was ignoring the Egyptian claims. Bevin had said: "There would be no attempt to appease the Egyptian government at the expense of the Sudanese people. Whether they take this matter to the Security Council or anywhere else, we cannot go any further than the offer we have made."[25] This last remark was a reference to the Sidky–Bevin protocol of 1946.

The Egyptian claims and grievances stated in the letter to the United Nations were neither clear nor specific enough, which made it very difficult for the Security Council to carry out its duty of taking action in support of the Egyptian case, particularly as Egypt was demanding that the Council should resolve three controversial issues in one agenda. These issues were: (a) the question of Egyptian sovereignty over Sudan; (b) the immediate withdrawal of British troops from Egyptian territories as well as from Sudan; and (c) the revision of the 1936 treaty between Britain and Egypt.

Thus, when the UN secretary-general opened the proceedings, he invited the Egyptian prime minister to give an explanatory statement about the letter he had addressed to the Security Council. He was given the chance to present Egypt's case before the British made theirs. In two long speeches on 5 and 13 August 1947, Nokrashy enlarged on Egypt's letter to the UN secretary-general. In a speech lasting more than an hour he strongly attacked the British position in Egypt and Sudan. The main points of his speeches were as follows:[26]

Nokrashy maintained that the continued British occupation of Egypt and Britain's consequent interference in Egyptian domestic affairs put pressure on the Egyptian government and caused friction between the populace and the occupying forces. The increasing resentment of the people of the Nile Valley to the presence of British troops in the region for more than 65 years could no longer be ignored or stifled as in the past. The British military presence had led to bloodshed and loss of lives. Furthermore, Nokrashy argued, the Council should take into account the wider repercussions that this dispute might have beyond Egyptian frontiers.

Nokrashy argued that a strong Egypt, united with Sudan, would be able to act as a buttress of peace in the Middle East. He demanded that the British forces be immediately withdrawn from the Suez Canal Zone. The British occupation of Egypt since 1882 was evidence of British imperialistic aims in Egypt itself, Nokrashy said, emphasizing that it was a flagrant disregard of international law by the British government. Britain had been the first to violate the Convention of London of 1840 and other agreements which recognized Egyptian sovereignty and territorial integrity. Despite repeated assurances by British statesmen that the Bristish occupation of Egypt was only temporary, it was still in force. At the same time Nokrashy defended the 1922 Declaration of Independence, saying that it stemmed from Egypt's national aspirations which resulted in a nationwide uprising forcing Britain's hand.

With regard to Sudan, Nokrashy alleged that the unity of the Nile Valley was indisputable and had been officially recognized in the past by the British government. He described the present line dividing Sudan from Egypt, which was devised and implemented by the British, as purely artificial. Nokrashy claimed that the unity between Sudan and Egypt was based on agricultural, industrial and commercial interests, with both Egyptians and Sudanese relying on the water of the Nile. He defended Egyptian penetration in Sudan as it had been accomplished by peaceful and natural means between the peoples of the Nile who shared a common language and culture. Under the rule of Muhammad Ali, Egypt and Sudan formed a single political unit under a single central authority. This was also confirmed by the Ottoman sultan's firmans which recognized Egyptian sovereignty over Sudan. This sovereignty received international recognition after 1840 including recognition by Britain.[27]

Egypt attacked the Anglo-Egyptian Condominium Agreement of 1899 which it described as out of date. It also attacked British policy in Sudan because the British administration had, Nokrashy said, monopolized Sudanese affairs. In particular, the governor-general of Sudan had always been a British official and had in fact appointed all higher and lower officials in the country in breach of the Condominium Agreement. At the same time, Britain had diverted to the Red Sea ports, trade from north Sudan which previously went through Egypt resulting in Sudan being cut off from Egypt. Egypt also maintained that Britain tried to cut off the spiritual relations between the two peoples. Nokrashy accused the British administration of dividing Sudan itself: Britain had attempted to separate the southern part of Sudan from the north because it wished to attach southern Sudan to the British colonies in East Africa.

Nokrashy Pasha emphasized that the historical relationships between the Egyptians and the Sudanese were internal domestic affairs which concerned only the two peoples. He contended that Britain had no right to interfere in those relationships.[28] With regard to the Anglo-Egyptian treaty of 1936, Nokrashy stressed that his country had given its loyal support and assistance to Britain and its allies throughout the Second World War. Egypt had confidently expected that after the war Britain would remove the limitations on Egypt's right to act as a free and sovereign state and that such restrictions would end.

He justified Egypt's position in demanding the revision of the 1936 treaty by claiming that Egypt had signed this treaty while under the stress and threats of that time. Since circumstances had changed, the treaty must be regarded as out of date. He also alleged that in 1936 when it signed the treaty Egypt was not a free state because of the occupation of its territories by the British forces. Britain had issued veiled threats and British negotiators had warned Egypt against the possible consequences of its failure to agree to the British demands.[29]

Egypt accused Britain of delaying a settlement because it hoped to retain its military bases in Egypt and Sudan in perpetuity. What was more, Britain had proposed a new treaty of alliance and military cooperation, a proposal which seemed to confirm Britain's desire to remain there. On the other hand, Egypt considered the recognition of the unity of the Nile Valley to be a central condition for any new agreement.[30] When the British delegation was finally forced to face this issue, Bevin recognized the Egyptian demand for the unity of Sudan and Egypt under the common crown of Egypt. This fact became public when Britain stated that it would only recognize as symbolic Egyptian sovereignty over Sudan. Britain insisted again that the Sudan should have the right to secede from Egypt in the near future. However, the Egyptian premier, Sidky Pasha, refused to sign with Bevin a document containing such an interpretation. On the other hand, the British governor-general of Sudan, Major-General Hubert Jervoise Huddleston, rejected the Sidky–Bevin protocol on Sudan and encouraged the Sudanese to oppose the agreement, so causing more disruption among the Sudanese.[31] Huddleston's active campaign against Egypt in Sudan was intended to cause a rift between the Sudanese and the Egyptians. Nokrashy Pasha concluded that, under these circumstances, there was no other course open to Egypt than to place the issue before the UN Security Council. Nokrashy hoped that the Council could take action on such a crucial matter. He also reminded the Council that Britain continued to occupy Egypt, which was a manifest contradiction of the conditions required by the resolution passed by the General Assembly and also of the UN Charter which embodied the principle of the sovereign equality of all nations and provided for a system of collective security to maintain world peace.

Thus, he said, Egypt would rely on juridical considerations since the function of the Council was to act as an international court of law and to preserve peace and security in the world. The Council, for its part, should take Egypt's view into consideration, bearing in mind that the political controversy between Egypt and Britain might threaten world peace. Further, the Council should not recognize the treaties – the Anglo-Egyptian agreements of 1899 and

1936 – as legal and should not allow anyone to deter it from its duty to solve matters.[32] In conclusion, Nokrashy expressed Egypt's confidence that the Council would solve the disagreements between the two countries.

Replying to Nokrashy's statement, Sir Alexander Cadogan, the British representative, put his government's case. He defended and justified the British presence in the region first in response to the letter which the Egyptian delegation had addressed to the UN secretary-general and secondly in response to Nokrashy's supplementary statement. In his opening speech, Cadogan said briefly that Egypt had brought this matter to the Security Council under Articles 33 and 37 of the UN Charter as a continuing dispute between the two countries which was likely to endanger international peace and world security. That statement, Cadogan contended, was false. No proof had been offered, he said, to show that the continuance of the British presence in Egypt was dangerous to world peace and security, unless the Egyptian government contemplated making it so.

Cadogan defended the British position on the legality and validity of the 1936 treaty with Egypt. He emphasized that there were many examples of similar treaties still in existence with periods of duration longer than that of the 1936 treaty and which provided for the stationing of troops. He quoted some examples to justify the presence of British forces in Egypt, saying, for instance, that under an agreement of 1941 the United States enjoyed the right to station forces in several bases on British territory for a period of 99 years. That did not mean that the United States infringed the principles of British sovereign equality. Another treaty, concluded in 1939, gave the United States the right, not merely for a period of years but in perpetuity, to control a zone ten miles wide within the territory of the Republic of Panama. Also, under the treaty of 1947 with the Republic of the Philippines, the United States had a 99 year lease on five major bases and ten auxiliary and training establishments in the Philippines. The Soviet Union, he added, had signed a treaty with China in August 1945 by which the Soviets acquired the right to maintain naval and air forces in Port Arthur for a period of 30 years. Another agreement, recently signed between Britain and Belgium, provided for a small number of British troops to stay on Belgian territory for the purpose of communications with the British Zone in Germany. That did not mean that Britain was infringing Belgian sovereignty, nor were the British infringing on Egyptian sovereignty when British forces were stationed in Egypt. Therefore, he concluded, there were no grounds for claiming that the treaty of 1936 was invalid.

In fact, he continued, the 1936 treaty itself afforded a complete answer to the claims which had been brought by Egypt. Article 8 of the treaty stated that the British forces should be stationed legally on Egyptian territory in the vicinity of the Suez Canal for a period of 20 years.[33] He concentrated his arguments principally on the legal issues of the validity of the 1936 treaty. He denied Egypt's claim that the people of Egypt desired the removal of British troops from Egyptian territory. This was not true, he said, and even if it were it would be of no benefit to change the agreement. Britain had leased bases to the United States for 99 years and that agreement, which had been concluded in wartime, was a useful mutual defence pact between the two countries. This case exactly paralleled the Egyptian one, he said. Britain could not now come to the Security Council and say that now that the war was over and the danger past, the agreement had become invalid and the British people now desired the removal of US forces from their country. Nor should it be forgotten, he said, that the British forces had saved Egypt from destruction by the Axis powers. Cadogan attacked Egyptian appeals to the United Nations and accused Egypt of having no justification for, or right to, revise the 1936 treaty since the duration of the agreement had not come to maturity, and in any case there was no agreement on its revision by one or other of the parties.

He accused Egypt of bringing an ill-founded claim before the Security Council. It was an entirely simple matter, he said, because the 1936 treaty was not only legally valid but had also been accepted by the Egyptian people and their parliament. Hence, the treaty did not constitute a violation of the General Assembly resolution of 14 December 1946 nor of any other principle of the UN Charter. In consequence, Egypt's case against Britain must be removed from the UN agenda.[34]

With regard to the Sudanese question Cadogan launched a strong attack on Egypt's demands in Sudan, and accused the Egyptian government of having its own interests in Sudan. Egypt was ignoring the dignity of the Sudanese and denying them the right to self-determination. Britain's presence in Sudan had no imperialistic motive, as Egypt had alleged. He laid the blame for the failure of the previous Anglo-Egyptian negotiations at Egypt's door and defended British policy in Sudan by claiming that His Majesty's Government had three basic aims: (a) the protection of Sudanese interests from outside interference; (b) the preparation of the Sudanese for self-government; and (c) the exercise of the right of the Sudanese to choose the future status of their country.[35]

Britain would have no objection if Sudan wished to unite with Egypt in the near future but the Egyptian government still insisted on limiting Sudan's choice and that Sudan should be under the Egyptian crown. In other words, he said, Egypt was not prepared to accord in the future to the Sudanese people the right of self-determination which Egypt had claimed for other Arab countries. He reminded Egypt that it was British action that had released Egypt from the Ottoman sultan's sovereignty, thus making Egypt an independent and sovereign country.[36]

So Britain devoted its argument principally to defending its military position in Sudan as legal in accordance with both the Condominium Agreement of 1899 and the 1936 treaty. The treaty itself provided, in Article II, for the continued legal British administration of Sudan with Egypt until the Sudanese were able to administer their country.[37] Finally he dismissed as weak and illogical Egypt's argument that the unity of Sudan and Egypt was based on the geographical unity of the Nile Valley. If that were true, then Egypt could claim also Ethiopia and Uganda. Even the Belgian Congo would have to be included in such a political argument for unity since the Nile derived most of its waters from these countries.

After the two disputant countries had presented their cases the issue was placed before Security Council members for debate. The Brazilian delegate was the first to comment: he pointed out that the Security Council's function was only to preserve peace among

United Nations members and to secure peace at the international level. The Anglo-Egyptian dispute, he said, did not contravene the UN Charter's principles. Brazil therefore recommended that Britain and Egypt should resume direct negotiations. If these failed to reach agreement on the revision of the 1936 treaty with regard to the evacuation of British forces from Egypt, either party would have the right either to seek the mediation of another party or to select other peaceful means to solve the dispute. The Security Council should be kept informed of the progress of these negotiations. On the question of Sudan the Brazilian delegate recommended that the matter be settled by the Sudanese themselves, rather than by other parties, in the near future.[38]

The Chinese delegate spoke next and advanced another proposal. China expressed its general sympathy with Egypt's aspirations to full independence. In his opinion the gulf between the Egyptian and British views about Britain's evacuation of Egypt was not wide since the Sidky–Bevin agreement provided for total evacuation by the end of 1949. Although that agreement had not been formally accepted, Britain had shown readiness to negotiate with Egypt on the complete evacuation of British troops. Therefore, China recommended to the Security Council that direct Anglo-Egyptian negotiations should be resumed in order to resolve the misunderstanding between Britain and Egypt. On the question of Egypt's desire to maintain unity with Sudan, China considered this to be reasonable and historically natural to Egypt, but the Security Council on the whole could not be party to anything which would prevent the Sudanese people from exercising the right of self-determination since the primary duty of the Security Council was to support the national aspirations of the peoples of the world. Thus the Chinese delegate supported the Brazilian recommendation.[39] Belgium also supported it and suggested that direct negotiations were possible between the two parties since normal methods of negotiation had not been at an impasse. If the next set of talks could not satisy either party, then the two countries may refer the dispute to the International Court of Justice.[40]

In contrast, the Soviet Union and Poland strongly supported Egypt's case in the UN debate. They claimed that the 1936 treaty was inconsistent with Article 103 of the UN Charter. They argued that it was the duty of the United Nations to assist peoples who wanted to achieve independence and exercise full sovereign rights. In their views, such aspirations were being thwarted by the outdated imperialistic treaties of the nineteenth century. The Soviet Union and Poland therefore demanded the immediate withdrawal of all British troops from the Nile Valley but they reserved judgement on the Sudan question since the wishes of the Sudanese people were not known. They urged the Security Council to take immediate decisions on the dispute between Britain and Egypt.[41]

The Australian representative suggested that the resumption of direct negotiations would settle the dispute and also lead to the settlement of other issues such as the Sudan question. Further, since the UN members were sympathetic to Sudan's right to self-determination, Australia recommended to the British and Egyptian governments that the Sudanese be included as a third party in the next round of negotiations which might then produce a fruitful result between the interested parties.[42]

The Columbian representative presented a different proposal. He called upon Britain and Egypt to resume direct negotiations, to set a date for the evacuation of British troops from Egypt and to terminate the joint Anglo-Egyptian administration of Sudan. This should be done with due regard to the principle of the self-determination of the Sudanese people. At the same time, he suggested that Britain and Egypt should keep the Security Council fully informed of the progress of the negotiations.[43]

The draft resolution put forward by Columbia was more specific than the Brazilian one in two respects. First, on the question of direct negotiations between the two parties, the Columbian delegate suggested setting a date for the British evacuation from Egypt, and, second, for the withdrawal of the British forces from the Nile Valley and the cessation of the Anglo-Egyptian administration in Sudan. Egypt welcomed the Columbian proposals, particularly the call for the termination of the British administration in Sudan, although the proposal did not specify the future of Egyptian sovereignty over Sudan. Britain, however, rejected the Columbian proposal because it was convinced that this formula would define the agenda for Anglo-Egyptian talks and might lead to the immediate termination of the British administration in Sudan – Britain still believed that the Sudanese were not yet capable of governing themselves. Therefore, when voting took place on the Columbian resolution, five countries (Brazil, China, Columbia, Syria and the United States) voted in favour and five (Australia, Belgium, France, Poland and the Soviet Union) abstained. The United Kingdom, in accordance with Article 27 of the UN Charter, did not participate in the voting.[44]

Thus, it became obvious to Egypt that without the support of the United States at the United Nations Britain could not secure conclusive results, and no draft resolution was adopted, though the issue remained on the agenda. In an exceptional move, the Syrian representative to the United Nations, Fares al-Khouri, who was also the acting president of the Security Council, made a moving appeal to Sir Alexander Cadogan requesting that Britain should make a friendly gesture by telling the Council that Britain did not intend to keep its forces in the Nile Valley indefinitely. He also stated that it was the wish of the UN General Assembly that, in accordance with the rules of the UN Charter, such practices as that by Britain in the Nile Valley should not continue. Syria hoped that Britain would take the matter seriously without specific invitation or recommendation to do so by the Security Council. He wished, he said, that Britain would adopt a similar attitude to that which it adopted in 1946 with respect to the Lebanon and Syria. Britain at that time helped propose a resolution for the independence of the two countries. If Britain were to initiate such action again, the entire dispute with Egypt would be solved without difficulty. Syria also called for an immediate evacuation of British troops from Egypt and described the 1936 treaty as an obstacle to the improvement of Anglo-Egyptian relations. Further, Syria indicated that the International Court of Justice was not the place to deal with this kind of dispute between countries. Finally, Syria asked Britain to be more flexible over Egypt's demands.[45]

The British representative responded by stating that Britain would pay heed to the Syrian requests and would study all the arguments which had been put forward during the UN debate. Sir Alexander Cadogan promised to urge His Majesty's Government to act on these recommendations soon. At the same time, Cadogan asked the president of the Security Council to remove the Egyptian case from the United Nations agenda.[46] Thus, the Security Council's meeting dealing with the Anglo-Egyptian dispute ended inconclusively. The president of the Security Council announced, however, that the Egyptian case would remain on the UN agenda until the Council decided to remove it.[47]

Before concluding this chapter, I will elaborate on a few points concerning the Sudanese observers to the United Nations and attempt to explain why they did not participate in the debate on the future of their country. The Sudanese delegation was representing the two major political parties in Sudan – the Umma and the Ashiqqa – which were available for consultation at Lake Success. Although the Australian representative to the United Nations suggested that the Sudanese be consulted during the debate, they were conveniently avoided by all the debating representatives. This can perhaps be explained by saying that their case was fairly understood by the Security Council and that their involvement would not have contributed anything to the Sudanese cause. All the representatives at the Security Council unanimously maintained the right of the Sudanese to determine the future status of their country.

In the introduction, I questioned Egypt's reasons for taking its claim to the United Nations knowing that the attempt might fail. First, the king and the government may have thought that Egypt had nothing to lose by following this course of action, which might win the country international sympathy and the support of a UN resolution. However poorly conceived this action might have been, domestic developments within Egypt at that time might explain it. By referring the Anglo-Egyptian dispute to the United Nations, the Egyptian government perhaps hoped to halt the tide of popular discontent, at least temporarily, and to divert people's attention from the government's failure to grasp the opportunity offered by the Sidky–Bevin protocol which had brought the two countries close to a favourable agreement, at least with respect to Egypt's full independence.

Nahhas Pasha, the leader of the strong Wafd Party, who was on better terms with the British than his opponent Nokrashy, realized what the king and Nokrashy were planning. He sent a cable to the UN Security Council[48] in which he tried to discredit Nokrashy before the United Nations indicating that there was disagreement within Egypt with respect to the issue before it. Second, Nahhas wanted to make clear to the Wafdists their position on the issue. As the chief Egyptian architect of the 1936 treaty, Nahhas's stance reinforced the legal validity of that treaty which could be revised only with the consent of both the British and Egyptian governments. Nahhas Pasha was keen to weaken Nokrashy's government (which was a minority government) so that he himself could become prime minister.

Generally speaking, the transfer of the Anglo-Egyptian dispute to the international arena was mistimed. The world community, in particular the West, was unlikely to view the Anglo-Egyptian dispute as an important issue in 1947 because supporting the Egyptian demand in the United Nations would have weakened the allies' strategic position in the Middle East. This would have given the Soviet Union, which could not be trusted, an opportunity to fish in troubled waters. Egypt's location was considered to have strategic significance for counter-attacking possible communist activity in the region, which was considered of vital interest to the Western nations.[49]

The Egyptian government, if it really hoped for a favourable resolution from the UN Security Council, must have misunderstood the position, because it was world security that was the UN's primary concern, particularly during the Cold War between the new superpowers. It was also not to be expected that the United Nations would establish a precedent by passing resolutions contradicting an existing legal treaty, in this case the 1936 Anglo-Egyptian Treaty of Friendship and Alliance. As the British representative to the United Nations had said in his presentation to the Security Council, there were many relationships similar to that which existed between Britain and Egypt and which had not been brought to the United Nations for revision, or for discussion by other states.

The Egyptian government should not have expected a favourable response from the Security Council. Nokrashy Pasha in particular, who was a professional lawyer, ought to have known that Egypt's case did not have a good chance at the United Nations. Nokrashy returned home empty-handed.[50]

Notes

1. Richard Hill, *Egypt in the Sudan 1820–1881* (London, Oxford University Press, 1959), pp. 5–7.
2. *Ibid.*, p. 79
3. Ronald Robinson and John Gallagher, *Africa and the Victorians*, pp. 79–83.
4. *Ibid.*
5. Report from British Embassy in Cairo to Foreign Office, 7 January 1946, PRO/FO 371/62944.
6. *Ibid.*
7. *Ibid.*
8. *al-Ahram*, 27 October 1946.
9. Foreign Office Report, June 1947, PRO/FO 371/62954.
10. Ministry of Defence Secret Report, July 1947, PRO/FO 371/62955.
11. Sudan Government Independence Front, Memorandum, Khartoum to UNO, 27 April 1947, PRO/FO 371/62944.
12. *Ibid.* See also M. B. Omner, *Revolution and Nationalism in the Sudan* (London, Collings, 1974), pp. 176–9.
13. *Ibid.*
14. *Ibid.*, pp. 185–91.
15. R. Mitchell, *The Society of Muslim Brothers* (London, Oxford University Press, 1969), pp. 107–13.
16. *al-Wafd al-Masri*, 17 July 1949.
17. Parliamentary Debates [Commons], 1947, vol. 428, cols 295–6.
18. Cable from Khartoum to UNO, 27 April 1947, PRO/FO 371/62978.
19. British Governor-General of Sudan Secret to Foreign Office, June 1947, PRO/FO 371/62981.
20. Secret Meeting between Egyptian Prime Minister and Ambassador, Cairo, 17 February 1947, PRO/FO 371/69262.
21. Campbell to Bevin, Tel. 33, 25 July 1947, PRO/FO 371/63708.
22. *Ibid.*
23. *al-Ahram*, 11 August 1947.
24. From Prime Minister, Cairo, to Secretary-General of United Nations, 8 July 1947, PRO/FO 371/62955.
25. From Foreign Office to Alexandria, Cable 47, 22 February 1947, PRO/FO 371/63366.
26. Nokrashy Pasha's Speech to the Security Council, 5 August 1947, PRO/FO 371/62980.
27. *Ibid.*
28. *Ibid.*
29. *Ibid.*

30. Nokrashy Pasha's Speech to the Security Council, 11 August 1947, PRO/FO 371/62980.
31. *Ibid.*
32. *Ibid.* See also *al-Ahram*, 17 October 1947.
33. Cadogan's Speech to the Security Council, 5 August 1947, PRO/FO 371/62978.
34. *Ibid.*
35. Cadogan's Speech to the Security Council, 11 August 1947, PRO/FO 371/62978.
36. *Ibid.*
37. British Embassy in Cairo to Foreign Office, Tel. 2107, 26 June 1947, PRO/FO 371/62978.
38. From New York to Foreign Office, Tel. 107, 13 August 1947, PRO/FO 371/62981.
39. From New York to Foreign Office, Tel. 121, 14 August 1947, PRO/FO 371/62982.
40. *Ibid.*
41. From New York to Foreign Office, Tel. 4, 17 August 1947, PRO/FO 371/62982.
42. *Ibid.*
43. *Ibid.*
44. From New York to Foreign Office, Tel. 731, 13 August 1947, PRO/FO 371/62982.
45. Foreign Office Minutes on Anglo-Egyptian dispute at the United Nations, January 1948, PRO/FO 371/62983.
46. *Ibid.*
47. From New York to Foreign Office, Tel. 801, 19 August 1947, PRO/FO 371/629882.
48. Cable from Nahhas Pasha, the Leader of the Egyptian Wafd Party, to the Secretary-General of the United Nations, 29 July 1947, PRO/FO 371/62981.
49. Cabinet Conclusion, December 1945, PRO/FO 371/62943.
50. M. Heikal, *Mudhakkirat fi 'l-siyasah al-misriyya*, vol. 2 (Cairo, 1980), pp. 50–7.

3

The Palestine War of 1948 and its Effects on Anglo-Egyptian Political Relations

Following Egypt's failure to obtain a favourable resolution from the United Nations concerning its dispute with Britain, the UN General Assembly on 29 November 1947 passed Resolution 181 concerning the partition of the Arab land of Palestine. The UN's action resulted from Britain's abandonment of its mandate over Palestine and referral of the case to the United Nations. In response to this resolution, Egypt and other Arab states became involved in the Palestine War of 1948. This war complicated the already hostile Anglo-Egyptian relations and delayed the much needed negotiations to settle the dispute between Britain and Egypt.

In this chapter I will describe the developments which led to Britain's involvement in Palestine and Egypt's participation in the Palestine War, and examine how these developments affected Anglo-Egyptian relations during the period under study.

It would be impractical to attempt a thorough investigation of the Palestine crisis here. I will therefore give only a brief historical background that will help to explain the events which interest us.

British involvement in Palestine began in 1917 when Arthur James Balfour, the British foreign secretary, made the following declaration in order to win Jewish support during the First World War:

> His Majesty's Government views with favour the establishment in Palestine of a national home for the Jewish people, and will use their best endeavours to facilitate the achievement of this object, it being clearly understood that nothing shall be done which may prejudice the civil and religious rights of existing

> non-Jewish communities in Palestine or the rights and political status enjoyed by Jews in any other country.[1]

With this, which became known as the Balfour Declaration, the Zionist movement, which represented world Jewry, acquired a binding pledge of support for their efforts to establish a national home for the Jews in Palestine. It was not too long before this pledge became internationally recognized. France endorsed the Declaration in early 1918, and was soon followed by Italy and the United States.[2]

After the First World War Britain acquired the mandate over Palestine and, at San Remo in April 1920, this mandate was approved by the Council of the League of Nations. Britain, upon assuming its new position in Palestine, declared that neither the Arabs nor the Jews would be allowed to govern Palestine. Palestine would be ruled by the British government through a high commissioner and Sir Edwin Herbert Samuel was the first person to be appointed to this post. On assuming his responsibilities Samuel promptly set himself to the task of implementing the Balfour Declaration.[3] The world Zionist leaders were delighted with the British mandate system. They believed the British high commissioner in Palestine would be an advantage for the Jews and would provide them with material assistance regarding:

1. The implementation of the whole of the Balfour Declaration;
2. The recognition of the historical connection of the Jewish people with Palestine;
3. The establishment of a Jewish agency and its recognition as a public body for the purpose of advising the immigrant Jewish communities in Palestine;
4. The facilitation of Jewish immigration to the promised land, as the Jews believed it to be – a chosen land for a chosen people.[4]

With these conditions in mind, the Jews were convinced that the Balfour Declaration and the British mandate would enable them to establish a Jewish state in Palestine and that the mandate would facilitate the building of the foundation of that state by allowing unrestricted Jewish immigration into Palestine and economic expansion.[5]

The Arabs in general and the Palestinians in particular rejected the whole idea of the Balfour Declaration and the British mandate on the grounds that they contravened the terms of the League of Nations Covenant and were therefore legally invalid. Therefore, in 1919, under the leadership of Haj Amin al-Hussaini – the Mufti (religious legislator) of Jerusalem – protests and outbreaks of violence took place in Palestine for the first time against the influx of Jewish immigrants and the British mandate. Britain responded by suppressing the rebellion and arresting its leaders, forcing them to flee the country and leave the Palestinians without qualified leadership.[6] Disturbances continued in Palestine while unrestricted numbers of Jewish immigrants continued to flow into the country.

The 1930s witnessed a dramatic increase in violence between the Palestinian inhabitants who wanted to maintain the Arab character of Palestine, and the Jewish immigrants who became a sizeable minority with political goals and greater economic advantages.[7] These disturbances led eventually to the declaration of the Palestinian revolution in 1936.[8]

As hostilities between the two communities increased, Britain became aware of the real danger. The British government decided in early 1939 to restrict further immigration of Jews to Palestine in an attempt to restore order and maintain peace in the country. In May 1939, Britain introduced the document which became known as the "White Paper" which legitimized and recognized Arabs' rights in Palestine, banning in the meantime the selling and purchasing of land belonging to the Arabs to non-Arabs.[9] This attempt, however, failed to do much to maintain order or enforce law in the country.[10] When the Jewish leaders in Palestine realized that Britain would not completely satisfy their wishes, they began to search for another great power that would patronize them and promote their claims in Palestine.[11] Subsequently, the Jewish leaders began to shift their energy and efforts to the United States which they well exploited in the Biltmore Conference in May 1942.[12] This Zionist conference (held in the Biltmore Hotel, New York city) concluded that the Jewish State should exist in Palestine and that the Jews must be ready to fight the Arabs, if not the British, in order to attain their Jewish national home. This was strongly expressed by David Ben-Gurion and Moshe Sharet, the most radical Jewish leaders in Palestine.[13]

This explained why the new Jewish immigrants in Palestine had organized themselves under the guise of a Jewish agency when in fact they were well-trained militants organized for the purpose of defending the Jewish settlers. This organization was known as the Haganah. It continued to operate as an underground organization and was illegal from the point of view of the British mandate in Palestine. By the end of the Second World War, the Haganah had increased its membership and included scores of ex-soldiers who were trained and had fought in East Europe.

The Haganah became a military organization and built up stores of arms and ammunition which were obtained either by illicit purchases or by theft from the camps of allied forces in Palestine.[14] The Haganah became a powerful organization and was capable of spreading terror throughout the country. The Palestinians were also confronting violence with violence which made the British task of maintaining order almost impossible. Faced with this situation Britain decided to reappraise its role in Palestine. In early 1947 Britain's Labour government concluded that the mandate had proved unworkable in practice because neither the Arabs nor the Jews were happy with it. Ernest Bevin, the British foreign secretary, was convinced that by withdrawing British forces from Palestine, Britain would be able to maintain a friendly relationship with the Arabs as well as to restore law and order in Palestine.

The Arabs in Palestine, in Bevin's opinion, were able to defend themselves.[15] Subsequently, on 18 February 1947, Bevin announced in the House of Commons that Britain had decided to refer the Palestine question to the United Nations without recommending any particular solution for the problem.[16] Britain also announced that it would take no action which would not be agreeable to both the Jews and the Arabs. Thus, when the issue was put before the United Nations, Britain played a generally passive role and even abstained from voting after the General Assembly debate.[17] Britain declared that its forces would be evacuated from the whole of Palestine as rapidly as possible in order to save British lives which were threatened by the rising violence in the country.[18] On 15 May 1948 Britain formally terminated its mandated authority over Palestine without making any arrangements for the transfer of any authority in the country. That same day David Ben-Gurion proclaimed the establishment of the Jewish State of Israel.[19]

The Soviet Union was the first to recognize it. President Truman of the United States also recognized Israel as a new member of the family of nations, thereby assuring the security of its existence.[20] Furthermore, President Truman asked for a US $100 million loan for the new state during the reception for Chaim Weizmann (who later became the first president of Israel) at the White House on 20 May 1948.[21] Truman made his personal decision on US recognition of Israel without consulting the State Department or informing the US delegation to the United Nations. This was on the advice of his political campaign advisers who told Truman to expedite recognition of Israel so as to please the Jewish leaders in the United States and so gain their support in the forthcoming elections in 1948.[22]

After the UN General Assembly had issued Resolution 181 on 29 November 1947 concerning the partition of Palestine, the Egyptian government called for a meeting of the Arab League Council.[23] An emergency meeting was held in Cairo under the presidency of Secretary-General Abdel Rahman Azzam Pasha who announced that the Arab governments would take whatever steps were necessary to ensure that the UN resolution for the partition of Palestine would be rejected. The Arab League Council believed that the United Nations had no sovereignty over Palestine and that the provisions of its Charter did not allow it to partition its territory. Egypt in particular attacked the UN resolution and accused the United Nations of lacking good faith and a sense of justice for the Arab cause.[24]

Following the announcement of the birth of the Israeli state on 15 May 1948, the Arab League Council met again and decided, with the full support of Egypt, to go to war with the Jews in Palestine to forestall the establishment of an Israeli state. Azzam Pasha thought that the strategic position and the technical preparedness of the Arab forces were particularly favourable to the Arabs and that they would not have any great difficulties in achieving a swift military victory in Palestine. The Egyptian prime minister, Nokrashy Pasha, was of the same opinion. Subsequently Egypt decided to send its regular armed units into Palestine. Syria, Iraq, Lebanon and Jordan rushed volunteers to Palestine to reinforce the Egyptian forces.

King Farouk supported the idea of military intervention in Palestine not only because of the Arab League's decision but also because such a war was likely to restore his status as the defender of the Arab nation and the preserver of the Islamic faith in Palestine.[25] Farouk was also convinced that victory over Israel would win him credence within Egypt, helping him to restore his dwindling power and defeat his rivals in the Wafd Party and the Muslim Brotherhood organization. He also expected that this war would reduce the opposition to the already weakened Nokrashy who had just suffered defeat at the United Nations. The Palestine crisis, therefore, created a situation in Egypt that seemed likely to divert the attention of the masses and silence the opposition. It also offered an opportune moment to reinstate martial law in the country.[26]

Egypt played the largest part in the war against the newly born State of Israel. The Egyptian government expected that the war would not last longer than two weeks and that the Israeli forces would be defeated easily.[27] However, these expectations were far from the truth. The Israelis defeated the Arab states with Egypt suffering the greatest humiliation. The Egyptian defeat had a profound and immediate effect on Egypt's public life. Prime minister Nokrashy failed to conceal the disastrous course of the war from the Egyptian public. It became clear to many Egyptians, and in particular to the opposition in Egypt, that Nokrashy's government was ineffective. Opposition accusations of corruption in the administration and misappropriation of war funds soon surfaced.

The king and the government therefore failed in their attempt to use the war to eliminate opposition and win popularity in Egypt.[28] The Muslim Brotherhood organization, which had become considerable in Egypt, was most active in the anti-government campaign.

Its members accused the government of failing to protect Egypt's territories and defend the integrity of the Arab nation, especially after the Israeli forces succeeded in penetrating the Sinai peninsula.[29] The Israeli invasion of Egypt's territory resulted in a further deterioration of Anglo-Egyptian relations as a result of Britain's failure to respond to Egypt's demands for help during the war. Egypt demanded British assistance on the basis of Article 3 of the 1936 treaty which committed the two countries to aid one another in times of war or external aggression.[30]

Yet Britain did not react against Israeli aggression inside Egyptian territory during the Israeli campaign of December 1948, mainly because of US pressure against the use of Britain's military force stationed in the Suez Canal Zone against the new state. The United States did, however, intervene at an appropriate moment to stop the escalation of fighting in the area and asked Israeli leaders to withdraw from Egyptian territory and accept the proposed cease-fire. Their exhortations compelled the Israeli government, somewhat reluctantly, to agree to end the war against Egypt.

The United Nations also pressured Israel to withdraw from Egypt's territories and to accept the cease-fire.[31] The Egyptian government by now had realized that its military position had deteriorated critically. It therefore agreed to accept a cease-fire in early January 1949.[32] Immediately following the cease-fire the Egyptian and Israeli delegations began talks on the island of Rhodes with the presence of Ralph Bunche as the UN mediator and concluded an armistice agreement which was signed on 24 February 1949.[33] The Palestine War of 1948 came to an end and a Jewish state – Israel – with unspecified boundaries was born.

The Palestine War had caused considerable delay in the resumption of Anglo-Egyptian negotiations. Furthermore, Egypt's defeat in the war had two major consequences. First, fear of a regional danger and of the risk of war with Israel became a real factor and second, Egypt had proved incapable of defending its territories, especially the Suez Canal, against adversaries without external help. This caused the British government to reappraise its policy towards Egypt and convinced it that Britain should stay longer in the Suez

Canal Zone.[34] Egypt also came out of the war with heavy losses, in both military and financial terms. In addition, the Egyptian government found itself faced with serious domestic unrest. The reputation of the king and of his prime minister suffered considerably. They were held responsible for the failure and the mismanagement of the war and for the ignominious defeat at the hands of the Jews.[35]

Nokrashy Pasha was no longer credible as the leader of the government, particularly as the country was suffering from mounting political and economic problems such as the escalating cost of living as a result of the war. Nokrashy was also blamed for remaining silent and making no official attempts to resume the Anglo-Egyptian negotiations to end the Egyptian dispute with Britain.[36] This coincided with strong and growing demands for the withdrawal of British troops from Egypt as well as for unification with Sudan. These matters rendered Nokrashy unpopular and contributed to his eventual assassination on 28 December 1948.[37]

Following Nokrashy's death, the king immediately appointed the deputy prime minister, Ibrahim Abdel Hadi Pasha, as the new Egyptian premier.[38] Abdel Hadi assumed the office at an extremely critical juncture in the country's political history. His conclusion of a cease-fire with Israel had drawn serious criticism from the opposition who accused him of being as ineffective as his predecessor.[39] This reaction derived also from Abdel Hadi's strongly held view that there were more important issues to deal with than negotiations on Anglo-Egyptian relations. He announced that before considering the issues of the evacuation of British forces from Egypt and Egypt's unity with Sudan, he needed first to re-establish law and order in the country, to stabilize the government structure, and to find remedies for the financial predicament facing Egypt as a result of the Palestine War.[40]

Abdel Hadi's government was viewed by Egyptians as one of official terror and austerity, which had won for itself the unqualified hatred of the political opposition in the country.[41] Abdel Hadi's government ruled Egypt with the iron fist of the secret police.[42] It spread terrorist activities in the country and used force to threaten the opposition. For example, it was responsible for the assassination of Sheikh Hassan al-Banna, the Supreme Guide of the Muslim Brotherhood organization in Egypt,[43] on 13 February 1949.[44] During Abdel Hadi's tenure as prime minister, it became obvious to the Egyptian public that the assassination of political figures and arrests without obvious charges were official state policy. Nevertheless Abdel Hadi failed to restore the authority of the government or bring order to the country as demonstrations and turmoil continued to challenge the existing martial law.[45] The prime minister did not even spare the rich and powerful. His proposals for further taxation alienated him even from the élite. The new taxes were strongly opposed by the rich and the landed aristocracy who dominated the two houses of the Egyptian parliament and who held 90 per cent of the country's wealth.[46]

This measure made Abdel Hadi unpopular with the king who became convinced that his prime minister was the wrong man to deal with Egypt's problems. The king reached the point when he believed that the continuation of Abdel Hadi's government would seriously damage his own popularity.[47] He therefore dismissed Abdel Hadi Pasha's government on 26 July 1949, after it had been in office only five months.

In the face of growing unrest in the country, the king concluded that Egypt needed a national government capable of representing all the major political parties. He wanted to ensure that no single party could monopolize power during troublesome times; he was convinced that this divide-and-rule approach would give him a stronger grip on the country as a whole.[48] Subsequently, Farouk appointed Hussain Sirry Pasha as a temporary premier to lead a caretaker government until the general election which was to be held later in the same year.[49] Under instructions from the king, Sirry Pasha formed a government with Cabinet members from the four major political parties – the Wafd, the Saadists, the Watani and the Kotla. The Muslim Brotherhood organization, however, was excluded from participating in this government.[50] In order to restore people's confidence in the king and restore order in the country, Sirry announced in his first week in office that the government intended to abolish the martial law which had been imposed on the country since the Palestine War. His government released most of the political prisoners arrested by its predecessor.[51] In addition Sirry emphasized that his government would prepare for a general election within the following three months.[52]

Sirry promised to ensure just and free elections. At the same time, though Sirry's government would hold office for only a short period, he did not overlook the prime significance of the issues concerning Anglo-Egyptian relations. He therefore announced his government's readiness to negotiate with Britain so as to achieve Egyptian national aspirations.[53] The acting British ambassador in Cairo, E. A. Chapman Andrews, was informed of Egypt's wish to create a good atmosphere for the negotiations and remove all ill feeling in order to pave the way for a satisfactory agreement.[54] Sirry also made it clear to the British that the king himself was still interested in restoring Anglo-Egyptian relations to normality.[55] Britain responded positively to Egypt's request. The acting British ambassador assured Egypt's new premier that Britain looked forward to finding a satisfactory formula for the continuation of friendly relations with Egypt based on mutual interests.[56] Although this initiative was taken, actual Anglo-Egyptian negotiations did not take place because Sirry's short term in office allowed insufficient time for a settlement.

Sirry Pasha kept his promise to the Egyptian people: the elections were held and constitutional liberties were protected. The election resulted in a Wafdist victory and Sirry Pasha tendered his government's resignation to the king in late December 1949.[57] The Wafdist victory was mainly due to Nahhas's pledge to secure complete withdrawal of British troops from the country as well as the unity of the Nile Valley. Nahhas Pasha once again became prime minister of Egypt in early January 1950. He announced that his government was ready to resume negotiations with Britain.[58] The course and consequences of these negotiations will be discussed in the next chapter.

In summary, Anglo-Egyptian political relations were directly affected by the Palestine War of 1948. This war not only caused a delay in Anglo-Egyptian negotiations for settling their dispute, but it also had a number of serious political repercussions between Britain and Egypt. Britain was portrayed as the cause of all evils. To begin with, Britain was seen as helping to create an enemy state in Egypt's backyard. This general feeling came as a result of Britain abandoning its mandate over Palestine after it had built up the foundation for its Jewish successors. Further, Britain was accused of refusing to fulfil its commitment towards Egypt in accordance with the provisions of the 1936 treaty. Finally, the war had a serious impact on Egypt's economy which suffered from high war expenditure at the expense of the basic economic needs of the people which led to serious turmoil which shook the country in the following years.

Notes

1. Abd al-Latif al-Baghdadi (Egypt's vice-president 1958–66), *Mudhakkirat* [Memoirs], vol. 1 (Cairo, 1977) pp. 19–31. See also Fred J. Khouri, *The Arab–Israeli Dilemma* (New York, Syracuse University Press, 1968), pp. 57–61.
2. *al-Wafd al-Masri*, 5 December 1947.
3. *al-Ahram*, 9 June 1948.
4. Jewish Agency Report on Palestine to Foreign Office, January 1947, PRO/FO 371/61749.
5. *Ibid.*
6. Cabinet Discussion, July 1947, PRO/FO 371/61767.
7. Foreign Office Discussion, November 1947, PRO/FO 371/61961.
8. F. S. Northedge, *British Foreign Policy 1945–1961* (London, George Allen and Unwin, 1962), pp. 103–7.
9. *Ibid.*
10. Khouri, *The Arab–Israeli Dilemma*, p. 34.
11. Michael Dockrill and John Young, *British Foreign Policy 1945–1956* (Basingstoke, Macmillan, 1989), pp. 85–93
12. *Ibid.*
13. Khouri, *The Arab–Israeli Dilemma*, p. 34.
14. Foreign Office Secret Report, June 1948, PRO/FO 371/68632.
15. Kenneth Harris, *Attlee* (London, Weidenfeld & Nicolson, 1982), pp. 395–8.
16. Michael Dockrill, *British Foreign Policy*, pp. 85–93.
17. Harris, *Attlee*, pp. 395–8.
18. Cabinet Discussion, January 1947, PRO/FO 371/61931. See also *The Observer*, 7 April 1948.
19. From British Embassy in Washington to Foreign Office, Tel. 2405, 21 May 1948, PRO/FO 371/68649.
20. Harris, *Attlee*, pp. 394–7.

21. From Washington to Foreign Office, Tel. 2455: Reception of Dr Weizman at the White House, 24 May 1948, PRO/FO 371/68649.
22. Harris, *Attlee*, pp. 394–7. See also Dockrill, *British Foreign Policy*.
23. The Arab League was created partly as a result of the widespread Arab fear of growing Jewish political power in Palestine. It was an Egyptian idea and was approved by the British government. In late 1944 Abdel Rahman Azzam Pasha became the first Egyptian Secretary-General of the League. The League, however, failed to resolve the Palestine question. See Janice Terry, *The Wafd 1919–1952* (London, Third World Centre for Research and Publishing, 1982) and A. M. Gomaa, *The Foundation of the League of Arab States* (London, Longman, 1977).
24. *al-Ahram*, 22 December 1947.
25. *Ibid.*, 27 December 1947 and 5 January 1948.
26. *Ibid.* See also British Embassy in Cairo, Political Review, November 1948–January 1949, PRO/FO 371/73458.
27. Khouri, *The Arab–Israeli Dilemma*, p. 34.
28. PRO/FO 371/69120. See also R. D. Mitchell, *The Society of Muslim Brothers*, pp. 47–55.
29. From Haifa to Foreign Office, Tel. 1211, 31 December 1948, PRO/FO 371/75358.
30. *al-Wafd al-Masri*, 2 January 1949.
31. Alan Bullock, *Ernest Bevin, Foreign Secretary 1945–1951* (London, Heinemann, 1983). See also a Meeting between Truman and Ernest Bevin in Washington, March 1948, PRO/FO 371/68649.
32. Secret Report from the British Embassy in Cairo to Foreign Office, February 1949, PRO/FO 371/73458.
33. British Embassy in Cairo to Foreign Office, Tel. 113, 25 February 1949, PRO/FO 371/68681.
34. Cabinet Conclusion, February 1949, PRO/FO 371/73470.
35. British Embassy in Cairo, Egyptian Political Review, March 1949, PRO/FO 371/73478.
36. *Ibid.*
37. *al-Ahram*, 29 and 30 December 1948.
38. Confidential, British Embassy in Cairo to Foreign Office, n.d., February 1949, PRO/FO 371/73458.
39. *Ibid.*
40. *The Egyptian Gazette* (Cairo), 3 January 1949.
41. Confidential, British Embassy in Cairo to Foreign office, n.d., February 1949, PRO/FO 371/73458. *The Manchester Guardian*, 19 August 1949.
42. *al-Wafd al-Masri*, 17 January 1950.
43. The Muslim Brotherhood, or the Ikhwan al-Muslimin, was founded in early 1928 in Ismailiya by Sheikh Hassan al-Banna. The organization subsequently became an influential political party in Egypt in 1935–54. The primary objective of this organization was to return to the Islam of the Prophet Muhammad and his companions. The organization had considerable support among the Egyptians but mainly among the urban poor and students. Many of its members participated voluntarily in the Palestine war. See R. Mitchell, *The Society of Muslim Brothers*.
44. British Embassy in Cairo to Foreign Office, Tel. 917, 13 February 1949, PRO/FO 371/76463.

45. *al-Ahram*, 9 and 11 June 1949. See also *The Egyptian Gazette*, 7 July 1949.
46. British Ambassador Memorandum in Cairo to Foreign Secretary, February 1949, PRO/FO 371/80382.
47. From British Embassy in Cairo to Foreign Office, Tel. 1013, 2 August 1949, PRO/FO 371/80341.
48. British Embassy in Cairo Secret Report, December 1947, PRO/FO 371/72322.
49. British Embassy in Cairo to Foreign Office, Tel. 987, 4 August 1949, PRO/FO 371/80343.
50. *al-Ahram*, 4 August 1949.
51. *Ibid.*
52. *The Manchester Guardian*, 19 August 1949. See also *al-Balagh* (Cairo), 27 July 1949, 2 and 5 August 1949.
53. *Ibid.* See also *al-Ahram*, 15 September 1949.
54. *The Egyptian Gazette*, 29 September 1949.
55. *Ibid.*
56. British Embassy in Cairo to Foreign Office, Tel. 908, 2 September 1949, PRO/FO 371/80391.
57. *The Egyptian Gazette*, 14 January 1950.
58. British Embassy in Cairo to Foreign Office, n.d., 1949, PRO/FO 371/80397.

4

The Resumption of Anglo-Egyptian Negotiations and the Abrogation of the 1936 Treaty

The Palestine War of 1948 delayed Anglo-Egyptian negotiations for another sixteen months. Towards the end of 1949, following a period of extreme political unrest and serious economic difficulties, a general election took place in Egypt and the Wafd leader Nahhas Pasha returned to power. Nahhas succeeded in opening a new round of negotiations with the British which continued throughout 1950 and 1951. They again failed to resolve the dispute and as a result, Egypt unilaterally decided to abrogate the 1936 Anglo-Egyptian Treaty of Friendship and Alliance.

In this chapter I will discuss the developments which brought the Wafd Party back to power, examine the factors which contributed to the failure of the Anglo-Egyptian negotiations, and investigate the reasons for the subsequent decision to abrogate the 1936 treaty.

As described in Chapter Three, in late 1949, Sirry Pasha's caretaker government called a general election in Egypt. The Wafd Party won this election[1] and assumed power in January 1950. The Wafdist victory was expected for several reasons. First, the Wafd was considered the most organized and perhaps the wealthiest party in Egypt at that time. Its resources and good organization helped to whip up the necessary support in the 1949 election.[2]

In addition, the party claimed to have brought Egypt its independence in 1936, along with various political and socio-economic gains. Second, prior to the election, Nahhas Pasha and King Farouk had improved their relations. They reconciled their differences because they needed each other: Nahhas was anxious to return to power and the king wanted a strong party to take over the government and end the internal political strife. Secret contacts took place between the Wafd and the palace with the king offering royal support of the Wafd in return for the ending of their hostility against him.[3] He feared that continuation of the current chaos and ministerial instability might lead to a coup similar to the one carried out in Syria by Colonel Zaim.[4] The king also needed to enhance his reputation as a defender of Egypt's national demands and aspirations. Nahhas, having had a good relationship with the British, was thought able to bring to an end the Anglo-Egyptian dispute and thus fulfil the national aspirations of Egypt. Third, discontent with the recent political developments in the country won the Wafd the support of other political parties, including the Muslim Brotherhood and the Egyptian Socialist Party, which wanted to take revenge on the Saadist government for their severe treatment of them in 1946–9.[5] The Wafd's traditional cooperation with Britain did not seem to harm their cause. This was because Britain kept a low profile during the pre-election campaign and was careful to stick to a policy of non-intervention.

Of course, the British wanted Nahhas's return to power because he had previously shown willingness to cooperate with them. So British officials maintained a careful silence while Nahhas propagated his nationalist demands and campaign slogans, as they believed these to be for electoral purposes only.[6] Nahhas repeatedly stated that Egypt would not participate in any new defence plans with any other power, and that it would insist more than ever on the evacuation of British troops from Egyptian soil and on unity with Sudan. These campaign themes overshadowed the opposition's charge that Nahhas was pro-British.

On 12 January 1950, Nahhas Pasha formed a government and returned to power for the third time, with a majority controlling the Egyptian parliament.[7] The return of the Wafd Party under the leadership of Nahhas Pasha was welcomed by the British government,[8] which expected that its return would mean an end to the dispute between the two countries. Britain believed that it would be much easier to deal with Nahhas, whom it had dealt with before, than with a coalition of all Egyptian political parties. Its belief was founded on Nahhas's cooperative attitude in 1936 and 1942–4.[9]

The British government expected Nahhas to maintain this co-operative attitude and to understand its new policy for the defence of the whole Middle East. It further expected Nahhas to have a realistic appreciation of the changes that had taken place since the Second World War, and the threat that these changes posed to this vital area of the world, particularly the potential danger from the Soviet Union. Britain expected the Wafdist government to share its concerns for the protection of the Middle East, especially since Egypt, having the Suez Canal, was considered to be the most suitable country to act as a bastion of defence. Britain was convinced that its bases in Egypt were too important to be abandoned.[10]

Nahhas Pasha proved a disappointment to the British however. Their expectations that his policy would continue in Britain's favour were not fulfilled. Nahhas realized that he had been elected because of his promises and propaganda against the continued presence of British troops in Egypt and Sudan. So he became determined to free his country from the obligations and limitations of the 1936 treaty, which he had negotiated and signed. He was anxious to rid himself of the stigma of being pro-British.[11]

On the occasion of the opening of a new parliament on 16 January 1950, Nahhas Pasha declared that he would fulfil his government's promises and do everything in his power to hasten the withdrawal of British forces and to achieve the unity of Sudan and Egypt.[12] With the support of King Farouk, Nahhas Pasha emphasized that his government would do whatever it could to speed up British evacuation of the Nile Valley, and that Egypt would never lose sight of its goal of unity with Sudan. Egypt's insistence on speeding up negotiations for the settlement of problems between Egypt and Britain led to the start of a new round of informal talks between the two countries.

These began at the end of January 1950, when the British foreign secretary, Ernest Bevin, stopped in Cairo on his way back from the Colombo Conference in Ceylon[13] which had been initiated by the Commonwealth foreign ministers to provide financial aid and technical assistance to the developing countries of South and South-East Asia after the Second World War. Participants in this round of informal negotiations included Bevin, Nahhas and the Egyptian foreign minister, Muhammad Salah al-Deen. During the meeting Bevin surprised the Egyptians by his careful avoidance of any discussion of British evacuation from Egypt or of the Sudan issue. Instead he concentrated on matters concerning the improvement of Egypt's economy and the Egyptians' standard of living.[14] It became clear to Nahhas that the British Labour government was reappraising the conditions in Egypt, particularly after Britain and the United States had come to an understanding about the British military presence in the Suez Canal Zone. The US believed that the British presence was necessary to protect the region against possible communist penetration and to help to maintain peace between Israel and its Arab neighbours[15] and avoid the escalation of any conflict in the Middle East.

The Wafdist government, however, was still hoping to find a face-saving formula to fulfil its commitment to the Egyptian voters. The informal talks ended and the Egyptians made clear to Bevin their preference for the withdrawal of British troops from Egypt in the immediate future.[16]

On 17 May 1950, a new British ambassador, Sir Ralph Stevenson, was sent to Egypt to replace Sir Ronald Campbell. Stevenson wanted his government to find a formula for the settlement of the Anglo-Egyptian dispute to avoid tension between London and Cairo.[17] He had, however, no authority to do so on his own. In late May 1950, formal negotiations took place in Cairo. The British delegation consisted of Sir William Strong, the permanent under-secretary at the Foreign Office, Field Marshal Slim, chief of the imperial general staff and military adviser, and Ambassador Stevenson. The Egyptian government was represented by Nahhas, Salah Al-Deen, the foreign minister, and Mustafa Nasrat Bey, the minister of war and marine. At the first meeting, Field Marshal Slim emphasized that the special relationship between Britain and Egypt was based on both political and military interests. Egypt was asked to be aware that the main issue now was the regional security of the Middle East in which Egypt would play a pivotal role because of its strategic position and command of the Suez Canal.[18]

The Middle East had become more vital to Britain and the West for a number of reasons. First, there was a new awareness that access to Middle East oil (via Egypt) was essential for Britain's economic recovery after the Second World War. Second, Britain asked Egypt to consider seriously the new political dimension posed by the communist threat in the Middle East. Field Marshal Slim argued that Egypt might well be the first target of communist aggression.[19] However, Nahhas disagreed with Slim's argument.

Britain attempted to hammer its point home by quoting the example of the Korean War which was taking place at that time and in which the United States was engaged against the Soviet Union. This conflict had alerted the British and the Western allies to the political and military growth of the Soviet Union and China. The British wanted Egypt to understand that the events in Korea might be repeated in the Middle East.[20] That possibility was enough to convince the West that Britain's continued presence in the Suez Canal Zone was vital for Western global strategy.[21] The Egyptians, however, were not convinced by this new argument and continued to demand complete British withdrawal from Egypt and Sudan. Professor Janice Terry, in her book *The Wafd*, summed up this stalemate in Anglo-Egyptian negotiations thus: "Britain accused the Wafd of inflexibility and the Wafd accused the British of procrastinating and of imperialist designs."[22]

Obviously, there was much misunderstanding in this rather unsuccessful round of formal negotiations between the two parties. It became clear from the arguments and reactions that there was little hope of a satisfactory outcome. The Egyptians remained unwilling to differentiate between the political and military arguments put forward by the British.[23] While the Egyptian government stuck to its view that Britain's only concern was to hold on to Egypt for its own ends, Britain pleaded with it to adopt a more realistic view of the communist threat.[24] Field Marshal Slim explained that the British defence plan for the Middle East would be a new alliance between Britain and Egypt for defence of the whole region, with

Egypt as a full partner in the plan. Under this scheme the British presence in Egypt need not be seen as a military occupation, but merely as cooperation between the two countries in a time of peace. According to this plan, Egyptian forces would be expected to cooperate with British garrisons in the Suez Canal Zone in joint preparation for the defence of Egypt if danger threatened.[25] Furthermore, Slim warned that the Soviet Union was intent on penetrating Africa through Egyptian territories, and that Egypt had neither the military forces nor the experience to defend itself against the onslaught of a Soviet air attack. Consequently, Egypt would have no security at such a vital moment.[26]

Despite British justification of its defence plan for the region, Egypt rejected the British proposal for the defence of Egypt and other Arab countries. So this round of negotiations drew to a close without producing any significant results. Nahhas continued to insist on British evacuation while Britain remained convinced that the threat of communist aggression in the area was real.

At the second meeting, held in early June 1950, Nahhas opened the talks by rejecting the new British defence plan. For one thing, he told Field Marshal Slim, the Egyptian people would not accept it. The Egyptians were not convinced that the Soviets intended to attack them. In the meantime, Egypt was now unwilling to cooperate with Britain over the presence of British military forces in time of peace. Nahhas was convinced that the maintenance of a foreign army in peacetime on Egyptian land was simply another form of foreign control, and that by that route Egypt would never obtain its full independence.[27]

Commenting on Field Marshal Slim's suggestion that Egypt would be the target of a Soviet attack, Nahhas emphasized to the British negotiators that the cause of any such attack would be the very presence of foreign troops on Egyptian soil, which could constitute a pretext for aggression against Egypt. The continued presence of British forces in Egypt would thus be a permanent excuse for a Soviet attack on the area. Furthermore, the Egyptian premier argued, if the existence of a threat of war could justify the maintenance of British forces in Egypt, then the British occupation of the country would last forever, since the danger of war would never disappear. Nahhas pointed out that the danger of war had in the past come from Germany, then Germany and Italy, then Japan during the last world war. Now Britain believed that the threat of war would come from the Soviets. This argument would always be a vicious circle.[28]

Nahhas realized that his government would not survive long in office unless he was able to secure favourable terms of agreement from Britain. This compelled him to disagree with the new British defence plan. He now shared the views of the Egyptian people that the presence of British forces in Egypt would provoke a Soviet threat to Egyptian territory. He believed that the idea that the Soviet Union would attack Egypt without this provocation was only Western propaganda spread by the United States which exaggerated the communist threat to the region.[29] It would be very difficult, he said, to convince Egyptians that the presence of British troops was necessary to protect Egypt's sovereignty. Lastly, the Egyptian premier concluded that his government would be happy to discuss any plans for military cooperation with Britain on condition that British forces first evacuated the country. If Britain would really withdraw its forces, Egypt would consider a British plan for the defence of the Middle East. However, the Egyptians considered that the proposed new alliance, as it then stood, was no different from that provided for in the 1936 treaty.[30]

Nahhas Pasha reminded the British representatives that in the past Britain had often promised to withdraw its forces from Egypt. The latest promise had been made by the British foreign secretary, Ernest Bevin, to the former Egyptian premier Sidky Pasha in 1946 when Britain had promised to complete the withdrawal by the end of 1949. But Britain's promises had never been carried out. This had consequently weakened Egyptian faith in Britain on these matters. However, once Britain pulled out of Egypt, the Egyptian government and people would be most willing to work hand in hand with Britain against aggression in the area and for the protection of democracy.[31]

Nahhas applied tremendous pressure to persuade the British negotiators to understand the importance of the British evacuation for Egypt's national aspirations. He also emphasized that Egypt's loyalty would be far more useful to Britain in peace or war if both countries concluded a satisfactory agreement. The Egyptian officials would be happy if Britain would agree to supply the necessary weapons and modern equipment to strengthen Egypt's forces. This sort of military aid would enable Egypt to defend itself against attack and equip it to protect the Suez Canal which would be in the interest of all nations. It would also help Egypt to be a full partner with Britain in the defence of the region. At the same time, and significantly, the Egyptian premier made it clear that, in the event of an attack, British troops would be welcome in Egypt and would receive a guarantee from the Egyptian government of the provision of the necessary facilities in the country for the conduct of defence.[32]

It was clear that there was a fundamental difference between the British and Egyptian positions. Field Marshal Slim had difficulty in understanding the Egyptian national demands. He asked Egypt to consider Britain's military needs in the area. Britain was not ready to compromise on the evacuation of the Suez Canal Zone. The British Cabinet considered that the canal itself was of special interest to Britain and that Britain must control this vital waterway. Also, the British authorities in London – the Ministry of Defence and the chiefs of staff – had not yet decided what to do with £300-million worth of British military equipment which was stored in the Canal Zone.[33]

Thus, with these uncompromising attitudes the second official round of negotiations reached an impasse. In June 1950, Field Marshal Slim told Egypt that he was sure that if the British forces withdrew, Egypt would be the first target of a communist attack. Egypt would not be able to protect itself without the support of British forces stationed in the country. Egypt, however, did not share this view and said that the defence of Egypt depended upon the Egyptians themselves, quoting the example of the response to the Israeli campaign in Sinai in late 1948. Subsequently the negotiations ended in deadlock.

On 14 August 1950 another round of formal talks took place in Cairo. This time Britain was represented by Ambassador Sir Ralph Stevenson and Chapman Andrews, British minister at the British consulate in Alexandria. Egypt was represented by the foreign minister, Salah al-Deen, and the Egyptian minister of war and marine, Mustafa Nasrat Bey. On the direct instructions of Herbert Morrison, the acting British foreign secretary, the British representatives impressed on the Egyptians the importance of Egypt joining the Western powers in the defence of the Arab countries. The Egyptians, at the beginning of this round of negotiations, raised an important point: Salah al-Deen asked Sir Ralph Stevenson why the presence of the British forces in Egypt was necessary in time of peace, while British alliances with other countries were concluded only while there was a threat to peace. The British ambassador justified the presence of the British forces in Egypt by saying that Egypt had a unique geographical location because of its possession of the Suez Canal.[34] He added that this vital waterway and communication link was attractive to all maritime nations. He emphasized that it would be difficult for Britain to keep this vital canal open if it could not protect it. He drew an analogy with the Panama Canal, saying that the United States was solely responsible, by a treaty, for the defence of the Panama Canal and the United States' legal position in this regard would be the same as that of Britain with regard to the Suez Canal. This meant that Britain's purpose in Egypt was strictly for the protection of Egypt and its canal.[35]

To the Egyptians, this did not seem sufficient justification. The complete independence of Egypt was of more concern to the Egyptians than British interest in the Suez Canal. The Egyptians' experience during the last war had proved that the canal itself was not an essential strategic military zone and was not in time of war commercially vital to world trade. Most of the world's shipping during the war went via the Cape of Good Hope to the Far East without using the canal. The canal would be in the same situation again in any future war.[36] Consequently the Egyptian government rejected the British argument.

In response to British concern about the communist threat to the region, Egypt pointed out that the countries bordering the Soviet Union – Turkey and Iran – were not occupied at that time by any foreign troops. This did not put these countries under threat.

If the absence of a power meant an invitation to another power, then these two countries would be the first to be threatened by the communists. A Soviet invasion of Egypt would not be possible until the Soviet Union had swept through Iran. Even if Britain thought that retaining a location was necessary for reasons of global strategy, it would not need Egypt. Britain had already acquired a number of strategic bases in other states surrounding Egypt – Malta, Cyprus, Cyrenaica (in present-day Libya) and Jordan. These bases would enable Britain to deploy its troops as effectively as could result from its presence in Egypt if a counter-attack became necessary against communist aggression.[37]

The Anglo-Egyptian disagreement over the evacuation of British troops from Egypt was also complicated by the Sudan question. Egypt repeatedly insisted that its unity with Sudan was a legitimate aspiration of its people and asked Britain to recognize the legitimacy of this aspiration. Egypt argued that the two issues should not be separated, justifying its case by saying that all previous negotiations which had taken place in the past fifteen years had included the Sudan question. Therefore, Egypt considered that its unity with the Sudan and British evacuation from the Nile Valley constituted an indivisible demand in these present talks. Egypt emphasized that the Sudanese and Egyptians formed one nation and that there were no natural physical boundaries between them.[38]

From the start Britain refused to accept the Egyptian argument regarding Sudan. The British representatives preferred that the Sudan issue be excluded from the Anglo-Egyptian negotiations. Britain insisted that the Sudanese, like the Egyptians, had the right to become a free nation: the Sudanese should have the right to choose their future status without Egypt's interference. Thus, the Sudan issue must be treated as a separate question and the Sudanese must be viewed as a separate national community like any other nation. Britain pointed out that it was ready to support the legitimacy of the Sudanese right of self-determination as soon as it found a practical opportunity to do so.

These differences in objectives prevented the talks from producing any positive results. Consequently, the negotiations became more enmeshed, with yet more complications and misunderstandings between the two parties. Herbert Morrison accused Egypt in September 1950 of an uncompromising attitude because of its insistence on sticking to its demands and blamed Nahhas Pasha's Wafdist government for the lack of progress in the talks.[39]

In October 1950 Britain's decision to suspend financial aid and the exportation of British military equipment to Egypt brought relations between Cairo and London to an all-time low. Negotiations nevertheless dragged on throughout 1950 with no tangible progress on either side.

In early 1951 the Egyptian government made repeated attempts to resume direct formal negotiations, but to no avail. When Herbert Morrison succeeded Bevin as Britain's foreign secretary, Nahhas Pasha sent him a secret memorandum through the Egyptian ambassador in London.[40] In this crucial communication the Egyptian prime minister reminded Britain that as long as British troops remained in Egypt, the Egyptians would consider their country to be under occupation by a foreign power. Nahhas Pasha again tried to convince Britain that if any Egyptian government agreed to this occupation, the people of Egypt would not approve. The Egyptian people expected the British forces to be evacuated without delay especially since such an offer had been made frequently in the past. He emphasized that Britain must now seriously reconsider its relationship with Egypt, otherwise that relationship might not stay favourable. He further argued in all sincerity that gaining the support of the Egyptian people would be far more useful in protecting Britain's vital interests in the country than would the continued presence of British troops in the Suez Canal Zone. Nahhas Pasha also suggested that the difference of views between the two countries could be lessened if Britain observed the terms of the existing Anglo-Egyptian treaty. Egypt accused Britain of violating the treaty by maintaining many more than the permitted number of troops in the Canal Zone.[41]

Then Nahhas proposed new friendly relations with Britain on the following basis: first, British evacuation from the Nile Valley should be expedited and then, if this was achieved, Egypt would be ready to resolve its differences with Britain in a mutually respectful manner. Egypt also expected Britain to supply the Egyptian armed forces with modern weaponry, particularly for air defence. Egypt also needed British help in constructing airfields and improving its communications' systems so as to be able to protect itself from aggression. This would make Egypt willing to cooperate with the British armed forces on its own territory in the event of a threat to the security of the region, or whenever British interests in the area were endangered.[42] Finally, Egypt would be willing to discuss other British proposals as long as Britain would consider these Egyptian objectives.[43] Nahhas concluded that Egypt expected Britain to deal seriously with Egypt and reminded the British government that if it was not prepared to do so, Egypt might reluctantly take unwanted action which would risk damaging the traditional historical friendship between the two countries. Egypt praised the British Labour government's efforts to end the dispute, acknowledging that it had been sincerely anxious to achieve a satisfactory new settlement with Egypt.[44]

Although the Egyptian under-secretary for foreign affairs, Abdel Rahman Zaki Pasha, announced later, on 27 February 1951, that unless Britain agreed in principle to evacuate its forces, Egypt would not negotiate, he also described his country's position *vis-à-vis* Britain as frustrated by the lack of progress in the talks and described the 1936 treaty as an unsatisfactory basis for Anglo-Egyptian cooperation.[45] Meanwhile, *al-Dawa* (the Message) newspaper, the organ of the Muslim Brotherhood, as well as *al-Balagh*, a pro-Wafdist newspaper, expressed concern about an Egyptian settlement with Britain and called on the Wafdists to follow the example of the people of Iran who, under the leadership of Dr Muhammad Musaddiq, successfully challenged the British by nationalizing the Anglo-Iranian Oil Company in the spring of 1951.

Despite these developments, the Wafdist government hoped that the British Labour government would respond soon to Egypt's demands. But Morrison adopted delaying tactics. He was instructed to get a better bargain for Britain and to negotiate from a position of strength.[45] In other words, he was told to consider the British presence in the Suez Canal, the jugular vein of the British Empire, as a non-negotiable item in the negotiations. Retaining the canal was especially crucial for Britain which had already lost India. Attlee was also aware that the Middle East's agricultural resources could be easily developed in addition to the region's oil which was necessary for British industry and economic growth.[46]

In early April 1951, Morrison received the Egyptian ambassador in London, Omar Pasha, and informed him that he would like the Wafdist government to give Britain another six months to study the Egyptian proposal. However, a month later Britain proposed a new defence plan in which the Egyptian forces would cooperate with the British garrisons in the Canal Zone. This not very new idea was rejected outright by Egypt. As a result, the political relationship between London and Cairo became enormously complicated.[47]

Between May and October 1951, the British were preoccupied with the forthcoming general election. When, as a result of that election, held in late October 1951, the Conservatives came to power under the leadership of Winston Churchill, Anglo-Egyptian relations deteriorated further. Sir Anthony Eden, the new British foreign secretary, declared that his government could not meet Egypt's demands because these were not in Britain's interests.[48] This uncompromising statement left no opportunity for an alternative course of negotiation.

Churchill himself had repeatedly criticized the Labour government's policy towards Egypt for its weakness. The new British prime minister told his Cabinet, and correspondingly instructed the British Colonial Office, that Britain would not wish to relinquish the empire's dominance in the region. Churchill was convinced that Britain must hold primacy over the Middle East with the full cooperation of the United States.[49] Consequently, Britain suggested to the Egyptian government that Egypt might join the North Atlantic Treaty Organization (NATO)[50] as Turkey and Greece had done. Churchill was convinced that by joining NATO Egypt would gain what it needed from the West – economic and military aid. But by so doing, Egypt would have had to accept the continuing presence of British troops in the Suez Canal Zone. However, Churchill's calculations proved wrong: the Egyptian government totally rejected the British offer and described it as worse than the proposals made by the Labour government in its defence plan for the Middle East.[51] In response the British Conservative government tried repeatedly to intimidate Egypt by issuing warning statements. Churchill warned Egypt, for example, that he would hold it responsible for any breach of the peace and warned it of the damage that could result from abrogating those instruments of peace.[52] Egypt concluded that any further negotiations with the Conservative government would be futile. Britain's intransigent attitude towards Egypt made the Wafdist government lose hope of a favourable settlement.

Nahhas Pasha told the Egyptian parliament in mid-October 1951 that further Anglo-Egyptian discussions had become pointless. He blamed Britain for the consequences, saying that the Egyptian government had made tremendous efforts to persuade Britain to appreciate Egyptian national aspirations with regard to the evacuation of British troops and the unity with Sudan. These efforts had failed throughout all the negotiations.[53] Nahhas Pasha declared that it was now the duty of the government to fulfil its promises to the people. He explained that his government had officially broken off negotiations with the British because they had become fruitless and justified his action by saying that the Egyptians had suffered long enough in their attempts to reach a settlement with Britain. The Egyptian government, though it had negotiated patiently with Britain, had failed to achieve any results.[54] This was, he said, because the Conservative government's attempts to include Egypt in NATO made it evident that Britain, in cooperation with the United States, planned to retain a position of dominance in the region, so denying Egypt its complete independence.

On 8 October 1951, Nahhas made a crucial speech in the Egyptian Chamber of Deputies. He announced his intention to take action on the Anglo-Egyptian treaty in order to restore Egypt's honour and attain complete freedom. He declared that the 1936 treaty had outlived its purpose and that it had been concluded under circumstances of an actual threat of aggression. This threat no longer existed to justify the continued presence of large numbers of British troops in Egypt. The Egyptian prime minister concluded his speech with the remark: "It was for Egypt that I signed the 1936 treaty and it is for Egypt now that I ask you, the parliament, to denounce it."[55] Nahhas Pasha then asked the Egyptian parliament to endorse the abrogation of the 1936 treaty as well as the termination of the Anglo-Egyptian Condominium Agreement of 1899 on Sudan. The king of Egypt would now bear the title of "King of Egypt and Sudan". The Egyptian parliament approved the denunciation with an overwhelming majority; even the leaders of the opposition parties praised Nahhas on this occasion and gave the prime minister their full support on these issues.[56]

The Egyptian government's decision to denounce the 1936 treaty and the Condominium Agreement was justified by the following arguments:

1. Britain was held responsible for having violated the 1936 Anglo-Egyptian Treaty of Friendship and Alliance and the 1899 Condominium Agreement for the administration of Sudan.
2. The British had monopolized the administration of Sudan even to the extent of making appointments of junior members of the Sudanese administration. Britain repeatedly denied Egypt any rights in Sudan.
3. Britain maintained ten times the number of troops in the Suez Canal Zone permitted under the 1936 treaty.
4. The 1936 treaty committed both countries to defending each other in case of outside aggression but Britain denied Egypt any help during the invasion of Egyptian territory by the Israelis in 1948.
5. Britain, contrary to the terms of the 1936 treaty, denied Egypt the supplies of arms and equipment necessary for its defence. Britain had always blocked Egypt's opportunities to purchase arms from other Western countries – Belgium, the United States and France.[57]
6. Britain failed to accept the Egyptian demands made on the basis of Egyptian national aspirations. It advanced unrealistic theories to prolong its occupation of the Suez Canal. Britain even wanted

to establish a military government in the Canal Zone in addition to the existing legitimate government of Egypt.[58]

7. Britain failed to negotiate in good faith with the Egyptians a revision of the 1936 treaty.

In response, Britain condemned the Egyptian government's abrogation of the 1936 treaty as illegal because it was a unilateral denunciation of an international agreement. The British government maintained that the treaty still had five years to run and was recognized by international law and members of the world community of nations. Britain also condemned the Egyptian action regarding the Condominium Agreement. It similarly described this action as unilateral and illegal and reiterated that Britain intended fully to support the governor-general of Sudan, Sir Robert Howe, in administering the country in accordance with the 1899 agreement. Meanwhile, Britain would accelerate its present policy of attaining self-government for the Sudanese, leading to Sudan's self-determination in the near future.[59]

In conclusion, the Wafdist government returned to power in early 1950 as a result of its promises to fulfil the Egyptians' national aspirations for complete independence and unity with Sudan. The Egyptian people and the king of Egypt were determined to obtain these demands through negotiation with the British government. Any government in Egypt which could not accomplish those results was obviously destined to fail.

Perhaps Nahhas's promises during the elections were unrealistic, at least with respect to British evacuation and the complete independence of Egypt. Nahhas should not have had a problem accomplishing this because the British repeatedly made these offers to Nokrashy's previous government. However, the new British theory for the defence of the Middle East and its fears of communist penetration into the region had changed British strategy. Nahhas was caught between the rock and the hard place and was faced with difficult choices. He had to decide whether to hold to his government's commitment to the Egyptian electorate or to compromise and deliver a new agreement with Britain on British terms.

Nahhas decided to abandon his traditionally cooperative attitude towards the British, as he realized that to compromise with Britain would cost him dearly. He therefore opted for abrogating the 1899 and 1936 Anglo-Egyptian agreements – a move which strained Anglo-Egyptian relations almost to a state of war.

On 6 November 1951, Churchill declared that Britain would maintain its rightful position in the Canal Zone in spite of Egypt's illegal action. He said further that Britain would do its utmost to safeguard the canal as an international highway using, of course, no more force than would be necessary.[60]

Notes

1. The Wafd's success in the election was not due solely to its well-organized electoral campaign and its vast financial resources. The Wafd Party also benefited from the support of the Muslim Brotherhood and the Egyptian Socialist Party, which wanted to repay the Saadist governments for their severe treatment of them in 1946–9. Sirry's government, which was pro-British, also contributed to the spectacular victory of the Wafd. Two-thirds of the electorate of 4 million came out to vote. Furthermore, the Wafd Party considered itself the defender of Egypt's national independence. Nahhas Pasha was considered to be the direct descendant of Saad Zaghlul Pasha, the leader of the Wafd Party from 1919 to 1927. Lastly, the Wafd was believed to be more capable of dealing with the British than any other Egyptian party. For more details, see Rashid al-Barawi *Egypt, Britain and the Sudan* (Cairo, Renaissance Bookshop, 1952) and *The Egyptian Gazette*, *al-Wafd al-Masri* and *al-Ahram*, 15, 17 and 19 January 1950.
2. British Embassy in Cairo to Foreign Office, Tel. 1612, 17 December 1949, PRO/FO 371/96874.
3. *Ibid.*
4. Muhammad Abd al-Qader, *Mehnat al-dustur 1923–1952* (Cairo, 1983) pp. 170–5. See also *al-Masri*, 17 December 1949.
5. *The Egyptian Gazette, al-Masri* and *al-Ahram*, 15, 17 and 19 January 1950.
6. *al-Ahram*, 27 December 1949.
7. *The Egyptian Gazette*, 15 January 1950.
8. From Foreign Office to Alexandria, Tel. 1517, 12 January 1950, PRO/FO 371/96884.
9. Confidential British Embassy in Cairo to Foreign Office, September 1948, PRO/FO 371/73464.
10. *Ibid.*
11. *The Egyptian Gazette*, 7 January 1950.
12. *Ibid.*
13. *Akhbar al-Yawm* (Egyptian newspaper, Cairo), 17 January 1950.
14. Bullock, *Ernest Bevin, Foreign Secretary 1945–1951*, pp. 475–7.

15. Kenneth O. Morgan, *Labour in Power 1945–1951* (Oxford, Oxford University Press, 1984), pp. 470–5.
16. *al-Ahram*, 27 February 1952.
17. Memorandum, British Embassy, Alexandria to Foreign Office, August 1950, PRO/FO 371/80380.
18. From Foreign Office in Cairo, Tel, 1316, 17 May 1950, PRO/FO 371/80598.
19. A Meeting between the British and Egyptians, Cairo, 4 June 1950, PRO/FO 371/80447.
20. *The Times*, 23–5 June 1950.
21. Washington to Foreign Office, 29 June 1950, PRO/FO 371/86897. See also Cabinet Conclusion, 1950, CAB 129/62.
22. Janice Terry, *The Wafd 1919–1952*, p. 299.
23. A Meeting between the British and the Egyptians, Cairo, 4 June 1950, PRO/FO 371/80447.
24. *al-Ahram*, 13 July 1950. See also PRO/FO 371/80593.
25. *Ibid.* A Meeting held between Nahhas Pasha and Field Marshal Slim, Cairo, June 1950, PRO/FO 371/80593.
26. A Meeting between Nahhas Pasha and Field Marshal Slim, Cairo, 6 June 1950, PRO/FO 371/80451.
27. *Ibid.*
28. *Akhbar al-Yawm*, 22 July 1950.
29. Report from British Embassy in Cairo to Foreign Office, 27 August 1950, PRO/FO 371/80474.
30. *The Egyptian Gazette*, 7 September 1950. See also PRO/FO 371/80471.
31. *Ibid.* A Meeting between British Representative and Egyptian Government, 29 May 1950, PRO/FO 371/80471.
32. Ministry of Defence, Top Secret, London 1949, PRO/FO 371/80597. See also Cabinet Conclusion, n.d., CAB 129/63.
33. Top Secret, Ministry of Defence, London, n.d., 1949, PRO/FO 371/62954. See also Cabinet Conclusion, CAB 129/63.
34. Foreign Office to Cairo, Tel. 1089, 13 March 1951, PRO/FO 371/90130.
35. British Embassy in Cairo to Foreign Office, Tel. 1913, 17 August 1950, PRO/FO 371/80454.
36. Discussion between the British Embassy in Cairo and the Egyptian foreign minister, Cairo, January 1951, PRO/FO 371/90150.
37. *Ibid.*
38. *al-Ahram*, 13 November 1950.
39. From Foreign Office to Cairo, Tel. 980, 17 December 1950, PRO/FO 371/80383.
40. From Egyptian Prime Minister to British Foreign Office, A Secret Memorandum, n.d., 1950, PRO/FO 371/90154. See also PRO/FO 371/90131.
41. *Ibid.*
42. *Ibid.*
43. Report from British Embassy in Cairo to Foreign Office, August 1951, PRO/FO 371/90174.
44. *Ibid.*
45. PRO/FO 371/96974.
46. Francis Williams, *Ernest Bevin: Portrait of a Great Englishman* (London,

Hutchinson, 1952), pp. 258–60. See also Lord Morrison, *Herbert Morrison: An Autobiography* (London, Odhams Press, 1960).

47. Foreign Office Minutes, n.d., 1951, PRO/FO 371/90161. See also CAB 129/61.
48. *The Manchester Guardian*, 30 October 1951. See also PRO/FO 371/96974.
49. Cabinet Conclusions and the Chiefs of Staffs' Proposal, October 1951, PRO/FO 371/96877.
50. The pact initiating the North Atlantic Treaty Organization (NATO) was signed in Washington in spring 1949. Its main objective was to counter possible Soviet expansion, particularly in Europe. The United States became the main supplier to NATO member states, providing massive economic and military aid. Churchill expected that Egypt might agree to join the pact as Turkey and Greece had done. But in fact the United States did not want Egypt to join since it believed that if Egypt did so, the military balance of power between Egypt and Israel would tilt in Egypt's favour.
51. British Embassy in Cairo to Foreign Office, 9 September 1951, PRO/FO 371/ 90454.
52. *The Times*, 9 October 1951.
53. *Ibid.*
54. *al-Ahram*, 13 November 1951. See also PRO/FO 371/96845.
55. *The Egyptian Gazette*, 22 October 1951.
56. *Ibid.*
57. British Embassy in Cairo Minute to Foreign Office, n.d, PRO/FO 371/90174. See also PRO/FO 371/73495.
58. British proposal to establish military government in the Canal Zone, 1950, PRO/FO 371/80351 and 371/80357.
59. Statement by the British government regarding the abrogation of the 1936 treaty, November 1951, PRO/FO 371/90176.
60. Parlimentary Debates [Commons], 6 November 1951, vol. 493, col. 79.

5

Political Events Leading to the 1952 Military *Coup*

As a result of the failure of the Anglo-Egyptian negotiations and the abrogation of the 1936 treaty, bitterness and hostility between the British and Egyptian governments increased and Egypt suffered internal unrest. A number of governments were formed in 1951–2 but all failed to bring order to the country. Finally a military *coup d'état* took place: the Free Officers' movement ended the monarchist regime, took over the country, and changed the course of Anglo-Egyptian relations. In this chapter I shall discuss these political developments and examine the circumstances which brought about the new regime in Egypt.

Following Egypt's rejection of the new British strategy in the region and the British rejection of Egypt's demands for complete independence and unity with Sudan, the Egyptian government began to advocate and exercise violence. The Wafdist government, using the local media, started to encourage Egyptians to resort to force in confronting the British occupation in the Suez Canal Zone.[1] Anti-British demonstrations flared up in Cairo, Alexandria and in the Canal Zone cities, particularly in Ismailia and Port Said. This led to clashes between Egyptian demonstrators and British army patrols. On 16 and 17 October 1951, a serious confrontation took place at the Firdan Bridge near Kantara village which linked the Canal Zone with the Sinai peninsula.[2] In the climate of confrontation between Britain and Egypt, the Wafdist government encouraged the formation of liberation battalions and provided them with training facilities to prepare them for guerrilla warfare against the British forces in the Canal Zone.[3] At the same time, the minister of the interior, Sarag al-Deen Pasha, restored the properties and funds of the extremist

Muslim Brotherhood organization to allow it to resume its meetings and disseminate its publications freely.

The Wafdist government intended to gain the support of the Muslim Brotherhood in the struggle against Britain. The lifting of the ban on this organization was a clear indication that the Wafdist government was determined to solicit support from all political factions. In response to the Wafdist political gesture, the Muslim Brotherhood seized the opportunity to attack British installations in the Canal Zone. Its leader, Sheikh Hassan al-Hodeiby, issued a statement calling on his followers to intensify the campaign against the British.[4]

This turned relations between Egypt and Britain into a state of unofficial war. Demonstrations and strikes became daily occurrences in all the major cities.[5] Soon, enthusiastic students and youths, together with members of the Muslim Brotherhood, joined in resisting British occupation and in physically attacking British installations in the Canal Zone. They caused serious damage to British properties and utilities and kidnapped British soldiers who were stationed in the Canal Zone cities. These actions took place particularly in Ismailiya in late October and November 1951.[6] At the same time the Egyptian minister of social affairs, Ahmad Hussein, encouraged a new movement of non-cooperation with British forces in the Canal Zone. This resulted in the withdrawal of 80,000 civilian workers from their jobs and led to the British general headquarters at Fayid announcing in retaliation on 23 October 1951 that all transport of oil from the Suez Canal would be suspended.

In response to this announcement, the Egyptians retaliated by boycotting British goods and dismissing all British officials and teachers hired by the Egyptian government.[7] As a precautionary measure against British reaction to this decision, the Wafdist government appealed to wealthy Egyptians to provide financial assistance to the resistance and to guard against British retaliation. These moves encouraged the Muslim Brotherhood and other groups to carry out terrorist attacks against the British, particularly in the Canal Zone.[8]

During this time of violence the Wafd leaders were deeply implicated in corruption and mishandling of the administration. Their deliberate encouragement of troublemaking was intended to divert public attention away from the government's internal problems. However, their tactics did not go according to plan. The Wafd found that it could neither control the demonstrations nor stop the violence. The spread of violence against British targets only made the British more hostile to the Wafdist administration. During November and December 1951, Britain began to think that it must act decisively to alleviate, if not put an end to, the violence. Thus General George Erskine, commander of the British forces in the Canal Zone, on the instructions of the Conservative government, warned Egypt that Britain would meet the violence with force.

Britain held the Egyptian government responsible for any further breach of the peace and for any damage to British lives and property. But by this time the Wafdist government was unable to halt the wave of violence even if it had wanted to. Subsequently General Erskine decided to act. On 15 November 1951, his troops entered the village of Kafr Abdu because it was known to have housed armed Egyptian personnel and to be a centre for terrorist activities. They cleared the village and blew up 75 houses.

This British action antagonized Nahhas Pasha and in a broadcast to the nation he declared that Egypt would not stand idly by in the face of British horror and savagery; Britain would have to bear the far-reaching consequences of its actions.[9] Nahhas's broadcast fuelled the Egyptians' anger which in turn led to more terrorist attacks and more casualties among the Egyptians as well as damage to British property. Violence escalated particularly in December 1951 and early January 1952, resulting in even greater tension between London and Cairo. On 25 January 1952, General Erskine, who was convinced that the city of Ismailia was a main centre for the supply of arms and ammunition to the Egyptian resistance movement, decided to clear the city, as he had done in Kafr Abdu. He handed an ultimatum to the Egyptian deputy governor of Ismailiya demanding that all members of the local Egyptian police force should surrender their arms and evacuate the government building within a day.[10]

The Wafdist government protested strongly against the British demand and the minister of the interior Sarag al-Deen Pasha called it an irresponsible act by the British against innocent Egyptians. Hence, the Egyptians refused the British demand.[11] This British ultimatum created an embarrassing situation for the Wafdist government. It was interpreted as a humiliation of Egypt at the hands of the British commander in the Canal Zone. This naturally angered Sarag al-Deen Pasha who sent a telephone message to the deputy governor of Ismailia asking him to reject the British ultimatum and to encourage his police force to resist any attack.[12] Obeying this instruction the Egyptian police force refused to surrender its arms when it was faced by the British troops who surrounded the government building. On 25 January 1952 a battle between the two forces took place which ended with 50 Egyptian policemen killed and more than a hundred civilians wounded while the building was shattered to pieces as a result of heavy bombardment. There were no British casualties during this confrontation.[13] The date of 25 January has since become a memorial day for the Egyptian police.

The Wafdist government was well aware that Britain was behaving as if it had established complete sovereignty over Egypt. The British forces had imposed restrictions on civilian movement and were denying Egyptians free access to the Canal Zone and the Sinai peninsula. The British had also seized the Firdan Bridge which linked the Canal Zone with Sinai. Further, the British established a new requirement that the Egyptian government had to ask for permission 24 hours in advance when it needed to send supplies and food to Sinai where Egypt's army was stationed on the armistice frontiers with Israel.[14]

These hostile moves made the Egyptian Cabinet call an emergency meeting at which it unanimously decided to recall the Egyptian ambassador from London as a protest against British actions in the Canal Zone. The Wafdist government thought that the ambassador's recall would calm popular unrest and give it better control over the country. But the decision had the reverse effect and only agitated the Egyptian people still more against the British presence in the country.[15]

The Wafdist government found itself in a hopeless predicament where it could not do anything to restore order in the country or to prevent squads of guerrillas from attacking British targets, or even to control demonstrators in Cairo.[16] The Wafdist leaders knew well that if such activities continued they would eventually lead to the government's collapse and possibly anarchy throughout the country. They realized even more clearly that Egypt was not strong enough to declare an official war against Britain.

When news of the tragedy of Ismailia reached the capital on 26 January, spontaneous and unprecedented violence erupted in Cairo targeted against the British occupation.[17] That day marked the high point of violence during Wafdist rule. At that time central Cairo was burned down according to a Wafdist minister who witnessed the event.[18] Over 700 establishments were set on fire or destroyed. Thirty people were killed, including nine Europeans, and several hundred Egyptians were injured during the riots.[19] That day became known as "Black Saturday" and the riots as the "Cairo riots" during which over £4 million worth of British property and assets were destroyed in Cairo alone.[20]

These violent incidents and acts of sabotage brought the country to the verge of anarchy and led to the breakdown of order in the Egyptian capital. Martial law was introduced on 27 January 1952 and Nahhas Pasha was appointed military governor-general. A general curfew was imposed and supervised by military orders. This did not, however, satisfy the king's anger at his government's impotence and inability to maintain order in Egypt. On the evening of the same day the king dismissed Nahhas Pasha's government. The Wafdist government was accused of having failed to prevent the young demonstrators from damaging property and of having failed to restore order throughout the country during the past months. The Cairo riots constituted a turning-point in Egyptian political history since at that time neither the king nor the government was able to control the situation. Conditions in the Canal Zone continued to deteriorate as guerrilla activities against the British forces escalated.[21] Subsequently the king called on Ali Maher Pasha to form a new government.

Ali Maher was known to be the most adroit politician in Egypt and the one most able to deal with difficult situations, according to Sir Ralph Stevenson, the British ambassador.[22] On 28 January 1952

Ali Maher formed a government whose priority was to restore public order and to arrange for the security of Cairo and the Canal Zone cities. He hoped to prevent any further escalation of violence and aimed to manifest goodwill towards both his people and the British. At the same time Ali Maher declared that he would strive to achieve Egypt's independence and the unity of the Nile Valley.

Maher indicated that Egypt would not compromise its national objective – the unification of Egypt with Sudan. At the local level he asserted that he would take tough action against anyone found guilty of neglecting their duty to prevent violence or of participating in it. He promised compensation to those who had suffered losses during the recent riots. He also asked members of the young Egyptian nationalists and the resistance movement to immediately stop attacking British installations in the area.[23] He appealed to the Egyptian volunteers who participated in guerrilla warfare to withdraw from the Canal Zone and appealed to the workers in British bases to return to their regular jobs.

Ali Maher's moves indicated that he was eager to obtain a peaceful settlement with Britain through negotiation rather than through the policy of violence exercised by the previous government. Furthermore, Ali Maher reappointed Omar Pasha to his former position as Egypt's ambassador in London from where he had been recalled by the Wafdist government.[24] In the meantime, Ali Maher received the British ambassador at his request in a cordial and friendly manner on 7 February 1952. They discussed the possibility of reopening formal negotiations in an attempt to settle Anglo-Egyptian disagreements. Both parties agreed to begin with a clean sheet in the forthcoming talks and disregard the recent hostilities between Cairo and London.[25]

Ali Maher realized from previous experience that Britain would not yield to Egyptian pressure in order to gain a favourable agreement.[26] Furthermore he knew that in order to stabilize his government, he should first prove that Egypt would continue to maintain friendly relations with the West. The British, on the other hand, understood that they had to reassess their political approach towards Egypt.

Stevenson wrote a secret report to the Foreign Office indicating that if Britain did not compromise with Egypt it might lose another vital interest in the region as had happened in Iran. Also, Stevenson knew well that without resolving Anglo-Egyptian disagreements any Egyptian government would not be able to function well and administer Egypt's affairs.[27]

The British Cabinet had now concluded, especially after the Cairo riots, that it was no longer possible to stay in Egypt by force. The British Cabinet also praised the Egyptian government's action in restoring order in the Canal Zone and appreciated Ali Maher's initiative in suggesting the forthcoming negotiations to settle the dispute between London and Cairo in a peaceful manner.[28] Ali Maher's friendly gesture towards the British presence in Egypt caused Britain to respond similarly by ordering General George Erskine, commander of the British forces in the Canal Zone, to end military restrictions against the civilian population in the Canal Zone. General Erskine also released many Egyptians who had been captured and placed in custody during the latest anti-British campaign in the Canal Zone.

On 11 February 1952 the Foreign Office instructed Ambassador Stevenson and his staff in Cairo that the Egyptian suggestion regarding the coming negotiations would now receive most careful consideration from the British government with a view to ending the dispute peacefully at the earliest possible opportunity.[30] This sudden improvement in Anglo-Egyptian relations enabled Ali Maher's government to ease the tension between Cairo and London. It also encouraged the British embassy in Cairo to believe that a settlement might be more likely with Ali Maher's government than with the previous Wafdist government.[31]

Although the political climate seemed propitious for the course of Anglo-Egyptian relations to change from hostility to near friendliness, an internal issue between the king and his premier put a new obstacle on the path. The king insisted that before negotiations with Britain could be resumed, the Egyptian parliament had to be dissolved. The king wanted to acquire greater authority and to prevent any political party from influencing government policies.[32] Contrary to the wish of the king, Ali Maher was in favour of continuing parliament's role, believing that this would be necessary for the legitimacy of his government. The prime minister sought popularity for his government and hoped to minimize criticism from the Wafdist and other opposition parties.[33] The difference of opinion between the king and Ali Maher over the role of parliament developed into a crisis which resulted in Ali Maher's term of office being ended on 1 March 1952.[34] By provoking Maher's resignation King Farouk again failed to grasp the golden opportunity both to restore normal relations with Britain and to exploit the skills of a prime minister who had proved adept in handling internal political crises. The king's hesitation and the influence of his non-political personal friends made him morally weak and unable to handle crises.

After Ali Maher's resignation, Anglo-Egyptian relations and certain domestic matters were pushed to one side. The internal political situation in the capital was deteriorating and the Anglo-Egyptian settlement was postponed indefinitely. The king's personal power had diminished as a result of his weak judgement and the influence and advice of corrupt personal friends and foreign advisers – people such as Karim Thabet, Elias Andraos, and Pulli Bey, an Italian who had risen from being an electrician in the palace to a position of great influence in the organization of the king's private entertainment.[35] The king's corruption made him insensitive to the country's deteriorating economic and financial situation, especially the shortage of vital commodities.[36] In this context of political disarray in Egypt, a number of officers in the Egyptian army were diligently planning to rescue the country from its predicament. As the old regime became increasingly unstable, openings for political reform appeared. The Free Officers' movement in the army was looking for a suitable opportunity to play its crucial role in Egyptian political life. As the former Egyptian president, Anwar Sadat has stated, the advent of the revolution was just a matter of time.[37] Mohammad Heikal, the well-known Egyptian journalist, said the same.[38]

On 3 March 1952, the king called upon Ahmad Naguib al-Hilali Pasha – a 72-year-old Egyptian politician who had been minister of education during the 1937 and 1942 Wafdist governments but had broken with the Wafd Party during the 1949 elections – to form a government of his own. Now Hilali formed a government after agreeing with the king on the dissolution of the parliament and the suspension of the chamber of deputies.[39] Hilali, who lacked Ali Maher's political vision, incurred the contempt of the Egyptian nation by his acquiescence to the king's wishes. As a result, his government was too weak to deal effectively with the country's pressing problems. He occupied himself, with the king's support, in persecuting prominent political figures, particularly Wafdists such as Sarag al-Deen Pasha, whom he blamed for the Cairo riots.[40] He also persecuted Ahmad Hussein, the leader of the Egyptian Socialist Party,[41] who was accused of direct involvement in the latest troubles. Few young Egyptians and students were spared persecution because of their participation in the Cairo riots. Worse still, Hilali made no attempts at reconciliation with other Egyptian political leaders with the result that his government plunged further into unpopularity.

Hilali Pasha also initiated a programme to eradicate the corruption[42] which was widespread and deeply-rooted amongst the Egyptian political élite, including the Wafdists. However, these measures generated serious disagreements with the king. Farouk did not favour Hilali's anti-corruption campaign as he personally received huge amounts of money in return for personal favours to many people. For instance, Ahmad Abboud, a famous Egyptian businessman, frequently paid the king money in order to avoid paying taxes. Farouk was largely responsible for corruption as his regime was firmly based on favour as opposed to merit.[43] As a result Hilali also clashed with the king over the revision of the procedure of exceptional promotions in the civil service. The prime minister tried hard to persuade the king to dismiss his foreign and personal advisers and asked the king directly to restrain his personal friends from interfering in official government business. These requests annoyed Farouk who had repeatedly told Hilali that he would not allow him to pursue his programme to eradicate corruption if this were to affect his personal friends.[44] The king believed that this would damage his reputation and consequently threaten his throne. His personal friends, who naturally opposed Hilali's clean-up policy, put pressure on the king to dismiss Hilali.[45]

While the Egyptian government and the king were arguing over internal administrative matters, the Egyptian people were impatiently waiting for the Anglo-Egyptian dispute to be settled. Hilali's government had shown no sign of striking a deal with Britain regarding the evacuation of British forces from Egypt. The British embassy considered Hilali to be an aged prime minister with ill-health who lacked political support. Stevenson did not expect Hilali's government to last long in power.[46]

Thus, Britain could not depend on him as a negotiating partner. This discouraged the British from resuming formal negotiations with him. The resulting inaction once again drove the Egyptian people to take their frustrations onto the streets of the capital. They demonstrated against the British presence in the country as well as against the deteriorating economic conditions.[47] Groups at all levels became discontented with the current political conditions: peasants, workers, the middle classes and the intellectuals, all showed evidence of growing discontent towards the government. The situation in Egypt became ripe for change, and reform was inevitable.

The Free Officers of the army exploited these circumstances well. They were in the best position to conduct their *coup d'état* against the existing regime. Even the British embassy in Egypt was expecting this *coup*. In more than ten political reviews between November 1951 and April 1952 describing the internal situation in Egypt, the embassy in Cairo drew attention to the prevailing poverty in the country, the people's awareness of widespread corruption, and concluded that a revolution might erupt any time.

The embassy also pointed out that King Farouk had become an obstacle to the ending of Britain's dispute with Egypt. The embassy held the king responsible for the country's latest troubles and blamed him for not reaching an agreement with Britain.[48] The king's personal life and behaviour, unbecoming to a head of state, consisted of gambling and an endless round of entertainment, which diminished his popularity with his people as well as with Britain, and had reduced his influence to its lowest ebb. His defeat in the war against Israel in 1948 and the recent turmoil in the country made him especially unpopular and his incompetence in dealing with the British during 1951 when he permitted the abrogation of the 1936 treaty, had made him an undesirable head of state. This led the Free Officers to believe that Britain might not intervene to save his throne in the event of a *coup d'état*.

Following Hilali's expected dismissal on 3 July 1952, a new government was formed by Hussein Sirry Pasha. Sirry was not new to government: he had been prime minister in 1942 and 1944. He agreed to form the government only if the king accepted his terms which were: first, that his government would not be considered a temporary government;[49] second, that the king's personal friends and advisers would not interfere in government affairs; and third, that Hilali's programme of eradicating corruption in senior government posts would be allowed to continue.

The king accepted in principle Sirry's conditions. Meanwhile, Sirry repeatedly reminded Farouk that the priority of his government would be to repair the damage done to Egyptian politics by previous irresponsible governments. At the same time his government would prepare a suitable climate for the resumption of Anglo-Egyptian negotiations for a complete settlement with Britain.[50]

Sirry made a positive gesture towards reconciliation with the other political parties in order to enhance his government's position. He released Sarag al-Deen, the former Wafdist minister of the interior, as well as many others, from internment camps. He also announced on 7 July 1952 that his government intended to reform the electoral law and prepare for the election of a new parliament on the basis of a healthy democracy.[51] He also emphasized that his government would follow a sound economic reform policy which would lead to improved living standards. He intended to focus on agricultural production since he believed that agriculture was the backbone of Egypt's economy.

Sirry's promises however came a little too late. While the British embassy in Cairo thought that Sirry's government might be able to bring the Anglo-Egyptian dispute to a satisfactory conclusion,[52] the Egyptian Free Officers' movement[53] had lost every vestige of hope in the bankrupt old regime. It believed that the time was now ripe for a *coup d'état*.[54] Unfortunately King Farouk again quarrelled with his new prime minister over an administrative issue. The king objected to Sirry's wish to fill a vacant position in the Cabinet. Sirry wanted to appoint a minister of war and marine – a post which had remained vacant since the previous government of Hilali – rather than assume this post himself.[55]

Sirry wanted to assign this ministerial position to someone who would win him the support of the army and his choice fell on General Muhammad Naguib. This general enjoyed a reputation for honesty and was popular among both senior and junior officers of the army. Sirry believed that this appointment would maintain the army's discipline and loyalty to the government. He therefore proposed Naguib's name to the king for the post of minister of war and marine. But the king rejected the proposal because of an incident in December 1951, when General Naguib had become head of the Officer's Club contrary to the wish of the king who wanted General Hussein Amer to assume the post.[56] Naguib had won the election overwhelmingly due to support from junior officers in the army.

Later, when Sirry Pasha recommended General Naguib for the post of minister of war and marine the king again insisted on appointing General Hussein Amer instead. General Amer was unpopular with army officers who considered him unprofessional because of his lack of military background.[57] As a result of this conflict with the king over the ministerial appointment, Sirry Pasha decided to tender his resignation on 19 July 1952.

After his customary hesitation the king accepted Sirry's resignation two days later. On this same day the king called Hilali Pasha to once again form a government. This was only four weeks after the resignation of Hilali's previous government. Before accepting the offer, Hilali laid down certain conditions designed to solve the Cabinet crisis over the minister of war and marine portfolio. After prolonged bargaining, the king agreed to accept any conditions considering that the time was so critical. The king and Hilali decided to appoint Colonel Ismail Sharine – the king's brother-in-law – to the vacant Cabinet position.[58] However, the king's attempt to settle these internal political disputes came too late to rescue his throne from the danger of the imminent revolt.

These rapid developments might well have been the immediate signal for the army officers to act against the existing regime. Following Sirry's resignation, the Free Officers had already decided to launch their *coup d'état* and these recent events rallied General Naguib to their cause. The general already knew of the intended move against the king, as he was invited by Gamal Abdel Nasser, the leader of the Free Officers, eight days before the *coup d'état* to become their official leader (front man), but did not accept until after the crisis over the portfolio of the minister of war and marine had passed. Despite his sympathy with the Free Officers' demands (for the improvement of their financial status and supply of modern equipment), General Naguib had not intended to overthrow the monarchy. He merely wanted to hold a mass demonstration to force the king to comply with the army's demands without recourse to direct military action.[59] However, following the dispute over the ministerial appointment and the resignation of Sirry's government, General Naguib reviewed his position. Meanwhile, Gamal Abdel Nasser and his friends succeeded in convincing General Naguib of the need for the *coup d'état*. They convinced him that the country was ready to accept it. Furthermore, Naguib had heard from his friends in the palace that the king and Hilali's government would soon transfer him to a less influential post in the Egyptian army. This, along with the government decision to appoint Ismail Sharine as minister of war and marine (a man who, in Naguib's opinion, would not be able to do the job) influenced Naguib's decision to support the Free Officers' plan.

The deteriorating political situation as well as the dispute over the ministerial post left the road clear for the Free Officers to act against the regime and to accelerate their plans for a *coup*. In the late afternoon of Tuesday 22 July, immediately after the government had announced the appointment of Sharine as the new minister of war and marine, the Free Officers decided to act.[60] That same afternoon, Hilali's government announced that it had just received information about a possible conspiracy in the Egyptian army led by a group of young officers. The government did not take any action, however, believing that these officers were not intending to overthrow the monarchy or the government. Yet, only a few hours later the *coup d'état* was in motion. By the early morning of Wednesday 23 July 1952, unusual troop movements were noticed in Cairo. The Egyptian chief of staff, General Haidar Pasha, immediately called a number of senior officers for consultation. They met at the Abbassia Barracks in central Cairo to discuss the movement of troops. By the time General Haidar and his advisers met, the Free Officers' movement was already well advanced in its operation and had been joined by a significant proportion of the Cairo garrison. Shortly before 3 a.m. on Wednesday 23 July, the Free Officers surrounded Abbassia Barracks and arrested the assembled senior officers who did not put up any resistance.

By 7 a.m. General Naguib and the Free Officers were sure that their operation had been successful and that there was no risk of resistance or bloodshed. By then the rest of the army in the capital and virtually all the police officers were cooperating well with the military movement and facilitated the action of the *coup* leaders in occupying Egypt's National Bank and the Egyptian Broadcasting Station and in patrolling the city.[61] By 8 a.m. a proclamation was broadcast from Cairo on behalf of General Naguib, with an announcement by Lieutenant Anwar Sadat, one of the twelve members of the Free Officers' movement, justifying the Free Officers' action, claiming that the army had been forced to take its own measures to end interference in its affairs. The movement would redress Egyptian officers' grievances and would restore constitutional life in the country. It would purge the government offices of corruption and, most importantly of all, the Egyptian army would guarantee enforcement of law and order throughout the country and would protect all foreigners and their properties in Egypt.[62]

The Free Officers did not ignore or underestimate the British reaction to their *coup*. They considered the chance that British forces might intervene and for this reason informed the British embassy in Cairo at the beginning of their operation. They informed the embassy that what was about to happen in Egypt would be a purely internal affair. They also asserted that the Egyptian army would remain responsible for the protection of British personnel and properties.[63] At the same time, the Free Officers addressed a message to the British forces through the United States embassy. They claimed that their action had internal significance only and that the Egyptian army would respect the Anglo-Egyptian agreements. They also warned that any attempt by British military forces to intervene in their action would be considered as an interference in the country's domestic affairs which would have serious consequences.[64] The British embassy responded through the British military attaché in Cairo as the ambassador was on holiday. The military attaché gave assurances that Britain had no intention of interfering in the internal affairs of Egypt. Britain, he said, would intervene without hesitation only if it became necessary to protect British lives and property.[65] The Americans were also well-informed of the *coup* by the Free Officers.[66] The United States was concerned to avoid bloodshed between the British and Egyptian forces and, meantime, wanted the new Egyptian regime to be friendly to the West.[67]

Hilali's government collapsed during the afternoon of Wednesday 23 July after being in office for less than 24 hours.[68] General Naguib had already appointed himself as commander-in-chief of the Egyptian army. He demanded from the king (who was in Alexandria as usual during the summer) the appointment of Ali Maher Pasha as prime minister. He also demanded the dismissal of all the king's favourite friends and of the king's nominees from appointments in palace affairs. These nominees included Karim Thabet, Elias Andraos and Pulli Bey. The king yielded to the first of these demands but jibbed at the second concerning the dismissal of his nominees. However, by the evening of 24 July Ali Maher Pasha had formed his second government three months after the termination of his previous one.[69] He took the oath of allegiance in Alexandria and began his government duties under the watchful eye of the army.

It was a clever manœuvre by the *coup* organizers to choose Ali Maher as prime minister.[70] This sent a clear signal to the British in particular, and the West in general, that the new regime was a friendly one. Ali Maher was known to be welcome in the West. The new premier retained the portfolios of foreign affairs, war and marine, and the interior ministry. He was virtually a one-man Cabinet.

On 25 July 1952 General Naguib arrived in Alexandria with a substantial force of tanks, artillery and supporting troops to ask King Farouk to abdicate.[71] The king had already been in close touch with the United States ambassador, Jefferson Caffrey, since the beginning of the *coup* (particularly after the British declined to intervene to stop the *coup*). The king now wanted to save his life which he realized was in danger. He appealed to the United States ambassador to intervene but neither the British nor the Americans wanted to protect the monarchy despite several appeals from the king on 24 and 25 July. General Naguib, however, took every precaution to ensure the king's safety and, later, his quiet departure from Egypt. The new regime banned all demonstrations in the country. General Naguib met King Farouk in his palace in Alexandria and presented him with the Free Officers' demands and conditions. The king agreed to all of them.[72]

Early the next day, 26 July, Ali Maher Pasha met the king and conveyed to him the army's final demands that he should abdicate by noon in favour of his infant son, Prince Ahmad Fouad. He was also asked to leave the country that same day. Farouk agreed at once and punctually left the country together with his wife, three daughters and infant son. They boarded the royal yacht, *Mahroussa*, and sailed for Italy.[73] At his departure Farouk was accorded full military honours in a ceremony befitting a king's dignity. The ceremony was attended by Prime Minister Ali Maher, General Naguib, and the United States ambassador in Cairo.[74] Farouk's last act was to sign a decree appointing a Regency Council of his own selection; his son Ahmad Fouad was proclaimed the king of Egypt and Sudan.[75] The terms of this decree were not made public and were indeed never to see the light of day. Farouk left Egypt to live in exile in Italy.

The king had passed from the scene of Egyptian public life quickly, leaving an impression of his irresponsibility in conducting the country's affairs during the past decade. His dictatorial policy, corrupt government and lifestyle unbecoming to a head of state, rendered him unfit to lead Egypt. Farouk was held responsible for the deterioration which brought about the military *coup* in Egypt.

The deterioration of Egyptian domestic political affairs during this seven-month period temporarily put the Anglo-Egyptian settlement into abeyance. Except for the communication between the Free Officers and the British during the past month, Anglo-Egyptian relations were relatively uneventful. The *coup* was entirely successful and the government's authority smoothly transferred to the Free Officers. They won overwhelming public support for their action from the early stages of the *coup*. The support came even from the old Egyptian political leaders who expressed their enthusiasm for the *coup* organizers.[76] As the Free Officers had seized power easily, they became eager to settle the major outstanding problems with Britain: the Sudan question and the evacuation of British troops from Egypt. In his first statement to the foreign press after the second week of the *coup*, General Naguib, the front man of the Free Officers, emphasized that these problems should be resolved quickly and, therefore, had major priority under the new Egyptian regime.[77]

Notes

1. *The Times*, 22 March 1952. See also PRO/FO 371/96884.
2. PRO/FO 371/96884.
3. *al-Wafd al-Masri*, 14 December 1951.
4. *al-Balagh* (Egyptian newspaper, Cairo), 20 December 1951. See also *al-Masr* 20 and 22 December 1951.
5. *Ibid.*
6. *Ibid.*
7. *al-Ahram*, 25 and 27 October 1951.
8. *al-Dawa* (Egyptian newspaper, Cairo), 23 and 24 November 1951.
9. From Foreign Office to Alexandria, Tel. 1142, 6 December 1951, PRO/FO 371/90121. See also Abd al-Rahman al-Rafi, *Muqadima thawra 23 yuliyo 1952* (Cairo, 1960).
10. *Ibid.*
11. *Ibid.*

12. *Ibid.* See also British Embassy in Cairo to Foreign Office, Tel. 119, 22 January 1952, PRO/FO 371/96862.
13. *Ibid.*
14. British Embassy in Cairo, Annual Published Reviews for 1951, 3 July 1952, PRO/FO 371/96845.
15. *Ibid.* See also *al-Masri*, 29 January 1952.
16. *Ibid.*
17. *Ibid.* See also *al-Ahram*, 29 January 1952.
18. Interview with Ahmad Abd Rabu Bey, Cairo, 17 February 1987. See also Muhammad Anis, *Hareeq al-Qahirah* (Cairo, Maktabat Madbuli, 1982).
19. British Embassy in Cairo, Annual political review for 1951, 22 July 1952, PRO/FO 371/96870.
20. British Embassy in Cairo, Tel. 718, 7 February 1952, PRO/FO 371/98670.
21. *Ibid.*
22. Muhammad Abd al-Qader, *Mehnat al-dustur 1923–1952*. See also *Akhbar al-Yawm*, 31 January 1952.
23. British Embassy in Cairo to Foreign Office, Tel. 519, 4 February 1952, PRO/FO 371/96873.
24. *al-Ahram*, 9 February 1952.
25. *Ibid.*
26. Ali Maher Pasha did not want a repetition of the past hostile relations with the British, particularly the incidents of June 1940 and 4 February 1942. In January 1942 Sirry Pasha's government had announced the rupture in diplomatic relations between Egypt and Vichy France as the British ambassador, Lord Killearn, asked Sirry to do. But Sirry had done so without consulting King Farouk about the decision. This led to Sirry's resignation as Farouk forced him out on 2 February 1942. Subsequently, on 4 February, Killearn surrounded the Abdin Palace in Cairo with British units. He then asked the king to submit to British demands or to abdicate. Farouk chose the former and accepted Nahhas Pasha as Egyptian premier. In fact, the main objective of the British action had been to get rid of Ali Maher Pasha. Maher had been the chief architect of Egyptian politics in 1936–42 and strongly influenced the king. Lord Killearn had become suspicious of Farouk and Maher for their sympathy with Germany. For more details, see Charles Tripp, 'Ali Maher Pasha and the Palace in Egyptian politics 1936–42: seeking mass enthusiasm for autocracy' (PhD thesis, School of Oriental and African Studies, University of London, 1984).
27. Stevenson to Foreign Office, n.d., 1951, PRO/FO 371/90136.
28. Cabinet Minute, March 1952, PRO/FO 371/90112.
29. Foreign Office Minutes, March 1952, PRO/FO 371/90123.
30. British Embassy in Cairo to Foreign Office, Tel. 1142, 7 February 1952, PRO/FO 371/90121.
31. *Ibid.* See also British Embassy in Cairo, Confidential Report, 1 April 1952, PRO/FO 371/96846.
32. Muhammad Abd al-Qader, *Mehnat al-dustur*, pp. 177–88.
33. *Ibid.* See also *al-Wafd al-Masri*, 9 March 1952.
34. *Ibid.* See also PRO/FO 371/96846.
35. British Embassy in Cairo, Confidential Report, 10 July 1952, PRO/FO 371/96879.

36. *Ibid.*
37. Anwar Sadat, *In Search of Identity* (London, Collins, 1978).
38. Muhammad Hassanein Heikal, *Abd al-Nasir wa'l-alam* (Beirut, 1972).
39. British Embassy in Cairo, Confidential Report, 10 July 1952, PRO/FO 371/96879.
40. *Ibid.* See also *The Egyptian Gazette*, 7 July 1952.
41. The Young Egyptian Party, or Egyptian Socialist Party, was the earliest youth movement to take shape in Egypt. A party of this name had existed as far back as 1910 but faded into insignificance after the First World War. The existing organization came into being in 1933 under the leadership of Ahmed Hussain. Later, Aziz Ali al-Masri Pasha accepted the honorary presidency of this organization. Its members, estimated to number 3,000–5,000, were mostly university students and graduates. Like that of the Muslim Brotherhood its programme was one of extreme nationalism based upon the denunciation of the presence of all foreign troops in Egypt. Ahmed Hussain was imprisoned in 1941 but released in 1944 on condition that he pursued a pro-Wafd policy. For the next few years the Egyptian Socialist Party was indeed a faithful echo of the Wafd in contrast to its strongly anti-Wafd policy before Hussain's arrest. After the Wafd won the election, the socialists became once more extremist in outlook, and their members took part in anti-British action in Egypt and demanded a policy of non-negotiation with the British unless the latter evacuated the Nile Valley and accepted unity between Egypt and the Sudan. Hussain was minister of social affairs in the last Wafd government, in 1950–2. See Charles Tripp, 'Ali Maher Pasha and the Palace in Egyptian Politics' and PRO-file-62910.
42. British Embassy in Cairo to Foreign Office, Tel. 717, 27 July 1952, PRO/FO 371/96876.
43. British Embassy in Cairo, Secret Report to Foreign Office, n.d., PRO/FO 371/96876.
44. *Ibid.*
45. *Ibid.*
46. British Embassy in Cairo to Foreign Office, Tel. 871, 27 May 1952, PRO/FO 371/96877.
47. *The Egyptian Gazette*, 29 May 1952.
48. Egypt Fortnightly Summary Cairo to Foreign Office, 29 July 1952, PRO/FO 371/96885.
49. British Embassy in Cairo to Foreign Office, PRO/FO 371/96876. See also *The Observer*, 6 July 1952.
50. *Ibid.*
51. *The Egyptian Gazette*, 7 July 1952.
52. The "Free Officers" group came into existence in late 1949 as a result of the defeat of the Egyptian army at the hands of Israeli forces during the Palestine campaign of 1948. The junior officers who participated in the campaign became angry at the administration of the Egyptian army, particularly when they found out that the Palace and King Farouk's favourite friends were involved in the scandal of the defective arms supplied to the army causing casualties among Egyptian soldiers on the battle field. Most of the Free Officers in the movement were 1937–8 graduates of the military college during the Wafdist government's term of office. Some of the Free Officers had been supporters of the Wafd from the beginning since the Wafd government liberalized access to the military academy

in the sense of allowing middle-class men to join, whereas previously it had been restricted to the sons of the well-to-do. After the Egyptian government abrogated the 1936 treaty, the internal political system of Egypt was badly shaken, and the Free Officers came to think that the Egyptian army should play a predominant role in Egyptian politics. Because of his single-mindedness and excellent organizational ability Gamal Abdel Nasser became the most prominent figure in the movement. He was elected three times as leader of the Free Officers' movement since the organization was established. Nasser believed that the success of a *coup d'état* against the Egyptian monarchy would depend on the movement being led by a senior officer with special qualifications and high prestige and reputation. These qualities were found in General Naguib, who was actually invited by Nasser eight days before the *coup d'état* was launched to become the leader of the Free Officers. See PRO/FO 371/96879 and Vatikiotis, *A History of Egypt* and *Nasser and his Generation* (London, Croom Helm, 1978). See also Naguib, *Egypt's Destiny* (London, Gollanez, 1955).

53. British Embassy in Cairo, Confidential Report, 29 August 1952, PRO/FO 371/96881. See also Muhammad Naguib, *Mudhakkirat* [Memoirs] (Cairo, 1980), pp. 117–25.
54. Abdel-Latif al-Baghdadi, *Mudhakkirat*, vol. I.
55. *Ibid.*
56. *Ibid.*
57. British Embassy in Cairo, Confidential Report, 29 August 1952, PRO/FO 371/96881. See also Naguib, *Mudhakkirat*, pp. 117–25.
58. From Alexandria to Foreign Office, 28 June to 19 July 1952, PRO/FO 371/96884.
59. British Embassy in Cairo, Secret Report to Foreign Office, 19 August 1952, PRO/FO 371/96878. See also PRO/FO 371/96879.
60. Egypt Fortnightly Summary from Cairo to Foreign Office, 27 July 1952, PRO/FO 371/96847.
61. From Alexandria to Foreign Office, Tel. 1067, 23 July 1952, PRO/FO 371/96877.
62. *Ibid.*
63. British Embassy in Cairo, Confidential Report, 29 August 1952, PRO/FO 371/96881.
64. *al-Ahram*, 27 July 1952. See also PRO/FO 371/96881.
65. From Foreign Office to Cairo, Tel. 1072, 23 July 1952, PRO/FO 371/96877.
66. *al-Bayan* (UAE newspaper, Dubai), 17 October 1987.
67. From Alexandria to Foreign Office, Tel. 1067, 23 July 1952, PRO/FO 371/96877. See also U.S. Department of State, *U.S. Policy in the Middle East 1952–1953* (Washington DC, 1958).
68. British Embassy, Alexandria, to Foreign Office, Tel. 712, 24 July 1952, PRO/FO 371/96880.
69. From Alexandria to Foreign Office, Tel. 1079, 24 July 1952, PRO/FO 371/96877.
70. Ali Maher Pasha remained Egyptian premier until 7 September 1952. He was then forced to resign and was replaced by General Naguib because the Free Officers opposed him in every respect. Ali Maher refused to agree with the new agrarian reform which the Free Officers advocated. The maximum landholding was fixed at 200 feddans plus another 100 if the landowners had children. The rest of the land would be expropriated by the state without compensation and

then distributed among poor Egyptian farmers. Ali Maher insisted that the minimum landholding should be 500 feddans plus another 200 if the landowners had children and that, for the rest, the state should pay compensation to the landowners. This seemed to be more workable for the Egyptian economy from Ali Maher's point of view. The main objective of this reform was to put an end to the influence of the old Egyptian political leaders, especially the Wafdists; secondly, it was to improve the living conditions of the rural population; thirdly, it would divert capital from agriculture to industry; fourthly, it would raise agricultural output to feed the growing population. For more details see: J. Marlowe, *Four Aspects of Egypt* (London, Allen and Unwin, 1966) and Peter Beaumont and Gerald Black, *The Middle East: A Geographical Study* (London, Wiley, 1976).

71. Egypt Fortnightly Summary, Cairo to Foreign Office, 29 July 1952, PRO/FO 371/96885.
72. *Ibid.*
73. From Alexandria to Foreign Office, Tel. 1207, 26 July 1952, PRO/FO 371/96886.
74. *Ibid.*
75. Egypt Fortnightly Summary, Cairo to Foreign Office, 29 July 1952, PRO/FO 371/96885.
76. From Cairo to Foreign Office, Tel. 1118, 27 July 1952, PRO/FO 371/96887.
77. *al-Ahram*, 9 August 1952.

6

The Final Anglo-Egyptian Settlement

In this chapter I discuss the reasons for the success of the Free Officers in reaching a satisfactory agreement with Britain on both the question of Sudan and the British evacuation of Egypt while all the previous Egyptian governments had failed.

As soon as the new military regime assumed its responsibilities, it gave priority to the restoration of law and order which was achieved without much difficulty. Without wasting any time, General Naguib then expressed his desire to solve the two outstanding national problems: the Sudan and the evacuation of the British troops. He indicated that the new regime preferred to approach Britain in a friendly way rather than stir up mob violence against the British forces in the country. He opposed violence which had been the strategy of some of the previous Egyptian governments.[1] However, these pronouncements did not altogether halt attacks on the British base in the Suez Canal Zone.

Sir Anthony Eden, the British Conservative foreign secretary, welcomed Naguib's pragmatic approach. Eden was convinced that the new Egyptian government would soon be able to reach a satisfactory agreement with Britain.[2] But it was not the intention of the Foreign Office to make any definite proposal with regard to the outstanding issues. Britain wanted the initiative to come first from Egypt. While Eden was waiting for an approach, Naguib took some positive steps to open formal negotiations with Britain after having first thoroughly studied the two outstanding issues. The collapse of all previous Anglo-Egyptian negotiations over the Sudan question persuaded him to separate this thorny issue from the problem of evacuation.[3]

He wanted to solve the Sudan question before broaching any negotiations on the military issue. He therefore openly declared that, unlike previous governments, his government would no longer insist on Egyptian sovereignty over the Sudan. The new Egyptian government was now ready to concede the right of self-determination to the Sudanese in order to show goodwill to them if not to the British.

General Naguib himself was half Sudanese through his mother and he was born and educated in Sudan.[4] He invited the four main Sudanese political party leaders to Cairo in November 1952 to begin talks over the future of Sudan. Naguib agreed with the Sudanese political leaders that Egypt would, in principle, recognize and support Sudan's right to self-determination. In return the Sudanese political leaders would maintain the unity of their country.[5]

This encouraged the Sudanese political parties to accelerate the signing of a pact with Egypt in early January 1953 concerning the future independence of Sudan. In this pact it was agreed that Egypt and the Sudanese political parties would work towards the complete unity of Sudan as a single territory, using self-determination as the fundamental principle of such a policy. The Egyptian government and the Sudanese leaders further agreed that Sudan had the right to choose whatever form of government it wished.[6] Following the conclusion of this Egypt–Sudan agreement, Naguib immediately handed the British ambassador, Sir Ralph Stevenson, a memorandum on the future status of the Sudan. In this important memorandum, the Egyptian government proposed not only to accept self-determination for Sudan, but also to indicate that Egypt would not hesitate to help the Sudanese achieve their own political objectives. Basically, Egypt wanted the Sudanese to decide whether they wanted self-determination on the basis of the statute leading to Sudan's independence or union with Egypt.[7] The Egyptian memorandum also put forward a number of other significant proposals:

1. The Anglo-Egyptian administration of the Sudan should be liquidated over the following three years.[8] During this transitional three-year period, the Sudanese would be able to complete their independence and assume full government of their country.

2. The Sudanese people should have the right to exercise their self-determination in a free and neutral atmosphere without foreign interference.
3. During the transitional period, Britain and Egypt would draw up a draft constitution for the Sudan as a prerequisite for a general election for a permanent Sudanese parliament which would later decide the future of Sudan. It could then vote for either complete independence or for some kind of link with Egypt.
4. Britain and Egypt should undertake to respect the decisions of the Sudanese parliament concerning the future status of Sudan.
5. Britain should recognize all Sudanese territory from north to south as a single territory.
6. The British governor-general of Sudan, Sir Robert Howe, should be advised on the Sudan's administration during the three years of transition by a five-man commission consisting of one British, one Egyptian, two Sudanese, and one Indian or Pakistani representative. In the absence of the governor-general, the oldest of the two Sudanese on the commission should act in his place.[9]

These Egyptian proposals on the future status of Sudan were completely in line with the agreement signed between Naguib and the Sudanese political parties in Cairo.[10] The memorandum excluded all other issues and clearly renounced Egypt's claim to sovereignty in Sudan. The main reason for this sacrifice was the conviction of the majority in the military government that ultimately the future of Egypt's relationship with Sudan depended more upon the attitude of the Sudanese themselves than on Egyptian or British actions. There was nevertheless disagreement within the Egyptian military government over the issue. Major Salah Salem, the Egyptian minister of national guidance and Sudanese affairs was interested in keeping Sudan under Egyptian authority even if not united with Egypt. Colonel Nasser, the real leader of the Revolutionary Command Council, the all-powerful, twelve-member planning organization chaired by Naguib, opposed Salem. Nasser believed that Sudan was a burden upon Egypt and was convinced that Sudan should become independent despite Egypt's deep-seated interests and concern over the Nile waters. As it was Nasser (not Naguib) who took final decisions on behalf of the Revolutionary Command Council regarding all internal and external issues his decision regarding Sudan was final. Salah Salem's obduracy eventually led to his resignation in 1955 when it was widely rumoured that he had paid bribes to Sudanese politicians to solicit Sudanese votes for the union with Egypt. The other members of the new Egyptian military government were too pragmatic to assert Egypt's dubious right to a union with Sudan.

Sir Anthony Eden welcomed the Egyptian memorandum on the Sudan question and responded by saying that the new Egyptian regime offered Britain all that the British wanted for Sudan, and as a result was ready to negotiate with the Egyptian government on Sudan's self-determination.[11] Later Eden told the Cabinet that it would now be possible for Britain to reach an agreement with Egypt on the future of Sudan, which would then enable other outstanding problems with Egypt to be resolved.[12] He believed that there was now a great opportunity to improve Anglo-Egyptian relations. The Foreign Office praised and paid tribute to the courageous efforts of Naguib and his team, who had cut through the tangle of maladministration at home and tackled at the international level the disputes which were a legacy of previous Egyptian governments. In this congenial atmosphere of reciprocity prevailing simultaneously in London, Cairo and Khartoum, the British government instructed its ambassador in Cairo, Sir Ralph Stevenson, in early January 1953 to open preliminary talks with the Egyptians.[13] Accordingly, the talks with Egyptian officials resumed on a basis of trust and confidence.

The negotiators believed that this new round of negotiations would produce positive results. They made a serious bid to settle the outstanding disputes regarding the Sudan question. Both sides decided to work point by point through the Egyptian proposals for the Sudan. After the fifth preliminary round of talks which began in Cairo in mid-January 1953, the process of negotiation went quite smoothly and both parties gave precedence to solving the Sudan question. This was the first time that Anglo-Egyptian talks had concentrated solely on reaching a settlement of the Sudan problem. In past negotiations previous Egyptian governments had always combined the issue of unity between Sudan and Egypt with that of British evacuation of Egypt. This had been the source of conflict between the two countries for almost 30 years, after Britain had decided to expel the Egyptian administration from the Sudan[14] in 1924 as a result of the assassination of the sirdar of the Egyptian army and governor of the Sudan, Sir Lee Stack, in Cairo.

Although both parties were determined to solve the Sudan problem quickly, differences of opinion soon appeared when Stevenson insisted that Britain wished to retain special powers in Sudan. This British demand was allegedly made to protect the interests of the Southerners (the non-Muslim Sudanese) from the northern Sudanese.[15] These special powers meant that the southern part of Sudan would be under the special control of the British governor-general of the Sudan during the transitional period. In other words, the south would not be subject to the temporary Sudanese central government. Egypt completely rejected Britain's plan for southern Sudan and refused to recognize the special powers of the British governor-general.[15] The Egyptian negotiators insisted on an agreement on the Sudan based on Egypt's memorandum.[16] Naguib made it clear that Egypt was convinced that the memorandum would form the most suitable basis for an acceptable agreement for all parties concerned with the Sudan question.[17]

By the phrase "all concerned parties", Egypt was referring to the Sudanese in addition to the British and the Egyptians. The Egyptian agreement with the major Sudanese political leaders regarding the unity of Sudan and Sudanese self-determination strengthened Egypt's position and confidence. Time after time it adopted an uncompromising attitude towards Britain's demands regarding the south of Sudan. Negotiations slowed and the talks were eventually postponed. They resumed again in Cairo in late January 1953, however, but by early February had still not made any real progress.

The United States' ambassador to Egypt, Jefferson Caffrey, offered his mediation. Accordingly, Britain and Egypt asked the

United States, which had a friendly relationship with both countries, to act as a third party in the negotiations. The United States encouraged Britain, its greatest friend and ally, to make concessions to Egypt and to reach an agreement on the Sudan.[18] The United States was convinced that the Sudanese themselves had the right to decide their own country's future and that the Sudan should be a sovereign state. The new American Republican government believed that the settlement of the Sudan question between Britain and Egypt would help expedite the settlement of the remaining differences between the two countries, including the Suez Canal problem.

The Americans also indicated that a settlement would lead to an improvement in relations between other Western countries and Egypt, as a result of which Egypt might be persuaded to cooperate with NATO for the defence of the Middle East. Egypt, in particular, had an important strategic military location from the allies' point of view, and could act as a counterbalance to possible Soviet expansion in the region. The area was considered of vital interest to the allies following the end of the Second World War.[19]

For these reasons, the United States sincerely desired the speedy settlement of Anglo-Egyptian disagreements. The United States saw that maintaining the territorial unity of Sudan was an important issue.

The American mediation proved successful and an agreement was signed in Cairo in February 1953 by both Naguib and Stevenson concerning the self-government and self-determination of Sudan.[20] It also stipulated that at the end of the transitional period the Sudanese parliament would pass a resolution expressing its desire that arrangements for self-determination be put into action. This was exactly what happened later.

The Sudanese parliament voted unanimously for independence in late 1955 under the leadership of Ismail al-Azhari. Even before the British and Egyptians withdrew their forces, the Sudan officially became an independent republic on 1 January 1956, with Ismail al-Azhari as its first president. It should be remembered here that the Sudanese political party leaders also contributed to the achievement of the successful agreement. They were astute enough and had sufficient political experience to enable them to cooperate well to gain Sudan's self-determination and complete independence. At the same time they had kept a friendly relationship with both of the Condominium powers in the general interest of Sudan.[21]

The Egyptians, for their part, believed that the Sudanese would immediately ask Egypt for the union of the two countries after the British had left Sudan. Britain, on the other hand, expected that Sudan might well request to join the British Commonwealth. Both expectations were proved wrong. The Sudanese disappointed both Egypt and Britain by choosing to remain independent. Thus, the Anglo-Egyptian agreement on Sudan put an end to one of the long-standing disputes between the two countries. With the amicable settlement of this problem, which had been responsible for the failure of all the previous talks, it became obvious that a new era in Anglo-Egyptian relations had begun – an era in which both countries hoped for mutual understanding, trust and respect. This was expressed by Naguib who had played a major role in the negotiations leading to the agreement over Sudan. He said:

> The Sudan Agreement will open a new page in the old historic relations between Great Britain and Egypt, a page that will restore the confidence and trust between the two Governments, which will have favourable effects in the settling of the remaining issues between Britain and Egypt.[22]

However, the agreement on the Sudan could not have been reached if the military regime in Egypt had not been bold enough to break with the approaches and methods of previous governments, which had invariably combined the two issues in one single demand, and had insisted on the unity of the Nile Valley under Egyptian sovereignty, giving only partial self-government to the Sudanese within the framework of permanent union with Egypt.[23] The British government had always opposed the old Egyptian demand, because Britain had generally been interested for a long time to ensure that the Sudan should belong to the Sudanese.[24]

After the Sudanese agreement had been reached Egypt expected the Anglo-Egyptian negotiations to resume immediately for the settlement of the problem of the British military presence in Egypt. The military government was anxious to reach an agreement with Britain because the government's prestige and the political stability of the regime depended on securing the evacuation of foreign troops from the country.[25]

The Egyptian government had announced in an earlier statement in May 1953 that, unlike its predecessors, it did not wish to waste time by allowing the Anglo-Egyptian talks to drag on for years. Nasser, who was considered the most powerful figure in the government and who had also been behind the conclusion of the 1953 agreement, indicated that Egypt was now ready to hold talks with Britain on the question of the British military presence in the Suez Canal Zone. However, he warned that for the talks to succeed it was essential that Britain treated Egypt as a friend and not as it had done previously, in a manner reminiscent of nineteenth-century imperialism.[26] Nasser's point was that the world had changed and the nature and course of Anglo-Egyptian relations should also change. The tone of Nasser's statement annoyed the British minister of state at the Foreign Office, Selwyn Lloyd, who in the absence of the ailing foreign secretary, said on 12 May 1953 that Britain would not resume negotiations with the current Egyptian military regime until "terrorist" activities against the British installations in the Canal Zone had stopped completely.[27] Although attacks on British facilities had decreased considerably, further steps were taken by the Egyptian government to stop them.

The new Egyptian government had already made it clear that it did not intend to repeat the mistakes of previous Egyptian governments which had encouraged violence against British forces in the country. Moreover, the new regime in Egypt realized that its military power could not equal that of the British forces stationed in the Canal Zone. It therefore wanted to take firm action to stop guerrilla activity completely against British installations. It did succeed in stopping thefts of British property in the area, in particular thefts of machine-guns and ammunition from British stores.[28] Its success convinced the British Cabinet that the new regime in Egypt was stable and strong enough to end the Anglo-Egyptian dispute.

Meanwhile, the US president, Dwight Eisenhower, and the US secretary of state, John Foster Dulles, advised Britain that the Anglo-Egyptian controversy should now be brought to an end, and that in order to safeguard British interests in the region it had to compromise with Egypt and conclude a new agreement.

Britain, which had not yet fully recovered from the financial exigencies of war, was receiving US aid to help improve its economic position. Britain was also finding it hard to maintain all its forces in the Middle East even in peacetime. Thus, financial considerations made Britain think seriously about the American advice on the removal of its forces from Egypt. In addition, Britain, which could not defend the entire region against communist aggression on its own, was in dire need of US support. Hence, it was to be expected that Britain would consider seriously the US recommendations.

Britain also knew that the time had come to reach a new agreement with Egypt regarding the problem of the Suez Canal base as the 1936 treaty would expire in less than two years.[29] Furthermore, the British Ministry of Defence and the Chief of Staff Committee believed that the strategic value of the Suez base had decreased since the advent of nuclear weapons. At the same time they realized that the Suez base could not be adequately maintained without a large number of Egyptian labourers. The Egyptian workmen could not be expected to give their full cooperation and loyalty as long as their country continued to be occupied by British troops.[30] British military experts, therefore now favoured a new agreement with Egypt. In addition, most British MPs were also convinced that the time was right for the peaceful settlement of the Suez Canal issue and that a solution should be worked out without delay.[31]

The mutual desire to reach a new agreement on the Suez Canal issue encouraged the two governments to prepare well for a fresh round of negotiations. The first meeting was held in late June 1953. This time the talks were opened in Cairo and the meeting was attended, on the Egyptian side, by General Naguib, Colonel Nasser and Dr Mahmoud Fawzi, the foreign minister, and on the British side by Sir Ralph Stevenson, Michael Cresswell, minister at the British embassy in Cairo, and Sir Arthur Sanders, the commander-in-chief of the British forces in the Middle East. In this first round of talks both parties were eager to bring their dispute to a satisfactory conclusion.

The negotiations went smoothly and ended with Britain agreeing in principle to withdraw its troops from Egypt at the earliest possible opportunity.[32] During the talks, however, Egypt made a surprise demand that Britain's military installations and equipment should be transferred to Egypt directly following the British evacuation of the Suez base. Egypt also demanded that all British technicians who wished to remain on the base after the British evacuation should come under Egyptian control.[33] Although these demands seemed immoderate the British negotiators did not reject them and told the Egyptians that they would give their reply after consultation with their government.[34]

Despite this relative success, however, Anglo-Egyptian negotiations were delayed by the intensification of the struggle for power in Egypt and the rivalry between Naguib and Nasser over the leadership of the country. Nasser was accused by the powerful Muslim Brotherhood and the popular Wafd Party of being pro-Western. On the other hand, they were sympathetic to General Naguib. In the meantime there was serious disagreement among members of the Revolutionary Command Council over appointments to high positions in the government. Serious rivalries emerged between Salah Salem, Anwar Sadat, Gamal Salem and Kamal al-Deen Hussein. At the same time the absence of the British foreign secretary, Sir Anthony Eden, through illness, added to the problem, and the Anglo-Egyptian settlement was postponed for the rest of 1953.

During the power struggle in Egypt, Nasser emerged as the undisputed leader of the revolutionary regime, following his victory over General Naguib who was removed from his posts as president, prime minister and chairman of the Revolutionary Command Council on 25 February 1954.[35] As soon as this internal political feud was safely over, Nasser notified the British ambassador in Cairo that Egypt was ready to resume talks on the Suez issue. Nasser assured the ambassador that his government was ready to make certain compromises over points that Egypt had been stressing during the previous year and which concerned, in particular, the British military installations, equipment and the status of the British technicians who would remain in the Canal Zone base after the British military evacuation.[36]

Three weeks after the submission of the Egyptian proposal, the British ambassador in Cairo delivered Britain's response, stating that Britain was keen to resume talks with a view to reaching a satisfactory agreement as soon as possible on the presence of British troops in Egypt. In the meantime there were lengthy discussions in the British Cabinet on the future of British troops in Egypt and the Anglo-Egyptian settlement.

Britain was also in favour of an early settlement with Egypt, particularly as Egypt was now willing to compromise over its previous demands.[37] In addition there was a strong feeling among MPs that Britain's best interest in Egypt lay in reaching a new compromise agreement with the Egyptians.[38] The majority of members of the House of Commons shared the view of the Foreign Office which was convinced that as long as the Egyptians remained unhappy about the presence of the British troops in their country, the Suez base would be morally unacceptable to Egypt and militarily useless to Britain.[39] Such a situation might easily work against British interests, as had happened in Iran in the spring of 1951 during the Anglo-Iranian oil crisis. In addition, the Ministry of Defence and the Chiefs of Staff Committee addressed notes to the Cabinet stating their conviction that the Suez base was no longer tenable from a military point of view, especially in the age of nuclear warfare. The British prime minister, Sir Winston Churchill, who regarded himself as a military expert, agreed that the canal as a strategic military base could not be defended in a hostile environment.[40]

Britain concluded that the negotiations should be resumed as soon as possible in order to settle the Suez Canal issue peacefully. The Cabinet decided to appoint a delegation to be sent to Cairo under the leadership of Brigadier Anthony Head, the British secretary of state for war. The talks resumed in late March 1954 and after three sessions of negotiations had made some progress. The British delegation's stance was that the British forces should be pulled out of Egyptian territory and, at the same time, that Britain should seek a new agreement with Egypt. The British delegation then insisted on a number of conditions: to start with, the British insisted that the 4,000 British technicians who would remain in the Canal Zone to look after the British base (with all its equipment) in peacetime would continue to wear the uniform of the British army.[41] The Egyptians, however, were strongly opposed to British technicians appearing in military uniform in their country and as a result negotiations were held up for some time. The Egyptian negotiators believed that their military forces would view the wearing of British military uniforms as a sign that their country was still under British domination. At the same time, the appearance of British military uniforms would have an adverse psychological effect on the Egyptian people who would also consider it as a sign of the continued military occupation of their country. Secondly, the British negotiators insisted on a twenty-year agreement allowing for the 'reactivation of the base' in the event of an attack. This caused further disagreement, with Egypt being willing to accept only seven years.[42]

These differences of opinion between the British and Egyptian negotiators resulted in another postponement of the Anglo-Egyptian settlement. Once again the British negotiators assured the Egyptians that they would let them know their views after consultation with their government in London. Meanwhile, Nasser warned the British ambassador in Cairo (and repeatedly declared) that Britain should not expect Egypt to extend further accommodation and facilities to British troops in Egypt. Egypt could make the British soldiers' position in the country very uncomfortable if Britain intended to remain in Egypt permanently, he said.[43]

Nasser's statement came to the notice of some of the leaders of the British Commonwealth countries. India and Pakistan, who had recently gained independence from Britain, were sympathetic to the Egyptian cause. Jawaharlal Nehru, the Indian prime minister, and Muhammad Ali Jinnah, the Pakistani prime minister, who were at the time visiting London, advised Britain to be reasonable with the Egyptian government especially since the Egyptians had shown willingness to cooperate with Britain over its military bases on Egyptian territory.[44]

Meanwhile, the United States was giving attention to the Anglo-Egyptian dispute in relation to the Suez Canal issue, motivated especially by the growth of American interests in the region. The United States had friendly relations with both Britain and Egypt. It also had powerful influence over Britain which considered itself one of the closest allies of the United States and which had been dependent on the United States for aid since the 1940s. The United States had always encouraged both parties to end their dispute peacefully. At the same time, it put pressure on the British government to resolve the problem of the British base in Egypt. The US administration was convinced that Britain should now solve its outstanding problems with Egypt and believed that the time was ripe to reach a fresh agreement,[45] since the treaty of 1936 was due to expire in 1956 and Britain would then have to leave Egypt without an agreement. This was emphasized by the US secretary of state John Foster Dulles during his visit to Cairo in June 1954. According to Dulles, Britain's interests and those of the Western powers would be better served by an agreement with Egypt than by prolonging the discontent that was smouldering in the Middle East and might otherwise burst into flames.[46]

Dulles, who was a powerful secretary of state, believed that if the Suez dispute was successfully resolved, the last major obstacle in the way of creating a Middle East defence system would be removed. The Western powers would then be in an effective position to protect the region against Soviet penetration.

The American willingness and determination to end the Anglo-Egyptian dispute caused Britain and Egypt to be more conciliatory towards each other's suggestions. There were lengthy discussions at the Foreign Office. Selwyn Lloyd believed that the base had become a financial burden on Britain and the prime minister reckoned that the Suez Canal base had lost its strategic military importance due to the development of the H-bomb.

These calculations prompted Britain to compromise with Egypt and to agree in principle to end the dispute in a friendly manner. There was a general acceptance in London of the principle voiced by the British ambassador in Cairo that in order to safeguard

Britain's interests in the region Britain should seek another agreement with Egypt.[47] Thus, in order to bring the dispute to a successful conclusion, Britain decided in early July 1954 to send General Sir Brian Robertson, the former commander of the Middle East land forces and chairman of the British Transport Commission, to Cairo as the leader of the British negotiating team. On his arrival, Robertson announced that he had brought a fresh proposal regarding the settlement of differences between the two governments.

Robertson believed that a new agreement was possible and that the differences between Britain and Egypt could be solved on a mutually beneficial basis.[48] Thus the fourth round of the formal negotiations which were held in Cairo began in good faith between Nasser and Mahmoud Fawzi representing Egypt and Robertson and Stevenson representing Britain. After a third session of talks, both parties were of the opinion that a new agreement was necessary. Despite the amiable atmosphere, there were serious difficulties to overcome, particularly those relating to the issue of the number of British technicians remaining in the Suez base and the uniforms they should wear. Not least, there was also disagreement over the future of the British equipment and the "reactivation of the base". However, the differences did not seem as insurmountable as they had been previously. Both parties were anxious to end the dispute in a friendly way and much progress had already been made. Discussions were frank and cordial and aimed at reaching a mutual agreement.[49] The negotiations were productive, resulting in the initiation and preparation of a draft agreement in Cairo in late July 1954.

The agreement embodied the principles on which British forces would be withdrawn from Egyptian territory within twenty months of the signing of the agreement. As there was now hope of a settlement of outstanding issues between Britain and Egypt, Robertson left Cairo for final consultations with his government. At its first meeting in August 1954, the Cabinet approved the work of the British negotiators.[50]

In the same month the House of Commons endorsed the agreement with an overwhelming majority: 257 votes for and 25 against.[51] The Anglo-Egyptian agreement regarding the Suez base was not signed until 19 October 1954 in Cairo (see Appendix III). Nasser, a hard bargainer and shrewd statesman, had, through his diplomacy and persuasiveness, induced the British negotiators to reach an agreement almost entirely on Egypt's terms. Robertson's exploratory Cairo mission had also contributed to the success of the negotiations. The 1954 Suez Canal Base Agreement was hailed as a satisfactory compromise between Britain and Egypt. The signing of the agreement was an occasion of great rejoicing for the people of Egypt, particularly as the 74-year period of British domination had at last come to an end.

The Egyptian military rulers had, however, given ground on the question of the unity of Sudan and Egypt in return for full political independence. The new agreement was an achievement for Nasser, which he had accomplished in a very short time. On the occasion of the signing of the Suez agreement, Nasser announced:

> This is a turning-point in the history of Egypt. With this agreement, a new era of friendly relations between Egypt and Britain will begin, an era based on mutual trust, confidence and co-operation between Egypt, Britain and Western countries. This agreement will also contribute to the maintenance of peace and security in the Middle East. It is the biggest single achievement in Egypt's national aspirations to date. I must also pay a high tribute to the British side for their part in reaching the agreement. I want to mention in particular General Sir Brian Robertson and other British officials and members of the British embassy in Cairo for their friendly attitude towards Egypt. From now on, Egypt and Britain should get rid of the past mistrust of each other, in their hearts. We should start building up a new relationship with Britain on the solid basis of trust, which has been lacking in our relations for the past several decades. Finally, let us co-operate with Britain for the sake of Egypt and for world peace and international welfare.[52]

In this way the new agreement freed Egypt from the restrictions which were imposed on it by the 1936 treaty. Egypt was now able to draw up a new foreign policy based first on the safeguarding of its national interests, and secondly on protection of those of the

Arab world. The 1954 agreement strengthened Nasser's position as the undisputed leader of the Egyptian military government and revealed the defeat of the opposition forces, particularly the Wafdists and Muslim Brotherhood.

The Egyptian government was not the only party to believe that it had succeeded in signing a favourable agreement. Britain was even more delighted at having reached a successful conclusion to the treaty. Eden himself justified the 1954 agreement by comparing it with the 1936 treaty to which he was a signatory. He defended the new agreement in the House of Commons thus:

> The 1936 treaty allowed us to station troops in Egypt in order to fulfil an Anglo-Egyptian alliance for the joint defence of the Canal. That was the purpose of that treaty. We have no chance whatsoever of going to international arbitration and say, instead of doing that, we are going to maintain more than 80,000 troops in Egypt to do so. The case would be utterly indefensible, and noble friends, members would have to use the veto, not once, but almost every day.[53]

Accordingly, under the 1954 agreement, Britain obtained the legal right to stay in the Suez Canal Zone by consent, for the following seven years. During the last year of the agreement's duration, either government would have the right to consult with the other to decide what arrangements should be made regarding the future of the defence of the Suez Canal (see Article 12 in Appendix III) as well as of the 6,000 British servicemen who had the responsibility for running the existing British bases in the zone. Britain conceded the condition that British security personnel and technicians would wear civilian clothes. A further condition of the agreement was that instead of flying the British Union flag the British headquarters in the Canal Zone should bear a single identification, such as a badge, indicating that it remained under British military control.[54]

With this Britain had eliminated the main source of friction with Egypt[55] and had secured the safety of its employees and installations in the Canal Zone from any Egyptian threat. Furthermore, the agreement obtained for Britain the right to reoccupy the Canal Zone in the event of an attack on Egypt by any outside forces or on any of the Arab countries which were party to Arab collective security. Britain would also have the right of access to the Suez base in the event of an external threat to or attack on Turkey. Although Turkey was not a member of the Arab League, it was an important member of the NATO pact because the Western countries, especially the United States, considered Turkey to be of strategic importance as a buttress against the expansion of communist activities in the region. The whole of the Middle East was an area of the allies' influence.[56] In addition, the agreement gave Britain all it needed for the efficient operation of its base and also secured the Egyptians' assistance in the protection of British civil contractors employed on the Suez base. This included certain immunities for them from the jurisdiction of the Egyptian government. Finally, Britain obtained the right to use Egypt's Suez airfields. The Royal Air Force was able to fly over and land during reconnaissance flights and could also use Egyptian servicing facilities.[57]

It must be remembered that the circumstances this time were undoubtedly right and had contributed to the ending of the Anglo-Egyptian dispute. In particular, the new regime intelligently ended the dispute over Sudan which had been the single biggest stumbling-block in all previous negotiations. This compelled Britain to find a quick and peaceful solution to the dispute over its military presence on Egyptian territory.

Other reasons for the successful conclusion of the agreement included the fact that the 1936 Anglo-Egyptian Treaty of Alliance and Friendship was due to expire by the middle of 1956, when Britain would automatically have had to evacuate from Egypt. Britain would have had no legal right to remain there. Unless the Egyptian government agreed otherwise, Britain would have had to go to the United Nations to submit a request for arbitration for a renewal of the 1936 treaty, according to one of the articles of the treaty. It should also be remembered in this context that the United Nations had already debated the Anglo-Egyptian case in 1947 and that in that debate Egypt had strongly resisted Britain's demand for British troops to remain in Egypt as well as in Sudan. Although Britain had managed to avoid an embarrassing situation at that time, it might have again found itself trying to justify its position in Egypt in 1956. As times had changed since 1947, the general feeling at the United Nations might well have favoured the Egyptian position. This was particularly so since membership of the UN General Assembly in 1956 was dominated by the new nations of the Afro-Asian bloc, which without doubt, would have supported Egypt rather than Britain. Consequently, Britain might have found itself in a far less favourable position than that of 1947 and would have been leaving Egypt without an agreement.

Another factor was that the United States, through its embassy in Cairo, played an indirect role as mediator in the settlement by encouraging the two parties to end their dispute in a friendly way. This role was motivated by the growth of American economic and strategic interests in the Middle East.[58] The United States was interested in replacing the British domination in the region. Finally, the Suez Canal base itself had become a heavy financial burden for Britain. In order to maintain the base and run it efficiently Britain needed a huge amount of capital, over £50 million a year,[59] money which was badly needed at home. All these developments forced Britain to make concessions to Egypt and to agree to pull out of the country. Under the 1954 agreement, however, Britain had secured a respectable position in Egypt and earned the right of re-entry onto Egyptian soil in circumstances of threat of war in the region for the following seven years with the prospect that this right might be extended for a longer period. Furthermore, Britain retained its influence and prestige in the Arab world with which it traditionally had strong relations. Britain also secured vital interests in the Suez Canal, guaranteeing freedom of navigation for its ships.

The next chapter will discuss why Britain failed to comply with the terms of such a favourable agreement and why it invaded Egypt in 1956.

Notes

1. British Embassy in Cairo to Foreign Office, Tel. 916, 1 October 1952, PRO/FO 371/102726.
2. Anthony Eden, *Memoirs: Full Circle* (London, Cassell, 1960), vol. 3, pp. 240–2.

3. The Sudan Confidential Report, February 1953, PRO/FO 371/102727.
4. *Ibid.* See also Naguib, *Mudhakkirat*, pp. 117–37.
5. From British Governor of Sudan to the Foreign Office, Tel. 1017, 5 November 1952, PRO/FO 371/102791.
6. British Embassy in Cairo Report, n.d., 1952, PRO/FO 371/102728. See also Anthony Eden, *Memoirs: Full Circle*, pp. 242–7.
7. British Embassy in Cairo to Foreign Office. Tel. 611. 5 January 1952, PRO/FO 371/102729.
8. British Embassy in Cairo report. January 1953, PRO/FO 371/102730. See also Muhammad Naguib, *Egypt's Destiny*, p. 242.
9. *Ibid.*, pp. 242–7. See also The Sudan Confidential Report, Khartoum, n.d., 1952, PRO/FO 371/102726.
10. There were two main parties in the Sudan: the Umma Party, largely supported by members of Mahdiyya sect which had always favoured the creation of an independent Sudan, with British cooperation, and the National Unionist Party (NUP) – a coalition supported by the leaders of the Khatmiyya sect as well as other Sudanese political parties (see Chapter Two). The NUP was also in favour of Sudan's independence, despite its earlier support for an arrangement with Egypt. However, during 1954–5 relations between Cairo and Khartoum became cool because of Egyptian interference in Sudanese internal affairs. This included Ismail al-Azhari, the leader of the NUP, advocating Sudan's independence perhaps by pressure from the Sudanese public as well as other political leaders. This political development of the Sudan enabled the Sudanese to hoist their flag of independence in early 1956. See Peter Woodward, *Condominium and Sudanese Nationalism* (London, Rex Collings, 1979), pp. 136–47.
11. From Foreign Office to Cairo, Tel. 1070, 9 January 1953, PRO/FO 371/102725.
12. Cabinet Discussion, February 1953, PRO/FO 371/102731.
13. British Embassy Report in Cairo, n.d., 1953, PRO/FO 371/102730.
14. *Ibid.* See also P. M. Holt *A Modern History of the Sudan* (London, Weidenfeld and Nicolson, 1961), and Abdel Rahim Muddathir, *Imperialism and Nationalism in the Sudan* (Oxford, Clarendon Press, 1969), p. 213.
15. British Embassy in Cairo Confidential Report, January 1953, PRO/FO 371/1027331.
16. *Ibid.*
17. *Ibid.*
18. British Embassy in Washington to Foreign Office, Tel. 913, 12 February 1953, PRO/FO 371/102792.
19. *Ibid.* See also PRO/FO 371/102795.
20. *al-Ahram*, 13 February 1953.
21. British Embassy in Cairo, Top Secret to Foreign Office, March 1953, PRO/FO 371/108371.
22. British Embassy in Cairo, Political Review, July 1953, PRO/FO 371/102728. See also *The Egyptian Gazette*, 16 February 1953.
23. *Ibid.*
24. Foreign Office Minutes, March 1953, PRO/FO 371/108317.
25. British Embassy in Cairo to Foreign Office, Tel. 1709, 20 January 1954, PRO/FO 371/108214.

26. *al-Ahram*, 5–7 May 1953.
27. From Foreign Office to Cairo, Tel. 916, 12 May 1953, PRO/FO 371/102719.
28. From Foreign Office to Cairo Annual Political Review for August/September 1953, PRO/FO 371/118812.
29. Prime Minister's Minutes, November 1953, PRO/FO 371/113608.
30. Ministry of Defence and Chief of Staff Committee Memoranda, 26 March 1953 to Cabinet.
31. House of Common Debates, January 1954, PRO/FO 371/108345.
32. British Embassy in Cairo Political Review. June/July 1953, PRO/FO 371/102728. See also *The Sunday Times*, 13 June 1953.
33. *Ibid.*
34. British Ambassador Minutes, Cairo, June 1953, PRO/FO 371/102729.
35. *Ibid.* See also British Embassy in Cairo Report to Foreign Office, January 1954, PRO/FO 371/108617.
36. *Ibid.*
37. Top Secret, Prime Minister's Minutes, Egypt Canal Zone Base, n.d., PRO/FO 371/108417. See also PRO/FO 371/118861.
38. House of Commons Debates. February 1954, PRO/FO 371/108455.
39. *Ibid.* See also Foreign Office Minutes, March 1953.
40. The Chief of Staff Report to the Foreign Office, January 1954, PRO/FO 371/108417.
41. British Embassy in Cairo confidential report, May 1954, PRO/FO 371/108480.
42. *Ibid.*
43. British Embassy in Cairo to Foreign Office, Tel. 917, May 1954, PRO/FO 371/108481. See also *The Egyptian Gazette*, 9 June 1954.
44. Foreign Office Minutes, n.d., 1954, PRO/FO 371/102795.
45. British Embassy in Washington Report to Foreign Office, March 1954, PRO/FO 371/102779.
46. *The Manchester Guardian*, 7 July 1954. See also PRO/FO 371/102795.
47. British Ambassador Minutes in Cairo to Foreign Office, March 1954, PRO/FO 371/102799. See also Prime Minister's Minutes, Top Secret, Egypt, n.d., PRO/FO 371/108424.
48. *al-Ahram*, 2 July 1954. See also *The Egyptian Gazette*, 7 July 1954.
49. British Embassy in Cairo to Foreign Office, Tel. 713, 5 July 1954, PRO/FO 371/102799.
50. *Ibid.* See also Cabinet Conclusion, July 1954, CAB 129/65.
51. House of Commons Debates, 28–9, July 1954, PRO/FO 371/108455.
52. *al-Ahram*, Thursday 21 October 1954.
53. House of Commons Debates, 29 July 1954, PRO/FO 371/108455.
54. British Embassy in Cairo Report to Foreign Office, 29 June 1954, PRO/FO 371/118861.
55. House of Commons Debates, July 1954, PRO/FO 371/108455. See also Foreign Office Memorandum, April 1954,
56. *Ibid.*
57. House of Commons Debates, 29 July 1954, PRO/FO 371/108455.
58. From British Embassy in Washington to Foreign Office, Tel. 87, February 1953, PRO/FO 371/102779.

59. Prime Minister's Minutes, Top Secret, Egypt Canal Zone Base, PRO/FO 371/108417. See also PRO/FO 371/118861.
60. House of Commons Debates, 29 July 1954, PRO/FO 371/108455.

7

The Collapse of the 1954 Agreement and the Suez Crisis

In the previous chapter I discussed how the military regime in Egypt successfully settled the long-standing dispute with Britain over the problem of Sudan and the evacuation of British troops from Egypt. Following settlement of these outstanding issues, relations between London and Cairo improved. But this cordial relationship did not last long. In this chapter I will discuss the reasons for the growing unease in the relationship between Cairo and London, which eventually developed into open conflict in 1956. The Suez Canal Base Agreement of 1954, as discussed previously, was more favourable to Britain than to Egypt. While Britain was completely satisfied with the agreement, the Egyptian military government was strongly criticized by its opponents, the Wafdists and the Muslim Brotherhood, who both accused the new Egyptian regime of being too lenient with the British government. The Wafd and the Muslim Brotherhood attacked the 1954 agreement and claimed that there was no justification for concluding a new agreement with Britain, especially as the 1936 treaty was due to expire by the middle of 1956.[1]

Although the Egyptian government knew that the Suez agreement would be beneficial to Britain, it believed that the Western countries, particularly Britain itself, would help Egypt financially and militarily. The Egyptian government's aim was to improve the Egyptian economy and to modernize the army. After the Suez agreement had been concluded, Egypt immediately asked Britain for military aid. It had in fact been trying hard during the past seven months to persuade Britain to rearm the Egyptian army with modern British weapons. To Nasser's disappointment, however,

Egypt's request was denied: Britain said that British manufacturers could not now satisfy Egyptian demands and that in any case Egypt would not be able to pay for the arms in cash.[2]

Nasser now realized that Western countries, particularly Britain, had no intention of supplying the Egyptian army with modern equipment. France was hostile to the idea due to its belief that the new Egyptian regime of 1952 was creating far-reaching problems for the French colonies in North Africa. France was convinced that arms supplies to its North African colonies, particularly Algeria where the war of independence had started in 1954, had been arriving from Egypt. This had created many difficulties for the French in suppressing the Algerian rebels. These factors forced Nasser to ask the United States for supplies of modern weapons as well as for more American financial aid. Accordingly, in May 1955, Nasser sent a list of his military requirements to Raymond Hare, the US ambassador to Egypt. Hare promptly forwarded this to the US government, but the State Department postponed consideration of the Egyptian request for arms because of the pro-Israeli lobby which would oppose such a deal. Egypt concluded that it would not now be able to get sufficient arms from the United States to protect Egyptian territory from an Israeli attack.

The Israeli threat was a real concern following David Ben-Gurion's return from retirement in February 1955 and his assumption of the Israeli defence portfolio.[3] In the same week Israeli troops crossed the armistice line at the Gaza Strip and destroyed the garrison headquarters of the Egyptian army, killing 40 people and wounding 49 others.[4] This was the first major clash on the Israel–Egypt line since the armistice of February 1949. It led to increased tension in the area which influenced the course of events in the Middle East.[5] The conclusion of the Baghdad Pact[6] was a further irritant. Egypt considered that these two moves were intended to weaken the new Egyptian regime by shifting the leadership of the Arab countries from Cairo to Baghdad.[7] Moreover, Egypt believed that the Pact would pave the way for Western domination of the Middle East.

The opening of the historic Conference of African and Asian Nations at Bandung, Indonesia, on 18 April 1955 was a landmark in Egypt's foreign policy. Nasser attended the conference with a big Egyptian delegation which met with more than a score of non-aligned country leaders, most of whom had recently led their nations out of colonization to independence. During the conference, China's prime minister, Zhou Enlai, offered Egypt a supply of arms, and advised the Egyptian leader to turn towards the Soviet Union, with the suggestion that the communist bloc might help Egypt, particularly if Western countries continued to refuse to meet its demands.[8]

The Bandung Conference opened new horizons for Egypt. The Egyptian leaders discovered that Egypt's military needs might be met elsewhere. Nevertheless, Egypt still held out hope that the United States would respond to its demands. Nasser was still in touch with Raymond Hare whom he reminded on 27 June 1955 that Egypt was still awaiting the US response to its request for US aid and was still interested in a Western source of supply for the army. Egypt hoped that the US government would reconsider Egypt's request. The US secretary of state, John Foster Dulles, however, was convinced that the Egyptian regime was bluffing[9] and once again the United States refused to meet Egypt's request.

The failure of Nasser's government to obtain modern weapons from the Western powers during the preceding nine months led the Egyptian prime minister to announce publicly on 27 September 1955 that Egypt had concluded an arms' deal with Czechoslovakia and the Soviet Union for the supply of fighter aircraft, tanks, artillery and other heavy weaponry. Egypt would receive $250 million-worth of arms, to be paid for in Egyptian cotton at low interest rates over a decade or so. Within a few months, the arms, together with technicians, began to arrive in Egypt and Egyptian military officers were sent to the Soviet Union for training.[10] Naturally the announcement of the Czech–Soviet arms deal with Egypt provoked a shocked and hostile reaction in Washington and London as well as in Tel Aviv. (The Israelis had already protested about the 1954 agreement on the British evacuation from the Suez Canal Zone.) Ben-Gurion described the Egyptian arms deal as having only one aim: to destroy the state and people of Israel. He accused the Egyptian regime of preparing for an early war and an attack on Israel.[11] In Washington the arms deal struck Dulles and other State Department officials like a thunderbolt, as they feared that Egypt might become a communist satellite. The Soviet Union had vaulted over the Baghdad Pact. It had disregarded the Northern Tier countries and, after centuries of unsuccessful effort, had jumped brazenly and in strength right into the Middle East without any difficulty.

Britain became increasingly anxious about its position in the area, since it was still the predominant power in the Middle East and Africa. The introduction of Soviet influence into the region threatened Britain's entire position there and led Sir Anthony Eden to announce in November 1955 that the Arab states must support the Baghdad Pact against Soviet expansion in the Middle East. He also said that the hostility between Israel and its Arab neighbours must cease and that peace between the two parties should be reached.[12] But Eden did not clarify how such a peace might be achieved.

The United States and Britain were not the only powers to be concerned about the arms deal. The French government was also observing Egypt's role in the area. The French blamed Egypt for the escalation of fighting in the Algerian rebellion. Egypt was supporting the Algerian nationalist movement against France and Egypt's radio broadcasts and press attacked France's policy in Algeria. This led France to embark on a careful policy of appeasement towards Egypt in order to persuade it to stop its support of the Algerian rebels. For this purpose, the French foreign minister, Christian Pineau, visited Egypt in early March 1956. Pineau tried to reach a settlement on the Algerian question, but the Egyptian government told him that Egypt was not responsible for the Algerian rebellion.[13] The failure of Pineau's talks in Egypt infuriated the French government which as a result responded positively to an Israeli request for arms. Only two weeks after the Israeli request, France delivered 75 of the latest French *Mystère* fighter aircraft and other heavy military equipment to the Israeli army. This made the Israeli army far superior to that of Egypt.[14] The events in the area, the arms race between Egypt and Israel, and the enormous propaganda and political advantages gained by the Soviet Union, made the situation in the Middle East increasingly alarming for the West.

Since the beginning of the Egyptian revolution Egypt had been looking forward not only to modernizing its army but also to improving its economy by the building of the world's biggest dam, at Aswan on the Upper Nile, so as to increase the supply of water for irrigation to increase agricultural production and feed Egypt's rapidly expanding population.[15]

Following the overthrow of the monarchy, the young officers of the revolutionary government started planning Egypt's economic development. The question of the Aswan High Dam came up again. It continued to be discussed until 1954 when Nasser announced the decision to go ahead with the project. He described it as the cornerstone of Egyptian economic progress. The dam would provide Egypt with hydroelectricity and bring vast areas of desert into cultivation. Furthermore, over-year water storage would free the country from basin irrigation and eliminate fluctuations in the supply of irrigation water. All these factors would not only increase agricultural production, which still formed the backbone of the Egyptian economy, but would also benefit industry through the provision of electricity.

Such a scheme, the largest engineering project in the world at the time, was, however, fraught with difficulties. Egypt did not have the money to build the dam; it lacked the engineering skills to design and build such an enormous structure, and also lacked the huge quantity of modern technical equipment required for such a project. Assistance had to be sought from outside and the countries best qualified to provide it were those of the West, including the United States. Negotiations for the financing of the project began in early 1955 before the signing of the Baghdad Pact. Dulles and Eden eventually decided that the United States and Britain, together with a World Bank loan, would provide the necessary finance for the dam,[16] especially when they heard that the Soviet ambassador to Egypt, Daniel S. Solod, had offered Soviet help for the building of the dam during the negotiations for arms.

In response to this decision Nasser sent Dr Abdel-Moneim Kaissouny, the Egyptian finance minister, to Washington in November 1955. There he began negotiations with the president of the

World Bank, Eugene Black, and US and British representatives.[17] After protracted negotiations, the World Bank, the United States and Britain announced that they would guarantee the foreign currency requirement for the dam. In mid-December 1955 the United States declared its willingness to help Egypt with a grant of US$56 million for the first stage of the project. Britain followed suit with an offer of US$40 million and the World Bank with a loan of US$200 million. The whole project was estimated to require over US$1,000 million, much of this would consist of Egyptian currency.[18]

In December 1955, two days after Sir Anthony Eden and John Foster Dulles had officially announced the offer, the Soviet Union also announced that it hoped to participate in this humanitarian project in Egypt, unless Egypt's agreement with the Western countries specifically excluded it from doing so.[19] The United States and Britain at once reported that their offer of loans implied that the Soviet Union would not be included in the deal. Furthermore, Egypt was asked to accept the US and British recommendation for the execution of the project. First, Egypt should devote one-third of its domestic revenue for several years towards the cost of the dam project. Secondly, Egypt's resources should not be squandered on other projects. Thirdly, Egypt was required to impose controls to curb the growth of inflation which the immense expenditure of public money on the dam project would cause. Fourthly, contracts for the construction work were to be awarded on a competitive basis.[20] The Egyptian government considered these conditions to be very tough. They refused some of them from the beginning and described them as similar to those imposed by foreign powers during the Khedive Ismail's regime (1863–9) which had led to Britain and France becoming creditors to Egypt.[21] Egypt suspected that the West wanted to control the Egyptian economy again in the same matter.

The Egyptian ambassador in Washington, Ahmad Hussein, believed that the Aswan High Dam project would be successful and that the final deal should be signed between Egypt, the United States and Britain in early spring 1956. However, Hussein was recalled to Cairo in May 1956 for further consultation with his government regarding the West's conditions for the building of the dam. After long and extensive talks with Nasser, Hussein succeeded in persuading Nasser to abandon his position and accept the West's offer on its conditions.[22] The Egyptian ambassador returned to Washington and announced in early July 1956 that his government accepted the US and British conditions for financing the Aswan High Dam and that Egypt was ready to sign the deal.[23] Unfortunately when Hussein arrived for his appointment with Dulles on 16 July he was told that the secretary of state had changed his position as a result of the Czech–Soviet arms deal. The Egyptian ambassador was also told that the United States had concluded that the Egyptian economy could not withstand the economic strain of building the dam and as a result the United States was withdrawing its offer to finance the project. Dulles further justified the US withdrawal by saying that the Egyptian government had not yet reached an agreement on the Nile waters with Sudan. Finally, Egypt's ability to devote adequate resources to the project had now become uncertain.

Earlier, in the spring of 1956, Nasser had recognized the People's Republic of China and had reaffirmed Egypt's policy of non-alignment. But in John Foster Dulles's perception non-alignment was almost synonymous with communism, a fact which contributed to the US withdrawal of financial aid for the Aswan High Dam. The following day, Sir Anthony Eden announced Britain's withdrawal of its contribution. Consequently, the World Bank's offer collapsed.

These unexpected announcements came as a shock to the Egyptian leader, who at that time was in Yugoslavia (as Egypt's president) conferring with Marshal Tito and the prime minister of India, Jawaharlal Nehru. Not surprisingly Nasser's reaction was one of anger at what he called an insult to Egypt's dignity. Subsequently, on 26 July 1956, on the occasion of the fourth anniversary celebrations of the Egyptian revolution in Alexandria, Nasser delivered a rousing speech at the end of which he stunned his audience by proclaiming the nationalization of the Suez Canal Company. He declared that Egypt would build the Aswan High Dam from its own natural resources including the Suez Canal revenues. Egypt then by presidential decree turned the Suez Canal over to a special authority attached to the Egyptian ministry of commerce.[24]

Egypt described the nationalization of the canal as an internal Egyptian affair. It promised that the shareholders of the Suez Canal Company, who were mainly British and French, would be compensated. But this did not satisfy Sir Anthony Eden who was already convinced that President Nasser was a troublemaker as well as a dangerous threat to British interests in the Middle East and should be stopped.[25] However, apart from the nationalization of the Suez Canal Company, Egypt had not caused any damage to British and French interests, nor had it stopped British and French ships from passing through the canal, despite the refusal of British and French shipowners to pay the dues to the Suez Canal Authority. Furthermore, Egypt repeated that after the nationalization the canal would be operated in the interests of all those who used it. Egypt would continue to uphold the Constantinople Convention of 29 October 1888 which guaranteed freedom of navigation in the canal and stated that it would safeguard its independence and meet hostility with hostility.[26] The British government reacted violently against the nationalization of the Suez Canal Company with Sir Anthony Eden declaring the action illegal. The canal, he said, was of vital importance to the trade and prosperity not only of Britain but also of all Western countries. Therefore, it should not be left under the unfettered control of someone who could not be trusted.

Eden regarded Nasser as a potential threat to the British position in Egypt if not in the entire Middle East because of his opposition to the Baghdad Pact. He thought Nasser wished to bring about a progressive diminution of British influence in the Arab world and was determined to stop him.[27] He suggested that the administration of the canal should be under a system of international control which would guarantee freedom and safety for ships of all nations.

France's reaction against Egypt was even stronger than Britain's. France had already been angered by Nasser's government because of its support for Algerian nationalists. For this reason France asked Britain to act quickly against Egypt and offered Britain more than 100,000 troops from its 500,000 strong force in Algeria to fight against Egypt.[28]

In contrast the US reaction to the nationalization of the Suez Canal Company was less hostile than that of both Britain and France. The United States considered Nasser's action fully legal. Dulles declared that as long as there was no interference with navigation in the canal and no threat to international shipping, the United States did not share Anglo-French fears nor see any basis for military action against Egypt. In addition, the United States did not agree with British and French suspicions that Nasser was threatening Western interests in the Middle East and that he should be crushed.[29]

The Soviet Union expressed its fullest sympathy with Egypt and considered that the nationalization of the Suez Canal Company was legal and did not contravene international law. Further, the Suez Canal itself was an integral part of Egyptian sovereign territory. The canal had been built by the Egyptians and more than 200,000 Egyptians had died during its construction. At the same time, the Soviet Union reiterated its offer of assistance and economic aid.[30]

Britain and France became increasingly irritated at Nasser's behaviour and jointly decided that the only solution was to remove the Egyptian regime by force. They agreed in principle on military action against Egypt and threatened to use it.

Britain had already called up its military reserves in the Middle East and was concentrating its armed forces in Cyprus which had become Britain's main base in the region as the result of the British evacuation from the Suez Canal base. The French premier, Guy Mollet, and the British prime minister, Sir Anthony Eden, warned Nasser that force would be used if it became necessary to impose international control of the Suez Canal. Egypt however, chose to ignore these Anglo-French threats.[31]

President Eisenhower warned Britain and France that the United States would not provide either moral or material support for any military action against Egypt and disagreed totally with their plans against Egypt. The United States believed that Nasser was not the actual aggressor and that he was not a threat to peace or to Western interests in the area. The canal was still open, despite the Suez Canal Company having ordered its pilots to leave their jobs. The United States therefore expressed its hope that Anglo-French operations would not take place against Egypt. For this reason, President Eisenhower immediately sent Robert Murphy, the US deputy under-secretary of state, to London on 28 July. Murphy handed President Eisenhower's messages to Britain and France. These stated that the United States was giving careful and serious consideration to the Suez crisis. The United States warned its allies that a decision to use force against Egypt would be an unmitigated disaster for British and French interests in the Middle East.[32]

On 31 July Dulles flew from South America to London to participate in the talks. The tripartite meeting ended with a call for an international conference of those interested in the Suez Canal. This conference was held in London on 16–23 August 1956, to devise a means of peacefully solving the problem. Twenty-four countries were invited to the conference.[33] They were Egypt, Australia, Ceylon, Denmark, Ethiopia, West Germany, Greece, India, Indonesia, Iran, Italy, Japan, the Netherlands, New Zealand, Norway, Pakistan, Portugal, the Soviet Union, Spain, Sweden, Turkey, the United States, the United Kingdom and France. Israel was not invited. However, Egypt refused to attend and President Nasser announced that the conference had no right to discuss Egypt's internal affairs. Also Egypt would not negotiate any settlement under the threat of the use of force by Anglo-French forces. Greece also stayed out.

Egypt made a counter-proposal in the form of a conference of all 45 countries whose ships used the canal according to the Constantinople Convention of 1888 which guaranteed freedom of navigation through the Suez Canal.

At the London Conference, held at Lancaster House, Britain hoped that it would provide a decisive expression of opinion on the problem of the Suez Canal. The conference ended with an agreement to set up an international authority to administer the Suez Canal with Egypt. A five-nation committee, consisting of Australia, Ethiopia, Iran, Sweden and the United States, was formed and headed by the Australian prime minister, Sir Robert G. Menzies to persuade Egypt to comply. The Menzies Committee's mission was agreed to by Egypt on 28 August, and the Australian premier flew to Cairo and had a meeting with President Nasser. He warned Nasser that Britain and France were in earnest about the use of force and therefore urged Nasser to accept an international system for the control of the canal and to cooperate with this system. Nasser told Menzies that the threat of force from Britain and France would not dictate Egyptian policy.

This Anglo-French attempt to coerce Egypt by diplomatic pressure failed as Egypt refused to acquiesce to their demands.[35] Britain and France were convinced that the only way to solve the problem and to restore their rights over the canal was by the use of military force. Dulles, however, managed to persuade them to agree to another meeting in London. This was known as the "Second London Conference" and met on 19–21 September 1956. This was a conference of Suez Canal users and was inaugurated by 15 member states. Unfortunately the "Second London Conference" also ended without any clear conclusion being reached regarding a peaceful solution of the Suez crisis. President Nasser considered the conference as collective aggression.

Disillusioned by this conference[36] Britain and France believed that the United Nations might be able to put more diplomatic pressure upon Egypt to agree to place the canal under an international authority. Consequently both governments appealed to the United Nations on 23 September against Egypt's unilateral action in nationalizing the Suez Canal Company. Britain and France invited the president of the UN Security Council to call a meeting on 26 September and asked Dag Hammarskjöld, the UN secretary-general, to put the canal's operations under the control of an international agreement. At the United Nations a secret meeting was held between Egypt, France, Britain and the United States. As a result of these negotiations the foreign ministers of the four countries agreed that any settlement of the Suez Canal crisis would be in accordance with six agreed principles. These were unanimously adopted by the Security Council on 13 October. They were as follows:

1. There should be free and open transit through the canal without discrimination, overt or covert.
2. The sovereignty of Egypt over the canal should be respected.
3. The operation of the canal should be insulated from the politics of any country.
4. The manner of fixing tolls and charges should be decided by agreement between Egypt and the users.
5. A fair proportion of the dues should be allotted to development.
6. Unresolved disputes between the (old) Suez Canal Company and the Egyptian government should be settled by arbitration with suitable terms of reference and suitable provisions from the payment of sums found to be due.[37]

However, Britain and France considered that the six principles were meaningless in reality since Egypt still controlled the canal and collected the dues. The United Nations had no power to compel direct international control over the canal, particularly since the canal was still working satisfactorily under the Egyptian authority. Despite the fact that the Suez Canal Company had ordered its pilots to leave their jobs, and that the British and French governments had concluded that the only option was to resort to the use of force, Egypt maintained the canal in satisfactory operation.

It became clear that, from the beginning of the crisis, Britain and France had prepared for possible military action against Egypt, even if it meant that either of them had to act unilaterally. Furthermore, the British Cabinet instructed the chiefs of staff as early as 27 July 1956 to prepare the timetable for a possible military operation against Egypt. Britain called up its reservists who were to proceed to Malta and Cyprus by the first week of August 1956. At the same time Britain and France had already developed a joint plan for the invasion of Egypt. In addition, a meeting was held in Paris between Sir Anthony Eden, Selwyn Lloyd, Guy Mollet and Christian Pineau on 16 October in utmost secrecy and without any advisers present.

According to Eden's instructions, only two top British officials were to be brought into the secret plans with France.[38] It was in these secret plans that the question of Israel was mooted although Israel was not officially invited to act until ten days later. The original planning did not involve Israel but the Israelis were eager to participate for several reasons if Britain and France asked them to do so. Firstly, hostilities between Egypt and Israel had increased as a result of border raids. Secondly, Egypt strongly supported the Palestinian cause against the new Jewish settlers on Palestinian land. Thirdly, for eight years Egypt had maintained an economic blockade against Israel and had denied Israeli ships and cargoes the use of the Suez Canal. In addition, Egypt had blocked access to the Israeli port of Eilat by closing the Straits of Tiran. These actions were harming Israel's economy by forcing its ships to use the long route around the Cape to reach East Africa and Asia. Israel claimed the right to use the canal under the Constantinople Convention[39] and the Gulf of Aqaba under international law. Since the 1948 Palestine War, Egypt had refused to allow passage of Israeli ships through the Suez Canal and to ships of other nations which were bound for Israel despite a UN resolution passed in September 1951 permitting Israeli shipping through the Suez Canal and calling upon Egypt to end these restrictions. But Egypt disregarded this Security Council resolution. A further resolution calling upon Egypt to comply was put forward at the Security Council by New Zealand in 1954, but was vetoed by the Soviet Union.[40]

The Czech–Soviet arms deals with Egypt alarmed Israel since it could not now exclude an Egyptian attack on it in the future. Thus when Anglo-French preparations for an attack on Egypt was under way Israel became keen to join. The Israeli objective was mainly to cripple its strongest Arab neighbour before the Arab countries collectively acquired the strength to defeat it. Furthermore, the close relationship between France and Israel provided Israel with a golden opportunity to confront Egypt. France had also become the main supplier of modern arms to the Jewish state. In contrast, relations between France and Egypt were hostile because of Egypt's support for the Algerian cause. France and Israel were therefore both eager to disable Nasser's regime even before he nationalized the Suez Canal Company. On the British side, relations between

Britain and Israel were not at their best following the establishment of the Jewish state in 1948 in Palestine, particularly as the Israelis threatened Jordan which had had an alliance with Britain since 1946. This explains Britain's delay in recognizing the new State of Israel. In addition, Britain had already warned Israel that if Jordan were to be attacked Britain would go to war with Israel under the terms of the Anglo-Jordanian Treaty of 1946.[41]

In September 1956 France held secret meetings with Israel, and Britain soon accepted Israeli participation. Both France and Britain had assessed the value of Israeli assistance in a war against Egypt, and would use an Israeli attack on Egypt as a pretext for their military intervention. This is exactly what happened later. The Anglo-French military plan, known as "Operation Musketeer", at first provided for a large-scale British and French attack on Egypt from Alexandria and then an advance through Cairo to the Suez Canal Zone. But after Israel was invited into the Anglo-French plan, the operation was changed to a new plan, known as the "Musketeer Revised Plan", which was to be a direct assault on the Suez Canal Zone city of Port Said, followed by an invasion along the entire length of the canal. Israel would strike first. The British imperial chief of staff and the commander of the Anglo-French plan against Egypt, Sir Gerald Templer, strongly resisted the inclusion of Israel in the plan. Nevertheless, Israel was invited to a secret meeting with British and French officials on 22 October 1956 at Sèvres just outside Paris. The discussion resulted in a protocol called the Treaty of Sèvres. It became clear that the Israeli forces would not launch a full-scale attack alone on Egypt. According to the Anglo-Franco-Israeli Treaty of Sèvres, Israeli forces would strike by air, attacking Egypt in the early hours of 29 October and continuing the offensive until the Israeli forces reached Qantara, which was 15 miles east of the Suez Canal. Then the Israeli advance would stop before reaching the canal itself. Britain and France would be acting ostensibly to protect the canal from damage and would separate the combatants by issuing an ultimatum calling on Israel and Egypt to withdraw to ten miles from the canal. Egypt would have to accept the temporary British and French occupation of the Canal Zone; and Egypt's certain rejection of the ultimatum would provide the pretext for Britain to bomb Egypt.[42] This is what later took place. The Egyptian air force was completely destroyed on the ground at an early stage of the war and the city of Port Said was turned into rubble. More than 1,000 people were killed or injured.

The role of the French forces was to provide protection for Israel by covering the coastal defence of Eilat on the Gulf of Aqaba and to provide Israel with supplies and reinforcements of aircraft on the eve of the invasion. British and French forces would begin to land on 1 November, during the election in the United States, when the Americans would be preoccupied with election campaigning.

Consequently, on 29 October, the Israeli forces invaded Egyptian territory from the south and occupied the Gaza Strip, penetrating deep into the Sinai peninsula.[43]

When the news reached President Eisenhower at midday on 29 October the United States immediately asked the UN Security Council to consider steps for the immediate cessation of Israeli military activities against Egypt. President Eisenhower had already sent a message to Ben-Gurion on 25 October 1956 expressing US anxiety over Israel's mobilization, together with a warning to the Israeli leader against taking any forceful initiative in the area. The Israelis ignored Eisenhower's message. However, at the UN Security Council, the United States for the first time proposed a resolution which called Israel an aggressor and asked it to withdraw its forces from Egypt. Further the United States asked all members of the United Nations to refrain from force or threat of force in the area, and to withhold military, economic or financial assistance to Israel. But the American resolution was defeated by the French and British vetoes.[44]

In the morning of 30 October Mollet and Pineau flew to London determined to put the tripartite plan into motion at once. Later the same day, Britain and France issued their ultimatum to Israel and Egypt calling on both sides to stop all warlike action, to withdraw their forces to a distance of ten miles from the Suez Canal and, in the case of Egypt, to accept temporary occupation of the canal cities of Port Said, Ismailia and Suez by Anglo-French forces. Following the non-acceptance of these terms British and French troops would intervene within twelve hours in whatever strength was necessary to secure compliance.

This ultimatum was, of course, rejected by Egypt. Meanwhile the time stipulated by the ultimatum was running out and it expired on 31 October. The following day British aircraft based in Cyprus launched the first attack against Egypt, and by 4 November British and French forces had landed at Port Said and had advanced into the Canal Zone.

World reaction to the tripartite aggression against Egypt was strongly in Egypt's favour. In the United States in particular, both official and public reaction was intense, condemning its friends' actions. In Ottawa, the Canadian government issued a statement making it clear that Canada had not been consulted and regretting Britain's action.[45] The prime ministers of India, Ceylon and Pakistan signed a joint statement condemning the Anglo-French aggression.

On 5 November the Soviet premier Marshal Nikolai Bulganin sent strongly-worded messages to Eden, Mollett, and Ben-Gurion and condemned the aggressive actions against the sovereignty and integrity of Egypt. The communist leader gave a serious warning of the potentially dangerous consequences, and reminded them that the Soviet Union, as a great power, could not stand aside from this aggression against a peaceful country which was unarmed. Bulganin sent another message accusing France, Britain and Israel of unprovoked tripartite aggression. He reminded them of the position Britain or France would have been in if either of these countries had been attacked by a much stronger power with all kinds of sophisticated weapons whilst they were unarmed. He also questioned how they would have reacted if rockets had been used against them as had happened to Egypt. They would no doubt have called this a barbaric act. The Soviet Union was determined to use force to punish the aggressors and would draw from this crisis the appropriate prudent conclusion. The Soviet Union seriously warned the tripartite coalition against Egypt that the Soviets had the capability to use force against the aggressors and repeated again that the continuation of the war in Egypt could escalate into a Third World War.[46] This threat was not, however, taken seriously in London.

The US secretary of state, John Foster Dulles, in a speech at the United Nations, described the Anglo-French attack on Egypt as a grave error and inconsistent with the UN Charter. He called on the General Assembly on 2 November to introduce a resolution urging all parties involved in hostilities in the area to agree immediately to a cease-fire and halt the movement of military forces into the Canal Zone. The US resolution was passed by an overwhelming majority, with only Australia and New Zealand joining with Britain, France and Israel in opposing it.[47]

The reaction in the Middle East was naturally one of anger. Even the Iraqi government, which was not on good terms with Egypt, assured the Egyptian government that Iraq would send aid and support against this tripartite aggression. Iraq also broke off diplomatic relations with France and threatened to do the same with Britain. Saudi Arabia announced its intention to break off diplomatic relations with Britain and France and said it would also stop the sale of oil to both countries. Syria severed relations with both France and Britain and on 4 November three of the major oil-pumping stations of the Iraq Petroleum Company (IPC), in which Britain and France had shares, were destroyed, leading to oil and petrol rationing in France and Britain. Furthermore, on 2 and 3 November, more than seven ships were sunk in the canal by the Egyptians to block it, making the position of France and Britain even worse.[48]

On 1 November the United States and the Soviet Union agreed to the convening of a special emergency session of the UN General Assembly to discuss the crisis. Recourse to the Security Council was avoided to prevent Britain and France using their vetoes. Within days the General Assembly passed a US-sponsored resolution calling for a cease-fire and the withdrawal of the Anglo-French and Israeli forces from Egyptian territory. This initiative was to be taken to reopen the Suez Canal and secure the freedom of navigation through it. France and Britain refused to comply with the UN resolution, which angered the Soviet Union. The Soviets immediately put forward a note on 5 November to the United Nations as well as to the US president, suggesting that they employ naval and air forces to bring an end to the war in Egypt. Consequently, on the same day, the General Assembly met. During the meeting, Soviet representatives put forward a proposal for volunteers and military assistance for Egypt.[49]

It had become evident that the Soviets were contemplating some kind of independent action for which they wished to obtain cover. Therefore the White House immediately released a statement in reply to the letter from Bulganin in which President Eisenhower stated:

> The United Nations' resolution should be accepted urgently and unconditionally and Anglo-French forces should be withdrawn without any delay. Otherwise, the United States would join with the Soviet Union in the bipartite employment of their military forces to stop the fighting against Egypt. However, neither the Soviet Union's forces nor other military forces should enter the area except under a United Nations mandate.[50]

Although there was still bitter Egyptian civilian resistance in the Canal Zone cities, Dag Hammarskjöld announced that he had received a message that Israel and Egypt had accepted an unconditional cease-fire of military activities in the area. Meanwhile, on 6 November the Soviet government also asked the United Nations for an endorsement of a joint Soviet–US intervention, unless Anglo-French military operations were halted within twelve hours.

Thus, the strong US financial pressure, the Soviet threat and their joint condemnation of the Anglo-French aggressive war against Egypt, forced the British prime minister to hold an emergency Cabinet meeting on 6 November and announce that Britain would accept a cease-fire in the Canal Zone unless the British and French troops were attacked.[51] Consequently the Suez War ended, but the British and French forces remained in the zone for another six weeks until the total evacuation of their forces was completed on 21 December 1956.

Britain and France had virtually withdrawn without conditions[52] and without an agreement on the future of the Suez Canal.

Their forces were replaced by those of the United Nations. Furthermore, Britain began to face financial difficulties as a result of the blockage of the Suez Canal, as well as difficulties in obtaining oil supplies from the Western hemisphere, since the United States had refused to finance oil supplies to Britain and France. As a result the British Chancellor of the Exchequer, Harold MacMillan, announced on 12 November that the United Kingdom had lost over £330 million from the reserves during the two months to the end of October 1956. Britain was thus obliged to ask the International Monetary Fund for assistance to save the pound from further devaluation.[53] Meanwhile the Israeli forces did not in fact pull out from Sinai and the Gaza Strip until late February 1957, and then only as a result of President Eisenhower's pressure on the Israeli government.

The United States' threat to use economic sanctions against Israel compelled it to eventually withdraw from the Sinai peninsula and the Gaza Strip.[54] The Israelis gained little from the war, acquiring access to the Gulf of Aqaba through the Port of Eilat, admittedly a minor port for Israeli navigation with less than 5 per cent of Israeli goods passing through this waterway.

President Nasser announced that the Anglo-Egyptian Agreement of 1954 had now been terminated.[55] This was followed by a policy of "Egyptianization" designed to reduce foreign commercial influence in the country. British and French banks, insurance companies and industrial concerns were among the first to be affected in the nationalization programme. In the following years, this policy embraced every sector and private enterprise in Egypt. At the same time, in January 1957, the United Nations began a canal clearance operation with experts from Western countries (excluding Britain and France). Egypt announced that the clearance was to be carried out in three stages, with full navigability to be attained in spring of the same year.[56]

Notes

1. *Akhbar al-Yawm*, 17 January 1955.
2. From Foreign Office to British Embassy in Cairo, Tel. 1180, 29 May 1955, PRO/FO 371/119371.
3. David Ben-Gurion considered Nasser's regime as Israel's main enemy because Nasser's government strongly attacked the Jewish state in the press and through broadcasts. Ben-Gurion believed that the Egyptian government had to be punished until it realized the need to accept the existence of Israel.
4. British Embassy in Cairo, Confidential Report, March 1955, PRO/FO 371/119221. See also *The Egyptian Gazette*, 27 February 1955.
5. *Ibid.* See also Muhammad Hassanein Heikal, *Sanawat al-ghalayan* (Cairo, 1988) and *al-Enfijar* (Cairo, 1990).
6. The Baghdad Pact (the unofficial name for a defence treaty between Iraq and Turkey) was concluded on 24 February 1955 when Nuri al-Said was prime minister of Iraq. Pakistan later joined the organization. It was intended to complement NATO and the South-East Asia Treaty Organization (SEATO) but it worried Egypt which regarded Nuri al-Said as a pro-Western stooge. Iraq withdrew from the organization in 1958 after the Iraqi revolution. See PRO/FO 371/132920, 371/ 132926 and DEFE 5/69.
7. *Ibid.*
8. Muhammad Hassanein Heikal, *Milafat al-Suwais* (Cairo, 1989), pp. 117–25.
9. British Embassy in Washington to Foreign Office, Tel. 1510, 7 June 1955, PRO/FO 371/119070.
10. *al-Ahram*, from Nasser's speech to the public, 27 September 1955. See also British Embassy Report, Cairo to Foreign Office, PRO/FO 371/119721.
11. British Embassy in Cairo to Foreign Office, Tel. 613, 22 November 1955, PRO/FO 371/108717.
12. Foreign Office Minutes, December 1955, PRO/FO 371/112480.
13. From Cairo to Foreign Office, Tel. 719, 7 March 1956, PRO/FO 371/112337. See also *al-Ahram*, 9 March 1956.
14. Anthony Nutting, *No End of a Lesson: The Story of Suez* (London, Constable, 1967), pp. 88–9.
15. George Lenczowski, *The Middle East in World Affairs* (Ithaca, Cornell University Press, 1952), pp. 529–31. See also Heikal, *Sanawait al-ghalayan.*
16. *Ibid.*
17. *The Egyptian Gazette*, 7 November 1955, See also PRO/FO 371/112330.
18. Nutting, *Nasser*, p. 140.
19. From New York to Foreign Office, Tel. 918, 16 November 1955, PRO/FO 371/118075.
20. British Ambassador Memorandum in Cairo regarding Egypt's Aid, n.d. 1956, PRO/FO 371/119112.
21. Afaf Lutfi al-Sayyid Marsot, *A Short History of Modern Egypt* (Cambridge, Cambridge University Press, 1985), pp. 69–70.
22. British Ambassador Memorandum in Cairo regarding Egypt's Aid. n.d.1956, PRO/FO 371/119112.

23. British Embassy in Washington to Foreign Office, Tel. 9113, 17 July 1956, PRO/FO 371/125427.
24. *Ibid.* See also Lenczowski, *The Middle East in World Affairs*, pp. 527–9.
25. United States, Department of State, *The Suez Canal Problem* (Washington DC, Department of State Documentary Publication, no. 6392, 1956), pp. 34–6. See also *al-Ahram*, 27 July 1956.
26. Foreign Office Minutes, n.d., August 1956, PRO/FO 371/125429.
27. Prime Minister's Suez Memorandum following Egyptian nationalization, n.d., PRO/FO 371/125425. See also Heikal, *al-Enfijar*.
28. From Paris to London Secret Report, n.d., PRO/FO 371/125429.
29. From Washington to Foreign Office, Tel. 1613, 30 July 1956, PRO/FO 371/119080.
30. From Moscow to Foreign Office, Tel. 1033, 29 July 1956, PRO/FO 371/119079.
31. Nutting, *Nasser*, pp. 147–9.
32. From Washington to Foreign Office, Tel. 1613, 30 July 1956, PRO/FO 371/119080.
33. D. C. Watt, *Documents on the Suez Crisis* (London, Royal Institute of International Affairs, 1957), pp. 7–10.
34. *Ibid.*
35. Foreign Office Secret Report, September 1956, PRO/FO 371/125425.
36. *Ibid.*
37. From New York to Foreign Office, Tel. 175, 30 September 1956, PRO/FO 371/125399.
38. *Contemporary Record: The Journal of Contemporary British History*, vol I (London, Frank Cass, 1987).
39. Egypt considered that the Constantinople Convention of 1888 was still effective but did not apply to Israel because Israel did not exist as a state at the time it was drawn up.
40. From British Embassy in Cairo to Foreign Office, Secret Report, December 1954, PRO/FO 371/118731.
41. Suez Secret Memorandum on relations between the United Kingdom and France following the Egyptian nationalization, August 1956, PRO/FO 371/125427.
42. *Contemporary Record*, vol. I, 1987.
43. From Paris to London, Tel. 810, 29 October 1956, PRO/FO 371/112548.
44. From New York to Foreign Office, Tel. 919, 30 October 1956, PRO/FO 371/112548. See also PRO/FO 371/125425.
45. *Ibid.*
46. From Moscow to New York, Tel. 1347, 3 November 1956, PRO/FO 371/125482. See also PRO/FO 371/125425.
47. From New York to Foreign Office, Tel. 1055, 2 November 1956, PRO/FO 371/125223.
48. *al-Ahram*, 2 November 1956. See also Heikal, *Milafat al-Suwais*, pp. 117–19.
49. From New York to Foreign Office, Tel. 1113, 4 November 1956, PRO/FO 371/125223. See also PRO/FO 371/125425.
50. *Ibid.*
51. From Foreign Office to New York, Tel. 1090, 6 November 1956, PRO/FO 371/125223.

52. Prime Minister's Minutes, 10 December 1956, PRO/FO 371/125429.
53. *Ibid.*
54. Heikal, *Sanawat al-ghalayan*, pp. 92–9. See also US Department of State, *The Suez Canal Problem*.
55. *Ibid.*
56. For the definitive account of the Suez Crisis, see Keith Kyle, *Suez* (London, Weidenfeld and Nicolson, 1991).

Conclusion

Anglo-Egyptian relations during the period from 1947 to 1954 were characterized by misunderstandings and missed opportunities. No sooner had they improved at the time of an agreement forged between Britain and the new revolutionary regime in 1954, than they plunged into acrimony and finally into open conflict in 1956 invalidating that agreement.

After the Second World War the British Empire was in retreat, its contraction being signalled by the granting of full independence to India in 1947. This encouraged Egypt to make increased demands for Britain's evacuation from Egypt and for the unification of Egypt with Sudan.

Britain was reluctant to accede to these demands. The Suez Canal remained a vital element in British thinking, particularly as a great quantity of Middle Eastern oil was now passing through the canal on its way to supply British industry. British trade in the Middle East was still crucial for Britain's postwar economic recovery. This induced Britain to adopt delaying tactics over a settlement with Egypt. The Conservatives hoped that relations with Egypt need not be altered in the aftermath of the war.

Britain still expected to be able to dictate its terms in the Middle East. Egypt, on the other hand, was determined to emerge as a fully independent state. British intervention had freed it from the Ottoman Empire, and since 1922 it had possessed nominal independence but had still been treated in many ways as a British satellite. Its national ambitions included not only the desire for full independence but also the wish to incorporate the Sudan. The second of these ambitions impeded the achievement of the first and had eventually to be abandoned.

The failure of the old Egyptian regime to achieve a satisfactory settlement with Britain contributed to the domestic crisis in the country and played a part in the revolution which overthrew the monarchy.

King Farouk's refusal to accept the Sidky–Bevin protocol of 1946 as the basis of a new relationship with Britain caused Egypt to refer the disagreement with Britain to the United Nations in 1947. But this action did nothing to end the controversy and Egypt was disappointed with the outcome of the United Nations debate.

This led to the postponement of a settlement and worsened Egyptian relations with Britain. Other factors, such as the deteriorating situation in Palestine during 1948 which led to the first Arab–Israeli war, also contributed to postponing an Anglo-Egyptian settlement and further complicated attempts at a solution. Such developments also affected Egypt politically and economically.

By the early 1950s the Cold War was beginning to influence international attitudes towards Egypt. The two new world superpowers, the United States and the Soviet Union, wished to extend their influence over the Middle East because of the region's economic and military importance. Subsequently the competition between these two superpowers developed into a confrontation in the form of an undeclared war with each wishing to dominate the Middle East.

In January 1950, however, a new Wafdist government took office in Egypt under the leadership of Nahhas Pasha. He resumed negotiations with the British representatives in Cairo. But in June the British government reappraised its position in Egypt as a result of the Korean War, so delaying further the Anglo-Egyptian settlement.

The Truman administration in the United States backed this position. The United States considered itself to have assumed a definite military responsibility in the Middle East, both as a deterrent against a possible threat from the communist bloc to the region, and in order to keep the region's oil flowing to the West. Britain was also convinced that its military presence in Egypt was important to its strategy of military defence and would assist the preservation of peace and stability in the Middle East. But the Wafdist government expected to settle Anglo-Egyptian problems, so as to satisfy Egyptian national aspirations and fulfil their pledges to the Egyptian public concerning the evacuation of British troops and union with the Sudan. Unfortunately the Wafdist leaders failed to obtain any concessions from Britain. This put Nahhas's government in a difficult position and influenced him to abrogate the Anglo-Egyptian agreements in October 1951.

Following the abrogation of the treaty the domestic situation in Egypt deteriorated. Neither the king nor the government was able to control events. The abrogation of the treaty had numerous repercussions in Egypt: it undoubtedly shook the foundations of the Egyptian monarchy and destabilized the government which did not command legitimacy, and whose authority came under direct threat. This situation led eventually to the July 1952 military *coup d'état* and the removal of the old Egyptian regime.

The new Egyptian revolutionary regime had made a favourable impression on the British government. It repeatedly emphasized its desire to establish good relations with the West and its willingness to cooperate with Britain in finding ways to resolve the dispute. Accordingly the negotiations between the two governments resumed in Cairo in October 1952 and succeeded in solving the Sudan question in early 1953. The following year both governments were able to end the Anglo-Egyptian dispute by signing the historic evacuation agreement of 1954. Thus the British military presence in Egypt came to an end.

Nevertheless, after the 1954 agreement there remained an area of conflict. Eden asked Nasser to include Egypt in the British regional alliance, the Baghdad Pact, formed in 1955, and requested him to abandon his ambition for leadership in the Arab world. Nasser not only rejected membership of the Baghdad Pact but also showed his determination to reduce British influence in the region so as to further his own ambitions. Nasser's actions convinced Eden that he was pushing hard to reduce the pre-eminent British position in the region, which ran counter to British objectives in the Middle East.

At the same time, the Egyptian leader believed that improving Egypt economically and militarily was the only way to solve its problems. But the refusal of the West, especially of the United States and Britain, to supply Egypt with military and financial aid left Nasser with no option but to turn to the communist bloc for help. In consequence the Soviet Union became involved in Middle East politics for the first time. The Western allies had long prevented it from penetrating Middle East affairs.

Following Nasser's nationalization of the Suez Canal Company in July 1956, events then moved rapidly to the Suez crisis. Eden decided to use force against Egypt in order to topple Nasser's regime but he miscalculated in considering Nasser as a new Hitler rising in the Middle East.

The two superpowers were determined to resolve the Suez crisis through the United Nations and were able to bring the hostilities to an end. But Nasser emerged as the winner in this crisis which made him the undisputed leader of Egypt, if not of the entire Arab world, until his sudden death in September 1970.

Finally, the difficulties which Britain and Egypt experienced in finding a solution to their dispute derived from their incompatible aims. Britain's attempt to retain some of its pre-war power and to sustain its influence in the Middle East was incompatible with Egyptian nationalist ambitions in the pan-Arab context as well as with its desire to be a fully independent state.

British foreign policy found it difficult to resolve the contradictions involved in Middle East affairs. As a result, Britain lost a great opportunity to preserve much of its influence, especially in the Arab world. Its influence waned further after the Suez crisis, largely to Egypt's benefit.

APPENDIX I

DRAFT DECREE-LAWS ABROGATING THE 1936 TREATY

I

A draft decree-law abrogating the 1936 Treaty and its Annexes, and the Condominium Agreements of January 19 and July 10, 1899, regarding the administration of The Sudan.

We Farouk I King of Egypt.

Upon what has been submitted to us by the Council of Ministers.

We order the following:—

The following draft law is to be submitted in Our name to Parliament:—

Article I

Law No. 80, 1936, ratifying the Treaty of Friendship and Alliance between Egypt and Great Britain and which was signed in London on August 26, 1936, shall be rescinded. Thus, the provisions of this Treaty and the agreement attached thereto concerning exemptions and privileges enjoyed by the British Forces stationed in the Kingdom of Egypt, as well as the provisions of the Condominium Agreements of January 19 and July 10, 1899, regarding the administration of The Sudan shall cease to be operative.

Article II

Law No. 13 and Law No. 24, 1941, relative to exemptions and privileges referred to in the preceding Article are abrogated.

Article III

Our Ministers are hereby charged with the execution of this law, each in so far as he is concerned and with taking the necessary measures in this respect.

It will become operative as from the date of its publication in the "Journal Official".

Issued at Montazah Palace on
Al-Moharram 6, 1371 (October 7, 1951).
FAROUK

II

A draft decree-law inviting Parliament to amend the Constitution to decide the constitutional position of The Sudan and to define the title of the King.

We Farouk I King of Egypt.

After taking cognizance of Royal Decree No. 42, 1923, setting up a constitutional regime for the Egyptian state and of Articles 156 and 157 of the Constitution; and upon what has been submitted to us by the Council of Ministers.

We order the following:—

Article I

Parliament is invited to consider amending Articles 159 and 160 of the Constitution to decide the constitutional position of The Sudan and to define the title of the King.

Article II

The President of our Council of Ministers is hereby charged with the execution of this degree.

III

A draft decree-law providing that the King shall be titled King of Egypt and The Sudan.

We Farouk I King of Egypt.

After taking cognizance of Royal Decree No. 42, 1923, setting up a constitutional regime for the Egyptian State; of Articles 156 and 157 of the Constitution; of the decree issued on October 7, 1951, proposing the amendment of some provisions of the Constitution; and of the two decisions of Parliament approving the necessity of such amendment and the subject matter thereof.

We order the following:—

The following draft law is to be submitted in Our name to Parliament:—

Article I
Article 159 of the Constitution shall be cancelled and the following substituted:—

The provisions of this Constitution shall apply to all the Egyptian Kingdom. Although Egypt and The Sudan are one nation, the regime of rule in The Sudan shall be defined by a special law.

Article II
Article 160 of the Constitution shall be cancelled and the following substituted:—

"The King shall be titled King of Egypt and the Sudan."

Article III
The President of the Council of Ministers and the Minister of Justice are hereby charged with the execution of this law which will become operative as from the date of its publication in the "Journal Official".

IV

A draft decree-law providing that The Sudan shall have a special Constitution to be drawn up by a Constituent Assembly representing the inhabitants of The Sudan.

We Farouk I, King of Egypt and The Sudan.

After taking cognizance of Law of 1951, abrogating the Treaty of August 26, 1936, and its annexes and also abrogating the Condominium Agreements of January 19 and July 10, 1899, concerning the administration of The Sudan and also after taking cognisance of Article 159 of Royal Order No. 42, 1923, setting up a constitutional regime for the State of Egypt, amended by Law No. ..., 1951.

And upon what has been submitted to us by the Council of Ministers.

We order the following:—

The following draft law is to be submitted in Our name to Parliament:—

Article I
The Sudan shall have a special Constitution to be drawn up by a Constituent Assembly representing the inhabitants of The Sudan and shall be enforced as soon as sanctioned and promulgated by the King. The Constituent Assembly will also draw up an electoral law to become operative in The Sudan after its ratification and promulgation.

Article II
The rules and procedures of the Constituent Assembly shall be defined in a decree.

Article III
The Constitution referred to in Article I shall contain the following fundamental rules:—

(*a*) The establishment of democratic and representative rule in the country, whether the representative body consists of one Chamber or two. One of the two Chambers at least shall be entirely elective.

The King's prerogative to dissolve the representative body or the elected Chamber only, if the representative body is composed of two Chambers, a new general election shall be held within a short interval of time to ensure the continuance of parliamentary control over the executive authority.

(*b*) The separation of the legislative, executive and judicial authorities.
(*c*) The establishment of a Council of Ministers composed of Sudanese. The King ruling through his Ministers and having the right to appoint and dismiss his Ministers. The Ministers being jointly responsible to Parliament or to the elected Chamber, at least for the general policy of the Cabinet and each for his Ministry.
(*d*) The participation of the representative body with the King in practising the legislative authority including the introduction of legislation. Issuing of laws to be subject to approval by Parliament and sanction by the King.

The prior approval by the representative body of the levying of new taxes, their modification of abolition, floating of loans and the annual budget.

(*e*) The guarantee of the independence of the judicial authorities at all levels.

(*f*) The guarantee within the limits of the law of the rights of individuals, public and personal liberties, liberty of belief, freedom of opinion, liberty of the Press, liberty of meetings and of association.

Article IV

As an exception to the provisions of the preceding Articles, Foreign Affairs and matters of Defence, the Army and Currency, shall be exercised by the King throughout the country within the limits of Royal Order No. 42, 1923, establishing a constitutional government in the State of Egypt.

Article V

The President of our Council of Ministers is hereby charged with the execution of this law.

APPENDIX II

AGREEMENT ON SELF-GOVERNMENT AND SELF-DETERMINATION FOR THE SUDAN: BRITAIN AND EGYPT

12 February 1953[1]

Article 1

In order to enable the Sudanese people to exercise Self-Determination in a free and neutral atmosphere, a transitional period providing full self-government for the Sudanese shall begin on the day specified in Article 9 below.

Article 2

The transitional period, being a preparation for the effective termination of the dual Administration, shall be considered as a liquidation of that Administration. During the transitional period the sovereignty of the Sudan shall be kept in reserve for the Sudanese until Self-Determination is achieved.

Article 3

The Governor-General shall, during the transitional period, be the supreme constitutional authority within the Sudan. He shall exercise his powers as set out in the Self-Government Statute with the aid of a five-member Commission, to be called the Governor-General's Commission, whose powers are laid down in the terms of reference in Annex I to the present Agreement.

Article 4

This Commission shall consist of two Sudanese proposed by the two contracting Governments in agreement, one Egyptian citizen, one citizen of the United Kingdom and one Pakistani citizen, each to be proposed by his respective Government. The appointment of the two Sudanese members shall be subject to the subsequent approval of the Sudanese Parliament when it is elected, and the Parliament shall be entitled to nominate alternative candidates in case of disapproval. The Commission hereby set up will be formally appointed by Egyptian Government decree.

Article 5
The two contracting Governments agree that, it being a fundamental principle of their common policy to maintain the unity of the Sudan as a single territory, the special powers which are vested in the Governor-General by Article 100 of the Self-Government Statue shall not be exercised in any manner which is in conflict with that policy.

Article 6
The Governor-General shall remain directly responsible to the two contracting Governments as regards:

(*a*) external affairs;
(*b*) any change requested by the Sudanese Parliament under Article 101 (1) of the Statute for Self-Government as regards any part of the Statute;
(*c*) any resolution passed by the Commission which he regards as inconsistent with his responsibilities. In this case he will inform the two contracting Governments, each of which must give an answer within one month of the date of formal notice. The Commission's resolutions shall stand unless the two Governments agree to the contrary.

Article 7
There shall be constituted a Mixed Electoral Commission of seven members. These shall be three Sudanese appointed by the Governor-General with the approval of his Commission, one Egyptian citizen, one citizen of the United Kingdom, one citizen of the United States of America, and one Indian citizen. The non-Sudanese members shall be nominated by their respective Governments. The Indian member shall be Chairman of the Commission. The Commission shall be appointed by the Governor-General on the instructions of

the two contracting Governments. The terms of reference of this Commission are contained in Annex II to this Agreement.

Article 8

To provide the free and neutral atmosphere requisite for Self-Determination there shall be established a Sudanization Committee consisting of:

(*a*) an Egyptian citizen and a citizen of the United Kingdom to be nominated by their respective Governments and subsequently appointed by the Governor-General, together with three Sudanese members to be selected from a list of five names submitted to him by the Prime Minister of the Sudan. The selection and appointment of these members shall have the prior approval of the Governor-General's Commission;

(*b*) one or more members of the Sudan Public Service Commission who will act in a purely advisory capacity without the right to vote;

(*c*) the function and terms of reference of this Committee are contained in Annex III to this Agreement.

Article 9

The transitional period shall begin on the day designated as "the appointed day" in Article 2 of the Self-Government Statute. Subject to the completion of the Sudanization as outlined in Annex III to this Agreement, the two contracting Governments undertake to bring the transitional period to an end as soon as possible. In any case this period shall not exceed three years. It shall be brought to an end in the following manner. The Sudanese Parliament shall pass the resolution expressing their desire that arrangements for Self-Determination shall be put in motion and the Governor-General shall notify the two contracting Governments of this resolution.

Article 10

When the two contracting Governments have been formally notified of this resolution, the Sudanese Government, then existing, shall draw up a draft law for the election of the Constituent Assembly which it shall submit to Parliament for approval. The Governor-General shall give his consent to the law with the agreement of his Commission. Detailed preparations for the process of Self-Determination, including safeguards assuring the impartiality of the elections and any other arrangements designed to secure a free and neutral atmosphere, shall be subject to international supervision. The two contracting Governments will accept the recommendations of any international body which may be set up to this end.

Article 11
Egyptian and British military forces shall be withdrawn from the Sudan immediately upon the Sudanese Parliament adopting a resolution expressing its desire that arrangements for Self-Determination be put in motion. The two contracting Governments undertake to complete the withdrawal of their forces from the Sudan within a period not exceeding three months.

Article 12
The Constituent Assembly shall have two duties to discharge. The first will be to decide the future of the Sudan as one integral whole. The second will be to draw up a constitution for the Sudan compatible with the decision which shall have been taken in this respect, as well as an electoral law for a permanent Sudanese Parliament. The future of the Sudan shall be decided either:

(*a*) by the Constituent Assembly choosing to link the Sudan with Egypt in any form, or
(*b*) by the Constituent Assembly choosing complete independence.

Article 13
The two contracting Governments undertake to respect the decision of the Constituent Assembly concerning the future status of the Sudan and each Government will take all the measures which may be necessary to give effort to its decision.

Article 14
The two contracting Governments agree that the draft Self-Government Statute shall be amended in accordance with Annex IV to this Agreement.

Article 15
This Agreement and its attachments shall come into force upon signature.

Note

1. Great Britain, *Parliamentary Papers*, 1953, Treaty Series No. 47, Cmd. 8904.

APPENDIX III

AGREEMENT BETWEEN THE GOVERNMENT OF THE UNITED KINGDOM OF GREAT BRITAIN AND NORTHERN IRELAND AND THE EGYPTIAN GOVERNMENT REGARDING THE SUEZ CANAL BASE

Cairo, October 19, 1954[1]

The Government of the United Kingdom of Great Britain and the Government of the Republic of Egypt,

Desiring to establish Anglo-Egyptian relations on a new basis of natural understanding and firm friendship,

Have agreed as follows:—

Article 1

Her Majesty's Forces shall be completely withdrawn from Egyptian territory in accordance with the Schedule set forth in Part A of Annex I within a period of twenty months from the date of signature of the present Agreement.

Article 2

The Government of the United Kingdom declare that the Treaty of Alliance signed in London on the 26th of August, 1936, with the Agreed Minute, Exchanged Notes, Convention concerning the immunities and privileges enjoyed by the British Forces in Egypt and all other subsidiary agreements, is terminated.

Article 3

Parts of the present Suez Canal Base, which are listed in Appendix A to Annex II, shall be kept in efficient working order and capable of immediate use in accordance with the provisions of Article 4 of the present Agreement. To this end they shall be organized in accordance with the provisions of Annex II.

Article 4
In the event of an armed attack by an outside Power on any country which at the date of signature of the present Agreement is a party to the Treaty of Joint Defence between Arab League States, signed in Cairo on the 13th of April, 1950, or on Turkey, Egypt shall afford to the United Kingdom such facilities as may be necessary in order to place the Base on a war footing and to operate it effectively. These facilities shall include the use of Egyptian ports within the limits of what is strictly indispensable for the above-mentioned purposes.

Article 5
In the event of the return of British Forces to the Suez Canal Base area in accordance with the provisions of Article 4, these forces shall withdraw immediately upon the cessation of the hostilities referred to in that Article.

Article 6
In the event of a threat of an armed attack by an outside Power on any country which at the date of signature of the present Agreement is a party to the Treaty of Joint Defence between Arab League States or on Turkey, there shall be immediate consultation between Egypt and the United Kingdom.

Article 7
The Government of the Republic of Egypt shall afford overflying, landing and servicing facilities for notified flights of aircraft under Royal Air Force control. For the clearance of any flights of such aircraft, the Government of the Republic of Egypt shall accord treatment no less favourable than that accorded to the aircraft of any other foreign country with the exception of State parties to the Treaty of Joint Defence between Arab League States. The landing and servicing facilities mentioned above shall be afforded at Egyptian Airfields in the Suez Canal Base area.

Article 8
The two Contracting Governments recognize that the Suez Maritime Canal, which is an integral part of Egypt, is a waterway

economically, commercially and strategically of international importance, and express the determination to uphold the Convention guaranteeing the freedom of navigation of the Canal signed at Constantinople on the 29th of October, 1888.

Article 9

(*a*) The United Kingdom is accorded the right to move any British equipment into or out of the Base at its discretion.

(*b*) There shall be no increase above the level of supplies as agreed upon in Part C of Annex II without the consent of the Government of the Republic of Egypt.

Article 10

The present Agreement does not affect and shall not be interpreted as affecting in any way the rights and obligations of the parties under the Charter of the United Nations.

Article 11

The Annexes and Appendices to the present Agreement shall be considered as an integral part of it.

Article 12

(*a*) The present Agreement shall remain in force for the period of seven years from the date of its signature.

(*b*) During the last twelve months of that period the two Contracting Governments shall consult together to decide on such arrangements as may be necessary upon the termination of the Agreement.

(*c*) Unless both the Contracting Governments agree upon any extension of the Agreement it shall terminate seven years after the date of signature and the Government of the United Kingdom shall take away or dispose of their property then remaining in the Base.

Article 13

The present Agreement shall have effect as though it had come into force on the date of signature. Instruments of ratification shall be exchanged in Cairo as soon as possible.

In witness whereof the undersigned, being duly authorized thereto, have signed the present Agreement and have affixed thereto their seals.

Done at Cairo, this nineteenth day of October, 1954, in duplicate, in the English and Arabic languages, both texts being equally authentic.

(L. S.) Anthony Nutting
(L. S.) Ralph Skrine Stevenson
(L. S.) E. R. Benson

(L. S.) Gamal Abdel Nasser
(L. S.) Abdel Hakim Amer
(L. S.) Salah Salem
(L. S.) Mahmoud Fawzi

ANNEX I

WITHDRAWAL OF HER MAJESTY'S FORCES

(With Reference to Article 1 of the present Agreement)

Part A

1. In accordance with the provisions of Article 1 of the present Agreement, the following percentage of Her Majesty's Forces in Egypt on the 27th of July, 1954, shall have been withdrawn between that date and the dates indicated in the schedule below:

DATE	PERCENTAGE OF HER MAJESTY'S FORCES
Date of Signature of the Agreement plus 4 months.	22%
Date of Signature of the Agreement plus 8 months.	32%
Date of Signature of the Agreement plus 12 months.	54%
Date of Signature of the Agreement plus 16 months.	75%
Date of Signature of the Agreement plus 20 months.	100%

2. In connection with the above mentioned withdrawal, the Government of the Republic of Egypt shall afford all necessary facilities for the movement of men and material.

Part B

Procedure for Standing Machinery, Staff Contacts and Issue of Instructions to the Appropriate Egyptian and British Authorities to Facilitate Withdrawal

1. For the period of withdrawal mentioned in Article 1 of the present Agreement, the British and the Egyptian Authorities will each designate appropriate Headquarters in the Canal Area which will be responsible for the progressive transfer of responsibility for security or maintenance of installations from British to Egyptian control.

2. (*a*) The British Headquarters for this purpose will be the Headquarters British Troops in Egypt and the Headquarters No. 205 Group, Royal Air Force.

(*b*) The Egyptian Headquarters for this purpose will be the Headquarters Eastern Command.

3. The Headquarters mentioned in paragraph 2 will be the link between the British and the Egyptian Authorities on all details in connection with the transfer of responsibilities for the security and maintenance of installations from British to Egyptian control. The Headquarters will establish direct staff contacts as appropriate to carry out the task on the lines set out in this Annex. Through the medium of their respective Movements Staffs, they will arrange for all the facilities to be provided by the Egyptian Authorities for the British Forces under paragraph 2 of Part A of this Annex.

4. During the period of withdrawal, the Headquarters Eastern Command will gradually assume increasing responsibility for the control of the Canal Area as the commitments of the British Headquarters diminish.

5. The British Headquarters will draw up an outline programme of withdrawal from the various installations for which they are at present responsible. This programme will be discussed between the British and the Egyptian Headquarters so that the Egyptian Authorities may make plans accordingly for the progressive assumption of their responsibilities. The Egyptian Headquarters may propose in discussion minor modifications of dates, timing or areas concerned.

6. It is desirable that the transfer of responsibilities from the British to the Egyptian Authorities should be carried out by complete zones. But in cases where this is not possible, it is agreed, in the interests of ensuring a clear division of responsibility, that installations

and areas handed over will be of such a size as will avoid the mixing of British and Egyptian Forces and producing circumstances where responsibilities cannot be clearly defined.

7. Except as provided for in paragraph 8, the responsibility for the security and maintenance of an installation will not be transferred when:—

(*a*) the installation is still operated by British Forces; or

(*b*) the installation forms part of a larger installation still operated by British Forces.

8. When an installation is handed over to the Egyptian Authorities for security or maintenance the withdrawal of British Forces from such installation will be complete and likewise the assumption of responsibility for the security or the maintenance of the installation by the Egyptian Authorities will be complete. Nevertheless, the Egyptian Authorities agree that they will, on request by the British Headquarters, assume responsibility for the security of a particular installation while a limited number of British technical troops are still engaged within the installation. Such a request shall not be made unless the number of British guard troops available is inadequate to ensure security.

9. When an installation is to be handed over to the Egyptian Authorities for security or maintenance, the Egyptian Headquarters will be notified as far in advance as possible and a date for the handing over will be agreed between the British and the Egyptian Headquarters.

10. A hand-over document of each installation will be prepared by the British Forces in such detail as may be agreed between the British and the Egyptian Headquarters, and will be handed over to the Egyptian Authorities in advance of the transfer, so as to enable the Egyptian Authorities to assess the security and maintenance problems and to make appropriate arrangements to deal with them.

11. When any installation is handed over to the Egyptian Authorities for security or maintenance, all defence posts, emplacements, barbed wire fences, communications, perimeter lighting where applicable, and fire fighting equipment on an appropriate scale, connected with the protection of the installation will be handed

over by the British to the Egyptian Authorities. In addition all available information including data as to the pattern, number and location of mines will be handed over. In order to ensure a smooth and efficient transfer of responsibilities, the British Headquarters will provide all possible assistance and give advice, where required, particularly as regards mines.

12. When an installation, not listed in Appendix A to Annex II, is to be evacuated by British Forces, the Egyptian Headquarters will be notified as far in advance as possible.

13. During the period of withdrawal, British and Egyptian Forces will have unhampered use of the railways and main roads through each other's areas of responsibility. When large-scale movements are contemplated, previous notification will be given and the necessary traffic control arrangements made.

14. During the period of withdrawal, training areas will be agreed between the British and the Egyptian Headquarters.

15. In order to avoid interference between radio stations operated by the British Forces and the Egyptian Forces in the Canal Area during the period of withdrawal, the use of non-internationally registered radio frequencies in the Canal Area subject to coordination between the British and the Egyptian Headquarters.

Part C

Engagement and Security Screenings of Workers

The following provisions shall apply with respect to the engagement by the British Forces in the Suez Canal Area of technicians and personnel and other local labour (hereinafter referred to as "workers") and the security screening of those workers:—

1. Employment offices at Port Said, Ismailia, Suez and Zagazig will register workers for employment by British Forces.

2. The British Forces Labour Engagement Units will be placed to conform with the location of the Employment Offices mentioned in paragraph 1 and there will be full cooperation between these Units and Offices, and between the Central Labour Authorities of the British Forces and the Central Office of the Ministry of Social Affairs at Ismailia.

3. The British Forces Labour Engagement Units will give full details of occupational requirements when notifying vacancies to the Employment Offices.

4. Applicants registered at the Employment Offices will be screened by Officers of the Egyptian Ministry of the Interior.

5. If, however, the Security Officer of the British Forces considers that an applicant is undesirable, this fact will be notified to the Employment Office concerned. The reasons will also be notified whenever possible.

6. No worker will be engaged by the British Forces unless he has been registered at and submitted by an Employment Office after screening by the Officers of the Egyptian Ministry of the Interior.

7. The British Forces will trade-test applicants in skilled occupations as may be necessary and in accordance with present practice. If an applicant is not accepted, the Employment Office will be notified and brief reasons will be given.

8. Workers employed by the British Forces, who become redundant as withdrawal proceeds, will not be discharged until they have been considered for transfer to other units of the British Forces which may need additional workers in similar occupations. Notification of such transfers will be sent to the Employment Offices concerned. When notice of termination of services is given to a worker, notification will be sent to the appropriate Employment Office.

9. As and when the services of workers are terminated by the British Forces, such workers will, in accordance with the Civilian Employees Regulations of the British Armed Forces in the Suez Canal Zone, be paid the leaving indemnities due to them and be given their appropriate notice or alternatively wages in lieu of such notice.

10. The provisions of paragraphs 1 to 8 above apply to all workers, other than those of British nationality employed by the British Forces.

ANNEX II

ORGANIZATION OF THE BASE

Part A

1. For the purposes of the present Agreement, the following definitions shall apply:—

(*a*) "The Base" shall mean the installations listed in Appendix "A" to this Annex, including both land and buildings, but excluding the equipment therein.

(*b*) "British equipment" shall mean all movable property, including such property fixed to permanent foundations owned by the Government of the United Kingdom.

(*c*) "British technicians" shall mean the civilian personnel of British nationality employed in Egypt by the commercial firms in accordance with the provisions of paragraph 8 of this Part of this Annex.

(*d*) "Aircrafts under Royal Air Force Control" shall mean aircraft of Her Majesty's Forces and British civilian aircraft under charter to them.

2. (*a*) The Government of the United Kingdom shall have the right to maintain, and to operate for current requirements, the installations numbered as serials 1, 7, 8, 9, 10, 14, 16, 30 and 34 inclusive and 36 in the list at Appendix "A" to this Annex.

(*b*) Should the Government of the United Kingdom decide at any time no longer to maintain any of these installations they will discuss its disposal with the Government of the Republic of Egypt.

(*c*) The approval of the Government of the Republic of Egypt shall be obtained for any new construction in any of the installations mentioned in sub-paragraph (a) of this paragraph.

3. The Government of the Republic of Egypt shall maintain in good order each of the installations numbered as serials 2, 3, 4, 5, 6, 11, 12, 13, 15, 17 to 29 inclusive and 37 in the list at Appendix "A" to this Annex from the date on which the installation is handed over to the Government of the Republic of Egypt by the Government of the United Kingdom.

4. Within a period of twenty months from the date of signature of the present Agreement, the Government of the United Kingdom shall transfer to the Government of the Republic of Egypt ownership and possession of the installations and equipment listed in Appendix "B".

5. Following the withdrawal of Her Majesty's Forces, the Government of the Republic of Egypt as the sovereign government shall assume responsibility for the security of the installations and of all equipment contained therein, or in transit to or from the Base, in accordance with the provisions of Part "E" of this Annex.

6. For the purpose of maintaining and operating the installations referred to in paragraph 2 (a) above and the British equipment therein, the Government of the United Kingdom shall conclude contracts with one or more British or Egyptian commercial firms (hereinafter referred to as contractors).

7. (*a*) The Government of the Republic of Egypt shall give full support to the contractors who shall be afforded such facilities as may be required to enable them to carry out their tasks.

(*b*) The Government of the Republic of Egypt shall designate an authority with whom the contractors can cooperate in carrying out those tasks. This authority will be the General Officer Commanding Eastern Command, or any person delegated to act on his behalf.

(*c*) A Board of Management shall be appointed by the contractors and established in the Base to coordinate the contractors' activities.

8 (*a*) The contractors shall have the right to employ British technicians up to a total of 1,200 but not exceeding for those recruited outside Egypt a total of 800; as well as such Egyptian technicians and personnel, and such local labour engaged in Egypt as they may require.*

(*b*) The Government of the Republic of Egypt shall give facilities for the entry into and exit from Egypt of British technicians and their families.

9. The Government of the United Kingdom shall be afforded facilities for the inspection of the installations referred to in paragraph 2 (a) of this Part of this Annex, and the work being carried out therein. For this purpose, personnel, not exceeding eight in number, shall be attached to Her Majesty's Embassy in Cairo. In addition, personnel, not exceeding five in number, may be attached temporarily to Her Majesty's Embassy in Cairo.

Part B

Contractors and their Employees

1. Egyptian law shall apply to the activities in Egypt of companies and partnerships acting as contractors for the purposes of the present Agreement and to their personnel.

(*) British civilian technicians will be located at Abu Sueir Airfield and Fanara Flying Boat Station to assist in the servicing of aircraft under Royal Air Force control and in the take-off, flying and landing procedures in connection with the landing and servicing facilities mentioned in Article 7 of the present Agreement. So far as can be foreseen the number of such technicians located at Abu Sueir Airfield and Fanara Flying Boat Station will be 23.

2. Nevertheless, any such company or partnership having its head office and the office of its principal activity outside Egypt, and

having no other activities in Egypt at the date of signature of the Present Agreement, shall, with respect to its activities pursuant to the Present Agreement, enjoy the following exemptions:

(*a*) Such company or partnership shall not be required to effect any registration under the provisions of the Egyptian Commercial Register Law No. 219 of 1953 or be required to comply with the provisions of Articles 91, 92 and 93 of the Egyptian Companies Law No. 26 of 1954.

(*b*) Such company or partnership shall not be required to pay Egyptian tax on profits including the tax on the presumed distribution of dividends under Article 11 of Law No. 14 of 1939.

(*c*) With respect to British technicians recruited outside Egypt for the purposes of the present Agreement, any such company or partnership, as well as those technicians shall be exempt from the following Egyptian laws:—

(*i*) Individual Contract of Service Laws No. 317 of 1952 and No. 165 of 1953;

(*ii*) Law concerning Compulsory Insurance in respect of Workmen's Compensation No. 86 of 1942, Workmen's Compensation Law No. 89 of 1950 and Law on Compensation for Individual Diseases No. 117 of 1950, or any other Law which may require industrial insurance or compensation for industrial diseases; and

(iii) Law relating to Workers' Syndicates No. 319 of 1952.

3. References to laws in the preceding paragraph include any enactment replacing or amending these laws.

4. The Government of the Republic of Egypt express their willingness to consider sympathetically the grant of exemption from any law that may impede the performance by the contractors and their personnel of their tasks pursuant to the purposes of the present Agreement.

5. (*a*) With reference to paragraph 2, no activity shall be regarded as being outside the purposes of the present Agreement if it is done for the Government of the Republic of Egypt on their request.

(*b*) Subject to the consent of and on conditions agreed with the Government of the Republic of Egypt, a company or partnership referred to in paragraph 2 may, with respect to its activities pursuant to the present Agreement, continue to enjoy the exemptions referred to in paragraphs 2 to 4, notwithstanding any new activities in Egypt outside the purposes of the present Agreement.

6. Any company incorporated under the laws in force in the United Kingdom solely to act as a contractor for the purposes of the present Agreement and having its head office outside Egypt shall be treated in the same way and enjoy the same exemptions as companies and partnerships referred to in paragraph 2 notwithstanding that the office of the principal activity of such first-mentioned company may be in Egypt.

7. (*a*) In accordance with paragraph 2 (c) of Part A of this Annex, contractors may, subject to agreement with the Government of the Republic of Egypt, build houses in so far as the requirements of their personnel are not covered by existing accommodation.

(*b*) Contractors may also hire houses subject to such conditions as may be agreed between them and the lessors.

8. (*a*) Companies and partnerships incorporated or formed under the laws in force in the United Kingdom and engaged in activities pursuant to the present agreement and British technicians employed by such companies and partnerships shall, with respect to those activities, be accorded in Egypt treatment no less favourable than that accorded to the nationals, including companies and partnerships, of any other foreign country.

(*b*) The provisions of sub-paragraph (a) of this paragraph shall not be construed as conferring any right or privilege which is or may be accorded only to Arab League States.

9. Companies and partnerships engaged in activities pursuant to the present Agreement and their British workers, employees and personnel shall, with respect to those activities, be accorded treatment

no less favourable than that afforded generally to Egyptian nationals, including companies and partnerships. The provisions of this paragraph shall not confer any special privilege which is granted to Egyptian nationals in special circumstances.

10. Any service rendered or supply furnished from installations listed in Appendix "A" to this Annex or at Egyptian airfields in the Suez Canal Base area by contractors to Egyptian authorities or by Egyptian authorities to contractors will be at cost price, i.e., at a price composed of the cost of the materials consumed, the labour used and a due allowance for actual overhead expenses in providing the service or supply.

Part C

(With reference to Article 9 of the present Agreement)

1. The supplies held in the Base will consist of the categories listed in Appendix "C" to this Annex. After the end of the period of withdrawal, the level of supplies in each category shall not exceed the figure quoted in the schedule. Except with the consent of the Egyptian authorities, supplies in one category shall not be replaced by supplies of another category.

2. For the purposes of paragraph 1 above the contractors will, after the period of withdrawal, give the Egyptian Designated Authority information regarding the disposition, composition and amount of the supplies held in the installations.

3. The procedure to be followed with respect to the import and export of British equipment being moved into or out of the Base is set forth in Appendix "D" to this Annex.

4. The Government of the Republic of Egypt shall accord all necessary facilities for the storage and turnover of petroleum products to the contractor who maintains and operates the installations numbered as serials 30 to 34 inclusive in Appendix "A" to this

Annex as well as the storage capacity leased to him by the Government of the Republic of Egypt numbered as serial 35 in that Appendix. Petroleum products thus held on behalf of the Government of the United Kingdom shall be in accordance with paragraph 1 above.

Part D

Imports and Exports

1. British technicians recruited outside Egypt may, on first arrival, import into Egypt free of customs duty their personal effects and household goods. Members of one household may, on first arrival, import into Egypt free of customs duty personal effects and household goods belonging to other members of the same household.

2. (*a*) Provided that the supplies held in the Base do not exceed the level for which provision is made in paragraph 1 of Part C of this Annex, the contractors may import into Egypt and use for the purposes of the present Agreement, without licence, let or hindrance and free of any customs duty or any other dues or taxes. British equipment consigned by the Government of the United Kingdom which is either (i) within the categories of supplies referred to in that paragraph, or (ii) to replace equipment within any installation.

(*b*) Nevertheless, this exemption from customs duty, other dues and taxes shall not extend to:—

(*i*) any petrol, oil or lubricants used by the contractors;

(*ii*) any motor vehicles (other than tank transporters and their towing vehicles) used by the contractors outside the installations, or

(*iii*) any office furniture or office supplies imported and used by the contractors.

3. No property imported into Egypt in accordance with the

provisions of paragraphs 1 and 2 above shall be sold in Egypt unless Egyptian customs duty and all other dues are paid at the appropriate rate.

4. The Egyptian authorities shall permit, without licence, let or hindrance and without fee or other charge, the export by contractors of any British equipment now in the Base, imported into Egypt or manufactured in Egypt for the purposes of the present Agreement, and the export by British technicians recruited outside Egypt of any property imported into Egypt by them.

Part E

(With reference to paragraph 5 of Part A of this Annex)

Security

1. The installations shall receive from the Government of the Republic of Egypt as the sovereign Government the necessary measures for their security. Accordingly, the measures taken by the Government of the Republic of Egypt for the security of the installations handed over to the contractor shall not be less effective than those taken for the security of comparable Egyptian installations.

2. The measures to be taken by the Government of the Republic of Egypt for the security of installations handed over to the contractors shall include the upkeep of perimeter wires, perimeter lighting and defence posts and the provisions of defence stores, communications and other necessary measures. Material for the replacement or maintenance of such perimeter wires, perimeter lighting and defence posts shall be provided by the Government of the United Kingdom.

3. Without prejudice to the general principles mentioned above, the contractors shall:—

(*a*) take all reasonable measures necessary to prevent theft, sabotage and fire inside the perimeter of the installations, including the posting of internal security civilian guards; and

(*b*) in particular ensure that, as far as facilities permit, stores are kept under lock and key, and only the minimum in open stacks; and

(*c*) without prejudice to the provisions of sub-paragraphs (a) and (b) of this paragraph, comply with Egyptian general security regulations issued by the Egyptian Designated Authority and applicable to comparable Egyptian installations so far as they relate to the matters mentioned in those sub-paragraphs; in this connection the Egyptian authorities shall have the right to carry out inspections to ascertain that these regulations are complied with; and

(*d*) cooperate fully with the Egyptian authorities in the maintenance of the security of the installations.

4. The appropriate Egyptian authorities and the contractors shall jointly establish and enforce a pass system to cover the entry into and the exit from the installations of persons, vehicles, equipment and stores with a view to reducing the risk of loss or sabotage.

5. The Egyptian authorities, being responsible for the general security of equipment and stores during movement, shall be given 48 hours' notice when it is intended to move equipment or stores to or from installations except in cases where the Egyptian authorities agree to a shorter period of notice. Similar notification should be given to the Egyptian authorities in the case of stores awaiting movement at docks or railway sidings.

Part F

Engagement of Workers by Contractors and their Security Screening

The following provisions shall apply with respect to the engagement by contractors of technicians and personnel and other local labour (hereinafter referred to as "Workers") and the security screening of such workers:—

1. The Ministry of Social Affairs Employment Offices will provide full facilities to the contractors for the engagement of their workers.

2. The location of the installations will determine the Employment Offices with which contractors will cooperate.

3. The contractors will give full details of occupational requirements when notifying vacancies to the Employment Offices.

4. Workers engaged by contractors who have been previously employed by Her Majesty's Forces and have been screened by Officers of the Egyptian Ministry of the Interior will not be screened again, but all other workers previously employed by Her Majesty's Forces will be so screened before engagement by the contractors.

5. No worker, who has not previously been employed by Her Majesty's Forces or by a contractor, will be engaged by a contractor or be otherwise employed within an installation unless he has been registered at and submitted by an Employment Office after screening by Officers of the Egyptian Ministry of the Interior.

6. A worker who has already been trade-tested by Her Majesty's Forces or by another contractor may be engaged by a contractor in a similar occupation without further test. In the case, however, of a new applicant who is submitted to a contractor and is rejected after trade-testing, the Employment Office will be notified and brief reasons will be given.

7. The provisions of paragraphs 1 to 6 above apply to all workers, other than those of British nationality (who will be included in the agreed number of British technicians employed by the contractors).

Appendix B

(With reference to Paragraph 4 of Part A of Annex II)

The following are the installations to be transferred:—

(*a*) All the airfields in the Suez Canal Base area occupied by Her Majesty's Forces. These are situated at:—
El Firdan.
Ismailia, excluding the area of HQ MEAF stated in Serial 37 of Appendix A to Annex II.
Abu Sueir
Deversoir (excluding that part built on land which forms part of the concession of the Suez Maritime Canal Company)*
Fayid.
Kasfareet
Fanara (Flying Boat Station).
Kabrit
Shandur, and
Shallufa.

(*b*) Navy House, Port Said.

(*c*) Adabiya Port, including heavy cranes.

(*d*) Royal Navy Boom Depot, Adabiya.

(*e*) The Delta W. T. Station.

(*f*) Moascar.*

(*g*) Serials 2, 3, 4, 5, 6, 11, 12, 13, 15, 17–29 inclusive and 37 in the list of Installations in Appendix A to Annex II.

* Ownership and possession of Moascar Area shall be transferred under the terms of paragraph 4 of Part A of Annex II to the present Agreement with the exception of the possession of the area referred to under Serial 36 of Appendix A to Part A of Annex II (and shown and outlined on the site plan attached thereto) which shall be reserved rent free for the accommodation of British technicians during the period of the present Agreement.

Appendix C

(With reference to Paragraph 1 of Part C of this Annex)

Level of Supplies

Category Level

1. *Ammunition*, including all nature of ammunition, mines and explosives 50,000 (tons)
2. *Stores*, including bridging equipment, engineer and ordnance stores 300,000 (tons)
3. *Unarmoured Vehicles* 2,000 (number)
4. *Engineer Equipments*, including engineer plant and earth-moving equipments 500 (pieces)
   Railway Locomotives 30 (number)
   Railway Wagons 100 (number)
   Craft 3 (number)
5. *Air and Ground Fuels* 80,000 (tons)
6. *Petrol and Water Containers* 1,300,000 (jerricans)
7. *Equipment under Repair*
   Heavy and Light Armoured Vehicles 70 (number)
   Wheeled Vehicles 400 (number)
   Artillery Equipments 50 (number)
   Engineer Plant and Equipments 50 (number)
   Other Stores 1,500 (tons)

Appendix D

(With reference to paragraph 3 of Part C of this Annex)

Procedure for Clearance of British Equipment through Egyptian Ports

The following procedure shall apply with respect to the import and export of British equipment being moved into or out of the Base:—

1. Movement of British Equipment into or out of the Base shall take place in accordance with a Freight Movement Instruction issued to a contractor by the British authorities. A copy of the Freight Movement Instruction shall be given to the Egyptian authorities, in the case of British equipment moved out of the Base, before shipment takes place, and in the case of inward shipment before the arrival of the British equipment in Egypt. The Freight Movement Instruction shall contain details of the consignment, including the Freight Shipment Order number by which each item is identified. The Freight Shipment Order number shall be marked upon the items shipped.

2. British Equipment to be moved into or out of the Base shall, with respect to its transit between the Egyptian port and the installations concerned, be covered by a Convoy Note (in the case of road or inland water transport) or by a Railway Warrant, as the case may be. Copies of these documents, which shall bear the Freight Shipment order number of each item, shall be given to the Egyptian Designated Authority.

3. In the case of outward shipment, Foreign Requisitions shall be submitted by the contractors to a designated Freight Agent at the port of shipment. These requisitions shall contain the exact measurement of each item, and shall refer in each case to the Freight Shipment Order number. Copies of Freight Requisitions shall be given to the port authorities at the port of shipment.

4. Copies of Bills of Lading and of Ships' Manifests shall be available to the Egyptian port and customs authorities in the normal manner.

5. The designated Freight Agent shall, on behalf of the contractors, supply to the Egyptian port and customs authorities such information, documents and forms as are required to comply with the normal working procedure of these authorities.

6. Inspection by Egyptian authorities of British equipment moved into or out of the Base shall be in accordance with the following procedure:—

(*a*) In the case of imports, inspection shall normally take place at the port of entry into Egypt, and, in the case of exports, in the installation in which the British equipment to be moved is held.

(*b*) Inspection shall be carried out without unnecessary delay.

(*c*) After inspection clearance shall be given to the British equipment either by affixing a mark upon it or by the issue of a document.

(*d*) If articles arrive in tropical packing, the packages shall not be opened at the port of entry and shall be sealed by the Egyptian authorities.

Such articles shall be held on charge by the contractors in the installations. These articles shall not be unpacked unless in the presence of the Egyptian authorities.

(*e*) Packages containing such articles and bearing unbroken seals shall be cleared for re-export without being opened.

Note

1. PRO/FO-93-94 Treaties 1954.

Select Bibliography

Primary Sources

Unpublished Sources

Public Record Office, London:

(a) Cabinet Papers
(1952–1954)
CAB 129

(b) Cabinet Conclusions
(1952–1954)
CAB 129

(c) Chiefs of Staff Committee
(1952–1954)
DEFE

(d) Foreign Office
(1946–1957)
FO 371

(e) Prime Minister's Office
(1953–1954)
PREM 2

Published Documents

Hurewitz, J. C. *Diplomacy in the Near and Middle East, a Documentary Record: 1914–1956*, 2 vols., Princeton, NJ, Van Nostrand, 1956.

United States, Department of State, *Foreign Relations of the United States*, vol. II, Washington DC, 1960; *ibid.*, vol. VII, 1970.

United States Department of State, *The Suez Canal Problem. July 26– September 22, 1956,* Department of State documentary publication, no. 6392, 1956.

Watt, D. C. *Documents on the Suez Crisis*, London, Royal Institute of International Affairs, 1957.

Newspapers

al-Ahram (Cairo)
al-Akhbar (Cairo)
Akhbar al-Yawm (Cairo)
al-Balagh (Cairo)
al-Bayan (Dubai, UAE)
The Daily Telegraph
al-Dawa (Cairo)
The Egyptian Gazette (Cairo)
The Manchester Guardian
al-Masri (Cairo)
The Observer
The Sunday Times
The Times

Periodicals

British Society for Middle Eastern Studies Bulletin, vols. 10, 12, 14 (1987, 1988).

Contemporary Record: the Journal of Contemporary British History, London, Frank Cass, vols. 1, 5 (1987, 1988).

Foreign Affairs, New York, (1985, 1986).

Foreign Policy, vols. 64, 67 (1986, 1987).

International Affairs, London, published by Cambridge University Press for the Royal Institute of International Affairs, vol. 27 (1951), vol. 28 (1952), vol. 30 (1954), vols. 55, 56 (1979).

International Journal of Middle East Studies (*IJMES*), published under the auspices of the Middle East Studies Association of North America by Cambridge University Press, vols. 14, 16 (1984), vols. 22, 24 (1986).

The Middle East Journal, Washington DC, vol. 2 (1948), vol. 3 (1949), vol. 4 (1950), vol. 7 (1953), vol. 10 (1956).

Journal of the Royal United Services Institute, London (1956–7, 1958).

Interviews

Ahmad Abd Rabu Bey, Cairo, 9 January and 17 February 1987.

Fuad Sarag al-Deen Pasha, Cairo, 19 February 1987.

Professor Jamal al-Khali, Alexandria University, 19 and 20 January 1987.

Sheikh Yousef al-Qardawi, Doha, 10 October 1986.

Unpublished Theses

H. Rahman, 'Aspects of Anglo-Egyptian negotiations 1920–1936', MA thesis, University of Ottawa, Canada, 1977.

Charles Tripp, 'Ali Maher Pasha and the Palace in Egyptian politics 1936–1942: Seeking Mass Enthusiasm for Autocracy', PhD thesis, School of Oriental and African Studies, University of London, 1984.

Muhammad Sayed Ahmed, 'US-Egyptian relations from the 1952 revolution to the Suez Crisis', PhD thesis, School of Oriental and African Studies, University of London, 1987.

Books in Arabic

Anis, Muhammad. *Arba'a fibrayir 1942 fi ta'rikh Misr al-siyasi*, Beirut, 1972.

—*Hareeq al-Qahirah*, Cairo, Maktabat Madbuli, 1982.

al-Baghdadi, Abd al-Latif. *Mudhakkirat Abd al-Latif al-Baghdadi*, 2 vols., Cairo, 1977.

al-Bishri, Tariq. *Tarikh al-harakat al-siyasiya fi Misr, 1945–1952*, Cairo, 1970.

—*al-Muslimun wal Aqbat fi Misr*, Beirut, 1980.

al-Faqhi, Mustafa. *al-Aqbat fi al-siyasa al-misriyya. Makram Obeid wa dawruhu fi al-haraka al-wataniyya*, Cairo, 1985.

Hamrush, Ahmad. *Qissat thawrat 23 yulio*, 1952.

Hassan, Yusuf. *Mudhakkirat al-qasr wa dawruhu fi al-siyasa al-misriyya, 1922–1952*, Cairo, 1982.

Heikal, Muhammad Hassanein. *Abd al-Nasir wa'l-alam*, Beirut, 1972.

—*Mudhakkirat fi 'l-siyasah al-misriyya,* 3 vols., Cairo, 1980.

—*Qisat al-Suwais*, Beirut, 1980.

—*Li Misr la li Abd al-Nasir*, Beirut, 1985.

—*Sanawat al-ghalayan*, Cairo, 1986.

—*Milafat al-Suwais*, Cairo, 1989.

—*al-Enfijar*, Cairo, 1990.

Hussein, M. *Bashawat wa suber bashawat: Surat Misr fi asrayn*, Cairo, 1984.

Jalal, Yahya. *al-Wafd al-Misri 1919–1952*, Cairo, 1981.

al-Jamal, Shawki Atallah. *Tarikh Sudan Wadi al-Nil wa alaqatah bi Misr*, 3 vols., Cairo, 1969.

Muhammad, Z. Abd al-Qader. *Mehnat al-dustur 1923–1952*, Cairo, 1983.

Mahmoud, Asisi. *al-Ikhwan al-Muslimun*, Cairo, 1988.

Mohsen, Muhammad. *Khamsat ayyam hazat Misr*, Cairo, n.d.

Naguib, Muhammad. *Mudhakkirat* [Memoirs], Cairo, 1980.

al-Rafi, Abd al-Rahman. *Muqadima thawra 23 yuliyo, 1952*, Cairo, 1960.

—*Misr wal Sudan taht al-ihtilal al-biritani*, Cairo, 1983.

Ramadan, Abd al-Azim. *al-Jaysh al-misri fi al-siyasa*, Cairo, al-Hay'ah al-Misriyya al-Amma lil-Kitab, 1977.

al-Sabai, Bashir. *al-Wafd wal-ikhwan al-muslimun*, Cairo, 1986.

al-Sadat, Anwar. *Asrar al-thawrah al-misriyya*, Cairo, al-Dar al-Qawmiyah lil-Tibaah wa-al-Nashr, 1965.

El-Said, Rifaat. *Tarikh al-monadhamat al-yasariyya al-misriyya 1940–1950*, Cairo, 1976.

Sidky, Ismail Pasha. *Mudhakkirat* [Memoirs], Cairo, 1950.
Taha, Jad. *Maalim Tarikh Misr al-hadith wal-al-muasir*, Cairo, Dar al-Fikr al-Arabi, 1985.

Books in English

Abbas, Mekki. *The Sudan Question*, London, Faber and Faber, 1952.

Abdel Nasser, Hoda Gamal. *Britain and the Egyptian Nationalist Movement 1936–1952*, Reading, Ithaca Press, 1994.

Ahmed, J. M. *The Intellectual Origins of Egyptian Nationalism*, Oxford, issued under the auspices of the Royal Institute of International Affairs by Oxford University Press, 1960.

Anderson, M. S. *The Eastern Question*, Basingstoke, Macmillan Education, 1966.

Attlee, C. R. *Purpose and Policy*, London, Hutchinson, 1947.

—*As it Happened*, London, Odhams Press, 1954.

Baer, Gabriel. *A History of Land Ownership in Modern Egypt, 1800–1950*, Oxford, issued under the auspices of the Royal Institute of International Affairs by Oxford University Press, 1962.

al-Barawi, Rashid. *Egypt, Britain and the Sudan*, Cairo, Renaissance Bookshop, 1952.

—*The Military Coup in Egypt*, Cairo, Renaissance Bookshop, 1952.

—*Land Reform in Egypt*, Cairo, Renaissance Bookshop, 1960.

Barraclough, G. *Survey of International Affairs, 1956–1958*, Oxford, Oxford University Press, 1962.

Bartlett, C. J. *The Long Retreat: A Short History of British Defence Policy, 1945–70*, London, Macmillan, 1972.

—*British Foreign Policy in the Twentieth Century*, Basingstoke, Macmillan Education, 1989.

Beaumont, Peter and Black, Gerald H. *The Middle East: A Geographical Study*, London, Wiley, 1976.

Bell, J. Bowyer. *The Long War: Israel and the Arabs since 1946*, Englewood Cliffs, NJ, Prentice-Hall, 1969.

Berger, M. *The Arab World Today*, New York, Doubleday, 1962.

Berque, J. *The Arabs: Their History and Future*, London, Faber and Faber, 1964.

—*Egypt: Imperialism and Revolution*, London, Faber and Faber, 1972.

Bilankin, G. *Cairo to Riyadh Diary*, London, Williams and Norgate, 1950.

Blaxland, G. *Objective Egypt*, London, Muller, 1966.

Bowie, R. *Suez 1956*, London, Oxford University Press, 1974.

Braddon, R. *Suez: Splitting of a Nation*, London, Collins, 1973.

Brinton, J. Y. *The Mixed Courts of Egypt*, New Haven, Yale University Press, 1930.

Bullard, Sir R. *Britain and the Middle East*, London, Hutchinson, 1964.

Bullock, A. L. *The Life and Times of Ernest Bevin*, vol. II, London, Heinemann, 1960.

—*Ernest Bevin, Foreign Secretary 1945–1951*, London, Heinemann, 1983.

Burns, E. L. *Between Arab and Israeli*, London, G. G. Harrap, 1962.

Byrnes, J. F. *Speaking Frankly*, New York, Harper, 1947.

Campbell, J. C. *Defense of the Middle East, Problems of American Policy*, New York, published for the Council on Foreign Relations by Harper and Brother, 1960.

Cattan, H. *The Palestine Question*, London, Croom Helm, 1988.

Charmley, John. *Lord Lloyd and the Decline of the British Empire*, London, Weidenfeld and Nicolson, 1987.

Chatham House Study Group. *British Interests in the Mediterranean and Middle East*, London, issued under the auspices of the Royal Institute of International Affairs by Oxford University Press, 1958.

Childers, E. B. *The Road to Suez: A Study of Western Arab Relations*, London, MacGibbon and Kee, 1962.

Churchill, W. S. *The Second World War: The Grand Alliance,* vol III, London, Cassell, 1950.

Cohen, M. J. *Palestine: Retreat from the Mandate: The Making of British Policy, 1936–45*, London, P. Elek, 1978.

Collins, R. O. and Tignor, R. L. *Egypt and the Sudan*, Princeton, NJ, Prentice-Hall, 1967.

Connell, J. *The Most Important Country*, London, Cassell and Company, 1957.

Cooper, Chester. *The Lion's Last Roar: Suez 1956*, New York, 1978.

Cooper, D. *Old Men Forget*, London, Century, 1953.

Cromer, The Earl of. *Modern Egypt*, 2 vols., New York, Macmillan, 1909.

Darby, P. *British Defence Policy East of Suez, 1947–1968*, London, issued for the Royal Institute of International Affairs by Oxford University Press, 1973.

Darwin, John. *Britain, Egypt and the Middle East: Imperial Policy in the Aftermath of War 1918–1922*, London, Macmillan, 1981.

David, Carlton. *Anthony Eden: A Biography*, London, Allen and Unwin, 1981.

—*Britain: The Suez Crisis*, Oxford, Basil Blackwell, 1988.

Dawisha, A. L. *Egypt in the Arab World: The Elements of Foreign Policy*, London, Macmillan, 1976.

Dayan, Moshe. *Diary of the Sinai Campaign*, London, Weidenfeld and Nicolson, 1966.

Deeb, M. *Party Politics in Egypt: The Wafd and its Rivals, 1919–1939*, London, Ithaca Press for the Middle East Centre, St Antony's College, 1979.

Dockrill, Michael and Young John W., *British Foreign Policy 1945–56*, Basingstoke, Macmillan, 1988.

Eatwell, R. *The 1945–1951 Labour Government*, London, Batsford Academic, 1979.

Eden, Anthony. *Memoirs: Facing the Dictators*, London, Cassell, 1962.

—*Memoirs: Full Circle*, London, Cassell, 1960.

Evans, T. E. (ed.). *The Killearn Diaries, 1934–1946: The Diplomatic and Personal Record of Lord Killearn (Sir Miles Lampson)*, London, Sidgwick and Jackson, 1972.

Fabunmi, L. A. *The Sudan in Anglo-Egyptian Relations: A Case Study in Power Politics 1800–1956*, London, Longmans, 1960.

Feis, H. *From Trust to Terror: The Onset of the Cold War 1945–1950*, New York, Norton, 1970.

Finer, Herman. *Dulles over Suez: The Theory and Practice of his Diplomacy*, Chicago, Quadrangle Books, 1964.

Fisher, Sydney. *The Middle East: A History*, 3rd edn, New York, Knopf, 1979.

Fitzsimons, M. A. *The Foreign Policy of the British Labour Government 1945–1951*, Notre Dame, Ind., University of Notre Dame Press, 1953.

—*Empire by Treaty: Britain and the Middle East in the Twentieth Century*, London, Ernest Benn, 1965.

Galatoli, A. M. *Egypt in Mid-Passage*, Cairo, Urwand and Sons Press, 1950.

Ganin, Zvi. *Truman, American Jewry, and Israel, 1945–1948*, New York, Holmes and Meier, 1979.

Garbutt, P. E. *Naval Challenge, 1945–1961*, London, MacDonald, 1961.

Gilbert, M. *Winston S. Churchill 1945–1965*, vol. VIII, Boston, Houghton Mifflin, 1988.

Glubb, Sir J. B. *A Soldier With the Arabs*, London, Hodder and Stoughton, 1957.

Gomaa, A. M. *The Foundation of the League of Arab States*, London, Longman, 1977.

Gordon, M. R. *Conflict and Consensus in Labour's Foreign Policy 1914–1965*, Stanford, Ca., Stanford University Press, 1969.

Haddad, G. *Revolutions and Military Rule in the Middle East*, vol. 3, New York, R. Speller, 1965.

Harari, M. *Government and Politics of the Middle East*, Englewood Cliffs, NJ, Prentice-Hall, 1963.

Harris, C. P. *Nationalism and Revolution in Egypt*, The Hague, published for the Hoover Institution on War, Revolution and Peace, Stanford, Ca., by Mouton, 1964.

Harris, Kenneth, *Attlee*, London, Weidenfeld and Nicolson, 1982.

Hayter, Sir W. *The Diplomacy of the Great Powers*, London, Hamish Hamilton, 1960.

—*A Late Beginner*, 1966.

Heikal, M. H. *Cutting the Lion's Tail*, London, André Deutch, 1986.

Hill, R. A. *A Biographical Dictionary of the Anglo-Egyptian Sudan*, London, Clarendon Press, 1951.

—*Egypt in the Sudan 1820–1881*, London, Oxford University Press, 1959.

Hilton, Maj. Gen. R. *The Thirteenth Power*, London, C. Johnson, 1958.

Holt, P. M. *A Modern History of the Sudan*, London, Weidenfeld and Nicolson, 1961.

Hopwood, Derek. *Egypt, Politics and Society, 1945–1984*, London, Allen and Unwin, 1982.

Hoskins, H. L. *The Middle East*, New York, Macmillan, 1954.

Hottinger, A. *The Arabs, their History, Culture and Place in the Modern World*, London, Thames and Hudson, 1963.

Howard, H. *Turkey, the Straits and U.S. Policy*, Baltimore, Johns Hopkins University Press, 1974.

Howard, M. *The Mediterranean Strategy in the Second World War*, London, Greenhill Books, 1968.

Hull, C. *The Memoirs of Cordell Hull*, vol. II, New York, Macmillan, 1948.

Hurewitz, J. C. *Middle East Dilemmas: The Background of United States Policy*, New York, published for the Council on Foreign Relations by Harper, 1953.

—*The Struggle for Palestine*, New York, Greenwood Press, 1968.

Ibrahim, H. A. *The 1936 Anglo-Egyptian Treaty*, Khartoum, Khartoum University Press.

Issawi, C. *Egyptian at Mid-Century*, London, published under the auspices of the Royal Institute of International Affairs by Oxford University Press, 1954.

Jankowski, P. *Egypt's Young Rebels: Young Egypt, 1933–1952*, Stanford, Ca., Hoover Institution Press, 1975.

Jarvis, Maj. C. S. *Desert and Delta*, London, John Murray, 1938.

Khouri, Fred J. *The Arab–Israeli Dilemma*, New York, Syracuse University Press, 1968.

Kirk, G. *Survey of International Affairs, 1939–1946. The Middle East in the War*, London, Oxford University Press, 1952.

—*Survey of International Affairs: The Middle East 1945–1950*, London, Oxford University Press, 1954.

Kuniholm, B. R. *The Origins of the Cold War in the Near East:*

Great Power Conflict and Diplomacy in Iran, Turkey and Greece, Princeton, NJ, Princeton University Press, 1980.

Kyle, Keith. *Suez,* London, Weidenfeld and Nicolson, 1991.

Lacouture, J. and S. *Egypt in Transition*, London, Methuen, 1958.

Landau, J. M. *Parliaments and Parties in Egypt*, Tel Aviv, published for the Israel Oriental Society by the Israel Publishing House, 1953.

Lapping, B. *End of Empire*, London, Paladin, 1985.

Laquer, W. Z. *Communism and Nationalism in the Middle East*, New York, Praeger, 1956.

Lenczowski, G. *The Middle East in World Affairs*, Ithaca, Cornell University Press, 1952.

Lewis, B. *The Middle East and the West*, London, Weidenfeld and Nicolson, 1964.

Lewis, B., Pellat, C. H. and Schacht, J. (eds.). *The Encyclopaedia of Islam*, vol. II, 1965.

Liddell Hart, B. H. *Defence of the West: Some Riddles of War and Peace*, London, Cassell, 1950.

Little, T. *Modern Egypt*, New York, Praeger, 1967.

Lloyd, George A. *Egypt since Cromer*, 2 vols., New York, H. Fertig, 1933.

Louis, W. R. *Imperialism at Bay*, Oxford, Clarendon Press, 1977.

—*The British Empire in the Middle East 1945–1951*, Oxford, Clarendon Press, 1984.

Love, Kenneth. *Suez: The Twice-Fought War*, New York, McGraw-Hill, 1969.

Macmillan, Harold. *Riding the Storm 1956–1959*, New York, Harper and Row, 1971.

Mansergh, N. *Survey of British Commonwealth Affairs: Problems of Wartime Cooperation and Post-War Change, 1939–1952*, London, Oxford University Press, 1958.

Mansfield, P. *The British in Egypt*, London, Weidenfeld and Nicolson, 1971.

—*The Middle East: A Political and Economic Survey*, Oxford, Oxford University Press, 1980.

Marlowe, J. *Arab Nationalism and British Imperialism*, London, Cresset Press, 1961.

—*A History of Modern Egypt and Anglo-Egyptian Relations, 1800–1956*, 2nd edn, Hamden, Conn., Archon Books, 1965.
—*Four Aspects of Egypt*, London, Allen and Unwin, 1966.
Marsot, A. Lutfi al-Sayyid. *A Short History of Modern Egypt*, Cambridge, Cambridge University Press, 1985.
Miller, A. D. *The Arab States and the Palestine Question*, Washington D.C., Georgetown University, published by Praeger with the Centre for Strategic and International Studies, 1980.
Mitchell, R. D. *The Society of Muslim Brothers*, London, Oxford University Press, 1969.
Moncrieff, A. *Suez Ten Years After*, New York, Pantheon Books, 1967.
Monroe, E. *Bevin's Arab Policy: Middle Eastern Affairs*. Albert Hourani (ed.), St Antony's Papers, no. 11, Oxford, 1961.
—*Britain's Moment in the Middle East, 1914–1956*, London, Methuen, 1965.
Montgomery, B. L. *The Memoirs of Field Marshal the Viscount Montgomery of Alamein*, London, Companion Book Club, 1958.
Morgan, Kenneth O. *Labour in Power 1945–1951*, Oxford, Oxford University Press, 1984.
Morrison, Lord Herbert. *Herbert Morrison: An Autobiography*, London, Odhams Press, 1960.
Muddathir, A. R. *Imperialism and Nationalism in the Sudan, 1899–1956*, Oxford, Clarendon Press, 1969.
Muslih, M. Y. *The Origins of Palestinian Nationalism*, New York, Columbia University Press, 1988.
Nasser, Gamal Abdel. *The Philosophy of the Revolution*, Cairo, 1955.
Neff, D. *Warriors at Suez*, New York, Linden Press/Simon and Schuster, 1981.
Naguib, Muhammad. *Egypt's Destiny*, London, Gollancz, 1955.
Northedge, F. S., *British Foreign Policy 1945–1961*, London, George Allen and Unwin, 1962.
Nutting, Anthony. *No End of a Lesson: The Story of Suez*, London, Constable, 1967.
—*Nasser*, London, Constable, 1972.

Omner, M. B. *Revolution and Nationalism in the Sudan*, London, Collings, 1974.

Peacock, H. L. *A History of Modern Britain, 1815–1981*, London, Heinemann, 1974.

Porter, Bernard. *The Lion's Share: A Short History of British Imperialism 1850–1970*, London, Longman, 1975.

Potichnyi, P. J. and Shapiro, J. P. (eds.). *From the Cold War to Détente*, New York, Praeger, 1976.

Ramazani, R. K. *Iran's Foreign Policy, 1941–1973: A Study of Foreign Policy in Modernizing Nations,* Charlottesville, Va., University Press of Virginia, 1975.

Reynolds, P. A. *British Foreign Policy in the Inter-War Years*, London, Longmans, Green, 1954.

Richmond, J. *Egypt 1798–1952: Her Advance towards a Modern Identity*, London, Methuen, 1977.

Rifaat, B. M. *The Awakening of Modern Egypt*, London, Longmans, Green, 1947.

Robertson, Sir J. *Transition in Africa: From Direct Rule to Independence*, London, C. Hurst, 1974.

Robinson, Ronald and Gallagher, John. *Africa and the Victorians: The Official Mind of Imperialism*, London, Macmillan, 1981.

Rosencrance, R. N. *Defense of the Realm: British Strategy in the Nuclear Epoch*, New York, Columbia University Press, 1967.

Rubin, B. *The Great Powers in the Middle East, 1941–1947*, London, Frank Cass, 1980.

Russell, Sir T. *Egyptian Service 1902–1946*, London, John Murray, 1949.

Sadat, Anwar. *In Search of Identity*, London, HarperCollins, 1978.

Safran, N. *Egypt in Search of Political Community*, Cambridge, Mass., Harvard University Press, 1961.

Said, Edward. *The Question of Palestine*, London, Routledge and Kegan Paul, 1979.

Schonfield, H. J. *The Suez Canal in Peace and War 1896–1969*, Coral Gables, Fla., University of Miami Press, 1969.

Searight, S. *The British in the Middle East*, London, Weidenfeld and Nicolson, 1969.

Shibeika, M. *British Policy in the Sudan 1882–1902*, London, Oxford University Press, 1952.

Shinwell, E. *Conflict Without Malice*, London, Odhams Press, 1955.

Shuckburgh, Evelyn. *Descent to Suez: Diaries, 1951–56*, London, Weidenfeld and Nicolson, 1986.

Smith, G. *American Diplomacy during the Second World War, 1941–1945*, New York, Knopf, 1965.

Smith, P. A. *Palestine and Palestinians*, London, Croom Helm, 1984.

Snyder, W. P. *The Politics of British Defense Policy 1945–1962*, Columbus, Ohio State University Press, 1965.

Speiser, E. A. *The United States and the Near East*, Cambridge, Mass., Harvard University Press, 1947.

Stephens, R. *Nasser: A Political Biography*, New York, Simon and Schuster, 1971.

Strang, W., (1st Baron). *Home and Abroad*, London, André Deutsch, 1956.

El-Tayeb, S. *The Student Movement in the Sudan 1940–1970*, Khartoum, 1971.

Terry, J. Janice. *The Wafd 1919–1952*, London, Third World Centre for Research and Publishing, 1982.

Theobald, A. B. *The Mahdiya: A History of the Anglo-Egyptian Sudan, 1881–1899*, London, Longman, 1951.

Tripp, Charles. *Egypt Under Mubarak*, a SOAS Middle East Centre Study, London, Routledge and Kegan Paul, 1989.

Truman, H. S. *Memoirs: Years of Decisions*, vol. I, New York, 1956.

—*Memoirs: Years of Trial and Hope*, vol. II, New York, Hodder & Stoughton, 1956.

Vatikiotis, P. J. *Conflict in the Middle East*, London, Allen and Unwin, 1971.

—*The Egyptian Army in Politics*, Westport, Conn., Greenwood Press, 1975.

—*A History of Egypt from Muhammad Ali to Sadat*, Balimore, Johns Hopkins, 1980.

—*Nasser and his Generation*, London, Croom Helm, 1978.

Watt, D. C. *Great Britain and Egypt*, 1914–1936, 1914–1936, London, Royal Institute of International Affairs, 1936.

—*Britain and the Suez Canal*, London, Royal Institute of International Affairs, 1957.

Wavell, A. P., (1st Viscount). *Allenby in Egypt*, New York, Oxford University Press, 1944.

Wheare, K. C. *The Statute of Westminster and Dominion Status*, 5th edn, Oxford, Oxford University Press, 1953.

Williams, F. *Ernest Bevin: Portrait of a Great Englishman*, London, Hutchinson, 1952.

—*A Prime Minister Remembers; The War and Post-War Memoirs of the Rt. Hon. Earl Attlee*, London, Heinemann, 1961.

Wilmington, M. W. *The Middle East Supply Centre*, London, London University Press, 1971.

Wilson, H. M. *Eight Years Overseas, 1939–47*, London, Hutchinson, 1950.

Woodhouse, C. M. *Britain and the Middle East*, Geneva, E. Droz, 1959.

—*British Foreign Policy Since the Second World War*, London, Hutchinson, 1961.

Woodward, P. *Condominium and Sudanese Nationalism*, London, Rex Collings, 1979.

Zayid, M. Y. *Egypt's Struggle for Independence*, Beirut, Khayats, 1965.

Index